D1095984

Gunnerkrigg Court™

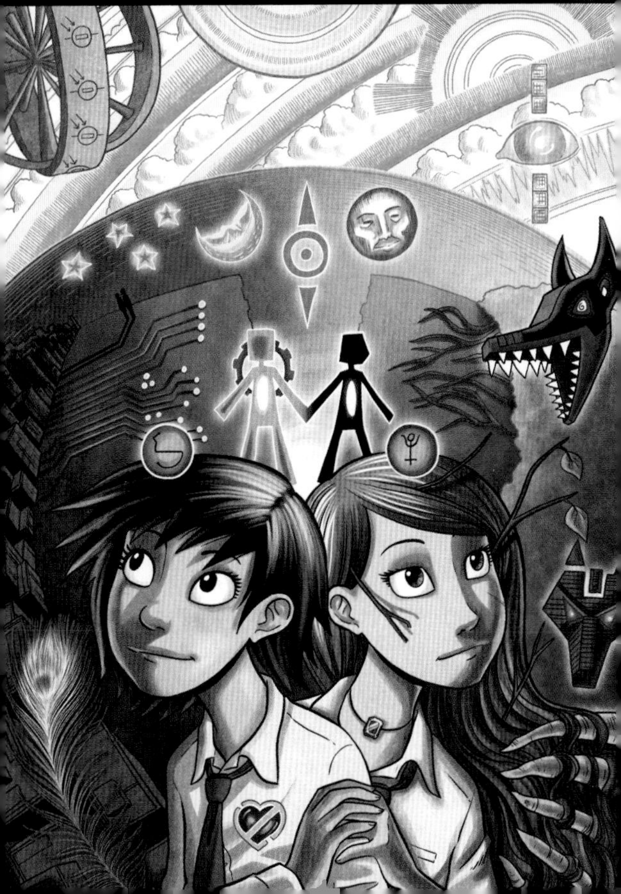

Gunnerkrigg Court Volume 4: Mate

Written & Illustrated by
Thomas Siddell

Taylor, *Editor*

Entertainment LLC
mmins, *President & COO*
mylie, *Chief Creative Officer*
ennedy, *Publisher*

Stephen Christy, *Editor-in-Chief*
Mel Caylo, *Marketing Manager*
Scott Newman, *Production Manager*

ed by **Archaia**

Entertainment LLC
ne Street, Suite 1010
geles, California, 90028
chaia.com

ARCHAIA
NEW STORIES. NEW WORLDS.

Gunnerkrigg Court™   Materia

Gunnerkrigg Court

Chapter 32:

From the Forest

She Came

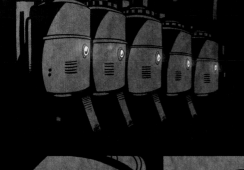

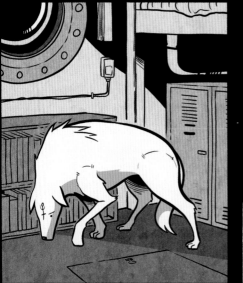

Clonk

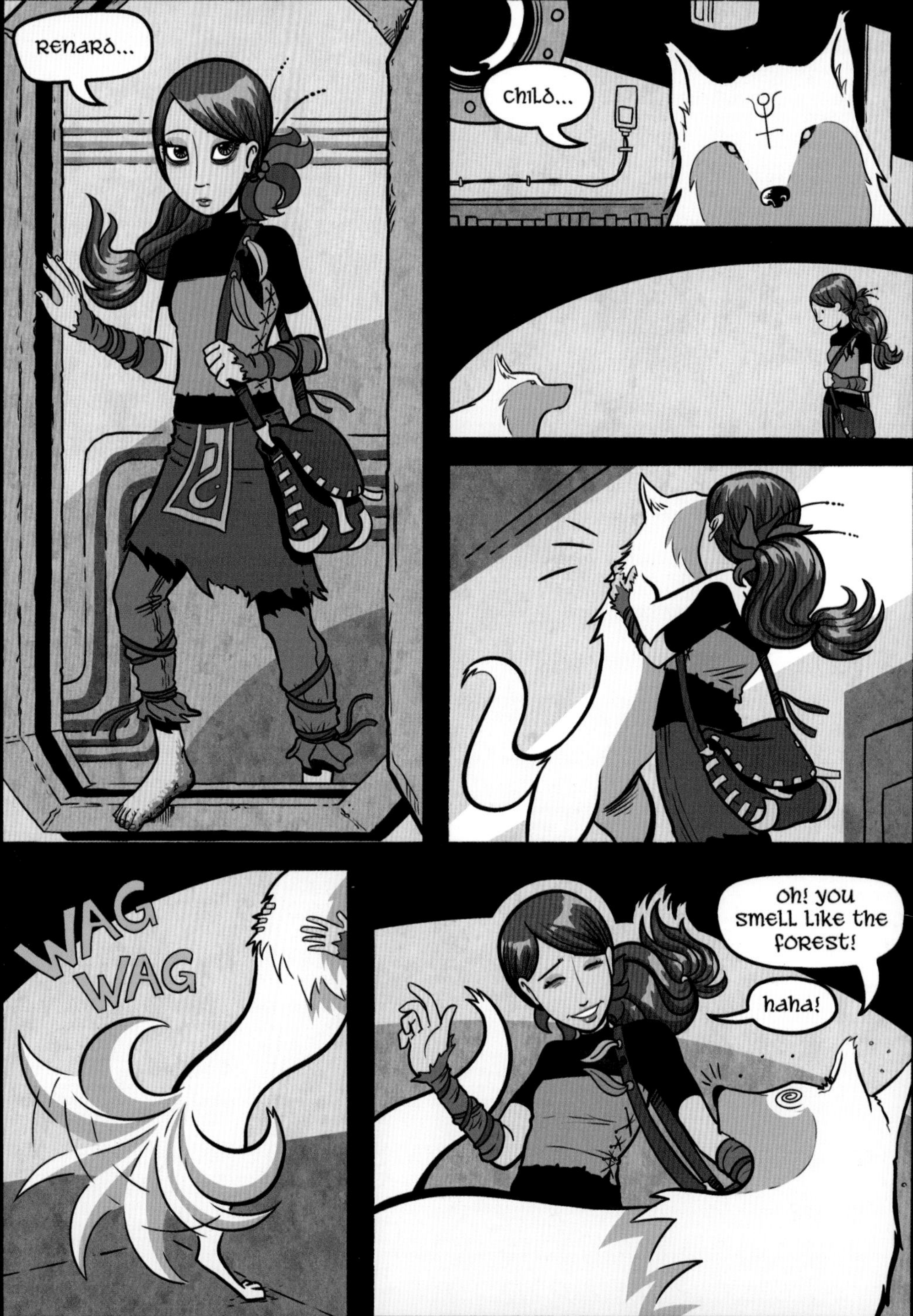

Renard...
Child...
WAG
WAG
Oh! You smell like the forest!
Haha!

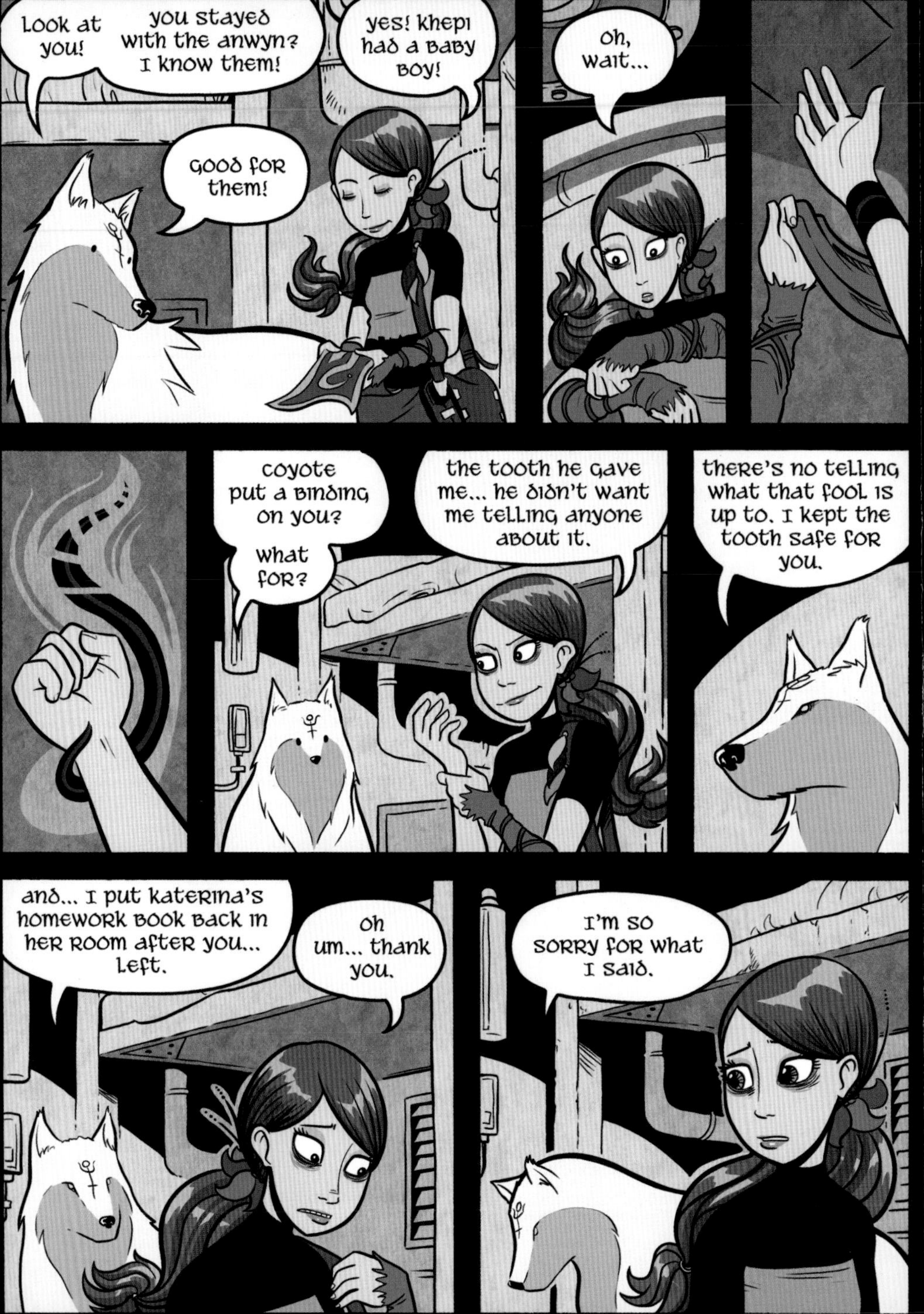
Look at you!
you stayed with the anwyn? I know them!
Good for them!
yes! khepi had a baby boy!
Oh, wait...
coyote put a binding on you?
what for?
the tooth he gave me... he didn't want me telling anyone about it.
there's no telling what that fool is up to. I kept the tooth safe for you.
and... I put katerina's homework book back in her room after you... left.
oh um... thank you.
I'm so sorry for what I said.

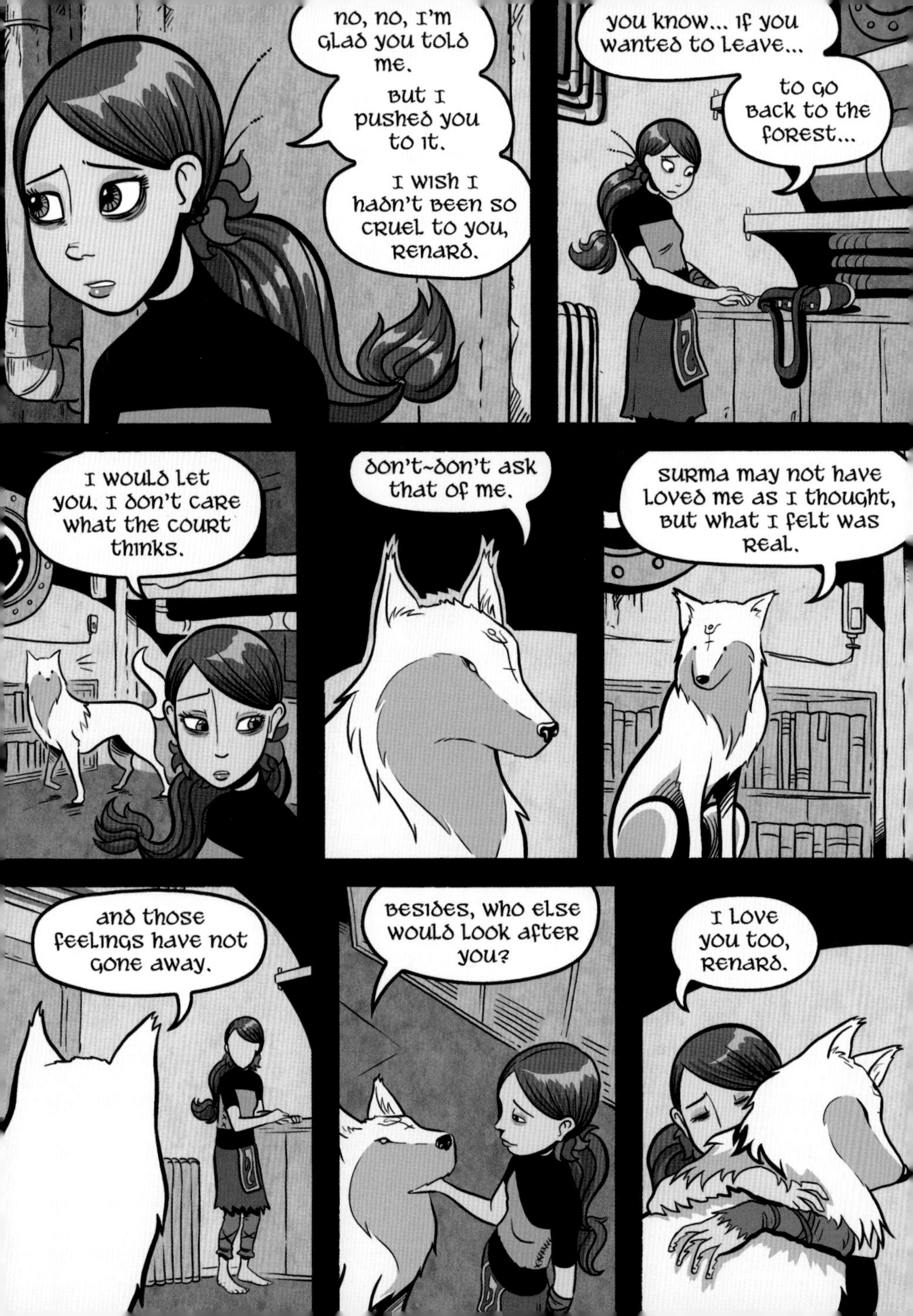
no, no, I'm glad you told me.
But I pushed you to it.
I wish I hadn't been so cruel to you, Renard.
you know... if you wanted to leave...
to go back to the forest...
I would let you. I don't care what the court thinks.
don't-don't ask that of me.
Surma may not have loved me as I thought, but what I felt was real.
and those feelings have not gone away.
Besides, who else would look after you?
I love you too, Renard.

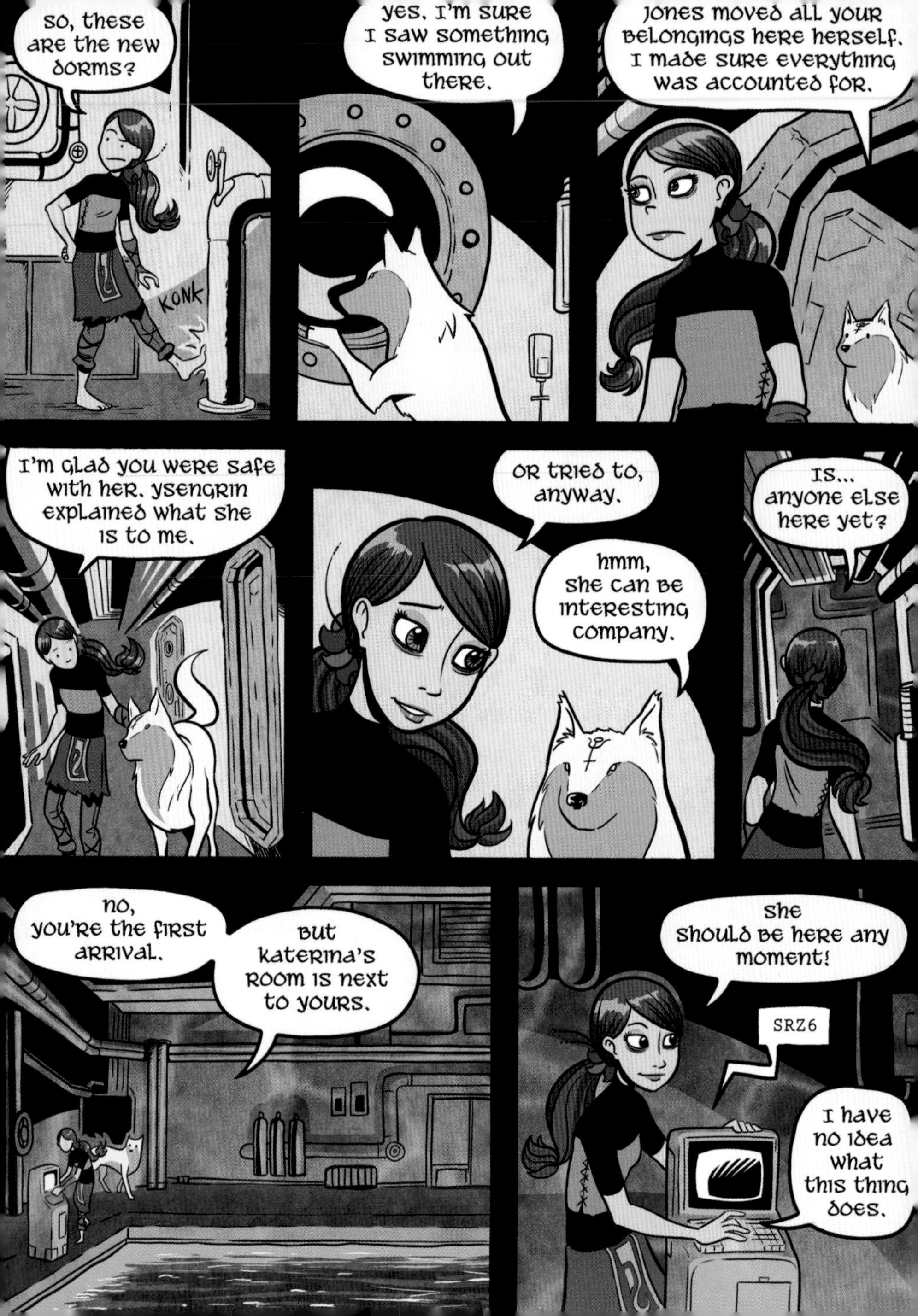
so, these are the new dorms?
KONK
yes. I'm sure I saw something swimming out there.
jones moved all your belongings here herself. I made sure everything was accounted for.
I'm glad you were safe with her. ysengrin explained what she is to me.
or tried to, anyway.
hmm, she can be interesting company.
is... anyone else here yet?
no, you're the first arrival.
but katerina's room is next to yours.
she should be here any moment!
SRZ6
I have no idea what this thing does.

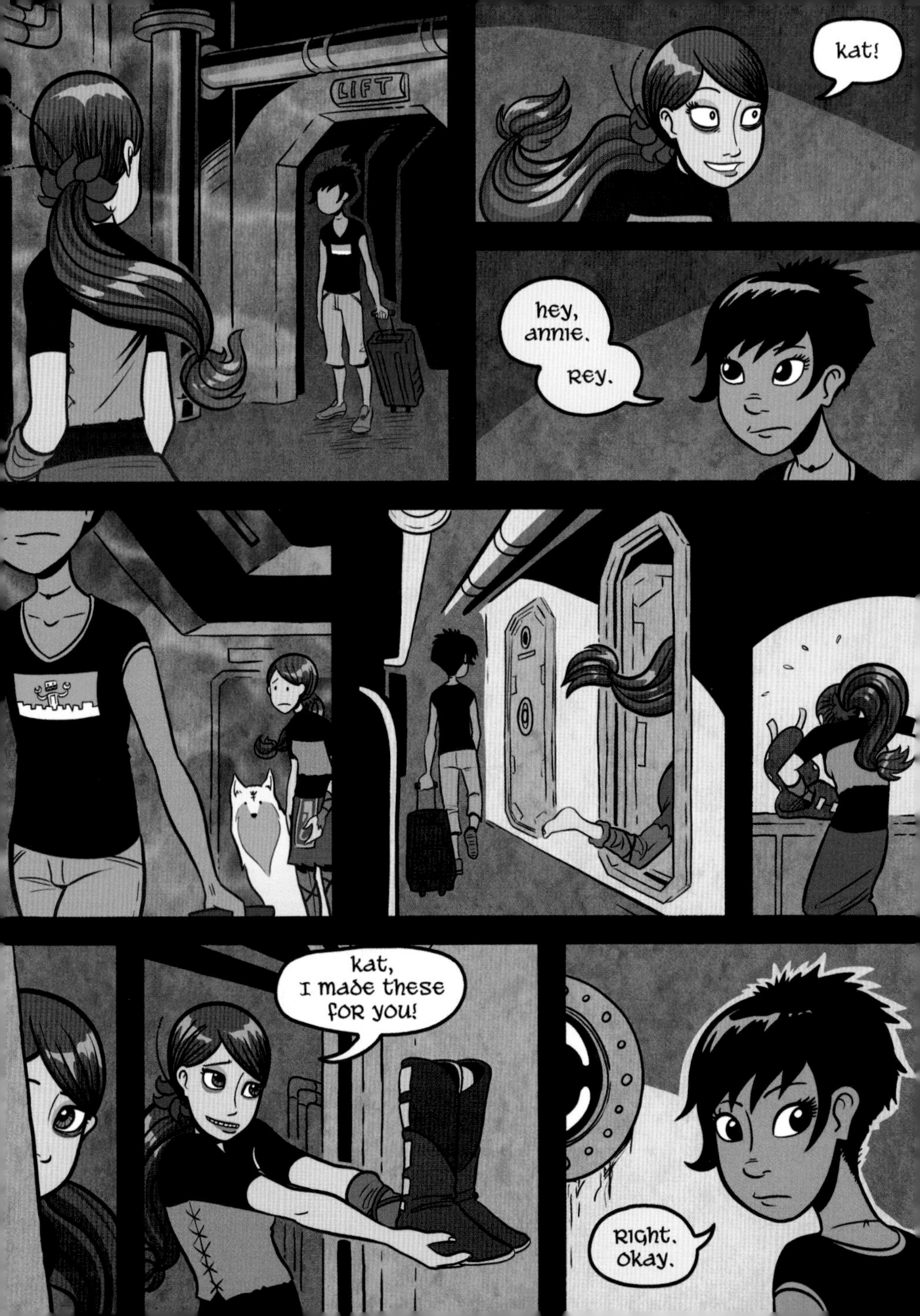
LIFT
kat!
hey, annie.
rey.
kat, I made these for you!
right. okay.

LOOK, I GOTTA GO GET MORE OF MY STUFF.

KAT... ARE YOU OKAY? I'M SO SORRY ABOUT THE SUMMER HOLIDAY.

DID YOU HAVE A NICE TIME?

ANNIE, WHEN I HEARD YOU RAN OFF, I WAS DEVASTATED.

THEN I HEARD... YOU KNOW, THE REASON YOU RAN OFF AND I WAS SO WORRIED.

THEN THAT JONES LADY SAID YOU WERE STAYING IN THE FOREST.

I FELT SO BAD. SO DID MY MUM. SHE THOUGHT IT WAS HER FAULT.

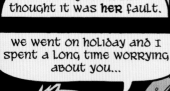

WE WENT ON HOLIDAY AND I SPENT A LONG TIME WORRYING ABOUT YOU...

BUT MAINLY I WISHED YOU WERE THERE WITH ME.

AND YOU KNOW... I EVEN FELT A LITTLE ANGRY THAT YOU'D DITCH LIKE THAT...

AND THAT MADE ME FEEL EVEN WORSE.

NOW I DON'T KNOW WHAT TO THINK.

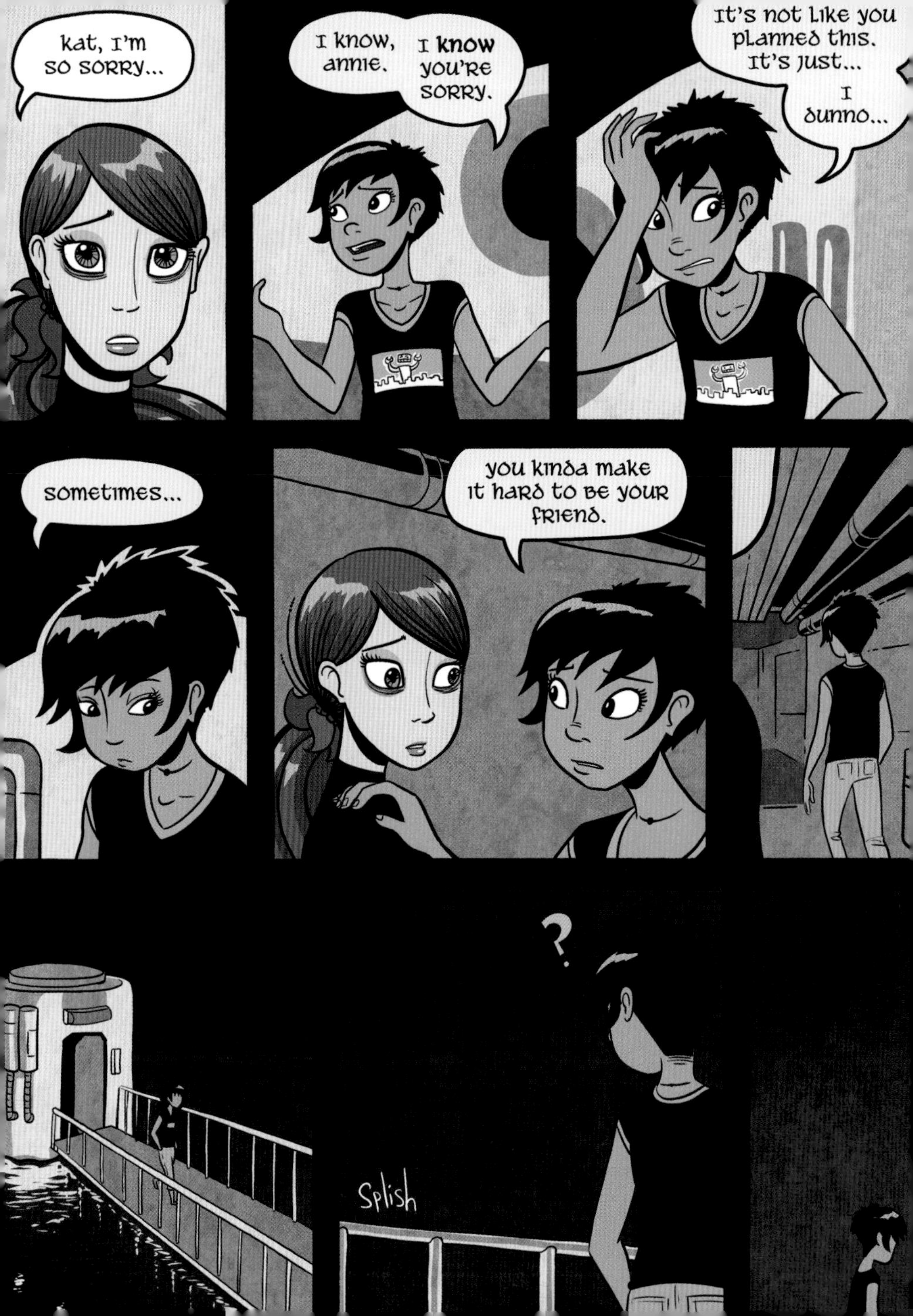
kat, I'm so sorry...
I know, annie.
I **know** you're sorry.
It's not like you planned this. It's just...
I dunno...
sometimes...
you kinda make it hard to be your friend.
?
Splish

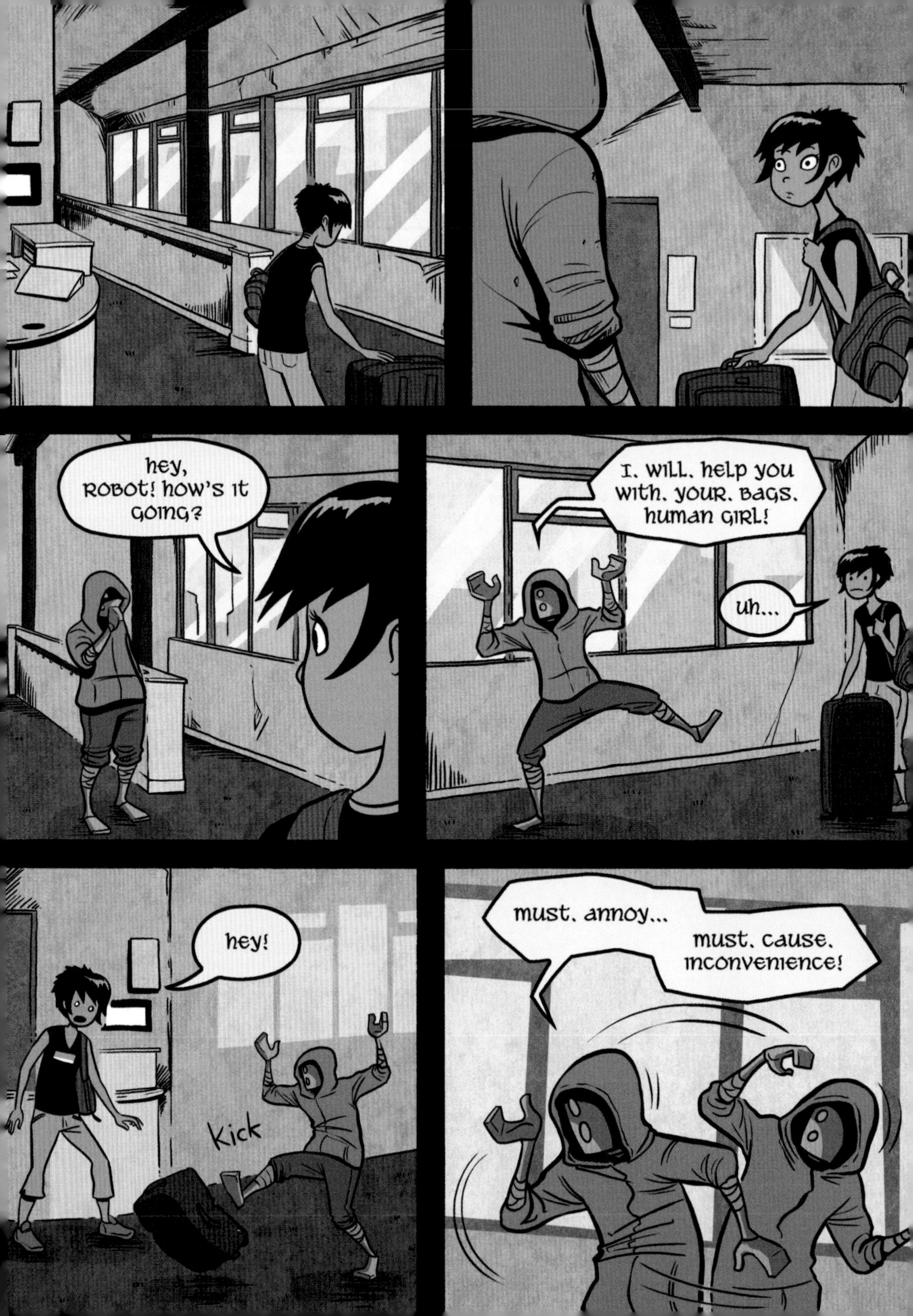
hey, ROBOT! how's it GOING?
I. WILL. help you with. YOUR. BAGS. human GIRL!
uh...
hey!
Kick
must. annoy...
must. cause. inconvenience!

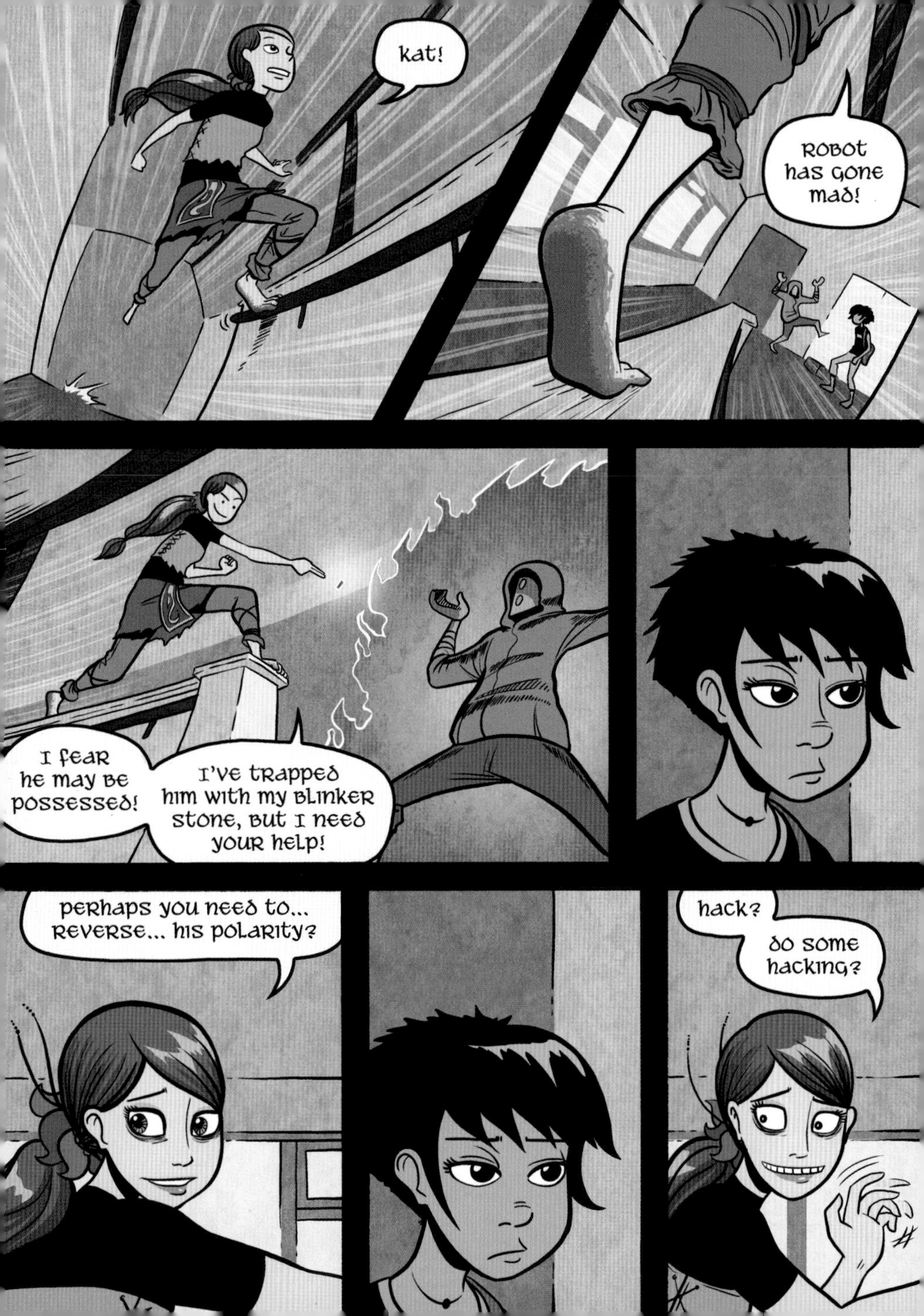
kat!
ROBOT has GONE mad!
I fear he may BE possessed!
I'VE tRapped him with my BLINKER stone, BUT I need yOUR help!
perhaps you need to... REVERSE... his polarity?
hack?
do some hacking?

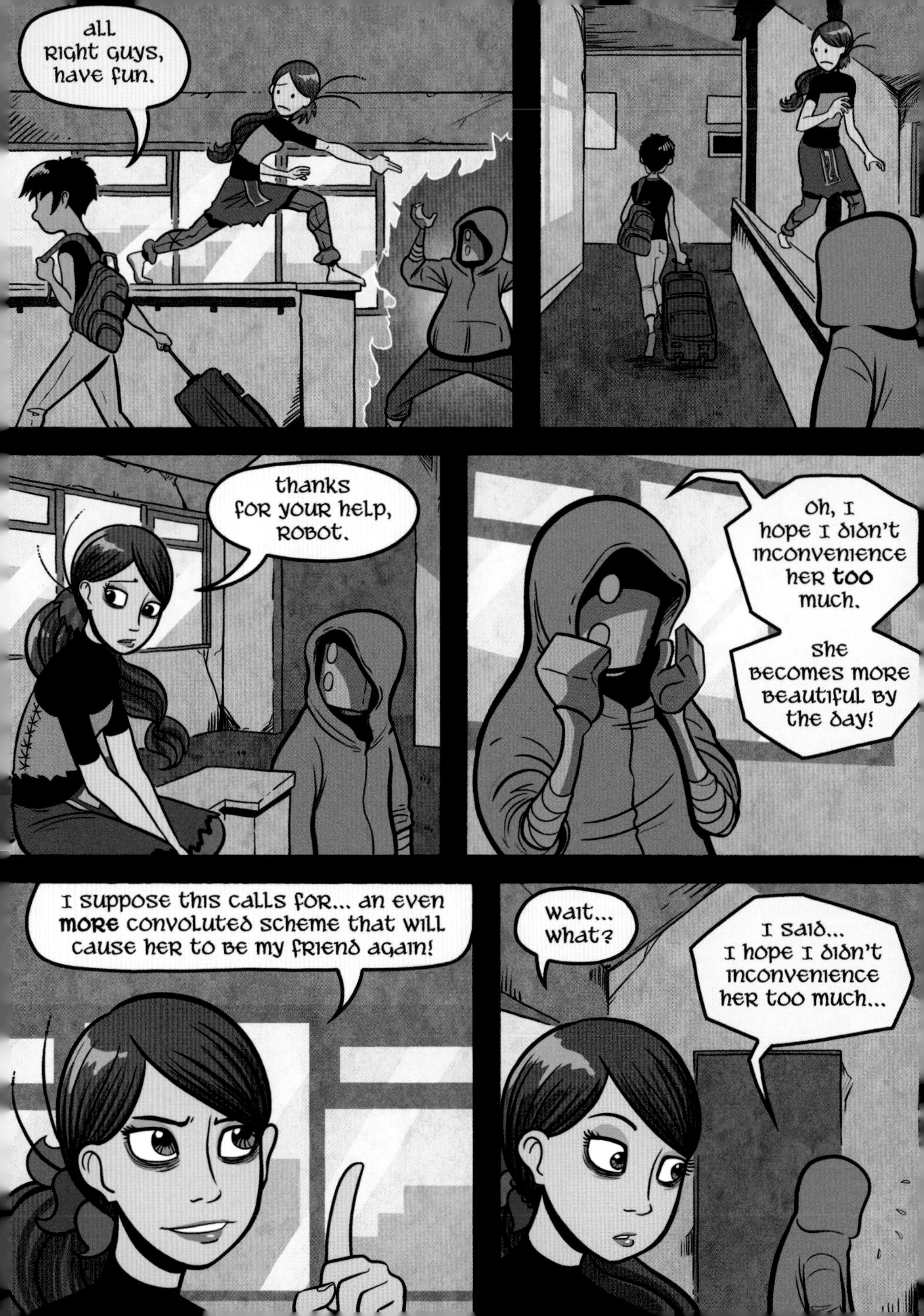
all Right guys, have fun.
thanks for your help, Robot.
Oh, I hope I didn't inconvenience her too much.
She becomes more beautiful by the day!
I suppose this calls for... an even MORE convoluted scheme that will cause her to be my friend again!
Wait... what?
I said... I hope I didn't inconvenience her too much...

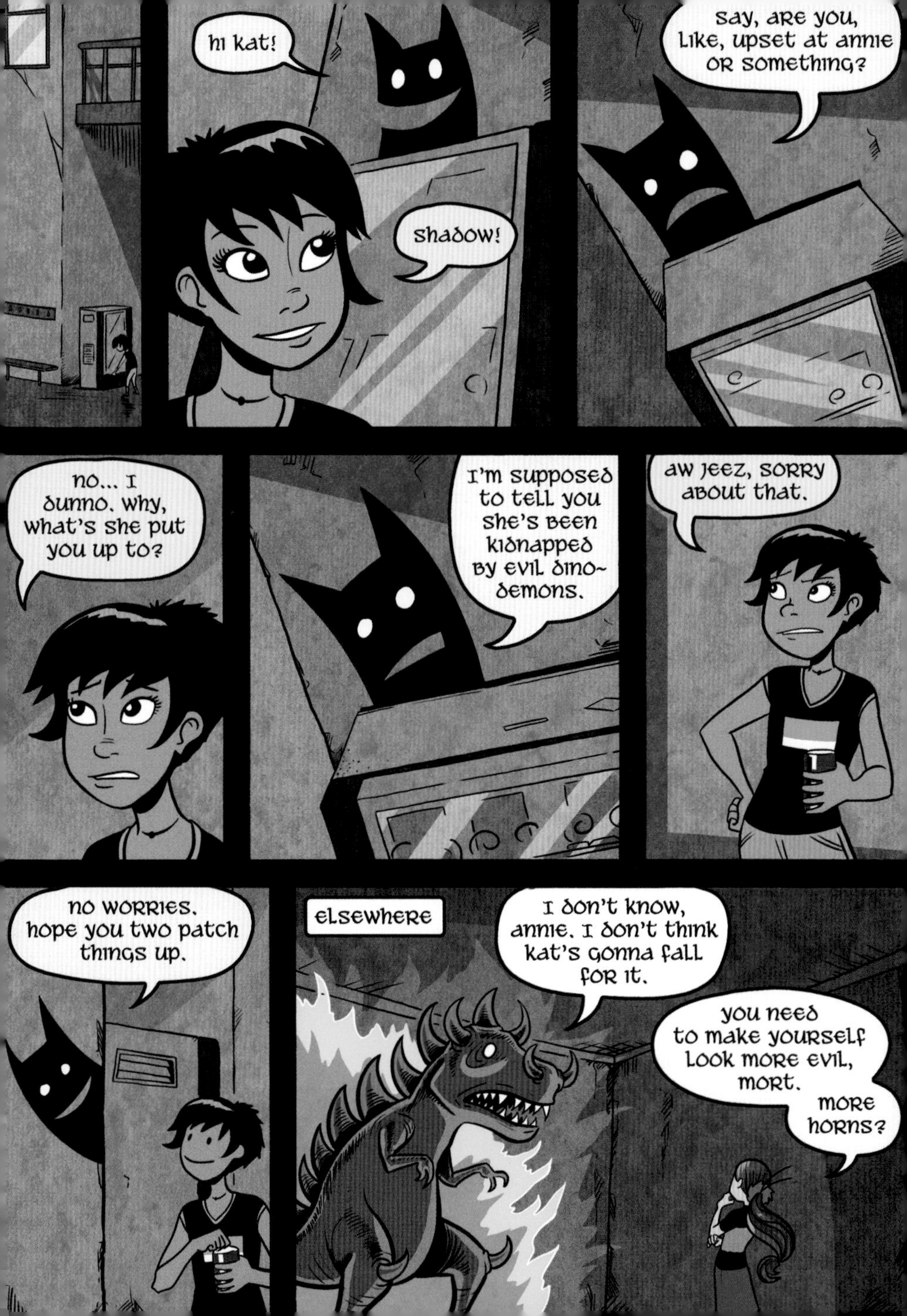
hi kat!
shadow!
say, are you, like, upset at annie or something?
no... I dunno. why, what's she put you up to?
I'm supposed to tell you she's been kidnapped by evil dino-demons.
aw jeez, sorry about that.
no worries. hope you two patch things up.
elsewhere
I don't know, annie. I don't think kat's gonna fall for it.
you need to make yourself look more evil, mort.
more horns?

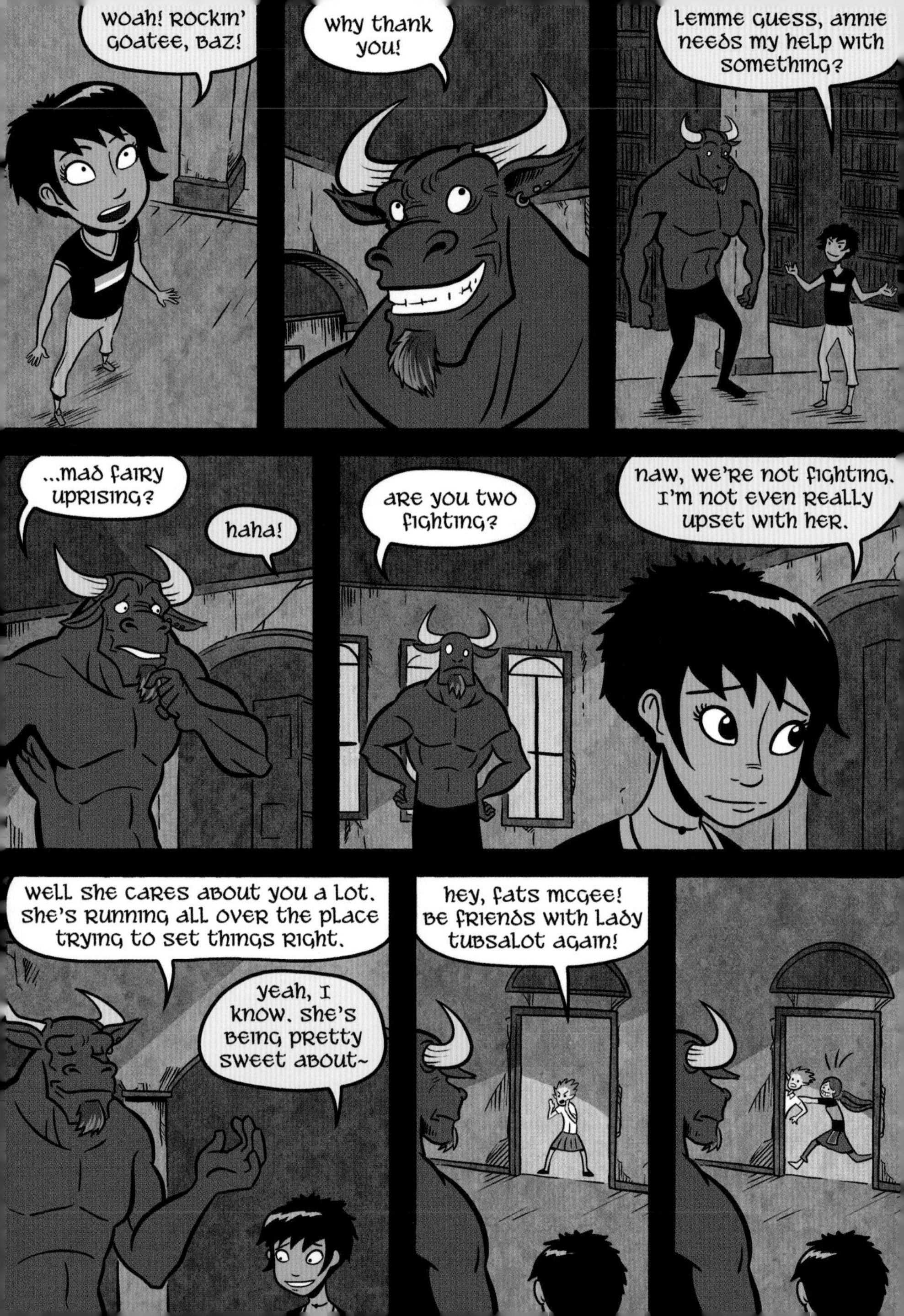
woah! Rockin' goatee, Baz!
why thank you!
Lemme guess, annie needs my help with something?
...mad fairy uprising?
haha!
are you two fighting?
naw, we're not fighting. I'm not even really upset with her.
well she cares about you a lot. she's running all over the place trying to set things right.
yeah, I know. she's being pretty sweet about~
hey, fats mcgee! be friends with lady tubsalot again!

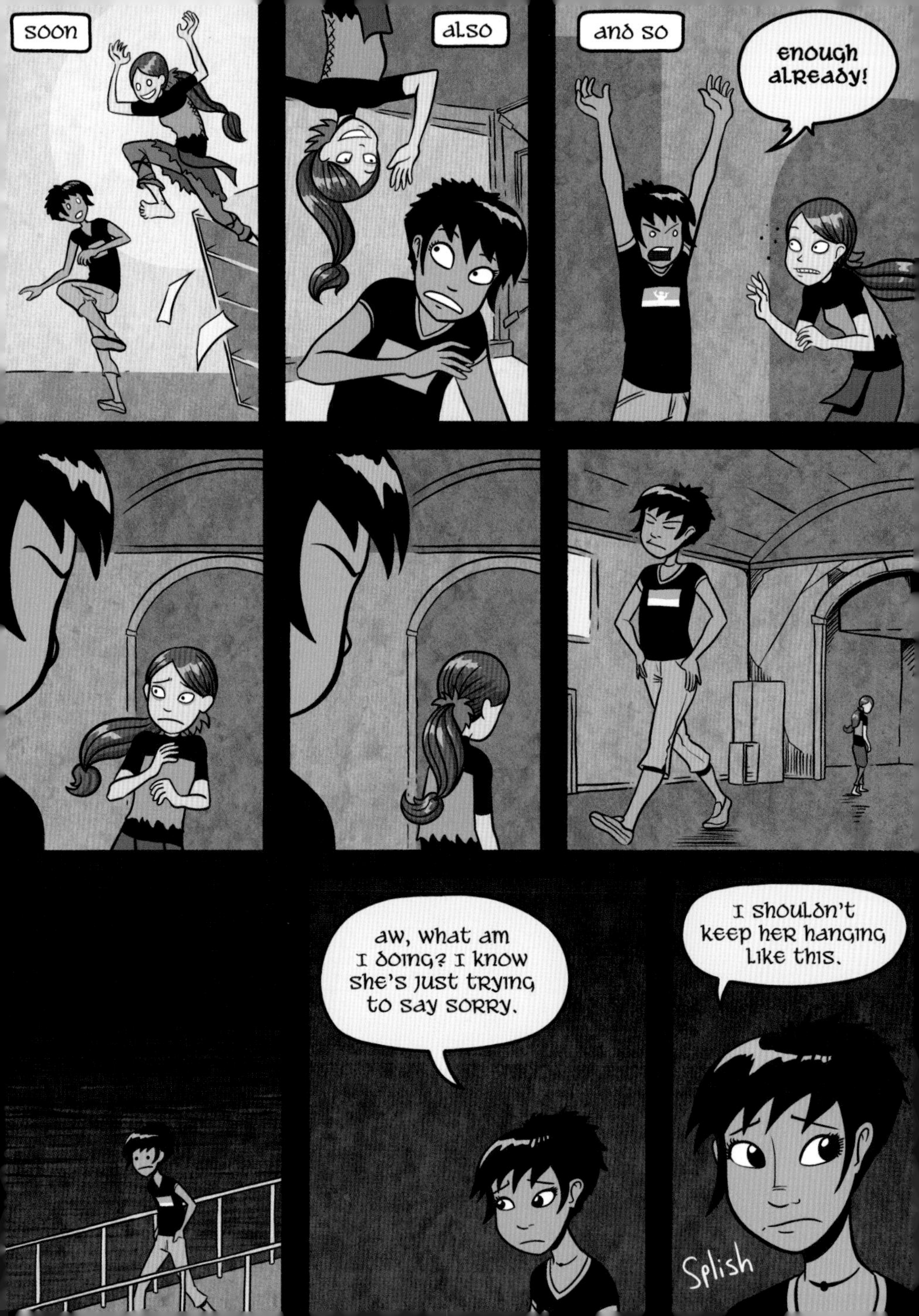
soon
also
and so
enough already!
aw, what am I doing? I know she's just trying to say sorry.
I shouldn't keep her hanging like this.
Splish

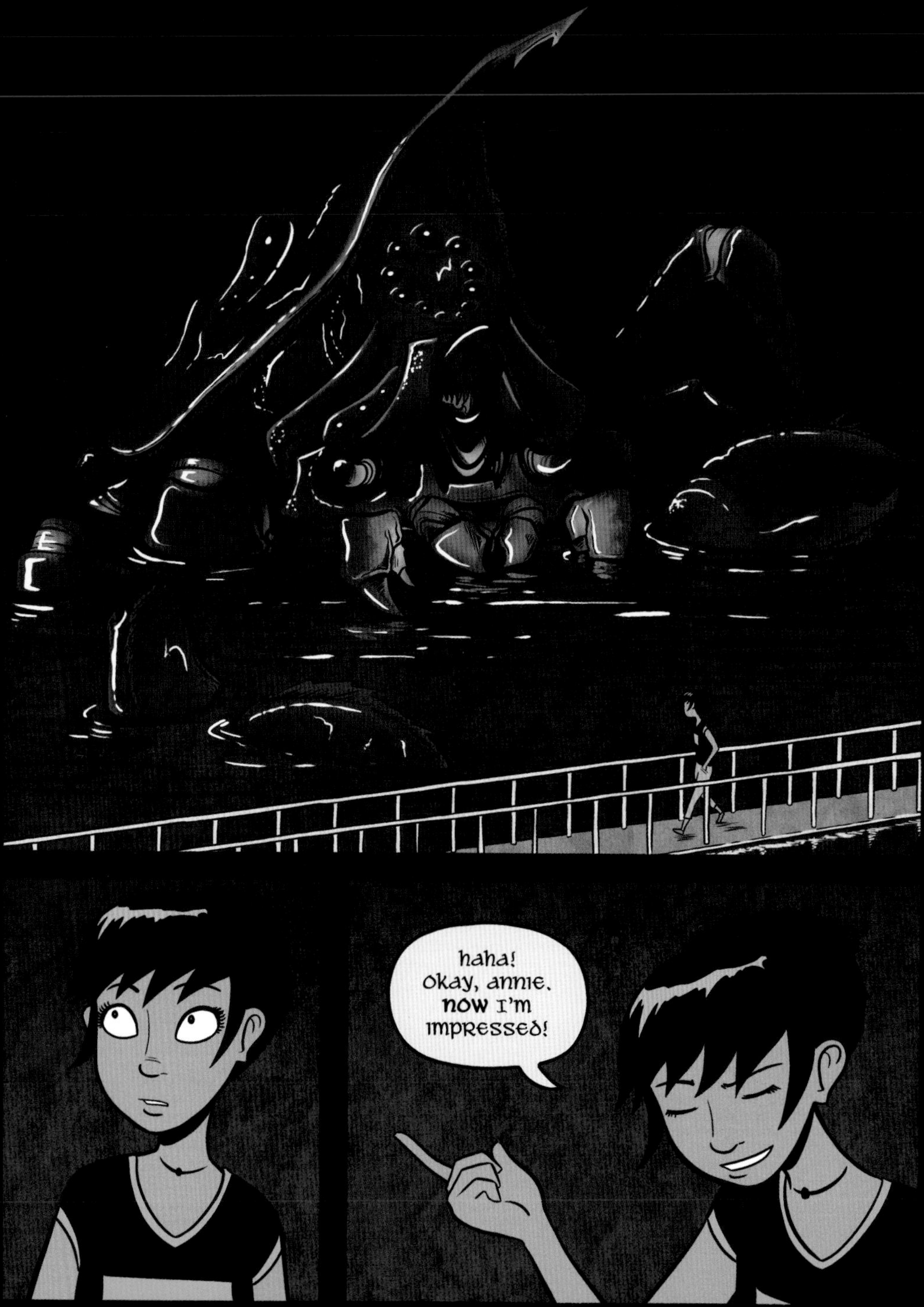
haha! okay, annie. now I'm impressed!

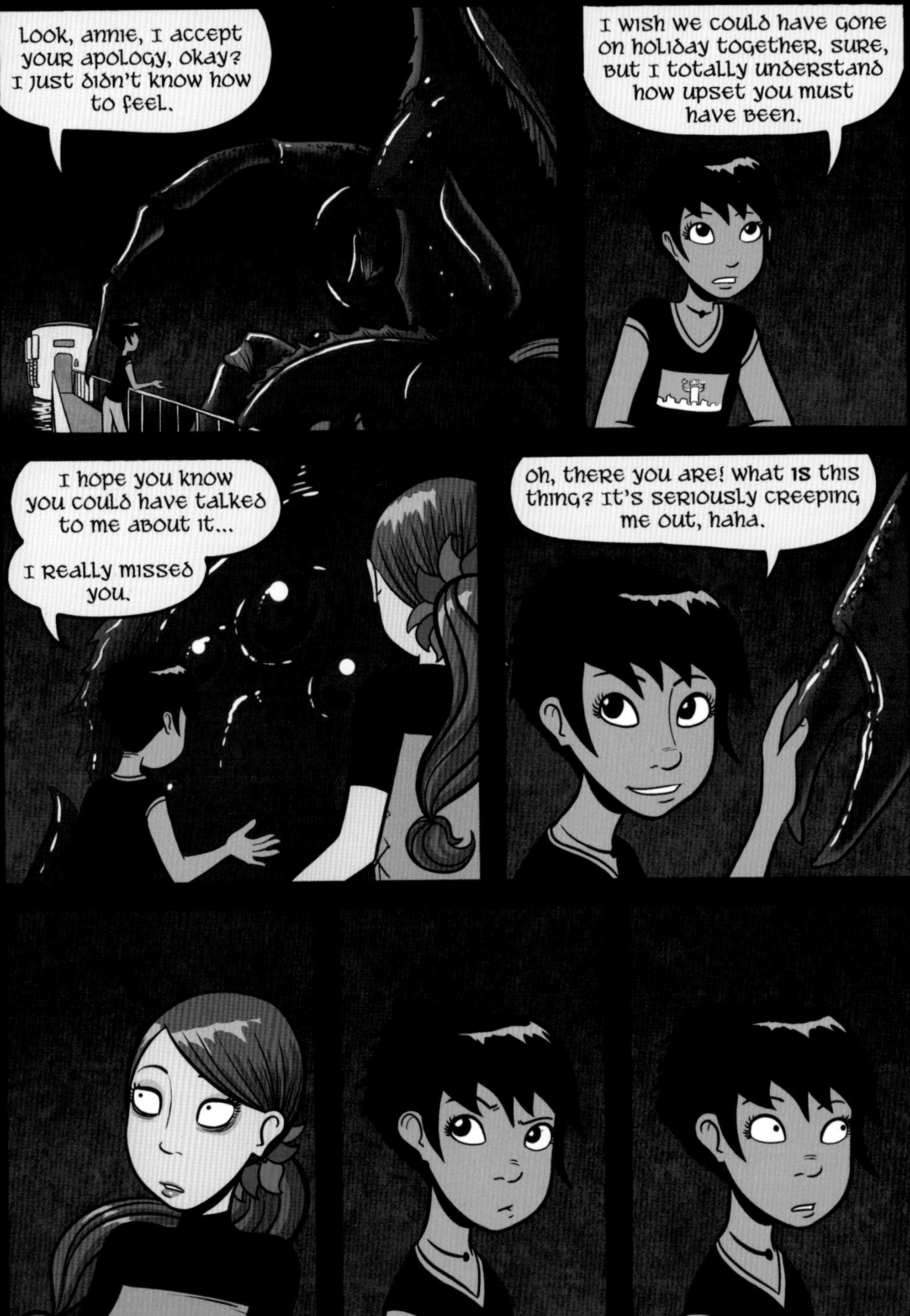
Look, annie, I accept your apology, okay? I just didn't know how to feel.
I wish we could have gone on holiday together, sure, but I totally understand how upset you must have been.
I hope you know you could have talked to me about it...
I really missed you.
Oh, there you are! What **is** this thing? It's seriously creeping me out, haha.

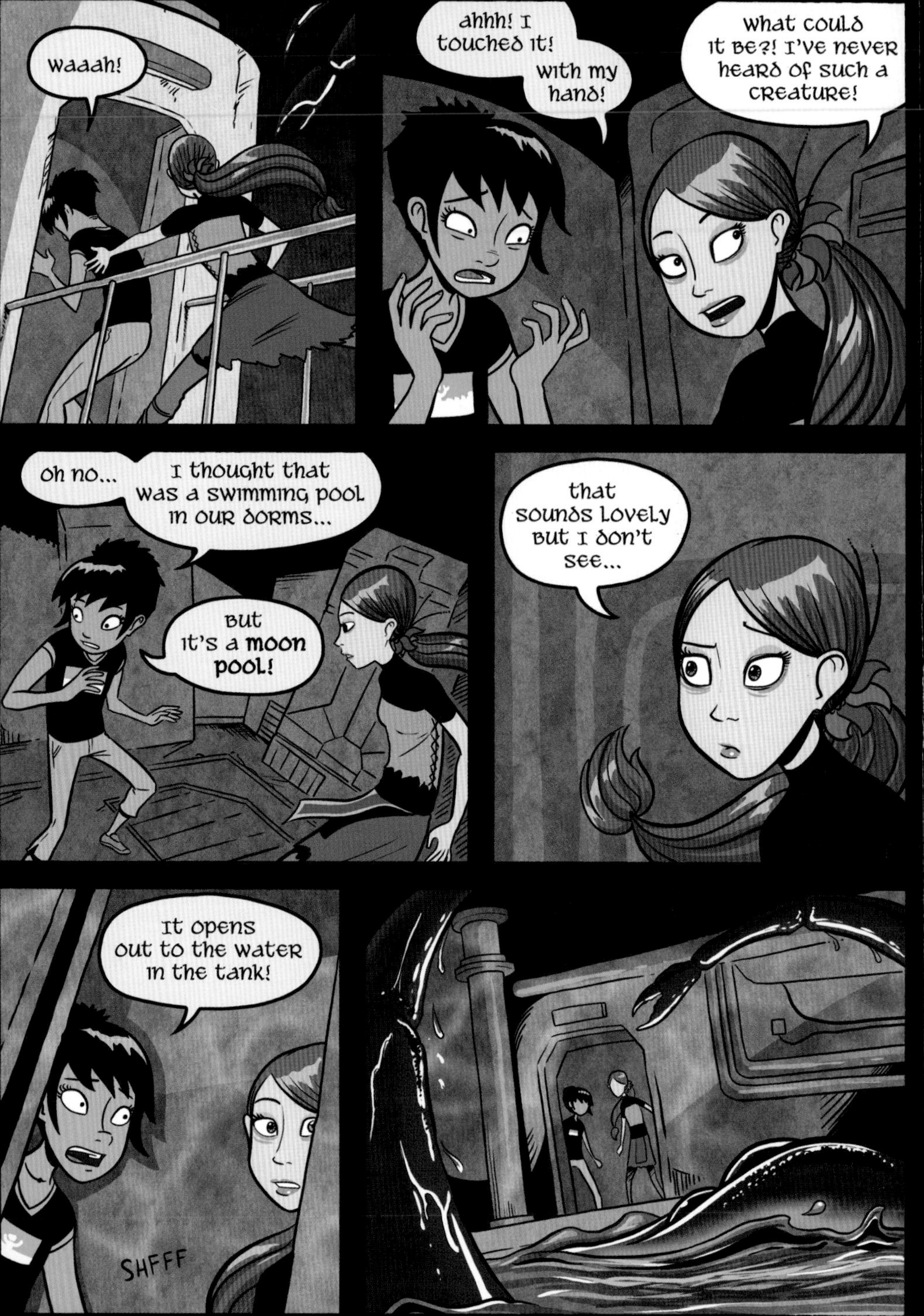
Waaah!
ahhh! I touched it!
with my hand!
What could it be?! I've never heard of such a creature!
oh no...
I thought that was a swimming pool in our dorms...
But it's a **moon pool!**
that sounds lovely but I don't see...
It opens out to the water in the tank!
SHFFF

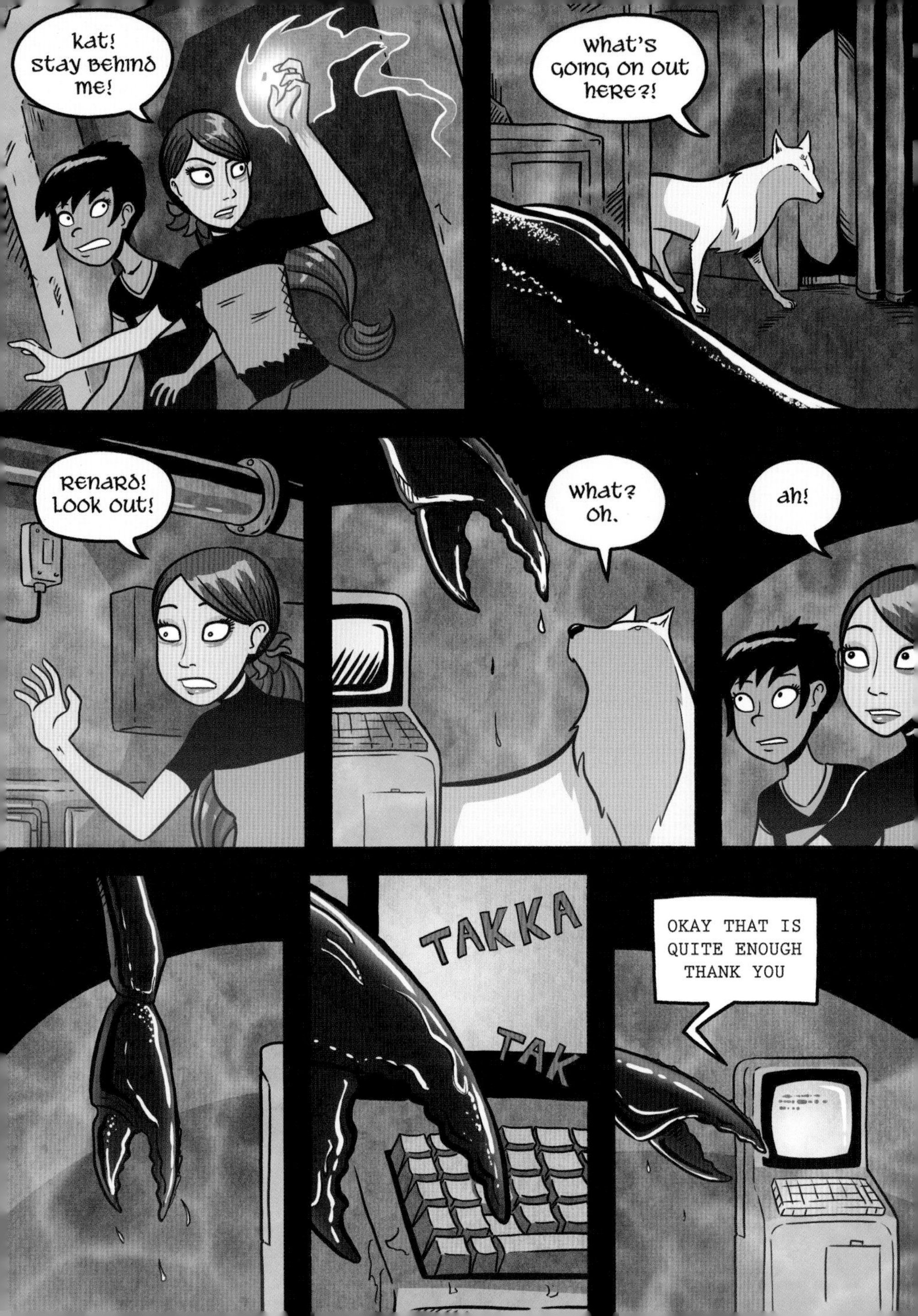
kat! stay behind me!
what's going on out here?!
Renard! Look out!
what? oh.
ah!
TAKKA
TAK
OKAY THAT IS QUITE ENOUGH THANK YOU

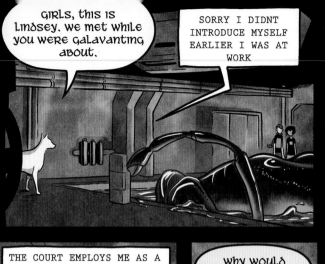

GIRLS, THIS IS LINDSEY. WE MET WHILE YOU WERE GALAVANTING ABOUT.

SORRY I DIDNT INTRODUCE MYSELF EARLIER I WAS AT WORK

YOU WORK HERE?

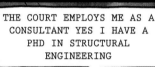

THE COURT EMPLOYS ME AS A CONSULTANT YES I HAVE A PHD IN STRUCTURAL ENGINEERING

WHY WOULD THEY UH... PUT YOU IN OUR TANK?

WELL TECHNICALLY YOU ARE IN MY TANK

I HELPED DESIGN YOUR DORMS I KEEP AN EYE ON THINGS MAKE SURE YOU HAVENT SPRUNG A LEAK HAHA

Tak Tak

THATS NOT LIKELY TO HAPPEN BY THE WAY

Tic-a-tac!
Tic!   Tac!

Tic Tac!

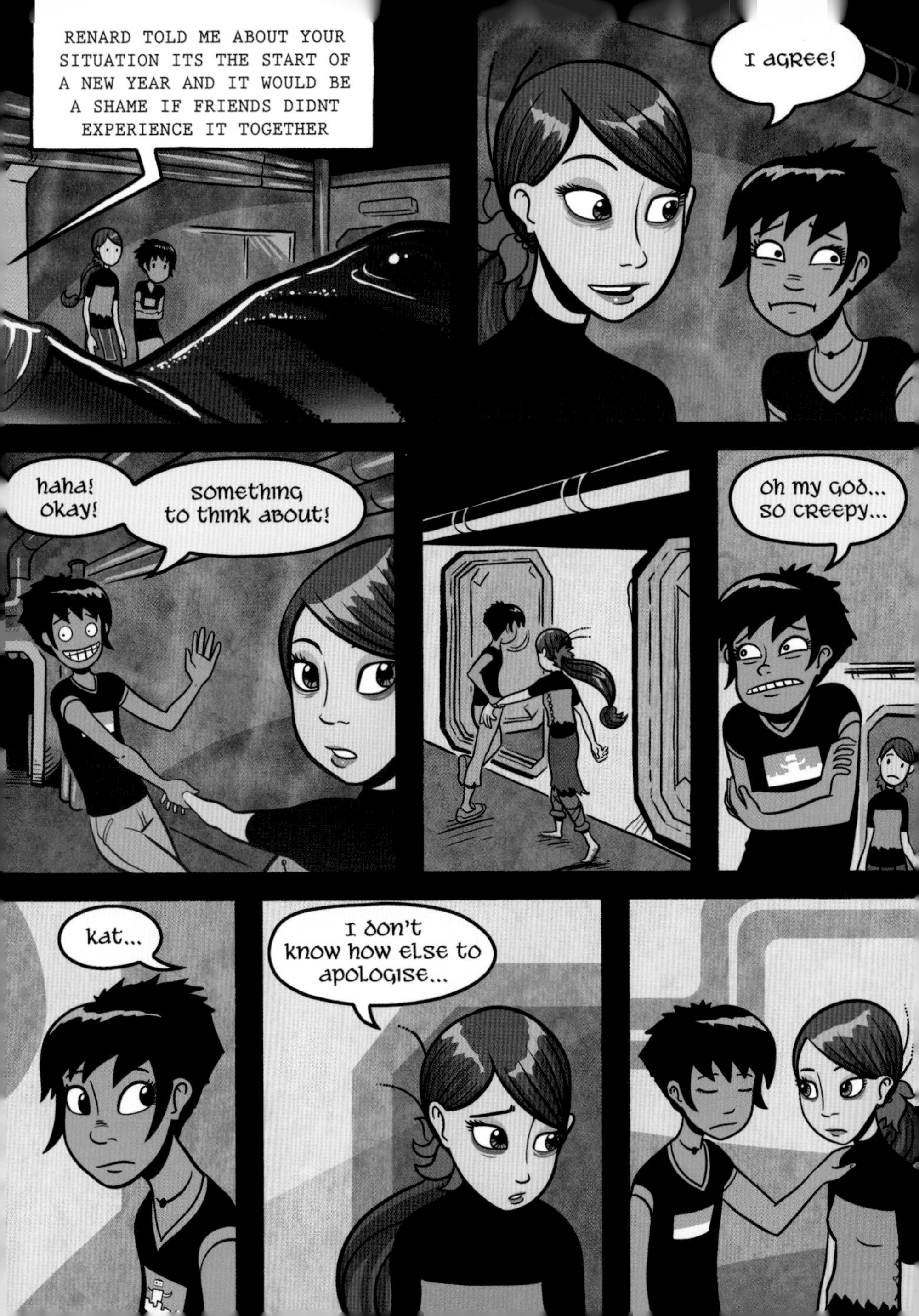
RENARD TOLD ME ABOUT YOUR SITUATION ITS THE START OF A NEW YEAR AND IT WOULD BE A SHAME IF FRIENDS DIDNT EXPERIENCE IT TOGETHER
I AGREE!
haha! Okay!
something to think about!
Oh my GOD... SO CREEPY...
kat...
I don't know how else to apologise...

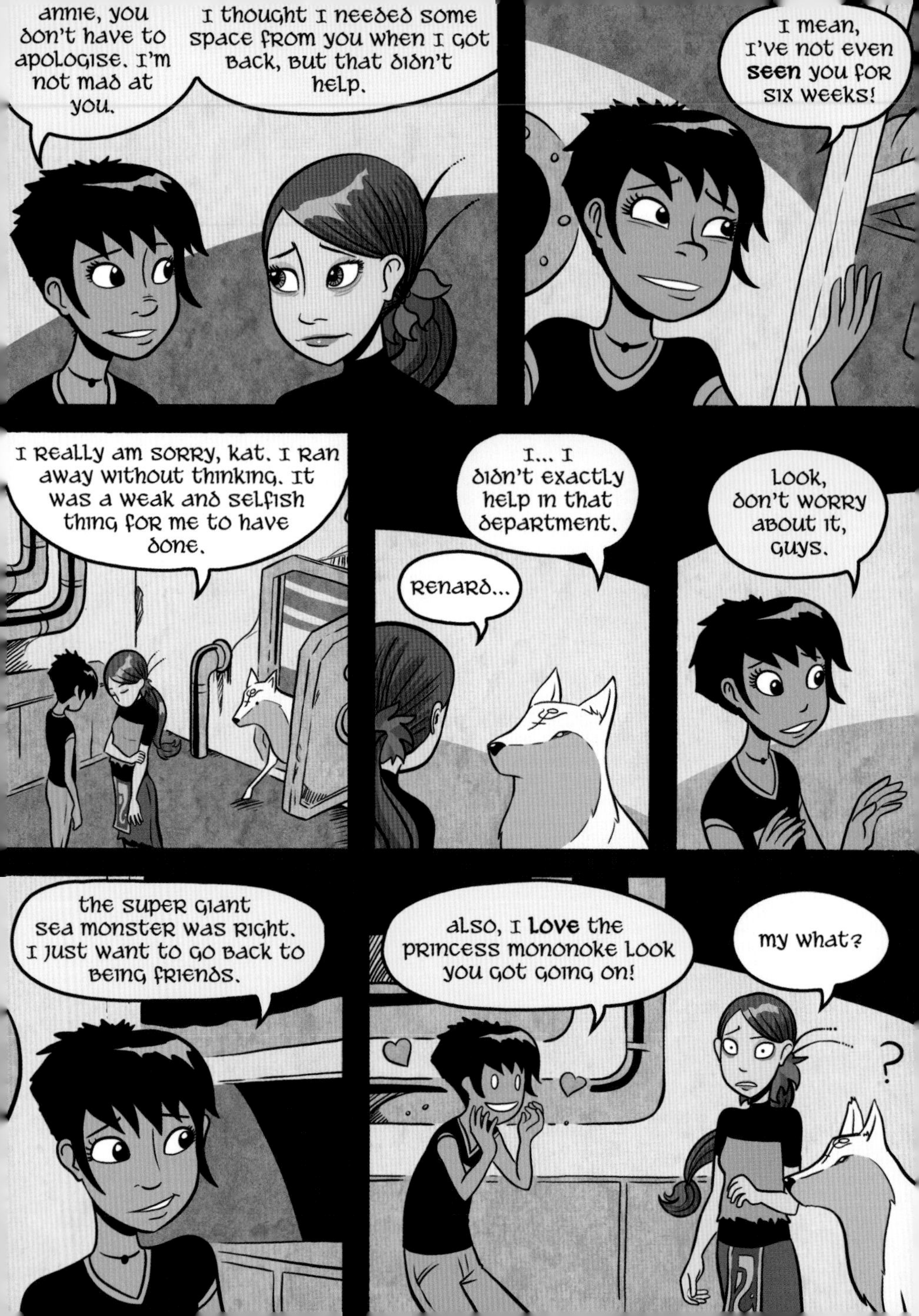
annie, you don't have to apologise. I'm not mad at you.
I thought I needed some space from you when I got back, but that didn't help.
I mean, I've not even **seen** you for six weeks!
I really am sorry, kat. I ran away without thinking. It was a weak and selfish thing for me to have done.
I... I didn't exactly help in that department.
Renard...
Look, don't worry about it, guys.
the super giant sea monster was right. I just want to go back to being friends.
also, I **love** the princess mononoke look you got going on!
my what?
?

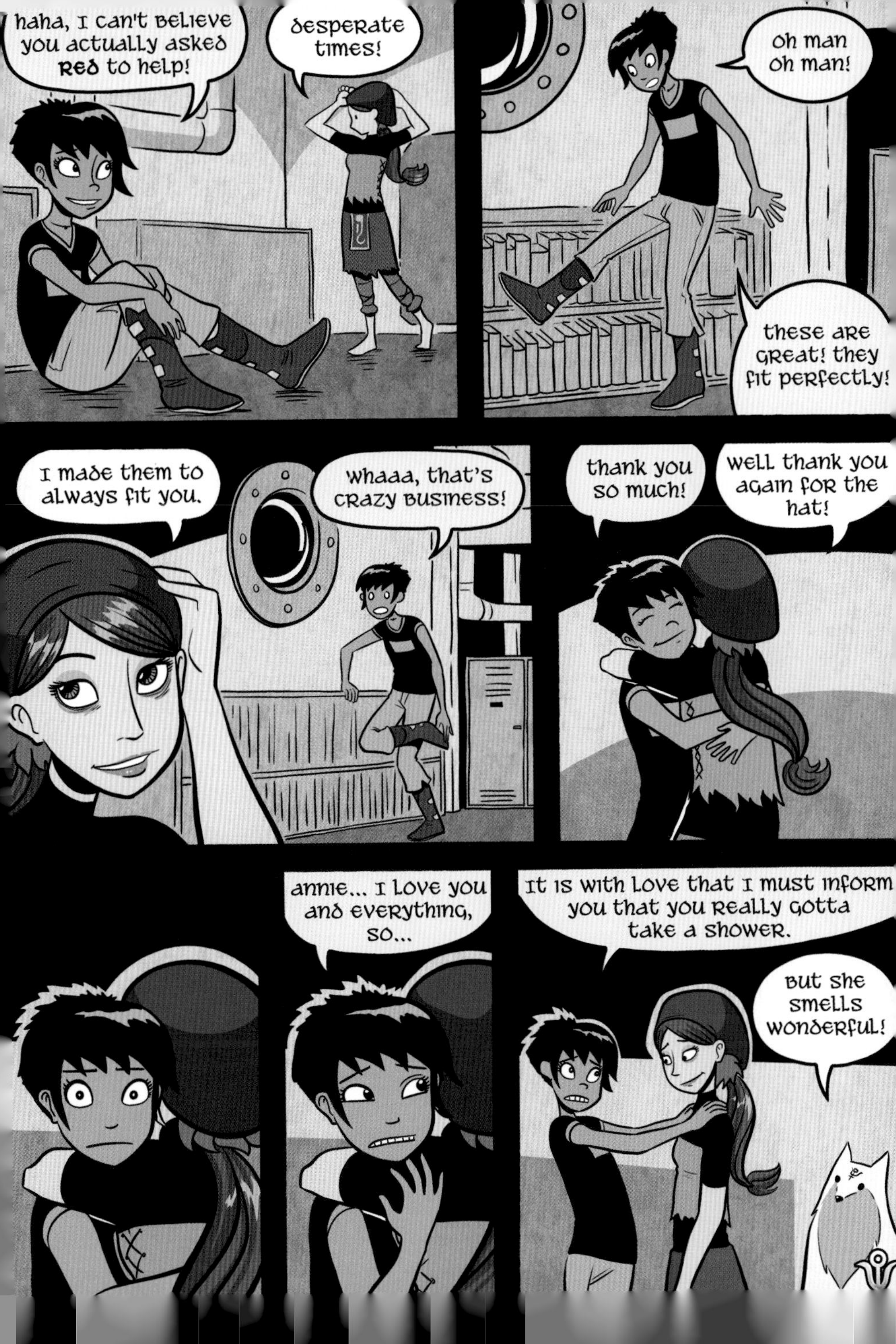
haha, I can't believe you actually asked Red to help!
desperate times!
Oh man oh man!
these are great! they fit perfectly!
I made them to always fit you.
whaaa, that's crazy business!
thank you so much!
well thank you again for the hat!
annie... I love you and everything, so...
It is with love that I must inform you that you really gotta take a shower.
But she smells wonderful!

WELCOME!

TO YEAR 9

Hello, new Year 9 students, and welcome back to school! Your dorm this year is a retrofitted, sub aquatic, deep sea oil drilling platform prototype. Please refer to the provided instructional manual for essential information on your new habitat. Above all, please be aware that your new dorm is

PERFECTLY SAFE!

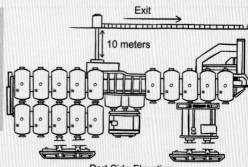

Exit

10 meters

Port Side Elevation

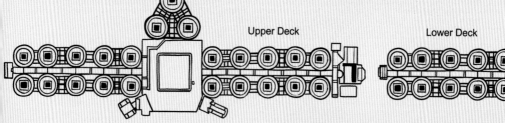

Upper Deck

Lower Deck

My name is LINDSEY!
I am what is known as a MEROSTOMATAZON.
You may see me now and then as I look after certain functions of your dorm, but please

DO NOT PANIC

In fact, I am happy to chat if you need anything, or are just feeling lonely!*

DID YOU KNOW:

- My Husband, Bud, looks after the boys' dorms!

- I have 47 eyes, and 15 not-eyes!

- A portion of my brain functions in a different dimension!

- I am an accredited couples therapist!

*I am unable to feel loneliness

Gunnerkrigg Court

Chapter 33:

Give and Take

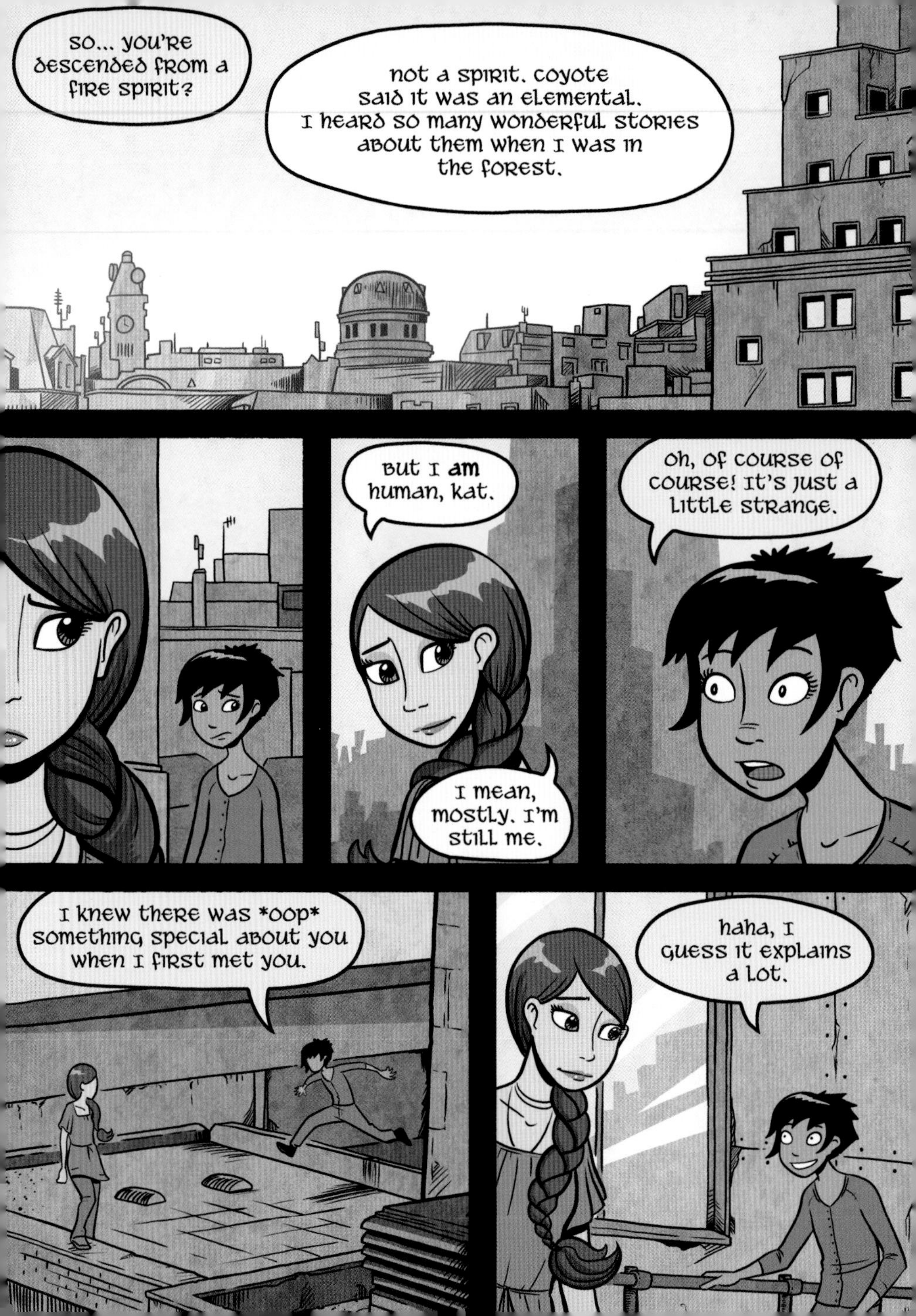
so... you're descended from a fire spirit?
not a spirit. coyote said it was an elemental. I heard so many wonderful stories about them when I was in the forest.
But I **am** human, kat.
I mean, mostly. I'm still me.
Oh, of course of course! It's just a little strange.
I knew there was *oop* something special about you when I first met you.
haha, I guess it explains a lot.

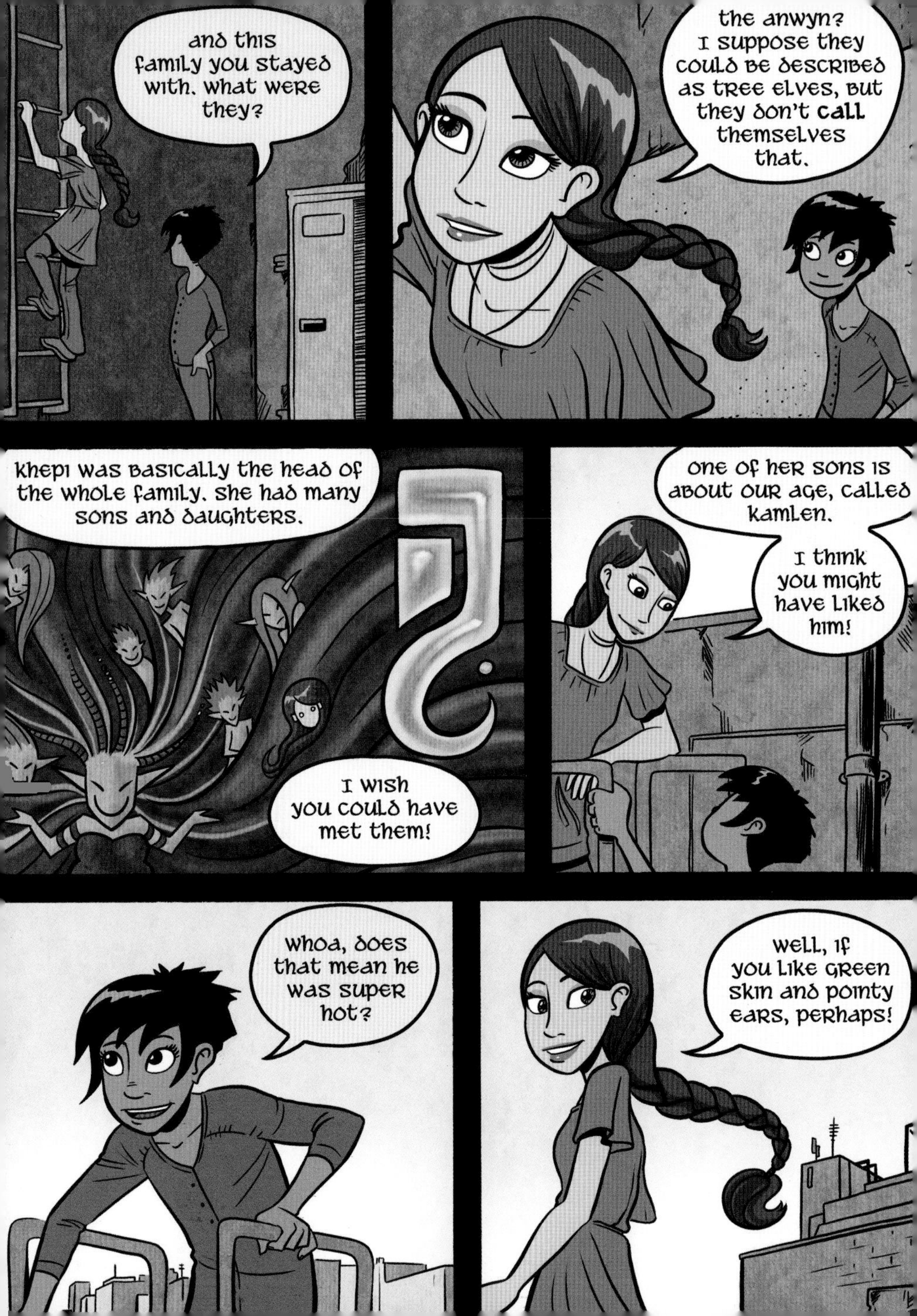
and this family you stayed with. what were they?
the anwyn? I suppose they could be described as tree elves, but they don't **call** themselves that.
khepi was basically the head of the whole family. she had many sons and daughters.
I wish you could have met them!
one of her sons is about our age, called kamlen.
I think you might have liked him!
whoa, does that mean he was super hot?
well, if you like green skin and pointy ears, perhaps!

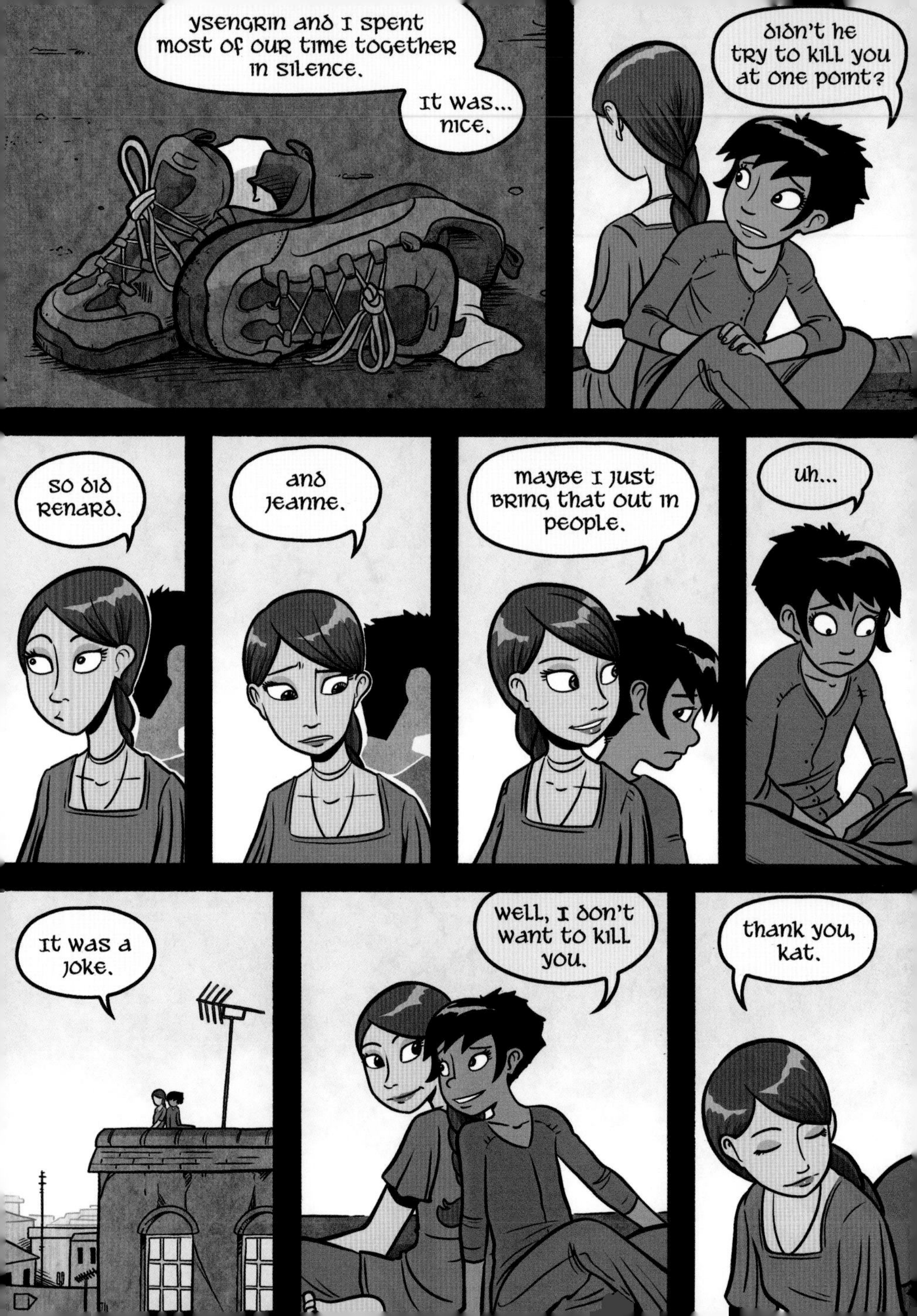
Ysengrin and I spent most of our time together in silence.
It was... nice.
Didn't he try to kill you at one point?
So did Renard.
And Jeanne.
Maybe I just bring that out in people.
Uh...
It was a joke.
Well, I don't want to kill you.
Thank you, Kat.

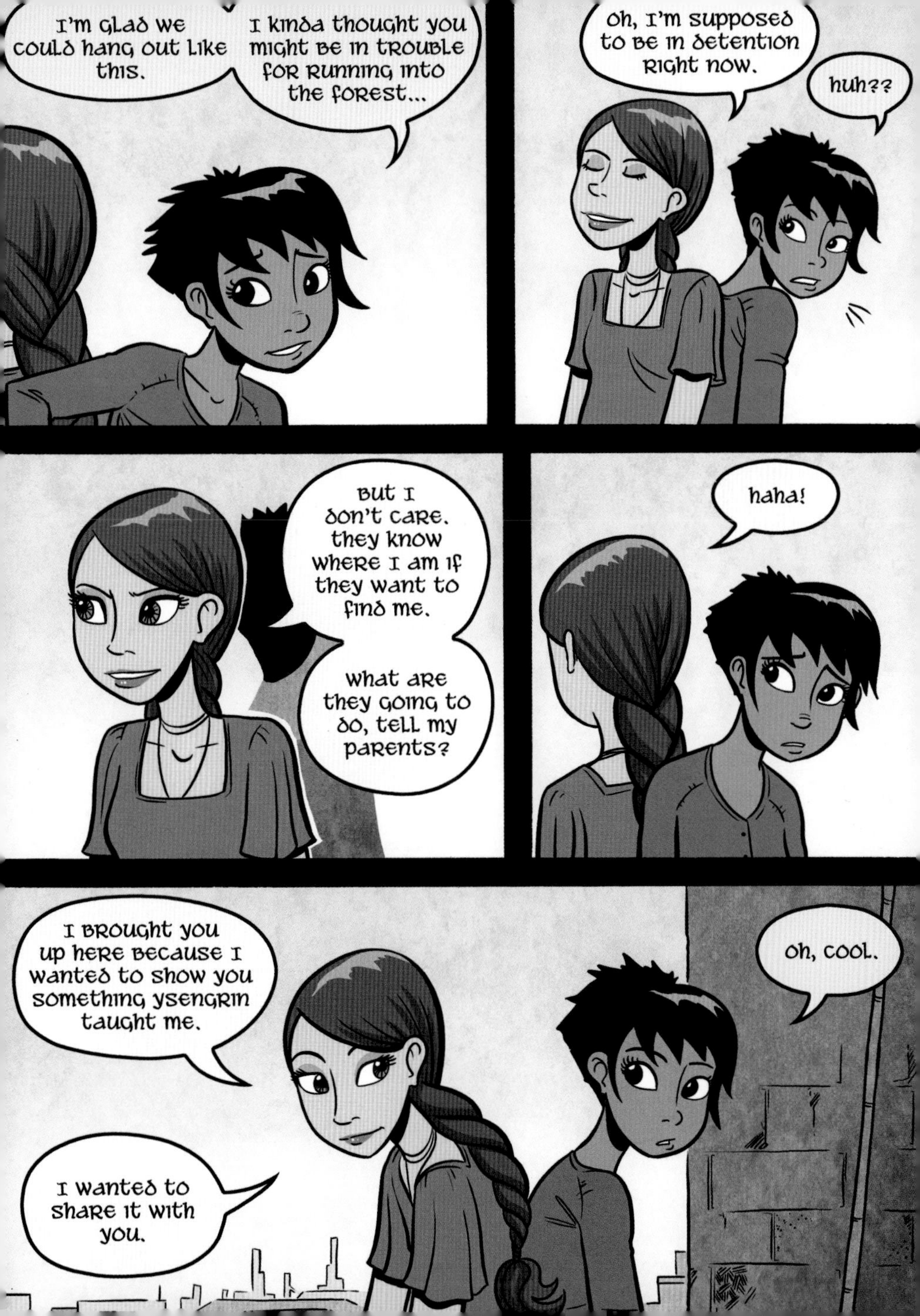
I'm glad we could hang out like this.
I kinda thought you might be in trouble for running into the forest...
Oh, I'm supposed to be in detention right now.
huh??
But I don't care. They know where I am if they want to find me.
What are they going to do, tell my parents?
haha!
I brought you up here because I wanted to show you something Ysengrin taught me.
Oh, cool.
I wanted to share it with you.

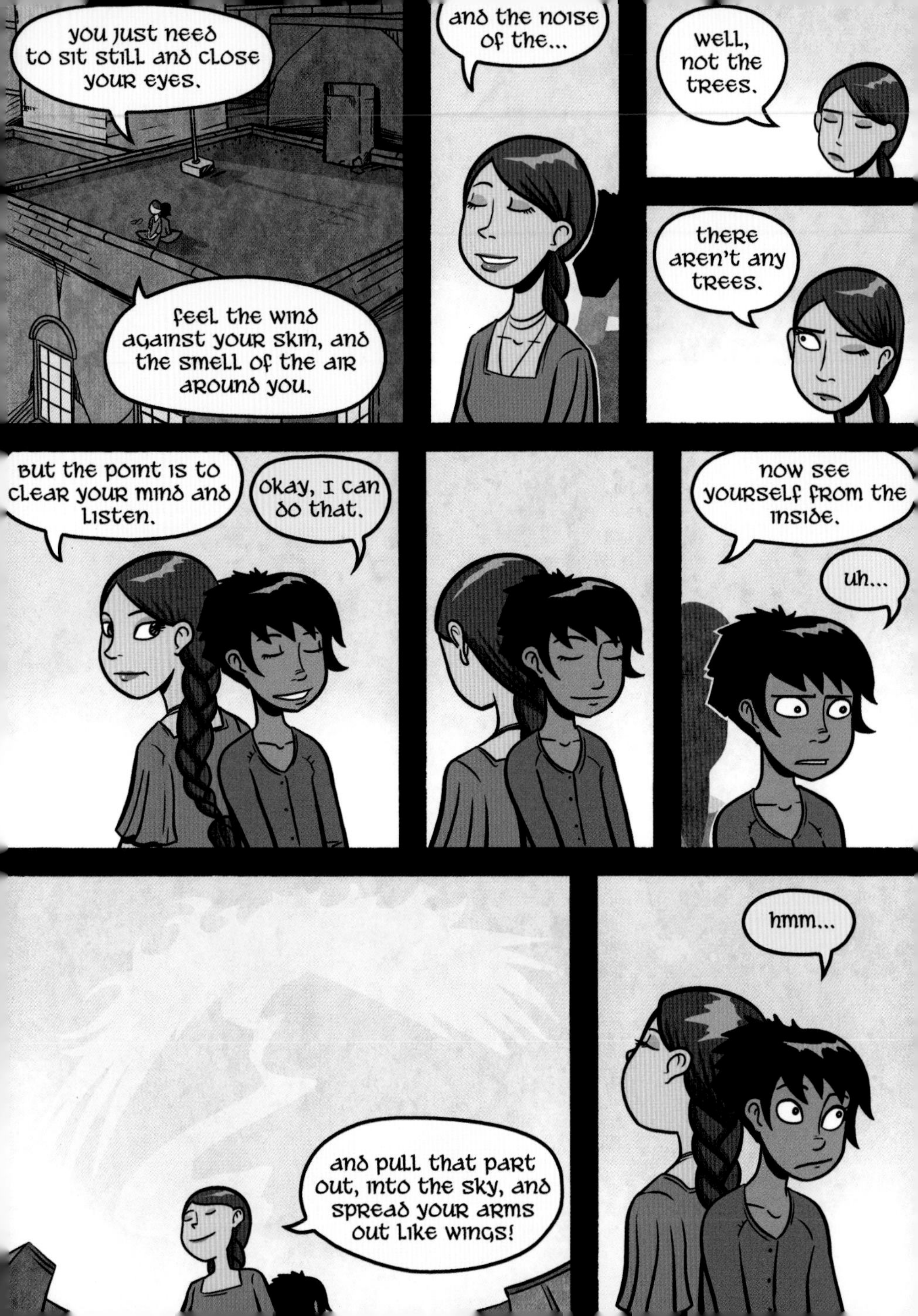
you just need to sit still and close your eyes.
feel the wind against your skin, and the smell of the air around you.
and the noise of the...
well, not the trees.
there aren't any trees.
but the point is to clear your mind and listen.
okay, I can do that.
now see yourself from the inside.
uh...
and pull that part out, into the sky, and spread your arms out like wings!
hmm...

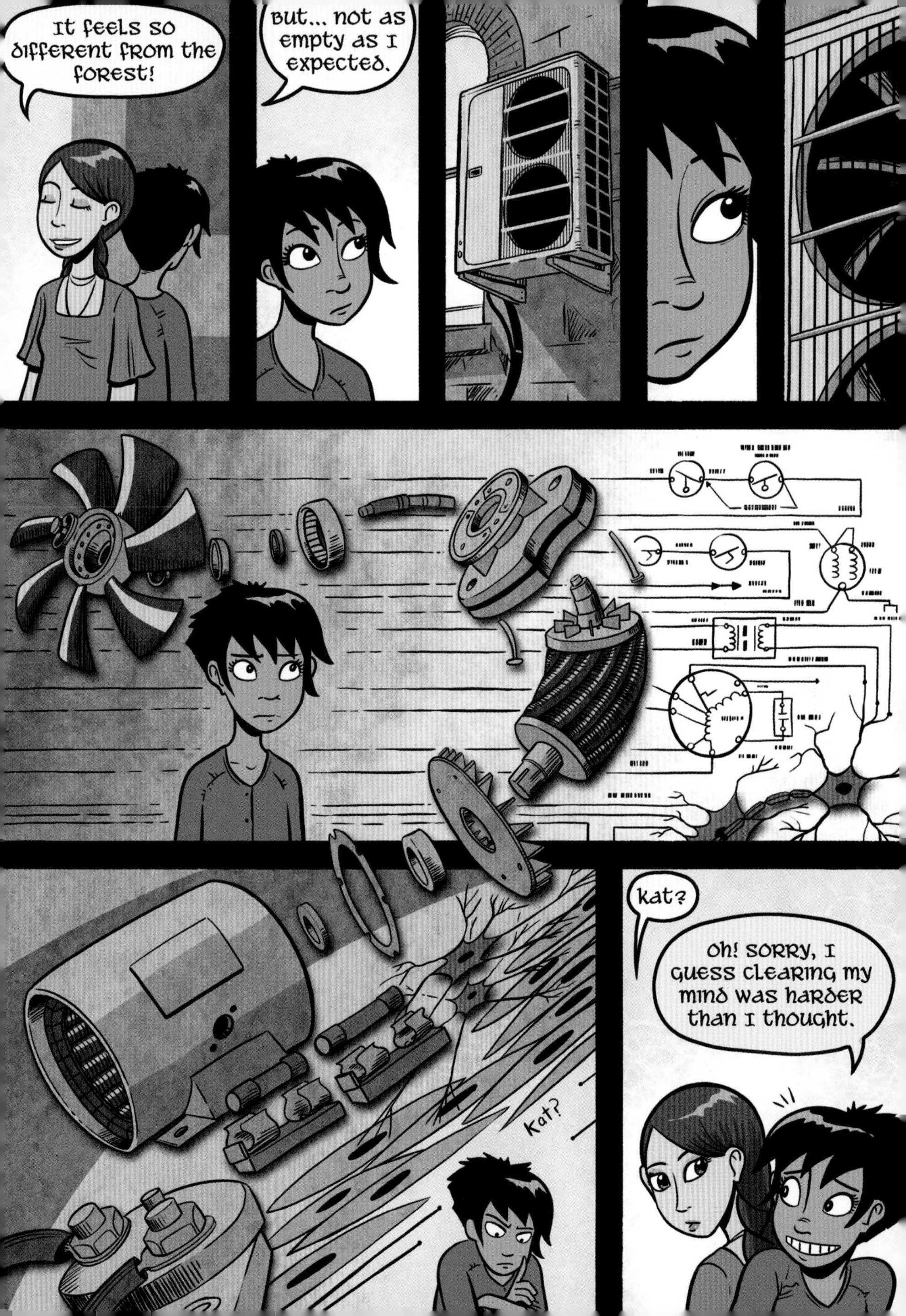
It feels so different from the forest!
But... not as empty as I expected.
Kat?
Kat?
Oh! Sorry, I guess clearing my mind was harder than I thought.

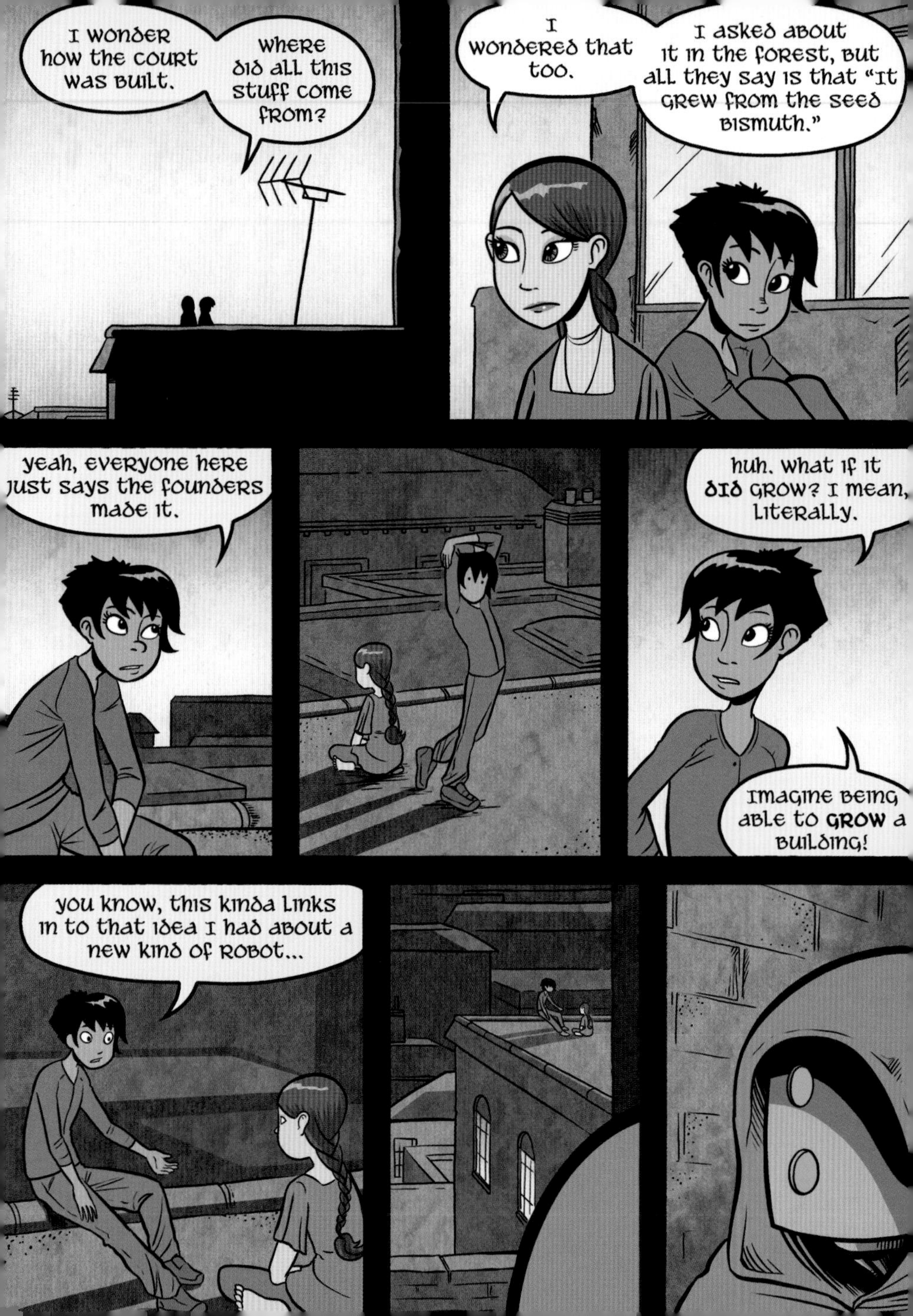
I wonder how the court was built.
where did all this stuff come from?
I wondered that too.
I asked about it in the forest, but all they say is that "It grew from the seed Bismuth."
yeah, everyone here just says the founders made it.
huh. what if it did grow? I mean, literally.
Imagine being able to grow a building!
you know, this kinda links in to that idea I had about a new kind of robot...

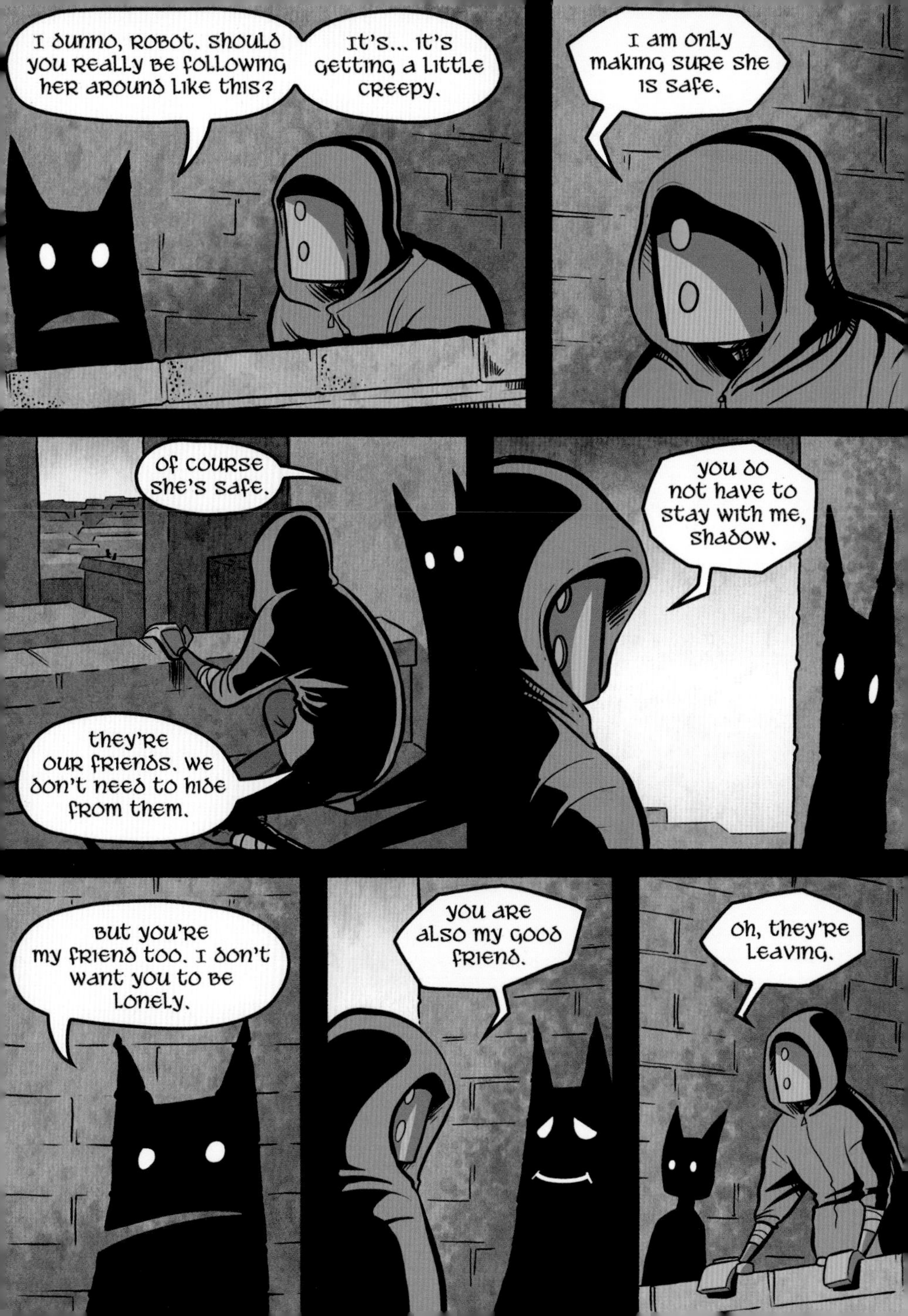
I dunno, Robot. Should you really be following her around like this?
It's... it's getting a little creepy.
I am only making sure she is safe.
Of course she's safe.
They're our friends. We don't need to hide from them.
You do not have to stay with me, Shadow.
But you're my friend too. I don't want you to be lonely.
You are also my good friend.
Oh, they're leaving.

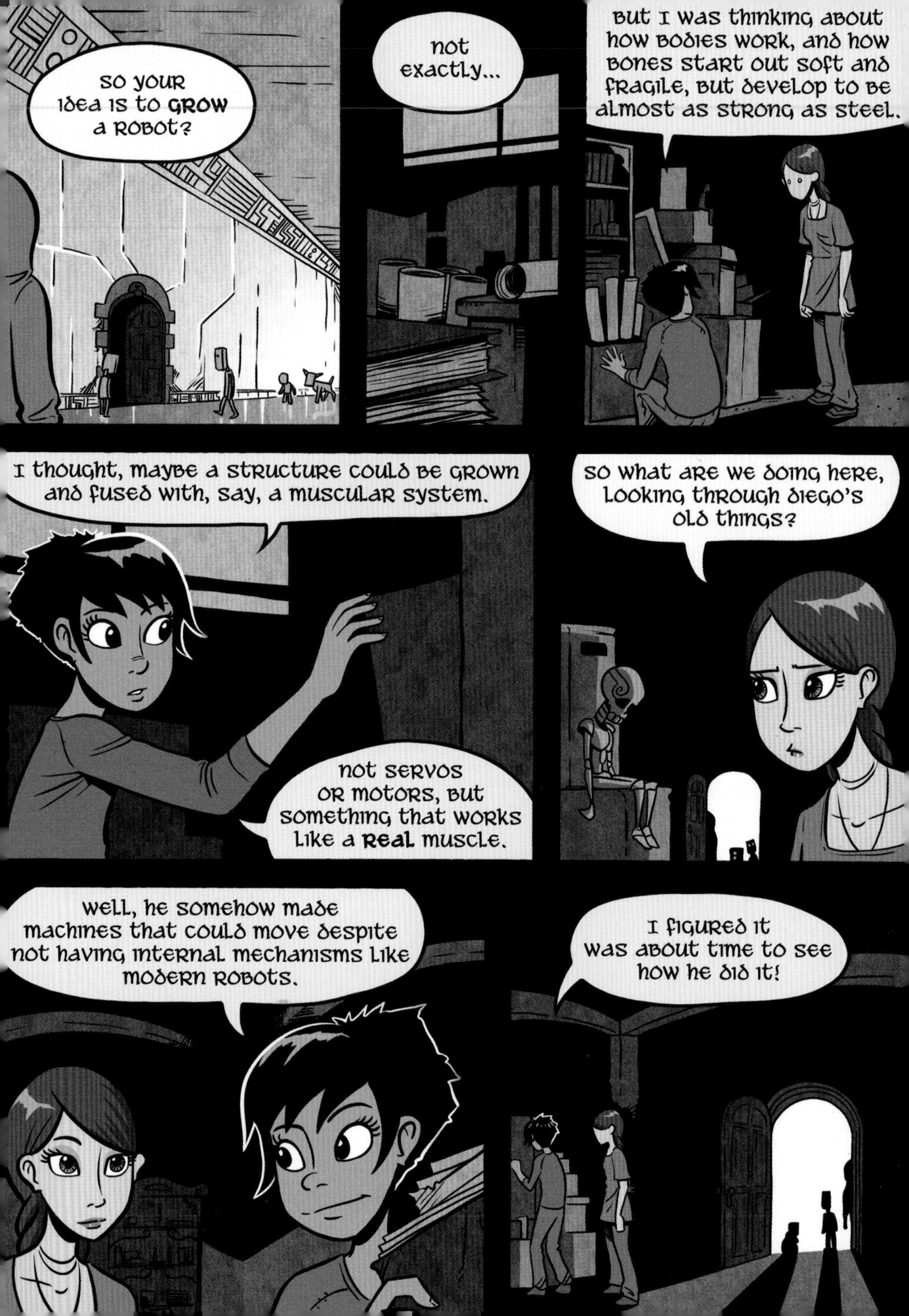
So your idea is to grow a robot?
Not exactly...
But I was thinking about how bodies work, and how bones start out soft and fragile, but develop to be almost as strong as steel.
I thought, maybe a structure could be grown and fused with, say, a muscular system.
Not servos or motors, but something that works like a real muscle.
So what are we doing here, looking through Diego's old things?
Well, he somehow made machines that could move despite not having internal mechanisms like modern robots.
I figured it was about time to see how he did it!

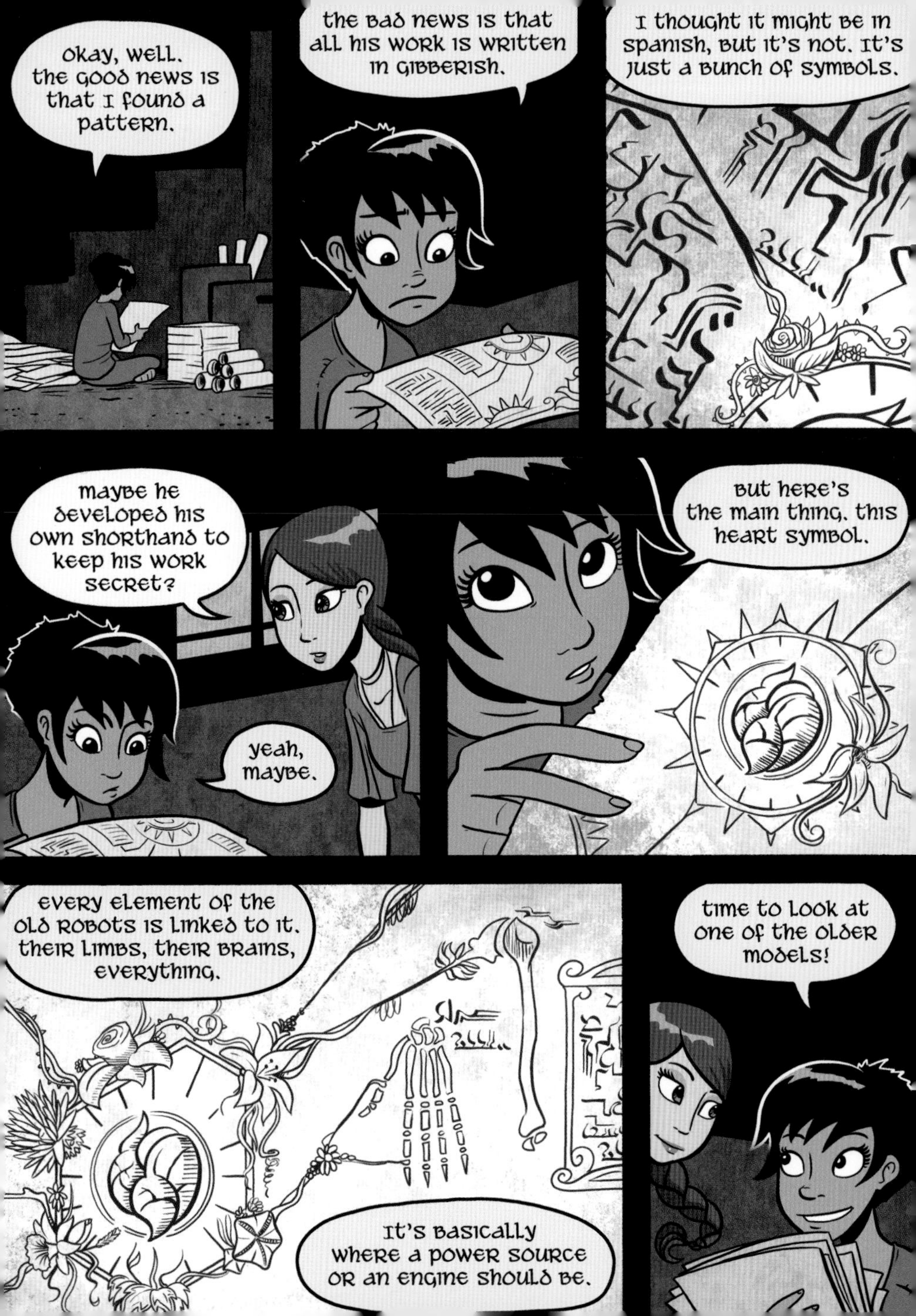

Okay, well. the good news is that I found a pattern.
the bad news is that all his work is written in gibberish.
I thought it might be in spanish, but it's not. It's just a bunch of symbols.
maybe he developed his own shorthand to keep his work secret?
yeah, maybe.
But here's the main thing. this heart symbol.
every element of the old robots is linked to it. their limbs, their brains, everything.
It's basically where a power source or an engine should be.
time to look at one of the older models!

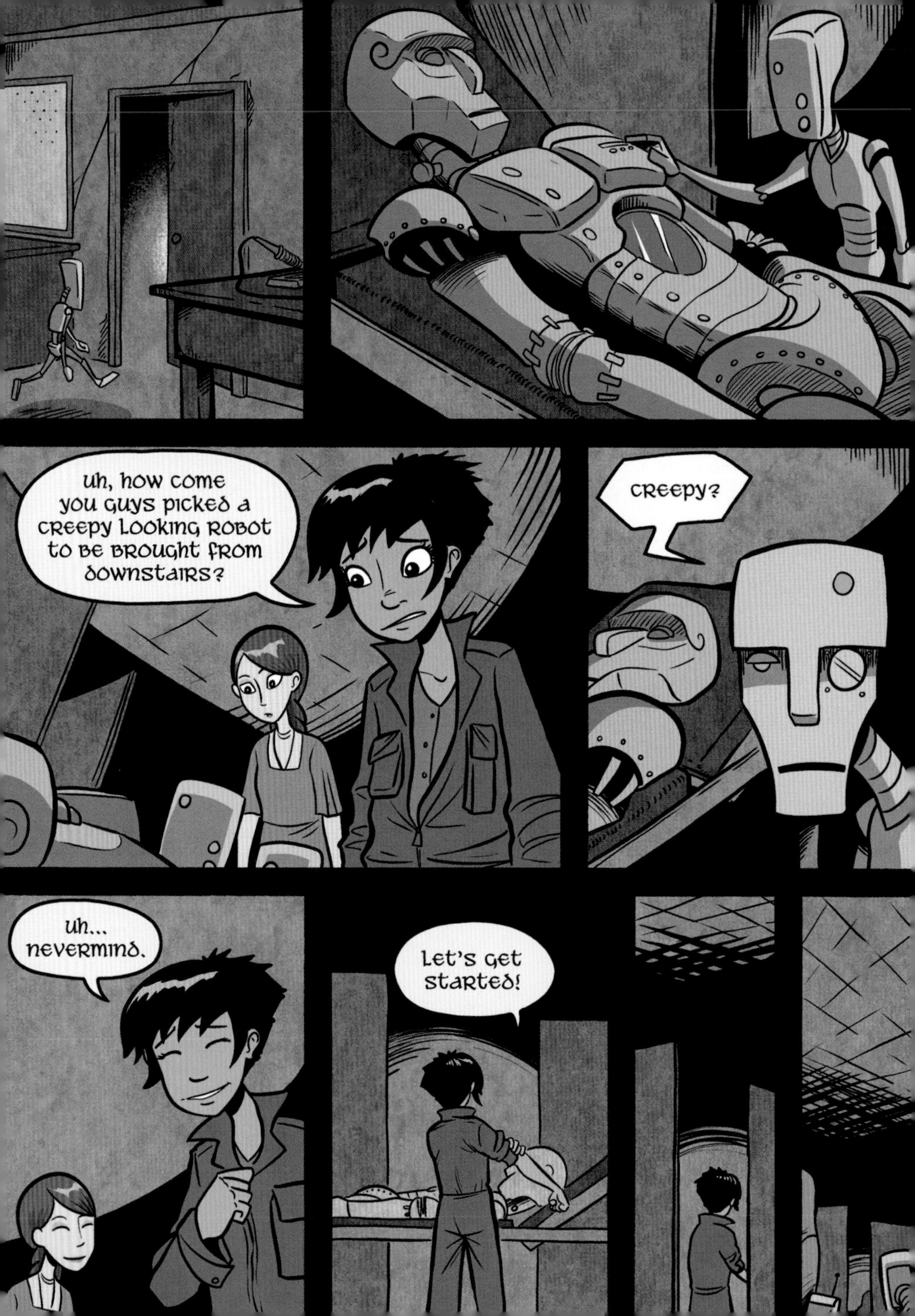
uh, how come you guys picked a creepy looking robot to be brought from downstairs?
creepy?
uh... nevermind.
let's get started!

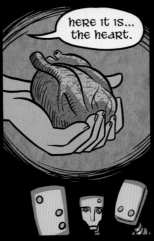
here it is... the heart.

It feels like a lump of ceramic, but...

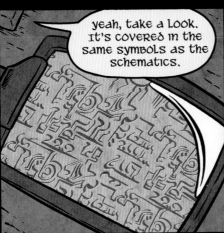
yeah, take a look. It's covered in the same symbols as the schematics.

It's beautiful...

yeah, but what is it for?

Kat... what if these are not really robots in the modern sense, but golems?

huh? wha?

a golem is inanimate matter brought to life with a set of instructions.

what if these hearts really do provide power, but through etheric means?

 **come on! golems are just... fairytales!**

they can't be real!

 **just as fire elementals can't be real?**

no! I didn't mean it like that!

haha, it's okay.

 **but... this would mean diego was a... magician, not a scientist.**

not necessarily.

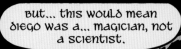

what are the modern robots if not inanimate material given life with the instructions in their software?

um, no offence.

none taken!

diego's work led to the creation of very real, tangible machines.

they may not be the SAME, but their inspiration came from him.

and you see the results before you now.

hmmm...

SEVERAL
DAYS PASS

YAAAWN!

UM...
MISS KAT.

HEY.

ABOUT THAT
OPERATING CODE YOU
ASKED US TO PRINT...

OH RIGHT, YEAH. I
FORGOT ABOUT
THAT.

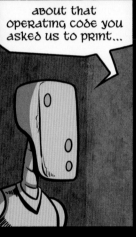

JUST IN TIME, TOO. I WAS RUNNING OUT OF IDEAS.
I GUESS YOU GUYS DID A BETTER JOB OF CREATING
YOUR OWN CODE BASED ON DIEGO'S DESIGNS
THAN I DID.

WHERE
IS IT?

HERE.

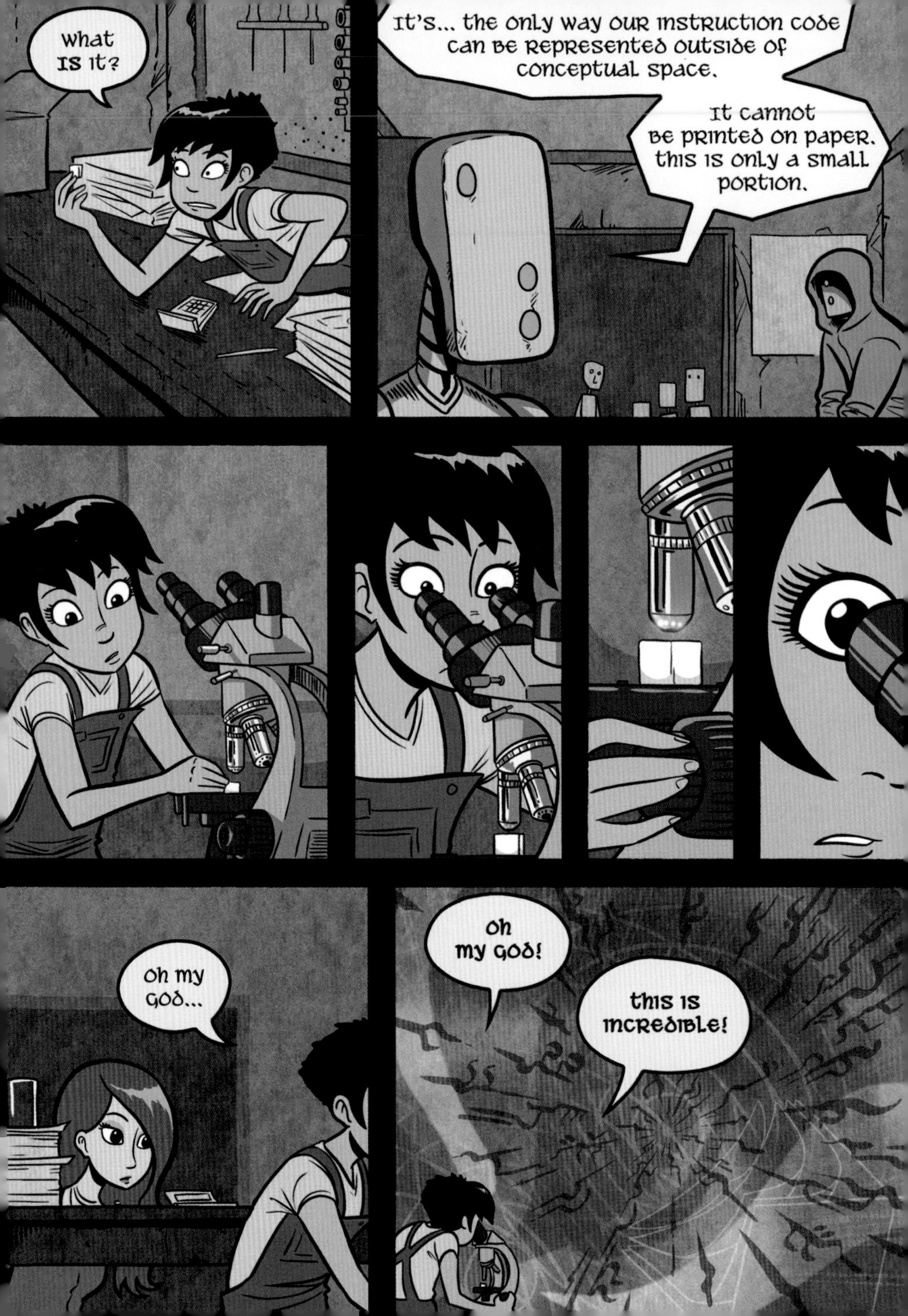
What IS it?
It's... the only way our instruction code can be represented outside of conceptual space.
It cannot be printed on paper. this is only a small portion.
Oh my god...
Oh my god!
this is incredible!

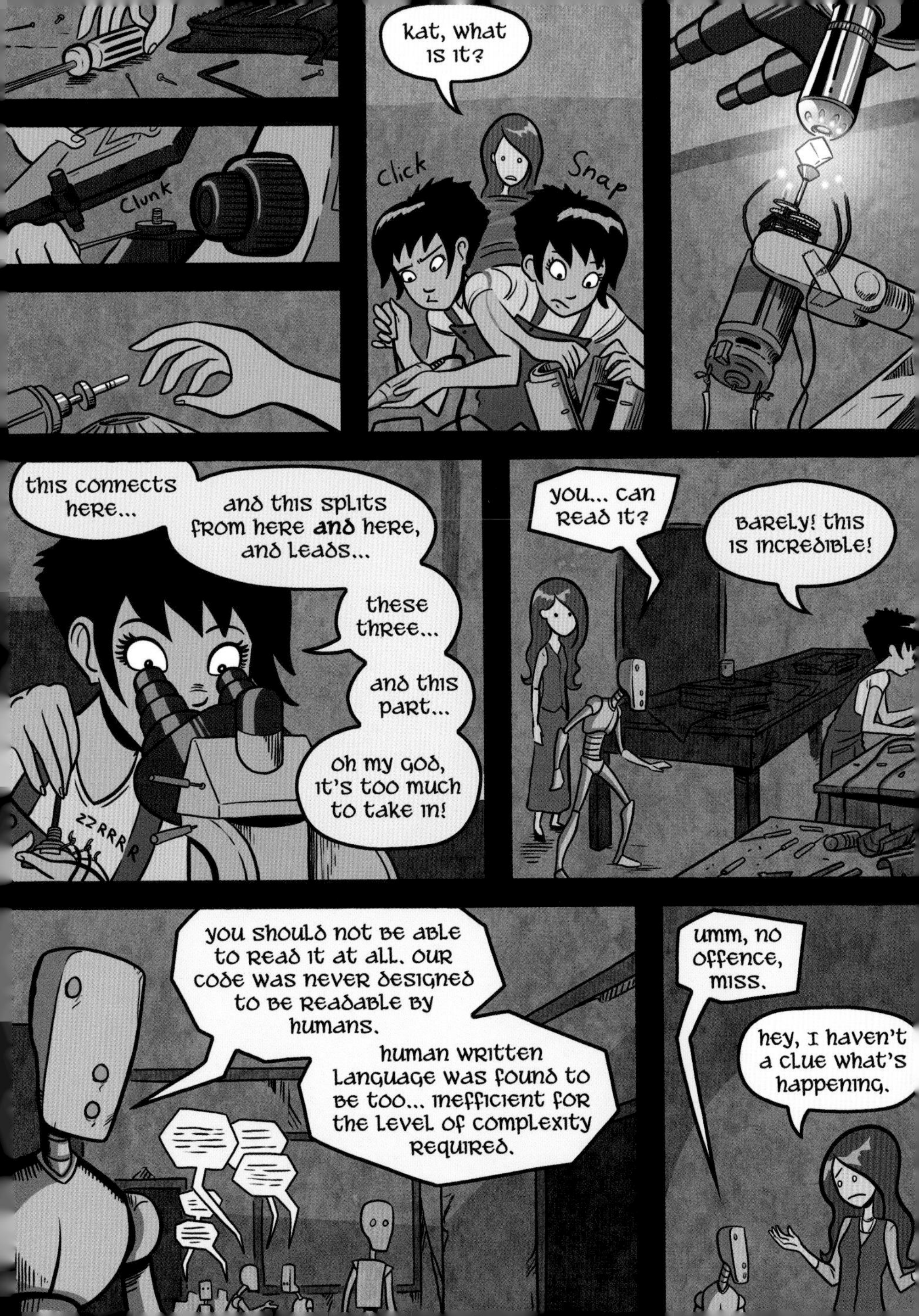
Clunk
kat, what is it?
Click
Snap
this connects here...
and this splits from here **and** here, and leads...
these three...
and this part...
oh my god, it's too much to take in!
ZZRRRR
you... can read it?
barely! this is incredible!
you should not be able to read it at all. our code was never designed to be readable by humans.
human written language was found to be too... inefficient for the level of complexity required.
umm, no offence, miss.
hey, I haven't a clue what's happening.

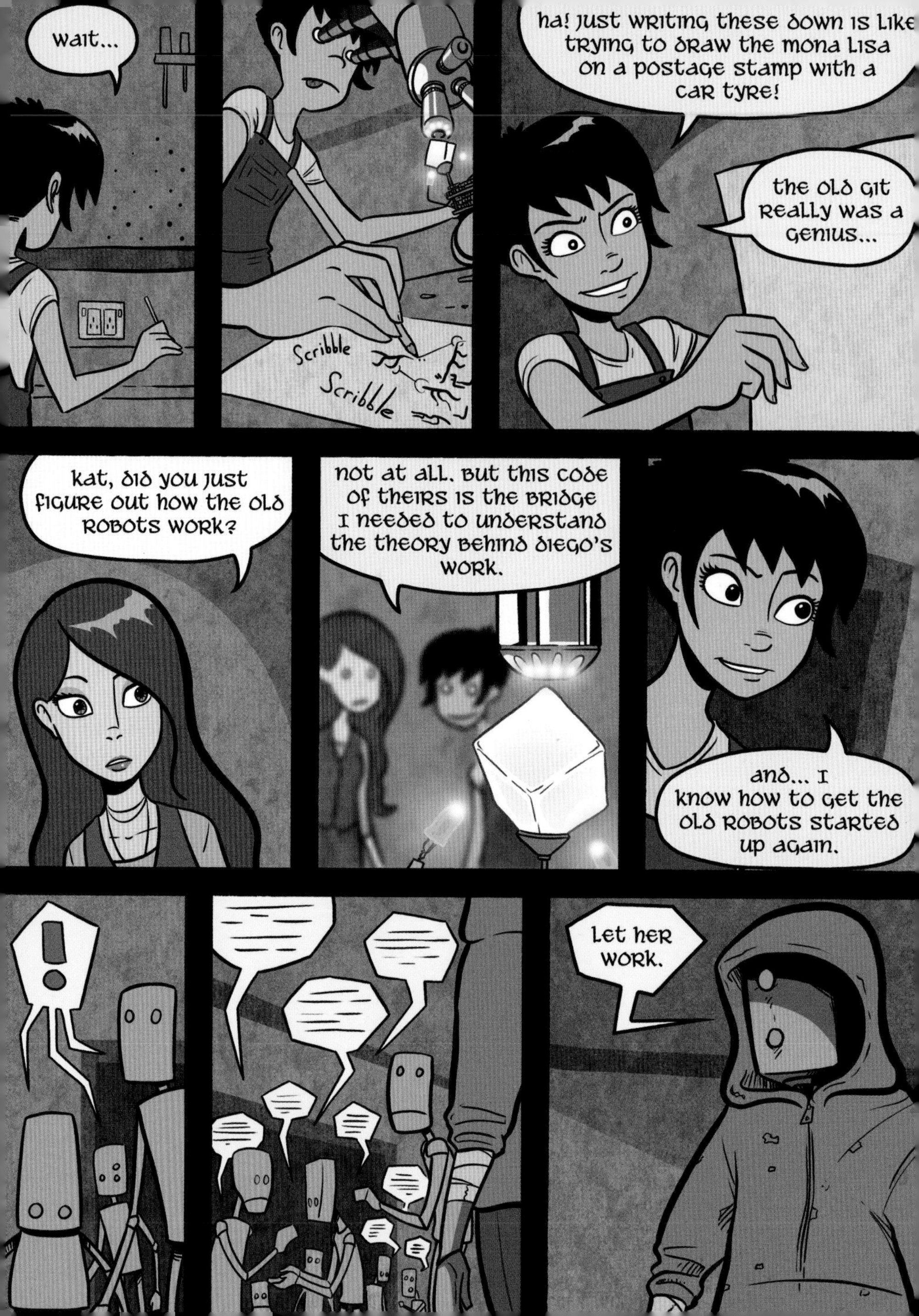
wait...
Scribble
Scribble
ha! just writing these down is like trying to draw the mona lisa on a postage stamp with a car tyre!
the old git really was a genius...
kat, did you just figure out how the old robots work?
not at all. but this code of theirs is the bridge I needed to understand the theory behind diego's work.
and... I know how to get the old robots started up again.
!
Let her work.

SEE, HERE. THIS TINY SCRATCH SEVERED THIS SYMBOL.

IT'S DEEP ENOUGH TO BE MORE THAN JUST SURFACE DAMAGE.

BUT? I THINK I CAN MAKE A BYPASS FOR IT...

I GUESS IT WAS ENOUGH TO SHUT DOWN THE ROBOT.

THERE...

I THINK THAT'S~

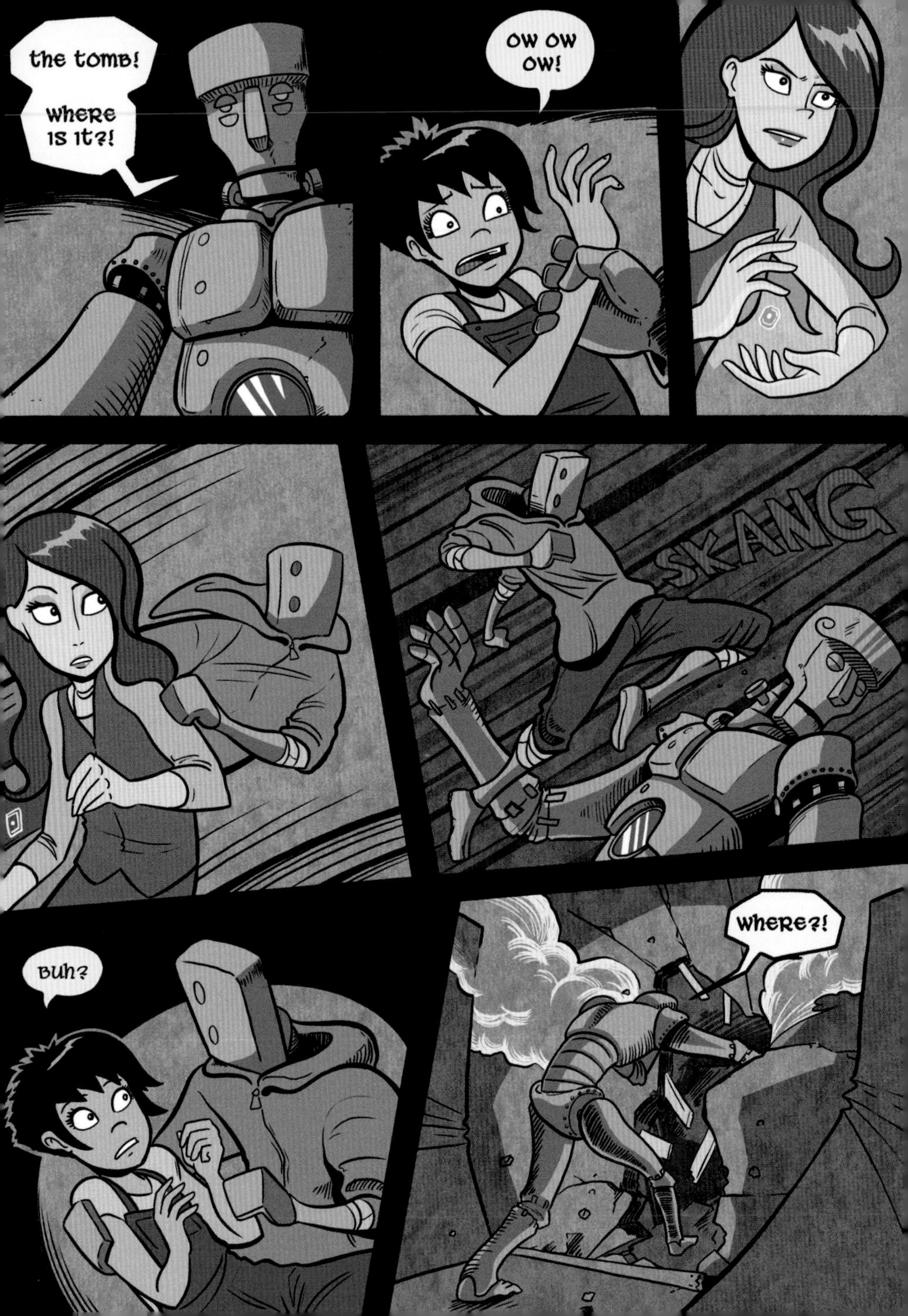
the tomb!
where is it?!
OW OW OW!
SKANG
BUH?
WHERE?!

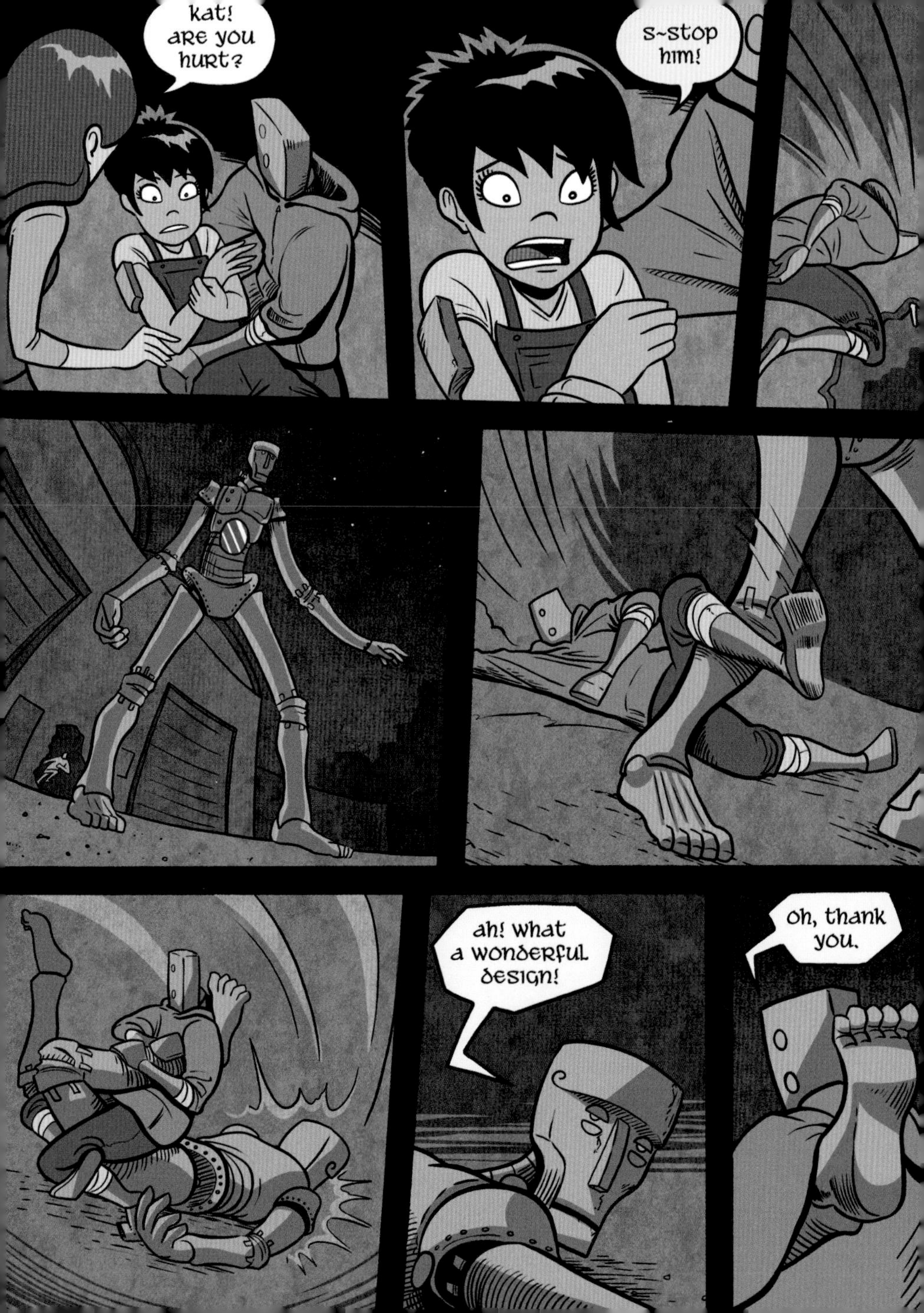
kat! are you hurt?
s~stop him!
ah! what a wonderful design!
oh, thank you.

that was awesome, robot.
a shadow man!
robot!
you are friends with this girl, also?
oh, how far you have come.
I apologise, miss. I was startled.
don't worry about it.
It's okay, robot.
please, can you tell me where the tomb is?

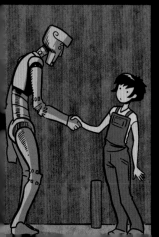

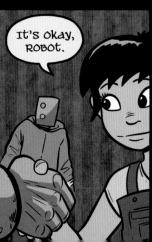

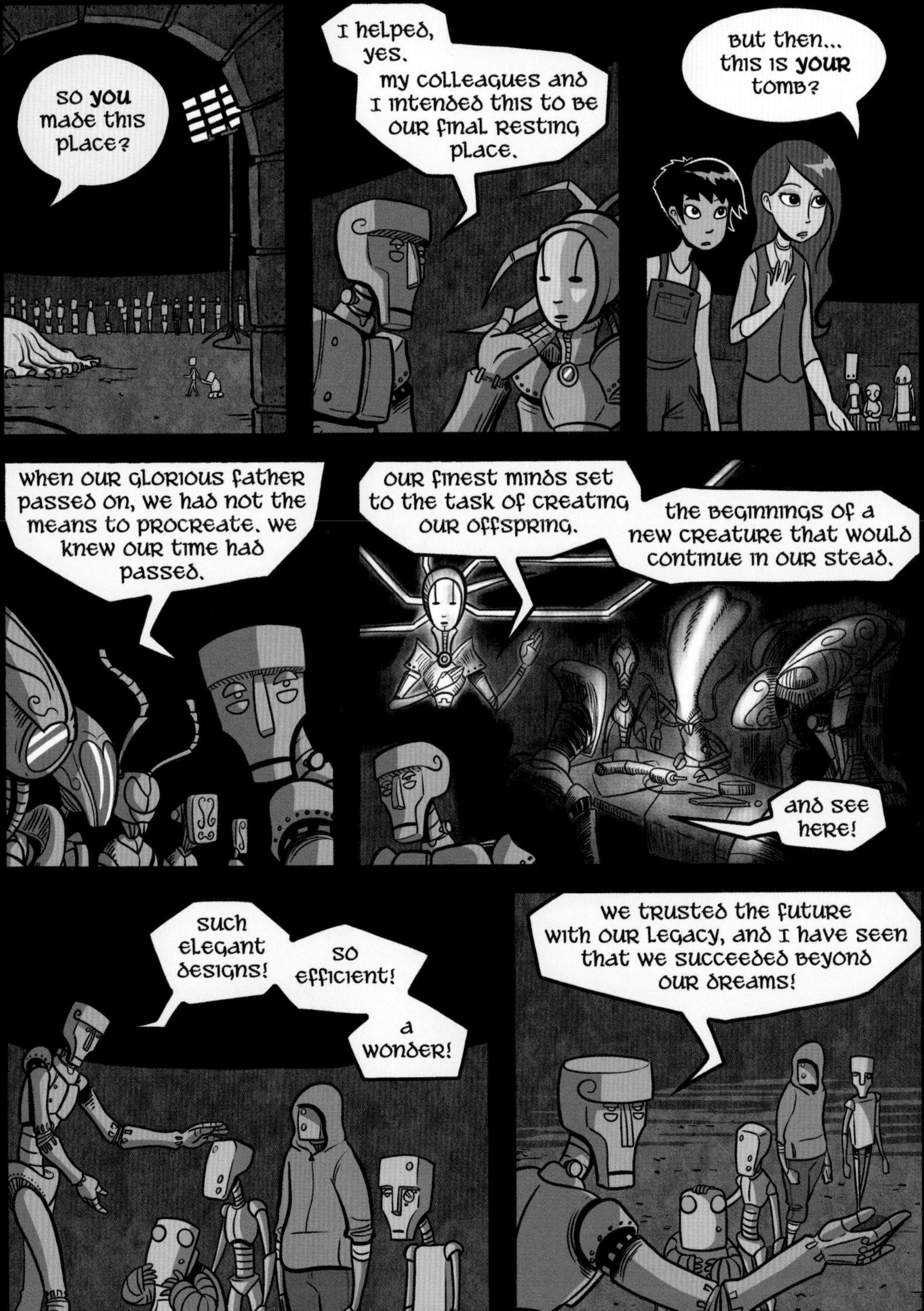
So **you** made this place?
I helped, yes.
My colleagues and I intended this to be our final resting place.
But then... this is **your** tomb?
When our glorious father passed on, we had not the means to procreate. We knew our time had passed.
Our finest minds set to the task of creating our offspring.
The beginnings of a new creature that would continue in our stead.
And see here!
Such elegant designs!
So efficient!
A wonder!
We trusted the future with our legacy, and I have seen that we succeeded beyond our dreams!

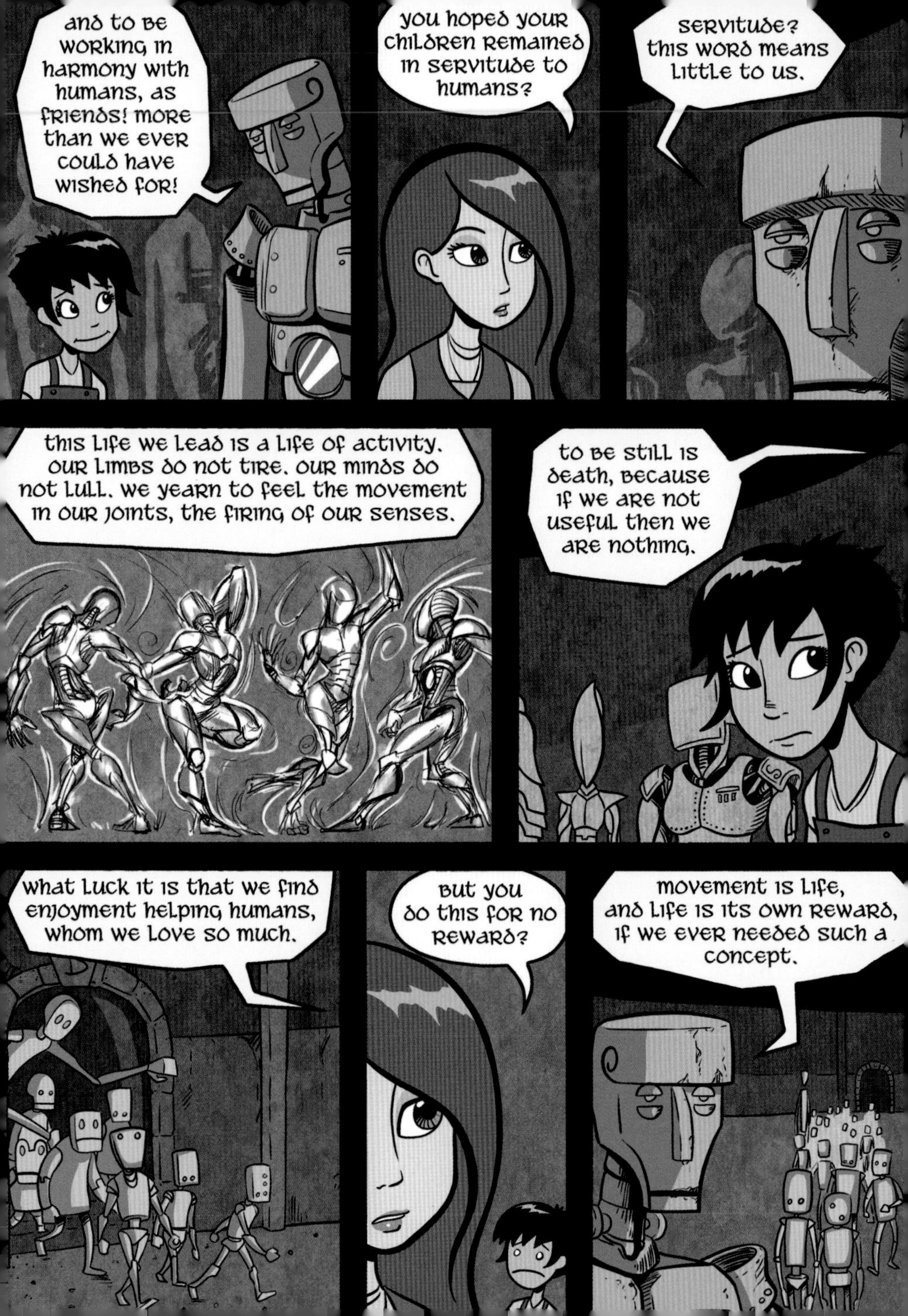
and to be working in harmony with humans, as friends! more than we ever could have wished for!
you hoped your children remained in servitude to humans?
servitude? this word means little to us.
this life we lead is a life of activity. our limbs do not tire. our minds do not lull. we yearn to feel the movement in our joints, the firing of our senses.
to be still is death, because if we are not useful then we are nothing.
what luck it is that we find enjoyment helping humans, whom we love so much.
but you do this for no reward?
movement is life, and life is its own reward, if we ever needed such a concept.

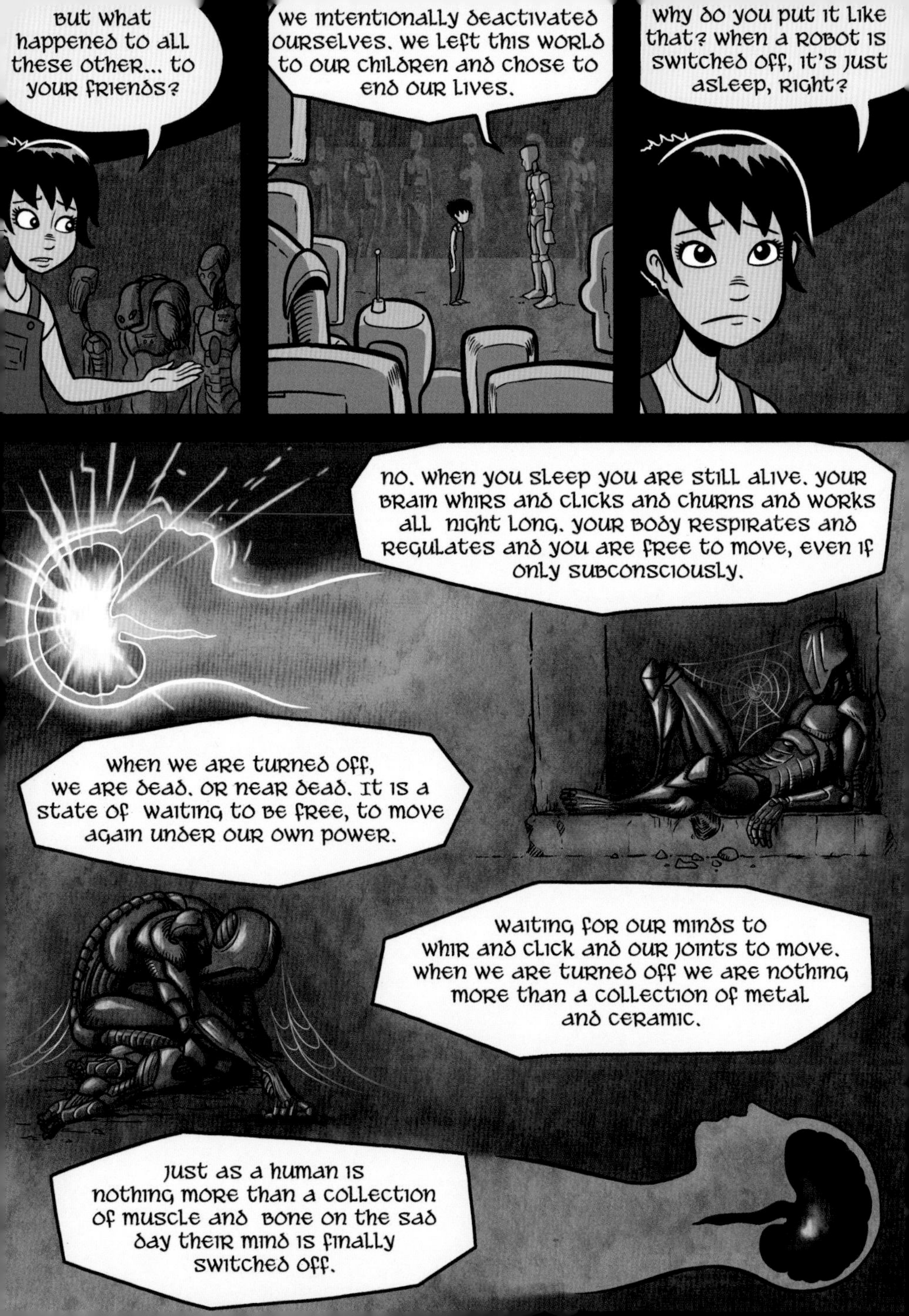
But what happened to all these other... to your friends?
We intentionally deactivated ourselves. We left this world to our children and chose to end our lives.
Why do you put it like that? When a robot is switched off, it's just asleep, right?
No. When you sleep you are still alive. Your brain whirs and clicks and churns and works all night long. Your body respirates and regulates and you are free to move, even if only subconsciously.
When we are turned off, we are dead. Or near dead. It is a state of waiting to be free, to move again under our own power.
Waiting for our minds to whir and click and our joints to move. When we are turned off we are nothing more than a collection of metal and ceramic.
Just as a human is nothing more than a collection of muscle and bone on the sad day their mind is finally switched off.

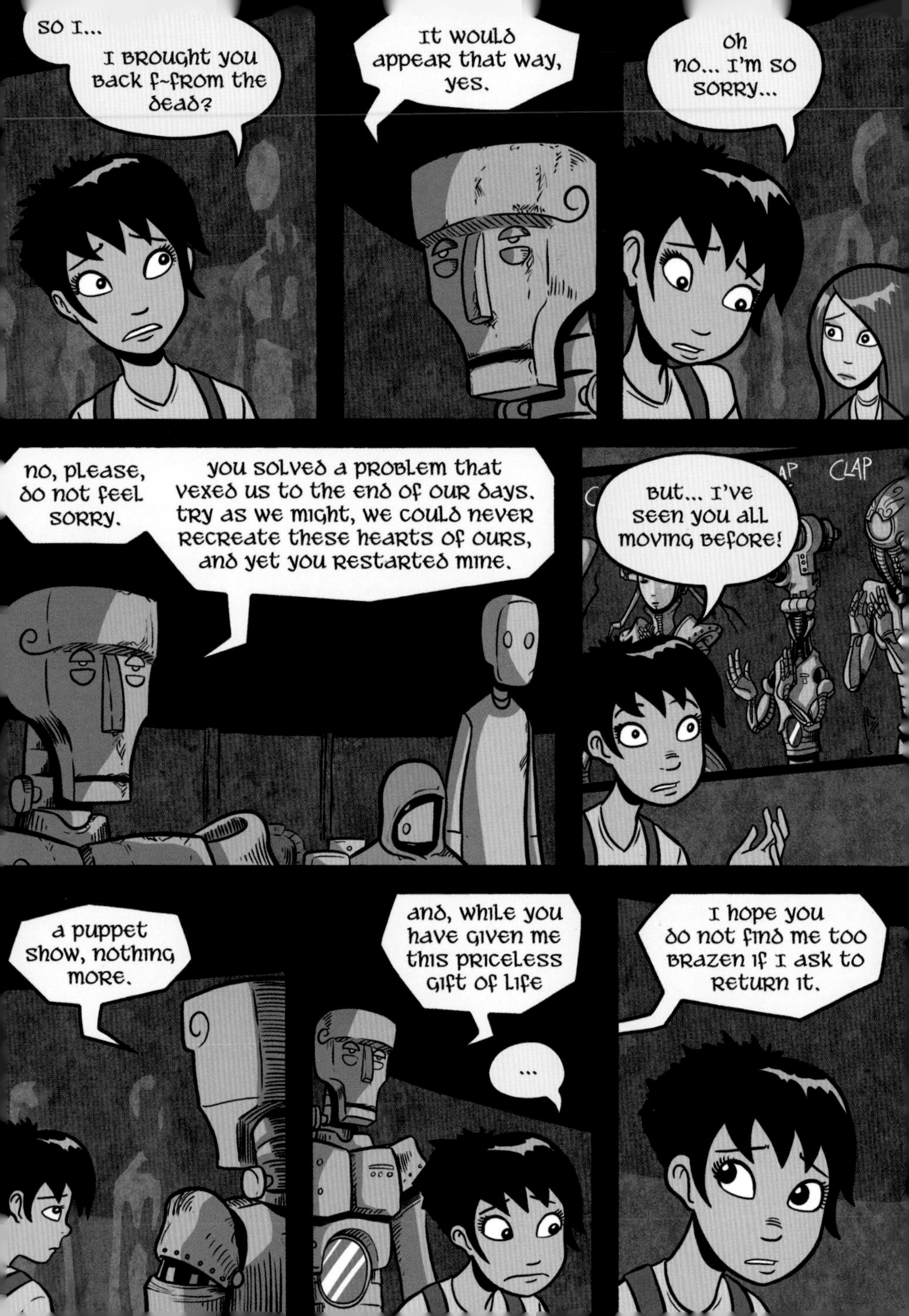
so I...
I brought you back f~from the dead?
It would appear that way, yes.
oh no... I'm so sorry...
no, please, do not feel sorry.
you solved a problem that vexed us to the end of our days. try as we might, we could never recreate these hearts of ours, and yet you restarted mine.
AP
CLAP
But... I've seen you all moving before!
a puppet show, nothing more.
and, while you have given me this priceless gift of life
...
I hope you do not find me too brazen if I ask to return it.

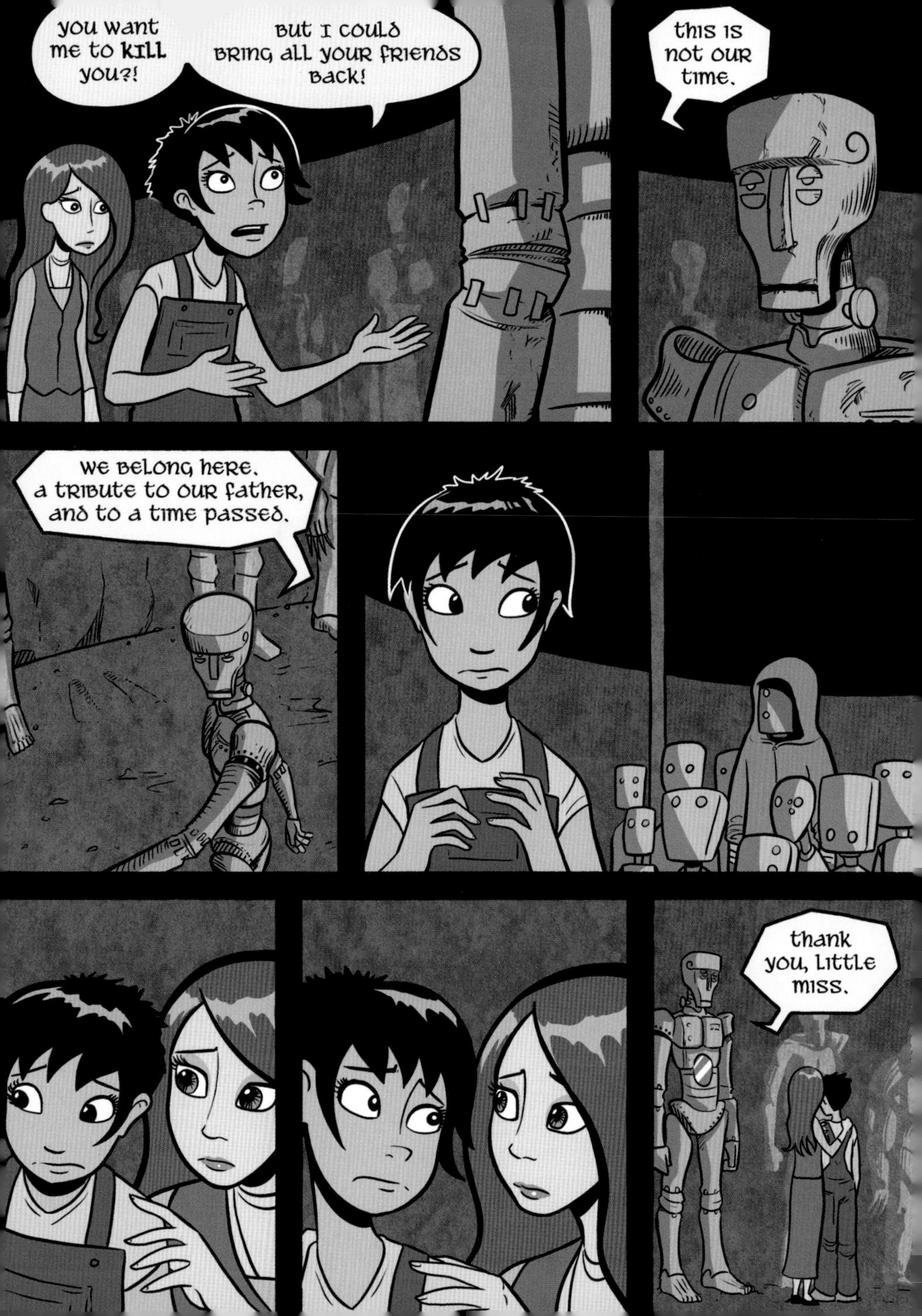
you want me to KILL you?!
But I could bring all your friends back!
this is not our time.
we belong here. a tribute to our father, and to a time passed.
thank you, little miss.

Wait, before you go.
Can you tell me how Gunnerkrigg Court was built?
The court?
It grew from the seed Bismuth.
But~
Please.
CRACK
I... think I need some fresh air...

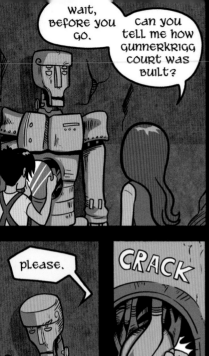

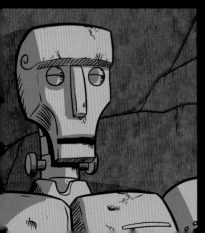

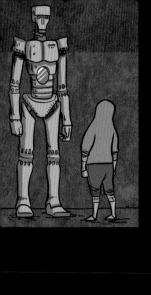

Let it be known

In this tomb of ancients, the angel called forth the spirit of the dead.

You see how easily she gave life.

And how easily she took it away.

Helping Hand

oh...

oh... ah... ROBOX.

I ~ I'm stuck.

did I... did I miss anything important?

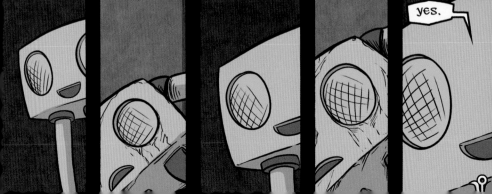

yes.

Gunnerkrigg Court

Chapter 34:

Faraway Morning
(and three short tales)

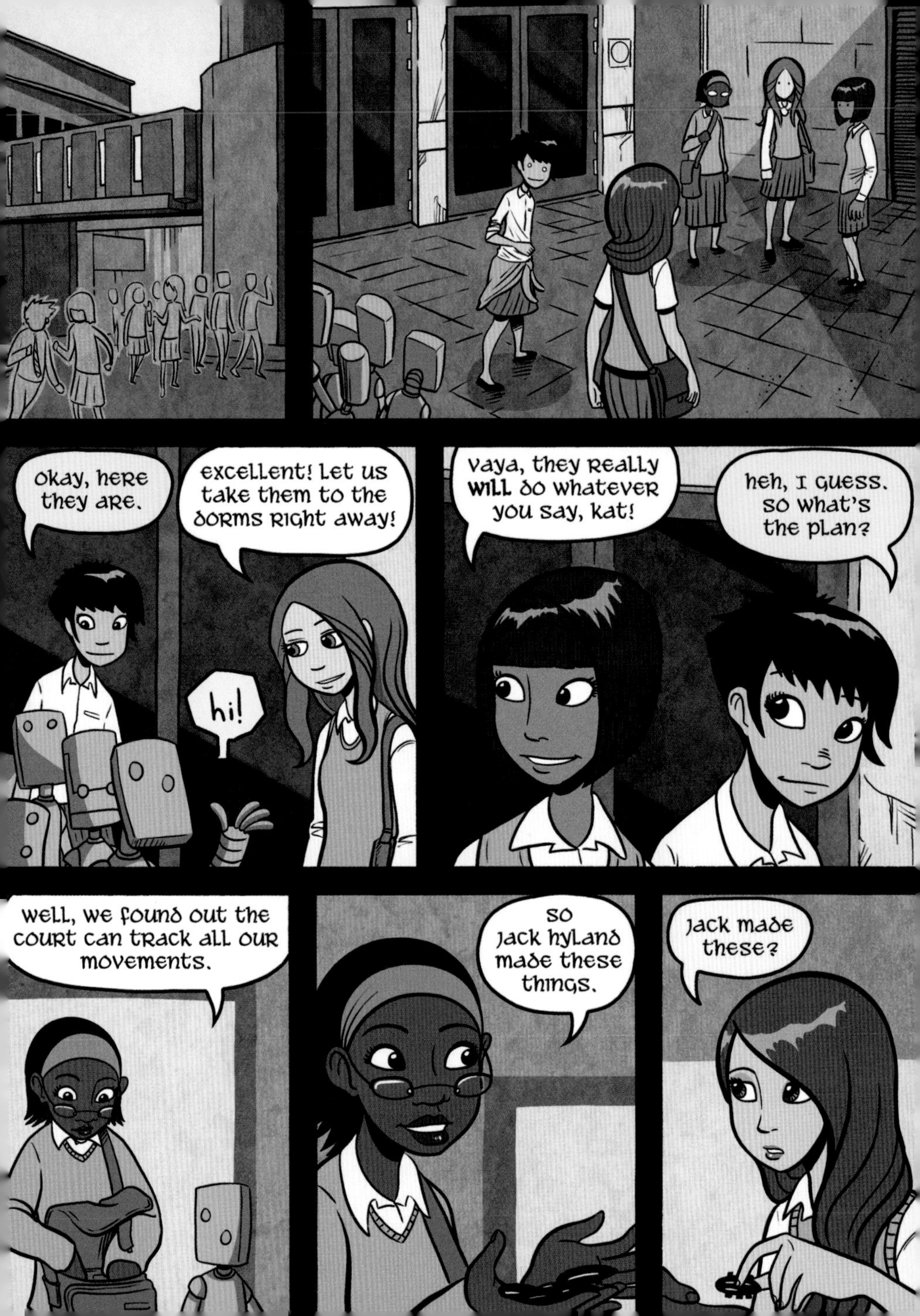
Okay, here they are.
Excellent! Let us take them to the dorms right away!
hi!
Vaya, they really **WILL** do whatever you say, Kat!
Heh, I guess. So what's the plan?
Well, we found out the court can track all our movements.
So Jack Hyland made these things.
Jack made these?

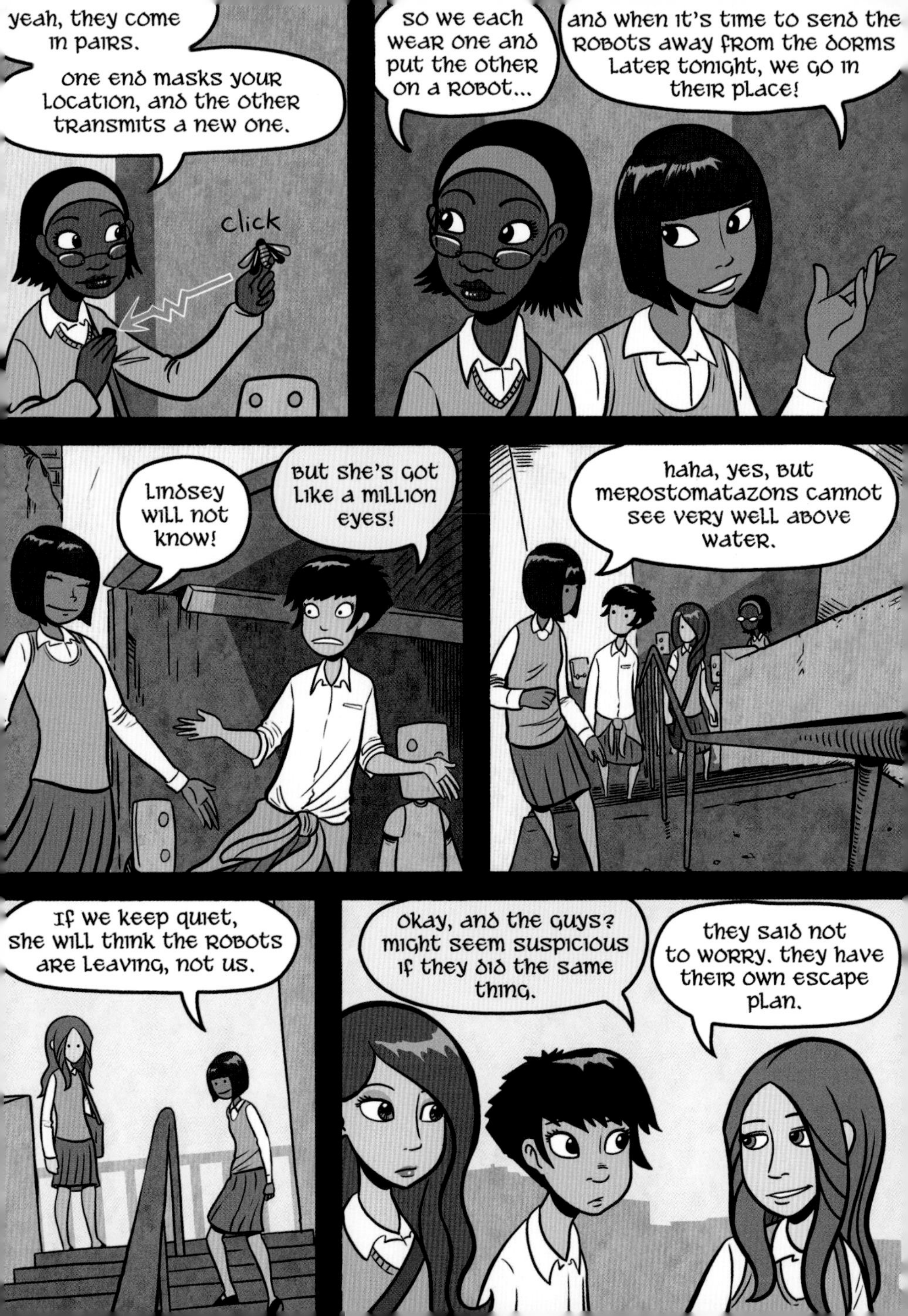
yeah, they come in pairs.
one end masks your location, and the other transmits a new one.
click
so we each wear one and put the other on a robot...
and when it's time to send the robots away from the dorms later tonight, we go in their place!
Lindsey will not know!
but she's got like a million eyes!
haha, yes, but merostomatazons cannot see very well above water.
If we keep quiet, she will think the robots are leaving, not us.
okay, and the guys? might seem suspicious if they did the same thing.
they said not to worry. they have their own escape plan.

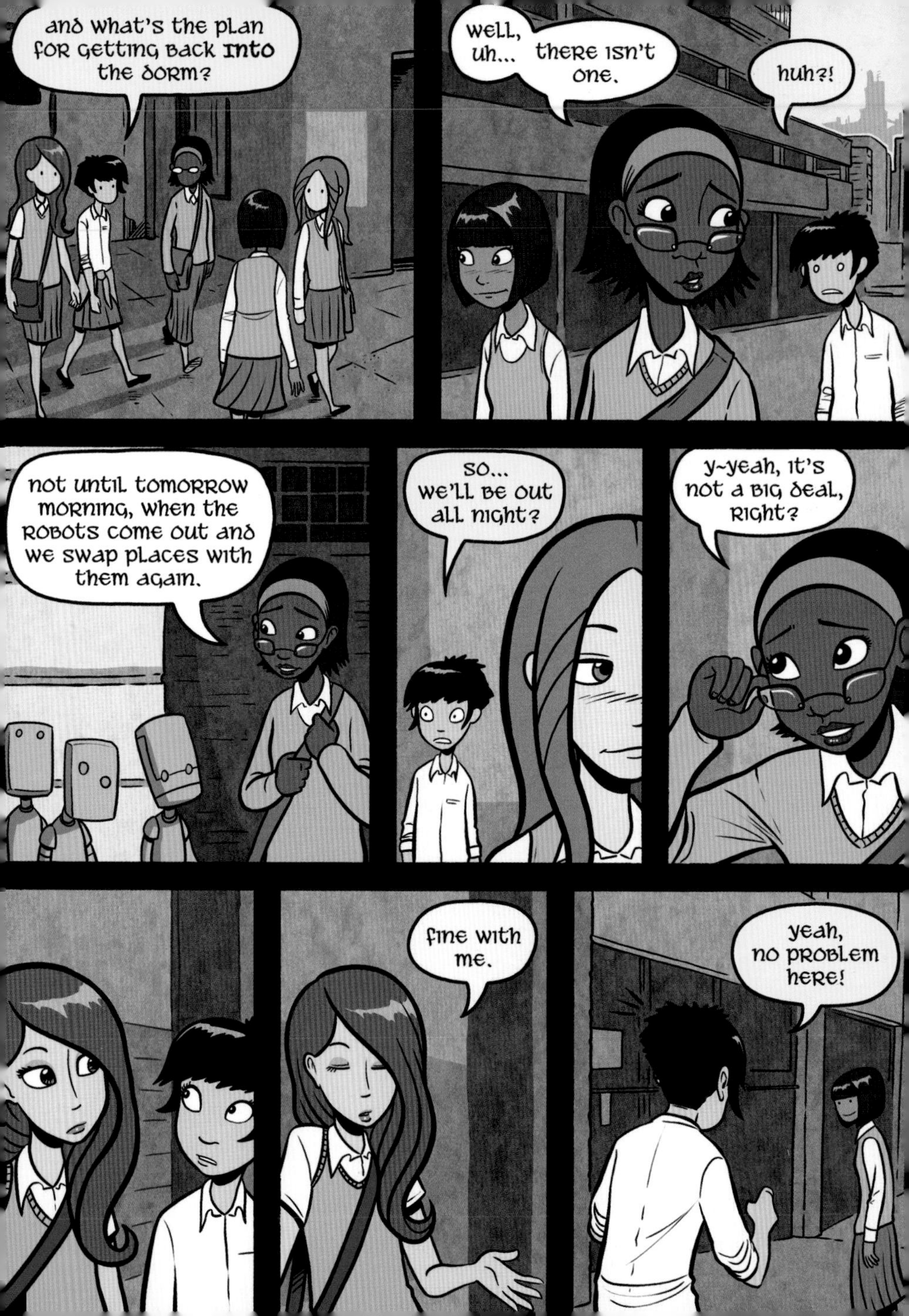
and what's the plan for getting back into the dorm?
well, uh...
there isn't one.
huh?!
not until tomorrow morning, when the robots come out and we swap places with them again.
so... we'll be out all night?
y-yeah, it's not a big deal, right?
fine with me.
yeah, no problem here!

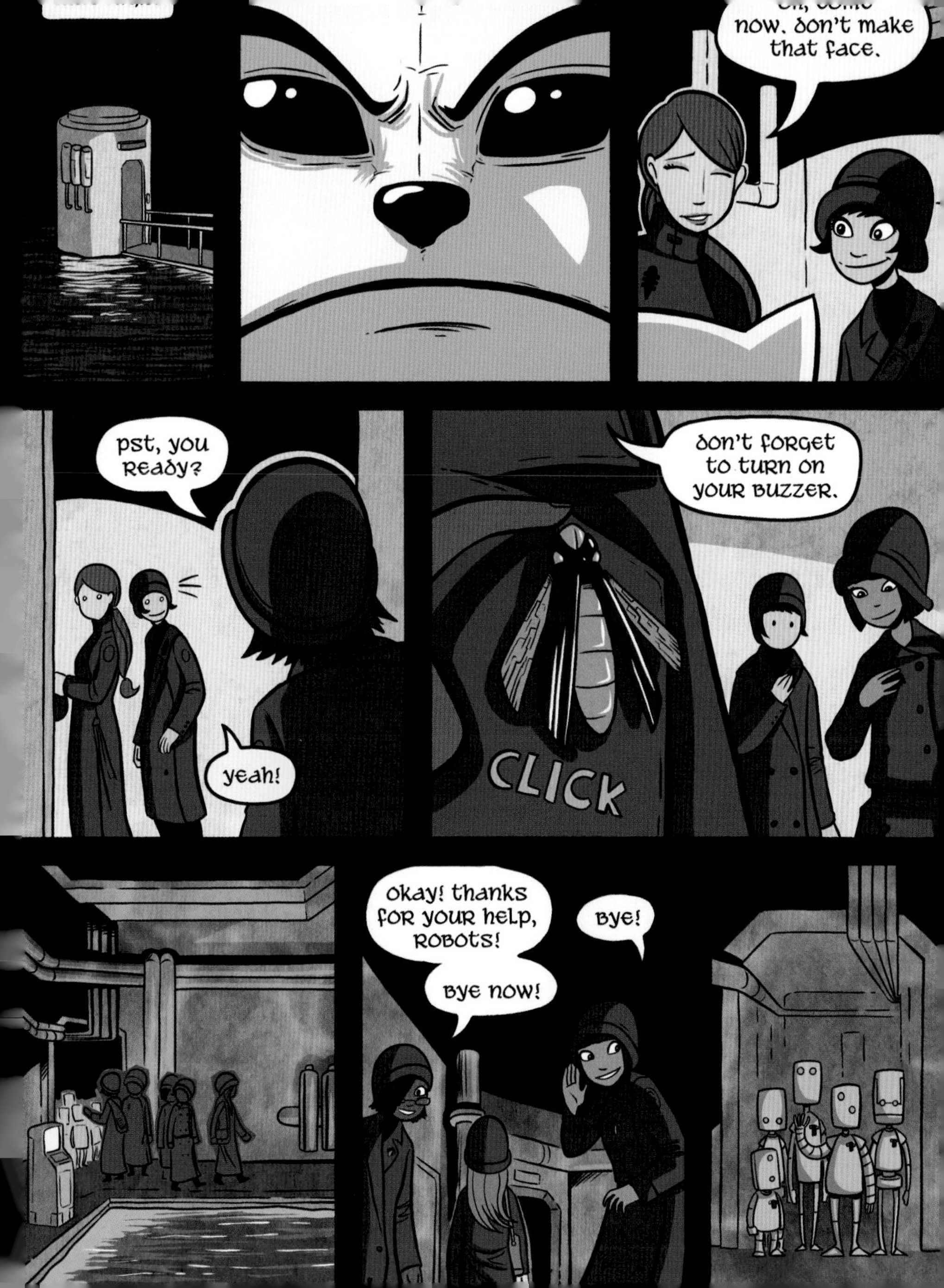
now. don't make that face.
pst, you ready?
yeah!
don't forget to turn on your buzzer.
CLICK
okay! thanks for your help, robots!
Bye!
Bye now!

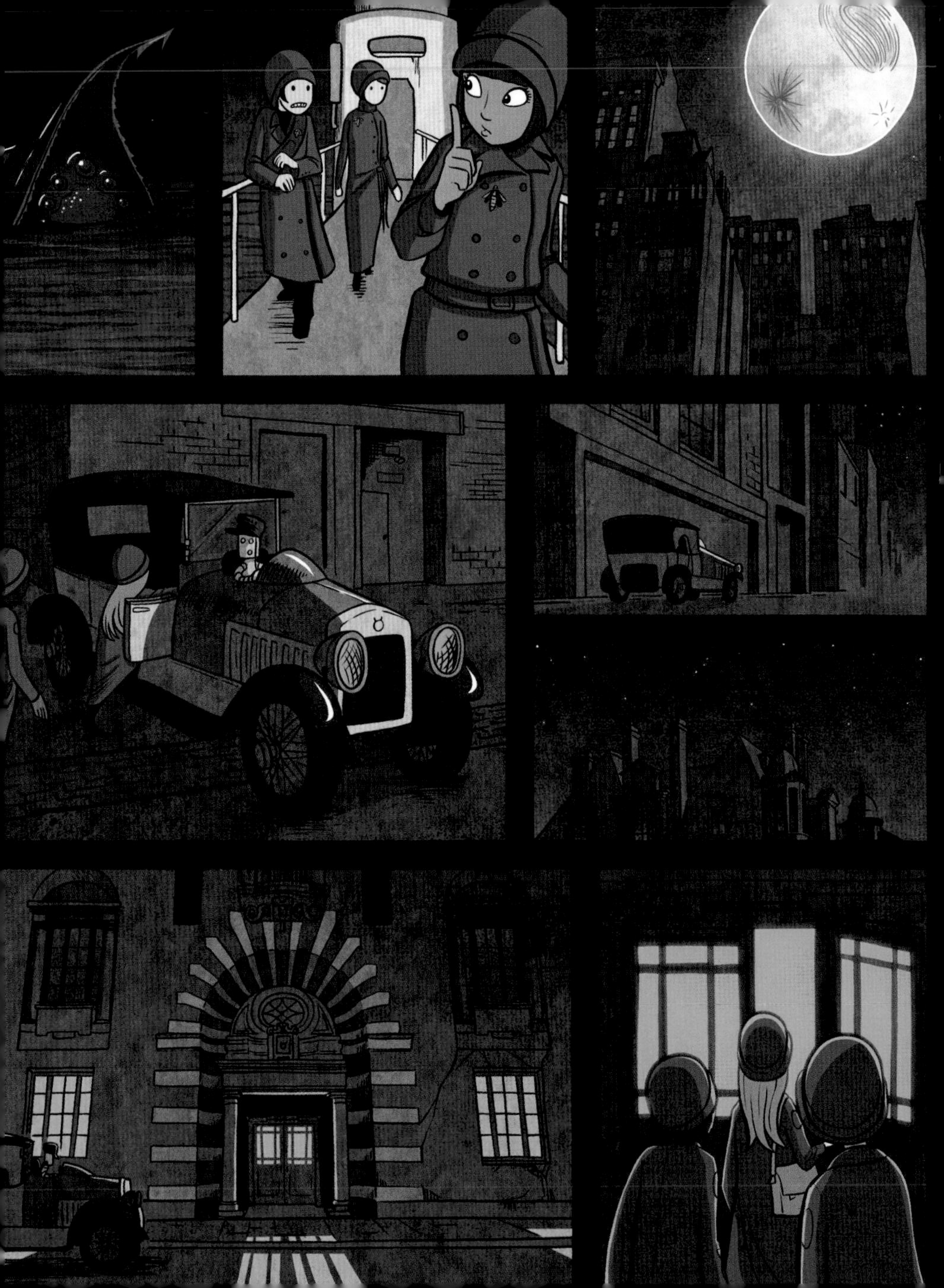

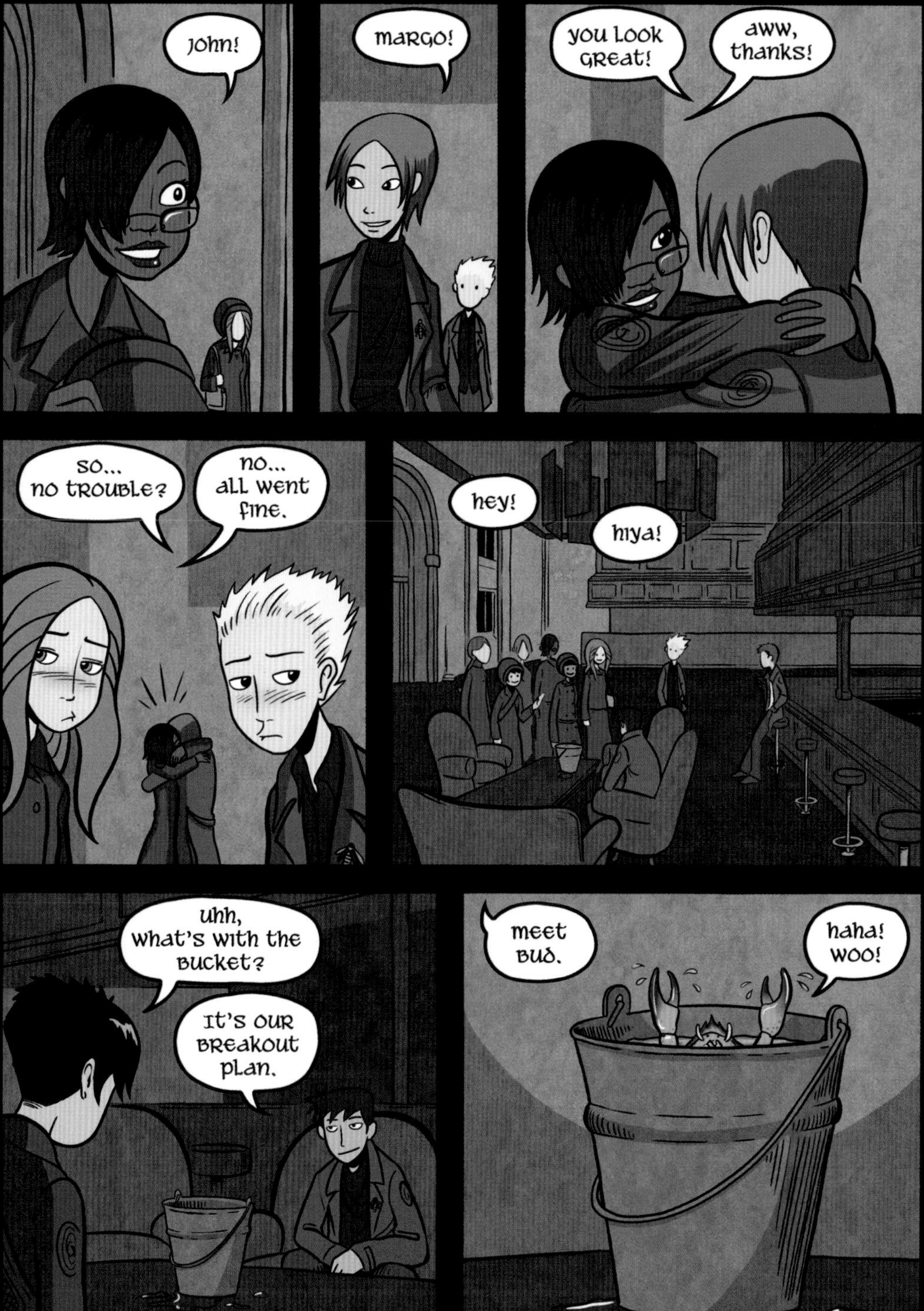
John!
Margo!
You look great!
Aww, thanks!
So... no trouble?
No... all went fine.
Hey!
Hiya!
Uhh, what's with the bucket?
It's our breakout plan.
Meet Bud.
Haha! Woo!

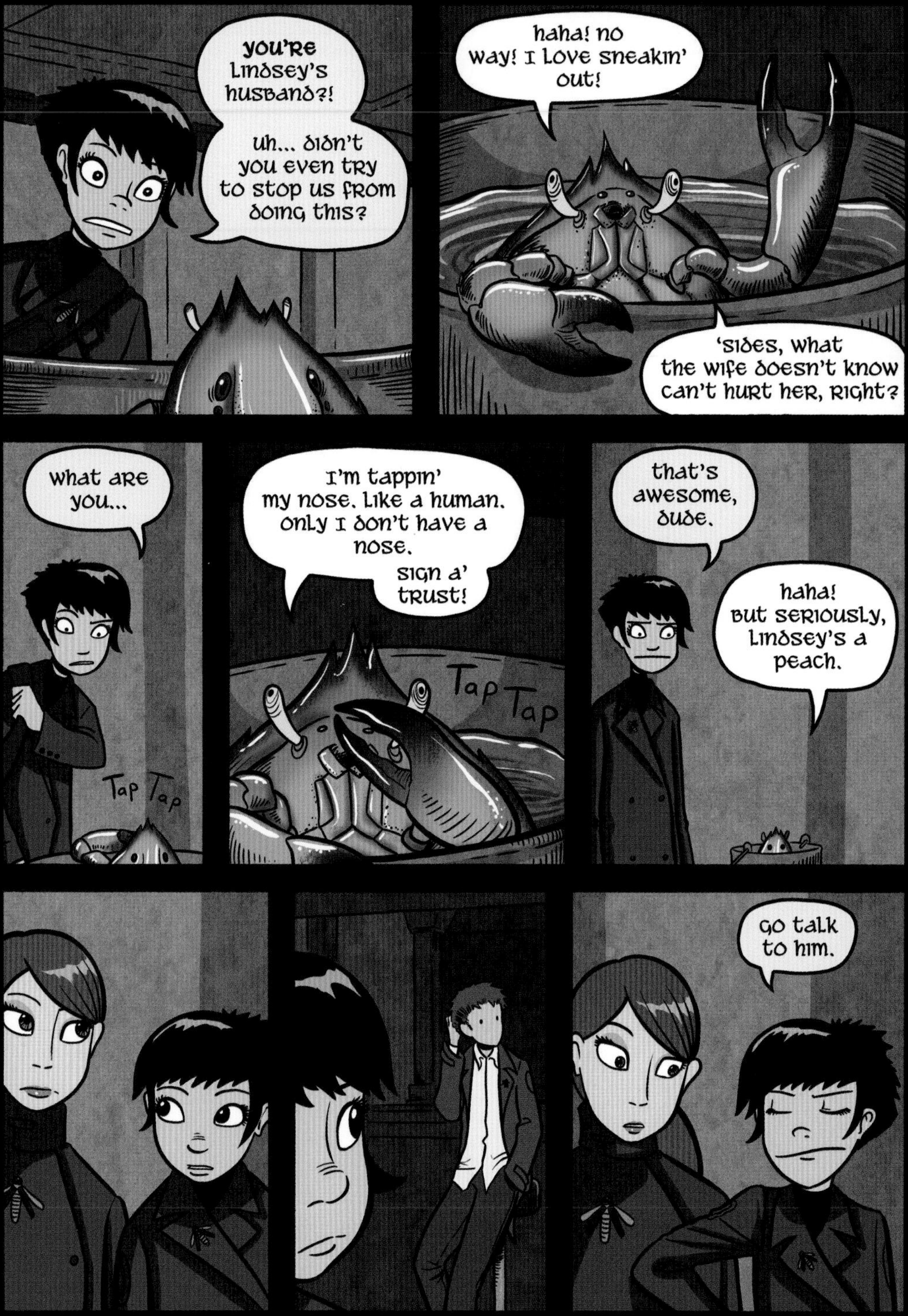
you're Lindsey's husband?!
uh... didn't you even try to stop us from doing this?
haha! no way! I love sneakin' out!
'sides, what the wife doesn't know can't hurt her, right?
what are you...
Tap Tap
I'm tappin' my nose. like a human. only I don't have a nose.
sign a' trust!
Tap Tap
that's awesome, dude.
haha! but seriously, Lindsey's a peach.
go talk to him.

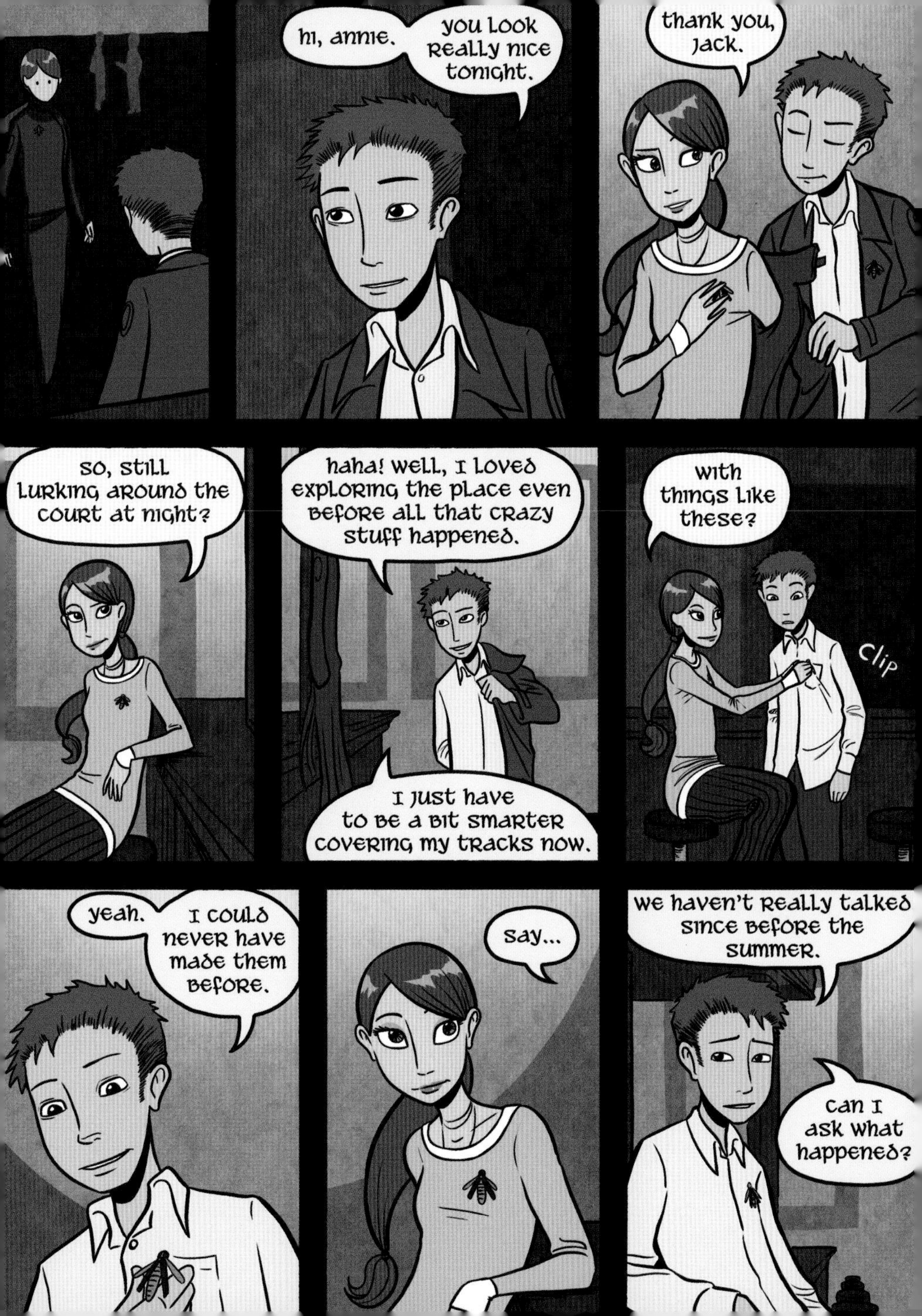
hi, annie.
you look really nice tonight.
thank you, jack.
so, still lurking around the court at night?
haha! well, I loved exploring the place even before all that crazy stuff happened.
I just have to be a bit smarter covering my tracks now.
with things like these?
Clip
yeah.
I could never have made them before.
say...
we haven't really talked since before the summer.
can I ask what happened?

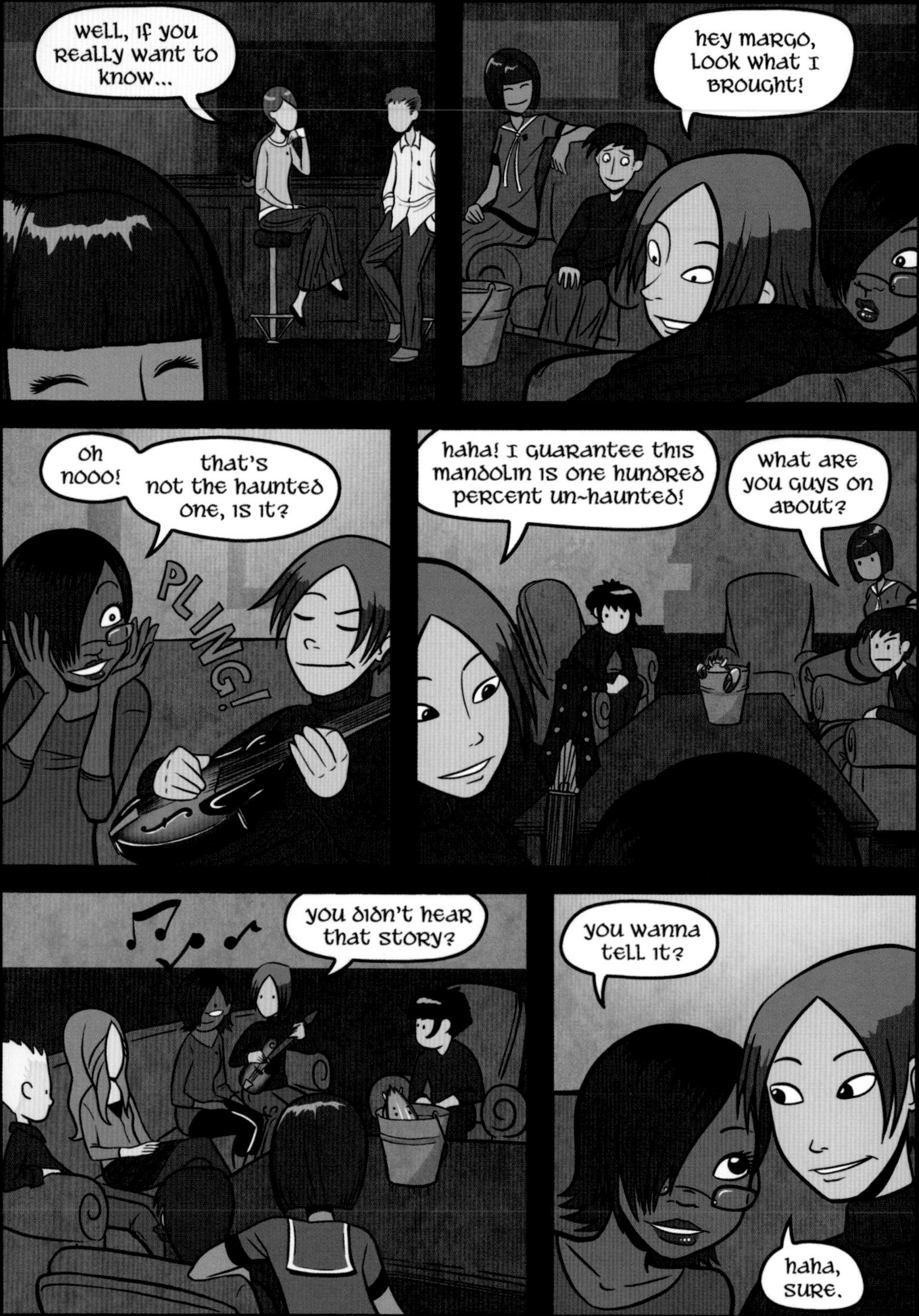
well, if you really want to know...
hey margo, look what I brought!
oh nooo!
that's not the haunted one, is it?
PLING!
haha! I guarantee this mandolin is one hundred percent un-haunted!
what are you guys on about?
you didn't hear that story?
you wanna tell it?
haha, sure.

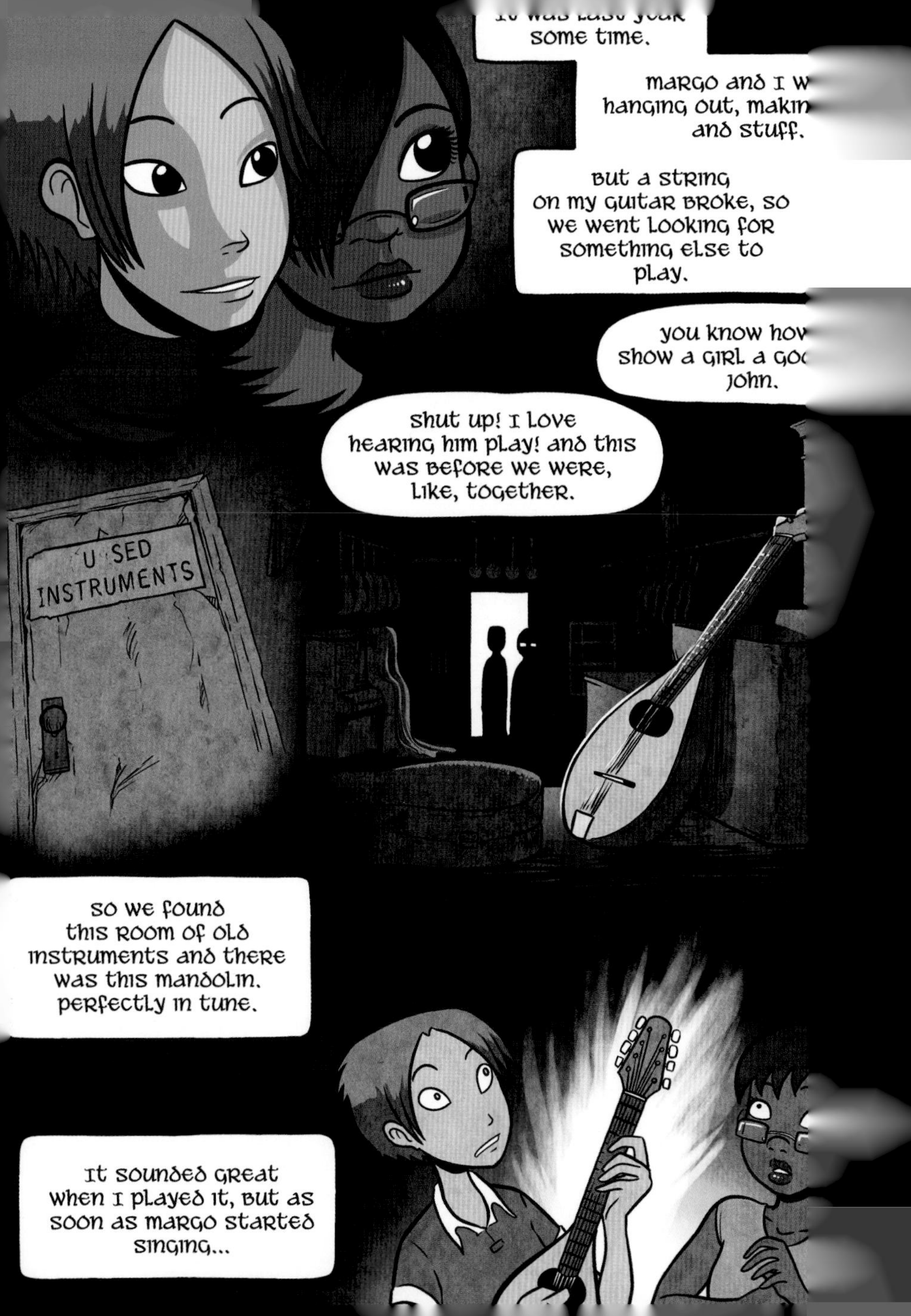
some time.
margo and I
hanging out,
and stuff.
But a string on my guitar broke, so we went looking for something else to play.
you know
show a girl a
john.
shut up! I love hearing him play! and this was before we were, like, together.
USED INSTRUMENTS
so we found this room of old instruments and there was this mandolin. perfectly in tune.
It sounded great when I played it, but as soon as margo started singing...

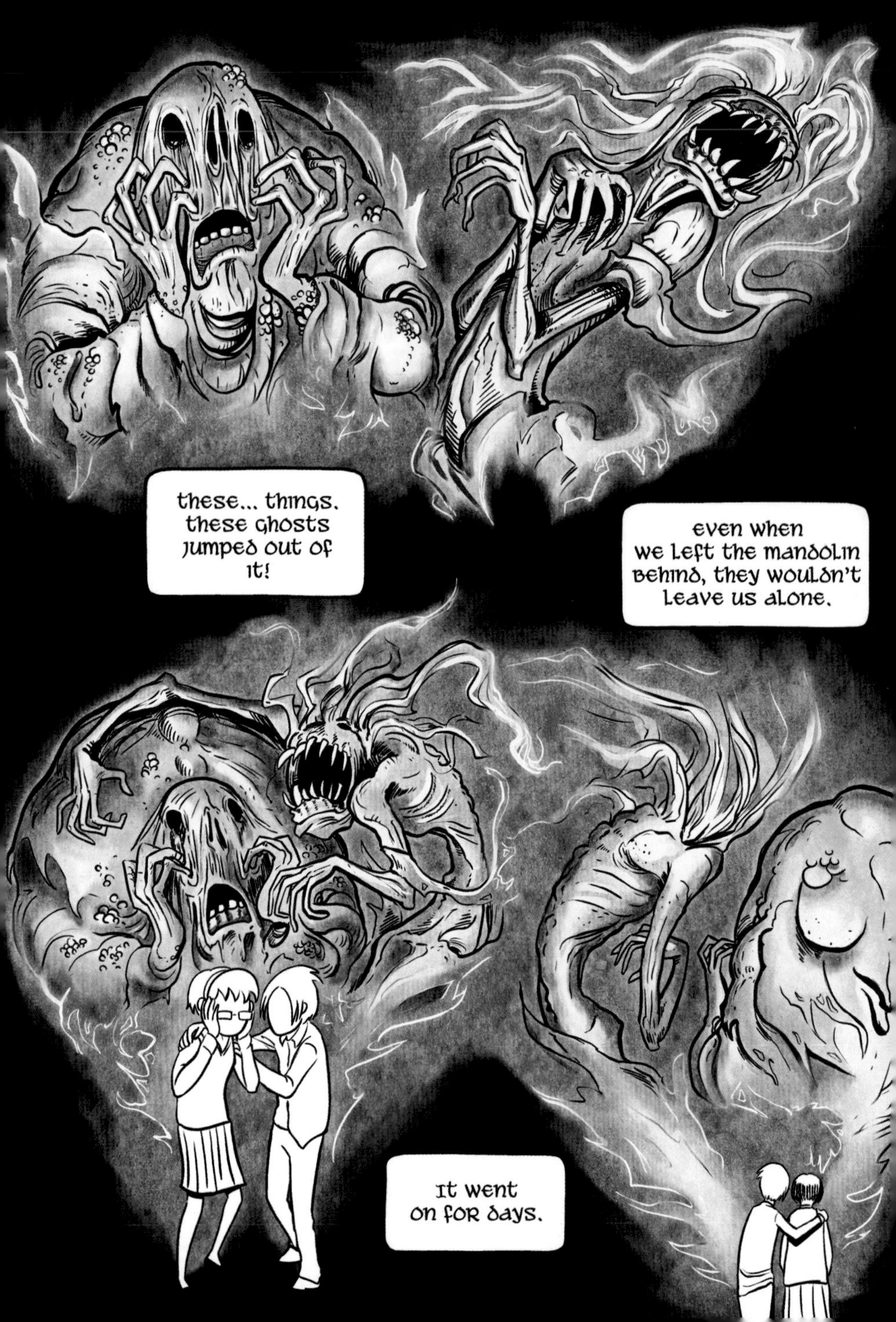
these... things, these ghosts jumped out of it!
even when we left the mandolin behind, they wouldn't leave us alone.
It went on for days.

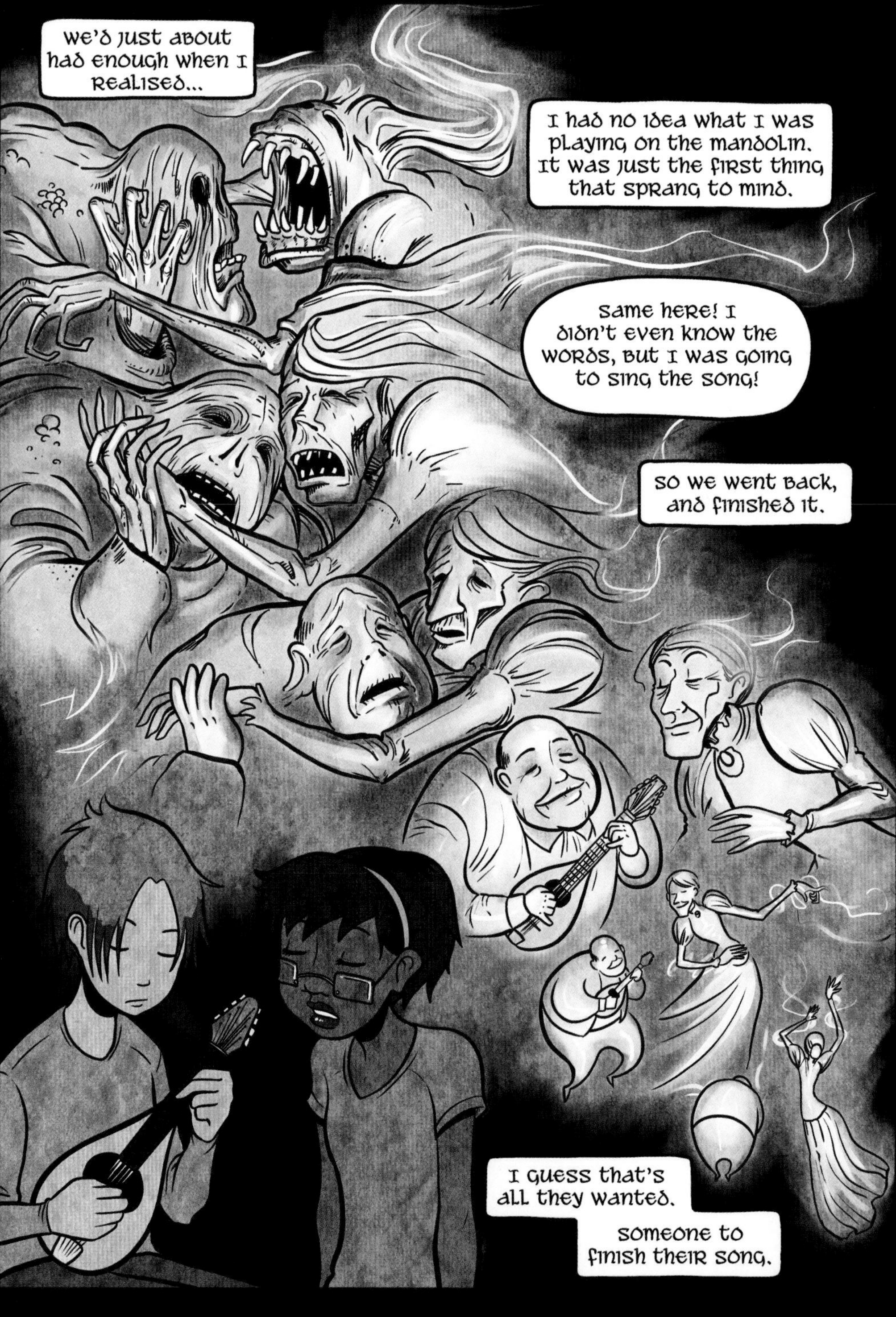
We'd just about had enough when I realised...
I had no idea what I was playing on the mandolin. It was just the first thing that sprang to mind.
Same here! I didn't even know the words, but I was going to sing the song!
So we went back, and finished it.
I guess that's all they wanted.
Someone to finish their song.

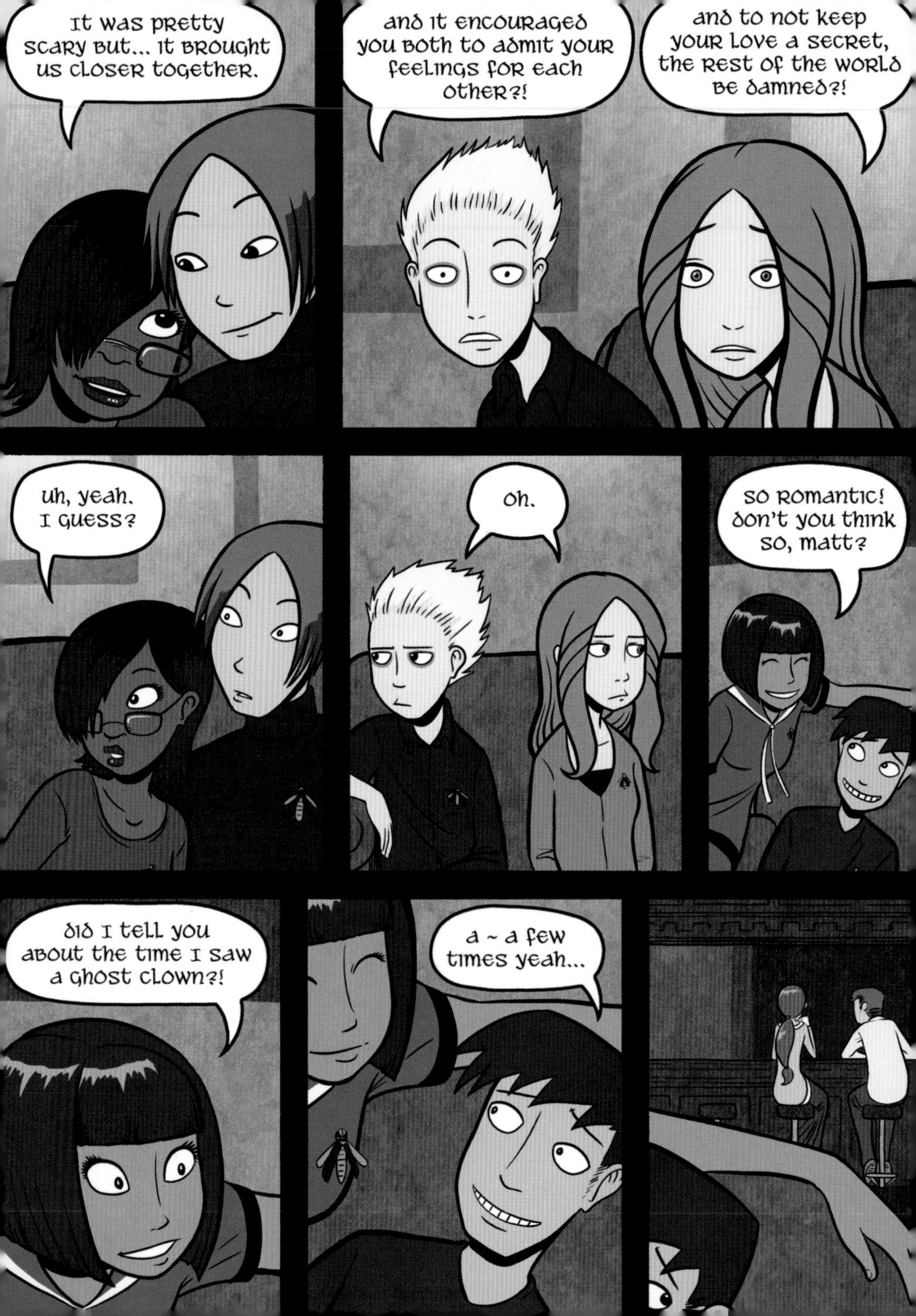
It was pretty scary but... it brought us closer together.
and it encouraged you both to admit your feelings for each other?!
and to not keep your love a secret, the rest of the world be damned?!
uh, yeah. I guess?
oh.
so romantic! don't you think so, matt?
did I tell you about the time I saw a ghost clown?!
a ~ a few times yeah...

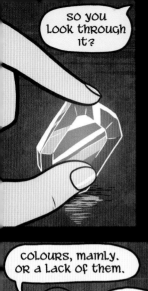

SO YOU LOOK THROUGH IT?

YES, IT'S LIKE A LENS OF SORTS.

WHAT DO YOU SEE?

COLOURS, MAINLY. OR A LACK OF THEM.

SOMETIMES I CAN SEE IF A PERSON HAS AN ETHERIC ABILITY.

HAHA, OH YEAH?

BUD, FOR EXAMPLE.

But the voltage across the cores would be way too low

HE'S ACTUALLY A VERY POWERFUL PSYCHIC.

HE'S FAR FROM BOUND BY THAT BUCKET HE'S IN.

On a metal-oxide semiconductor sure, BUT—

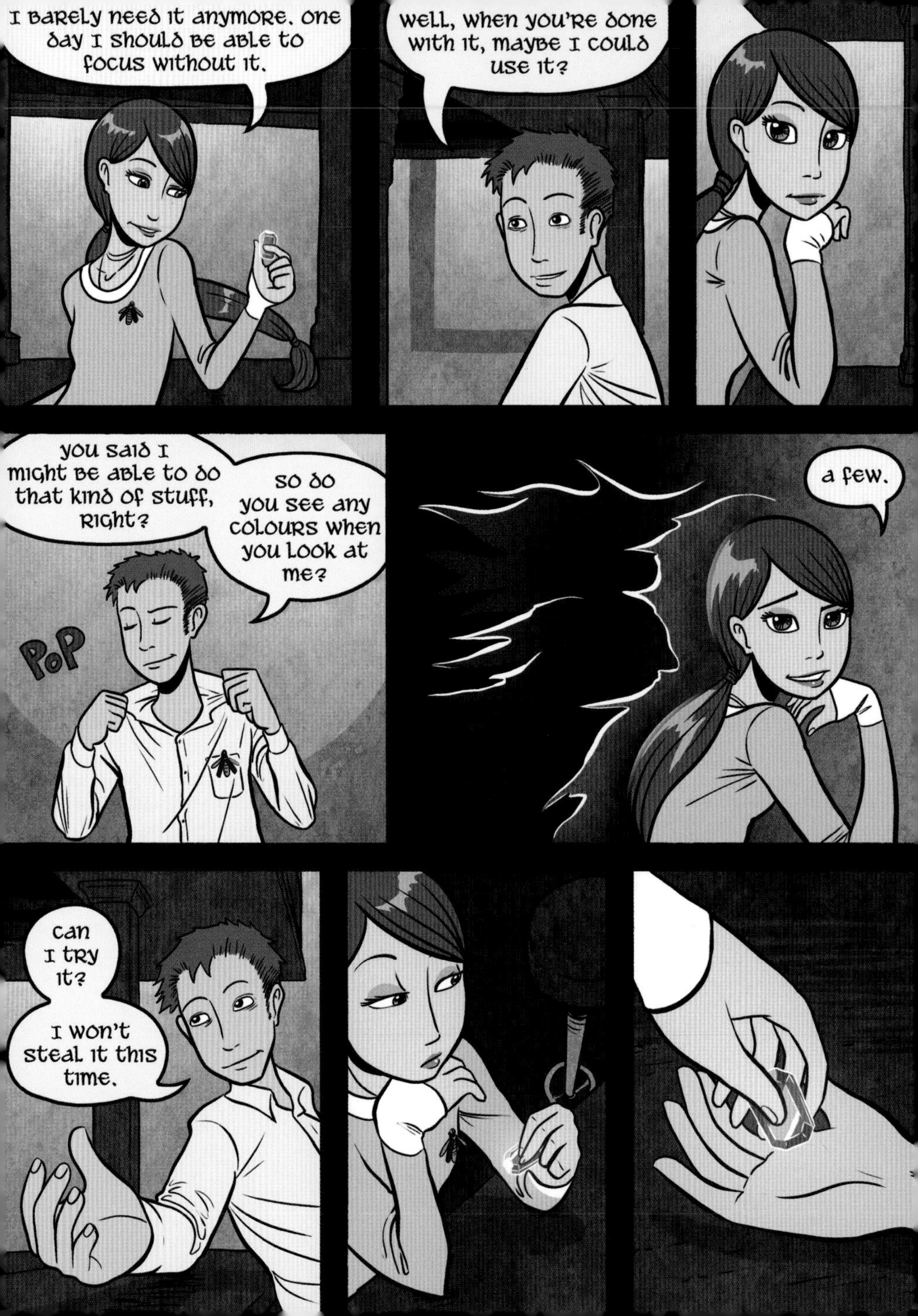
I barely need it anymore. One day I should be able to focus without it.
Well, when you're done with it, maybe I could use it?
You said I might be able to do that kind of stuff, right?
So do you see any colours when you look at me?
POP
a few.
Can I try it?
I won't steal it this time.

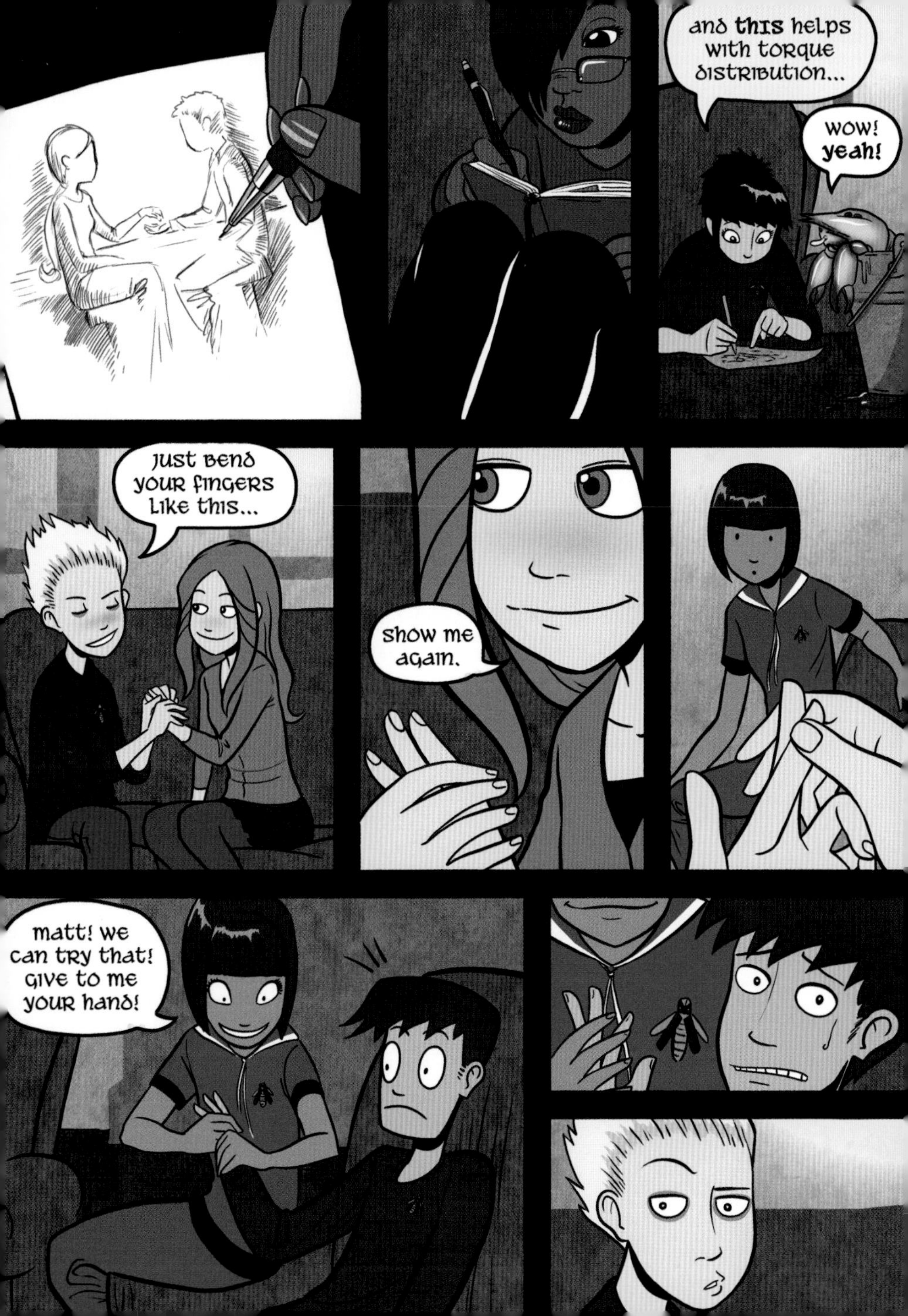
and **this** helps with torque distribution...
wow! **yeah!**
just bend your fingers like this...
show me again.
matt! we can try that! give to me your hand!

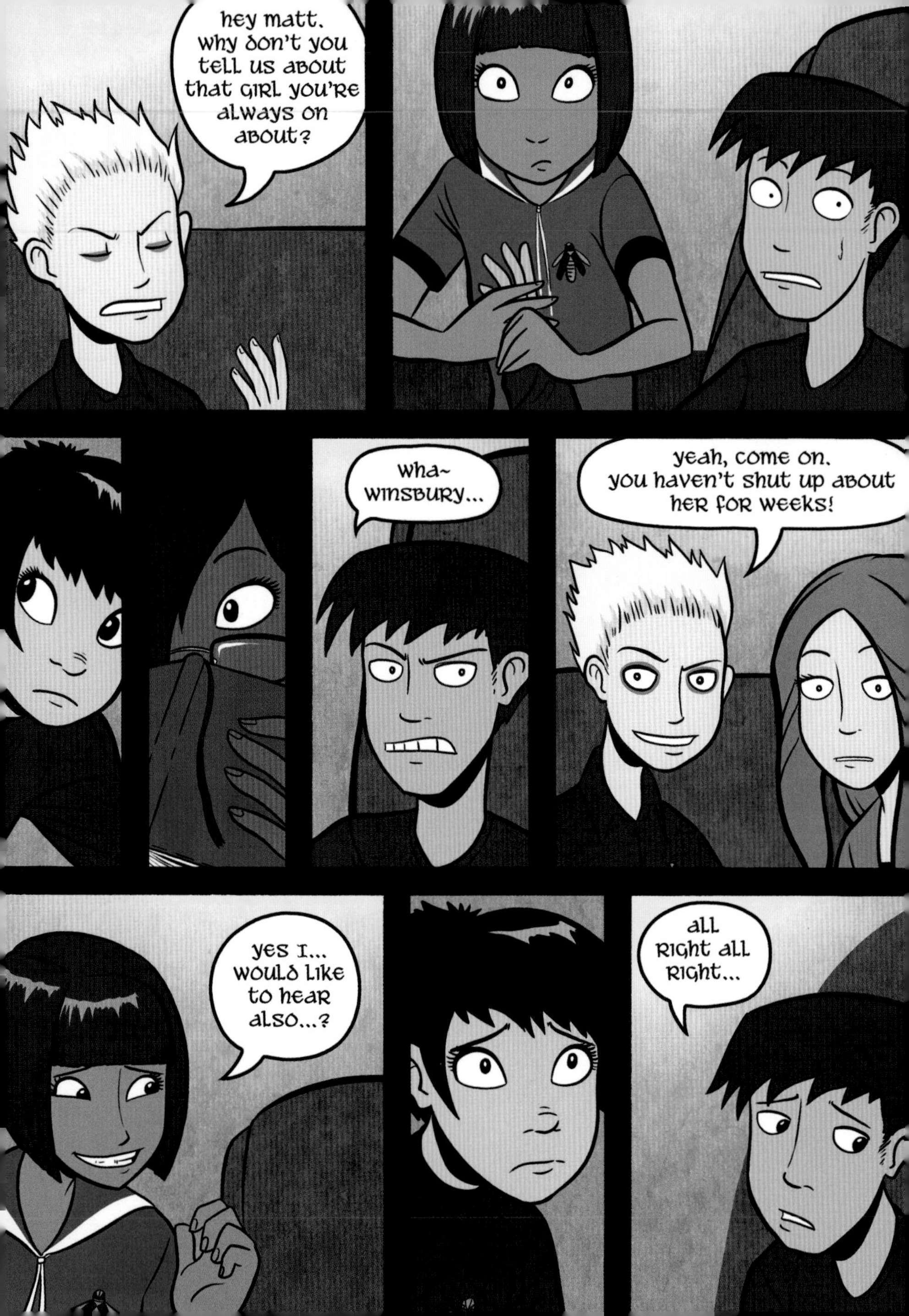
hey matt. why don't you tell us about that girl you're always on about?
wha~ winsbury...
yeah, come on. you haven't shut up about her for weeks!
yes I... would like to hear also...?
all right all right...

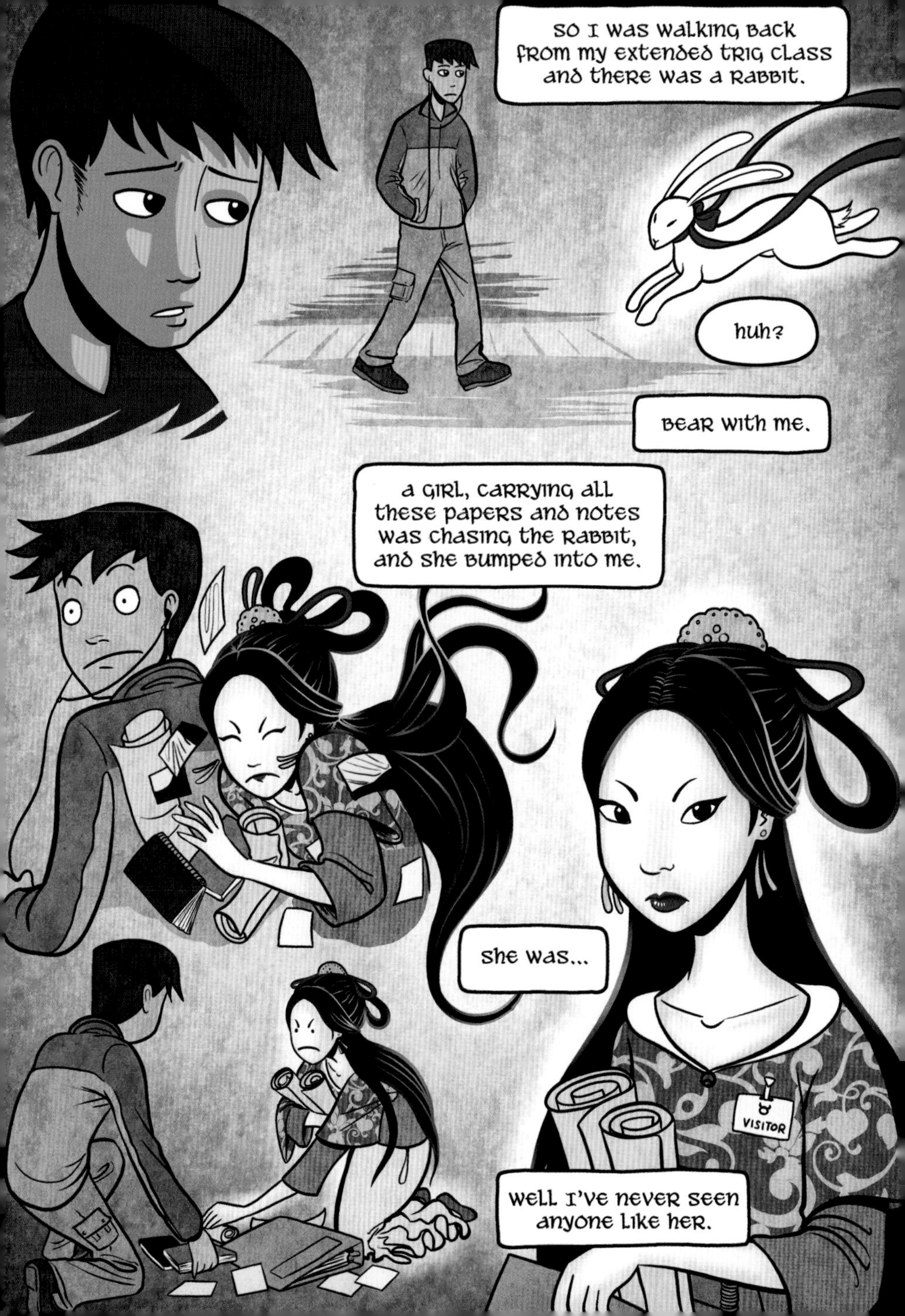
so I was walking back from my extended trig class and there was a rabbit.
huh?
bear with me.
a girl, carrying all these papers and notes was chasing the rabbit, and she bumped into me.
she was...
VISITOR
well I've never seen anyone like her.

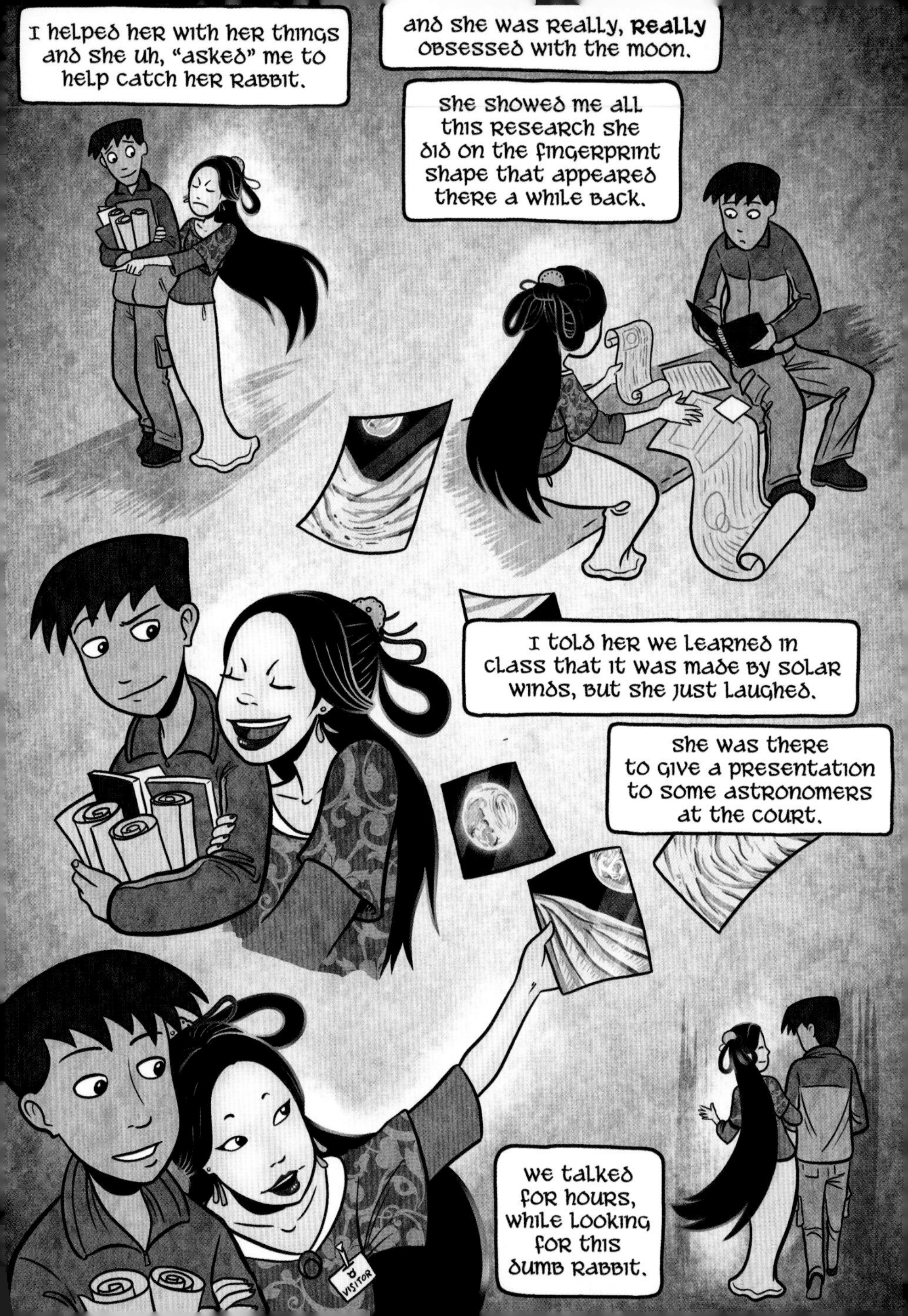
I helped her with her things and she uh, "asked" me to help catch her rabbit.
and she was really, **really** obsessed with the moon.
She showed me all this research she did on the fingerprint shape that appeared there a while back.
I told her we learned in class that it was made by solar winds, but she just laughed.
She was there to give a presentation to some astronomers at the court.
VISITOR
We talked for hours, while looking for this dumb rabbit.

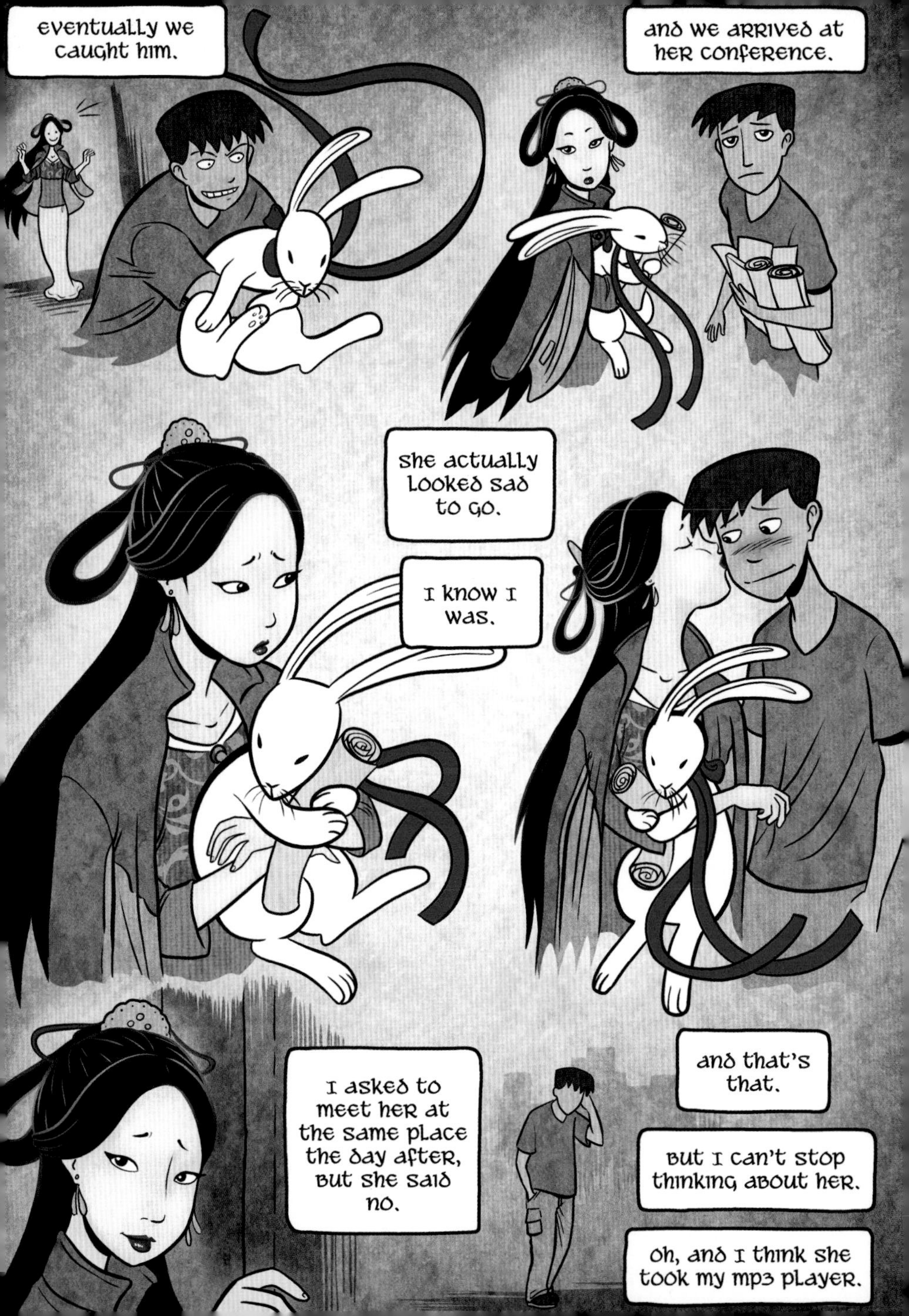
eventually we caught him.
and we arrived at her conference.
she actually looked sad to go.
I know I was.
I asked to meet her at the same place the day after, but she said no.
and that's that.
but I can't stop thinking about her.
oh, and I think she took my mp3 player.

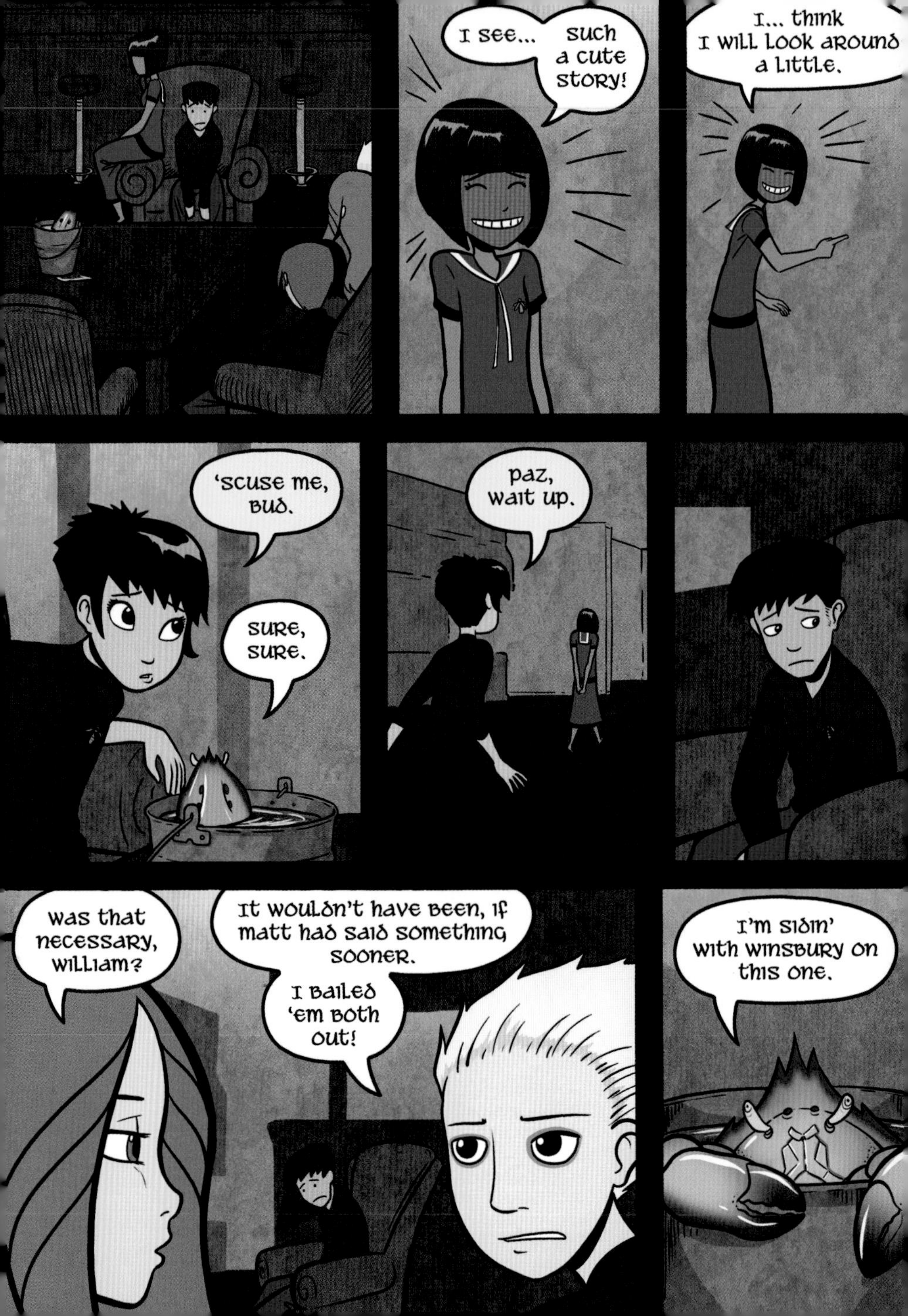
I see... such a cute story!
I... think I will look around a little.
'scuse me, bud.
sure, sure.
paz, wait up.
was that necessary, william?
It wouldn't have been, if matt had said something sooner.
I bailed 'em both out!
I'm sidin' with winsbury on this one.

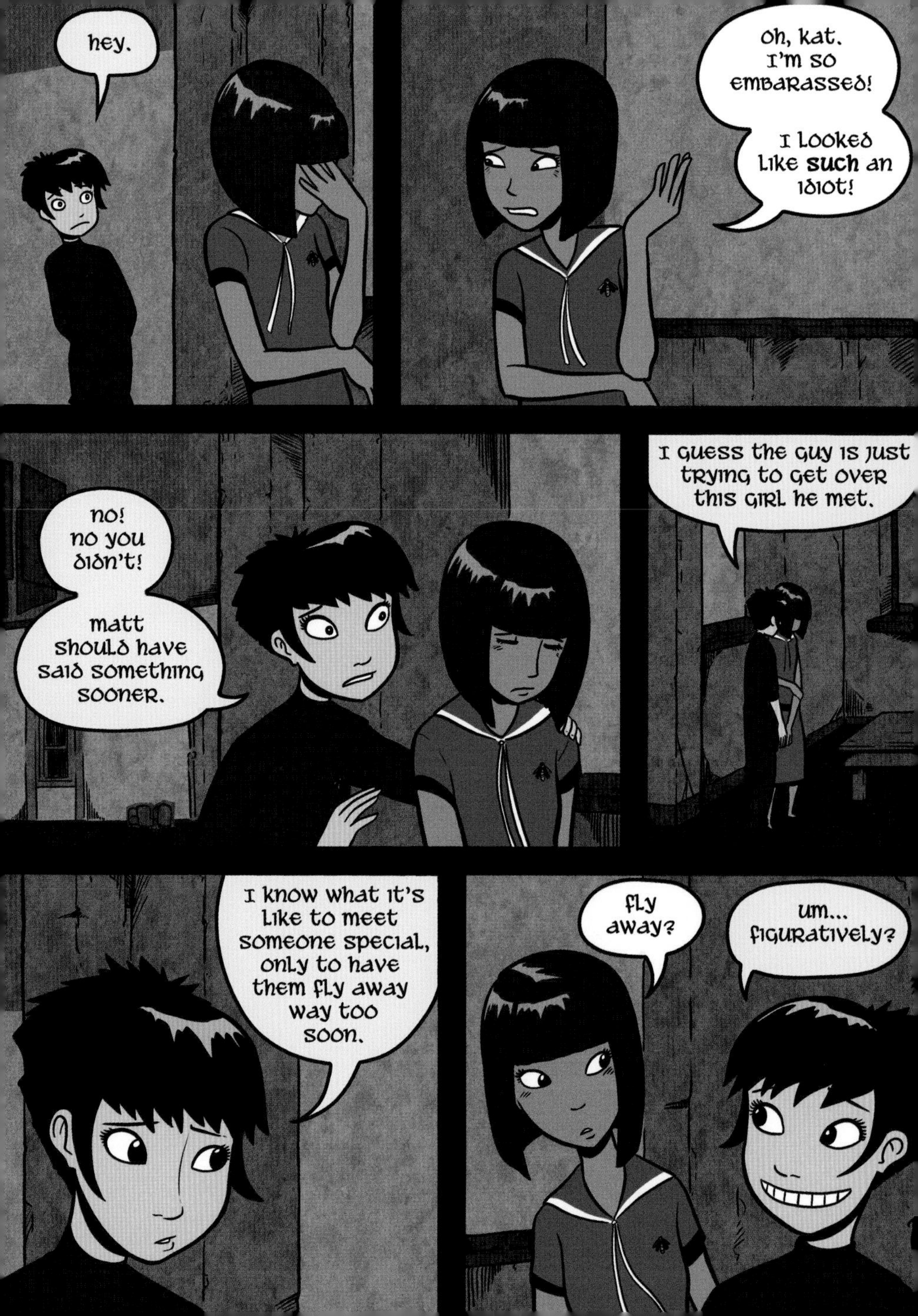
hey.
oh, kat. I'm so embarassed!
I looked like **such** an idiot!
no! no you didn't!
matt should have said something sooner.
I guess the guy is just trying to get over this girl he met.
I know what it's like to meet someone special, only to have them fly away way too soon.
fly away?
um... figuratively?

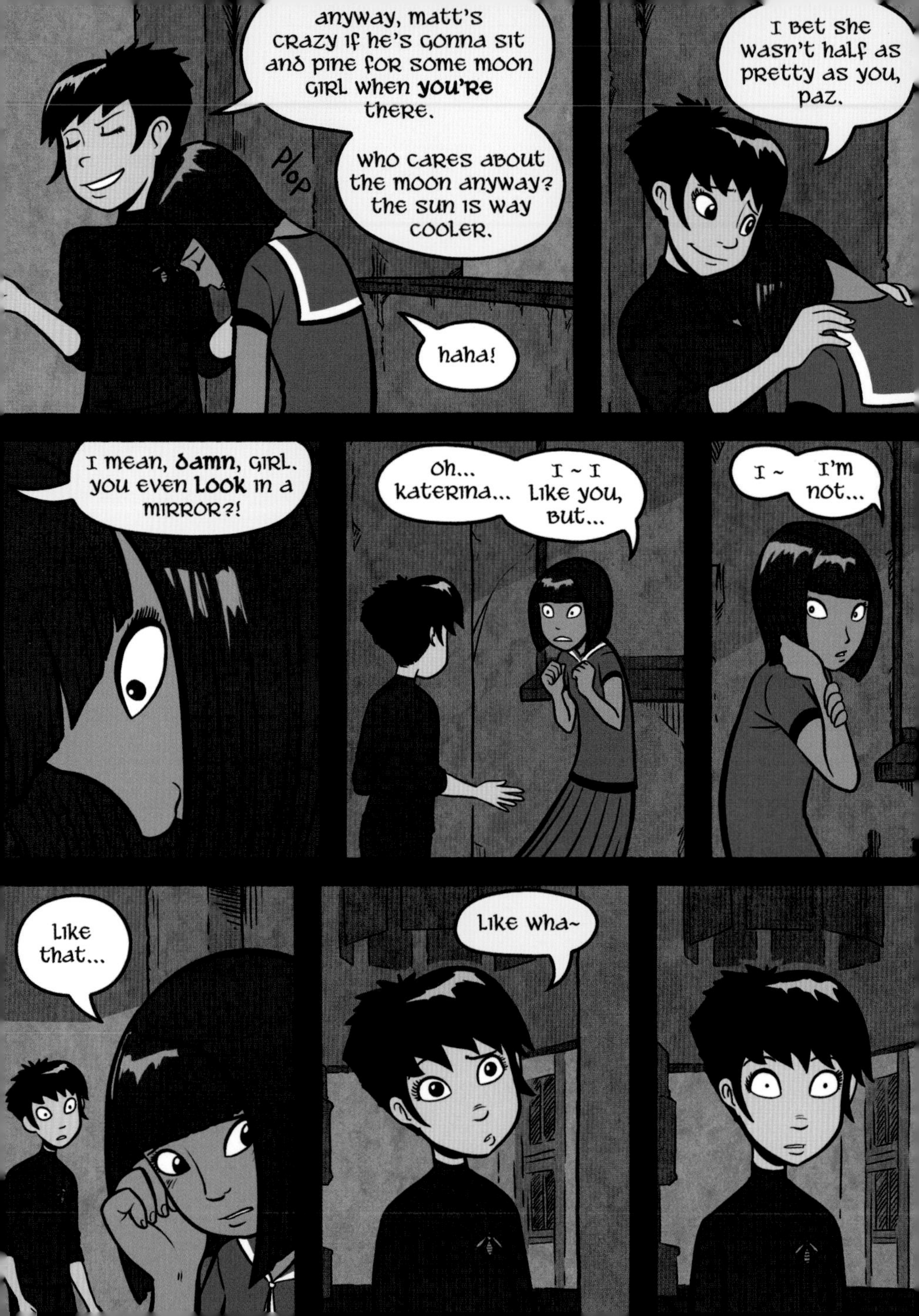
anyway, matt's crazy if he's gonna sit and pine for some moon girl when **you're** there.
who cares about the moon anyway? the sun is way cooler.
Plop
haha!
I bet she wasn't half as pretty as you, paz.
I mean, **damn**, girl. you even **look** in a mirror?!
Oh... katerina...
I ~ I like you, but...
I ~
I'm not...
like that...
like wha~

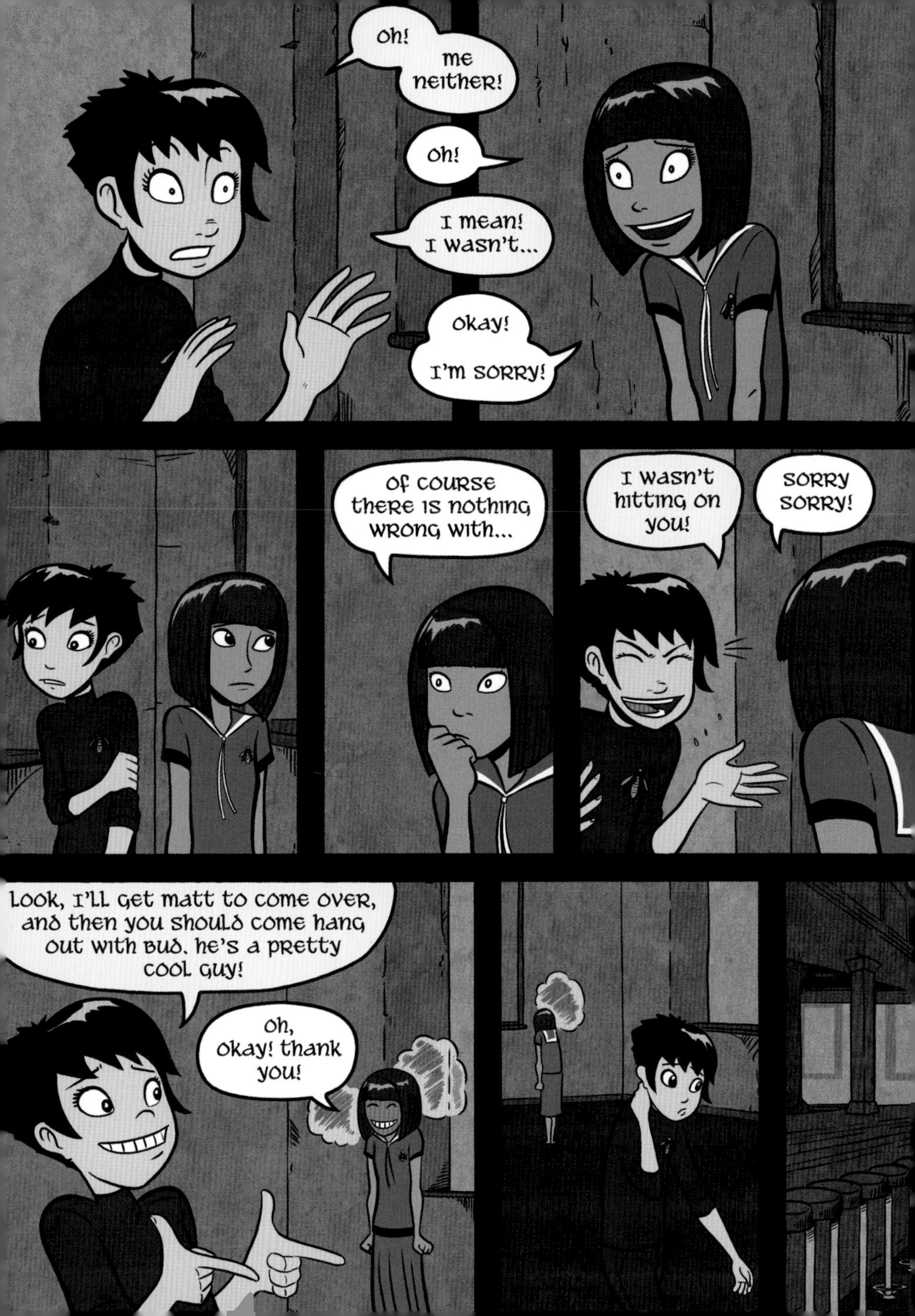
Oh!
me neither!
Oh!
I mean! I wasn't...
Okay!
I'm sorry!
Of course there is nothing wrong with...
I wasn't hitting on you!
Sorry sorry!
Look, I'll get Matt to come over, and then you should come hang out with Bud. He's a pretty cool guy!
Oh, okay! Thank you!

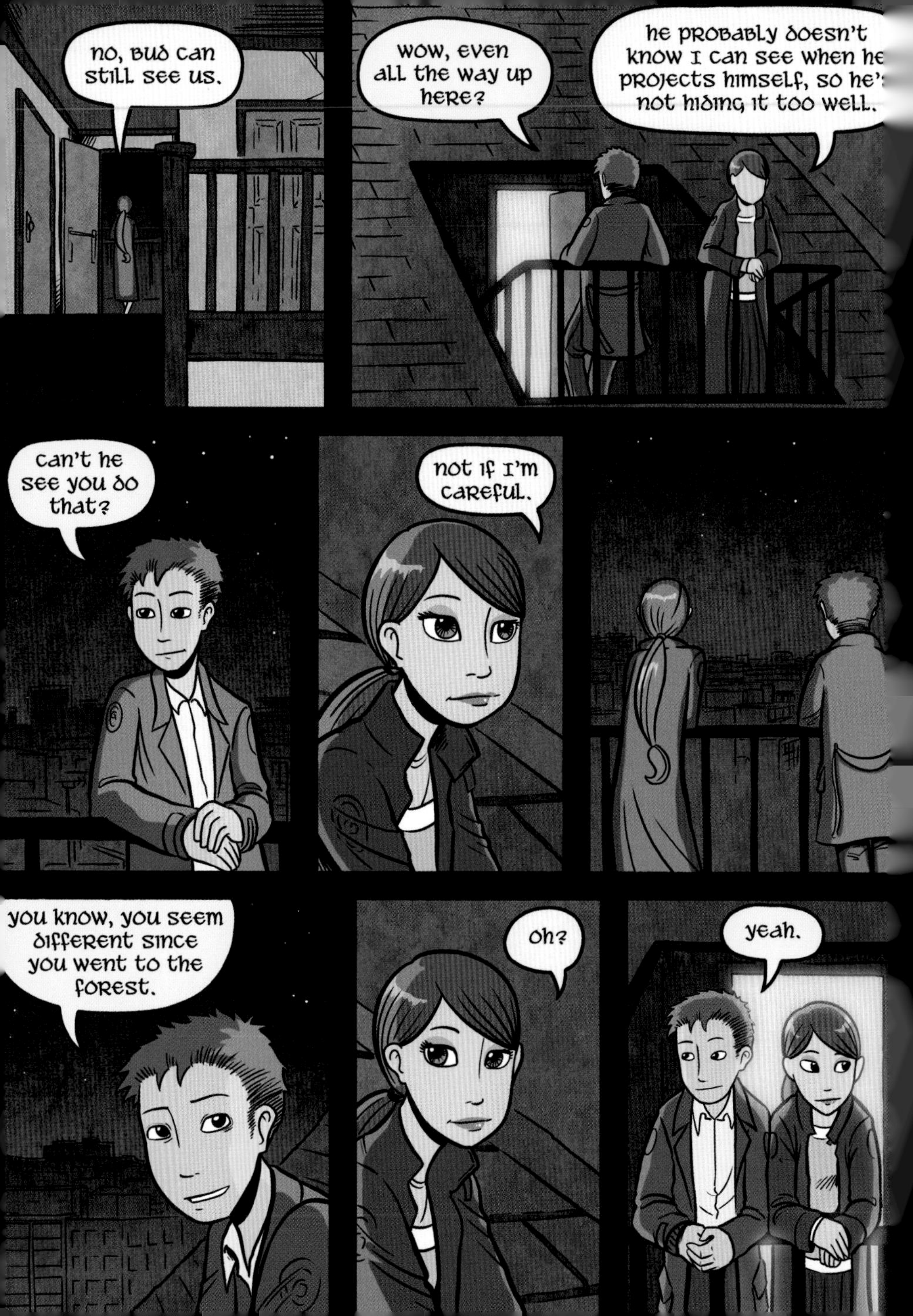
no, bud can still see us.
wow, even all the way up here?
he probably doesn't know I can see when he projects himself, so he's not hiding it too well.
can't he see you do that?
not if I'm careful.
you know, you seem different since you went to the forest.
oh?
yeah.

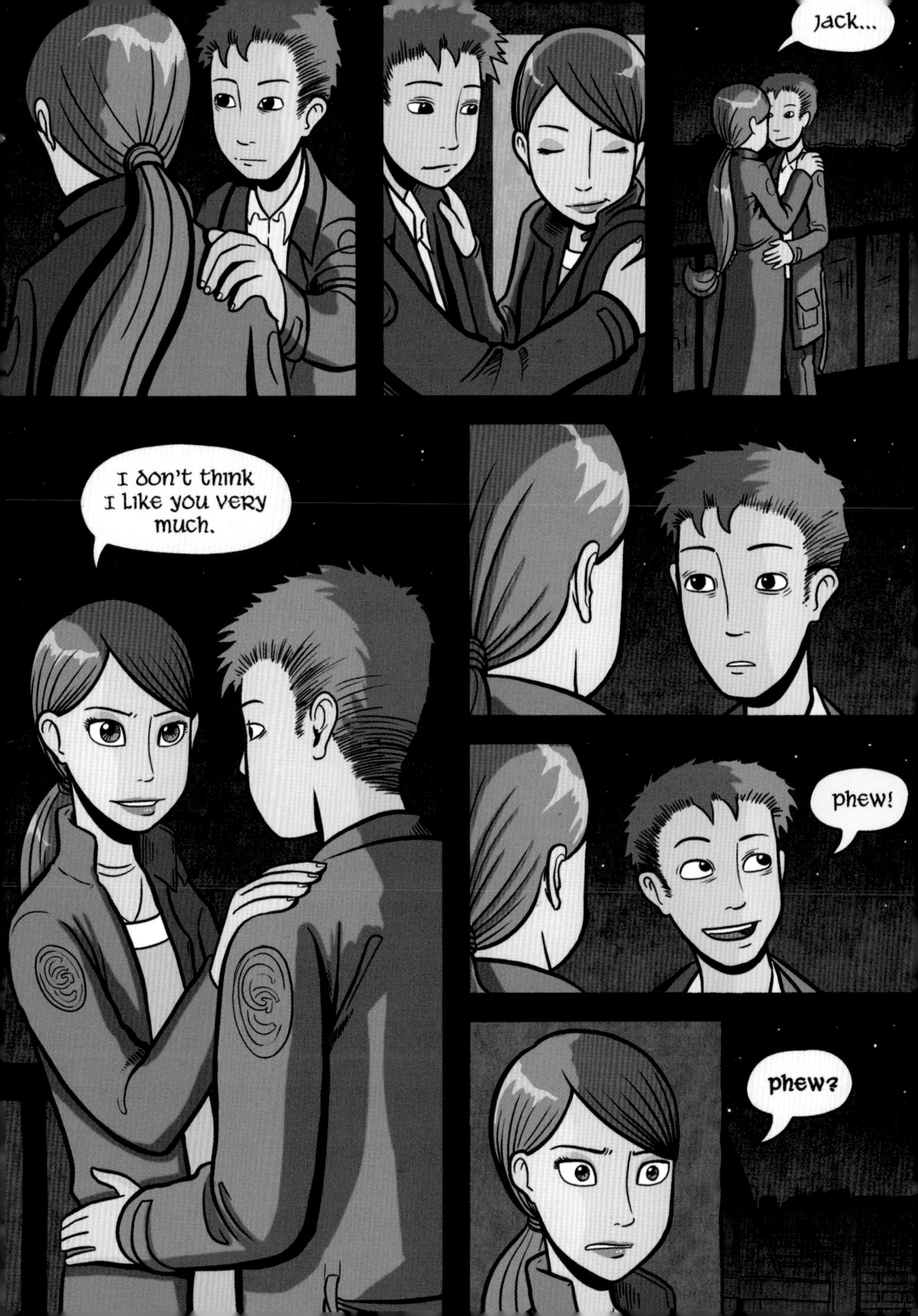
Jack...
I don't think
I like you very
much.
phew!
phew?

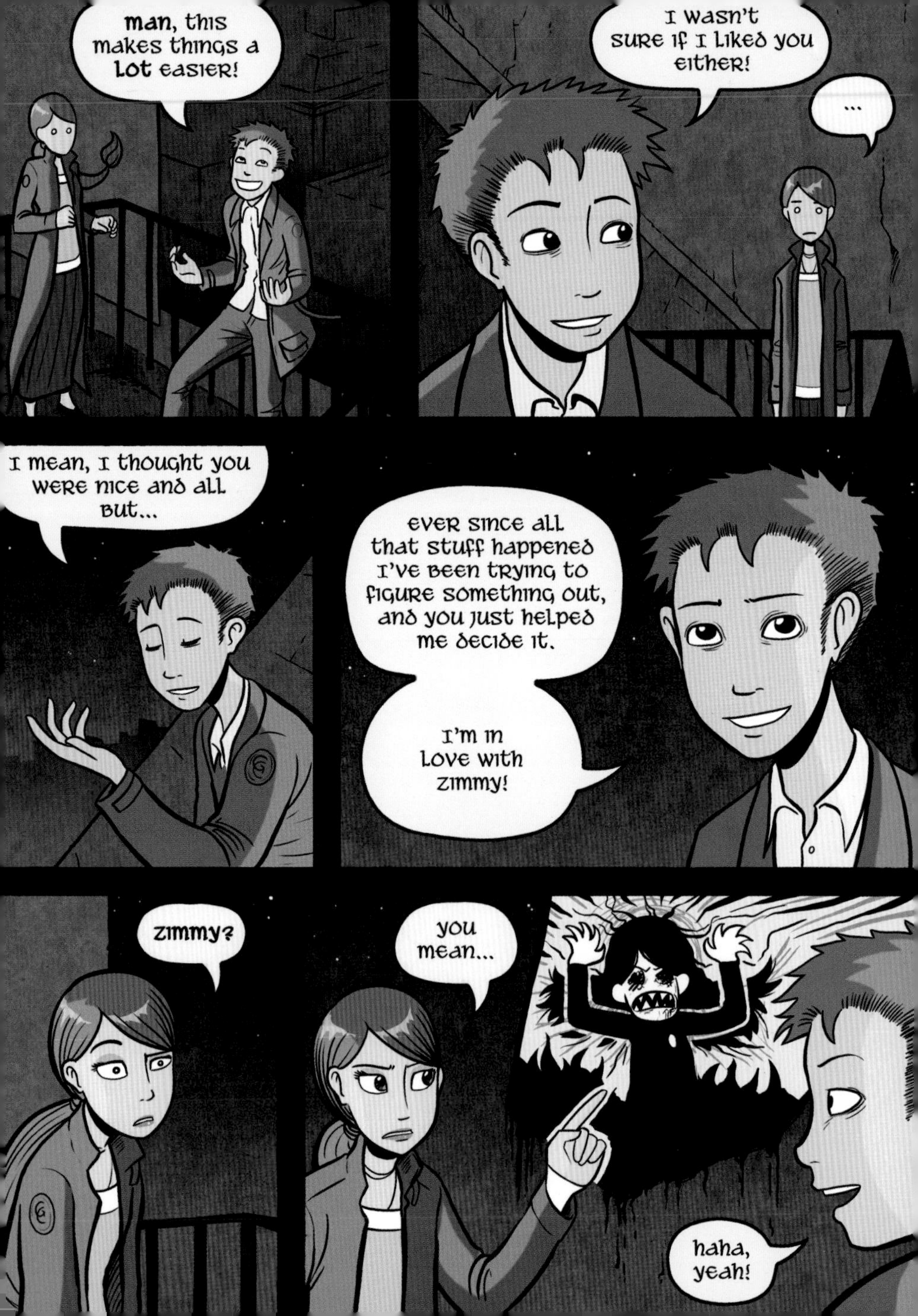
man, this makes things a lot easier!
I wasn't sure if I liked you either!
...
I mean, I thought you were nice and all but...
ever since all that stuff happened I've been trying to figure something out, and you just helped me decide it.
I'm in love with zimmy!
zimmy?
you mean...
haha, yeah!

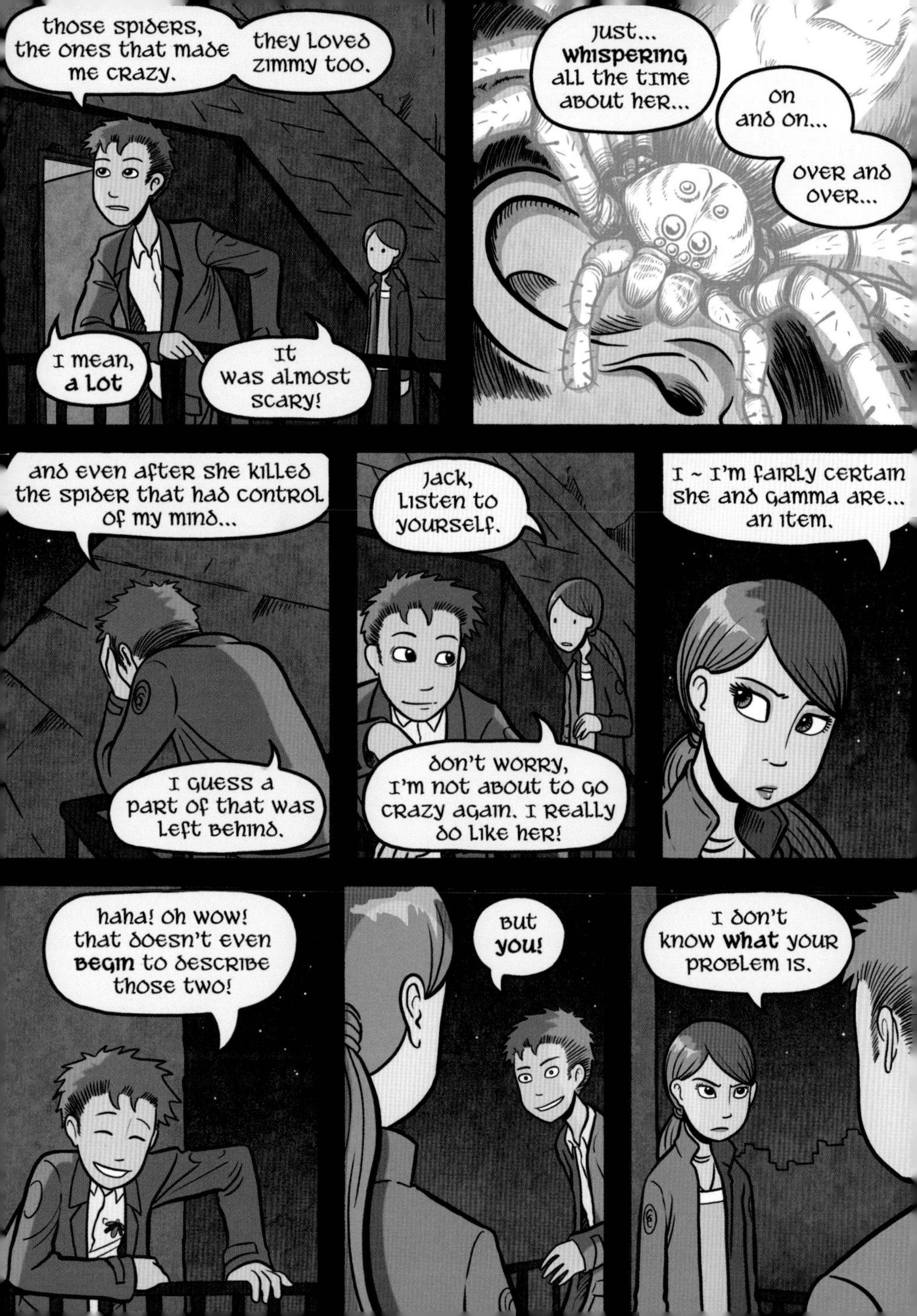
those spiders, the ones that made me crazy.
they loved zimmy too.
I mean, **a lot**
It was almost scary!
just... **whispering** all the time about her...
on and on...
over and over...
and even after she killed the spider that had control of my mind...
I guess a part of that was left behind.
Jack, listen to yourself.
don't worry, I'm not about to go crazy again. I really do like her!
I ~ I'm fairly certain she and gamma are... an item.
haha! oh wow! that doesn't even **begin** to describe those two!
But **you!**
I don't know **what** your problem is.

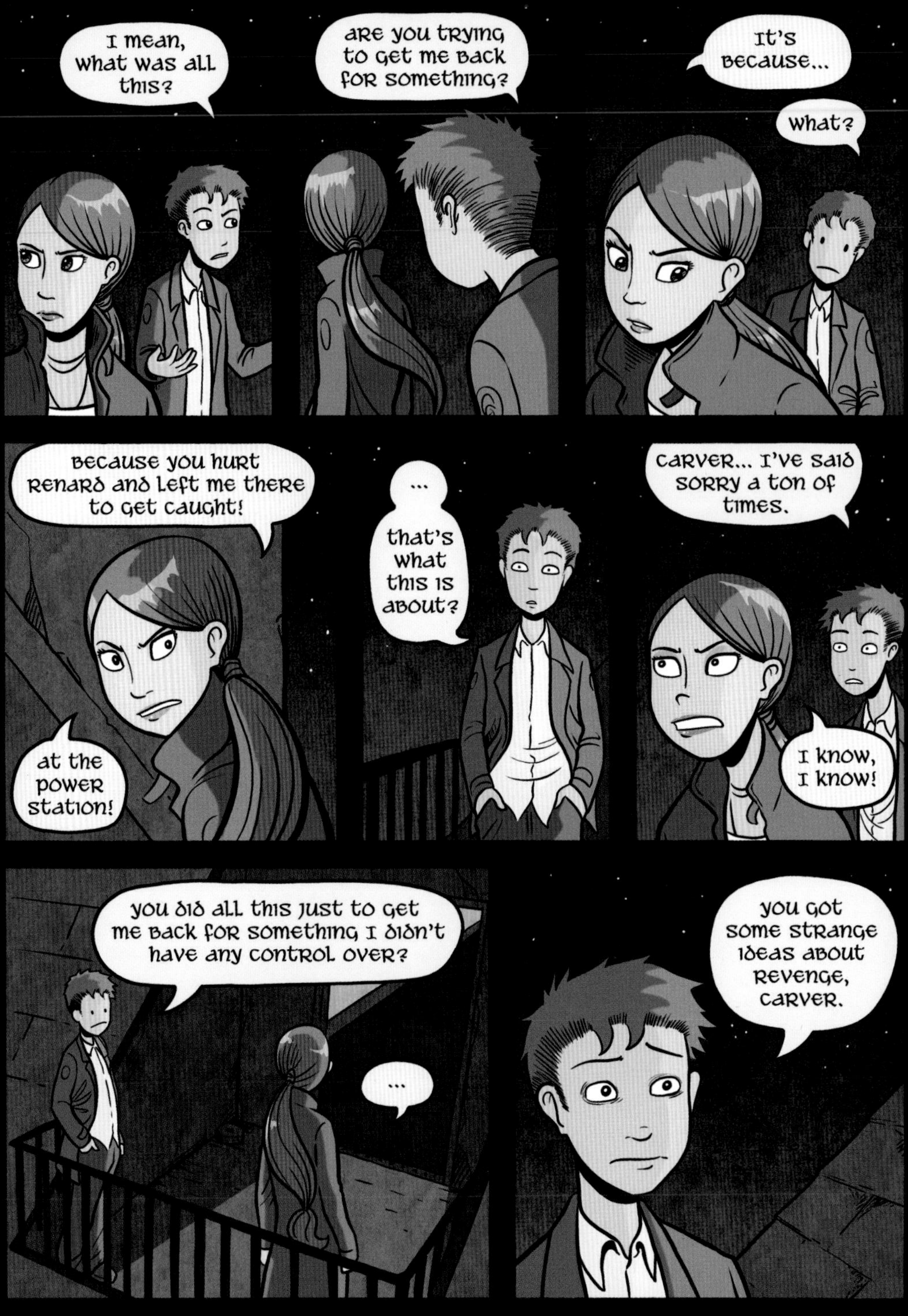
I mean, what was all this?
are you trying to get me back for something?
It's because...
what?
Because you hurt Renard and left me there to get caught!
at the power station!
...
that's what this is about?
Carver... I've said sorry a ton of times.
I know, I know!
you did all this just to get me back for something I didn't have any control over?
...
you got some strange ideas about revenge, Carver.

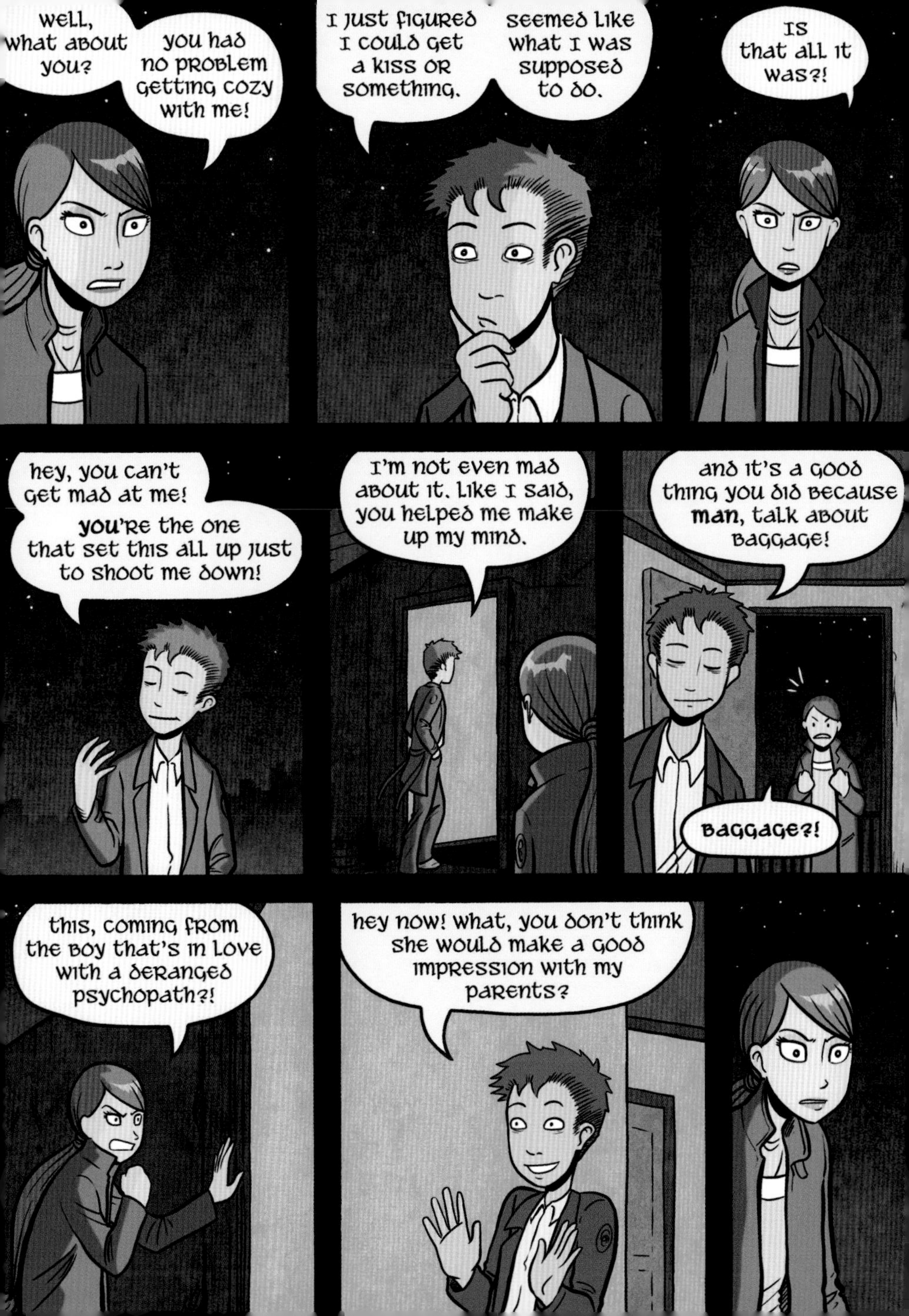
well, what about you?
you had no problem getting cozy with me!
I just figured I could get a kiss or something.
seemed like what I was supposed to do.
Is that all it was?!
hey, you can't get mad at me!
you're the one that set this all up just to shoot me down!
I'm not even mad about it. like I said, you helped me make up my mind.
and it's a good thing you did because man, talk about baggage!
baggage?!
this, coming from the boy that's in love with a deranged psychopath?!
hey now! what, you don't think she would make a good impression with my parents?

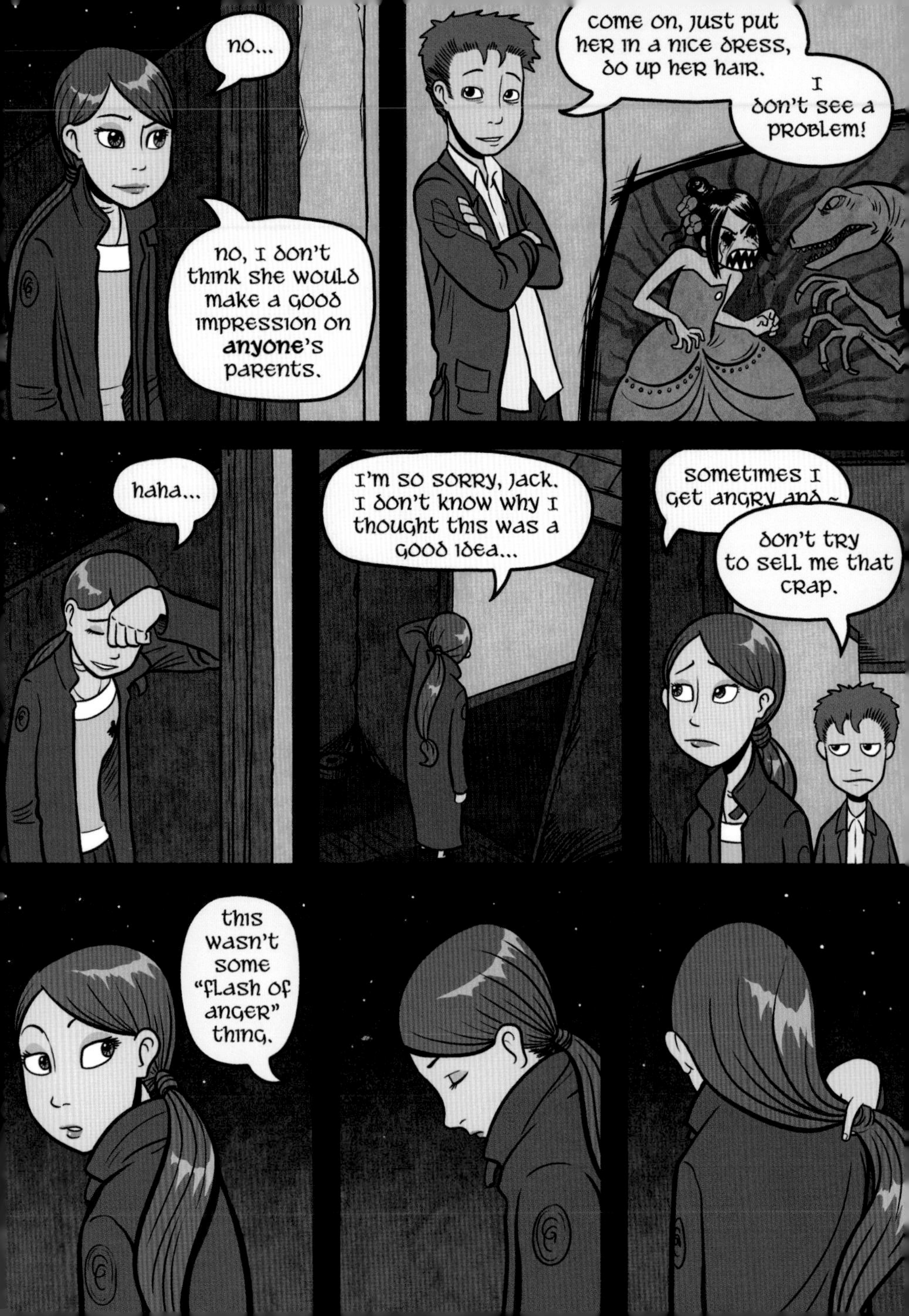
no...
no, I don't think she would make a good impression on **anyone**'s parents.
come on, just put her in a nice dress, do up her hair.
I don't see a problem!
haha...
I'm so sorry, Jack. I don't know why I thought this was a good idea...
sometimes I get angry and ~
don't try to sell me that crap.
this wasn't some "flash of anger" thing.

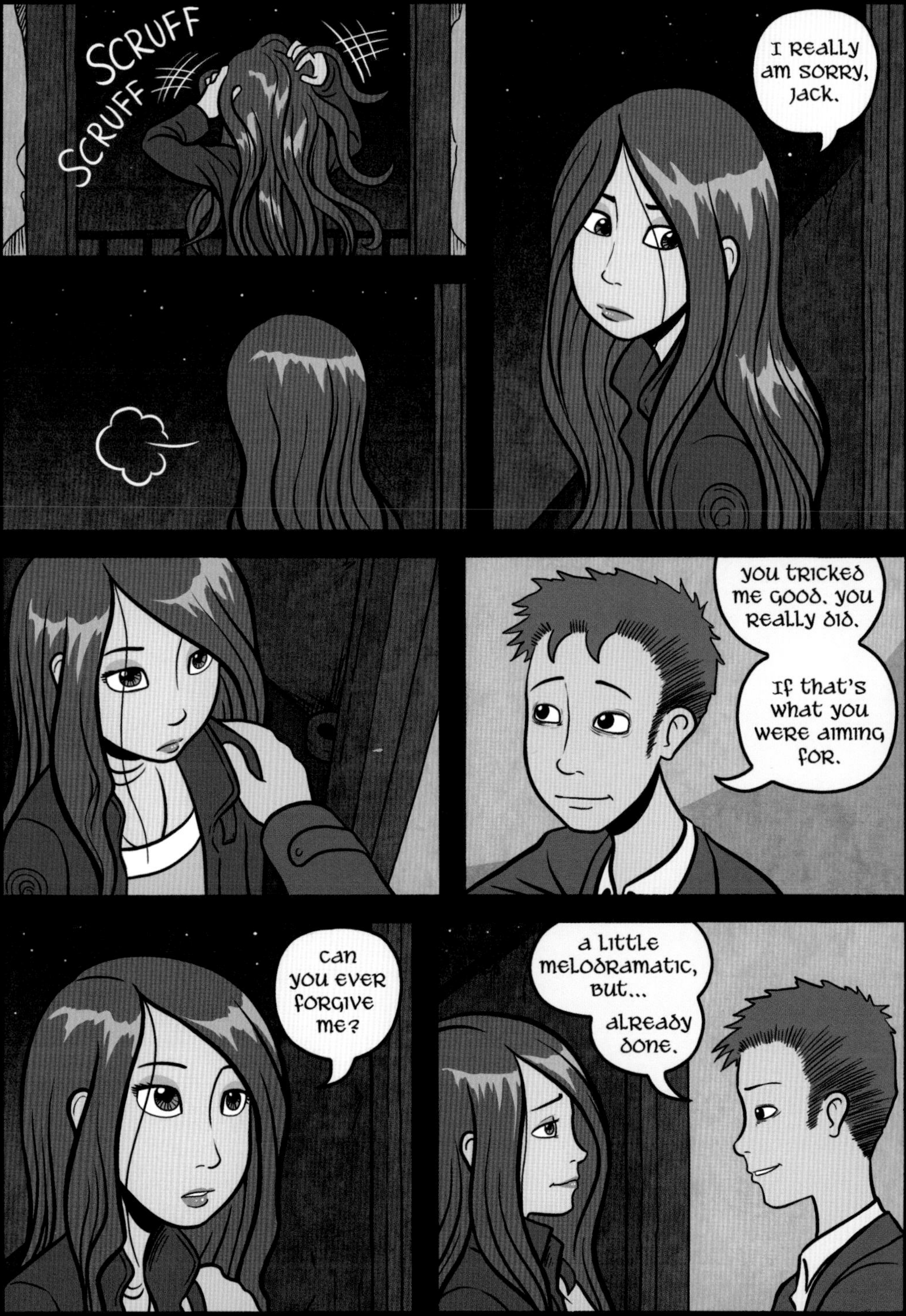
SCRUFF
SCRUFF
I really am sorry, Jack.
you tricked me good. you really did.
If that's what you were aiming for.
can you ever forgive me?
a little melodramatic, but...
already done.

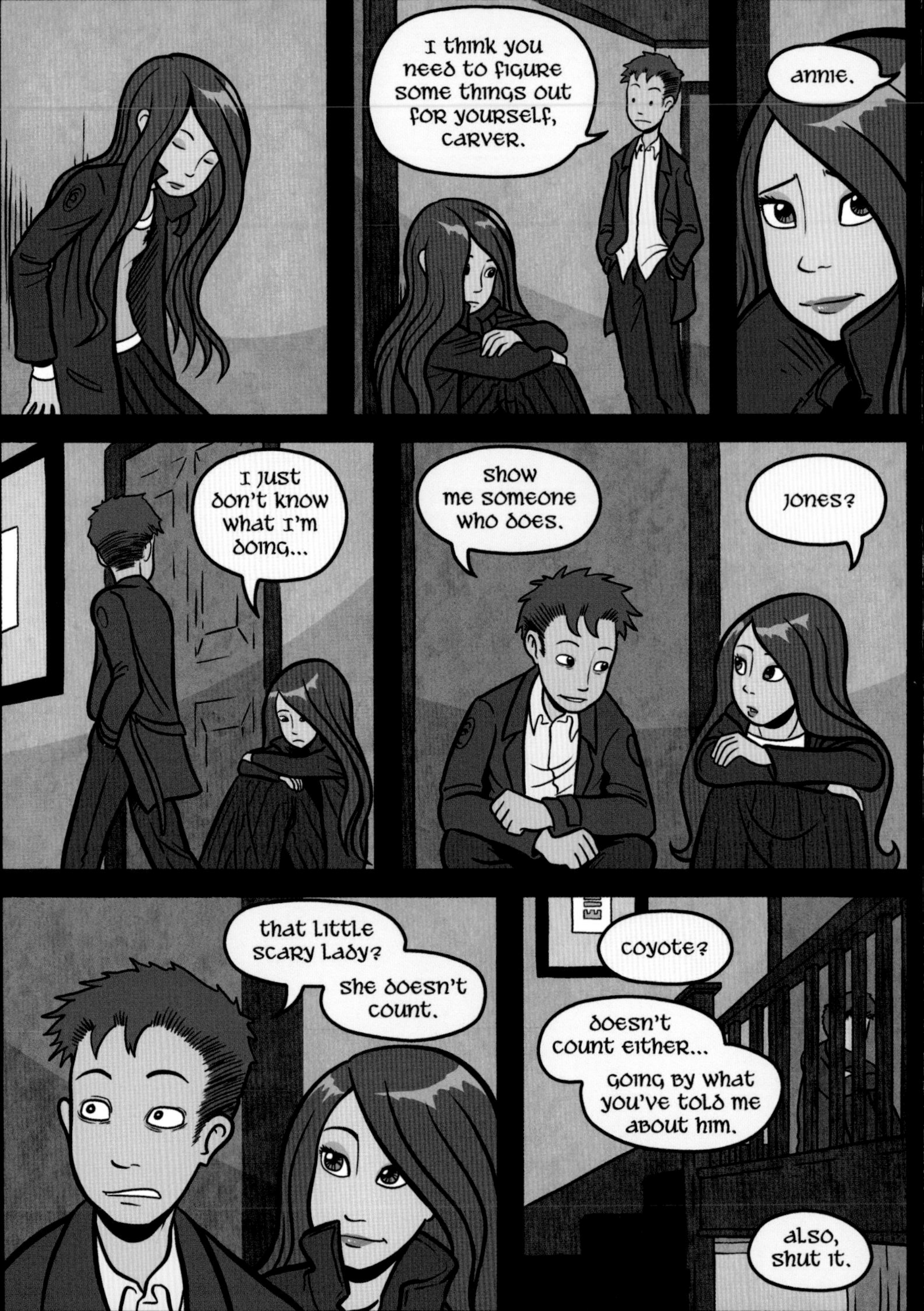
I think you need to figure some things out for yourself, Carver.
Annie.
I just don't know what I'm doing...
Show me someone who does.
Jones?
That little scary lady?
She doesn't count.
Coyote?
Doesn't count either...
Going by what you've told me about him.
Also, shut it.

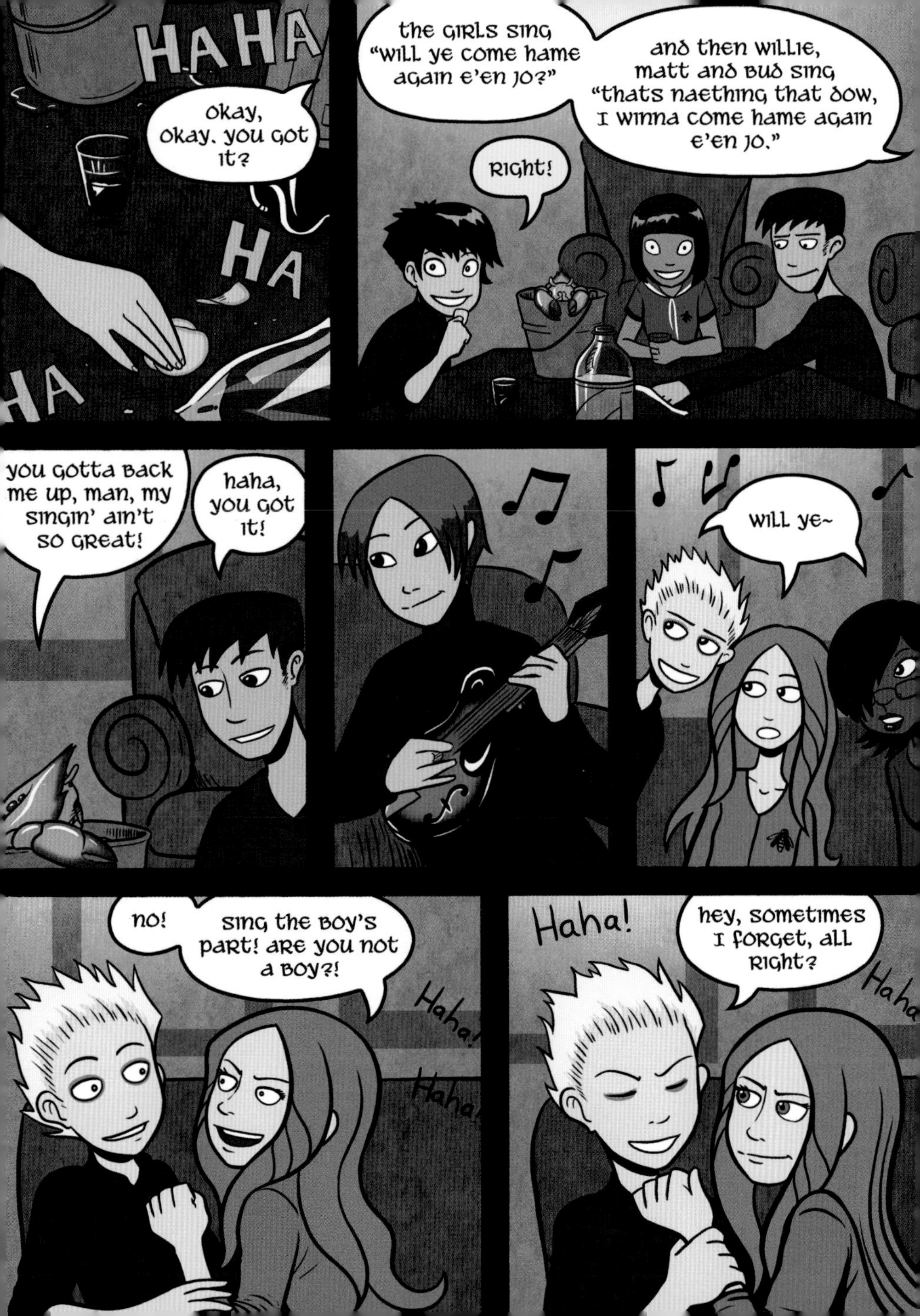
HAHA
Okay, okay. you got it?
HA
HA
HA
the girls sing "will ye come hame again e'en jo?"
and then willie, matt and bud sing "thats naething that dow, I winna come hame again e'en jo."
Right!
you gotta back me up, man, my singin' ain't so great!
haha, you got it!
will ye~
no!
sing the boy's part! are you not a boy?!
Haha!
Haha!
Haha!
hey, sometimes I forget, all right?
Haha

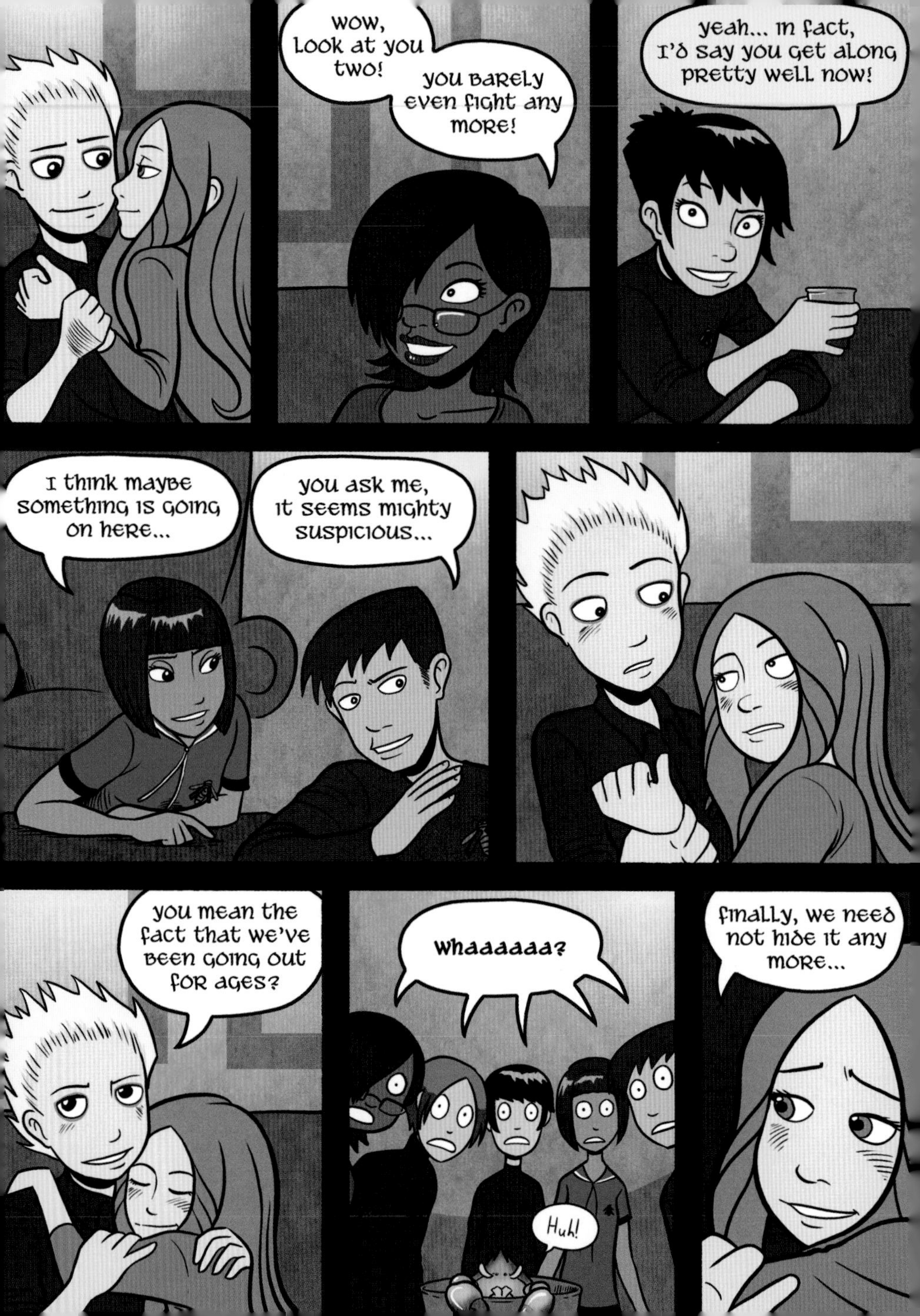
wow, look at you two!
you barely even fight any more!
yeah... in fact, I'd say you get along pretty well now!
I think maybe something is going on here...
you ask me, it seems mighty suspicious...
you mean the fact that we've been going out for ages?
Whaaaaaa?
Huh!
finally, we need not hide it any more...

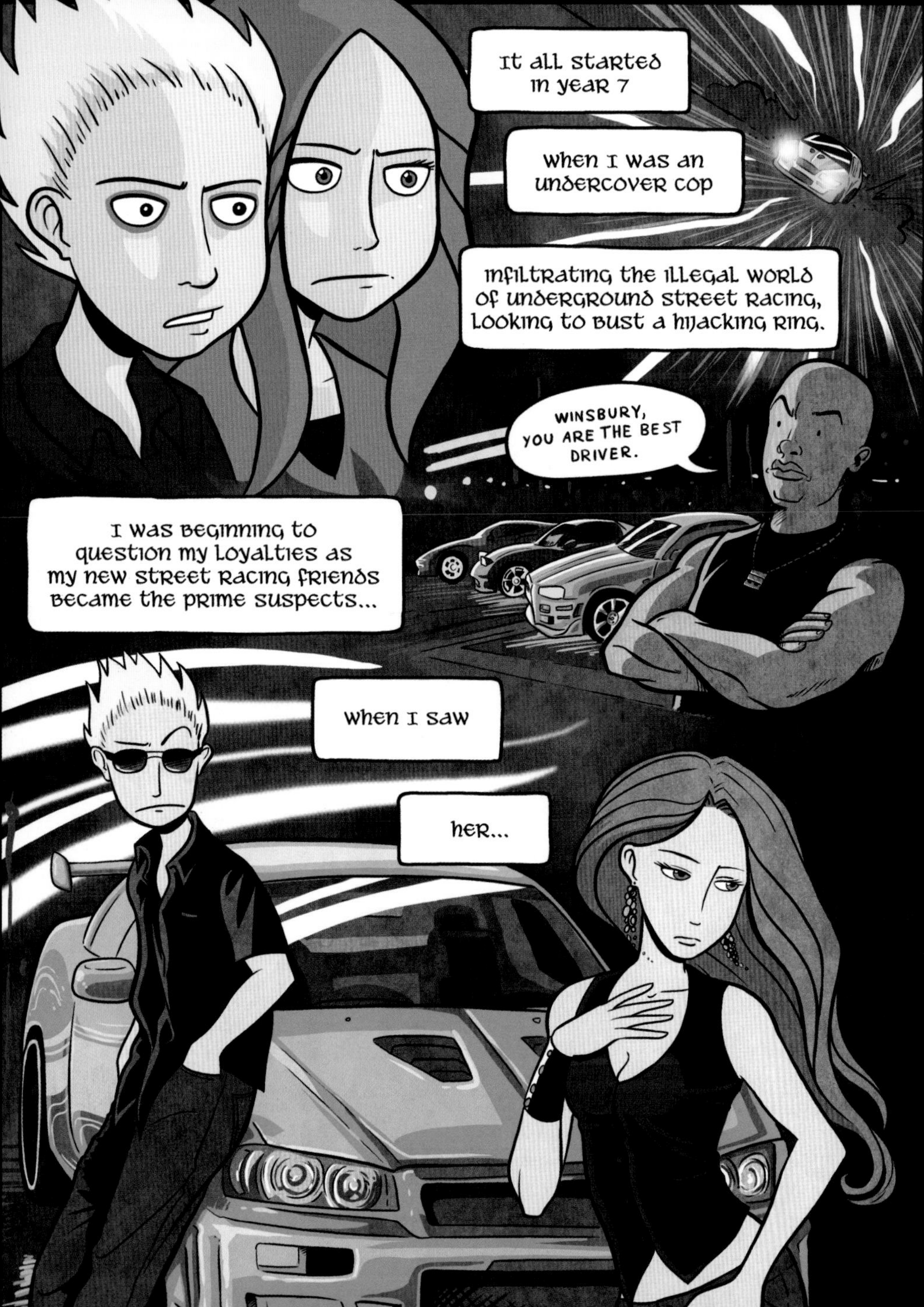
It all started in year 7
when I was an undercover cop
infiltrating the illegal world of underground street racing, looking to bust a hijacking ring.
WINSBURY, YOU ARE THE BEST DRIVER.
I was beginning to question my loyalties as my new street racing friends became the prime suspects...
when I saw
her...

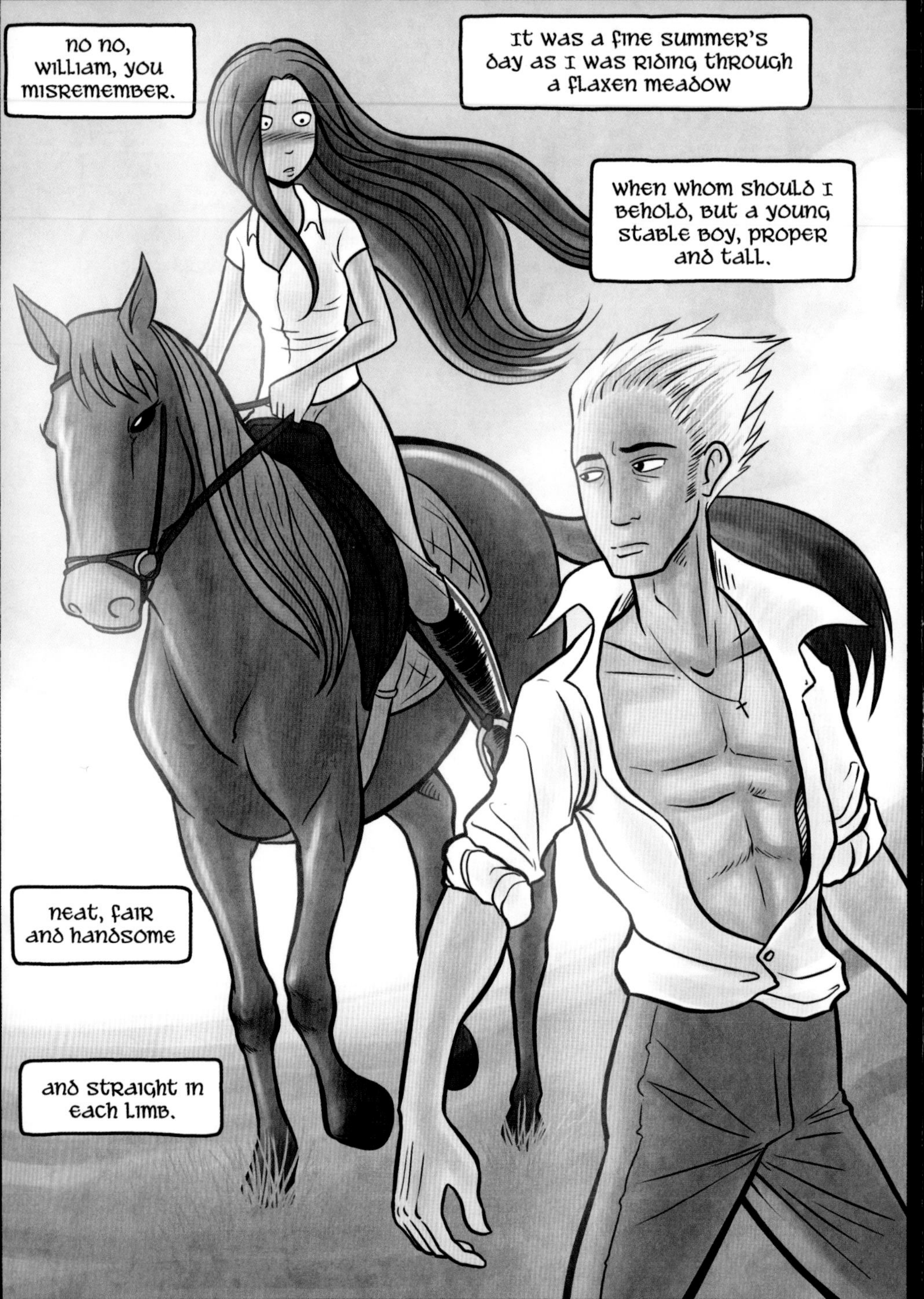
It was a fine summer's day as I was riding through a flaxen meadow
no no, William, you misremember.
when whom should I behold, but a young stable boy, proper and tall.
neat, fair and handsome
and straight in each limb.

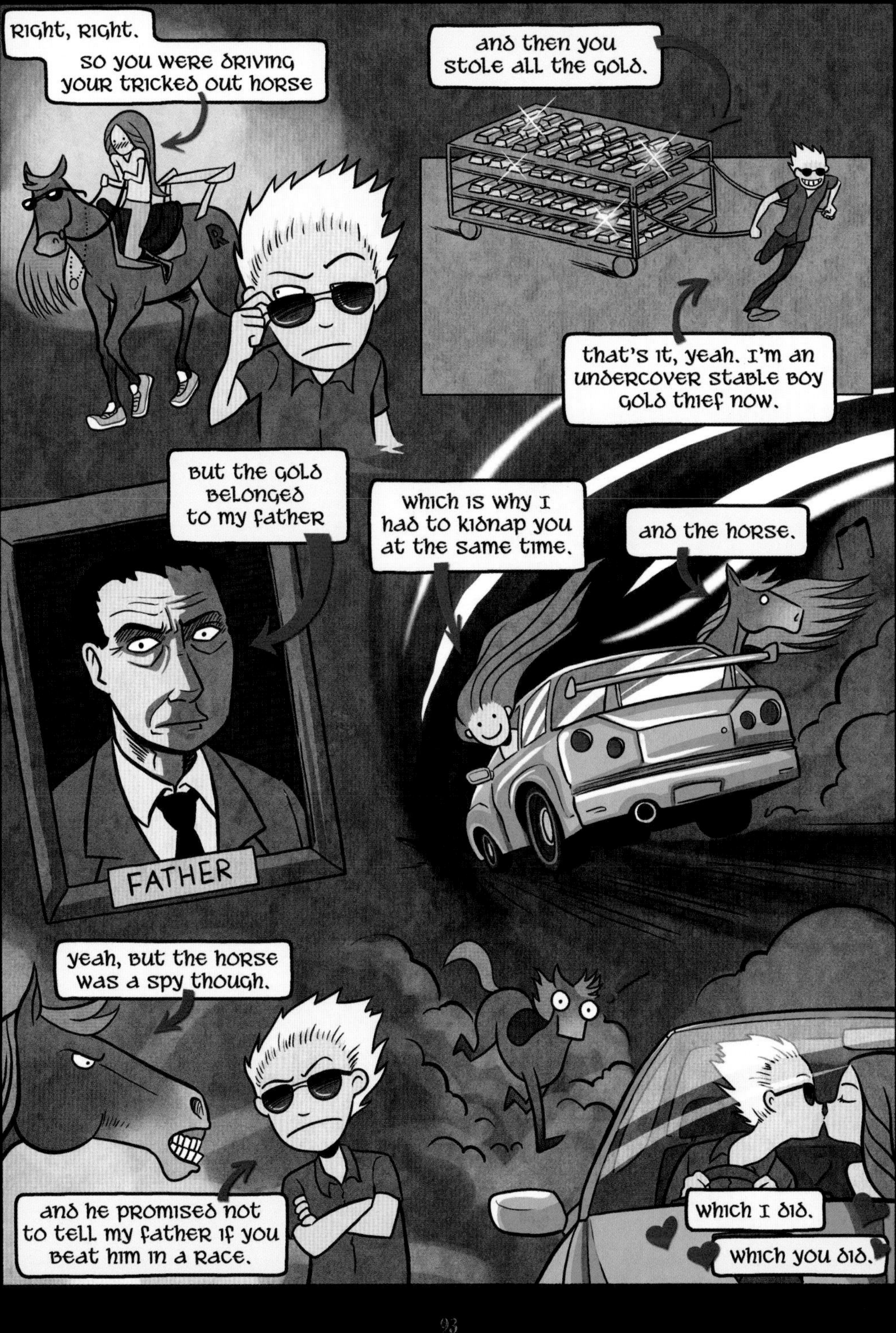
Right, Right.
so you were driving your tricked out horse
and then you stole all the gold.
that's it, yeah. I'm an undercover stable boy gold thief now.
But the gold belonged to my father
FATHER
which is why I had to kidnap you at the same time.
and the horse.
yeah, but the horse was a spy though.
and he promised not to tell my father if you beat him in a race.
which I did.
which you did.

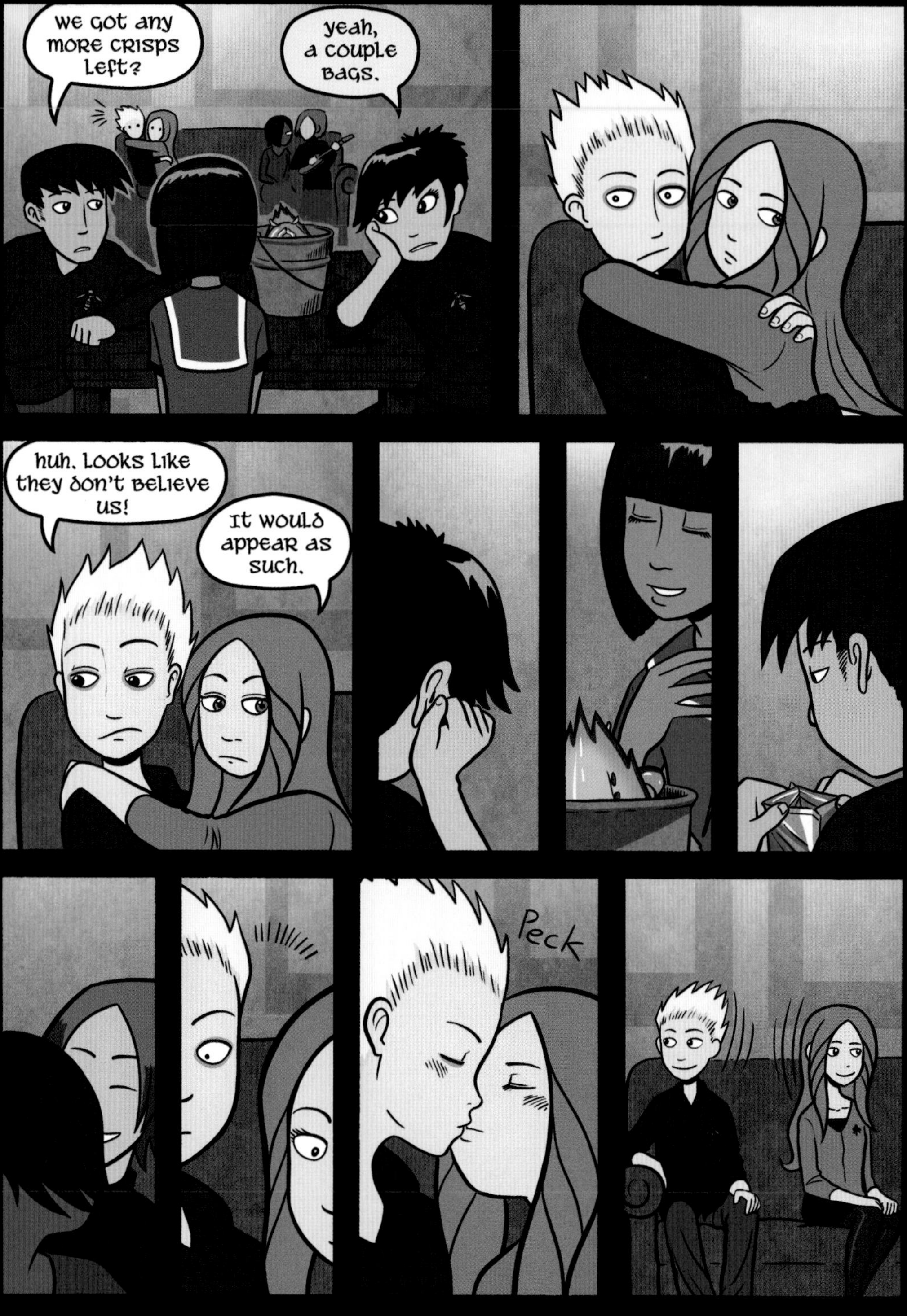
we got any more crisps left?
yeah, a couple bags.
huh. looks like they don't believe us!
It would appear as such.
Peck

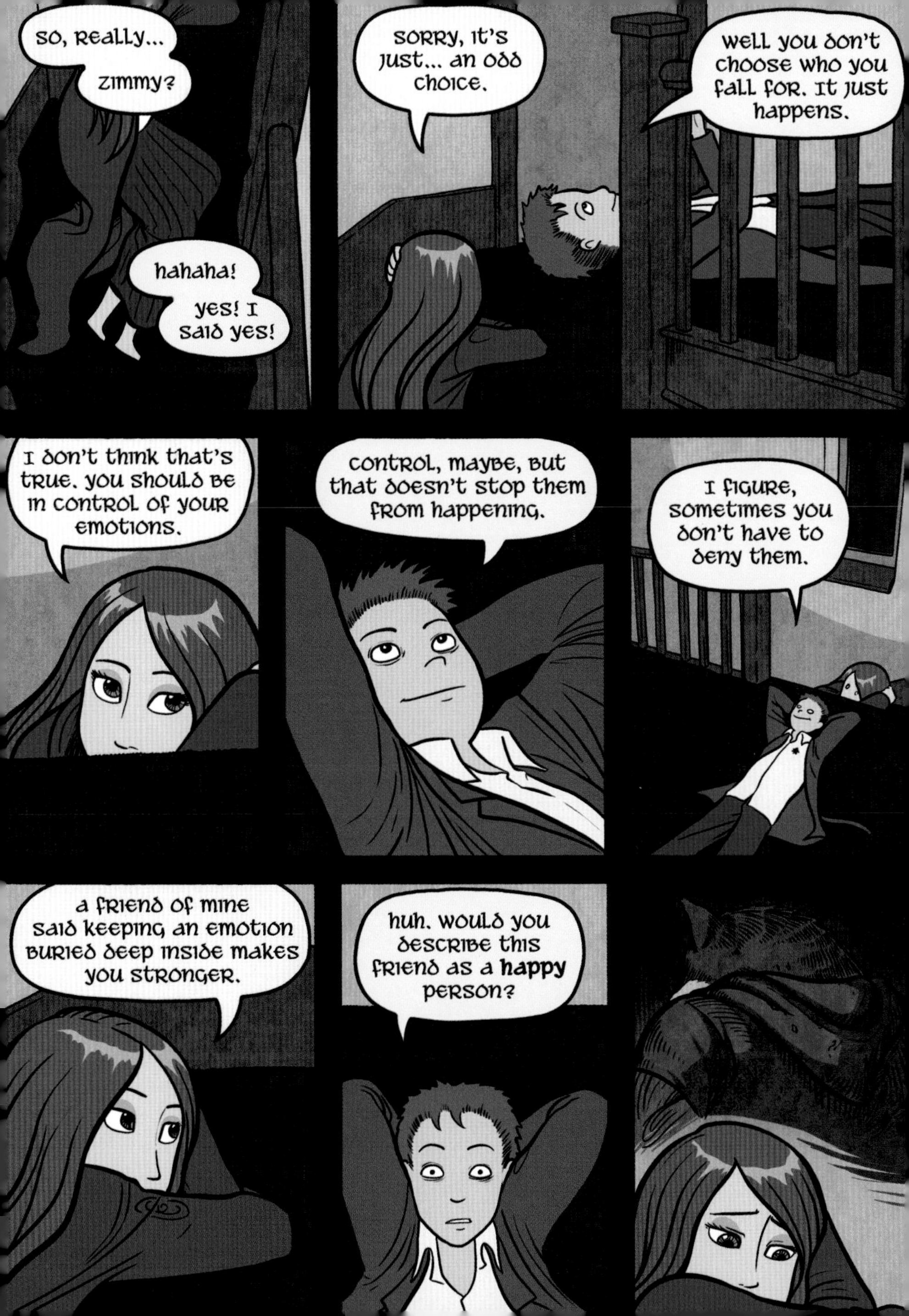
so, really...
zimmy?
hahaha!
yes! I said yes!
sorry, it's just... an odd choice.
well you don't choose who you fall for. it just happens.
I don't think that's true. you should be in control of your emotions.
control, maybe, but that doesn't stop them from happening.
I figure, sometimes you don't have to deny them.
a friend of mine said keeping an emotion buried deep inside makes you stronger.
huh. would you describe this friend as a **happy** person?

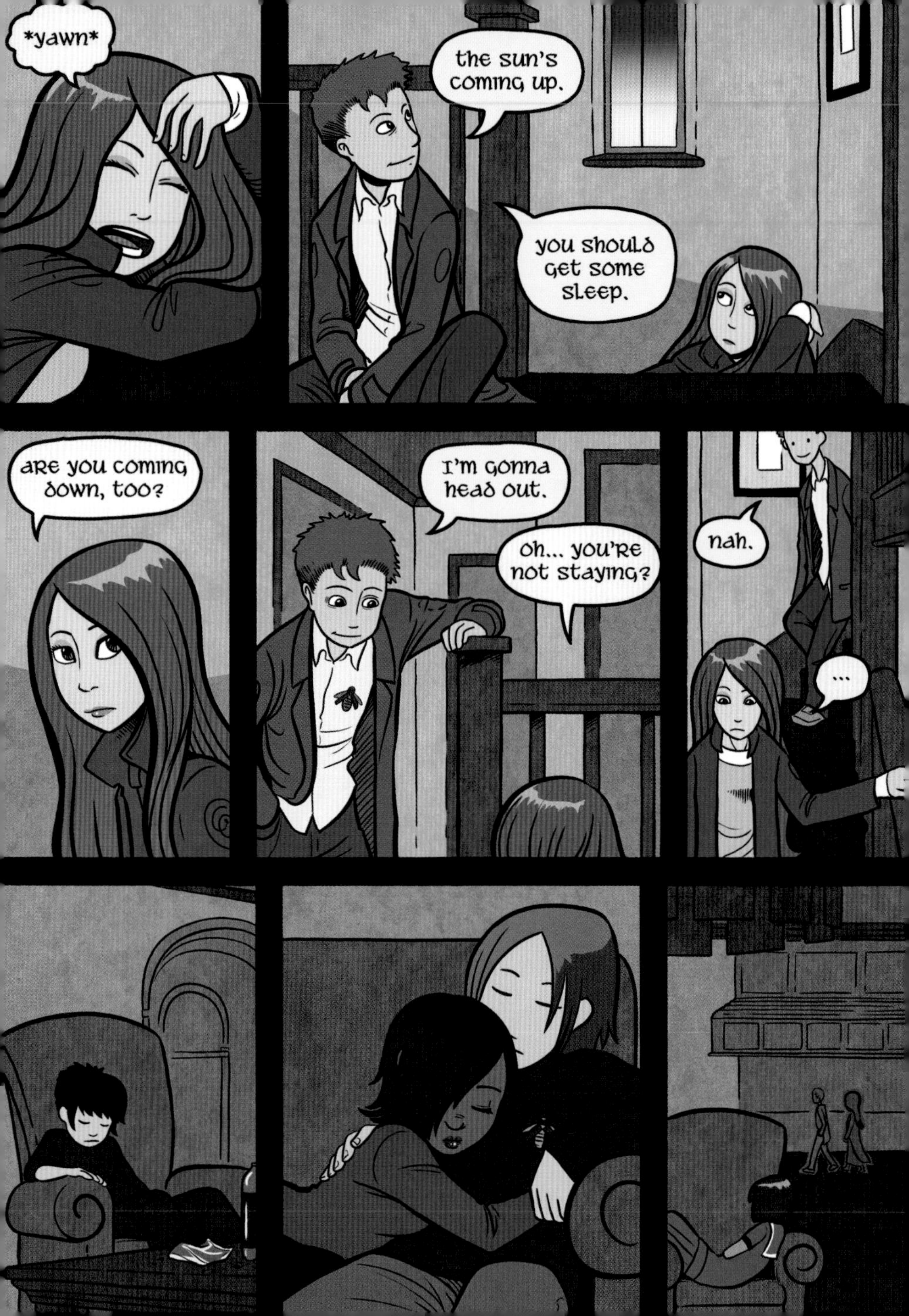
yawn
the sun's coming up.
you should get some sleep.
are you coming down, too?
I'm gonna head out.
oh... you're not staying?
nah.
...

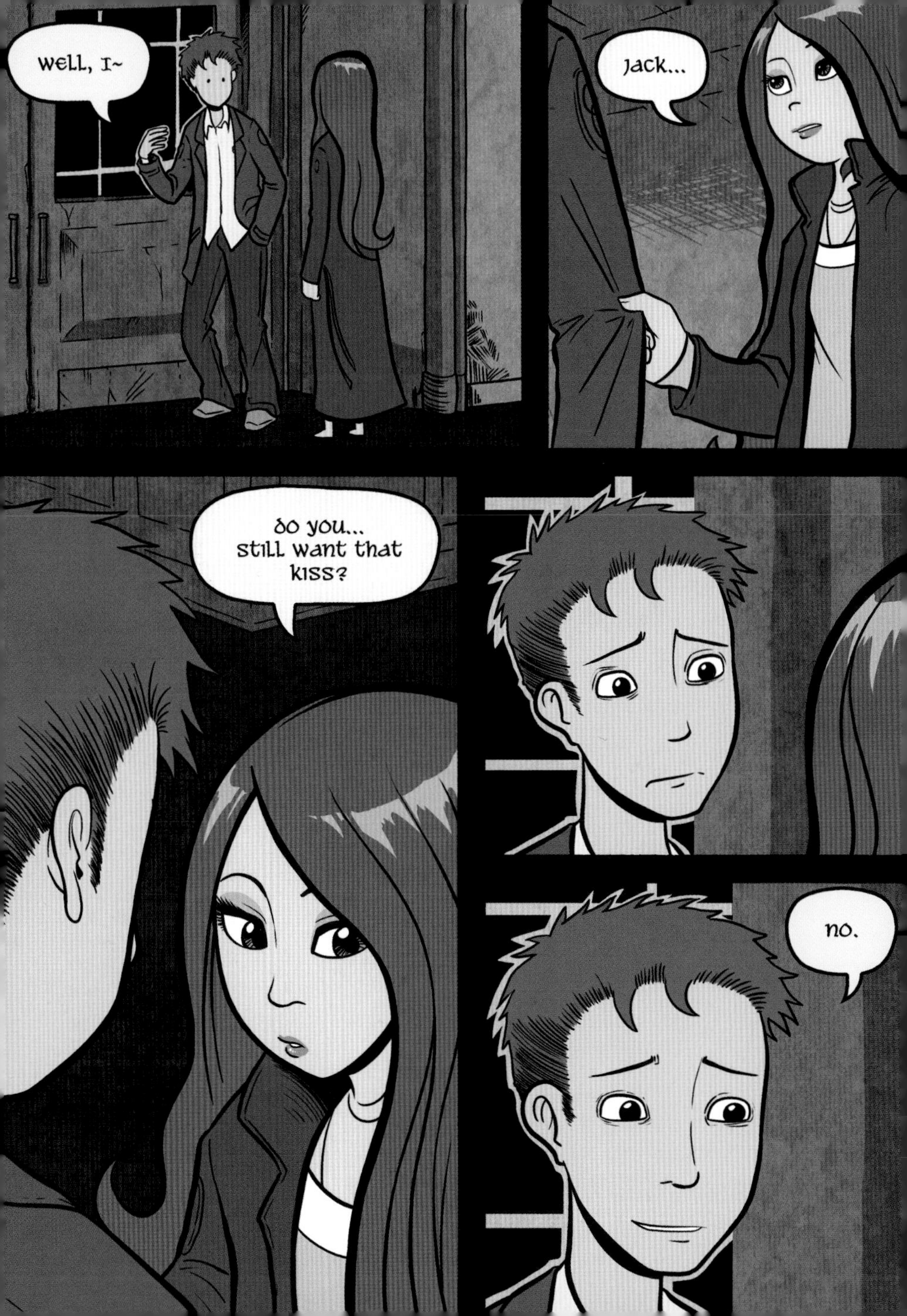
WELL, I~
JACK...
DO YOU... STILL WANT THAT KISS?
NO.

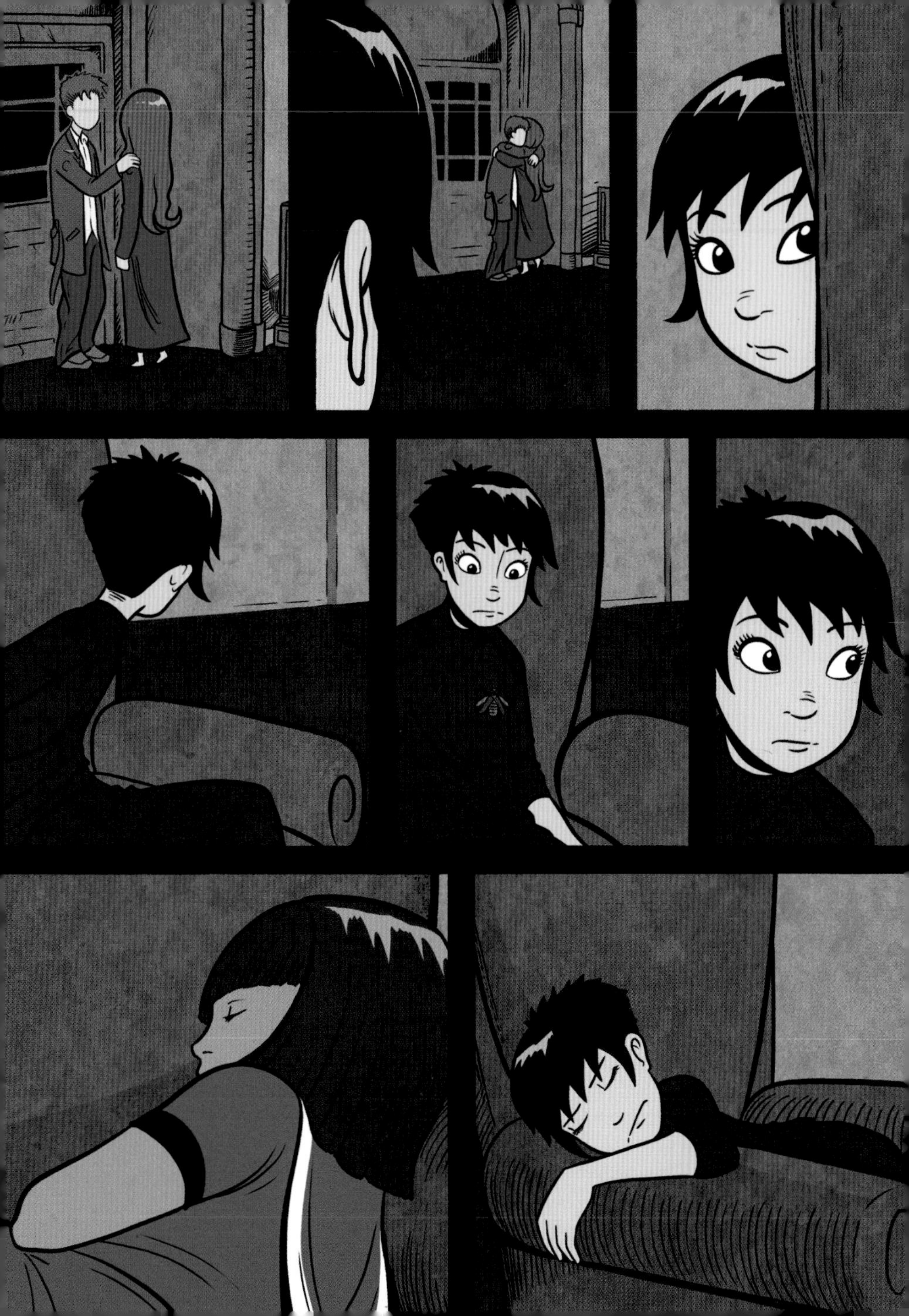

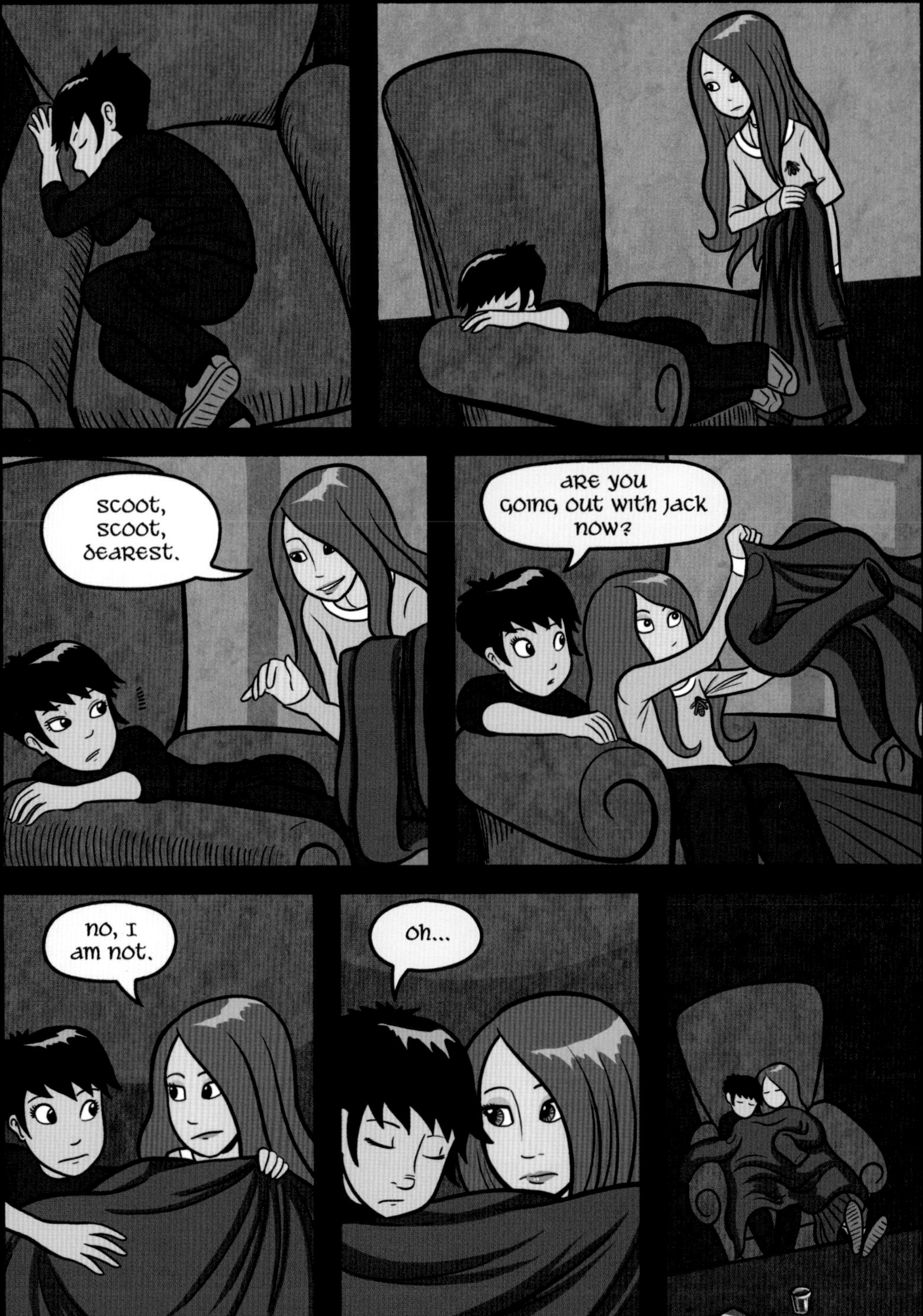
scoot, scoot, dearest.
are you going out with jack now?
no, I am not.
oh...

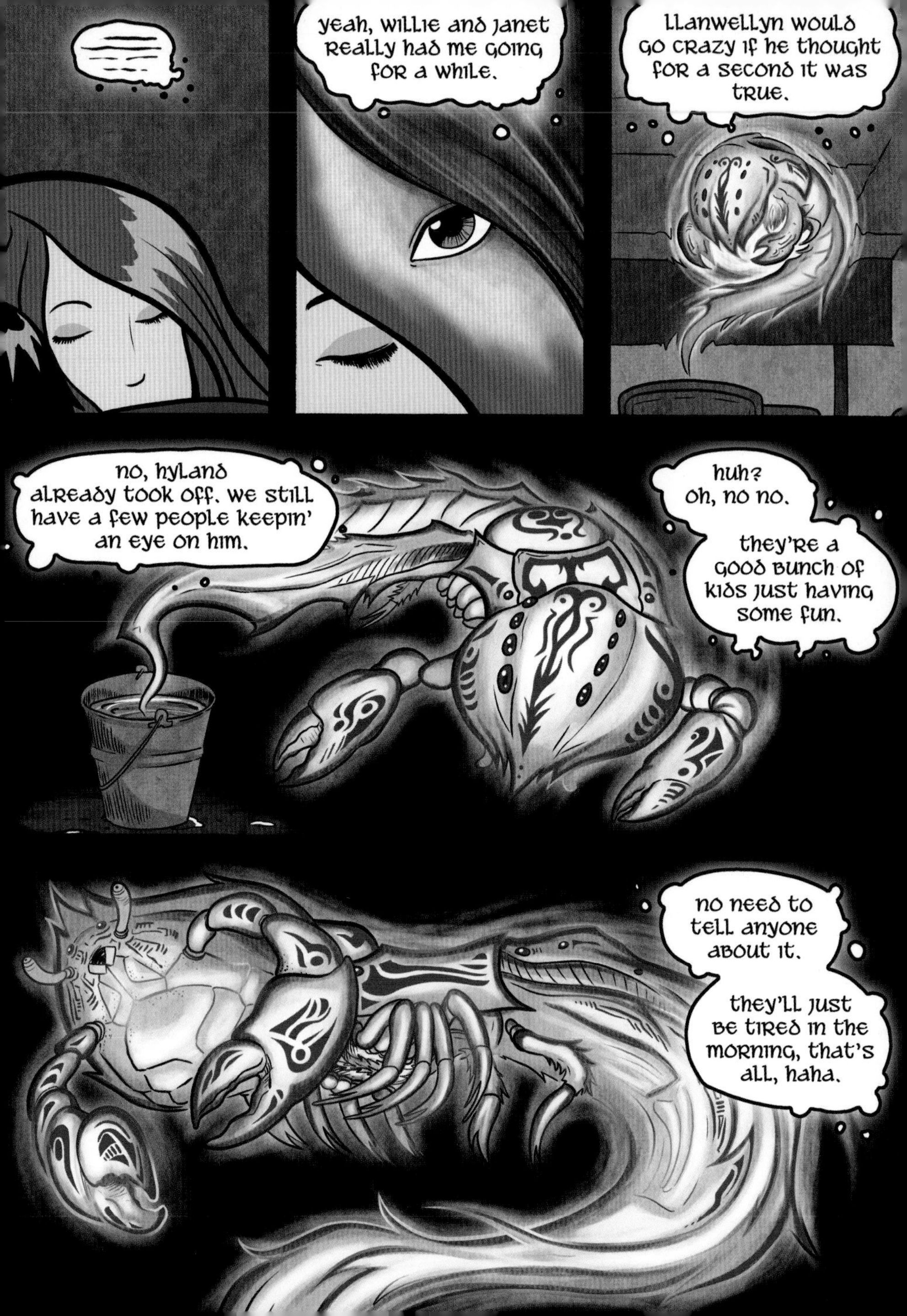
yeah, willie and janet really had me going for a while.
llanwellyn would go crazy if he thought for a second it was true.
no, hyland already took off. we still have a few people keepin' an eye on him.
huh? oh, no no.
they're a good bunch of kids just having some fun.
no need to tell anyone about it.
they'll just be tired in the morning, that's all, haha.

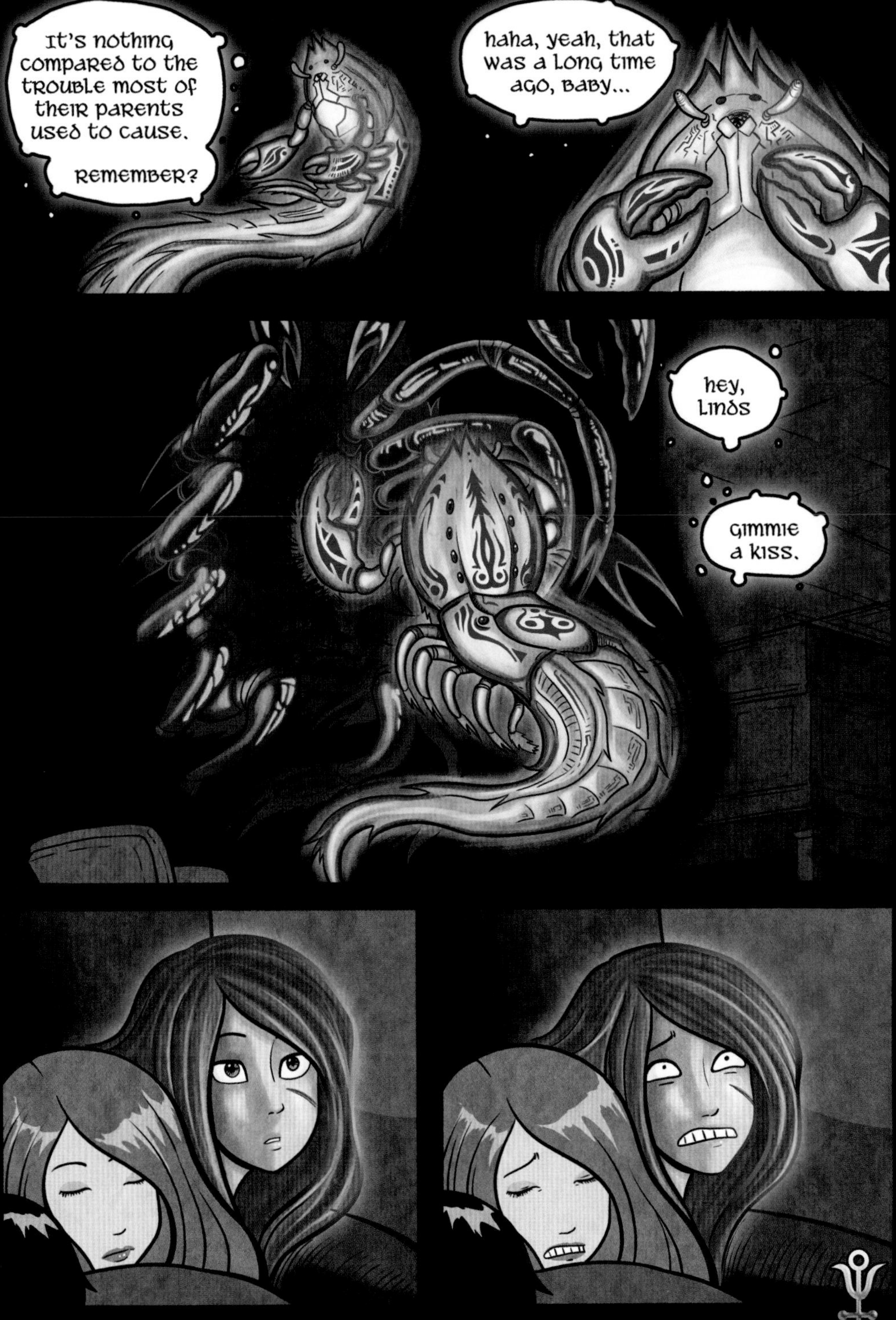
It's nothing compared to the trouble most of their parents used to cause.
Remember?
haha, yeah, that was a long time ago, baby...
hey, Linds
gimmie a kiss.

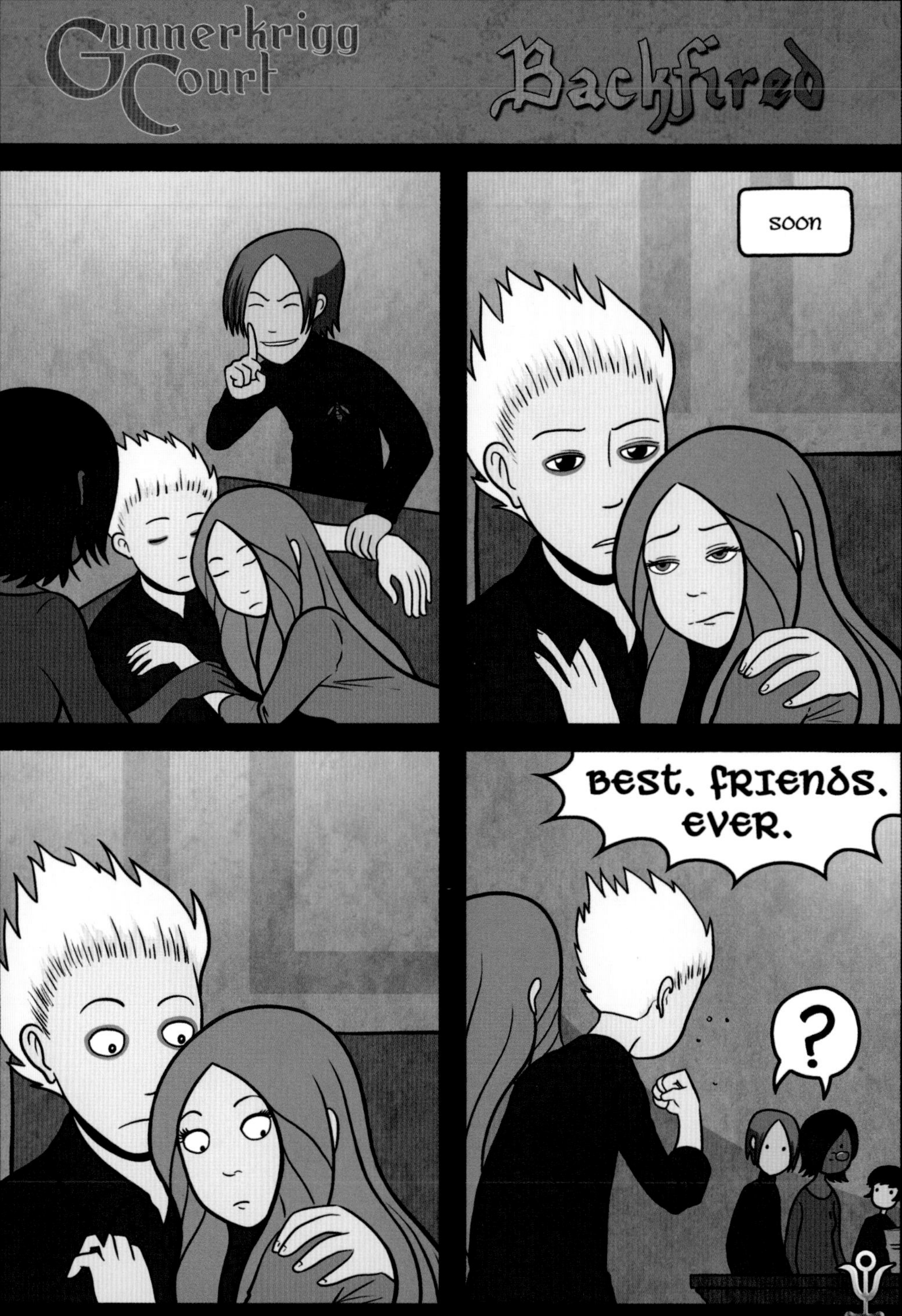
Gunnerkrigg Court
Backfired
soon
BEST. FRIENDS. EVER.
?

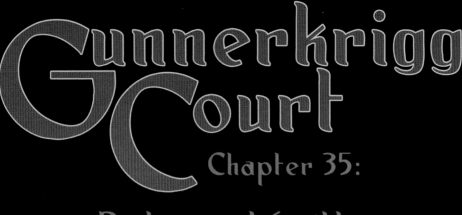

Gunnerkrigg Court

Chapter 35:

Parley and Smitty Are In This One

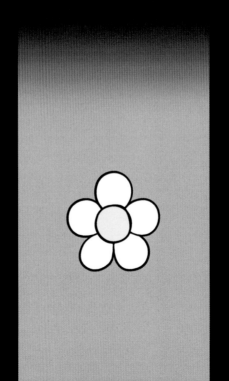

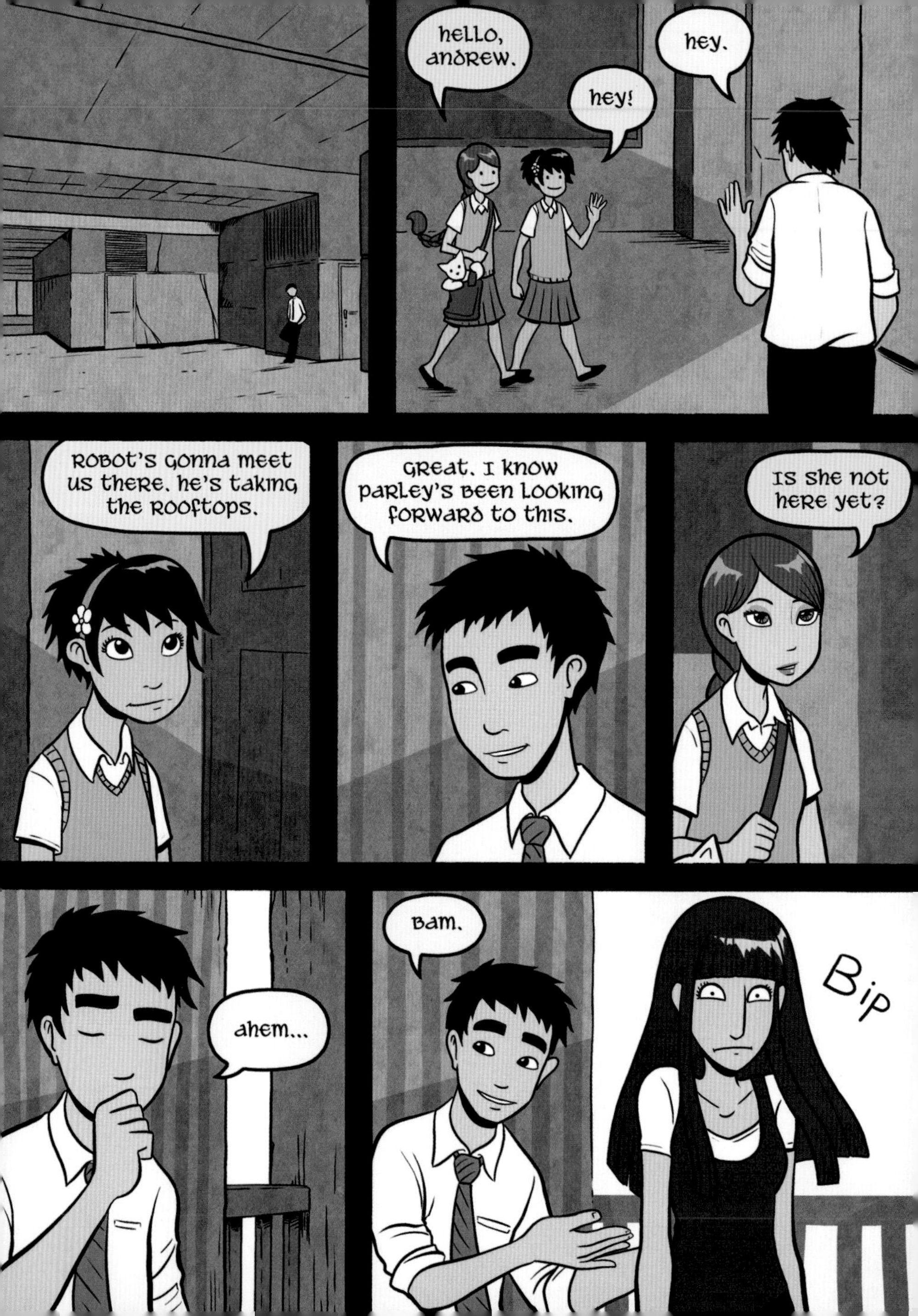
hello, andrew.
hey!
hey.
robot's gonna meet us there. he's taking the rooftops.
great. I know parley's been looking forward to this.
is she not here yet?
ahem...
bam.
Bip

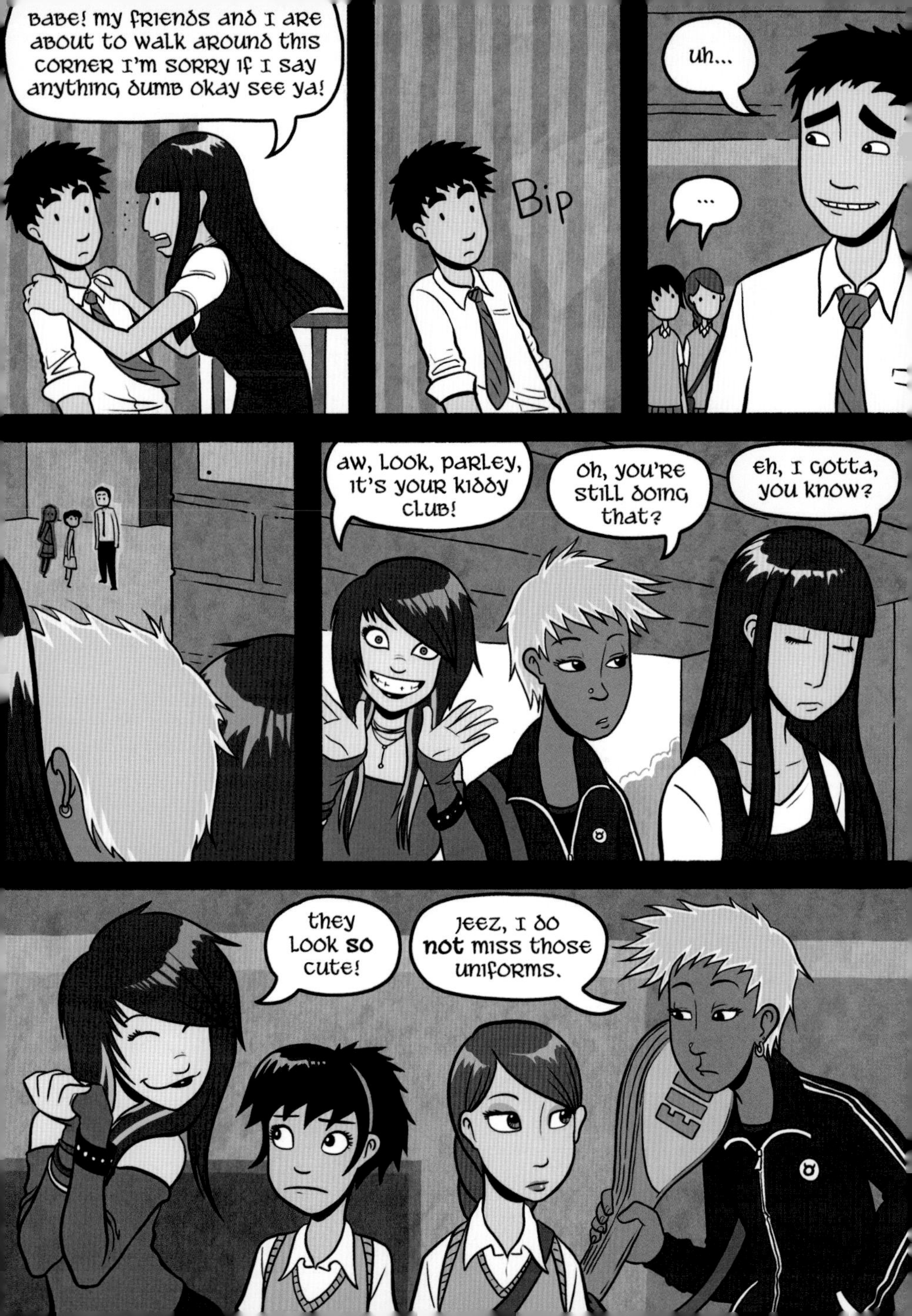
babe! my friends and I are about to walk around this corner I'm sorry if I say anything dumb okay see ya!
Bip
uh...
...
aw, look, parley, it's your kiddy club!
oh, you're still doing that?
eh, I gotta, you know?
they look **so** cute!
jeez, I do **not** miss those uniforms.

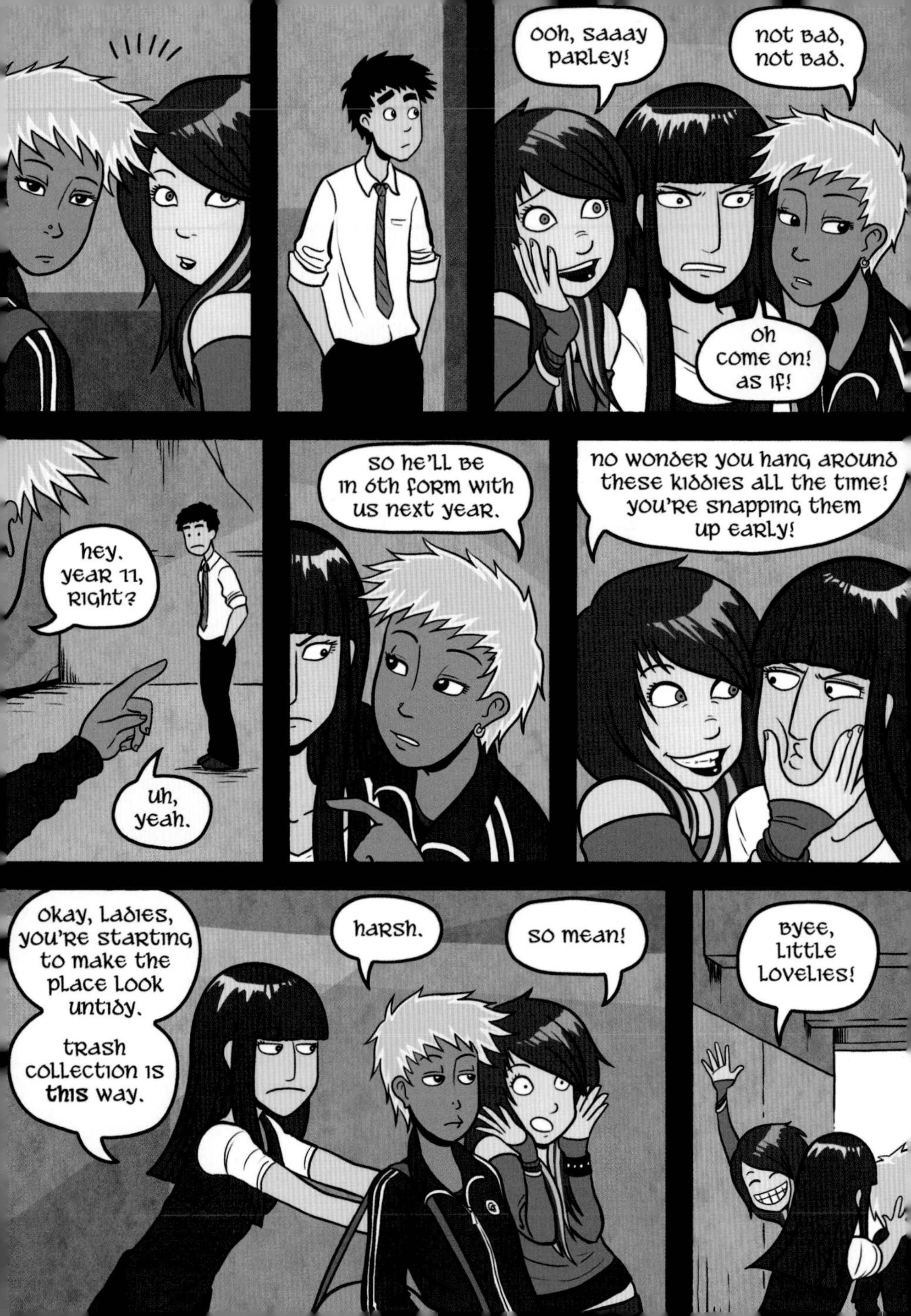

ooh, saaay parley!
not bad, not bad.
oh come on! as if!
hey. year 11, right?
uh, yeah.
so he'll be in 6th form with us next year.
no wonder you hang around these kiddies all the time! you're snapping them up early!
okay, ladies, you're starting to make the place look untidy.
trash collection is **this** way.
harsh.
so mean!
byee, little lovelies!

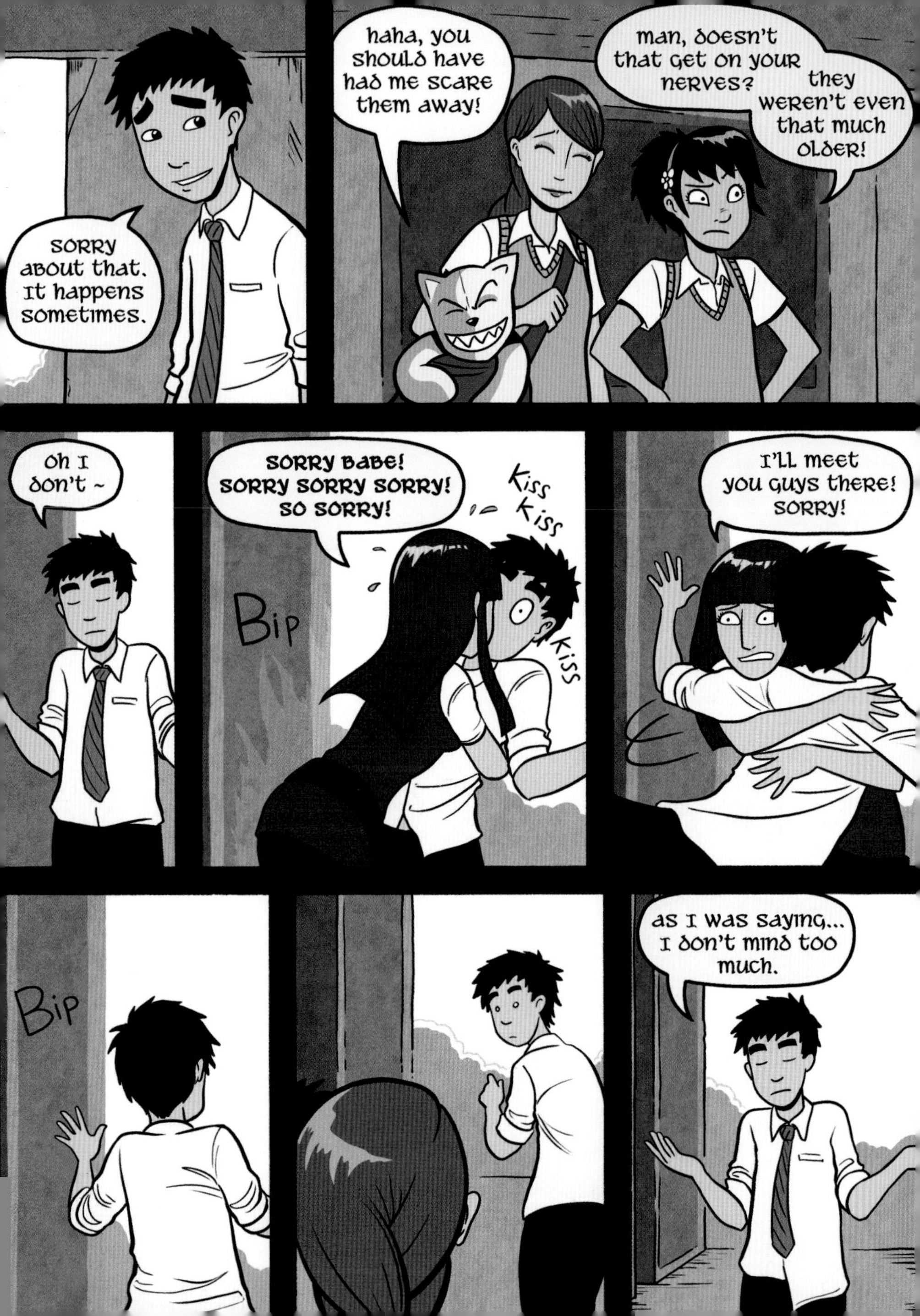
SORRY ABOUT THAT. IT HAPPENS SOMETIMES.
HAHA, YOU SHOULD HAVE HAD ME SCARE THEM AWAY!
MAN, DOESN'T THAT GET ON YOUR NERVES?
THEY WEREN'T EVEN THAT MUCH OLDER!
OH I DON'T ~
SORRY BABE! SORRY SORRY SORRY! SO SORRY!
Bip
Kiss Kiss
Kiss
I'LL MEET YOU GUYS THERE! SORRY!
Bip
AS I WAS SAYING... I DON'T MIND TOO MUCH.

IT'S OKAY, ROBOT, THE COAST'S CLEAR!

YEAH, I WOULDN'T MIND IF SHE WAS LESS EMBARASSED BY IT.

BUT I GUESS IT'S HARD BEING IN SIXTH FORM AND HAVING YOUNGER FRIENDS.

ESPECIALLY A YOUNGER BOYFRIEND.

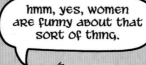

HMM, YES, WOMEN ARE FUNNY ABOUT THAT SORT OF THING.

RENARD IS THE RESIDENT LADIES EXPERT.

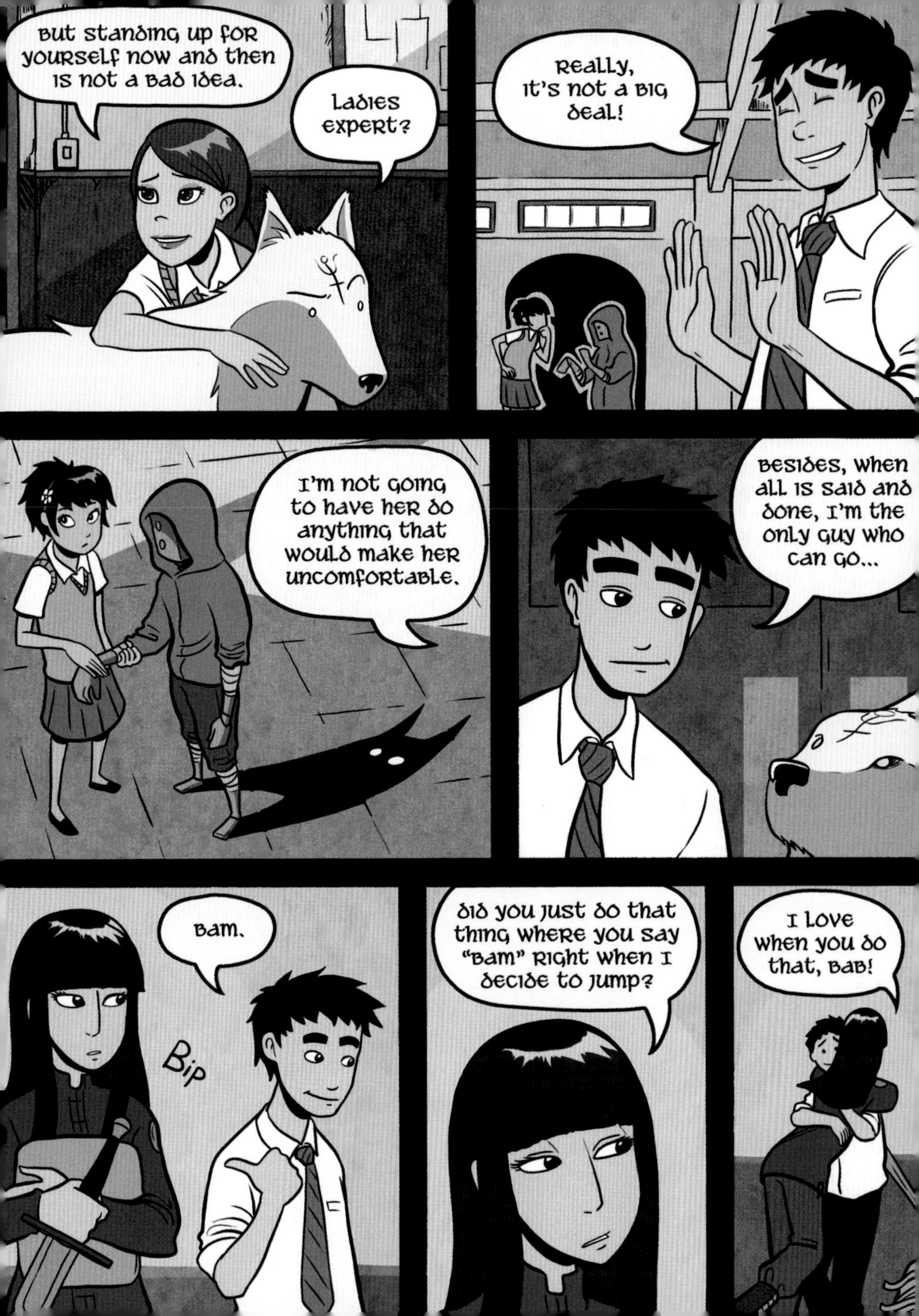
But standing up for yourself now and then is not a bad idea.
Ladies expert?
Really, it's not a big deal!
I'm not going to have her do anything that would make her uncomfortable.
Besides, when all is said and done, I'm the only guy who can go...
Bam.
Bip
Did you just do that thing where you say "Bam" right when I decide to jump?
I love when you do that, Bab!

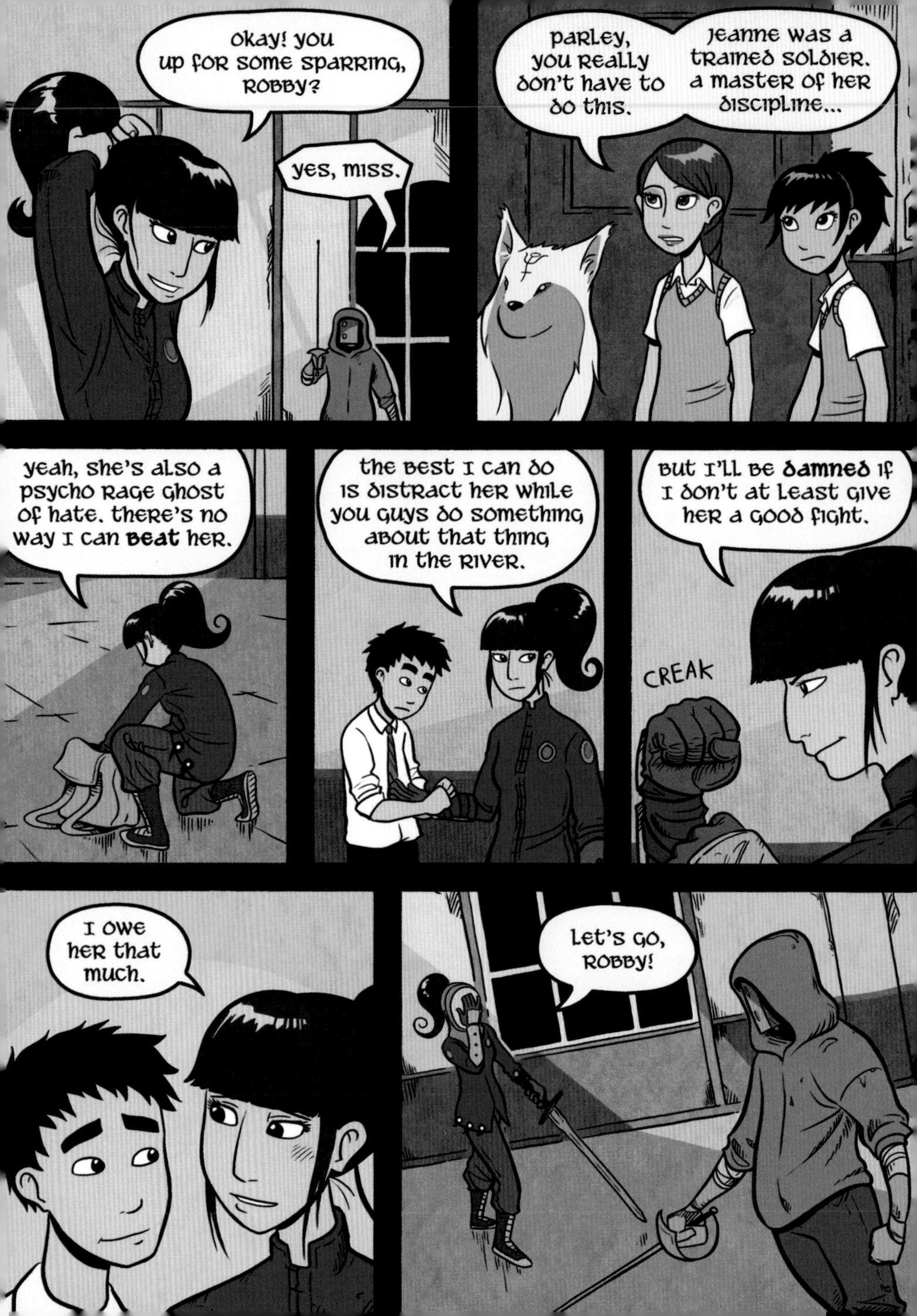
okay! you up for some sparring, robby?
yes, miss.
parley, you really don't have to do this.
jeanne was a trained soldier. a master of her discipline...
yeah, she's also a psycho rage ghost of hate. there's no way I can **beat** her.
the best I can do is distract her while you guys do something about that thing in the river.
but I'll be **damned** if I don't at least give her a good fight.
CREAK
I owe her that much.
let's go, robby!

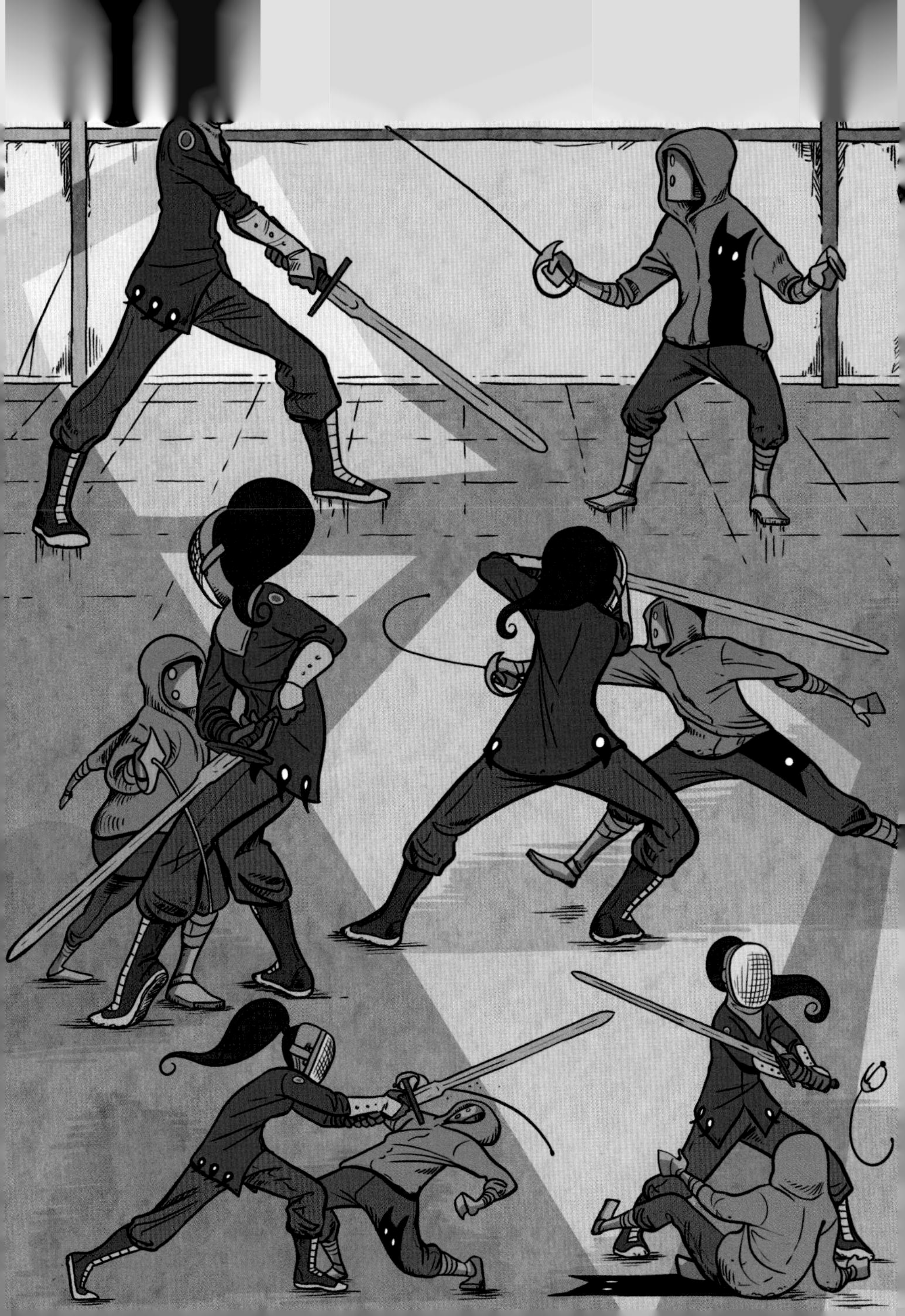

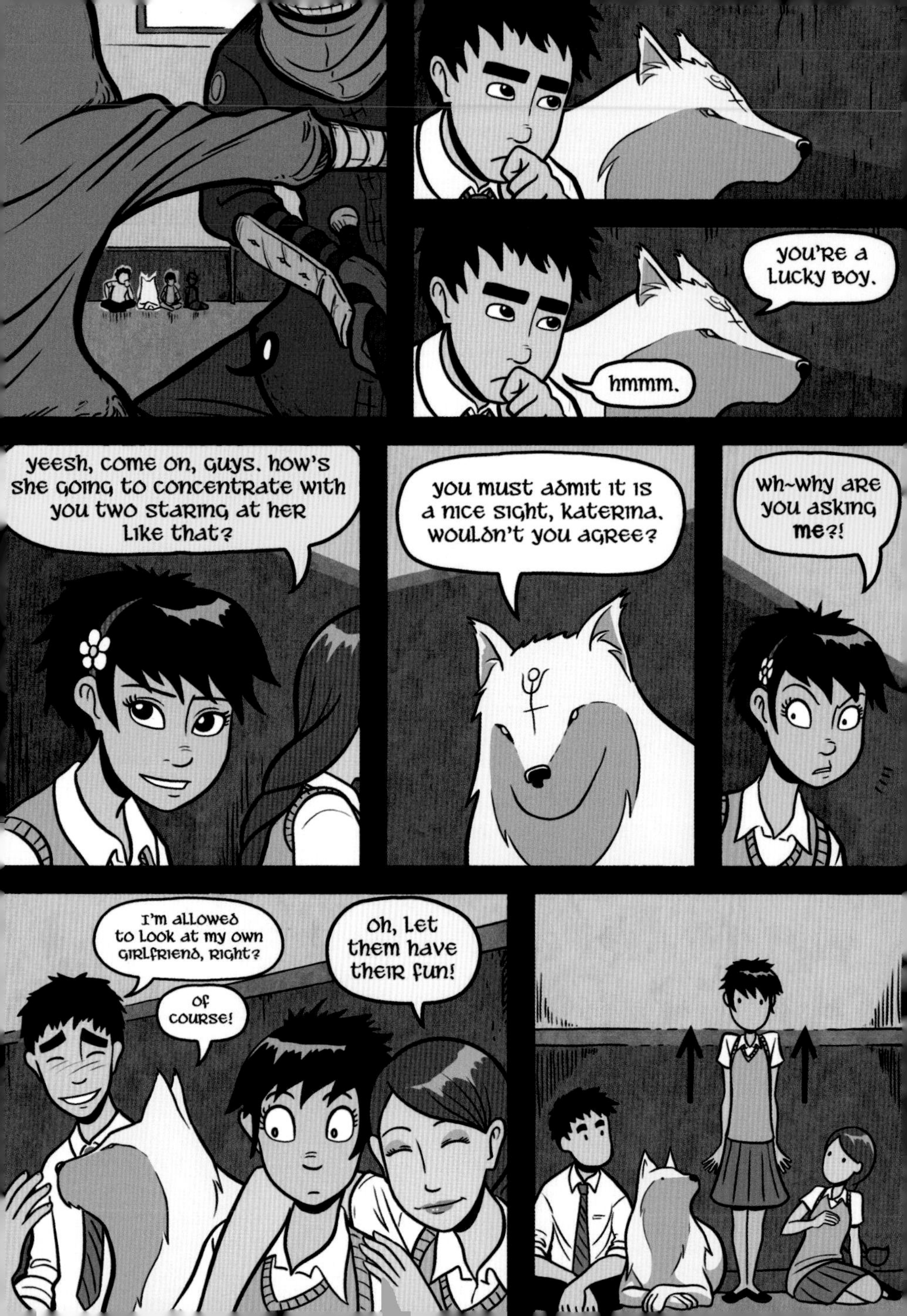
you're a lucky boy.
hmmm.
yeesh, come on, guys. how's she going to concentrate with you two staring at her like that?
you must admit it is a nice sight, katerina. wouldn't you agree?
wh-why are you asking me?!
I'm allowed to look at my own girlfriend, right?
of course!
oh, let them have their fun!

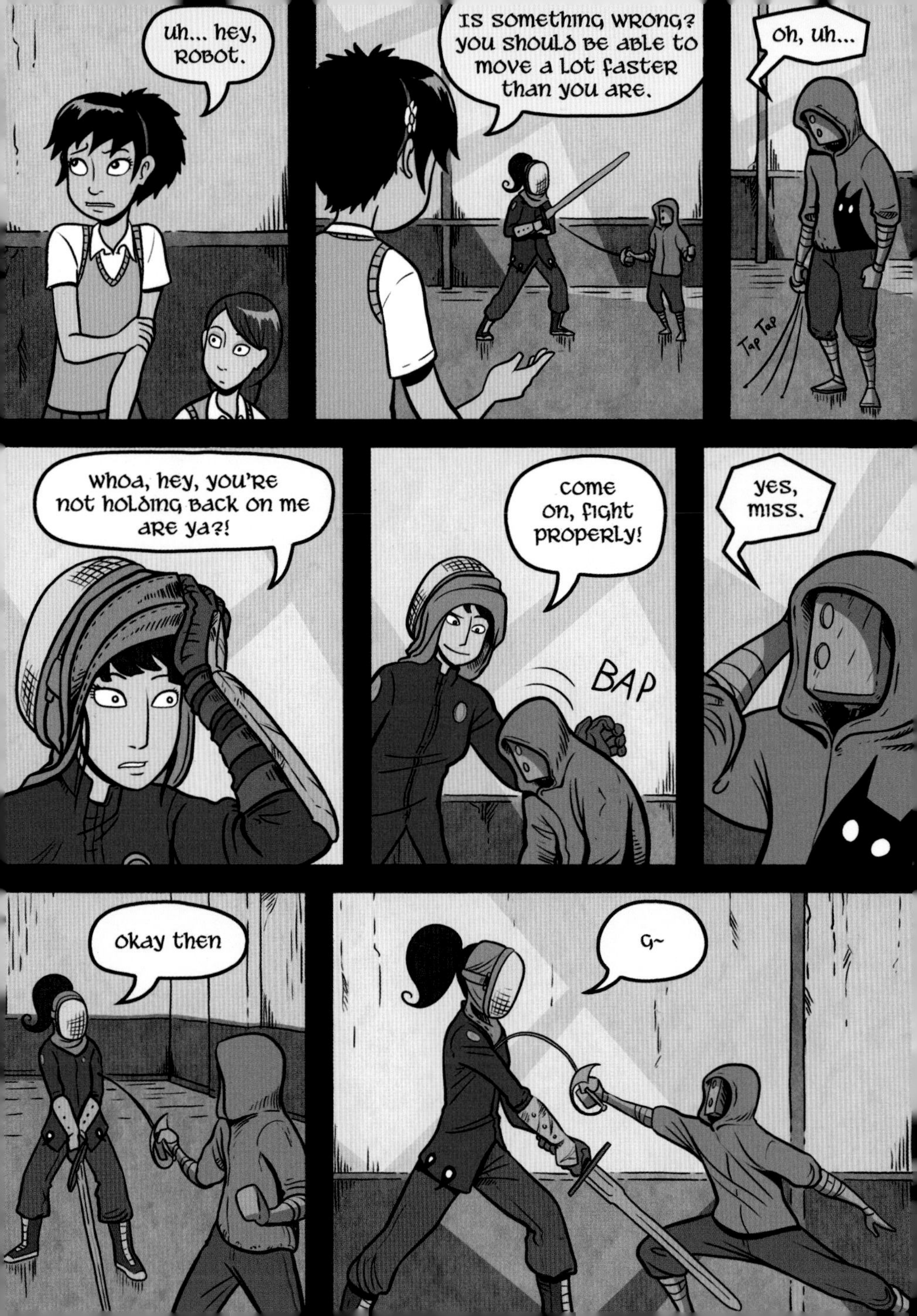
uh... hey, ROBOT.
IS something WRONG? you should be able to move a lot faster than you are.
oh, uh...
Tap Tap
whoa, hey, you're not holding back on me are ya?!
come on, fight properly!
BAP
yes, miss.
okay then
G~

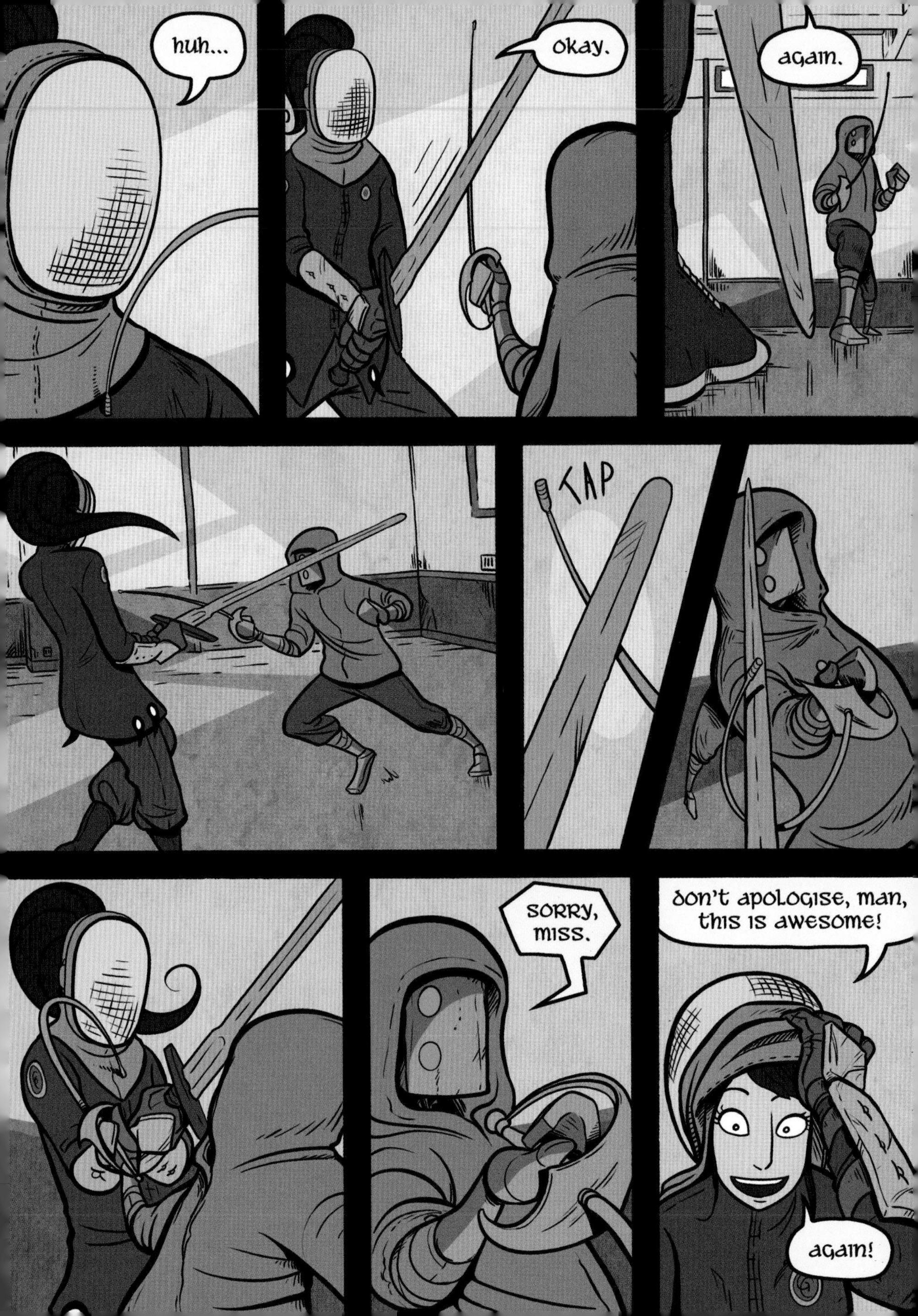
huh...
okay.
again.
TAP
SORRY, MISS.
don't apologise, man, this is awesome!
again!

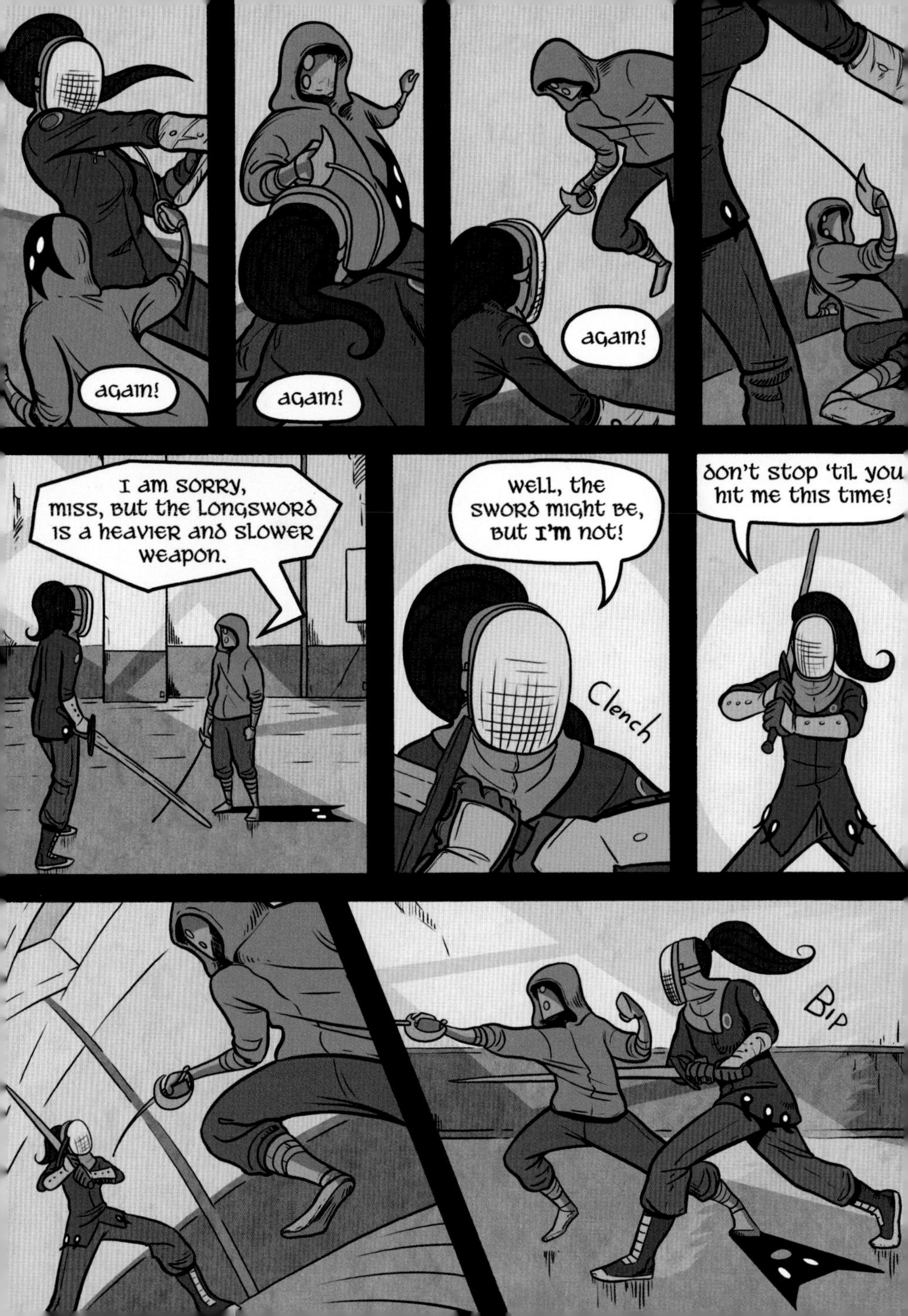
again!
again!
again!
I am sorry, miss, but the longsword is a heavier and slower weapon.
well, the sword might be, but I'm not!
Clench
don't stop 'til you hit me this time!
Bip

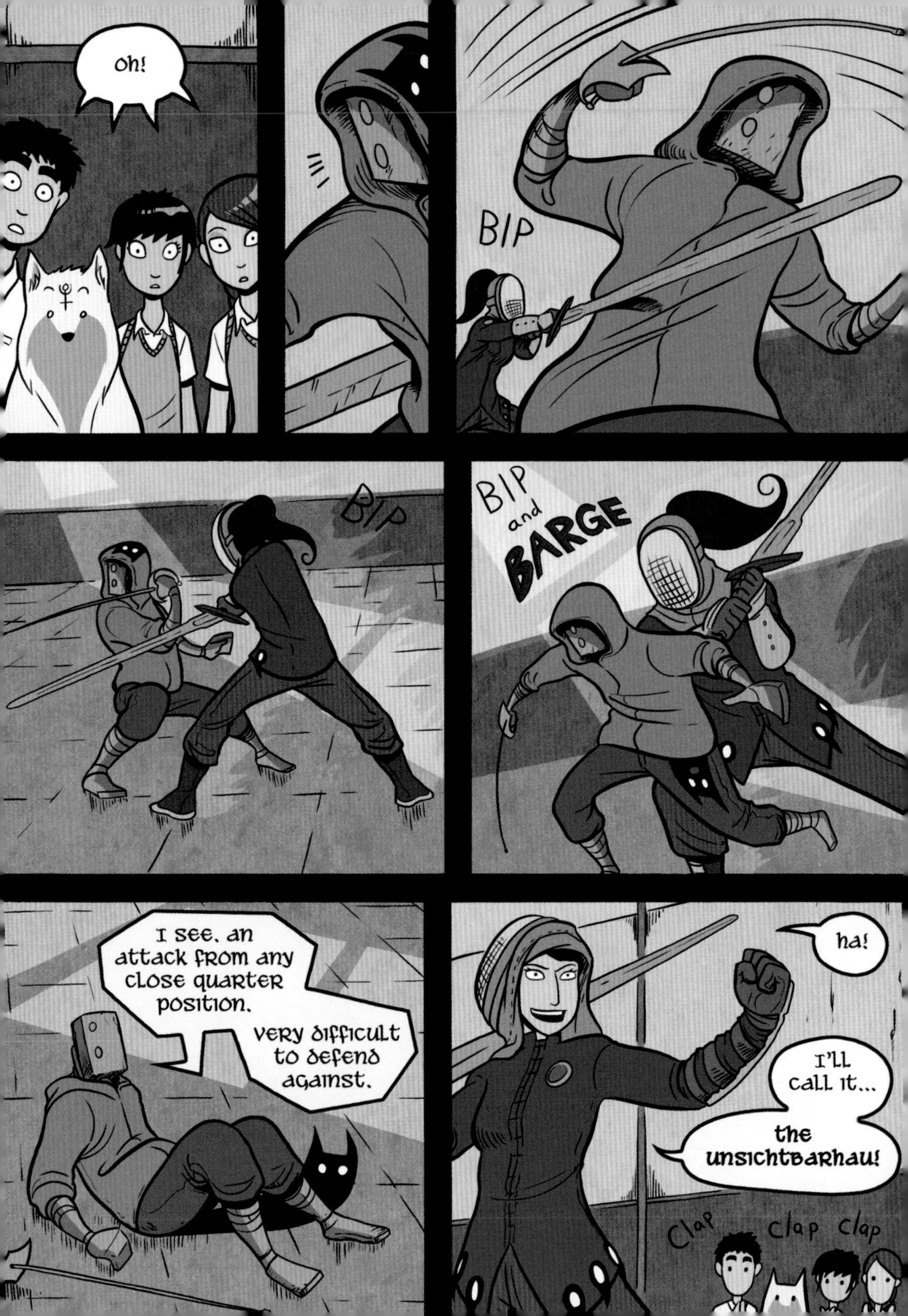

oh!
BIP
BIP
BIP
and
BARGE
I see, an attack from any close quarter position.
very difficult to defend against.
ha!
I'll call it...
the unsichtbarhau!
Clap
clap
clap

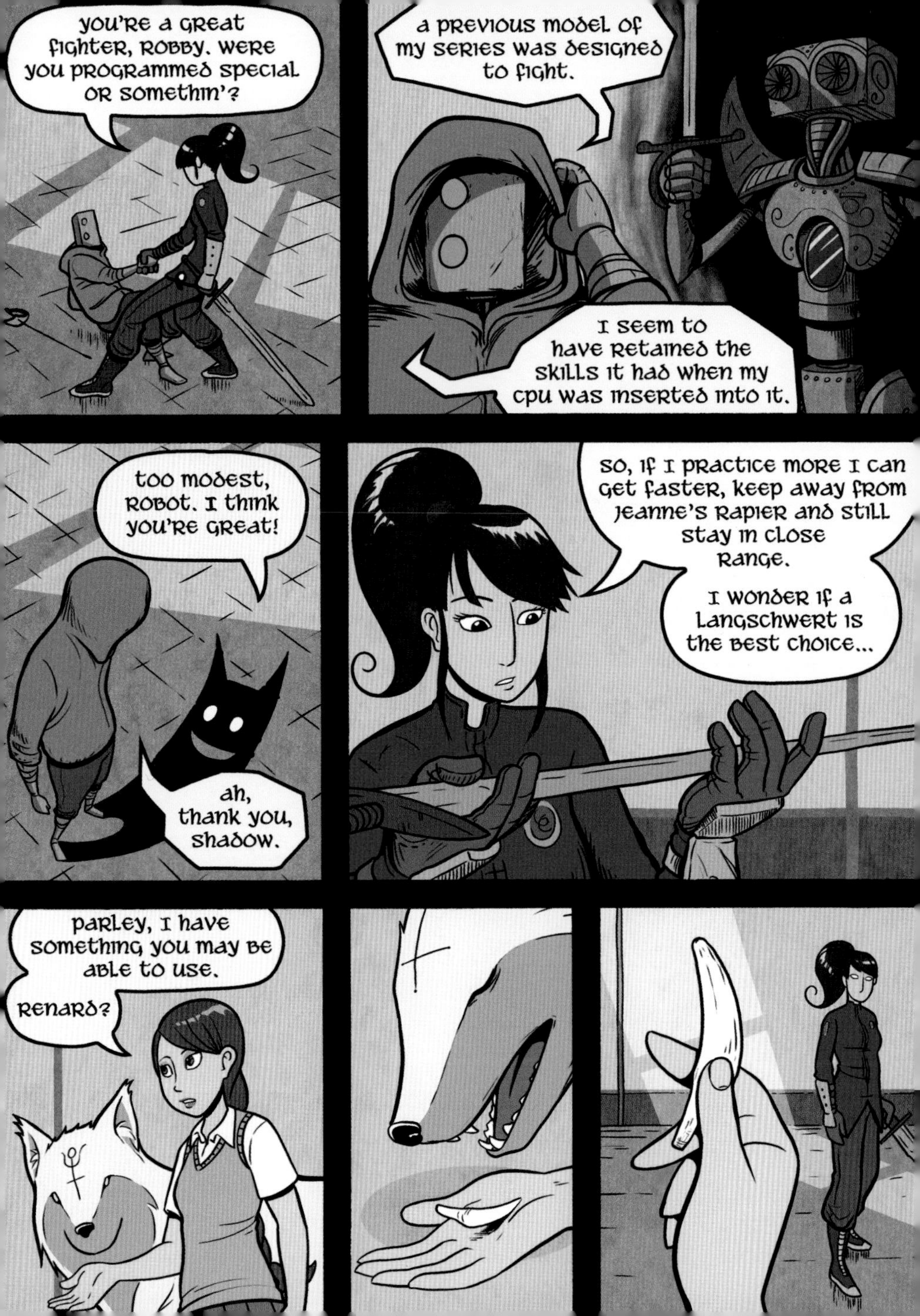
you're a great fighter, robby. were you programmed special or somethin'?
a previous model of my series was designed to fight.
I seem to have retained the skills it had when my cpu was inserted into it.
too modest, robot. I think you're great!
ah, thank you, shadow.
so, if I practice more I can get faster, keep away from jeanne's rapier and still stay in close range.
I wonder if a langschwert is the best choice...
parley, I have something you may be able to use.
renard?

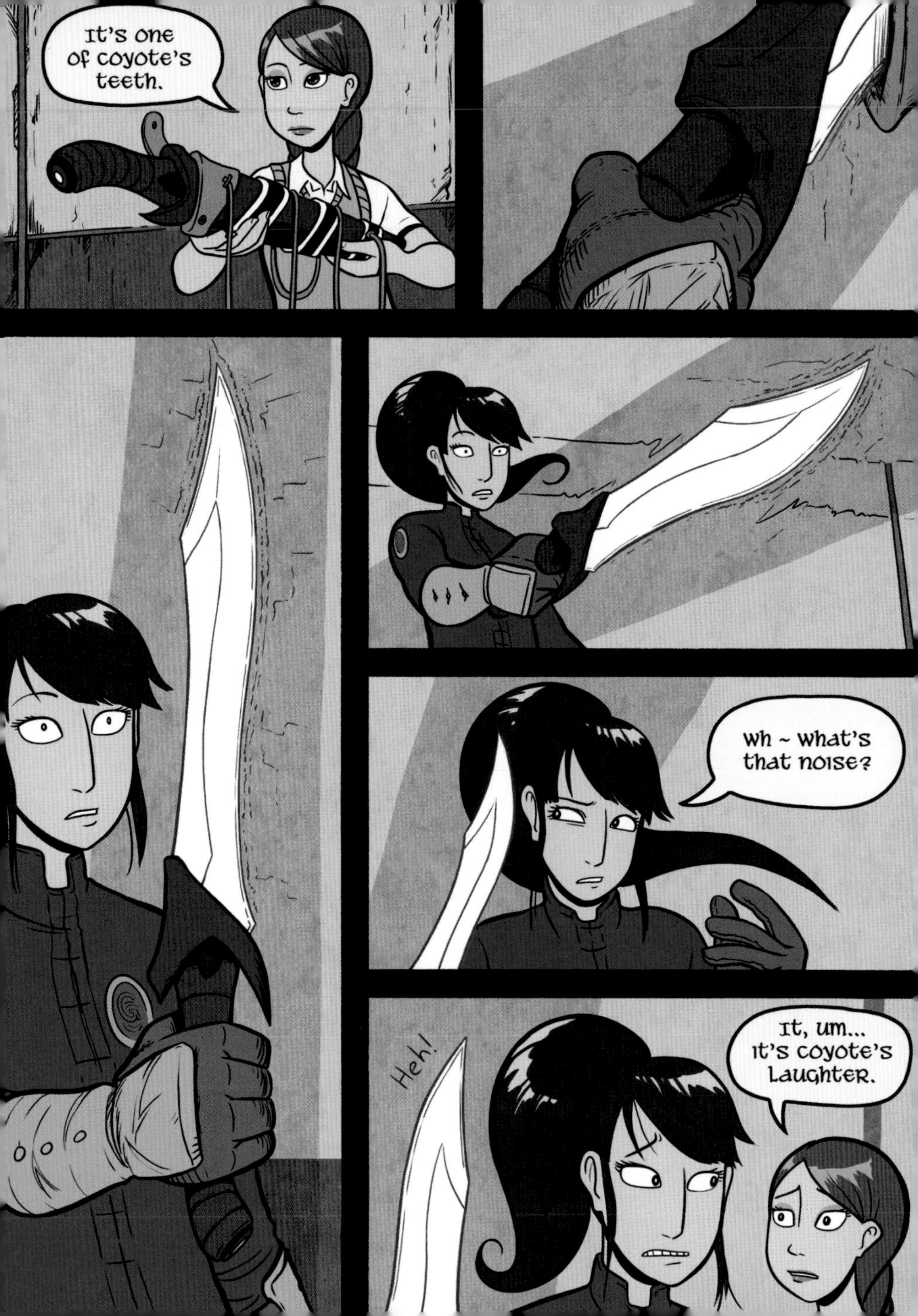
It's one of coyote's teeth.
Wh ~ what's that noise?
Heh!
It, um... It's coyote's laughter.

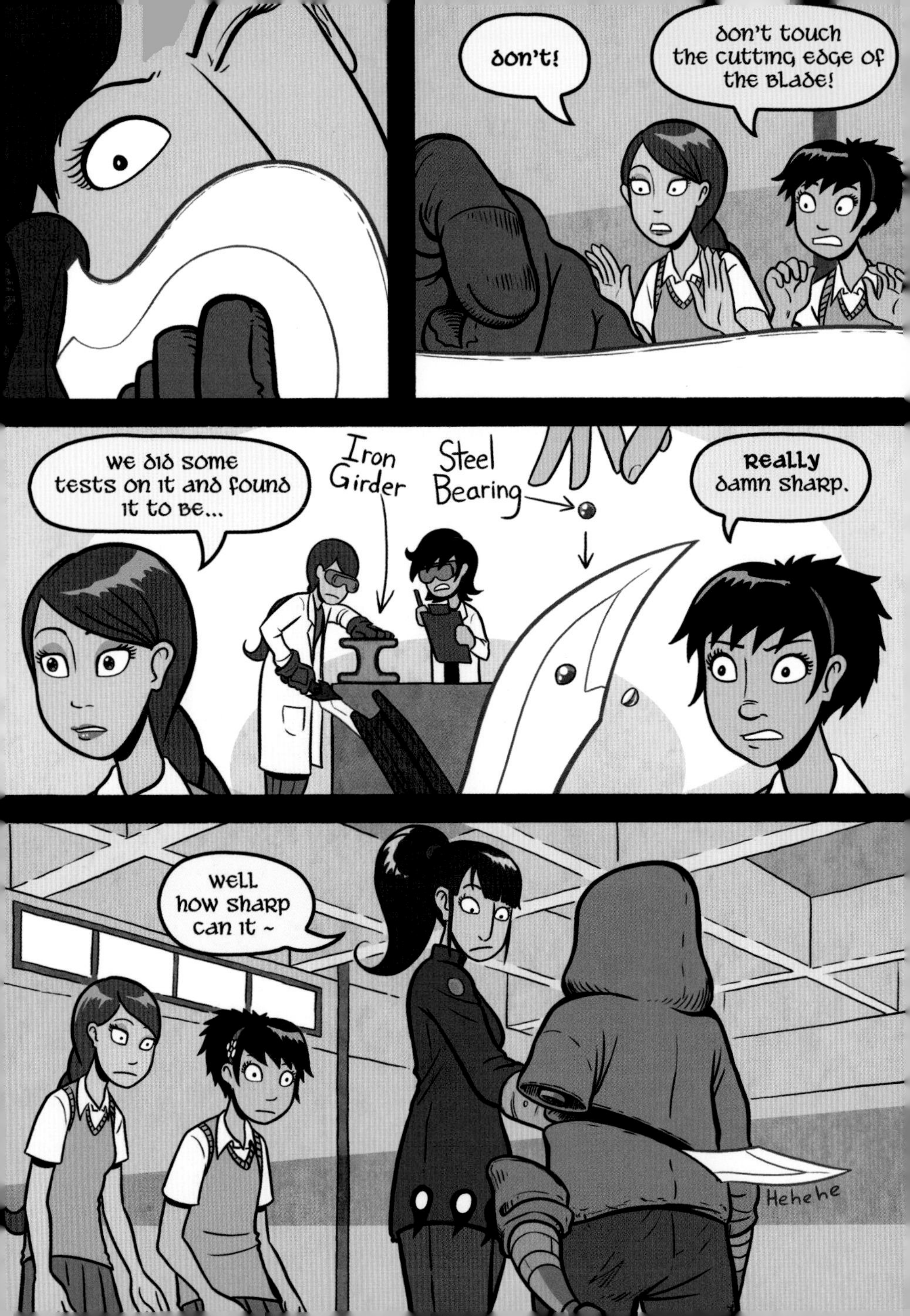

don't!
don't touch the cutting edge of the blade!
we did some tests on it and found it to be...
Iron Girder
Steel Bearing
Really damn sharp.
well how sharp can it ~
Hehehe

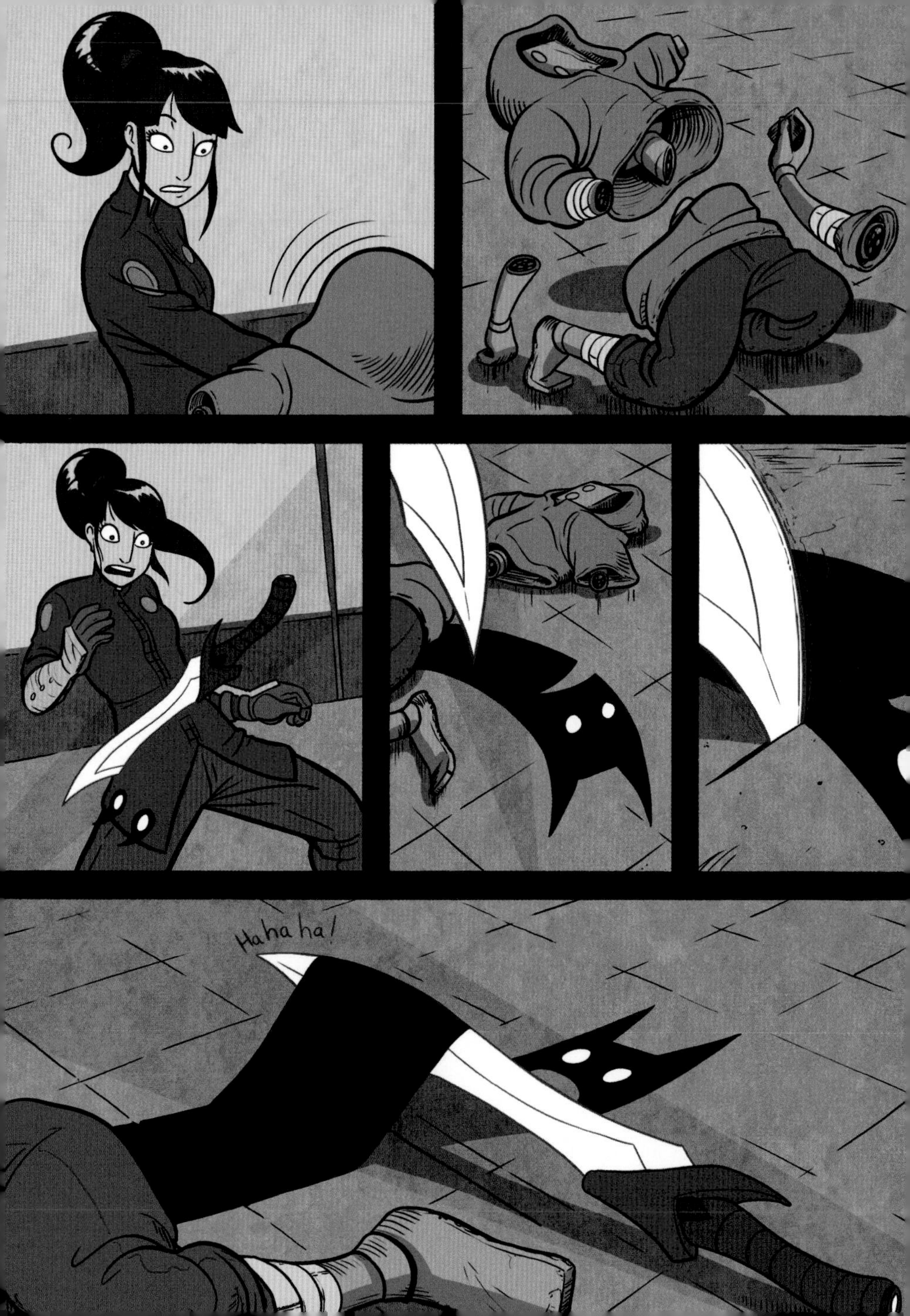
Ha ha ha!

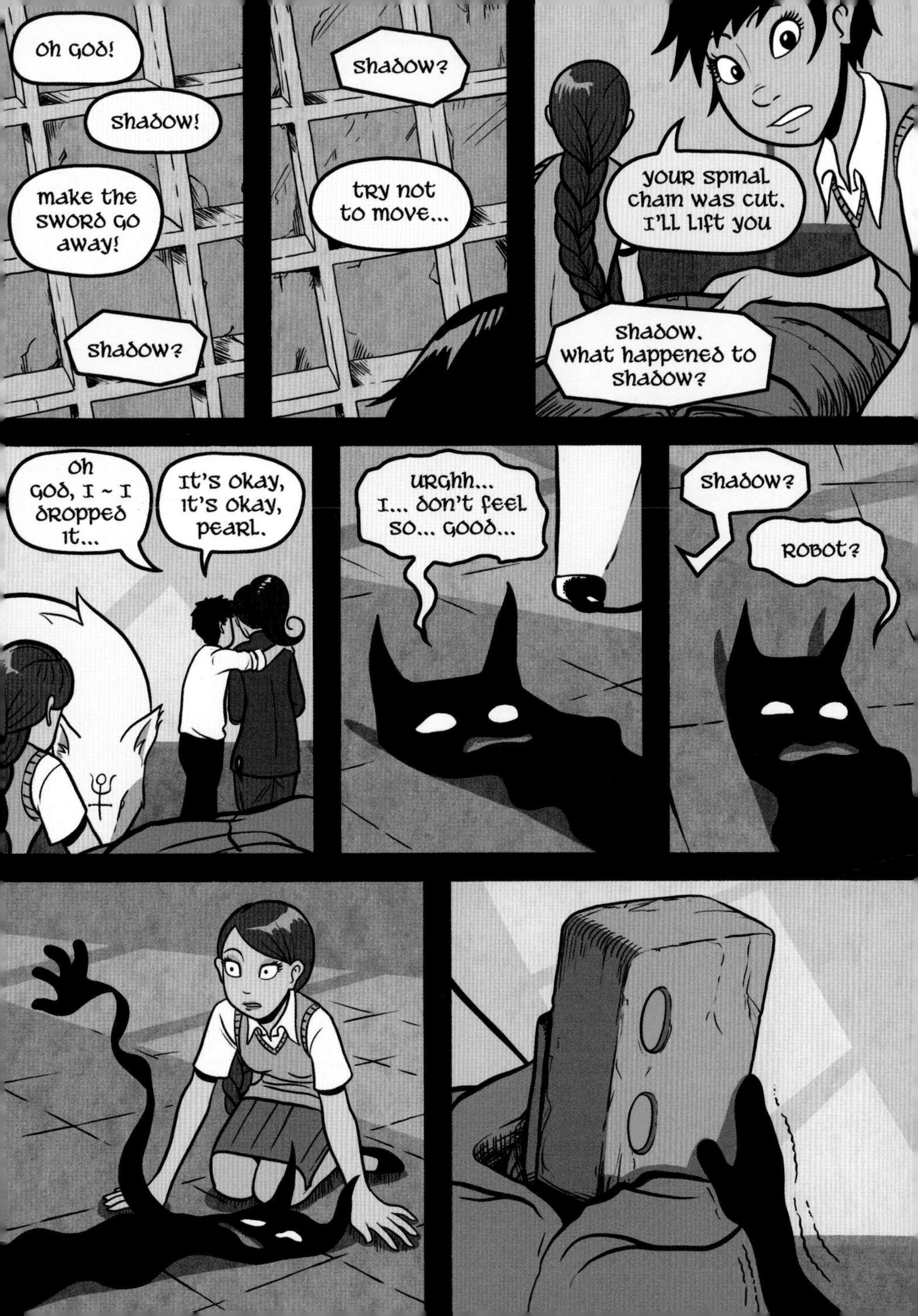
Oh GOD!
Shadow!
make the SWORD GO away!
Shadow?
Shadow?
try not to move...
your spinal chain was cut. I'll lift you
Shadow. what happened to Shadow?
Oh GOD, I ~ I DROPPED it...
It's okay, it's okay, Pearl.
URGhh... I... don't feel so... GOOD...
Shadow?
ROBOT?

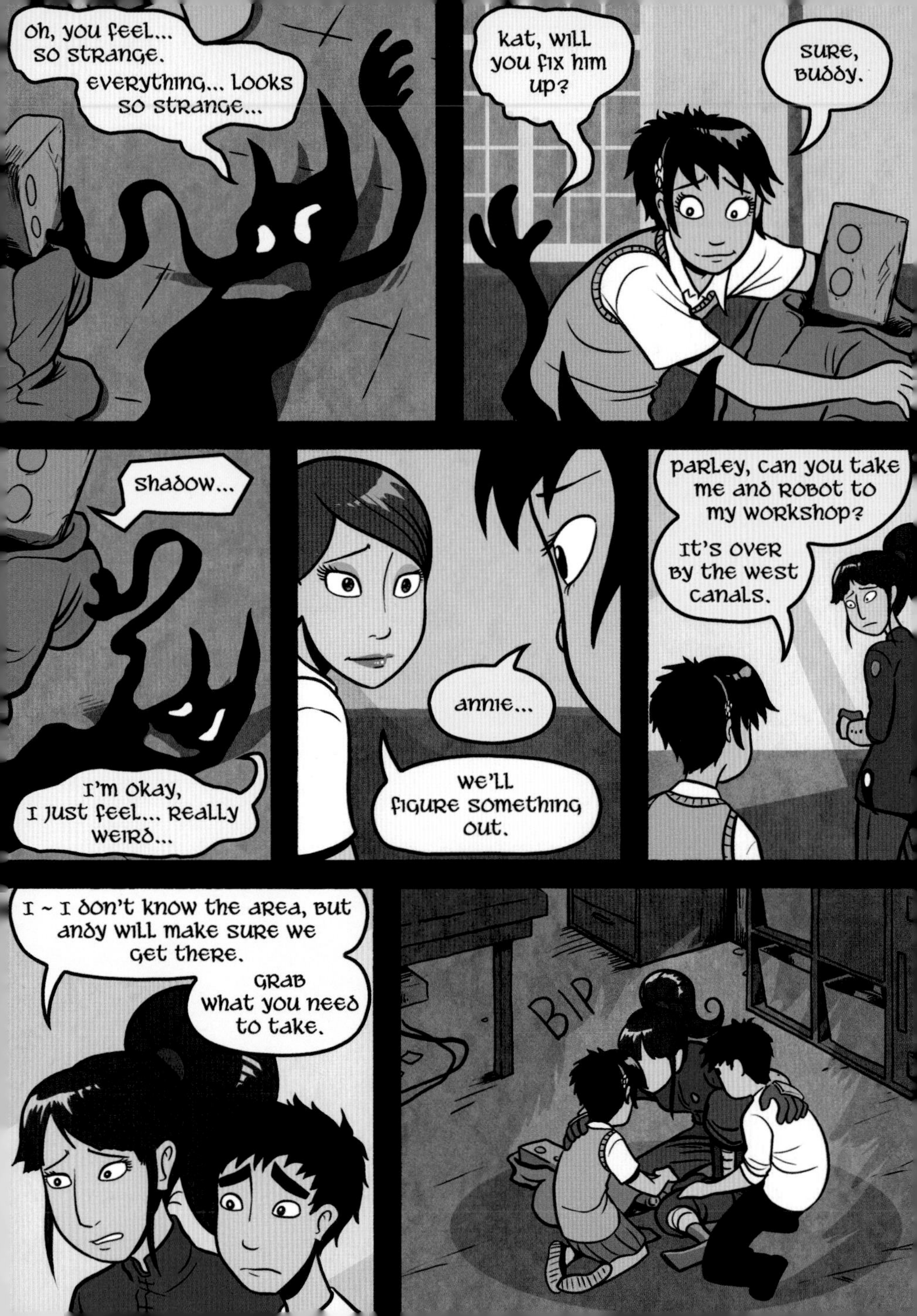
oh, you feel... so strange.
everything... looks so strange...
kat, will you fix him up?
sure, buddy.
shadow...
I'm okay, I just feel... really weird...
annie...
we'll figure something out.
parley, can you take me and robot to my workshop?
It's over by the west canals.
I ~ I don't know the area, but andy will make sure we get there.
grab what you need to take.
BIP

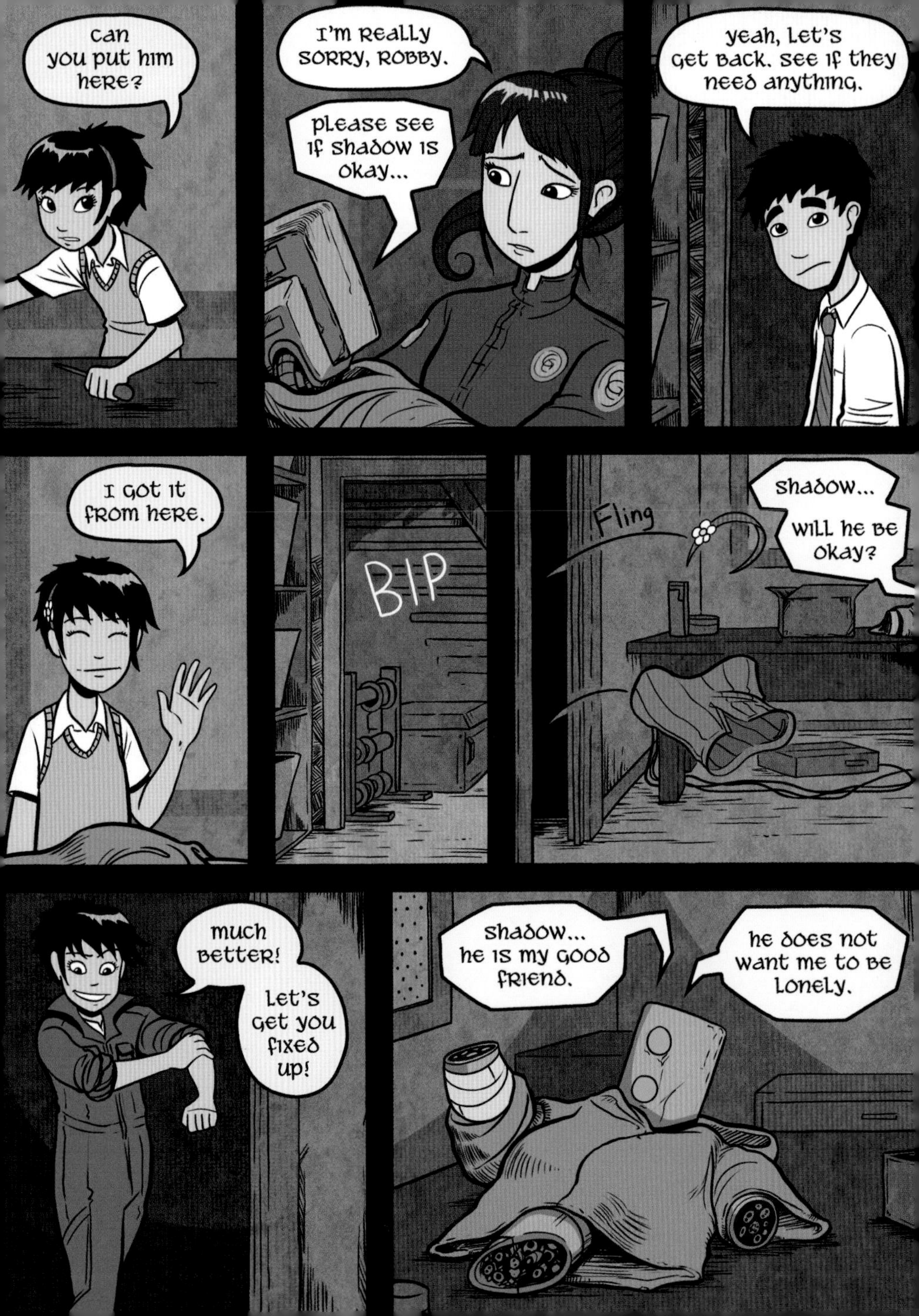
can you put him here?
I'm really sorry, Robby.
please see if shadow is okay...
yeah, let's get back. see if they need anything.
I got it from here.
BIP
Fling
shadow...
will he be okay?
much better!
Let's get you fixed up!
shadow... he is my good friend.
he does not want me to be lonely.

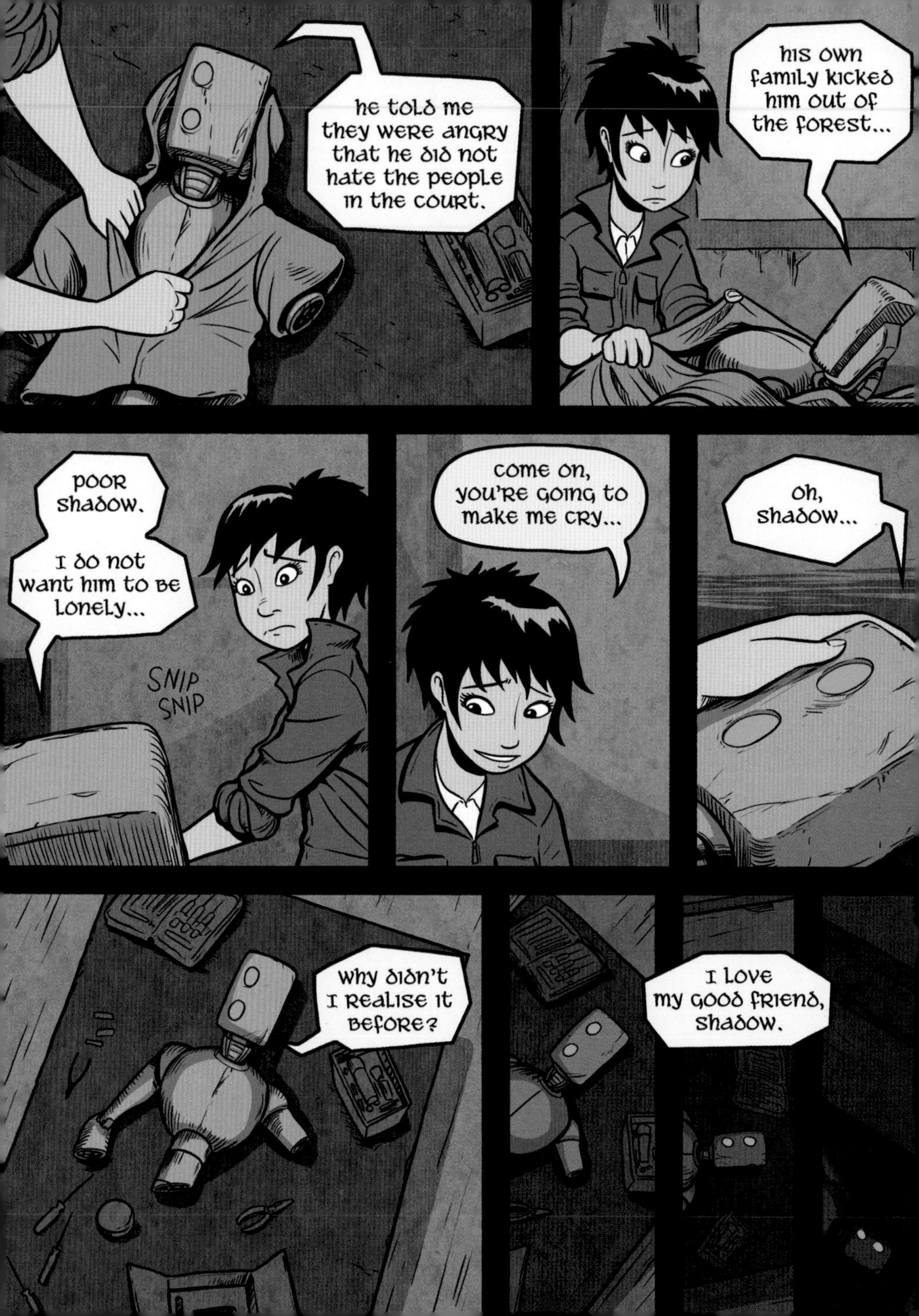
he told me they were angry that he did not hate the people in the court.
his own family kicked him out of the forest...
poor shadow.
I do not want him to be lonely...
SNIP SNIP
come on, you're going to make me cry...
oh, shadow...
why didn't I realise it before?
I love my good friend, shadow.

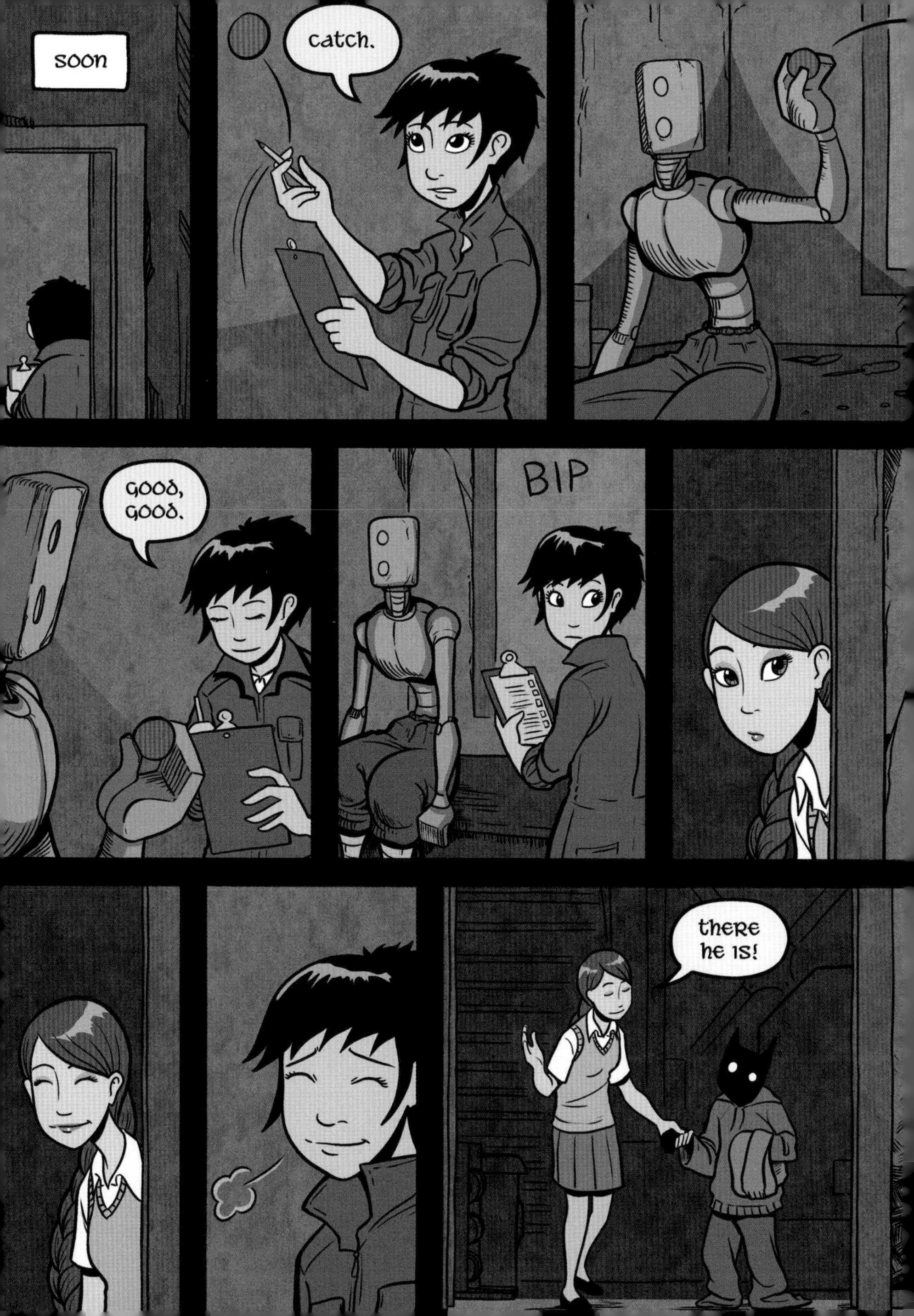
soon
catch.
good, good.
BIP
there he is!

Shadow, you are three dimensional now.

He was very worried about you, Robot.

I brought you a new jumper

I know you liked your old one.

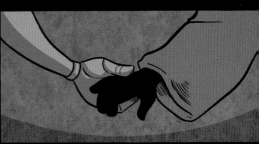

And look, I have a hood just like you!

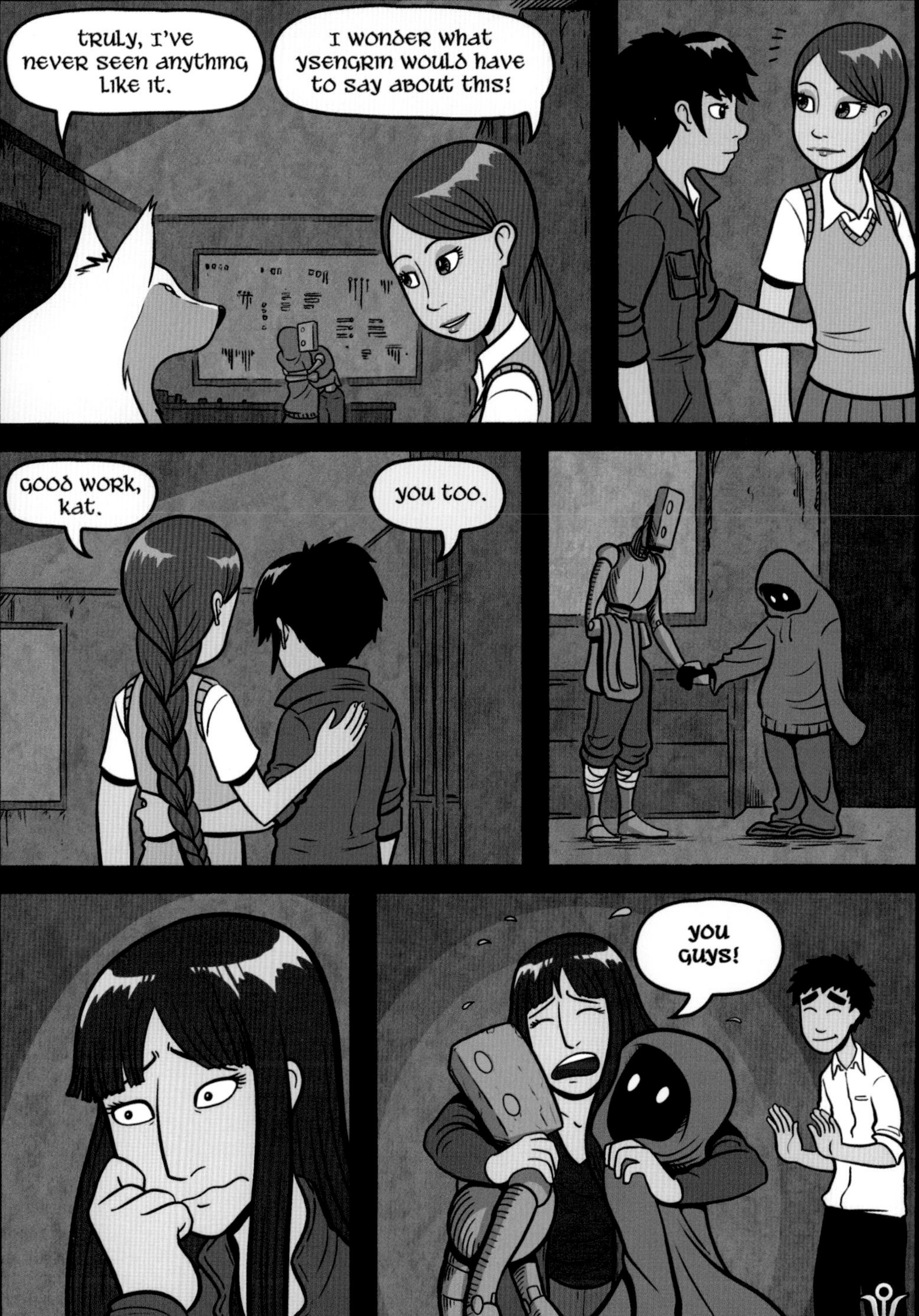
truly, I've never seen anything like it.
I wonder what ysengrin would have to say about this!
good work, kat.
you too.
you guys!

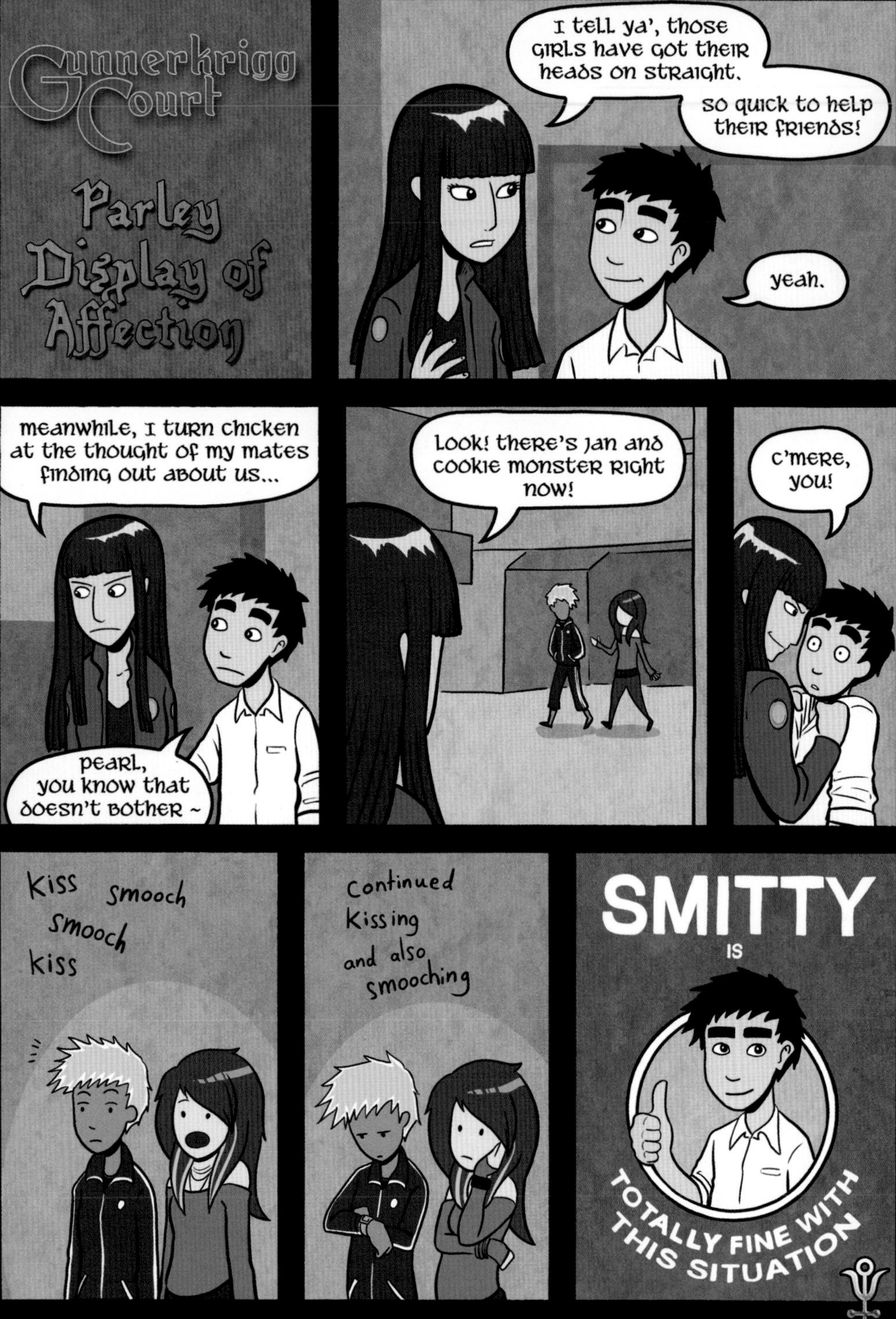

Gunnerkrigg Court
Parley Display of Affection
I tell ya', those girls have got their heads on straight.
so quick to help their friends!
yeah.
meanwhile, I turn chicken at the thought of my mates finding out about us...
pearl, you know that doesn't bother ~
look! there's jan and cookie monster right now!
c'mere, you!
kiss smooch smooch kiss
continued kissing and also smooching
SMITTY IS TOTALLY FINE WITH THIS SITUATION

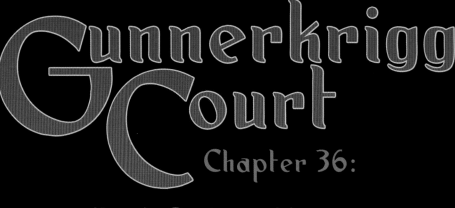

Gunnerkrigg Court

Chapter 36:

Red Gets a Name

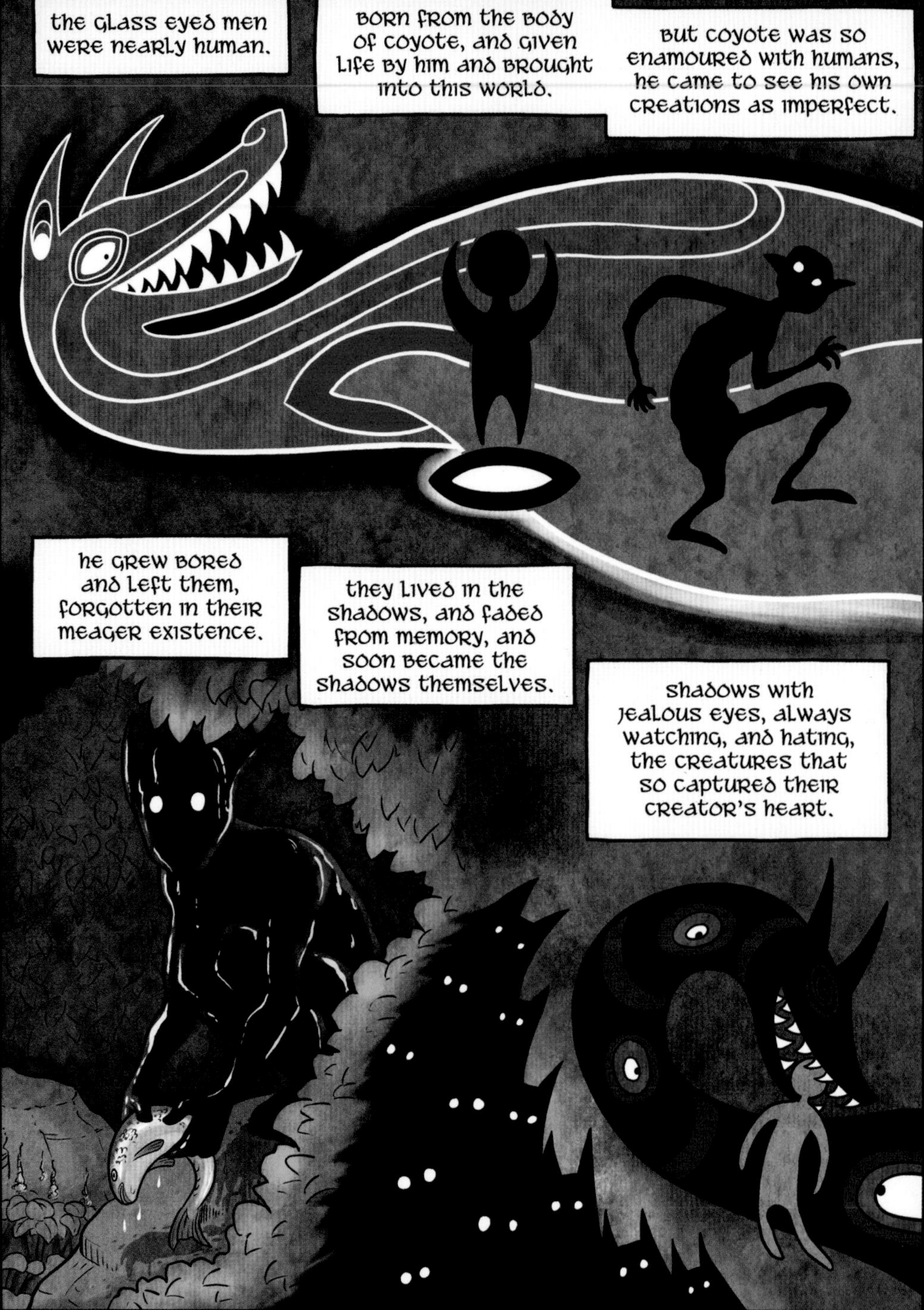
the glass eyed men were nearly human.
Born from the body of coyote, and given life by him and brought into this world.
But coyote was so enamoured with humans, he came to see his own creations as imperfect.
he grew bored and left them, forgotten in their meager existence.
they lived in the shadows, and faded from memory, and soon became the shadows themselves.
shadows with jealous eyes, always watching, and hating, the creatures that so captured their creator's heart.

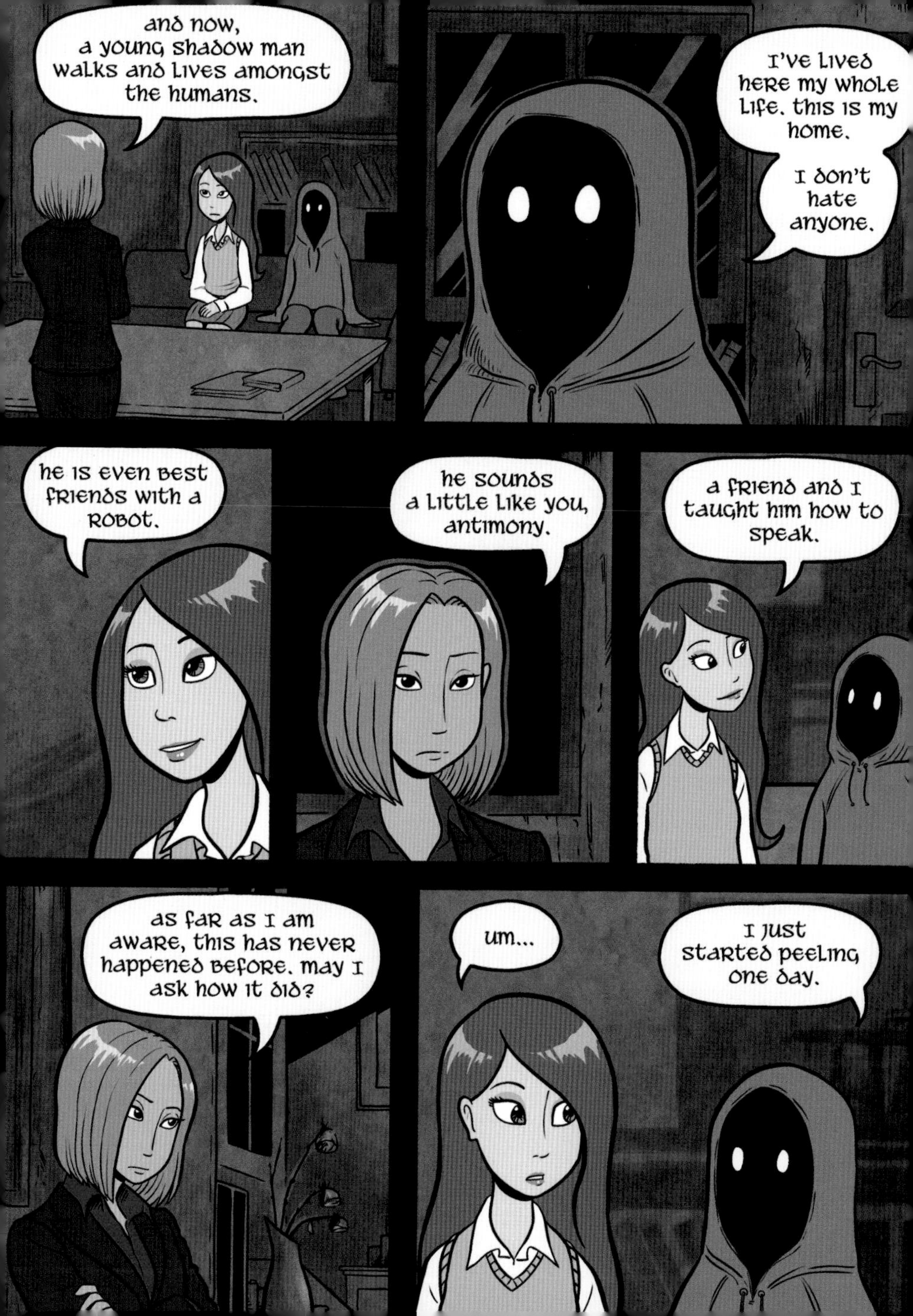
and now, a young shadow man walks and lives amongst the humans.
I've lived here my whole life. this is my home.
I don't hate anyone.
he is even best friends with a robot.
he sounds a little like you, antimony.
a friend and I taught him how to speak.
as far as I am aware, this has never happened before. may I ask how it did?
um...
I just started feeling one day.

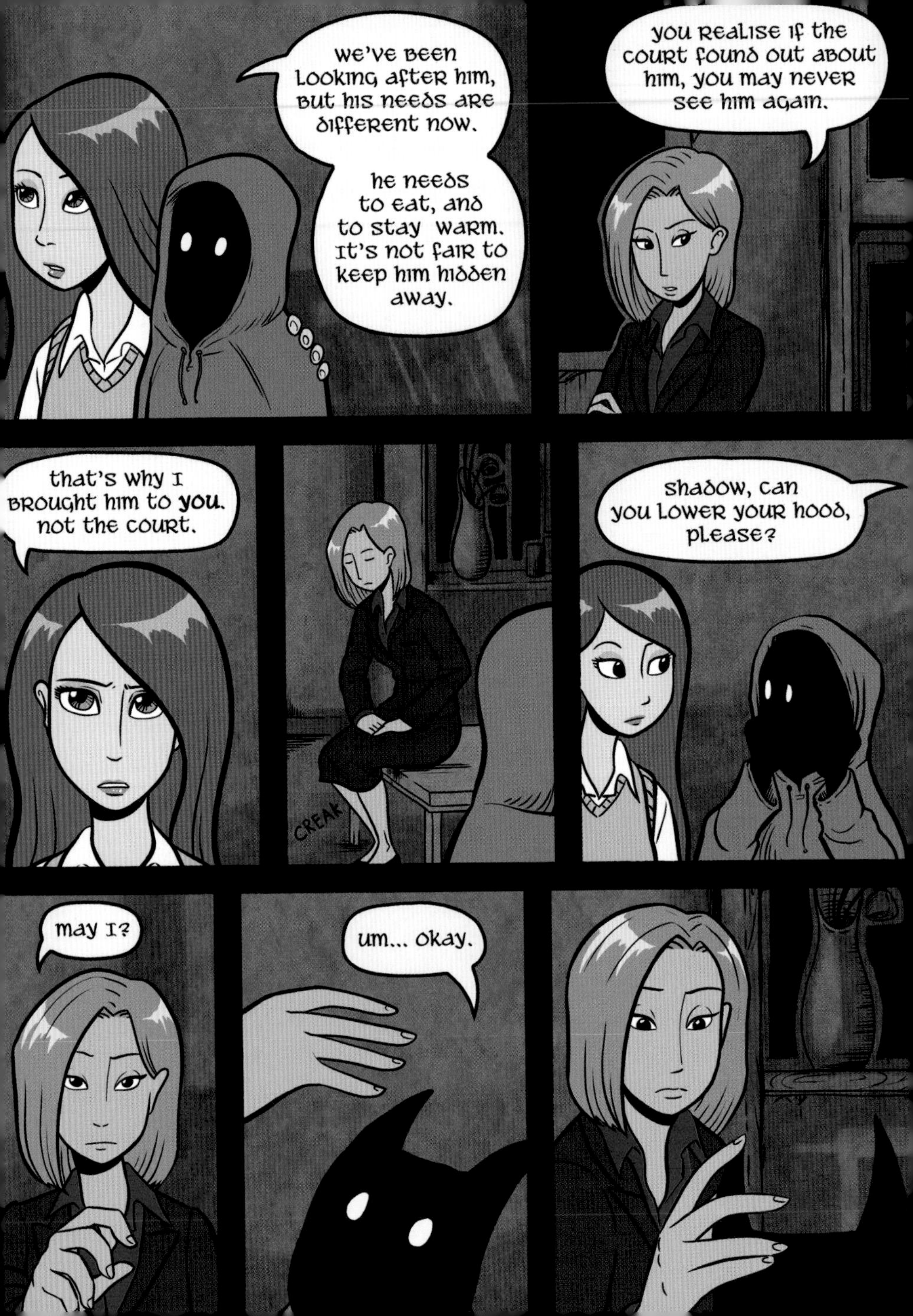
we've been looking after him, but his needs are different now.
he needs to eat, and to stay warm. It's not fair to keep him hidden away.
you realise if the court found out about him, you may never see him again.
that's why I brought him to **you**, not the court.
CREAK
shadow, can you lower your hood, please?
may I?
um... okay.

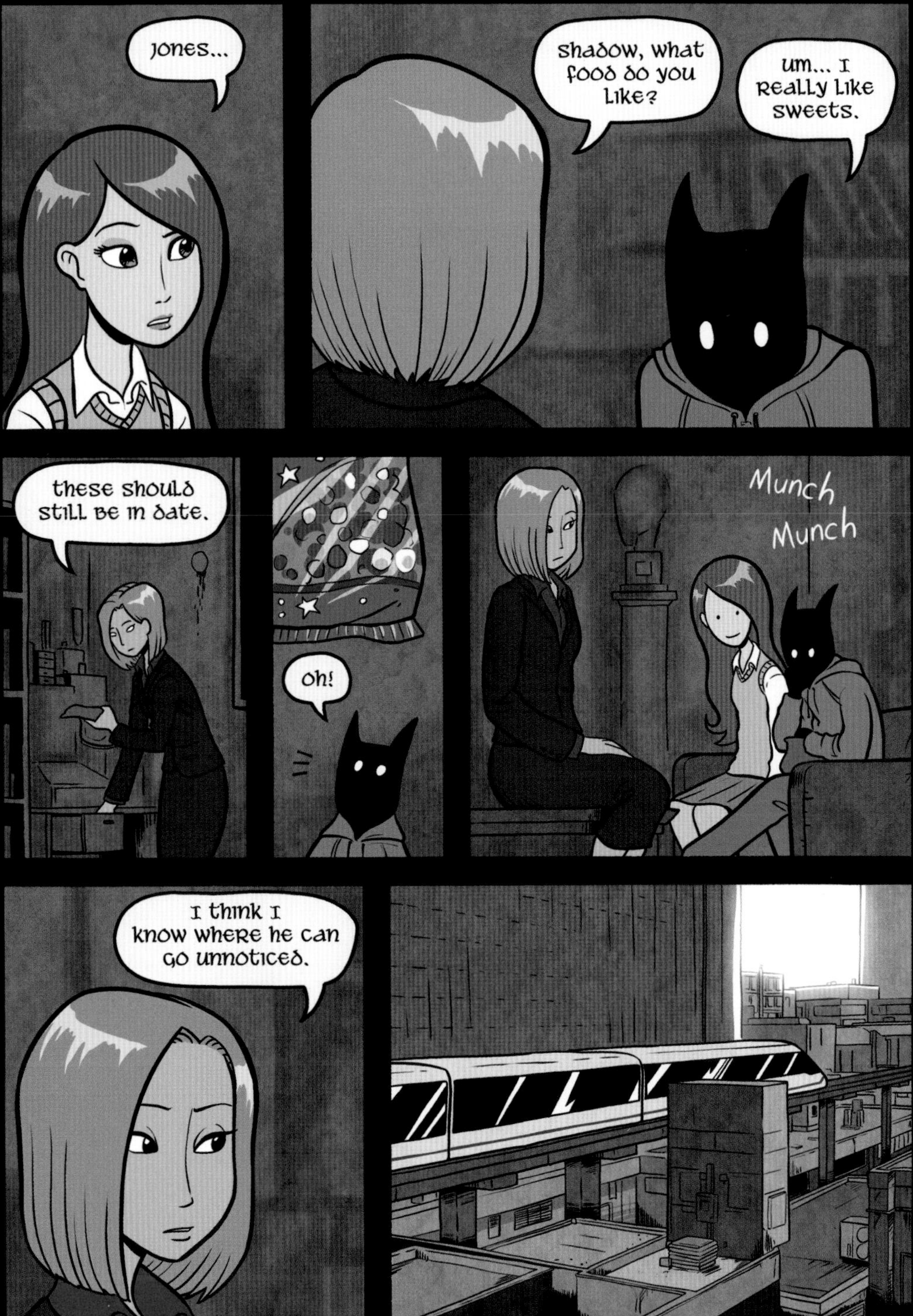
Jones...
Shadow, what food do you like?
Um... I really like sweets.
These should still be in date.
Oh!
Munch Munch
I think I know where he can go unnoticed.

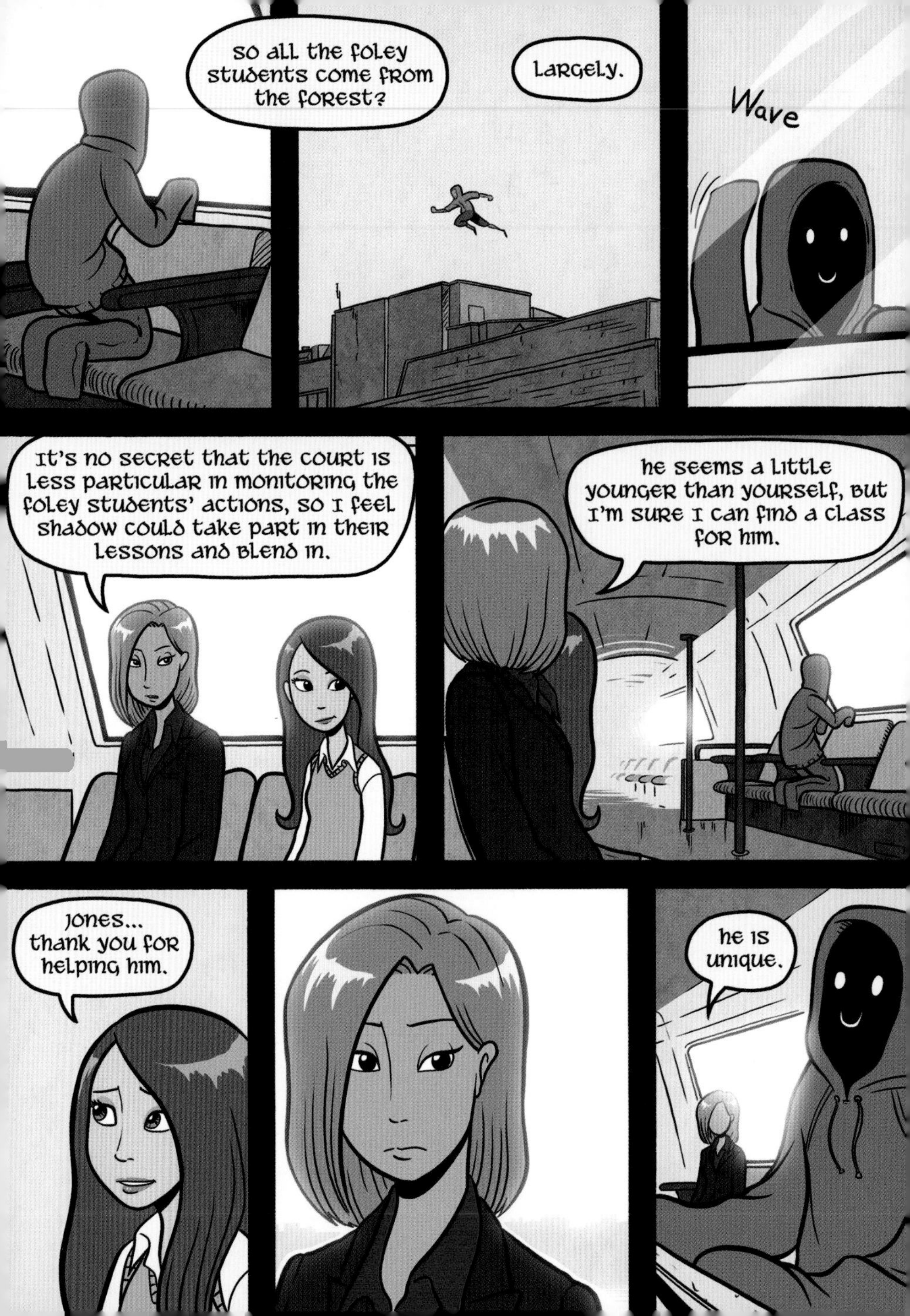
so all the foley students come from the forest?
Largely.
Wave
It's no secret that the court is less particular in monitoring the foley students' actions, so I feel shadow could take part in their lessons and blend in.
he seems a little younger than yourself, but I'm sure I can find a class for him.
jones... thank you for helping him.
he is unique.

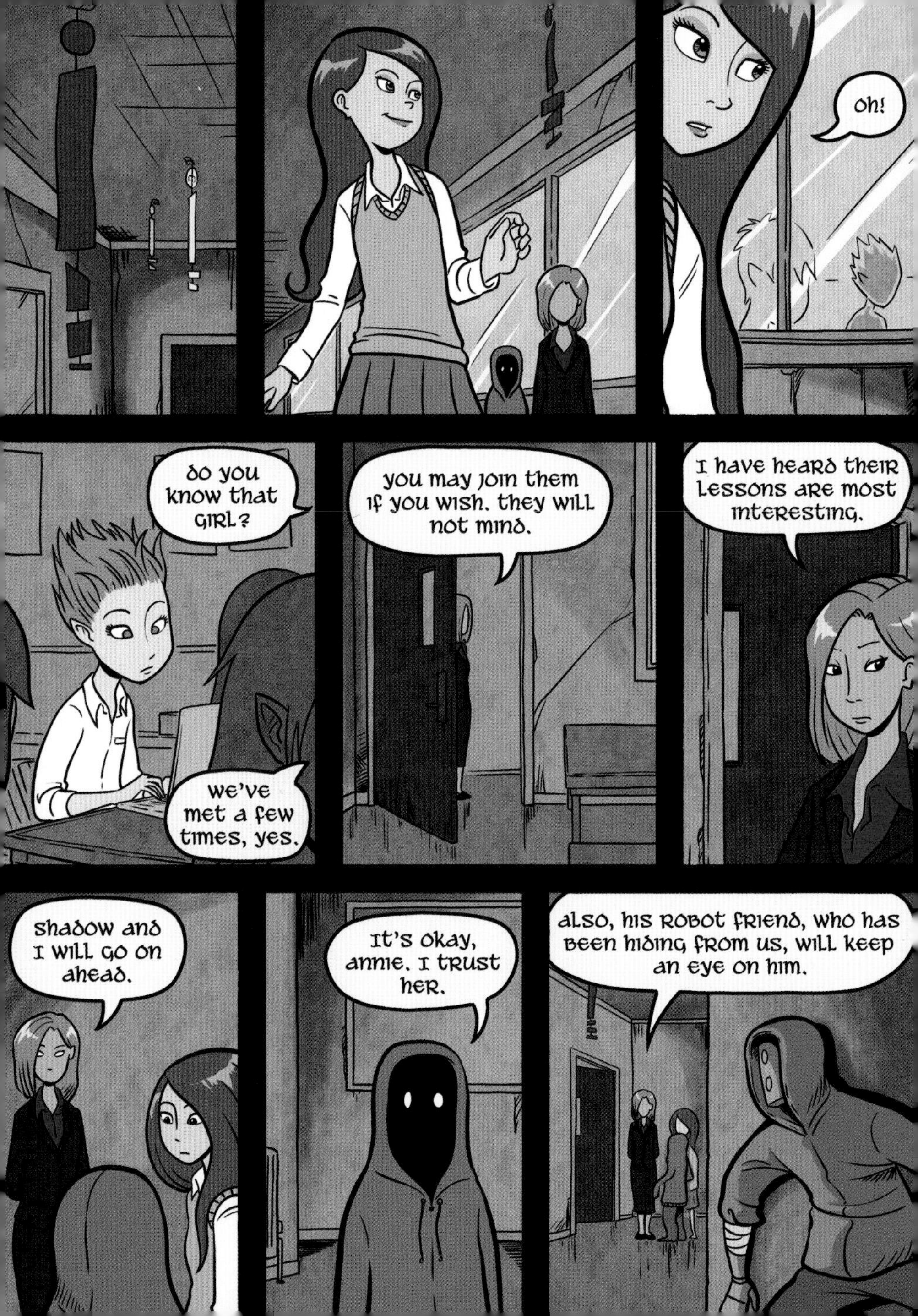
Oh!
do you know that GIRL?
we've met a few times, yes.
you may join them if you wish. they will not mind.
I have heard their lessons are most interesting.
shadow and I will go on ahead.
It's okay, annie. I trust her.
also, his robot friend, who has been hiding from us, will keep an eye on him.

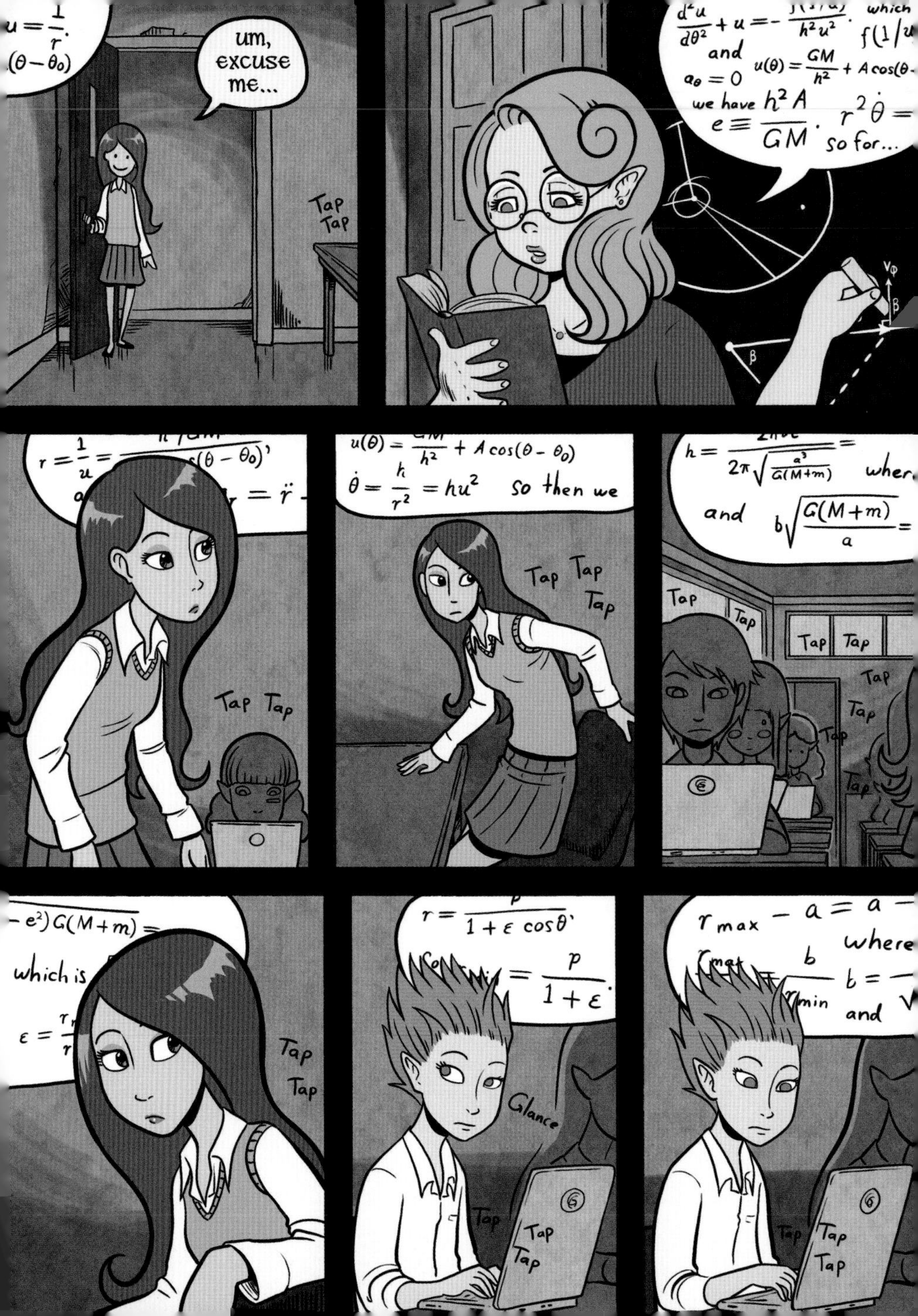

um, excuse me...
Tap Tap
and $a_\theta = 0$ $u(\theta) = \frac{GM}{h^2} + A\cos(\theta -$
we have $e \equiv \frac{h^2 A}{GM}$. so for...
β
Tap Tap
$u(\theta) = \frac{GM}{h^2} + A\cos(\theta - \theta_0)$
$\dot{\theta} = \frac{h}{r^2} = hu^2$ so then we
Tap Tap Tap
$h = \frac{2\pi ab}{2\pi\sqrt{\frac{a^3}{G(M+m)}}} =$ where
and $b\sqrt{\frac{G(M+m)}{a}} =$
Tap Tap Tap Tap Tap Tap Tap Tap
which is
Tap Tap
$r = \frac{p}{1 + \epsilon\cos\theta}$,
$= \frac{p}{1+\epsilon}$.
Glance
Tap Tap Tap
r_{max}
r_{min}
where
and
Tap Tap Tap

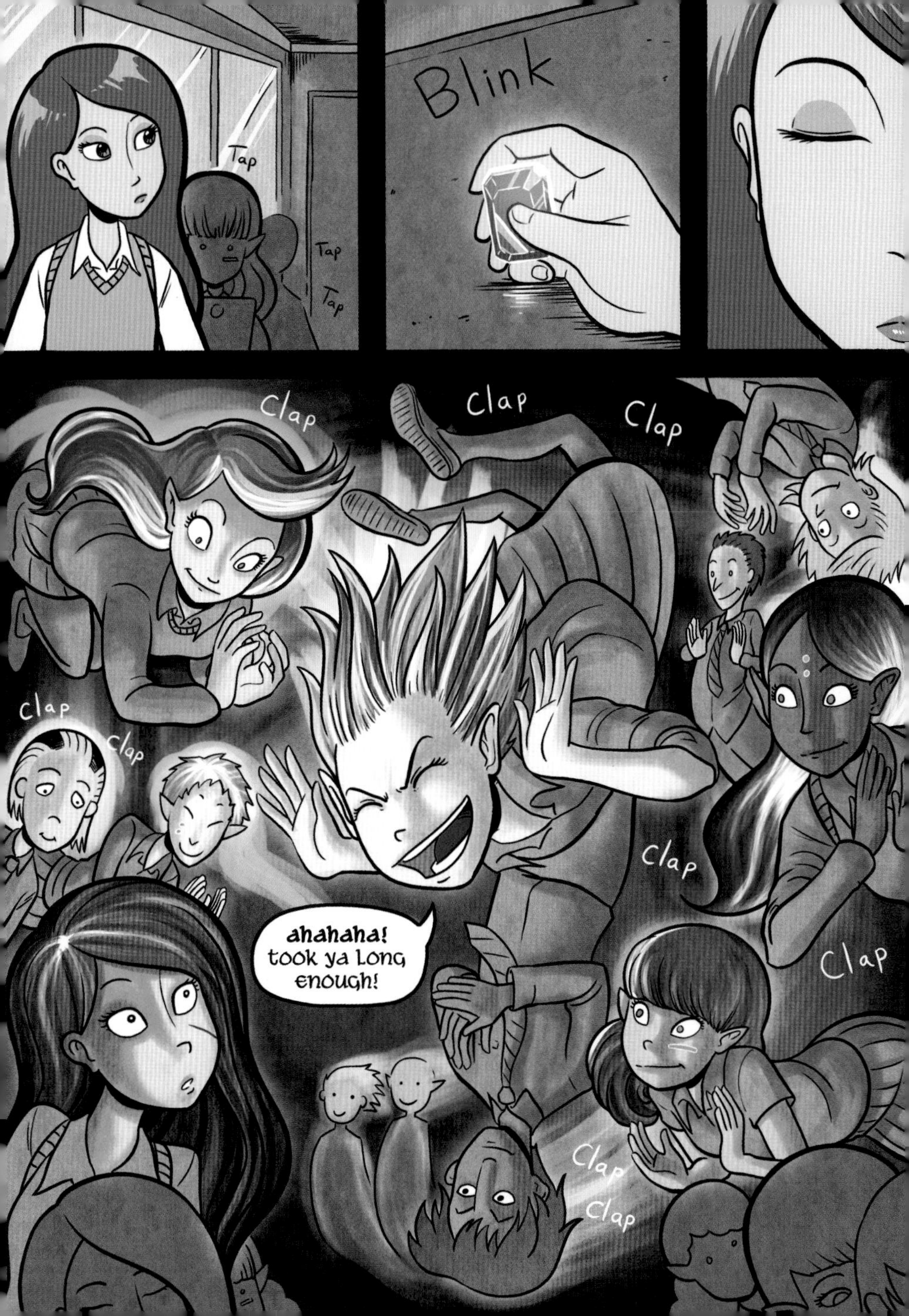
Tap
Tap
Tap
Blink
Clap
Clap
Clap
Clap
Clap
ahahaha! took ya long enough!
Clap
Clap
Clap
Clap

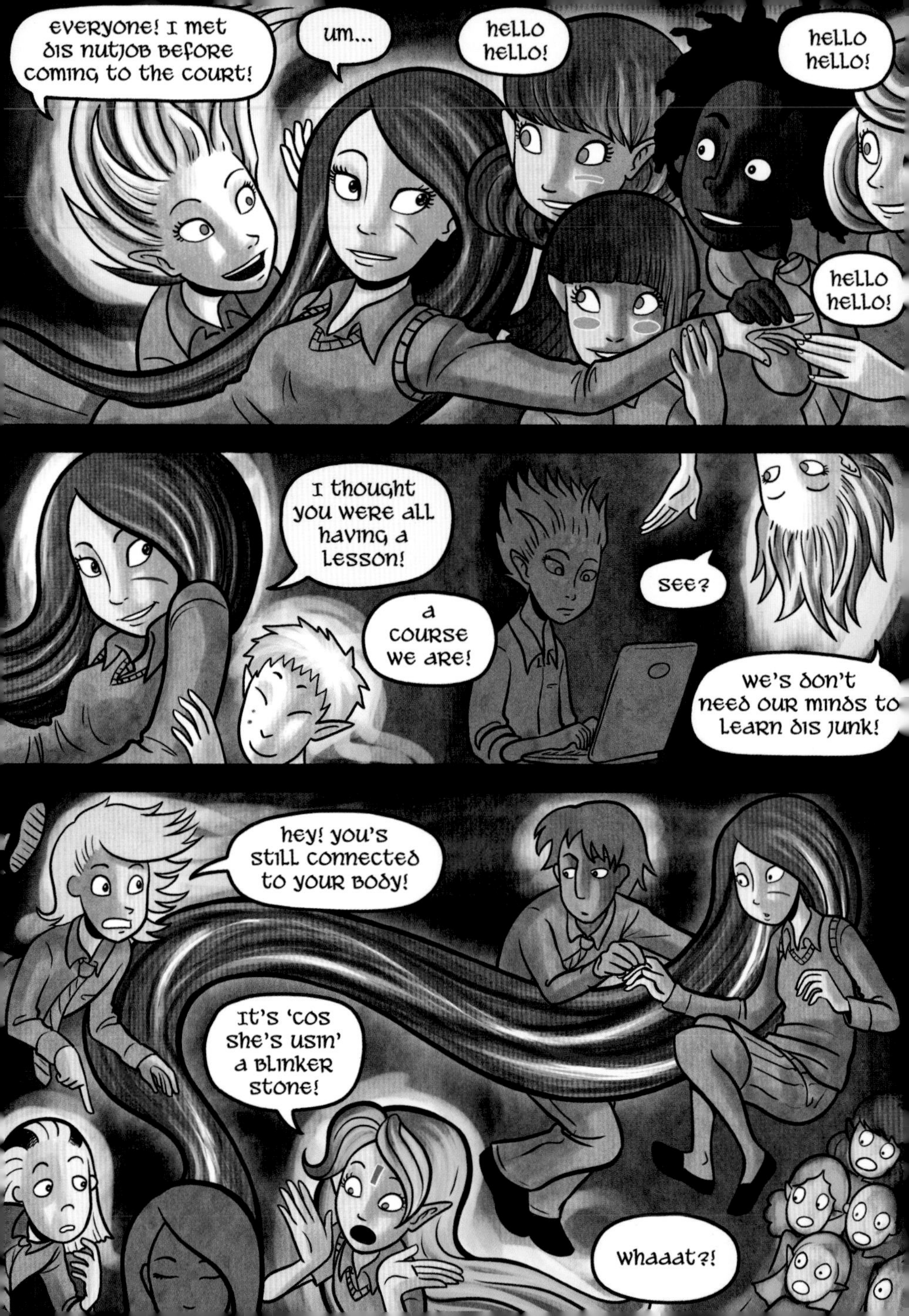
everyone! I met dis nutjob before coming to the court!
um...
hello hello!
hello hello!
hello hello!
I thought you were all having a lesson!
a course we are!
see?
we's don't need our minds to learn dis junk!
hey! you's still connected to your body!
It's 'cos she's usin' a blinker stone!
Whaaat?!

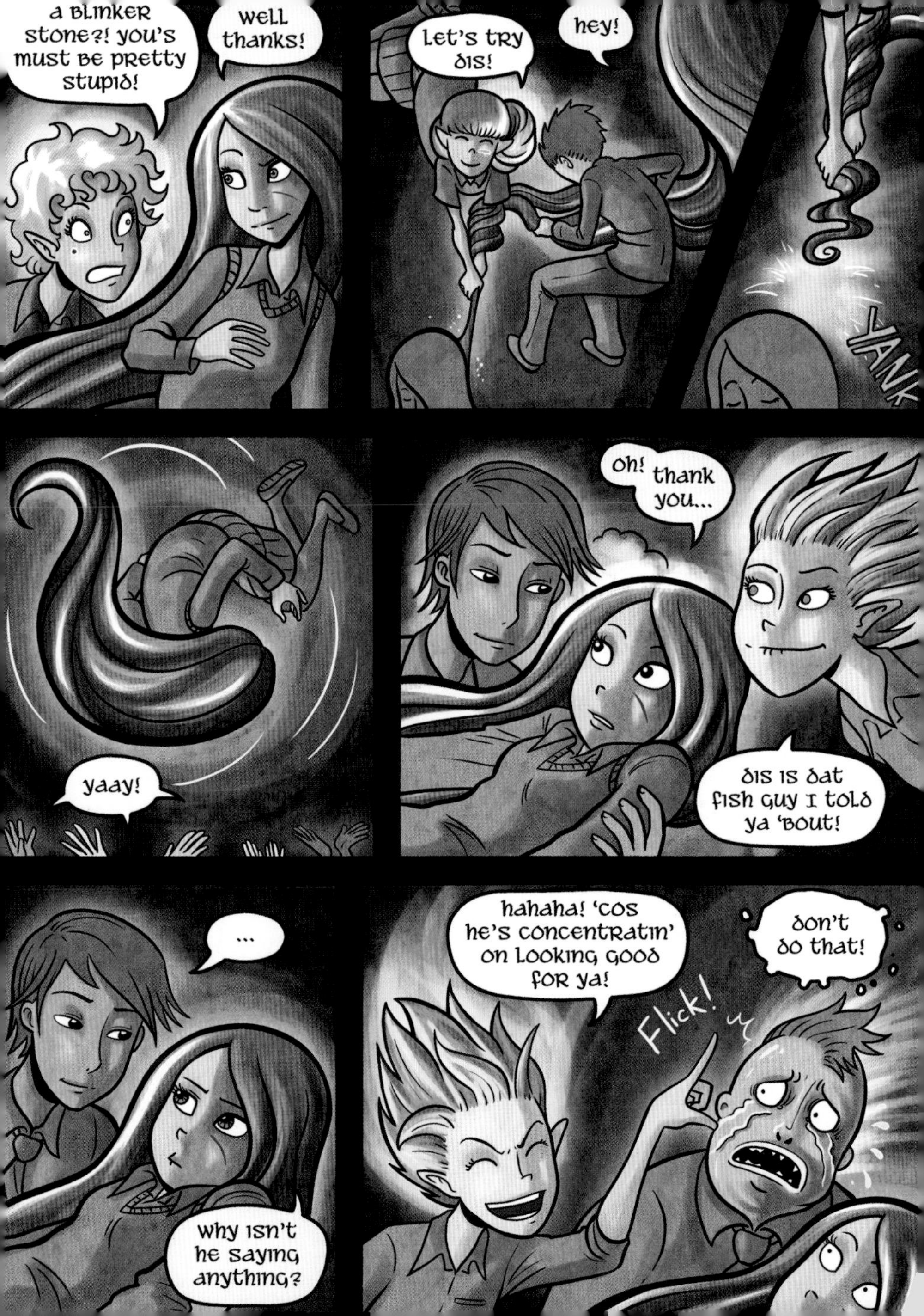
a BLINKER stone?! you's must be pretty stupid!
well thanks!
Let's try dis!
hey!
YANK
yaay!
Oh! thank you...
dis is dat fish guy I told ya 'bout!
...
why isn't he saying anything?
hahaha! 'cos he's concentratin' on looking good for ya!
Flick!
don't do that!

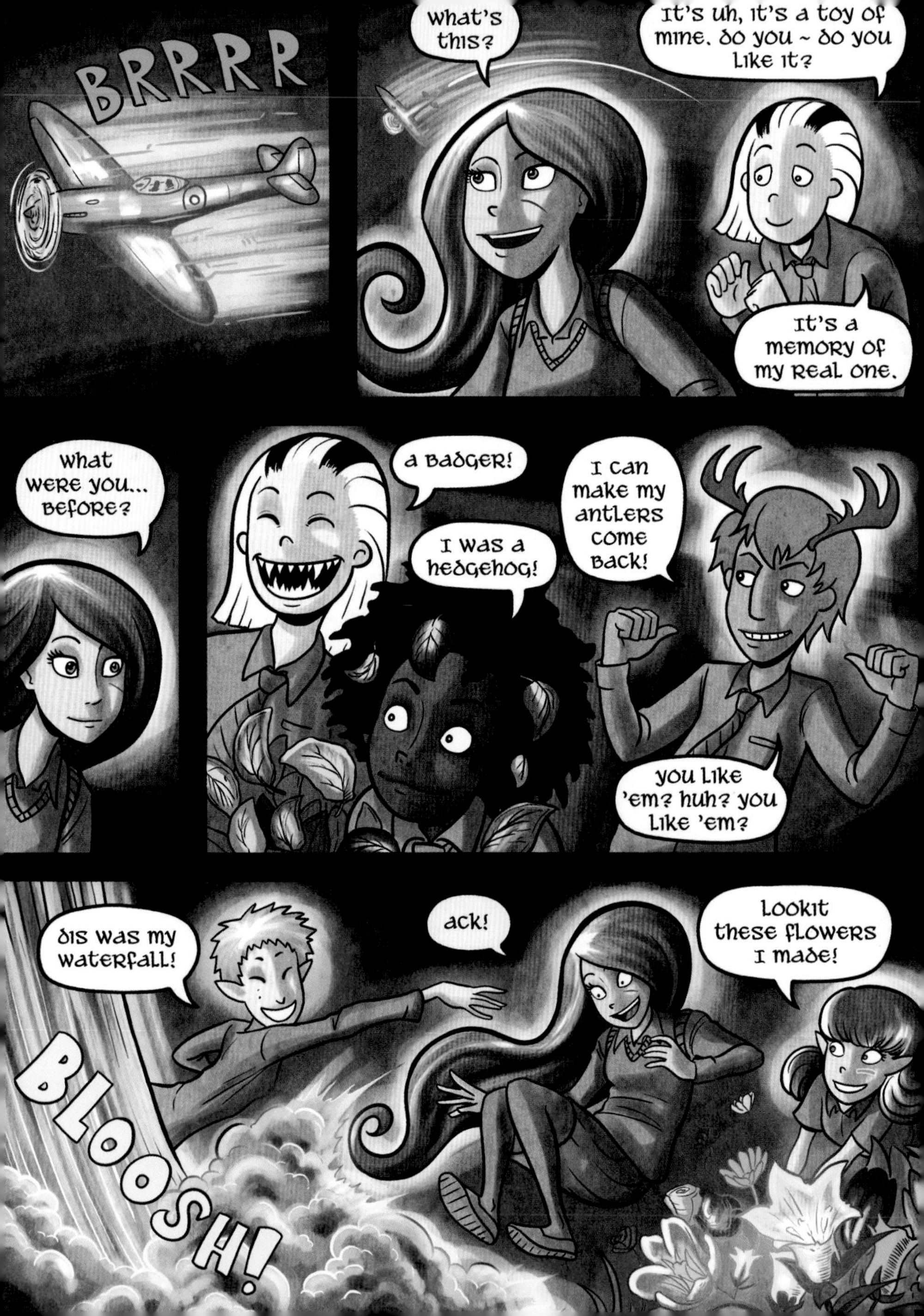
BRRRR
What's this?
It's uh, it's a toy of mine. do you ~ do you like it?
It's a memory of my real one.
What were you... before?
a badger!
I was a hedgehog!
I can make my antlers come back!
you like 'em? huh? you like 'em?
dis was my waterfall!
ack!
Lookit these flowers I made!
BLOOSH!

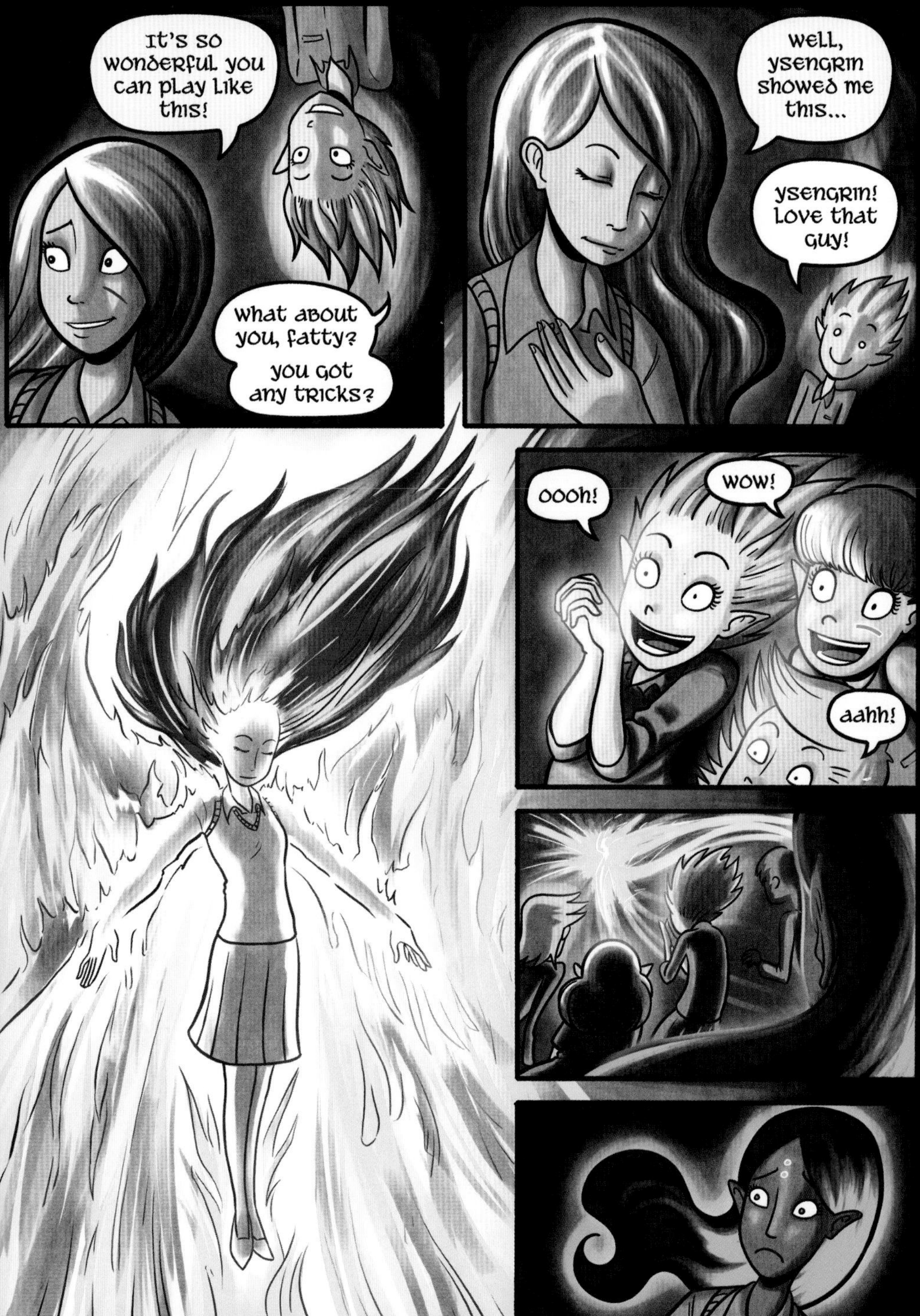
It's so wonderful you can play like this!
What about you, fatty?
you got any tricks?
Well, Ysengrin showed me this...
Ysengrin! Love that guy!
Oooh!
Wow!
Aahh!

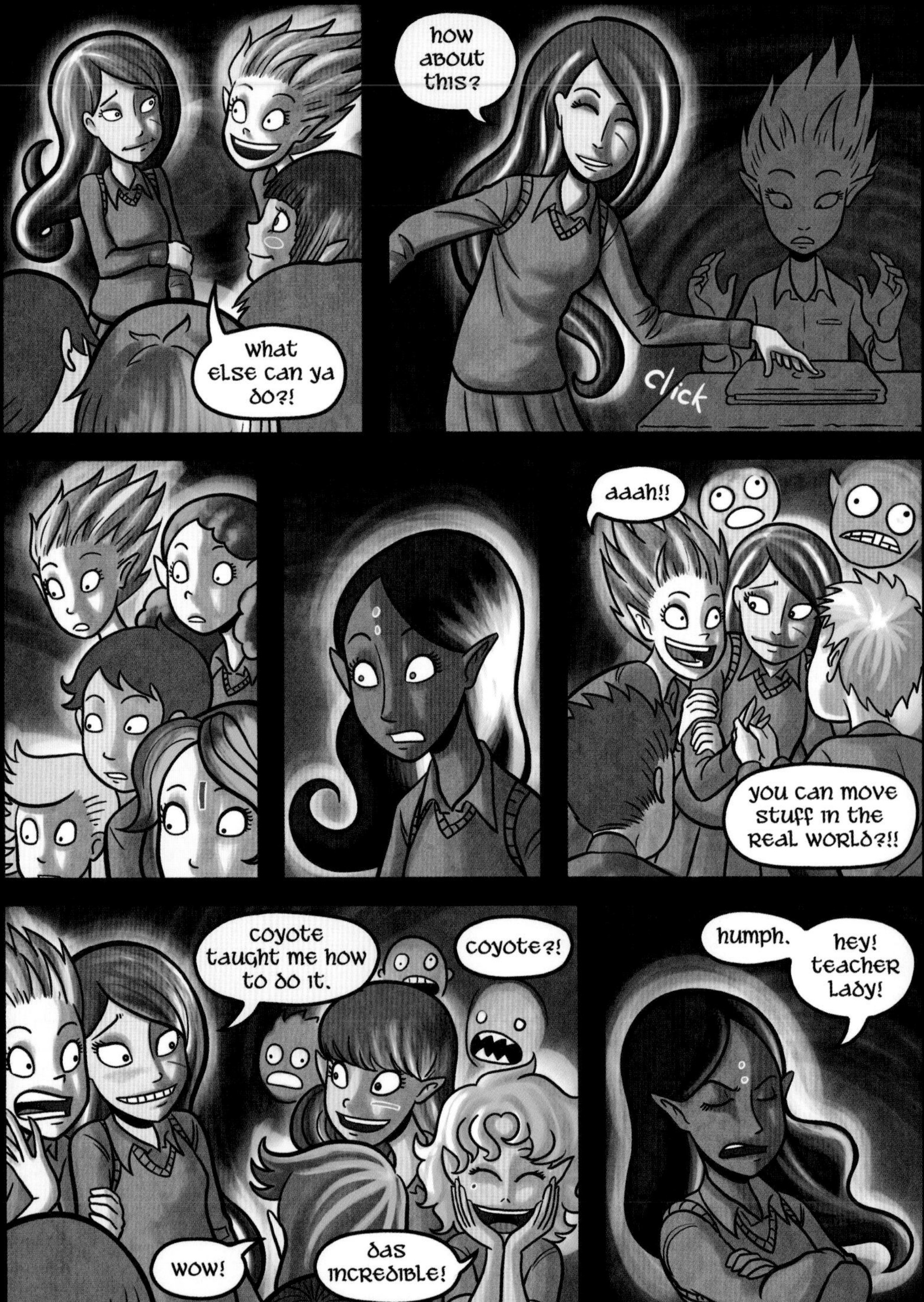
what else can ya do?!
how about this?
click
aaah!!
you can move stuff in the real world?!!
coyote taught me how to do it.
coyote?!
wow!
das incredible!
humph.
hey! teacher lady!

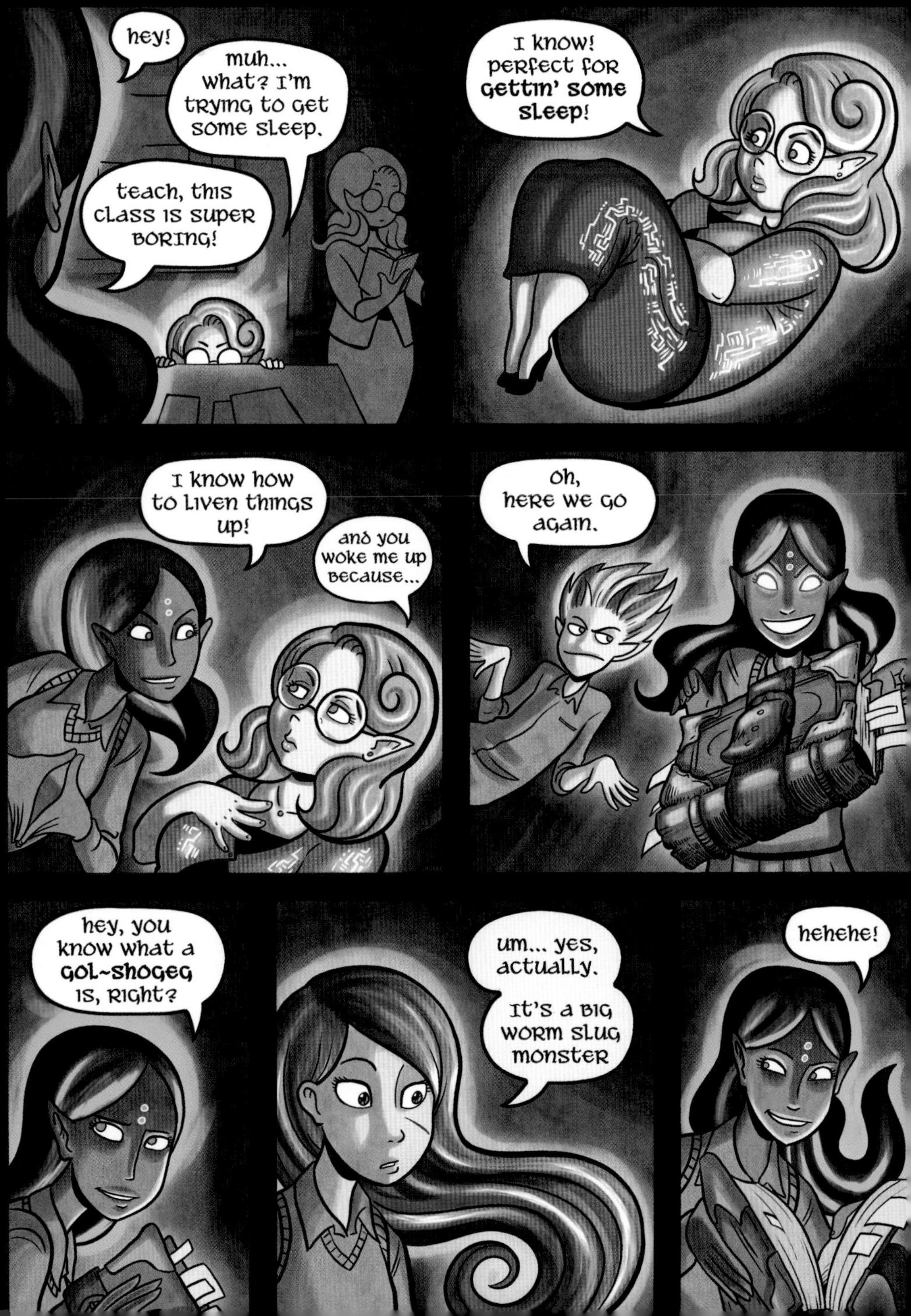
hey!
muh... what? I'm trying to get some sleep.
teach, this class is super boring!
I know! perfect for gettin' some sleep!
I know how to liven things up!
and you woke me up because...
oh, here we go again.
hey, you know what a gol-shogeg is, right?
um... yes, actually.
It's a big worm slug monster
hehehe!

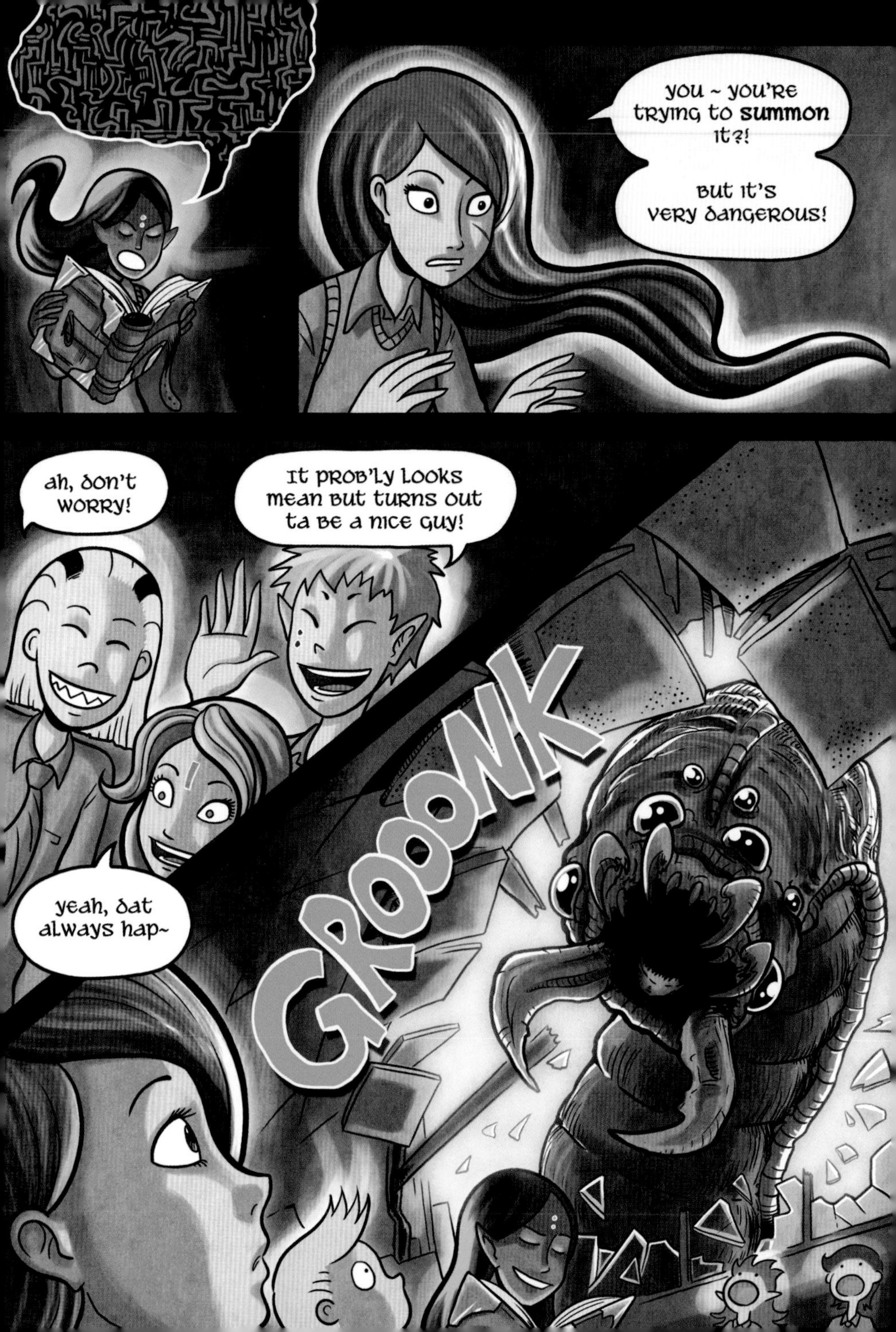
you ~ you're trying to **summon** it?!
But it's very dangerous!
ah, don't worry!
It prob'ly looks mean but turns out ta be a nice guy!
yeah, dat always hap~
GROOONK

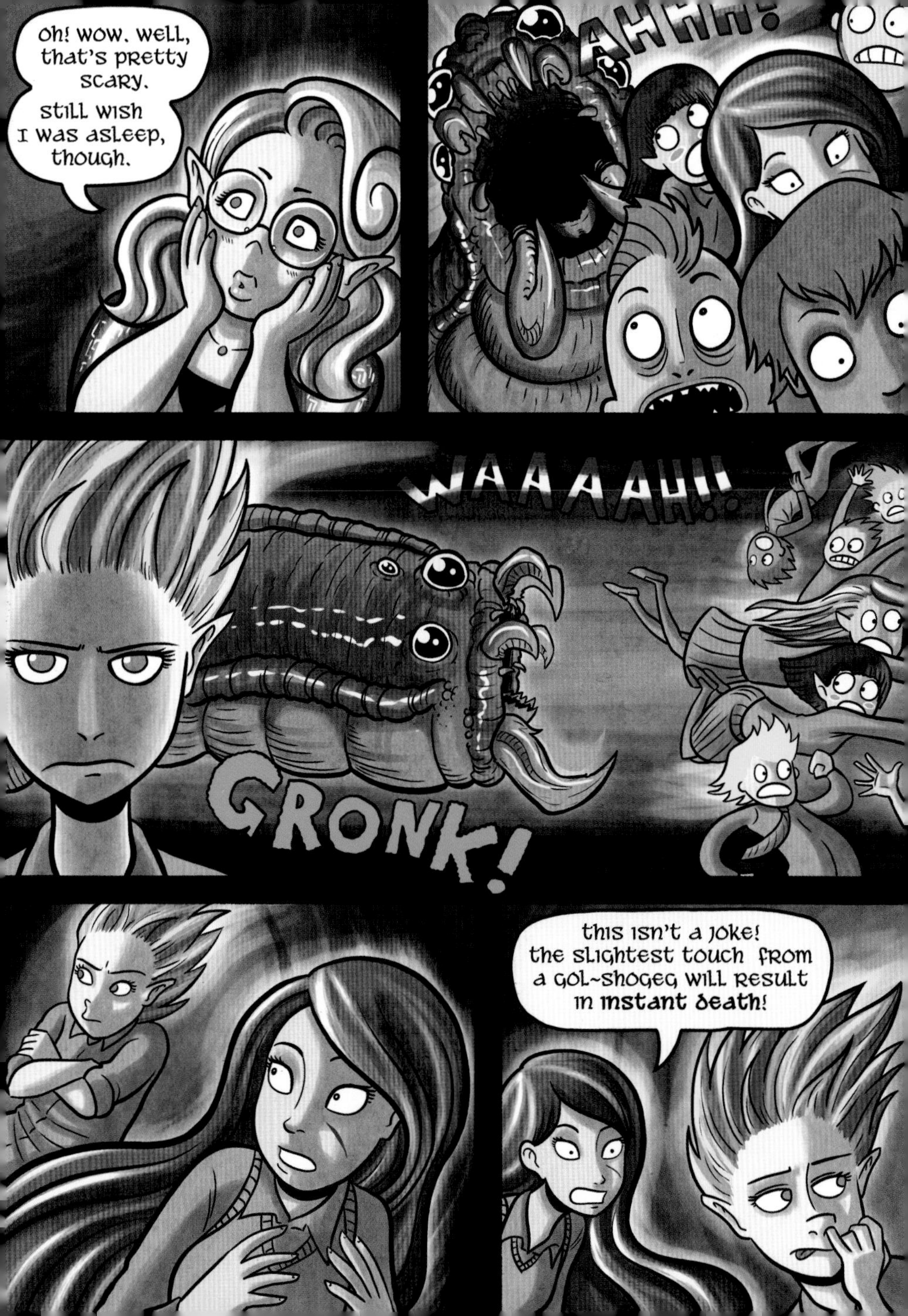
Oh! wow. well, that's pretty scary.
still wish I was asleep, though.
AHHH!
WAAAAAH!!
GRONK!
this isn't a joke! the slightest touch from a gol~shogeg will result in **instant death!**

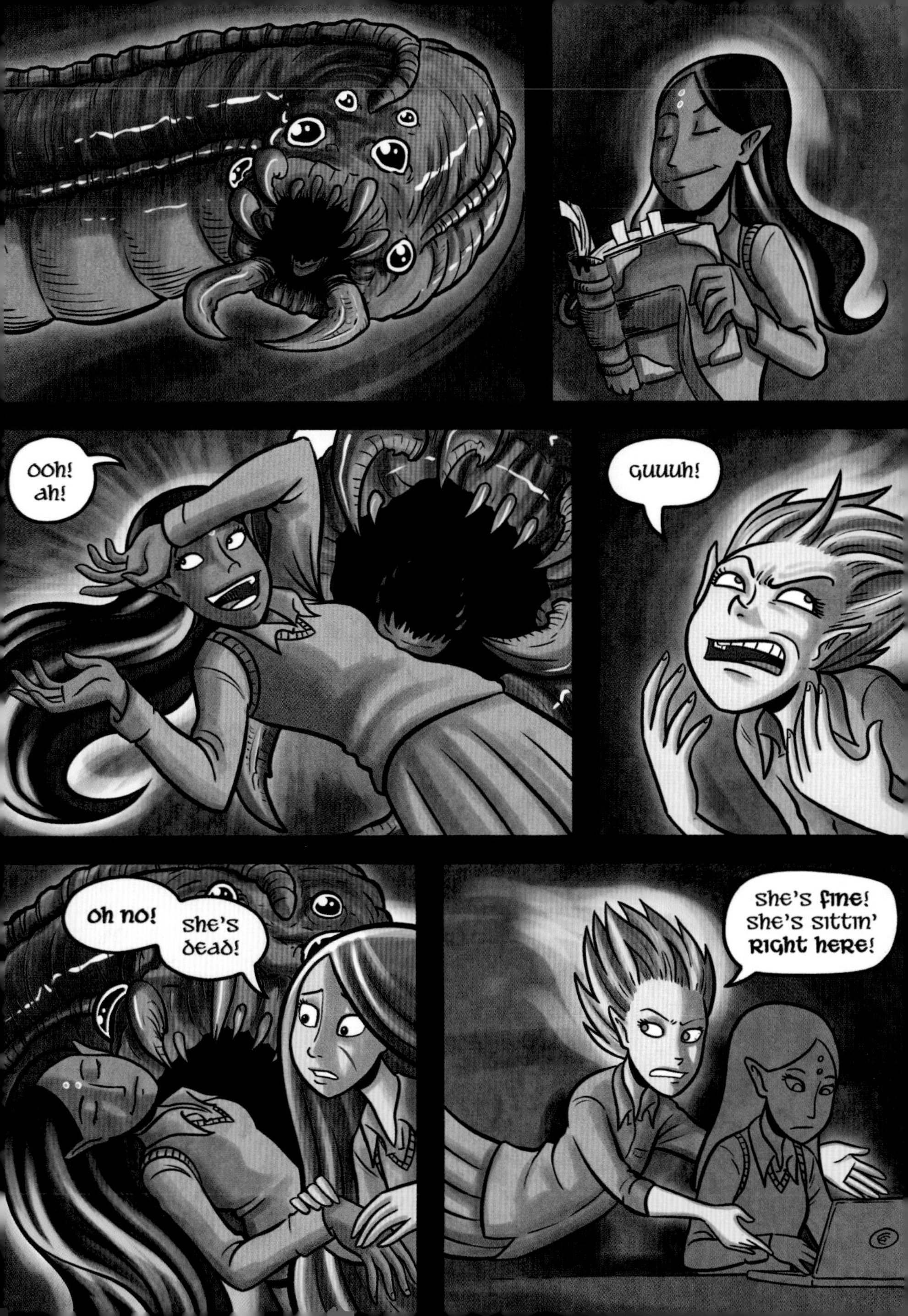
OOH! AH!
GUUUH!
OH NO!
SHE'S DEAD!
SHE'S FINE! SHE'S SITTIN' RIGHT HERE!

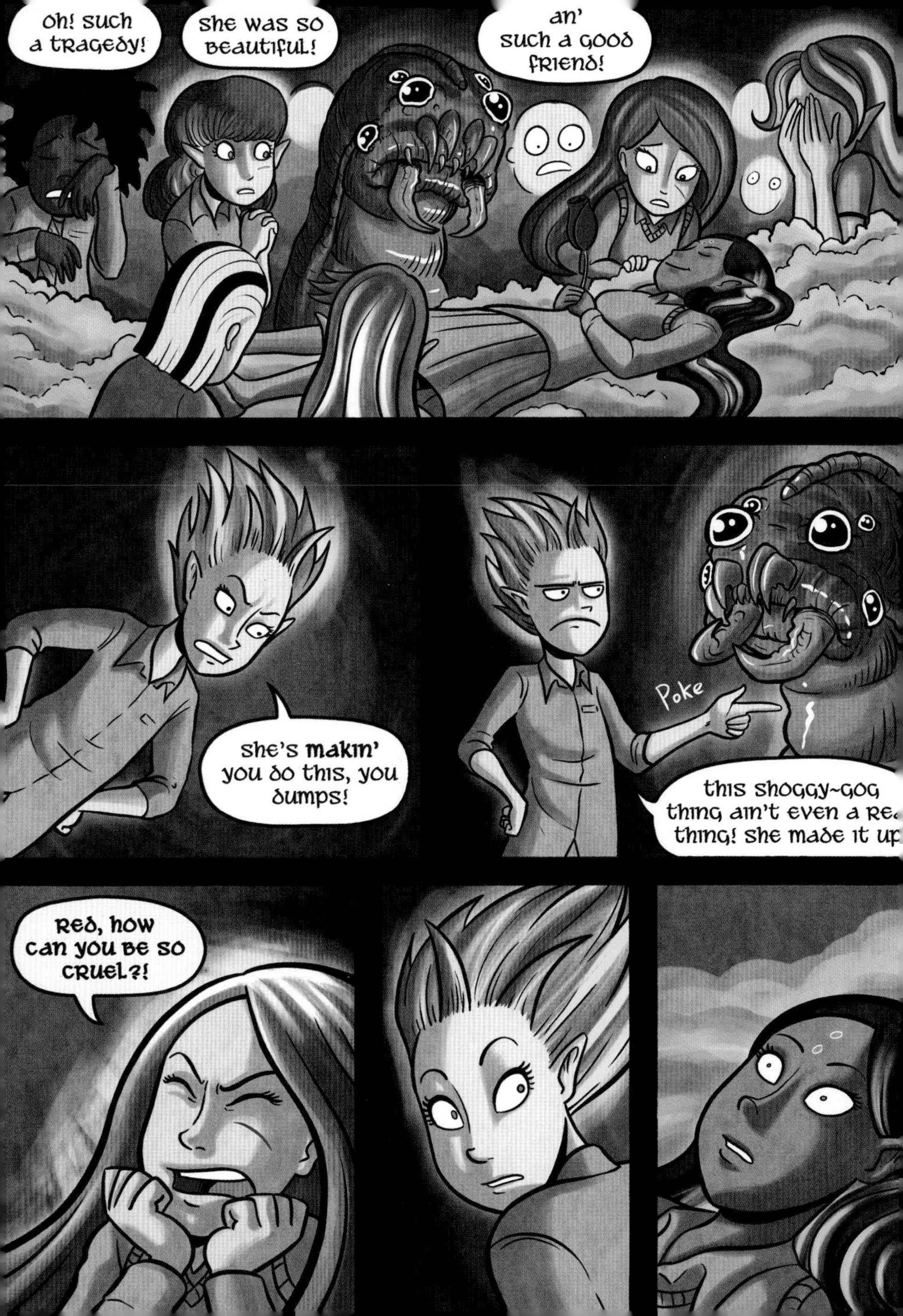

Oh! such a tragedy!
She was so beautiful!
an' such a good friend!
She's makin' you do this, you dumps!
Poke
This shoggy~gog thing ain't even a re. thing! She made it up
Red, how can you be so cruel?!

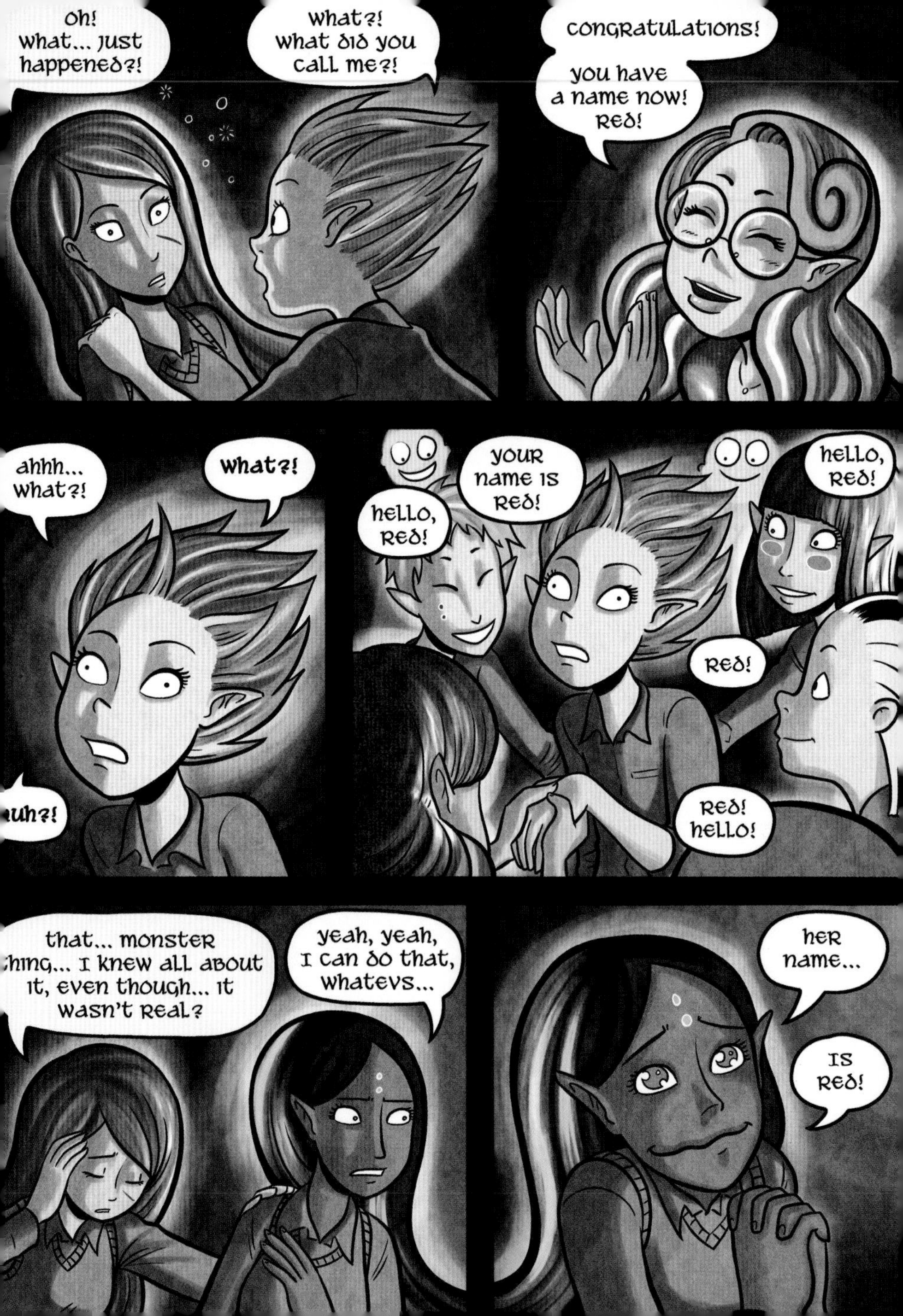
Oh!
what... just happened?!
what?!
what did you call me?!
congratulations!
you have a name now! Red!
ahhh... what?!
what?!
uh?!
your name is Red!
hello, Red!
hello, Red!
Red!
Red! hello!
that... monster thing... I knew all about it, even though... it wasn't real?
yeah, yeah, I can do that, whatevs...
her name...
is Red!

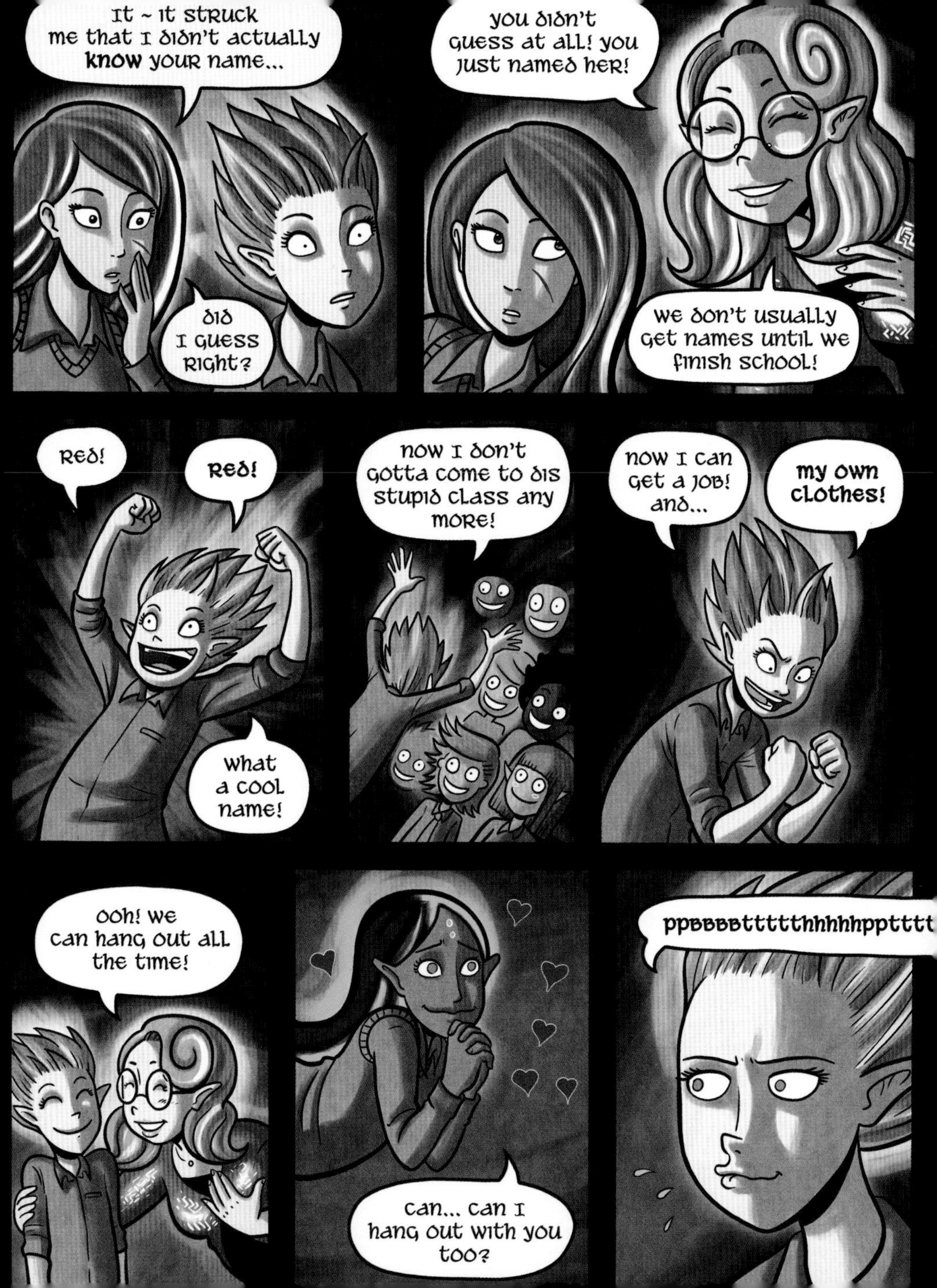
It ~ it struck me that I didn't actually **know** your name...
Did I guess right?
You didn't guess at all! You just named her!
We don't usually get names until we finish school!
Red!
Red!
What a cool name!
Now I don't gotta come to dis stupid class any more!
Now I can get a job! And...
My own clothes!
Ooh! We can hang out all the time!
Can... can I hang out with you too?
PPBBBBTTTTTHHHHHPPTTTT

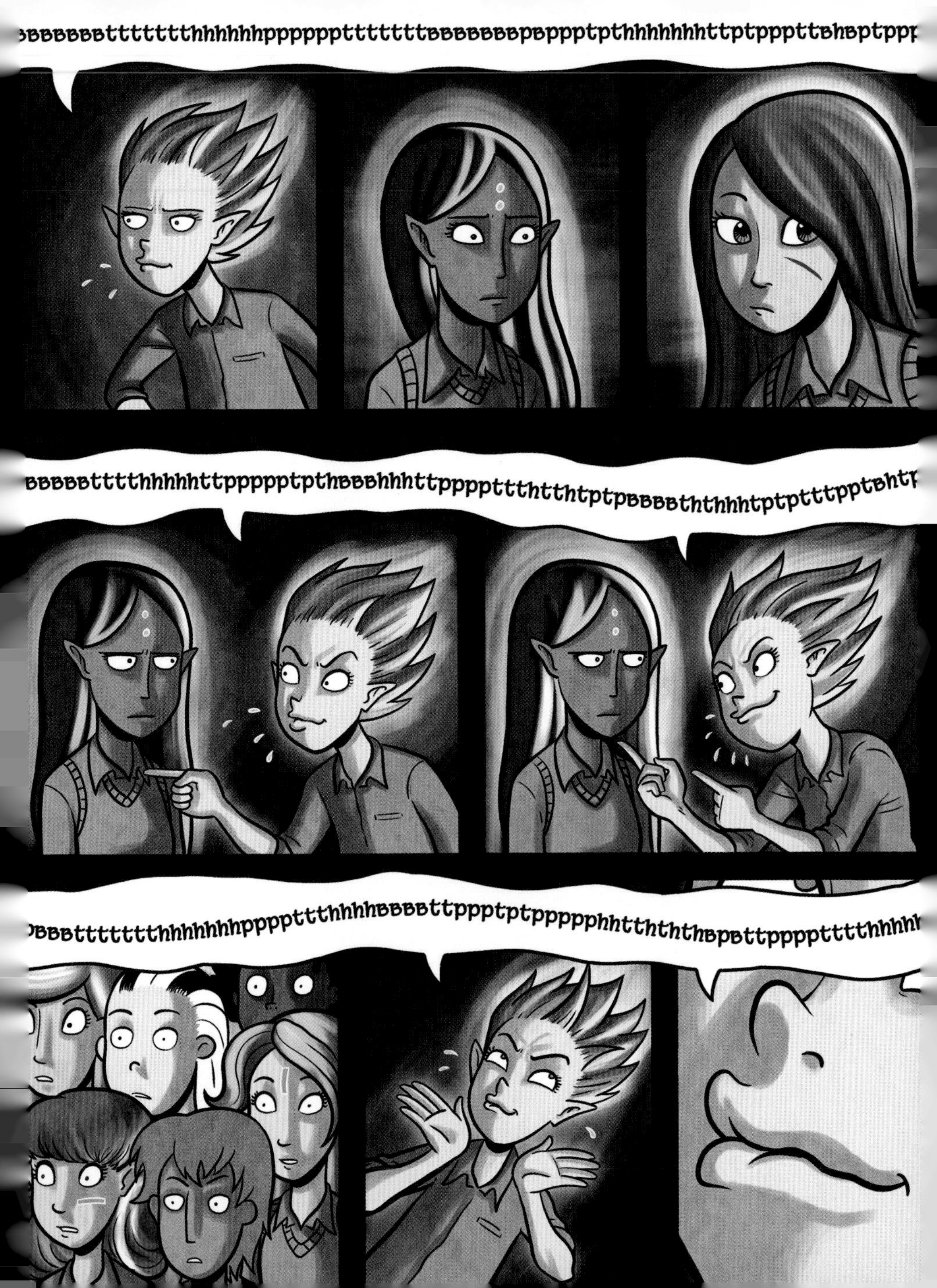
BBBBBBtttttthhhhhpppppttttttBBBBBBpBppptpthhhhhhttptppptt BhBptpp
BBBBBttttthhhhhttpppppptpthBBBhhhttppppttthtthtptpBBBBthththhtptptttpptBhtp
BBBttttttthhhhhhppppttthhhhBBBBttppptptppppphhththththBpBttppppttttthhhh

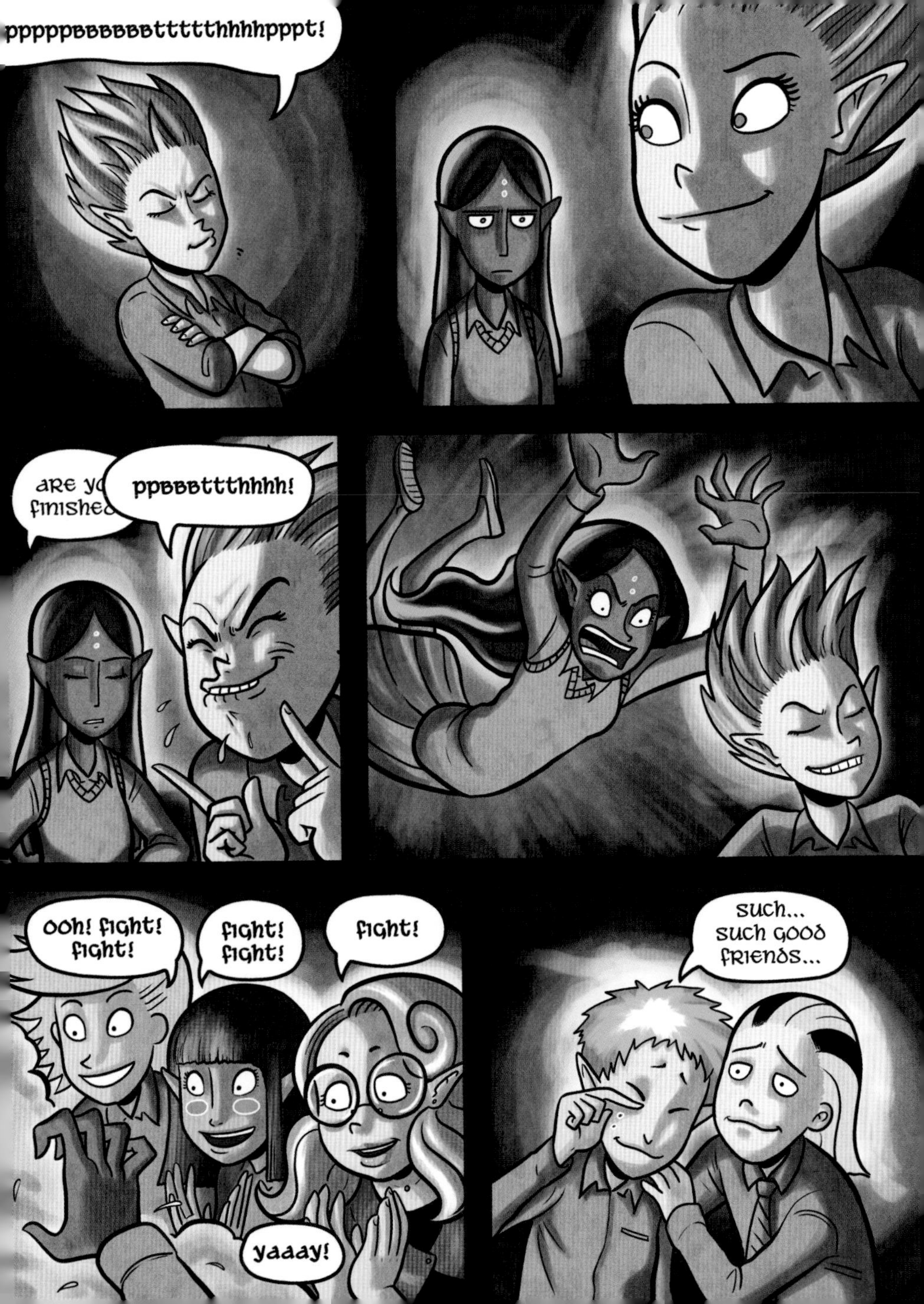
pppppbbbbbbttttthhhhpppt!
are yo… finished…
ppbbbtttthhhh!
ooh! fight! fight!
fight! fight!
fight!
yaaay!
such... such good friends...

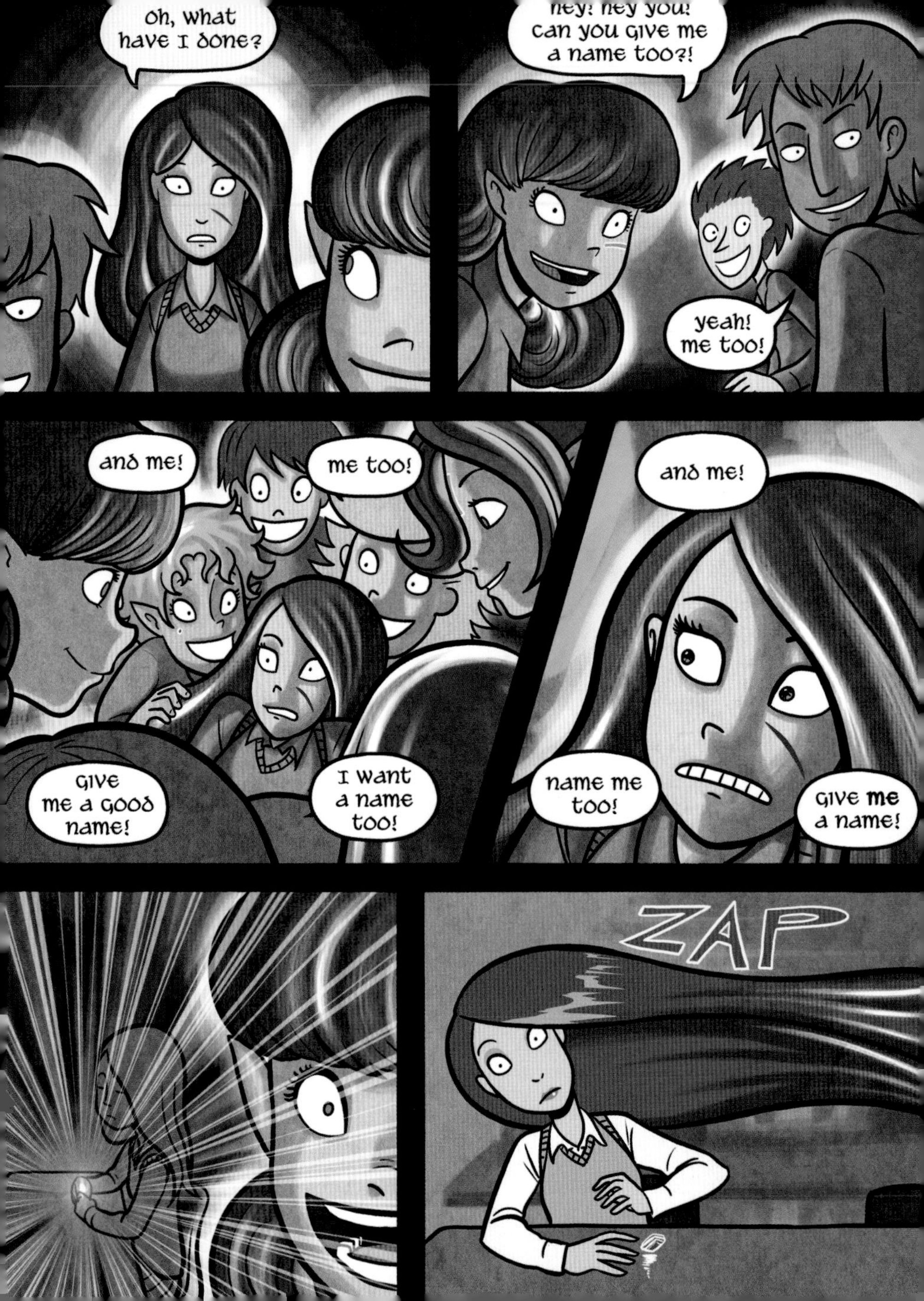

oh, what have I done?
hey! hey you! can you give me a name too?!
yeah! me too!
and me!
me too!
give me a good name!
I want a name too!
and me!
name me too!
give **me** a name!
ZAP

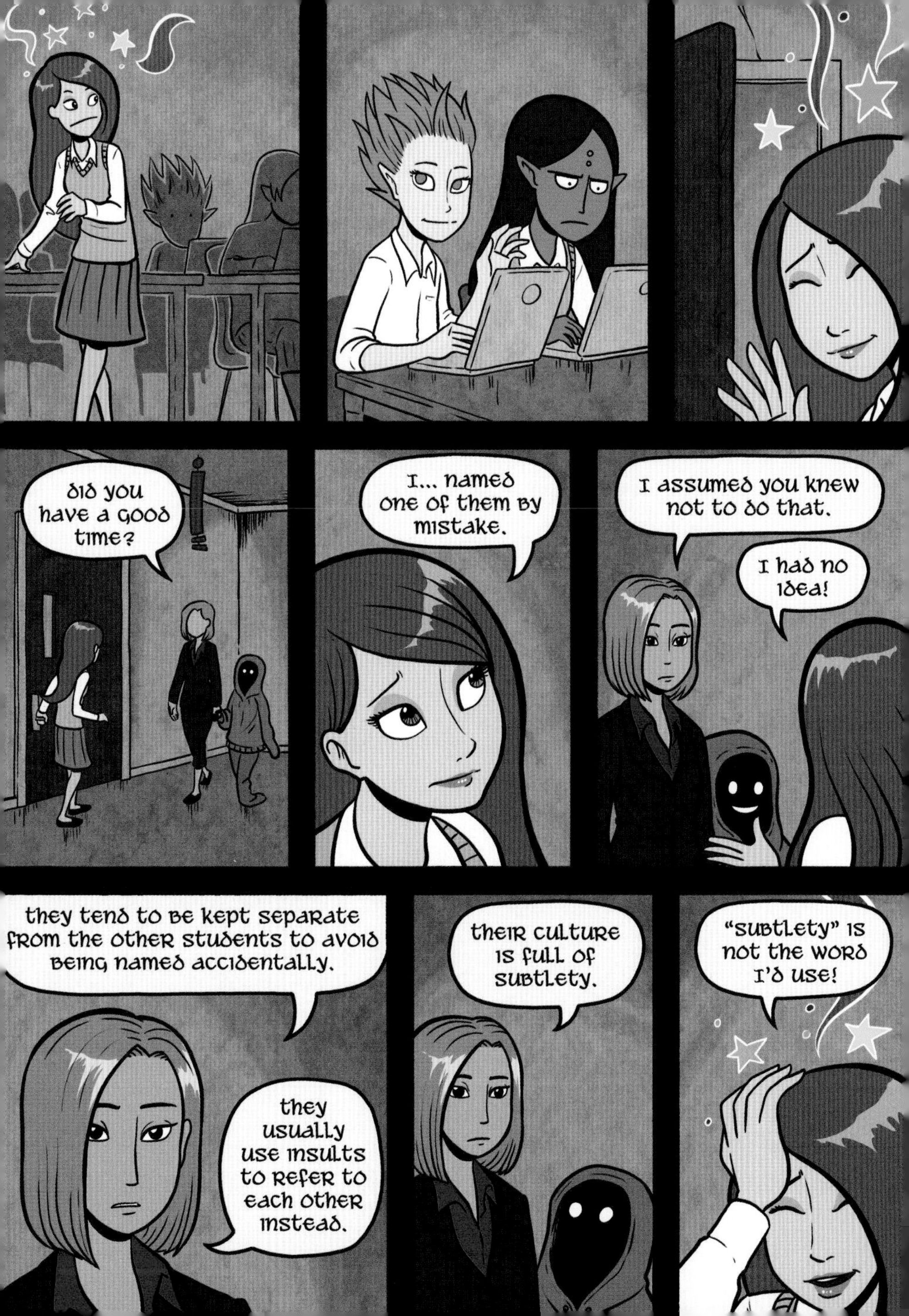
did you have a good time?
I... named one of them by mistake.
I assumed you knew not to do that.
I had no idea!
they tend to be kept separate from the other students to avoid being named accidentally.
they usually use insults to refer to each other instead.
their culture is full of subtlety.
"subtlety" is not the word I'd use!

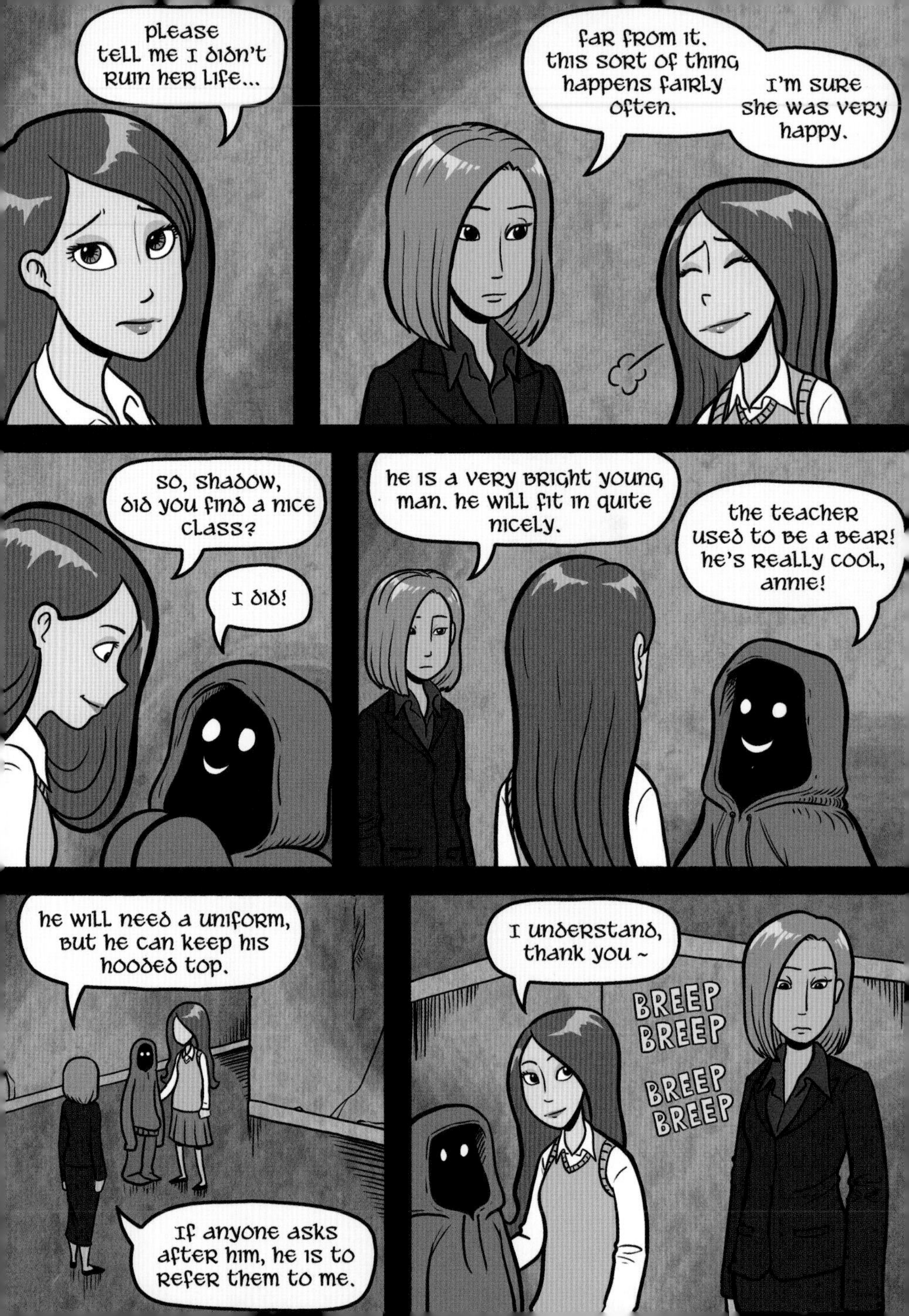
please tell me I didn't ruin her life...
far from it. this sort of thing happens fairly often.
I'm sure she was very happy.
so, shadow, did you find a nice class?
I did!
he is a very bright young man. he will fit in quite nicely.
the teacher used to be a bear! he's really cool, annie!
he will need a uniform, but he can keep his hooded top.
If anyone asks after him, he is to refer them to me.
I understand, thank you ~
BREEP BREEP
BREEP BREEP

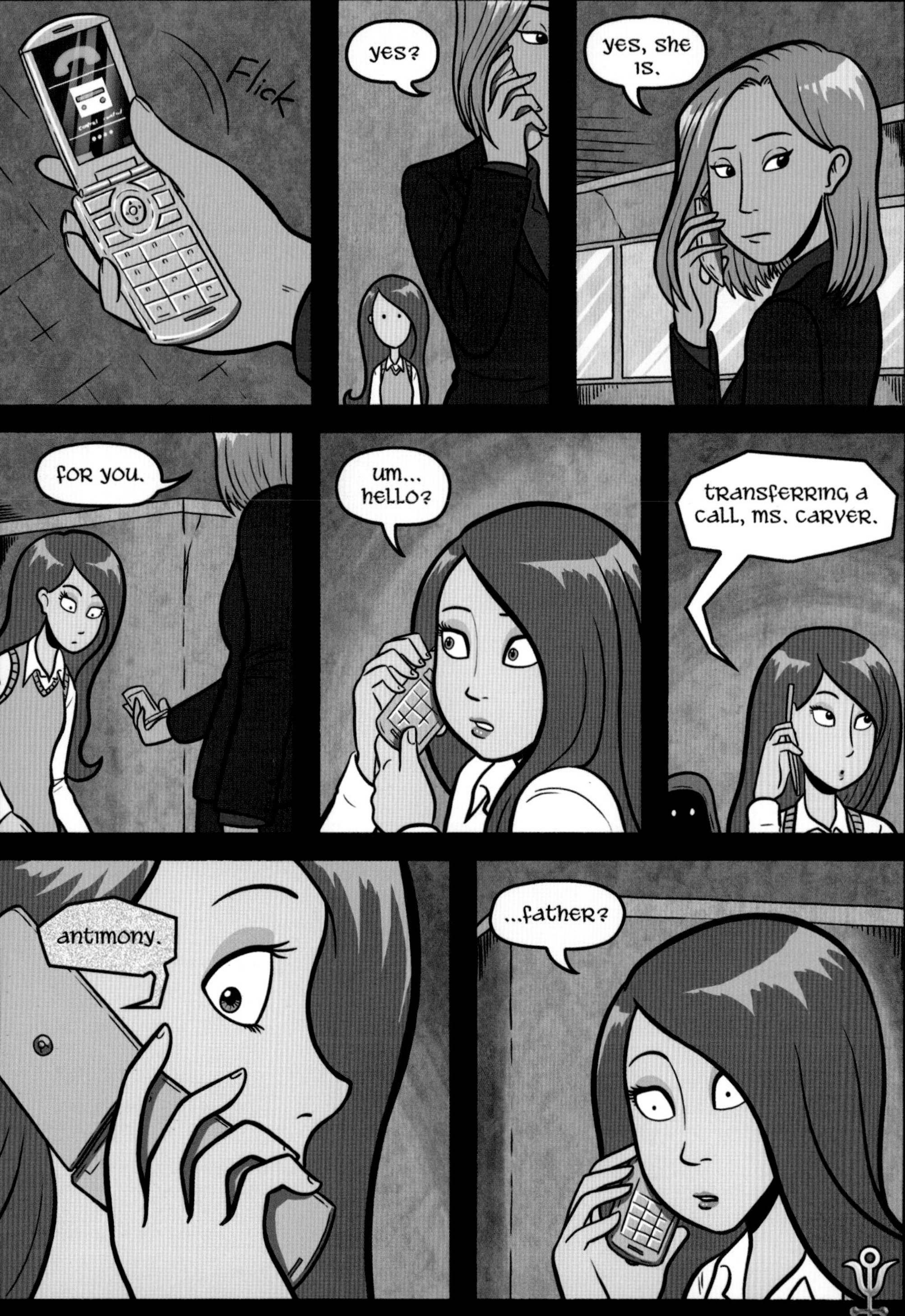

Flick
yes?
yes, she is.
for you.
um... hello?
transferring a call, ms. carver.
antimony.
...father?

Chapter 36 Character Guide

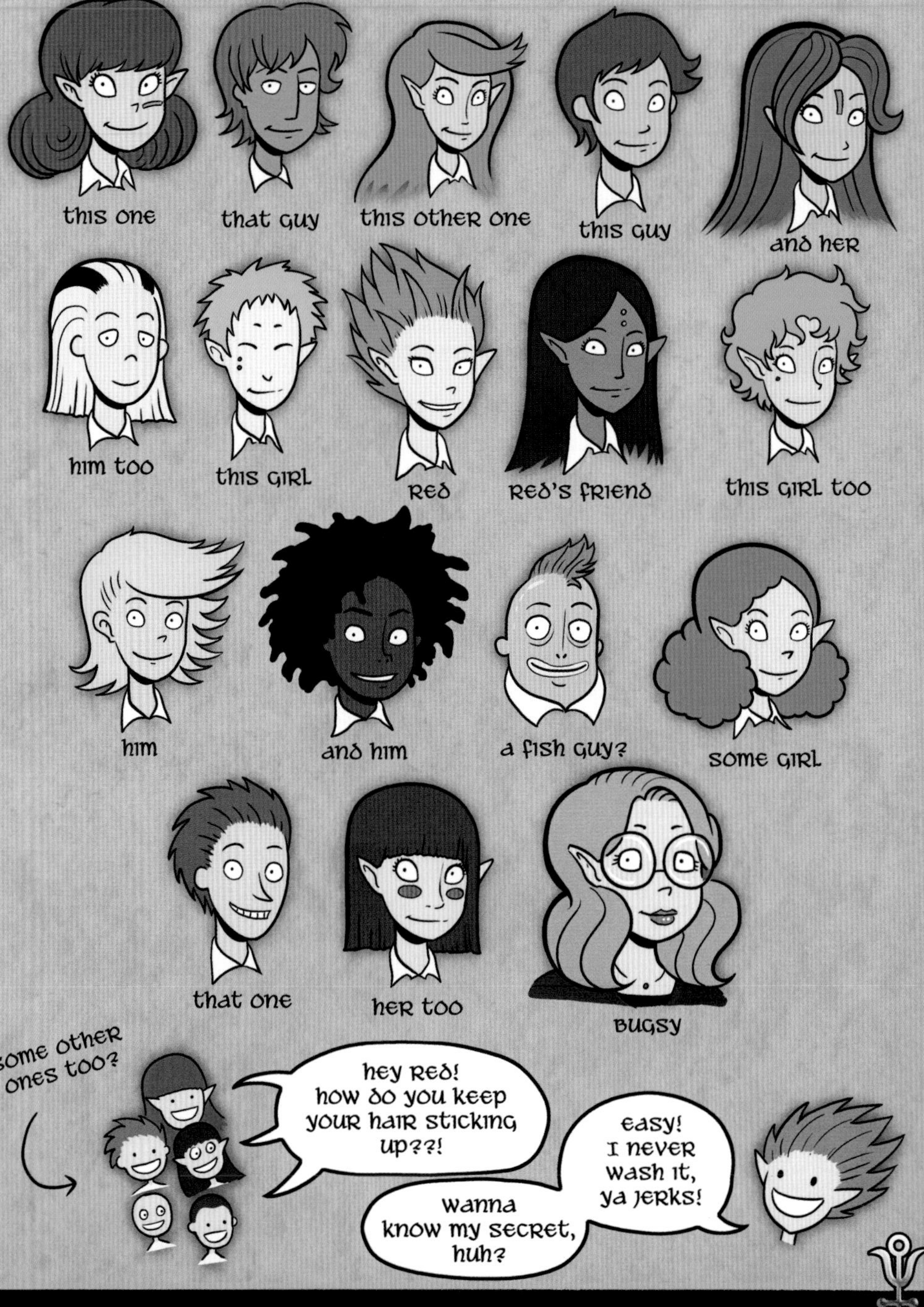
this one
that guy
this other one
this guy
and her
him too
this girl
Red
Red's friend
this girl too
him
and him
a fish guy?
some girl
that one
her too
Bugsy
some other ones too?
hey Red! how do you keep your hair sticking up??!
wanna know my secret, huh?
easy! I never wash it, ya jerks!

Gunnerkrigg Court

Chapter 37:

Microsat 5

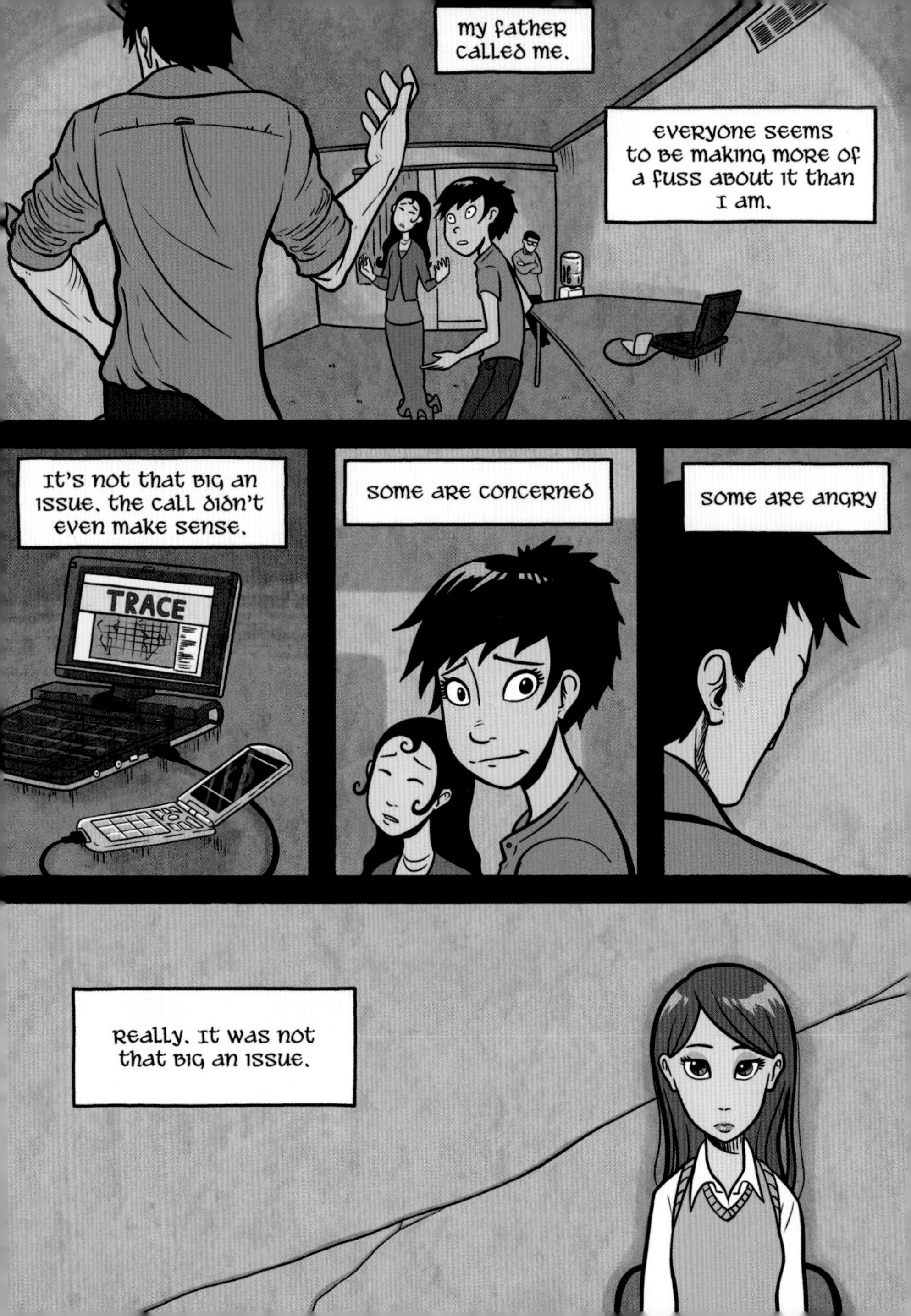
my father called me.
everyone seems to be making more of a fuss about it than I am.
It's not that big an issue. the call didn't even make sense.
TRACE
some are concerned
some are angry
Really. It was not that big an issue.

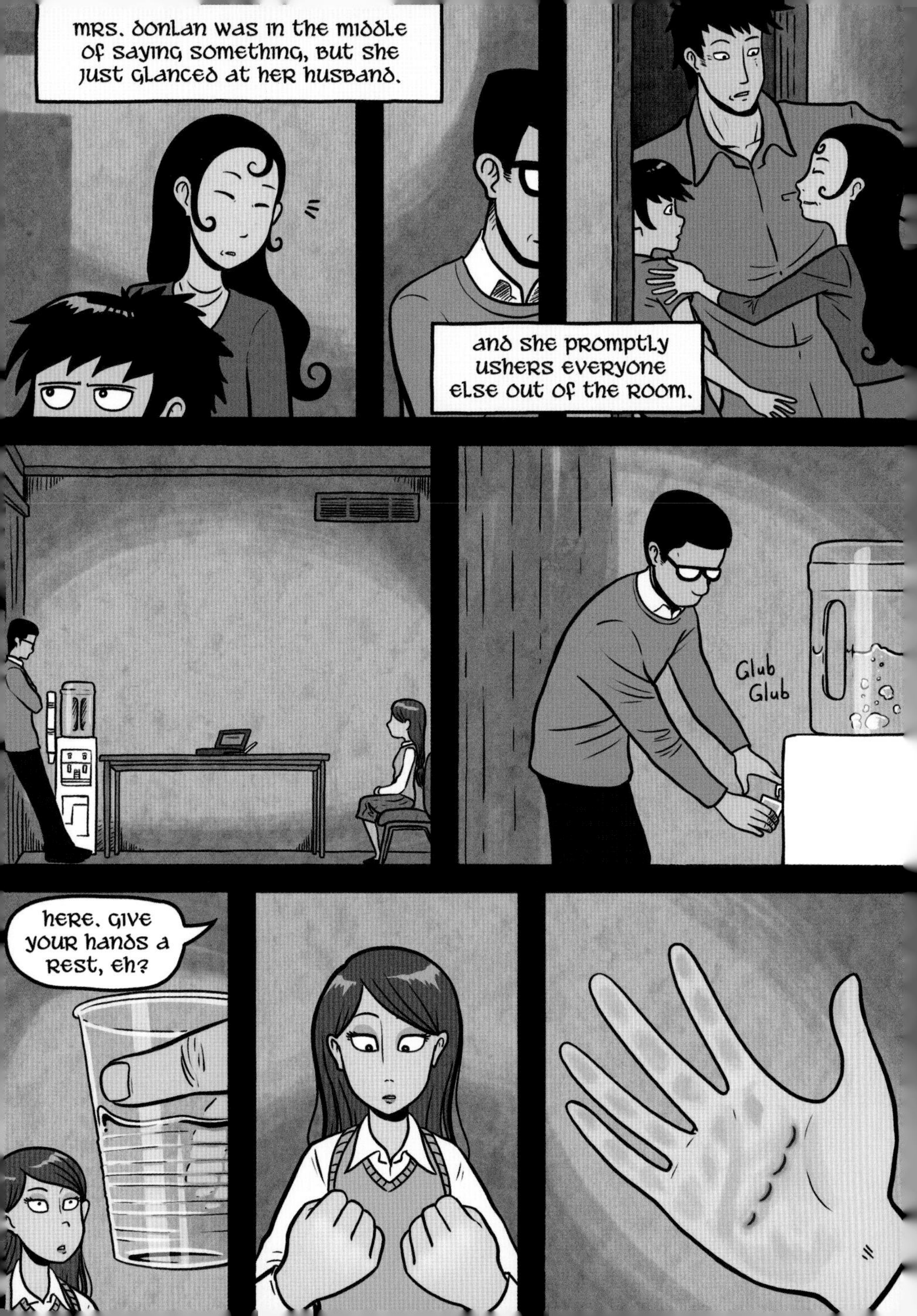
mrs. donlan was in the middle of saying something, but she just glanced at her husband.
and she promptly ushers everyone else out of the room.
Glub Glub
here. give your hands a rest, eh?

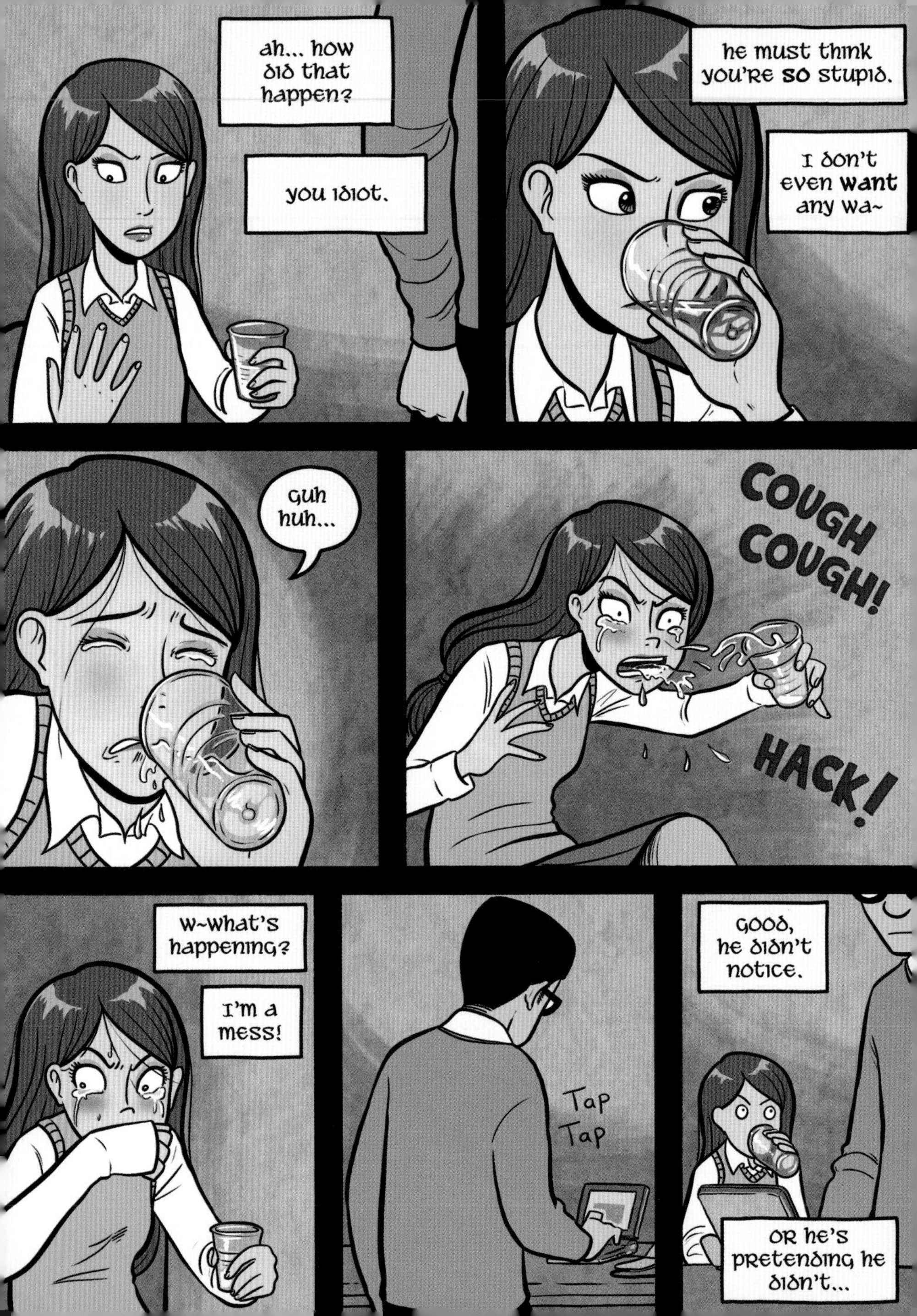

ah... how did that happen?
you idiot.
he must think you're **so** stupid.
I don't even **want** any wa~
guh huh...
COUGH COUGH!
HACK!
w~what's happening?
I'm a mess!
Tap Tap
good, he didn't notice.
or he's pretending he didn't...

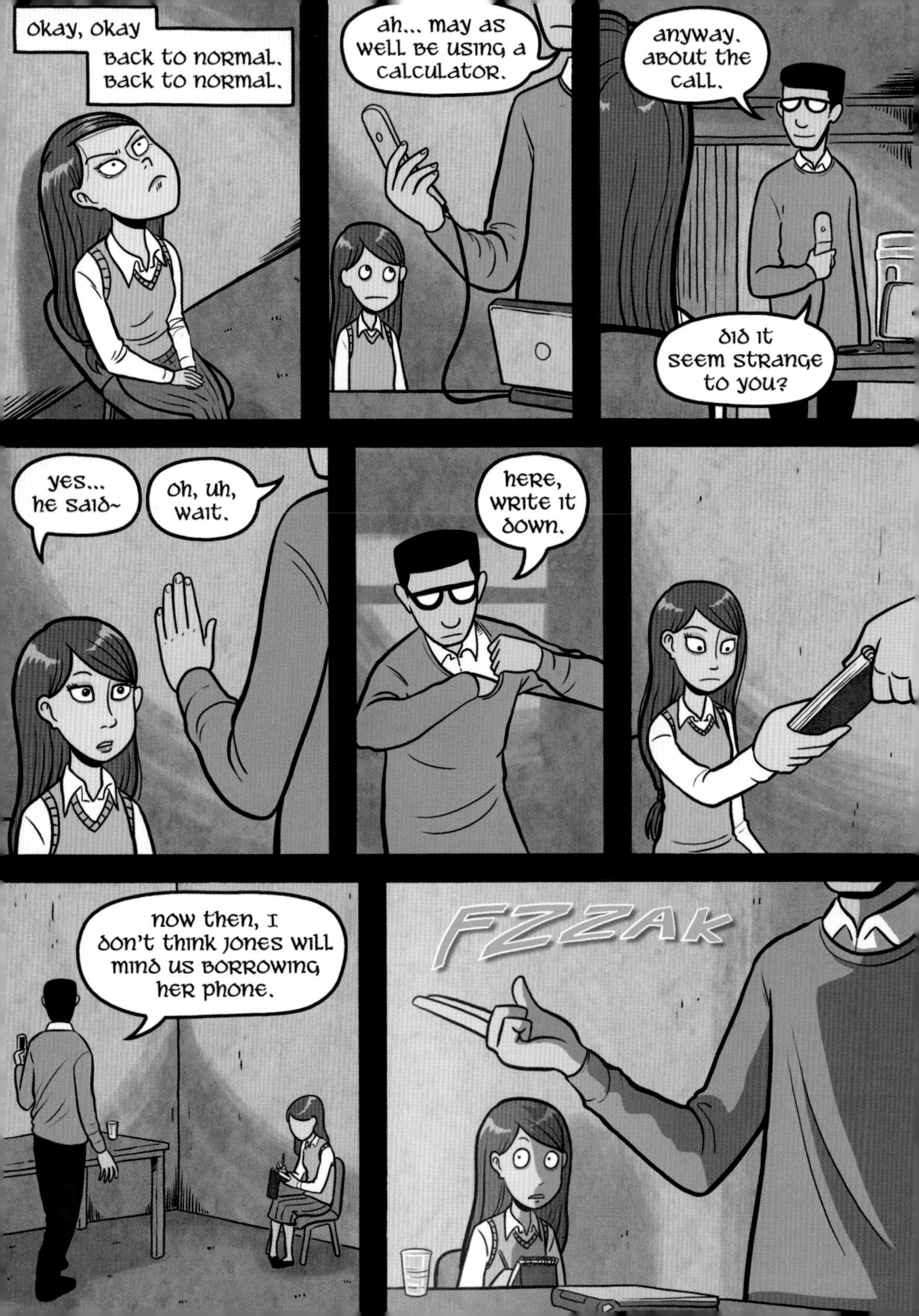
Okay, okay
Back to normal. Back to normal.
ah... may as well be using a calculator.
anyway. about the call.
did it seem strange to you?
yes... he said~
Oh, uh, wait.
here, write it down.
now then, I don't think Jones will mind us borrowing her phone.
FZZAK

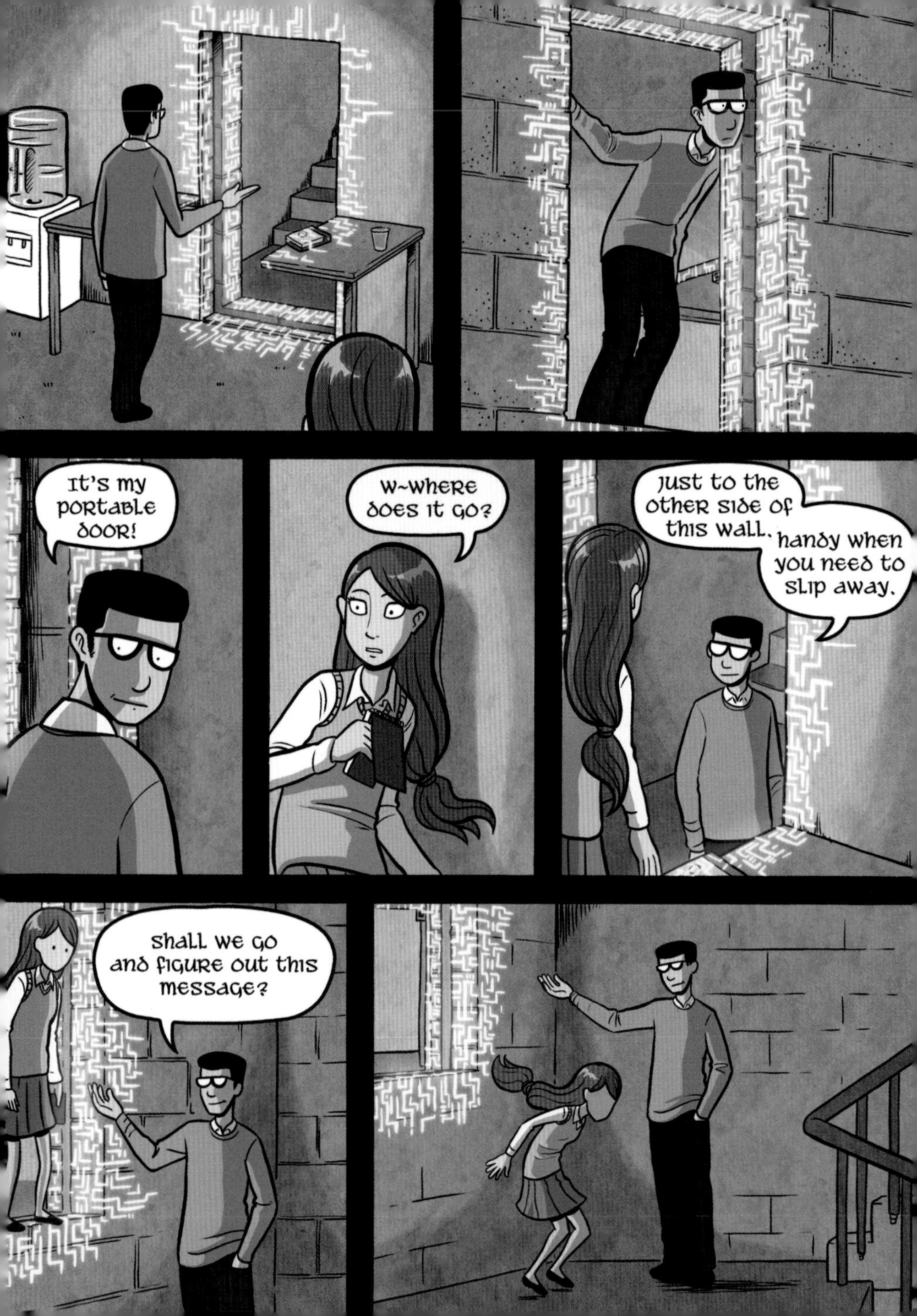
It's my portable door!
W-where does it go?
Just to the other side of this wall.
handy when you need to slip away.
shall we go and figure out this message?

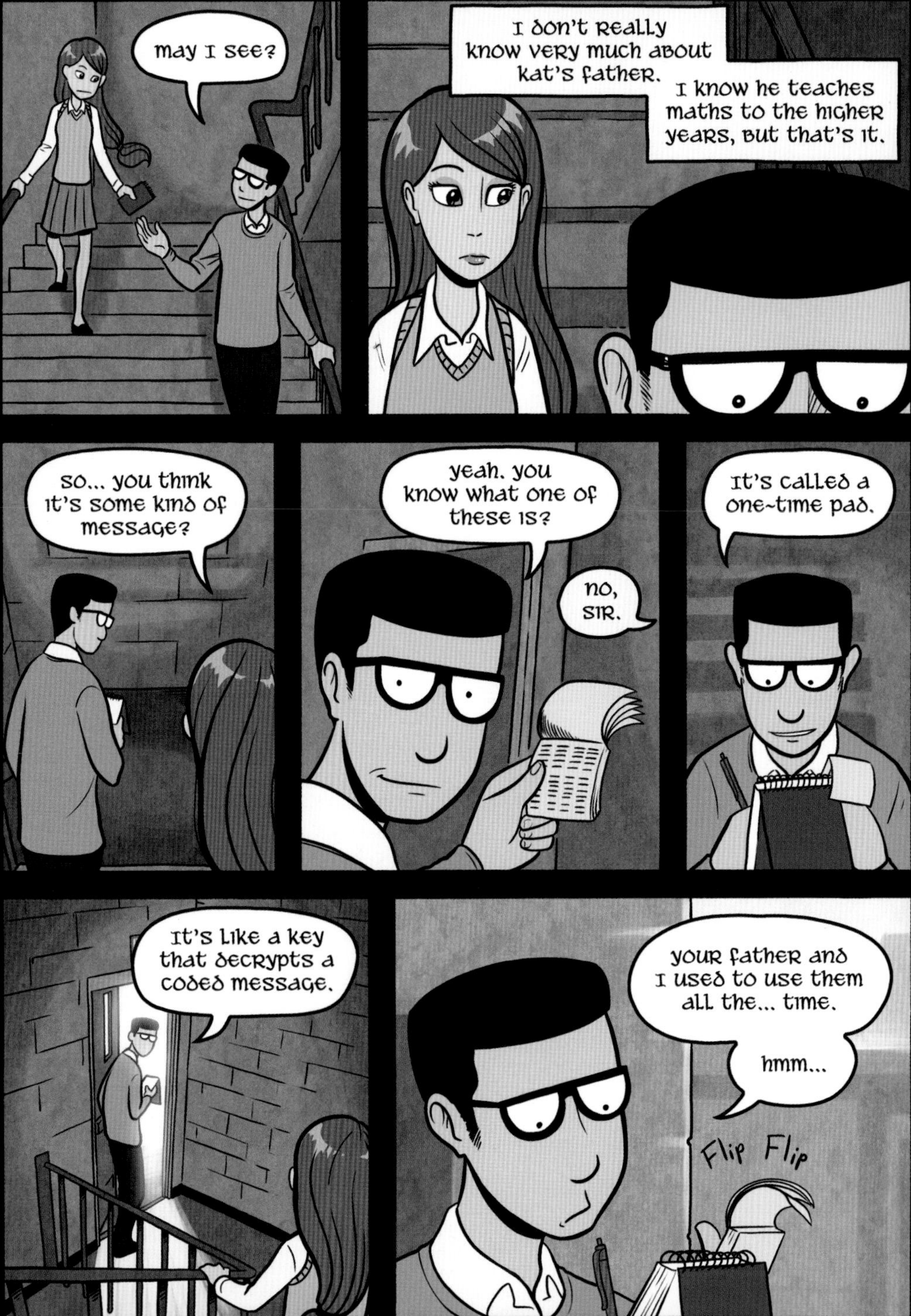
may I see?
I don't really know very much about kat's father.
I know he teaches maths to the higher years, but that's it.
so... you think it's some kind of message?
yeah. you know what one of these is?
no, sir.
It's called a one-time pad.
It's like a key that decrypts a coded message.
your father and I used to use them all the... time.
hmm...
Flip Flip

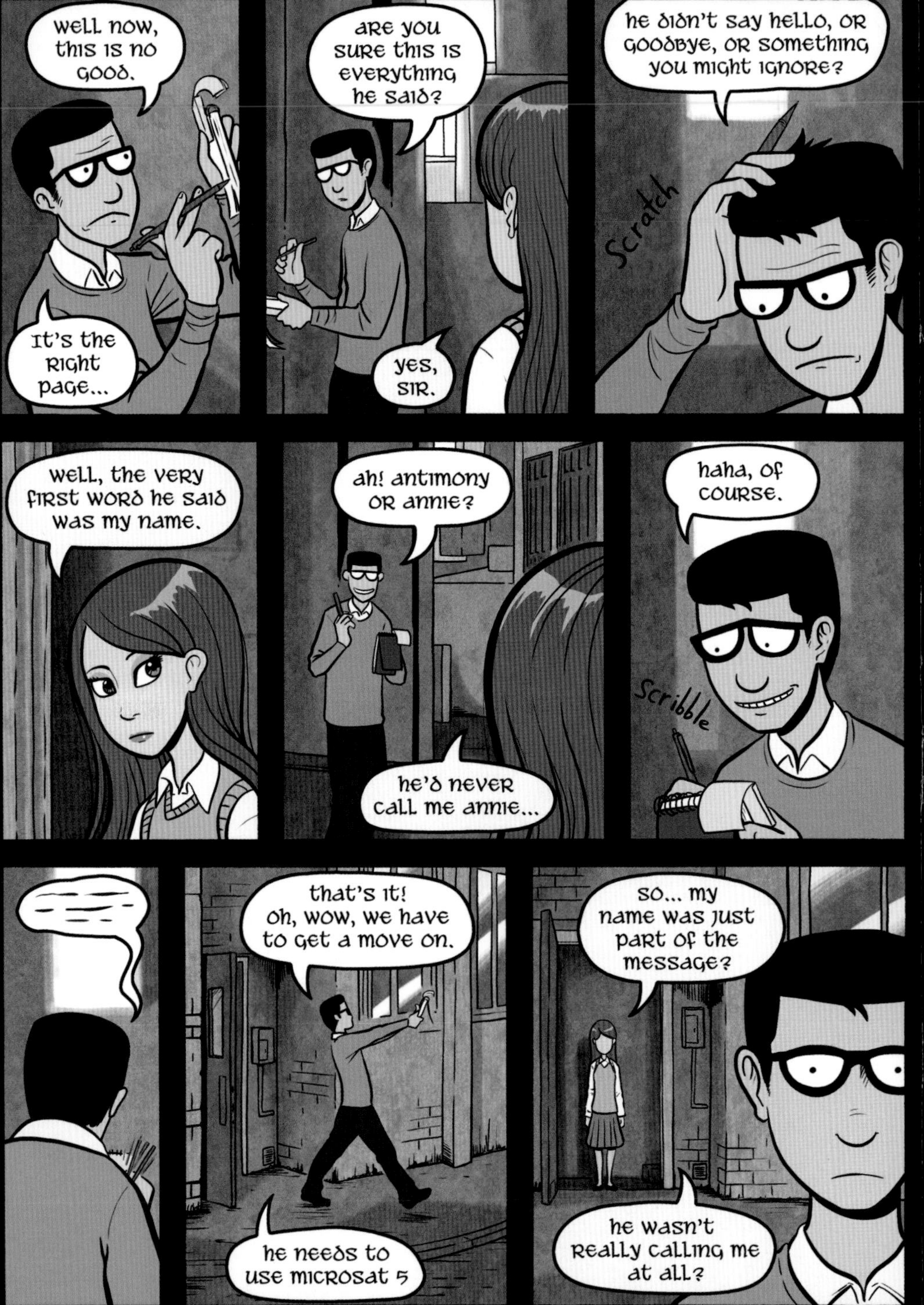
well now, this is no good.
it's the right page...
are you sure this is everything he said?
yes, sir.
he didn't say hello, or goodbye, or something you might ignore?
Scratch
well, the very first word he said was my name.
ah! antimony or annie?
he'd never call me annie...
haha, of course.
Scribble
that's it! oh, wow, we have to get a move on.
he needs to use microsat 5
so... my name was just part of the message?
he wasn't really calling me at all?

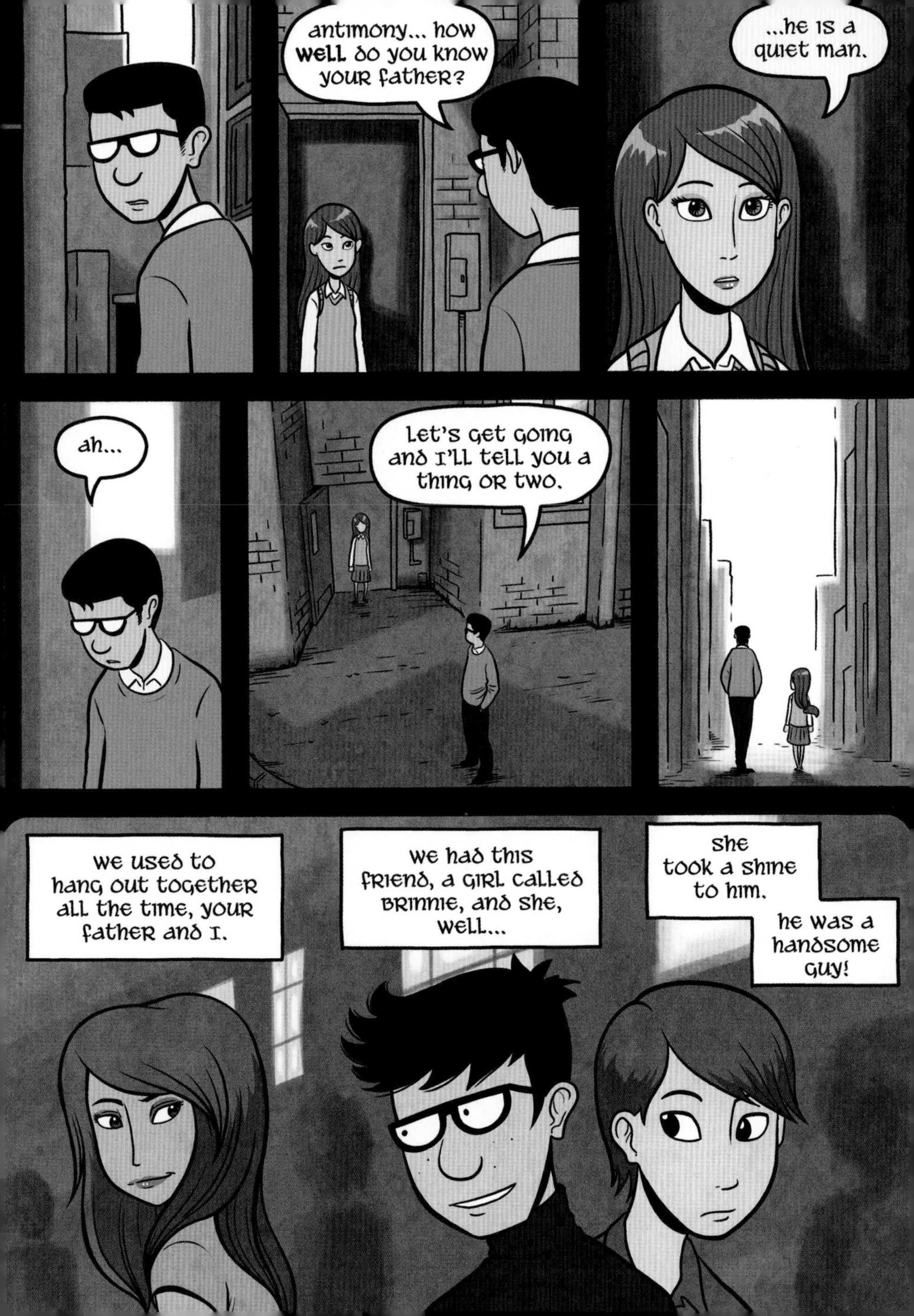
antimony... how WELL do you know your father?
...he is a quiet man.
ah...
Let's get going and I'll tell you a thing or two.
we used to hang out together all the time, your father and I.
we had this friend, a girl called Brinnie, and she, well...
she took a shine to him.
he was a handsome guy!

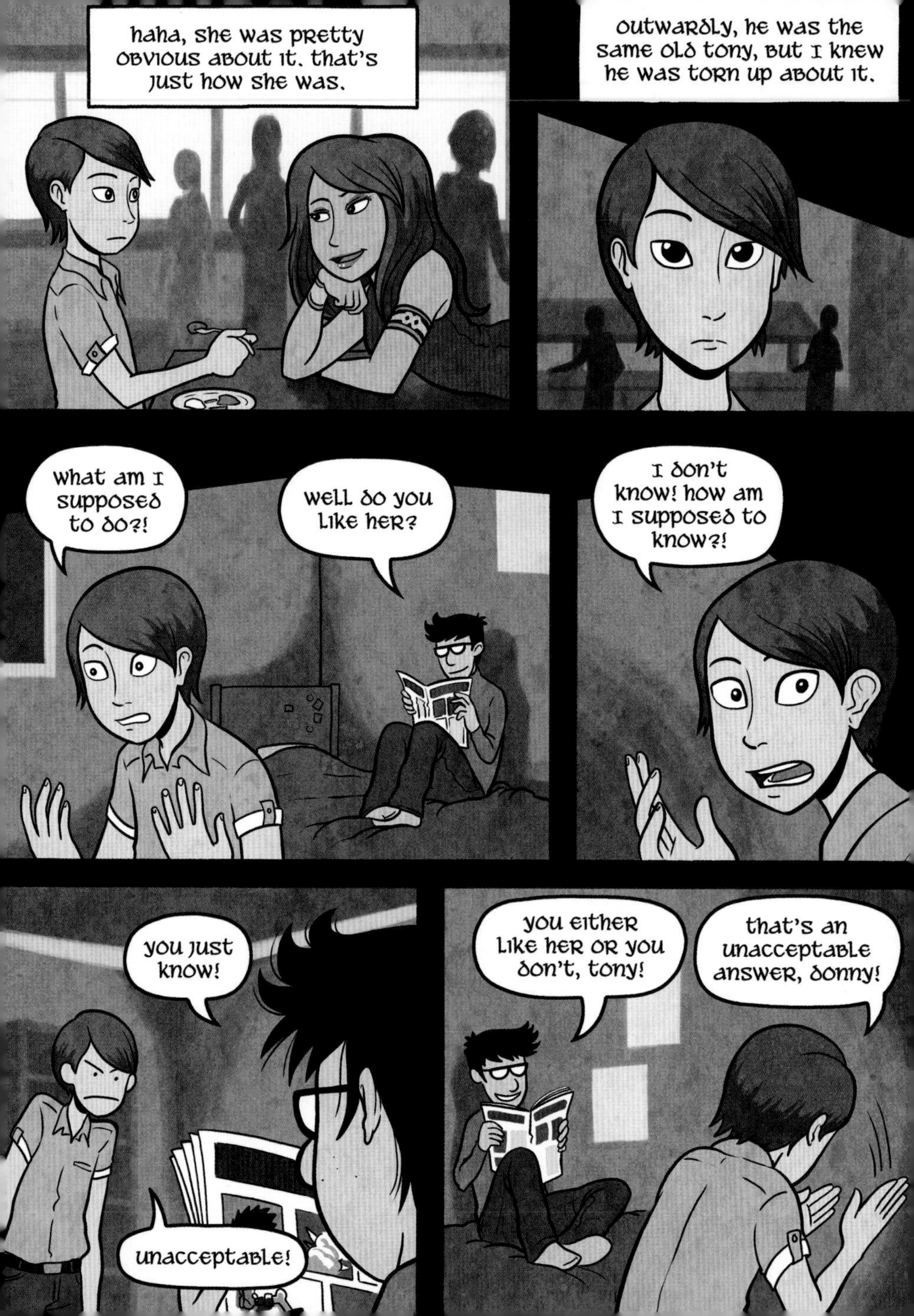
haha, she was pretty obvious about it. that's just how she was.
outwardly, he was the same old tony, but I knew he was torn up about it.
what am I supposed to do?!
well do you like her?
I don't know! how am I supposed to know?!
you just know!
unacceptable!
you either like her or you don't, tony!
that's an unacceptable answer, donny!

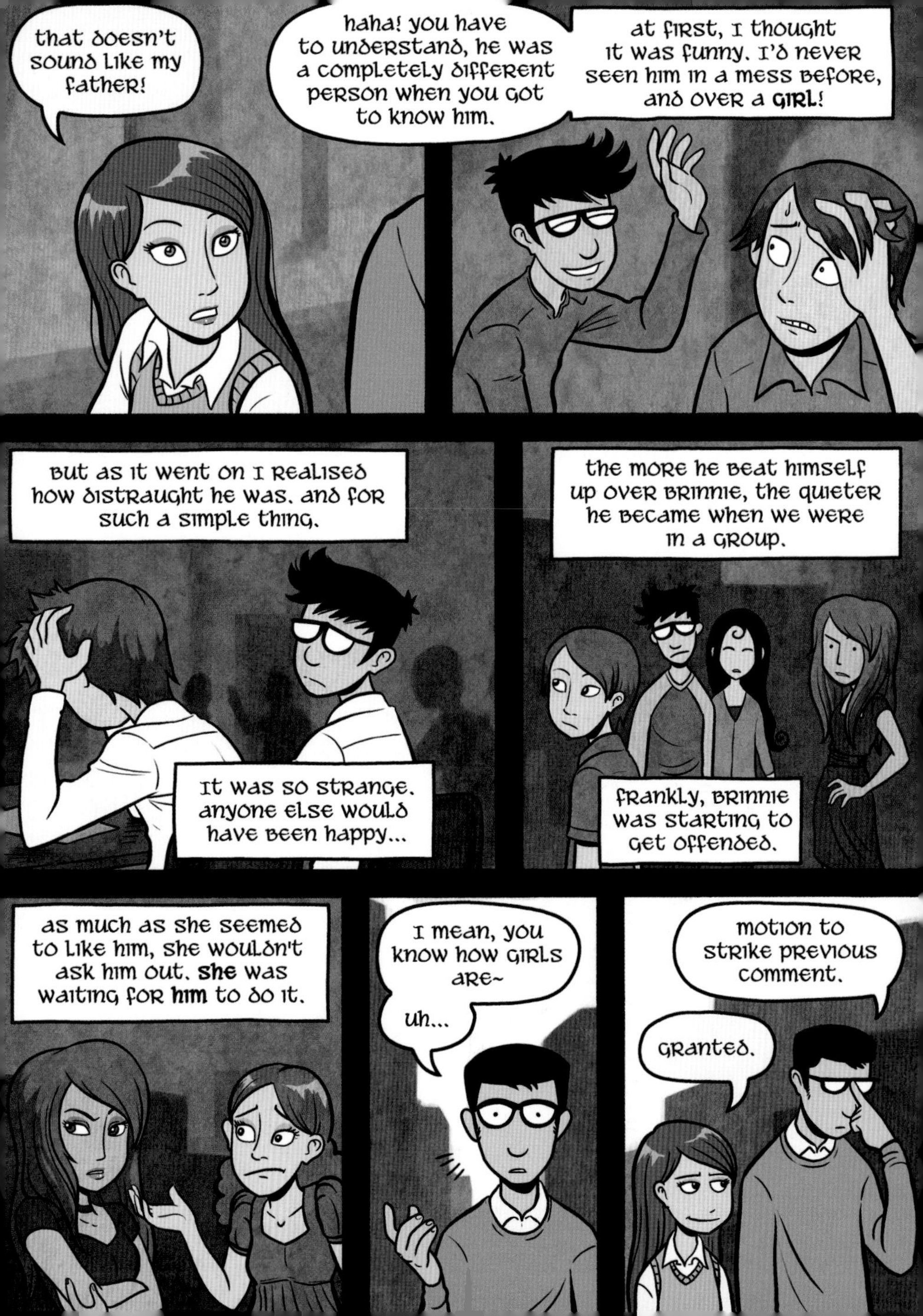
that doesn't sound like my father!
haha! you have to understand, he was a completely different person when you got to know him.
at first, I thought it was funny. I'd never seen him in a mess before, and over a **girl**!
but as it went on I realised how distraught he was. and for such a simple thing.
it was so strange. anyone else would have been happy...
the more he beat himself up over Brinnie, the quieter he became when we were in a group.
frankly, Brinnie was starting to get offended.
as much as she seemed to like him, she wouldn't ask him out. **she** was waiting for **him** to do it.
I mean, you know how girls are~
uh...
motion to strike previous comment.
granted.

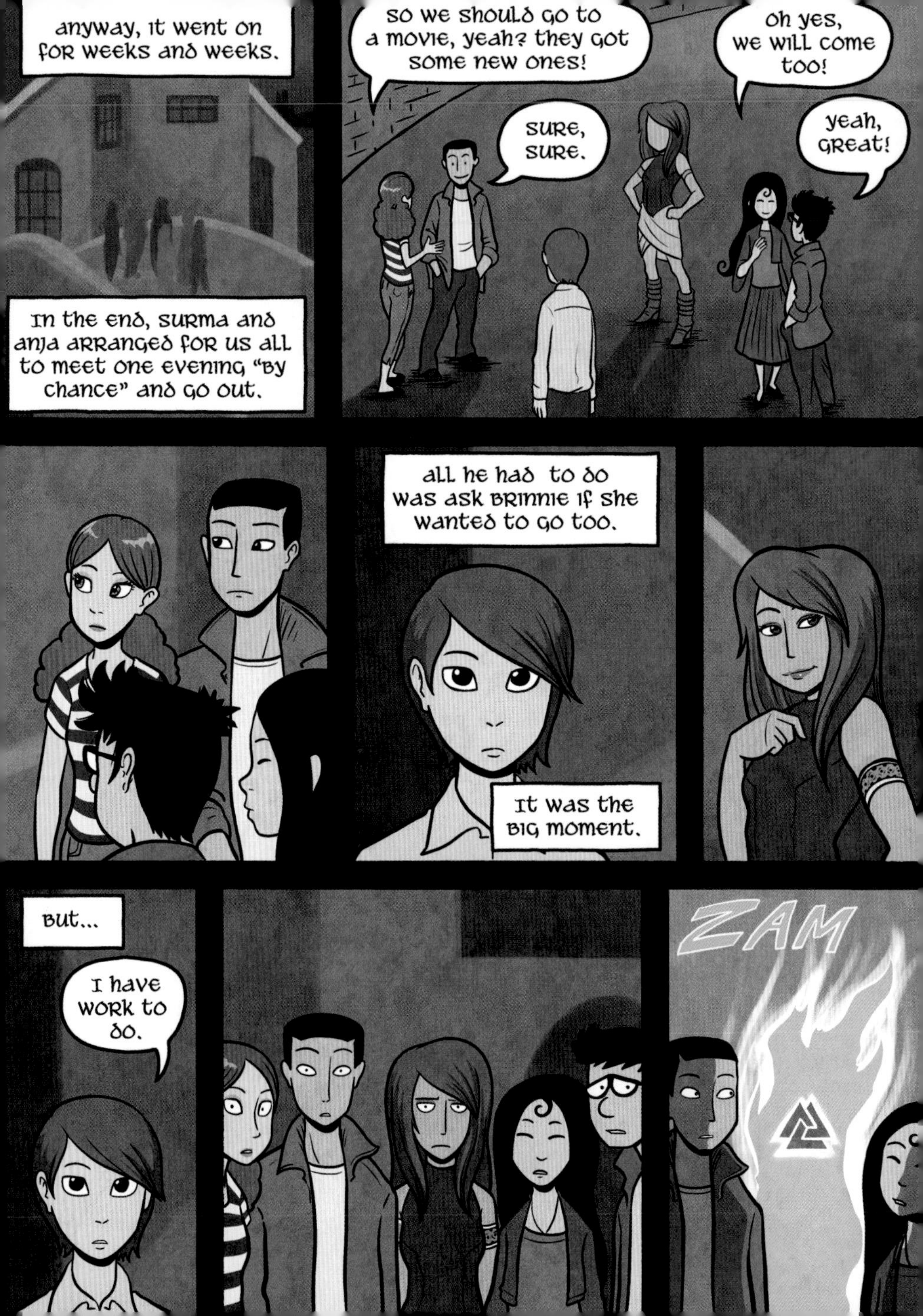
anyway, it went on for weeks and weeks.
In the end, surma and anja arranged for us all to meet one evening "by chance" and go out.
so we should go to a movie, yeah? they got some new ones!
sure, sure.
oh yes, we will come too!
yeah, great!
all he had to do was ask brinnie if she wanted to go too.
It was the big moment.
but...
I have work to do.
ZAM

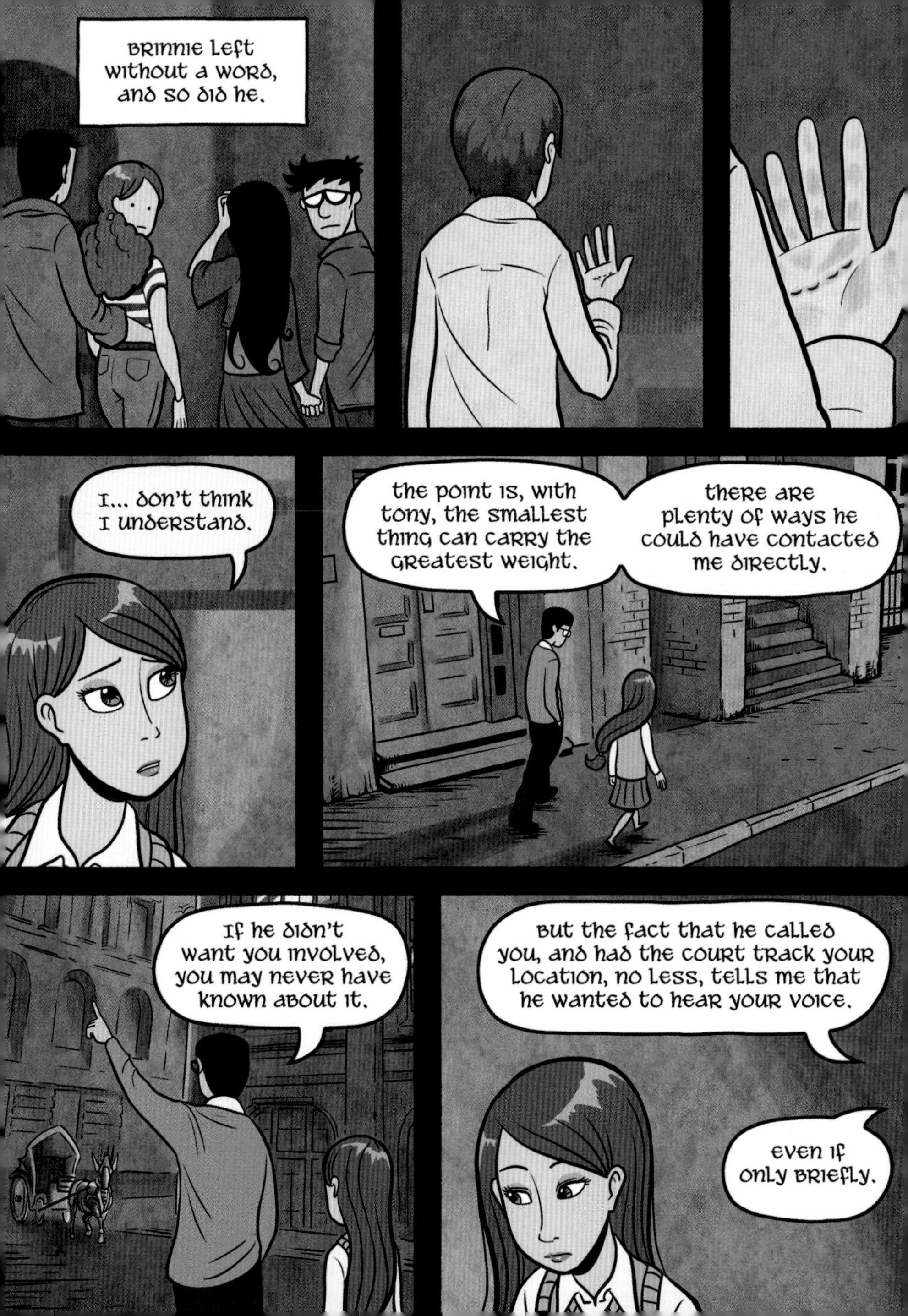
Brinnie left without a word, and so did he.
I... don't think I understand.
The point is, with Tony, the smallest thing can carry the greatest weight.
There are plenty of ways he could have contacted me directly.
If he didn't want you involved, you may never have known about it.
But the fact that he called you, and had the court track your location, no less, tells me that he wanted to hear your voice.
Even if only briefly.

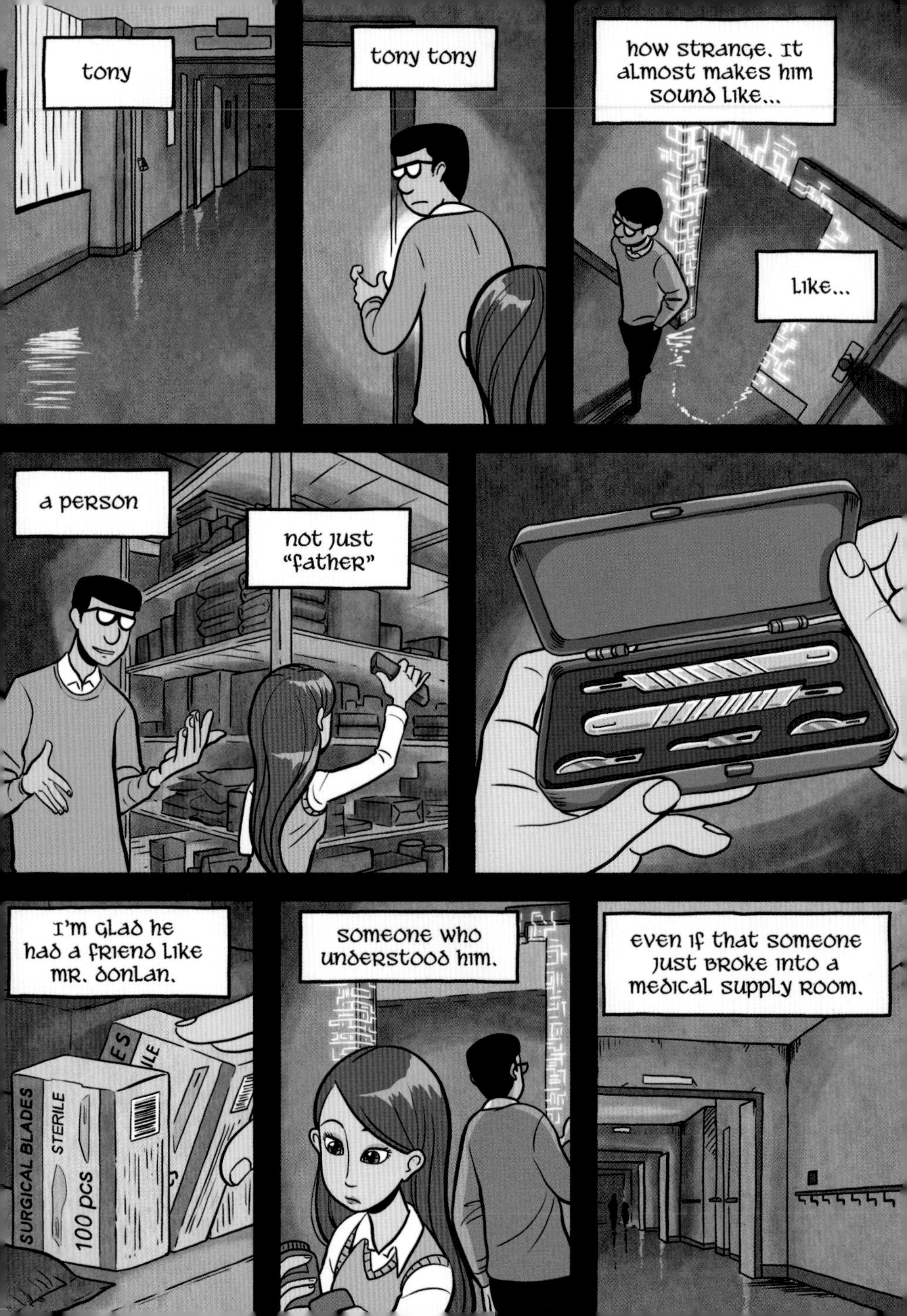
tony
tony tony
how strange. It almost makes him sound like...
like...
a person
not just "father"
I'm glad he had a friend like mr. donlan.
SURGICAL BLADES
STERILE
100 pcs
someone who understood him.
even if that someone just broke into a medical supply room.

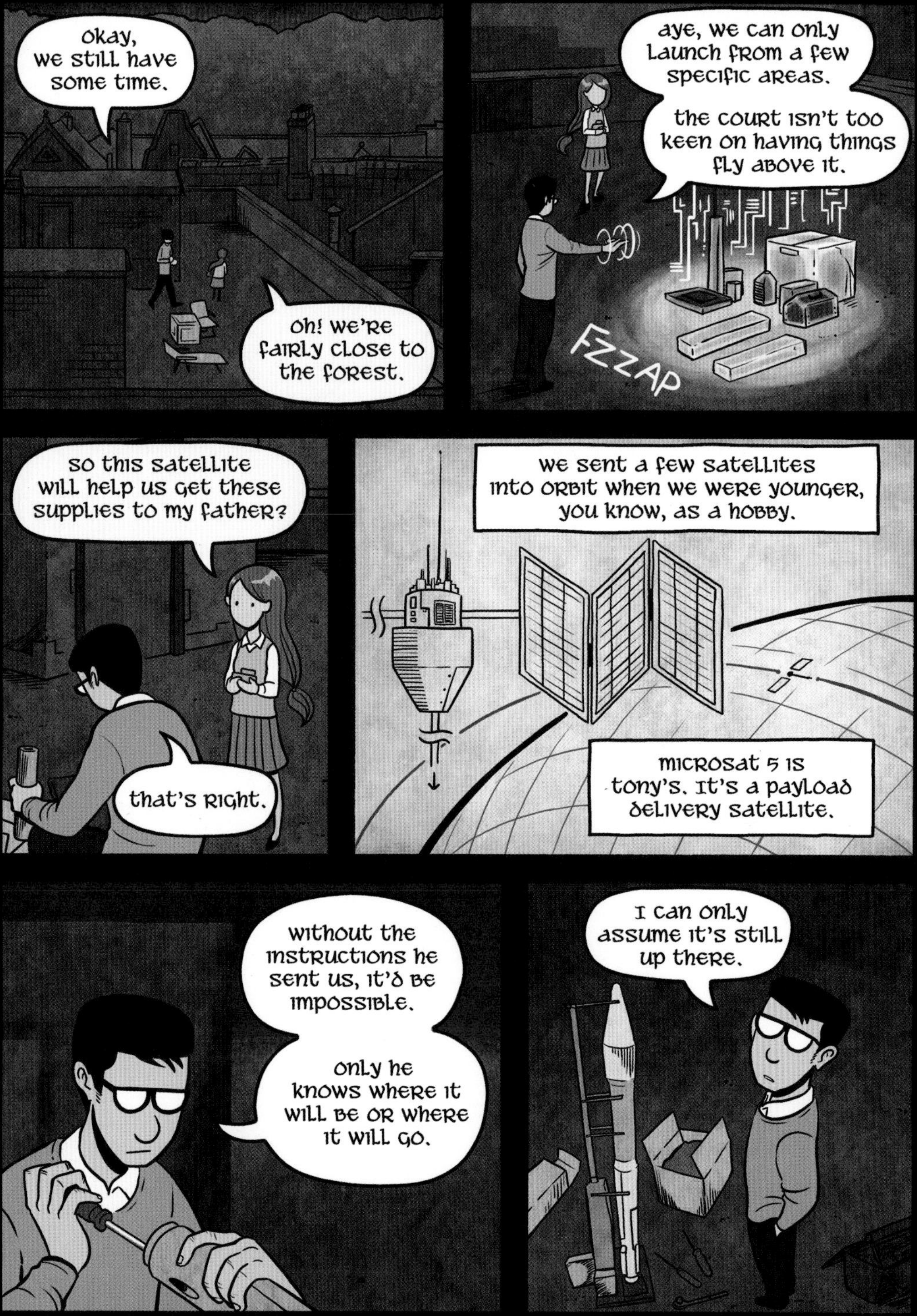
okay, we still have some time.
oh! we're fairly close to the forest.
aye, we can only launch from a few specific areas.
the court isn't too keen on having things fly above it.
FZZAP
so this satellite will help us get these supplies to my father?
that's right.
we sent a few satellites into orbit when we were younger, you know, as a hobby.
microsat 5 is tony's. it's a payload delivery satellite.
without the instructions he sent us, it'd be impossible.
only he knows where it will be or where it will go.
I can only assume it's still up there.

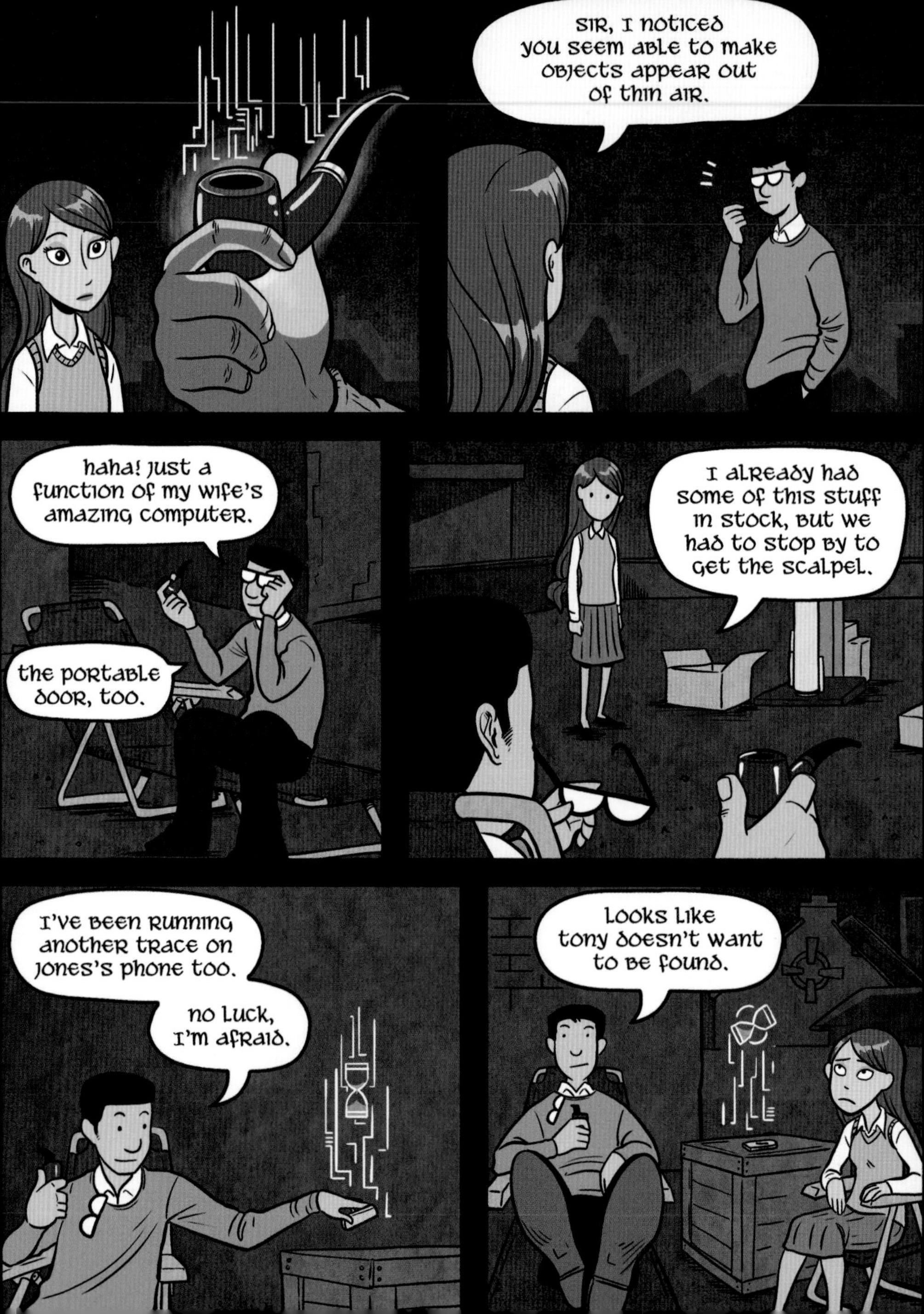
SIR, I NOTICED YOU SEEM ABLE TO MAKE OBJECTS APPEAR OUT OF THIN AIR.
HAHA! JUST A FUNCTION OF MY WIFE'S AMAZING COMPUTER.
THE PORTABLE DOOR, TOO.
I ALREADY HAD SOME OF THIS STUFF IN STOCK, BUT WE HAD TO STOP BY TO GET THE SCALPEL.
I'VE BEEN RUNNING ANOTHER TRACE ON JONES'S PHONE TOO.
NO LUCK, I'M AFRAID.
LOOKS LIKE TONY DOESN'T WANT TO BE FOUND.

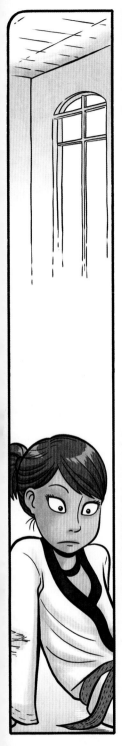

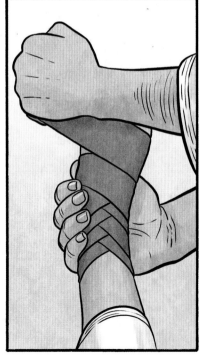

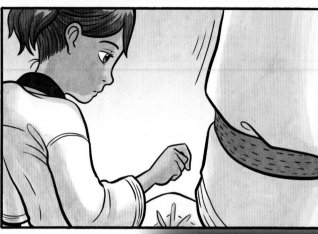
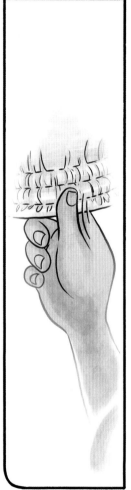

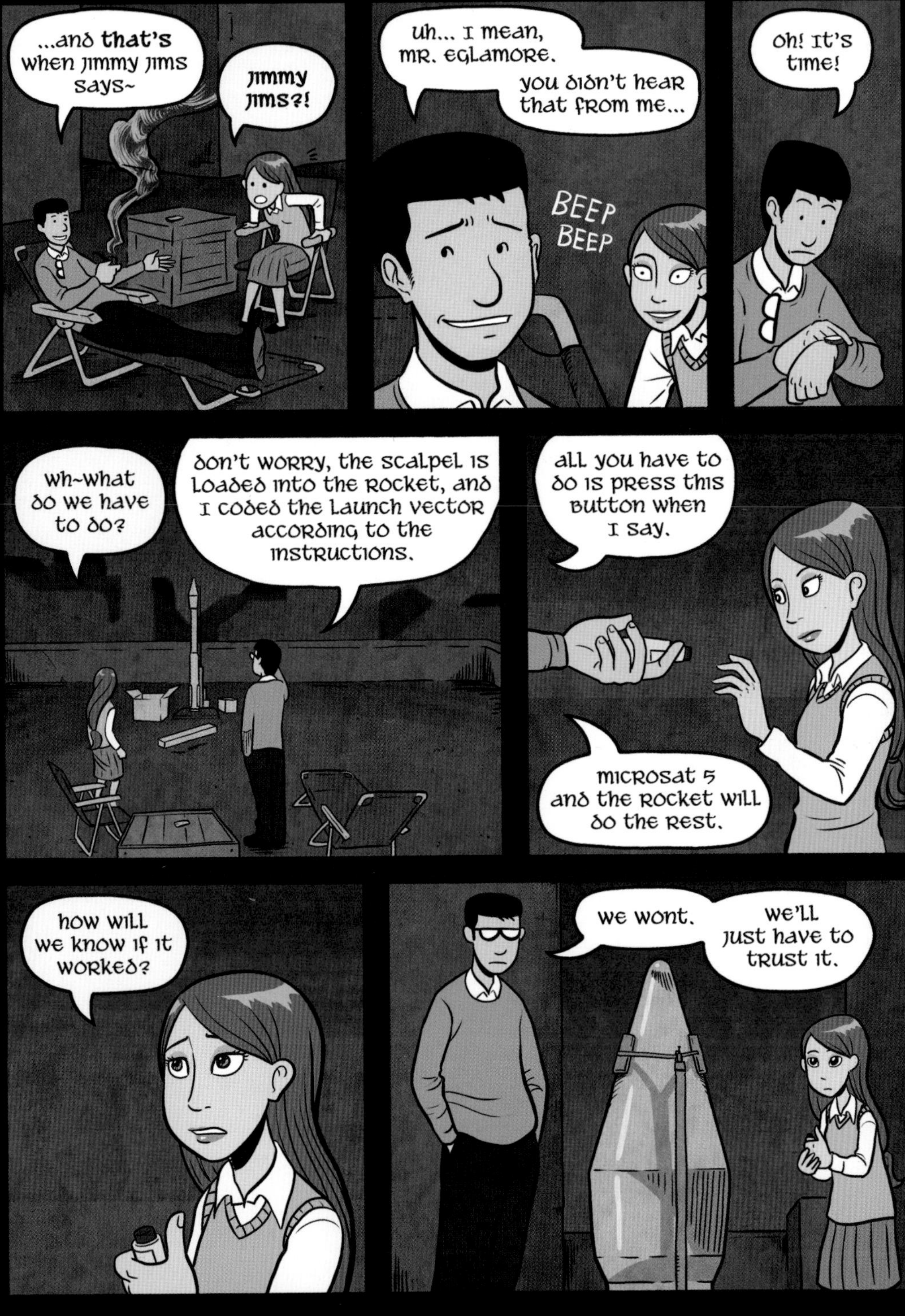
...and that's when Jimmy Jims says~
Jimmy Jims?!
uh... I mean, Mr. Eglamore.
you didn't hear that from me...
BEEP BEEP
Oh! It's time!
wh~what do we have to do?
don't worry, the scalpel is loaded into the rocket, and I coded the launch vector according to the instructions.
all you have to do is press this button when I say.
Microsat 5 and the rocket will do the rest.
how will we know if it worked?
we wont.
we'll just have to trust it.

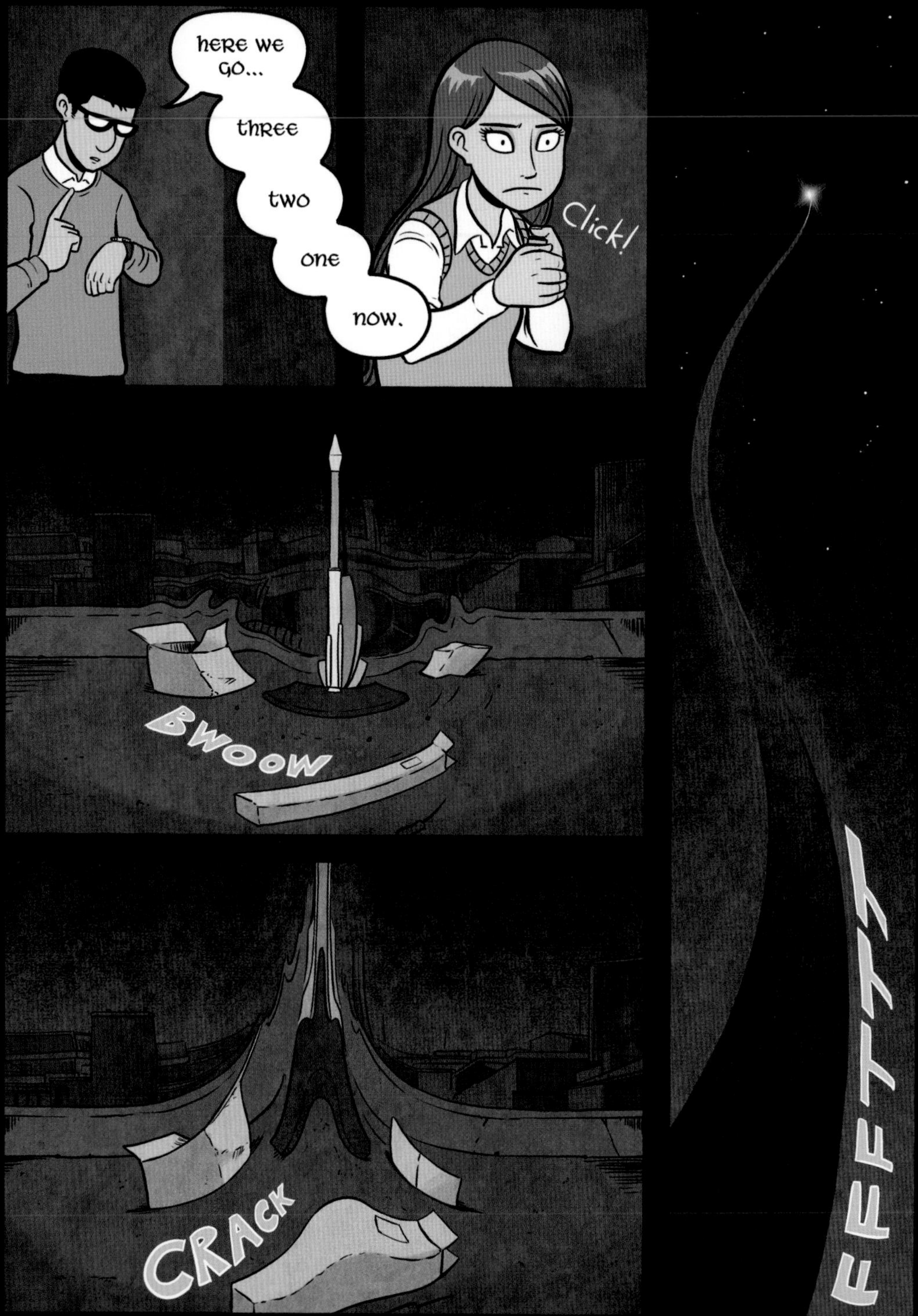
here we go...
three
two
one
now.
Click!
BWOOW
CRACK
FFFFTTTT

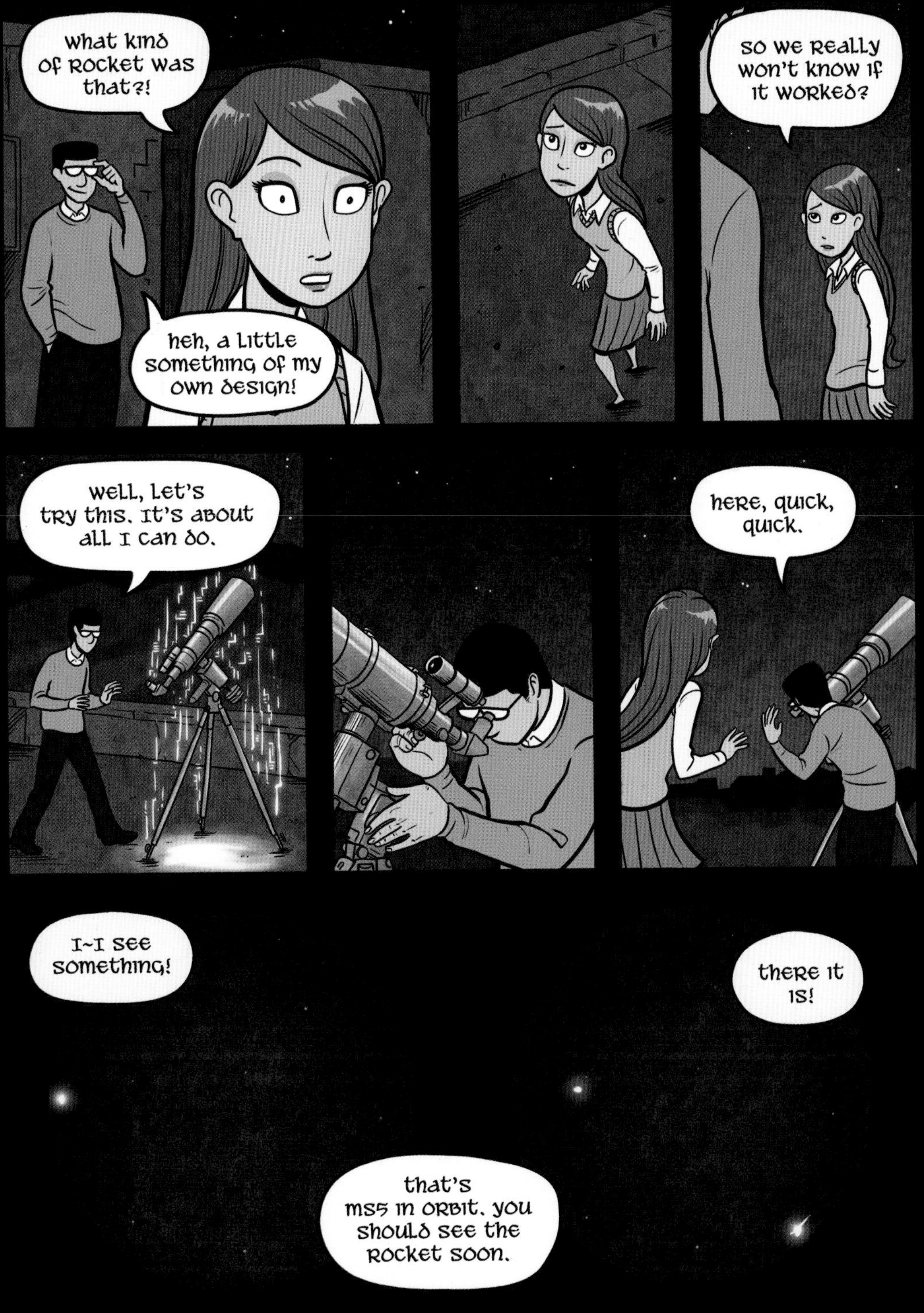
What kind of Rocket was that?!
heh, a little something of my own design!
so we really won't know if it worked?
well, let's try this. it's about all I can do.
here, quick, quick.
I-I see something!
there it is!
that's ms5 in orbit. you should see the Rocket soon.

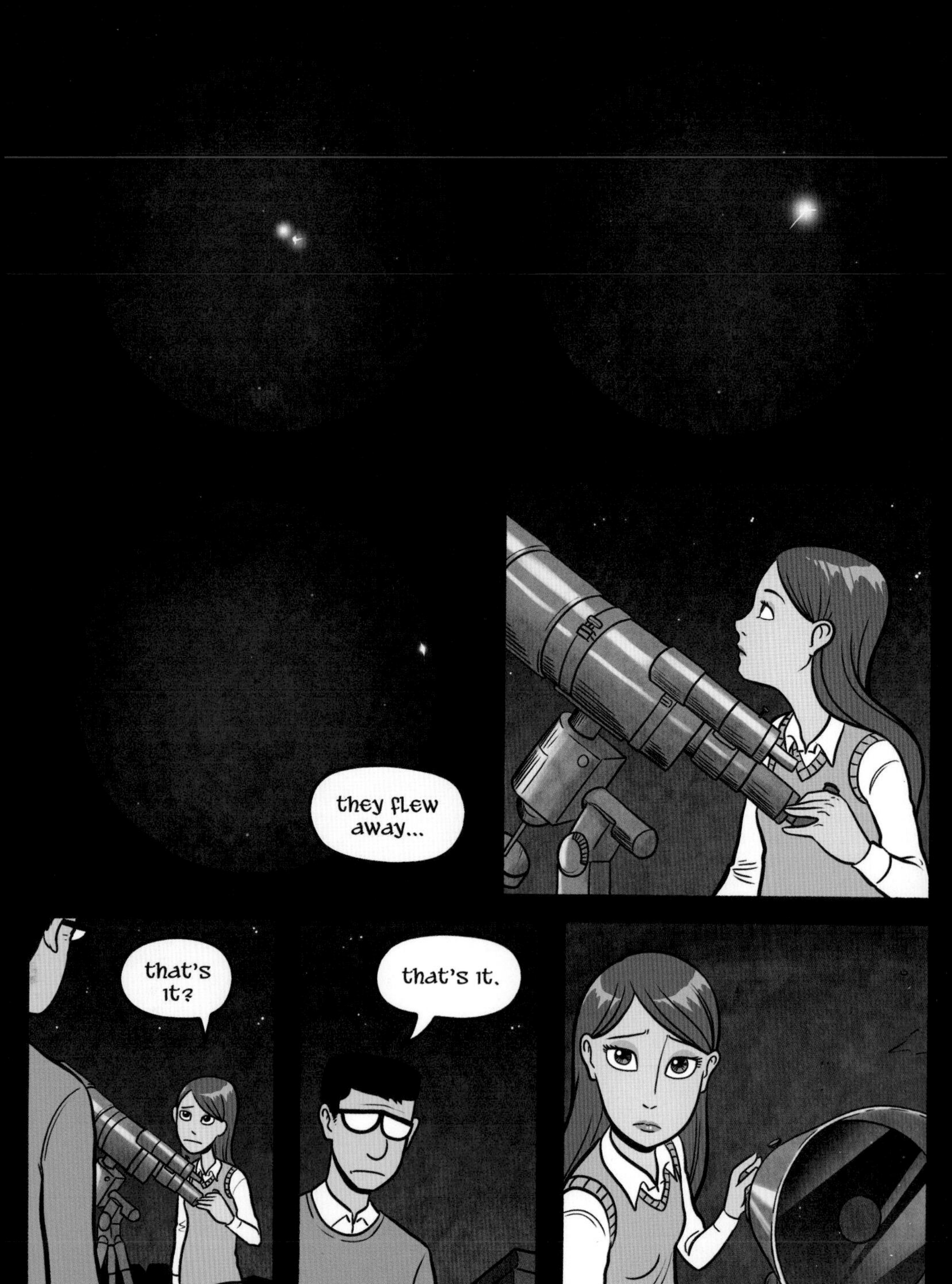
they flew away...
that's it?
that's it.

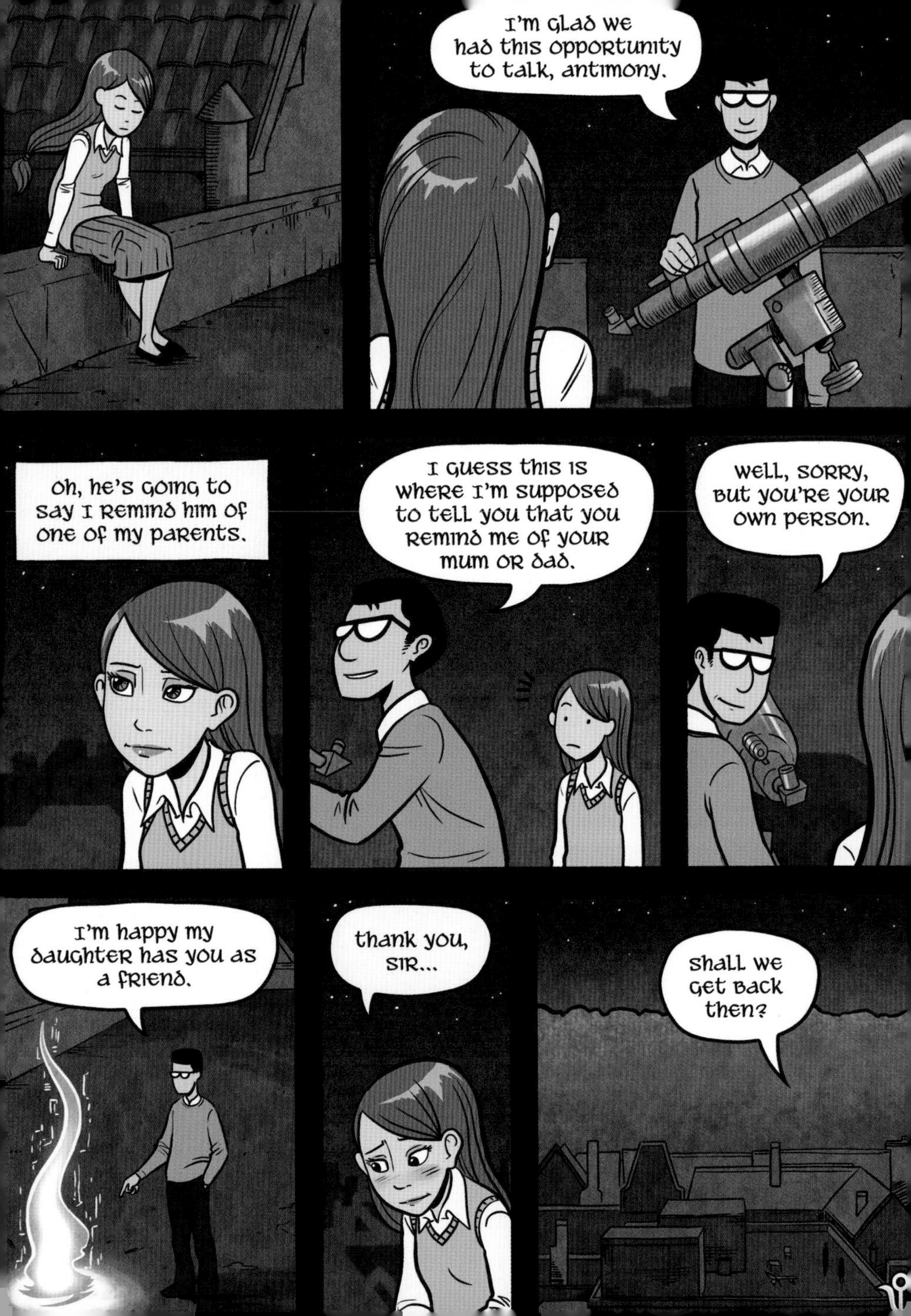
I'm glad we had this opportunity to talk, antimony.
Oh, he's going to say I remind him of one of my parents.
I guess this is where I'm supposed to tell you that you remind me of your mum or dad.
Well, sorry, but you're your own person.
I'm happy my daughter has you as a friend.
Thank you, sir...
Shall we get back then?

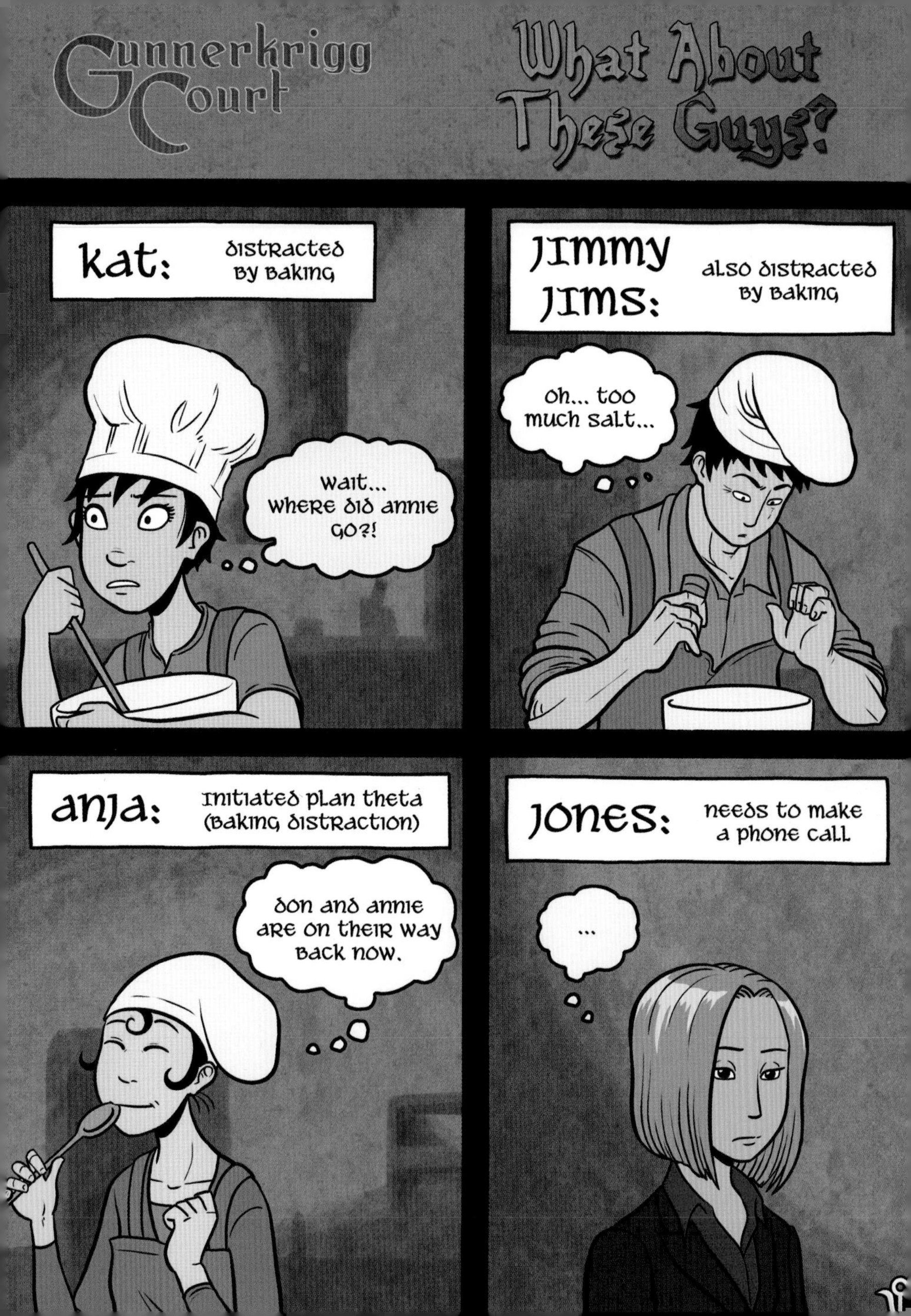

Gunnerkrigg Court
What About These Guys?
Kat: distracted by baking
Wait... where did Annie go?!
Jimmy Jims: also distracted by baking
Oh... too much salt...
Anja: initiated plan theta (baking distraction)
Don and Annie are on their way back now.
Jones: needs to make a phone call
...

Gunnerkrigg Court

Chapter 38:

Divine

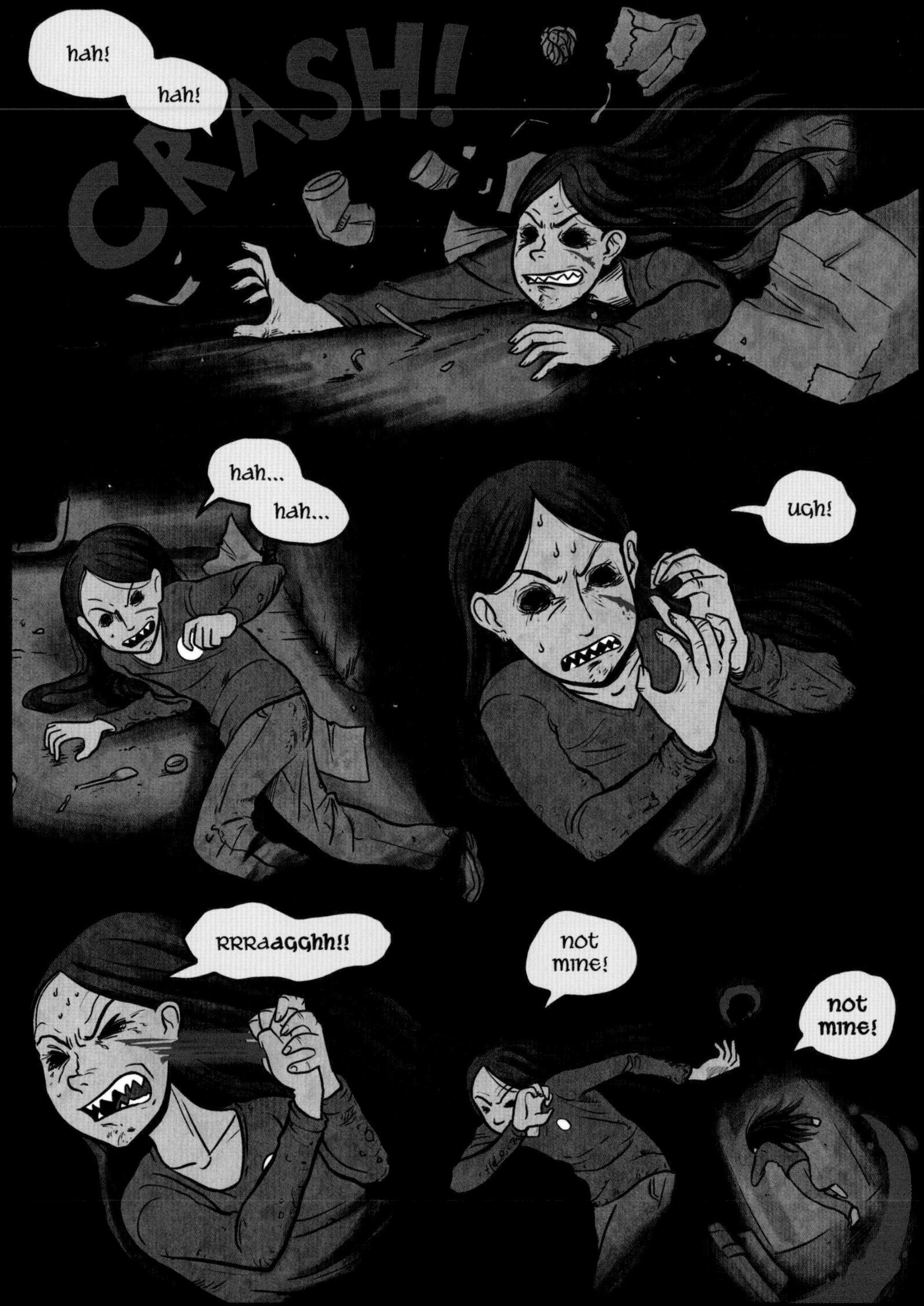
hah!
hah!
CRASH!
hah...
hah...
ugh!
RRRaaGGhh!!
not mine!
not mine!

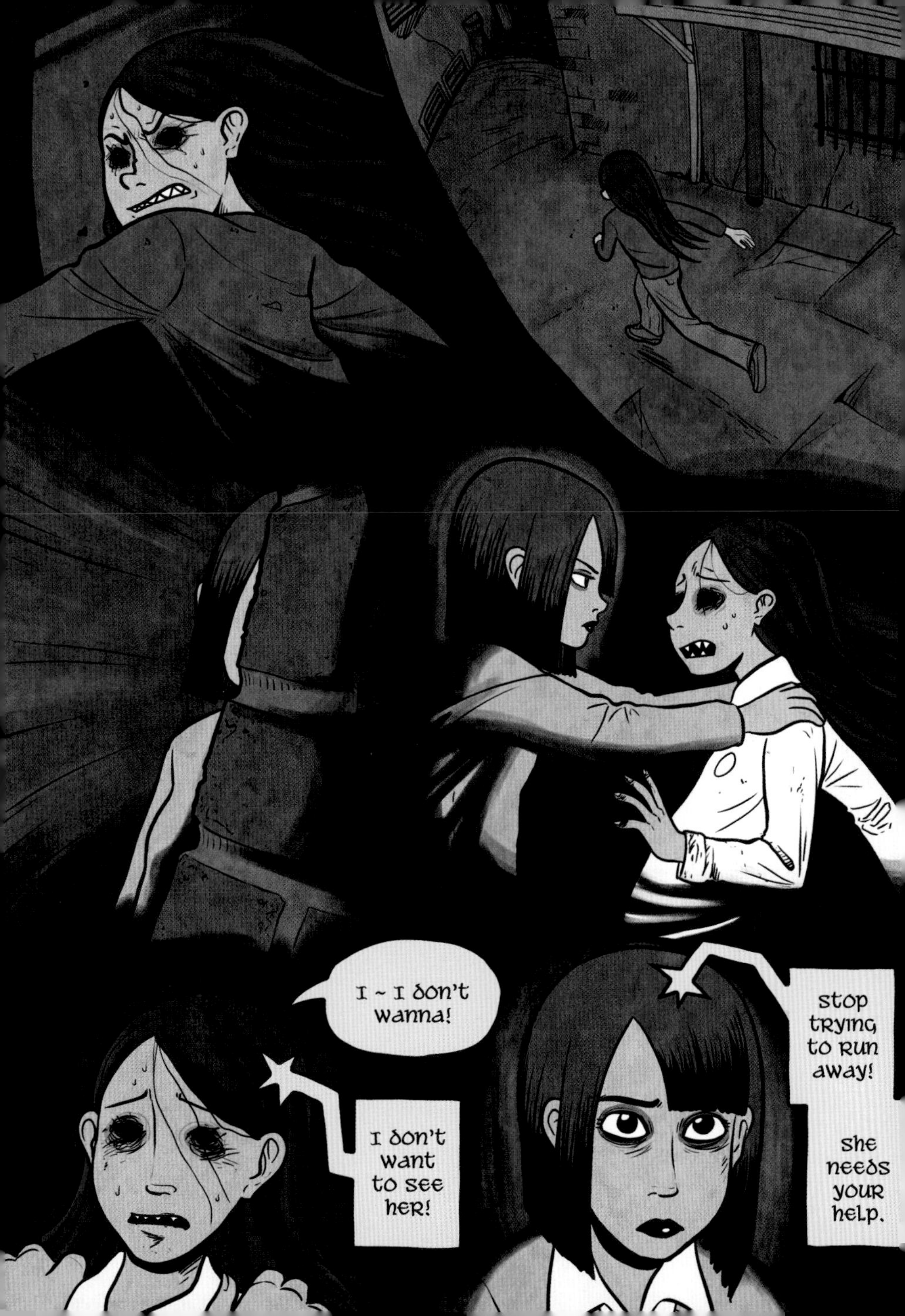

I ~ I don't wanna!
I don't want to see her!
Stop trying to run away!
She needs your help.

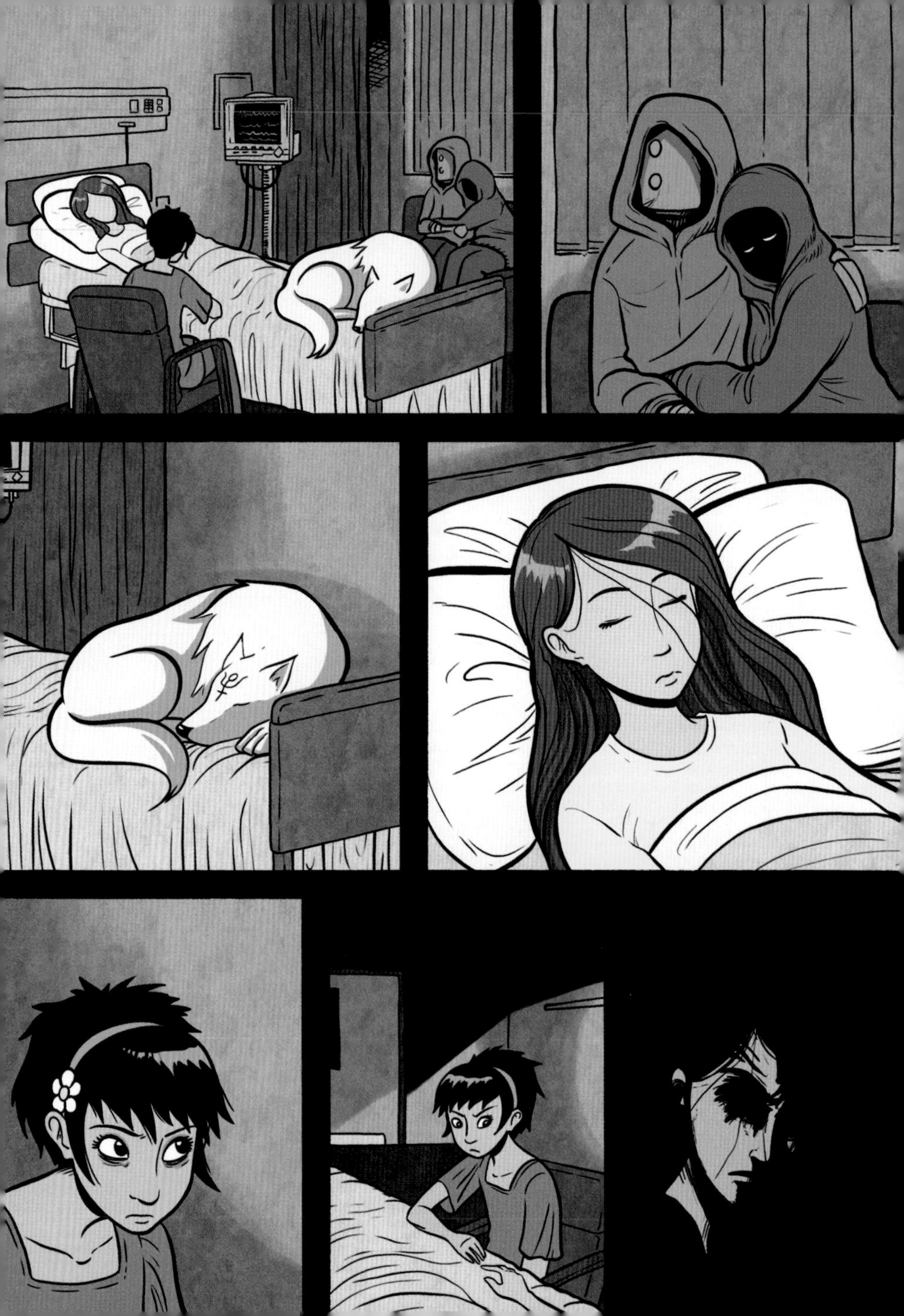

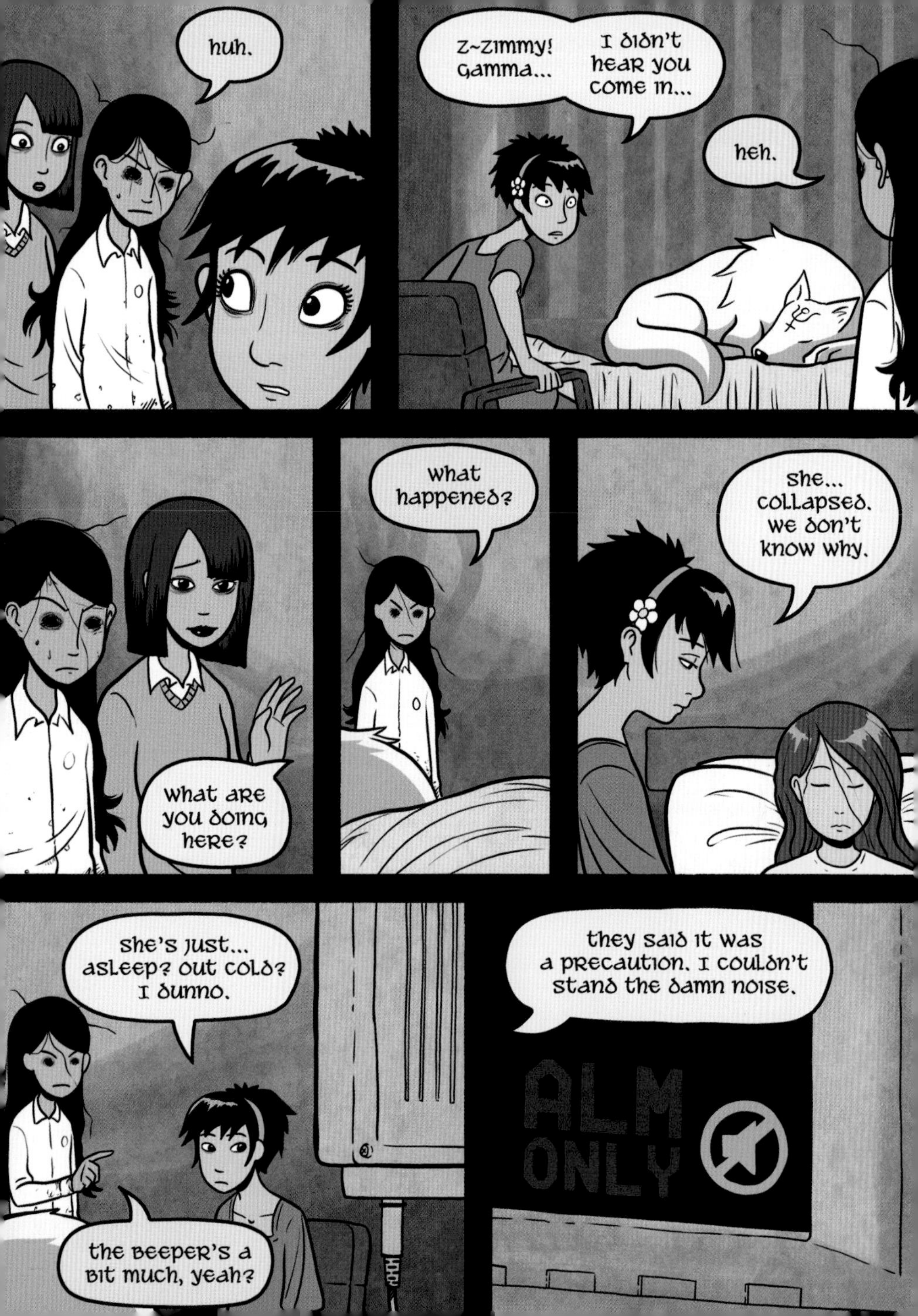
huh.
Z-Zimmy! Gamma...
I didn't hear you come in...
heh.
What happened?
What are you doing here?
She... collapsed. We don't know why.
She's just... asleep? Out cold? I dunno.
the beeper's a bit much, yeah?
they said it was a precaution. I couldn't stand the damn noise.
ALM ONLY

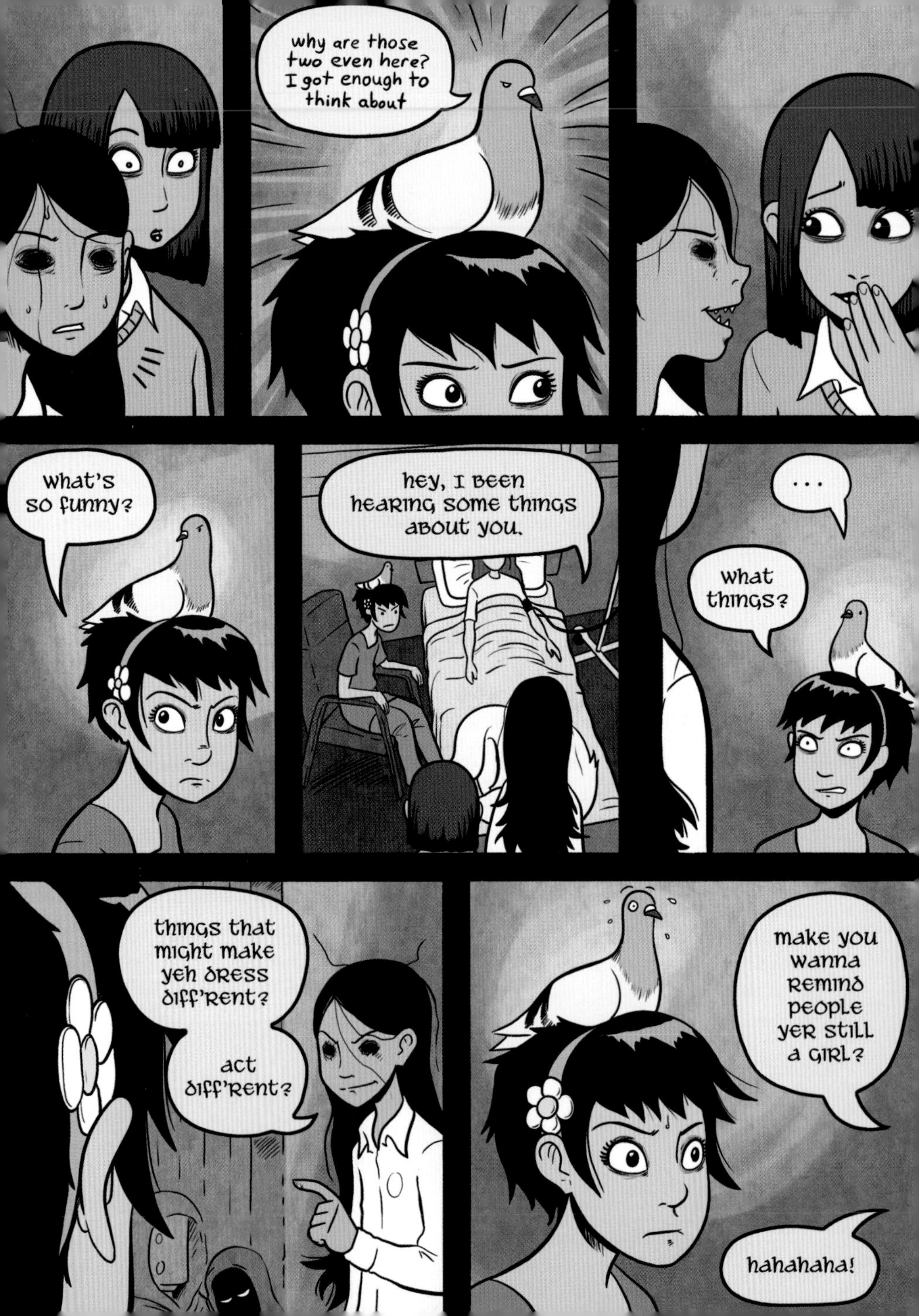
why are those two even here? I got enough to think about
What's so funny?
hey, I been hearing some things about you.
...
What things?
things that might make yeh dress diff'rent?
act diff'rent?
make you wanna remind people yer still a girl?
hahahaha!

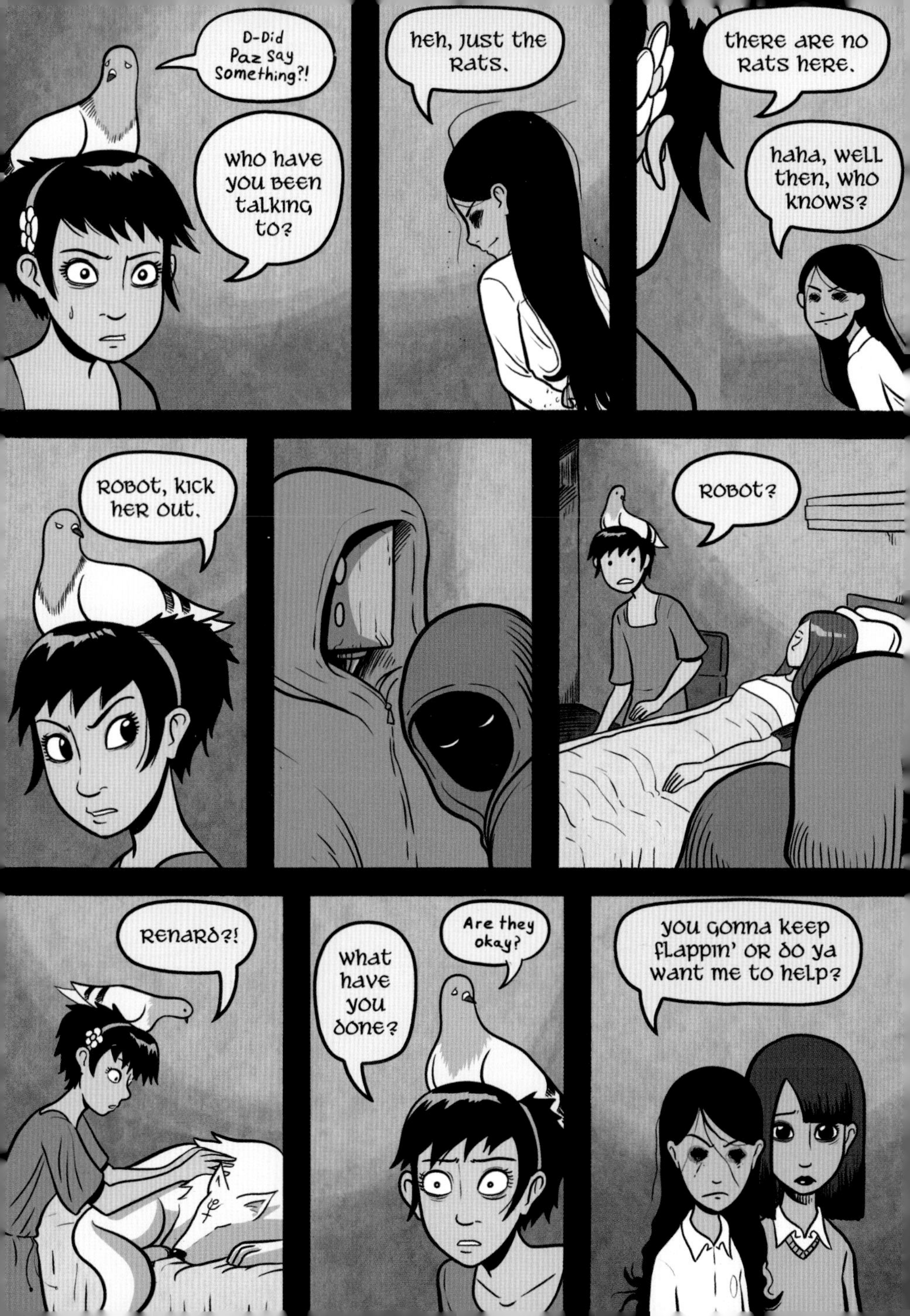
D-Did Paz Say Something?!
who have you Been talking to?
heh, just the Rats.
there are no Rats here.
haha, well then, who knows?
ROBOT, kick her out.
ROBOT?
RENARD?!
What have you done?
Are they okay?
you gonna keep flappin' or do ya want me to help?

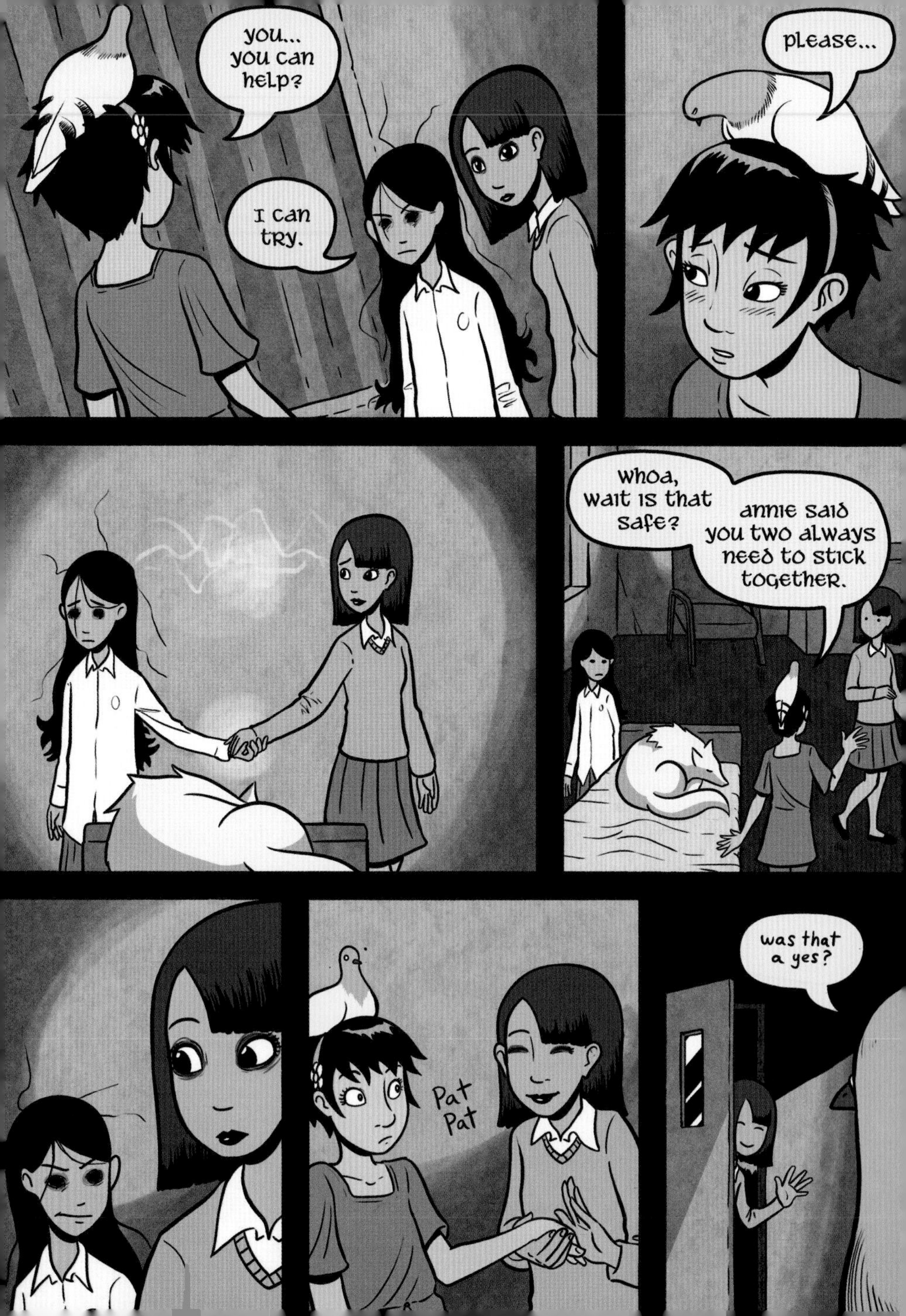
you... you can help?
I can try.
please...
whoa, wait is that safe?
annie said you two always need to stick together.
Pat Pat
was that a yes?

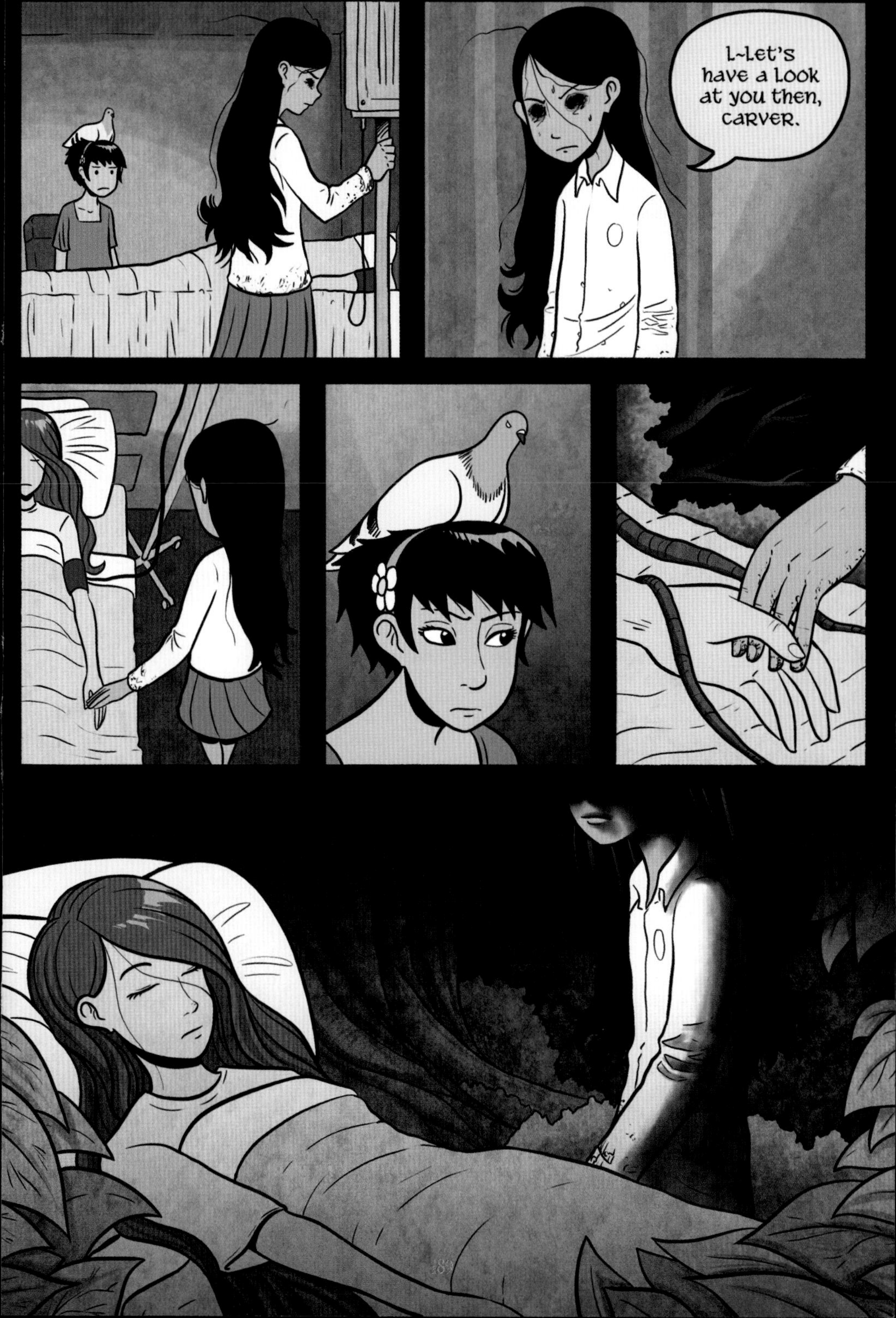
L-Let's have a look at you then, carver.

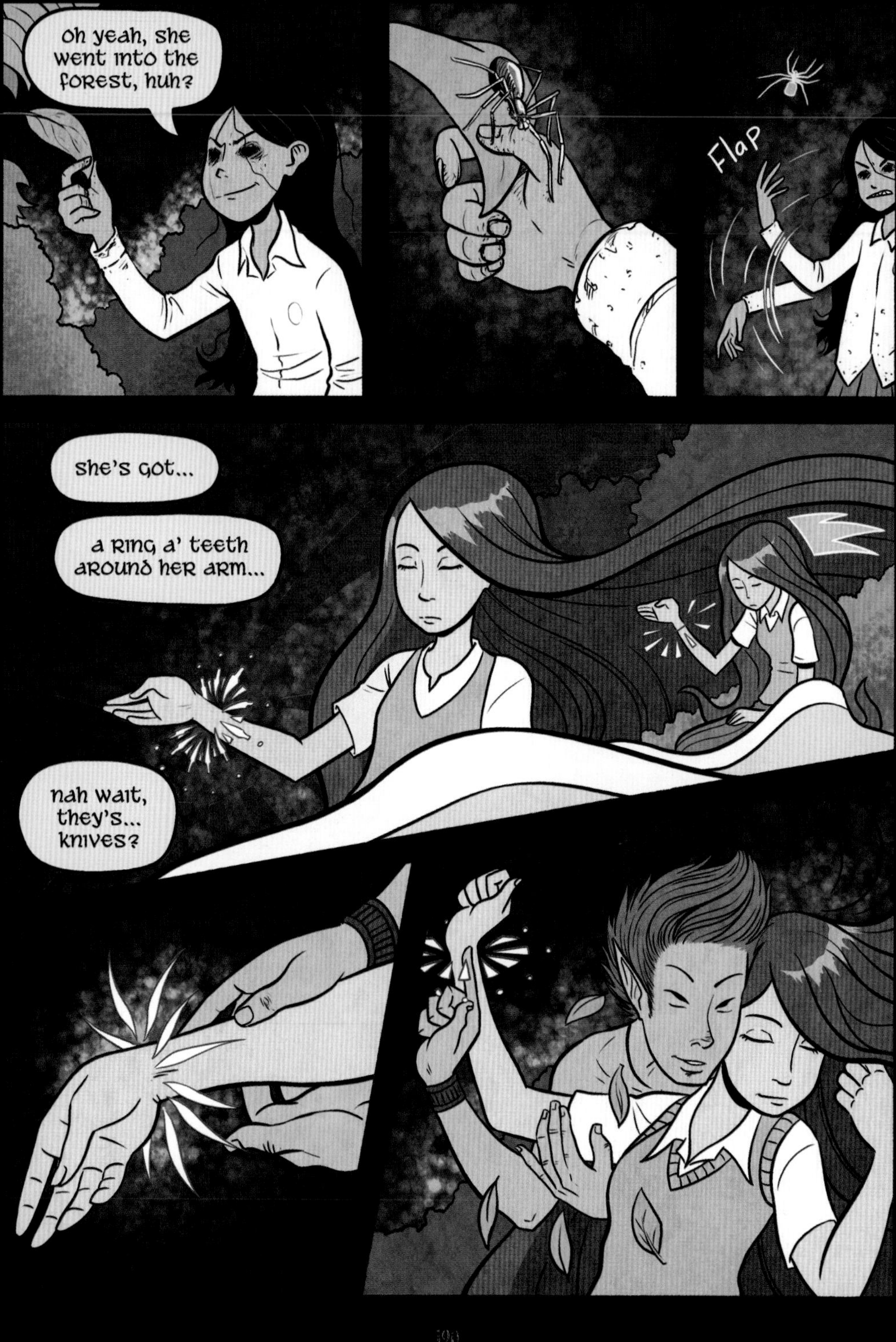

Oh yeah, she went into the forest, huh?
Flap
she's got...
a ring a' teeth around her arm...
nah wait, they's... knives?

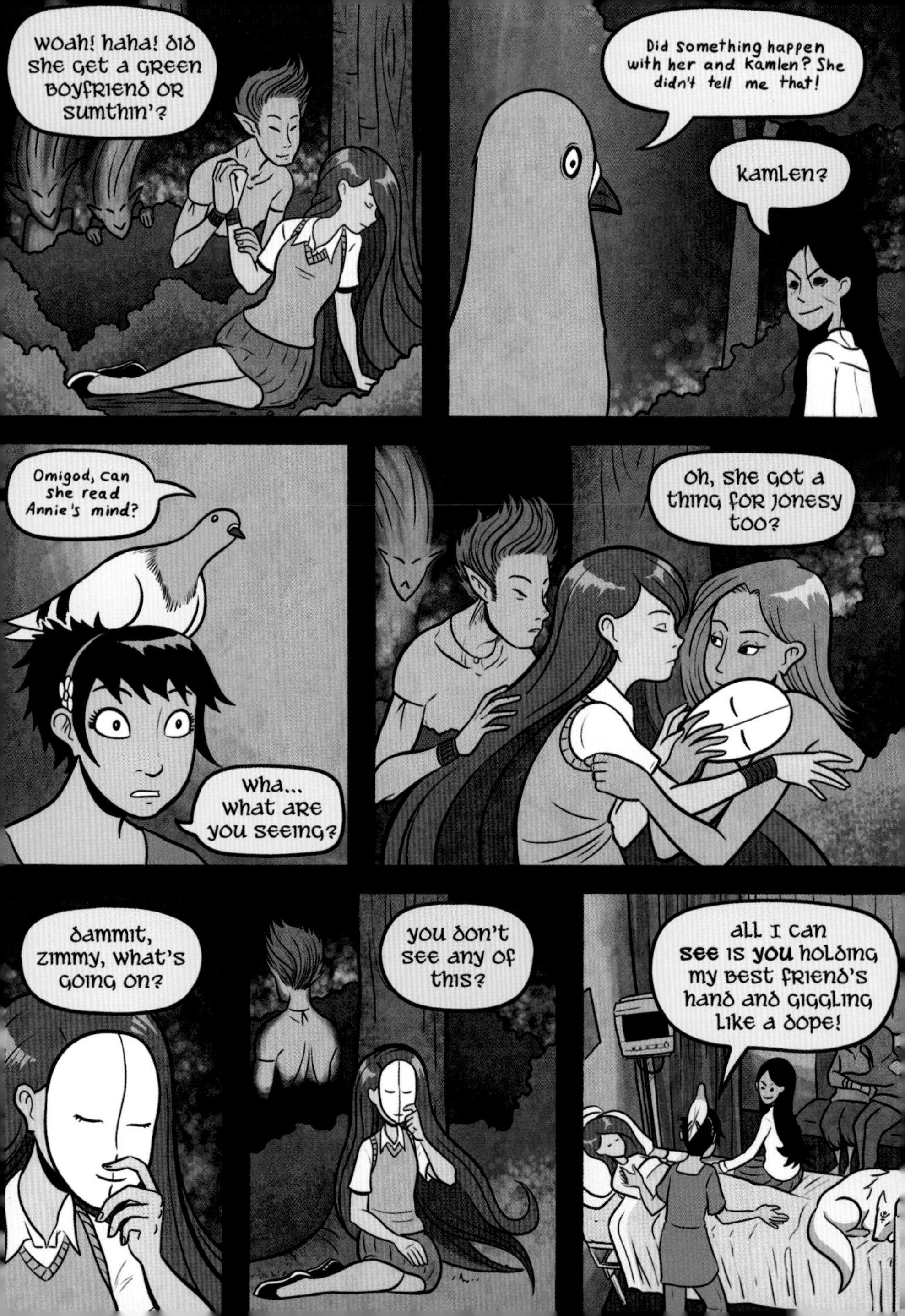
Woah! haha! Did she get a green boyfriend or sumthin'?
Did something happen with her and Kamlen? She didn't tell me that!
Kamlen?
Omigod, can she read Annie's mind?
Wha... what are you seeing?
Oh, she got a thing for Jonesy too?
Dammit, Zimmy, what's going on?
You don't see any of this?
All I can **see** is **you** holding my best friend's hand and giggling like a dope!

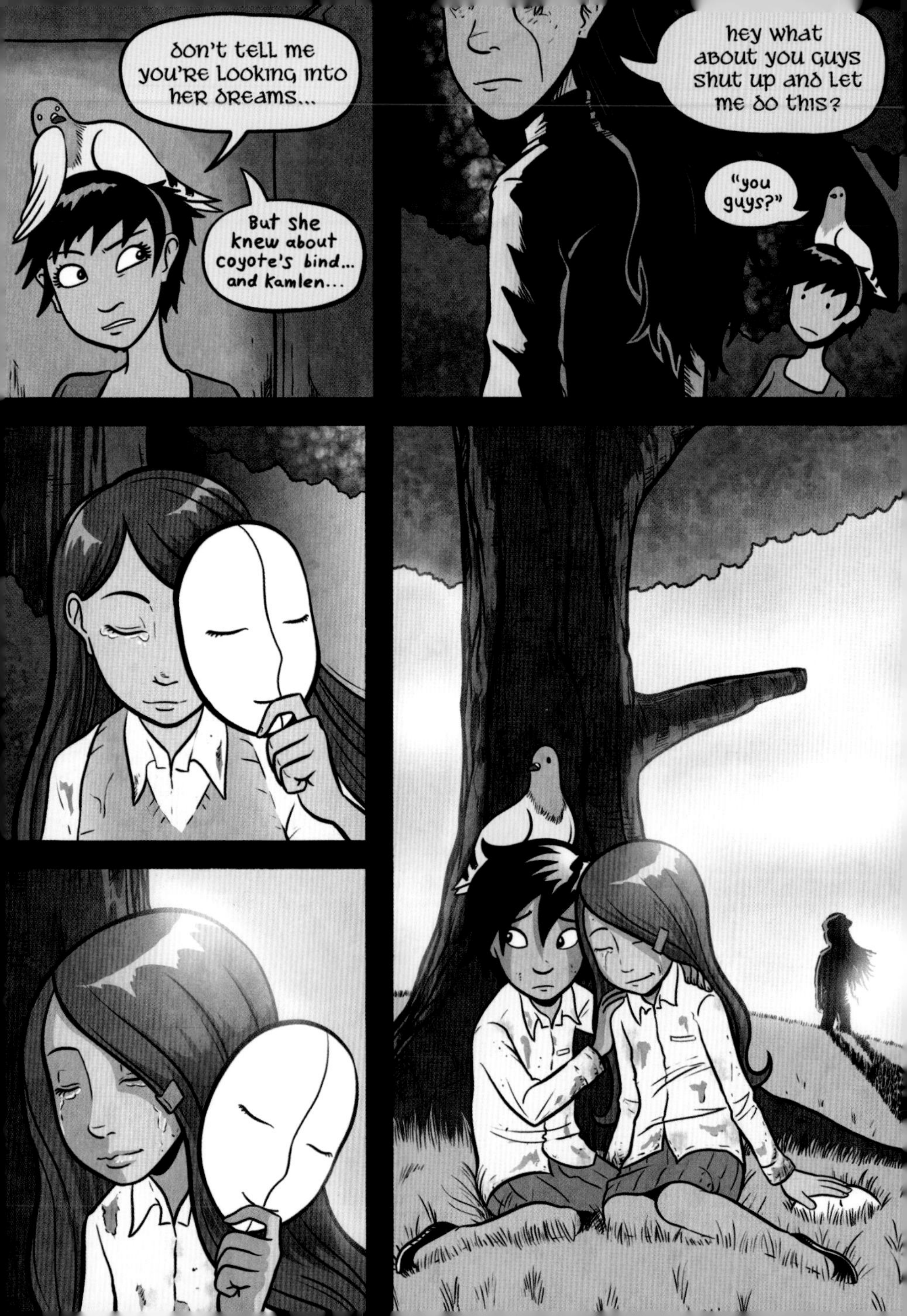
don't tell me you're looking into her dreams...
But she knew about coyote's bind... and Kamlen...
hey what about you guys shut up and let me do this?
"you guys?"

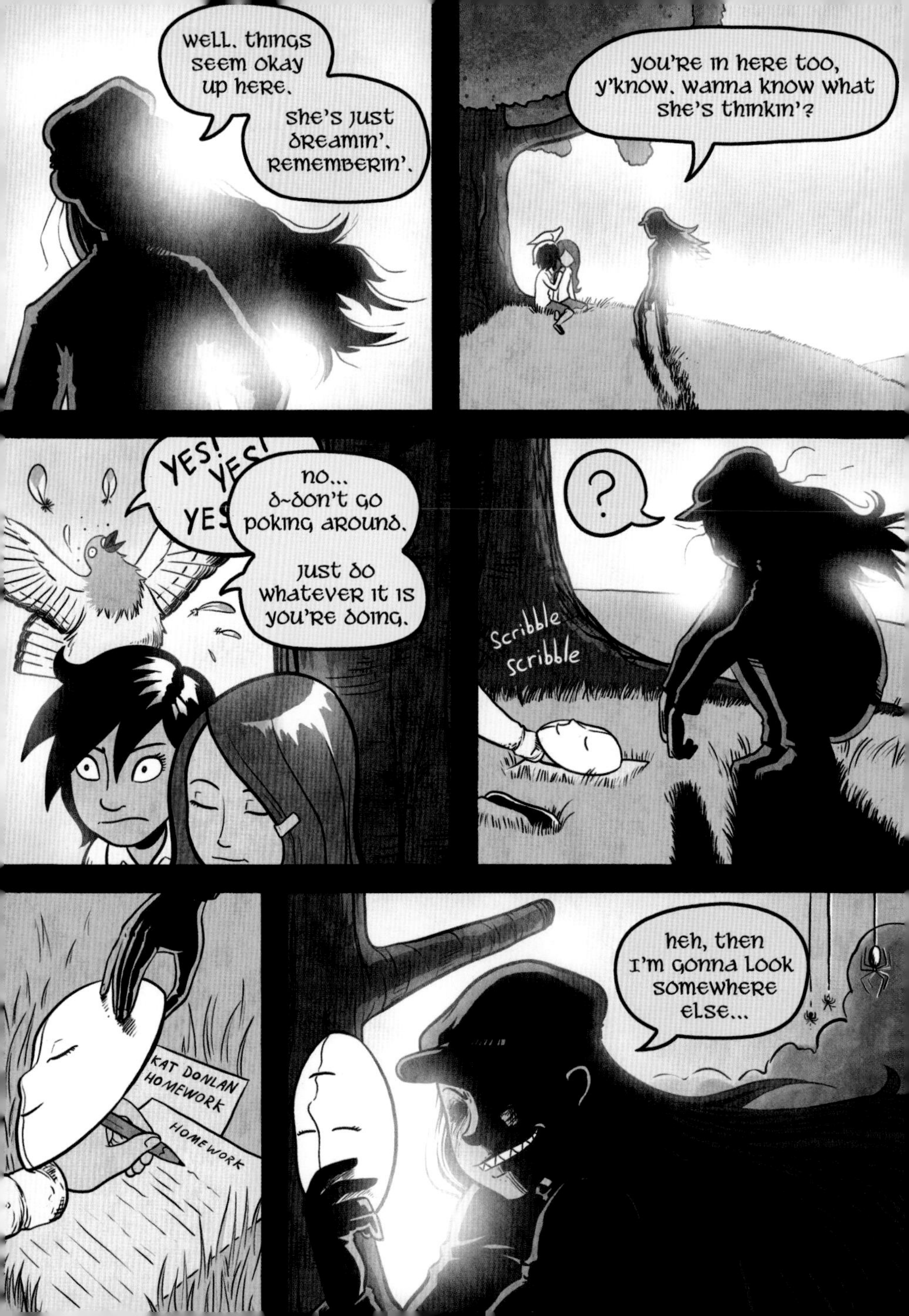

well, things seem okay up here.
she's just dreamin', rememberin'.
you're in here too, y'know, wanna know what she's thinkin'?
YES! YES! YES
no... d-don't go poking around.
just do whatever it is you're doing.
?
Scribble scribble
KAT DONLAN HOMEWORK
HOMEWORK
heh, then I'm gonna look somewhere else...

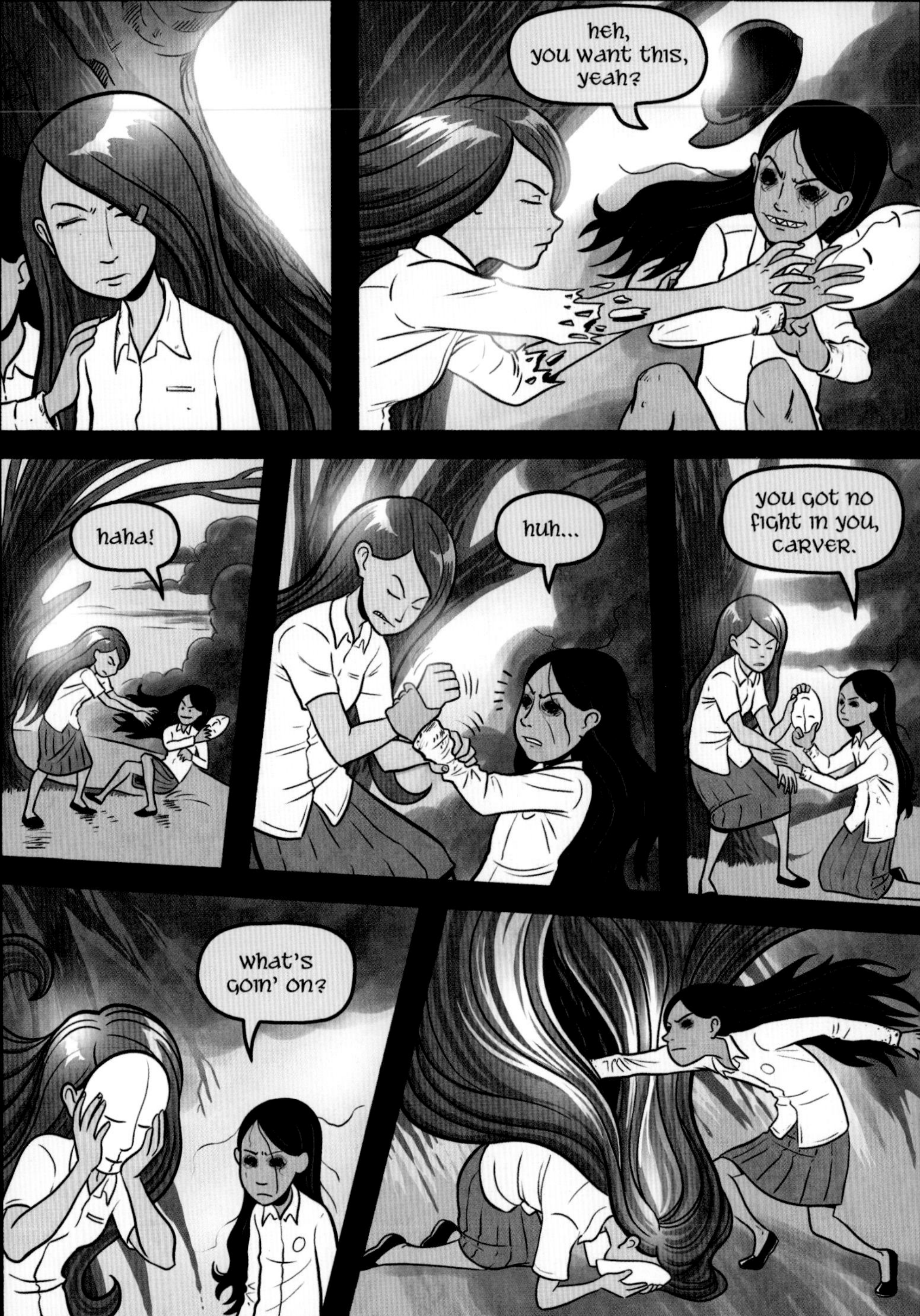
heh, you want this, yeah?
haha!
huh...
you got no fight in you, carver.
what's goin' on?

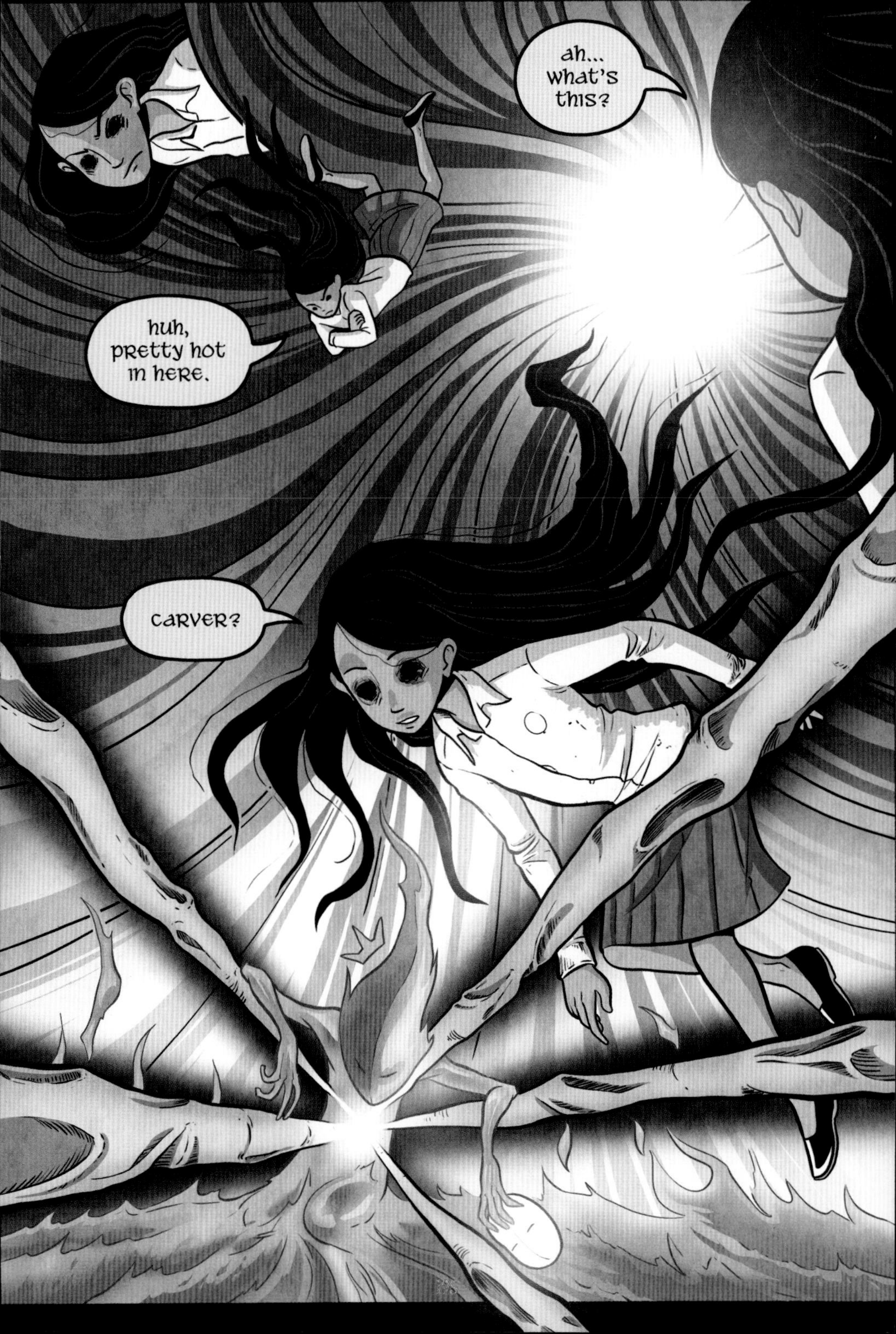
ah... what's this?
huh, pretty hot in here.
carver?

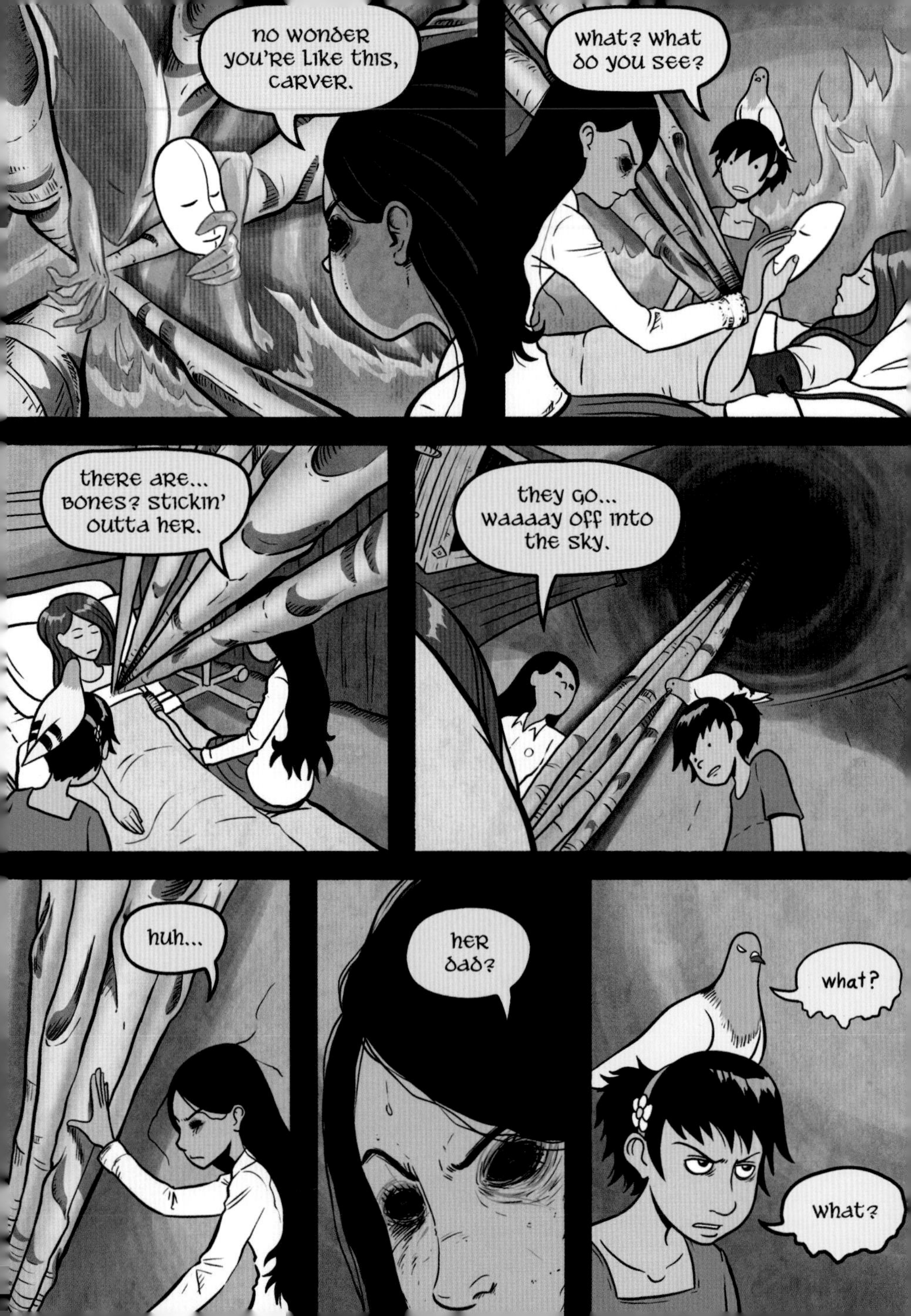
no wonder you're like this, carver.
what? what do you see?
there are... bones? stickin' outta her.
they go... waaaay off into the sky.
huh...
her dad?
what?
what?

What's the matter? Don't like him?
I HATE HIM! I HATE HIM!
...I never met the guy.
But she's always got an excuse for him, you know?
"Oh, he has his reasons."
"He must be doing something very important."
This is the second time she's ended up in an infirmary bed and he doesn't even know about it.
...
Well, I can't see where he is... but I can try to stop whatever he's doin'.

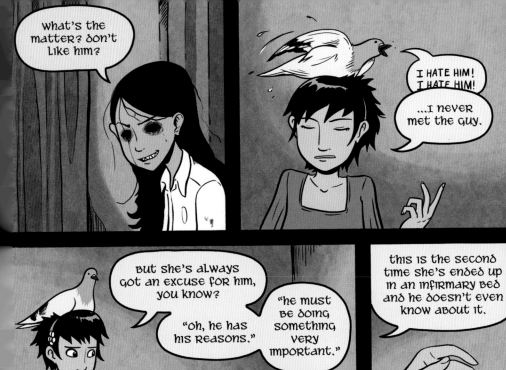

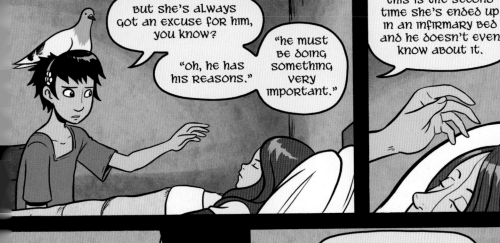

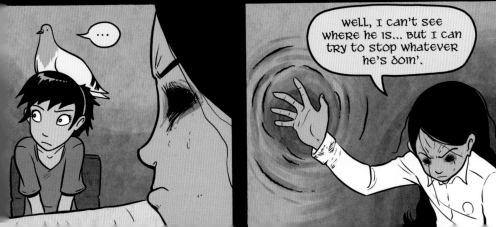

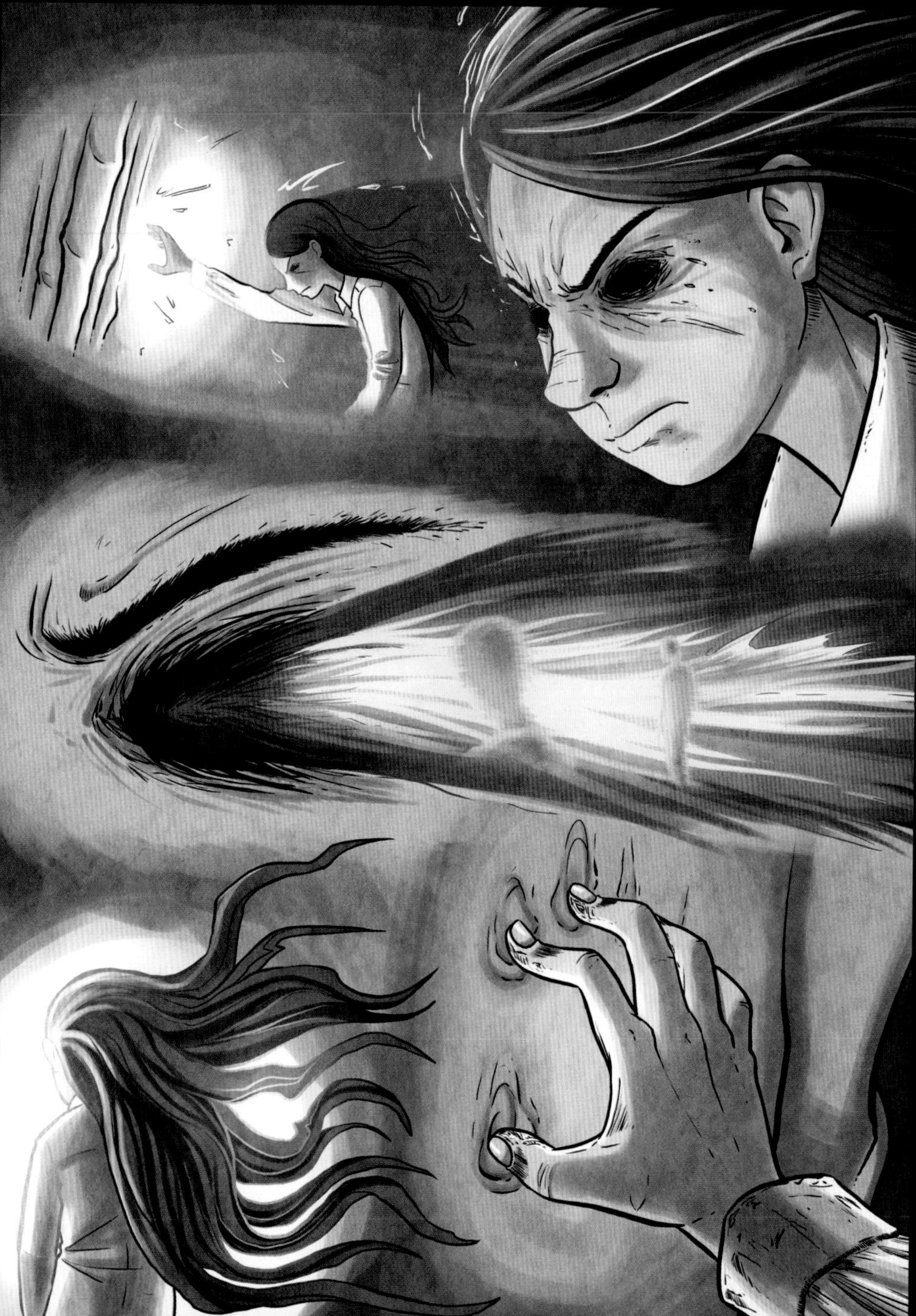

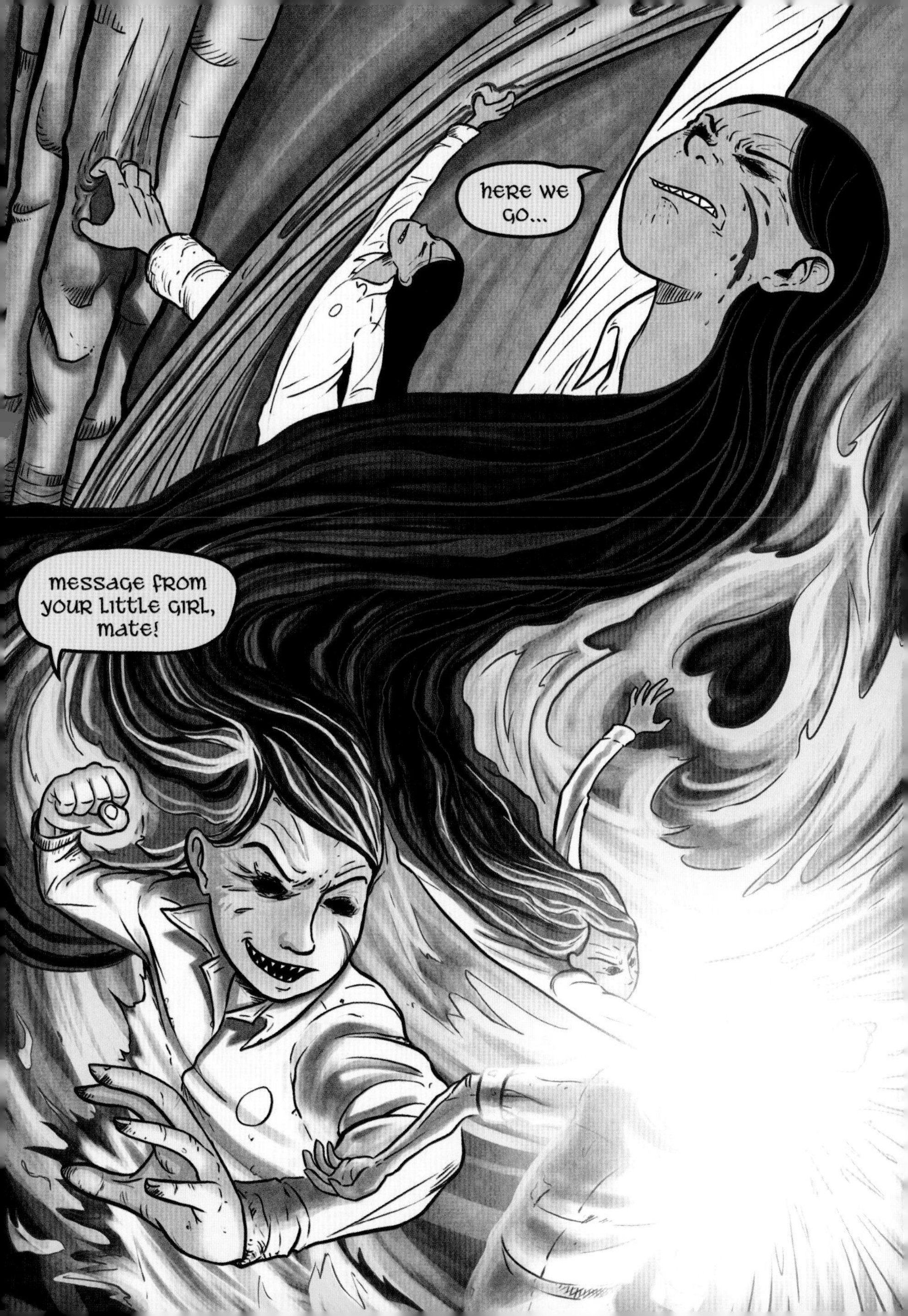
here we go...
message from your little girl, mate!

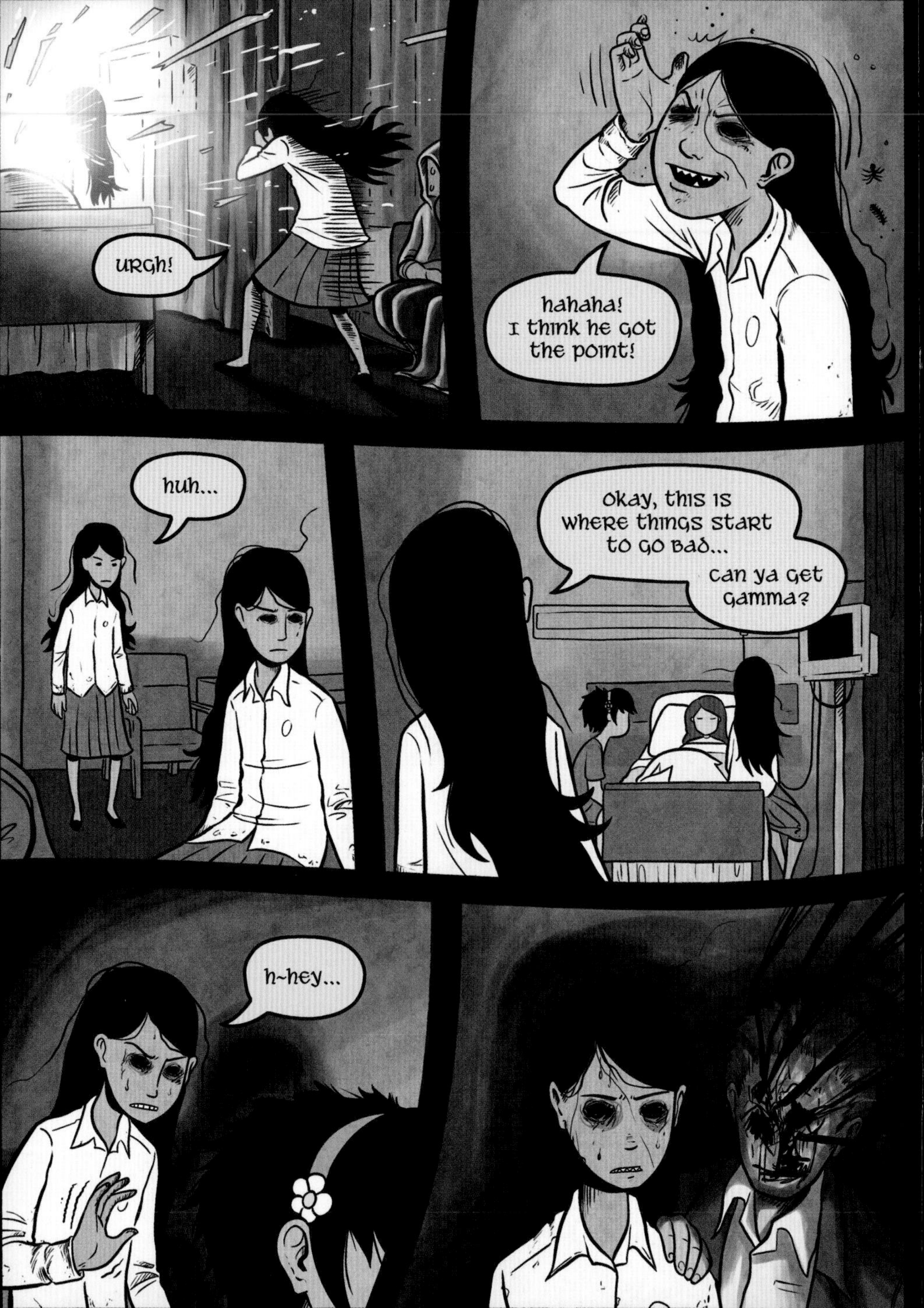
URGH!
hahaha! I think he got the point!
huh...
Okay, this is where things start to go bad...
can ya get gamma?
h-hey...

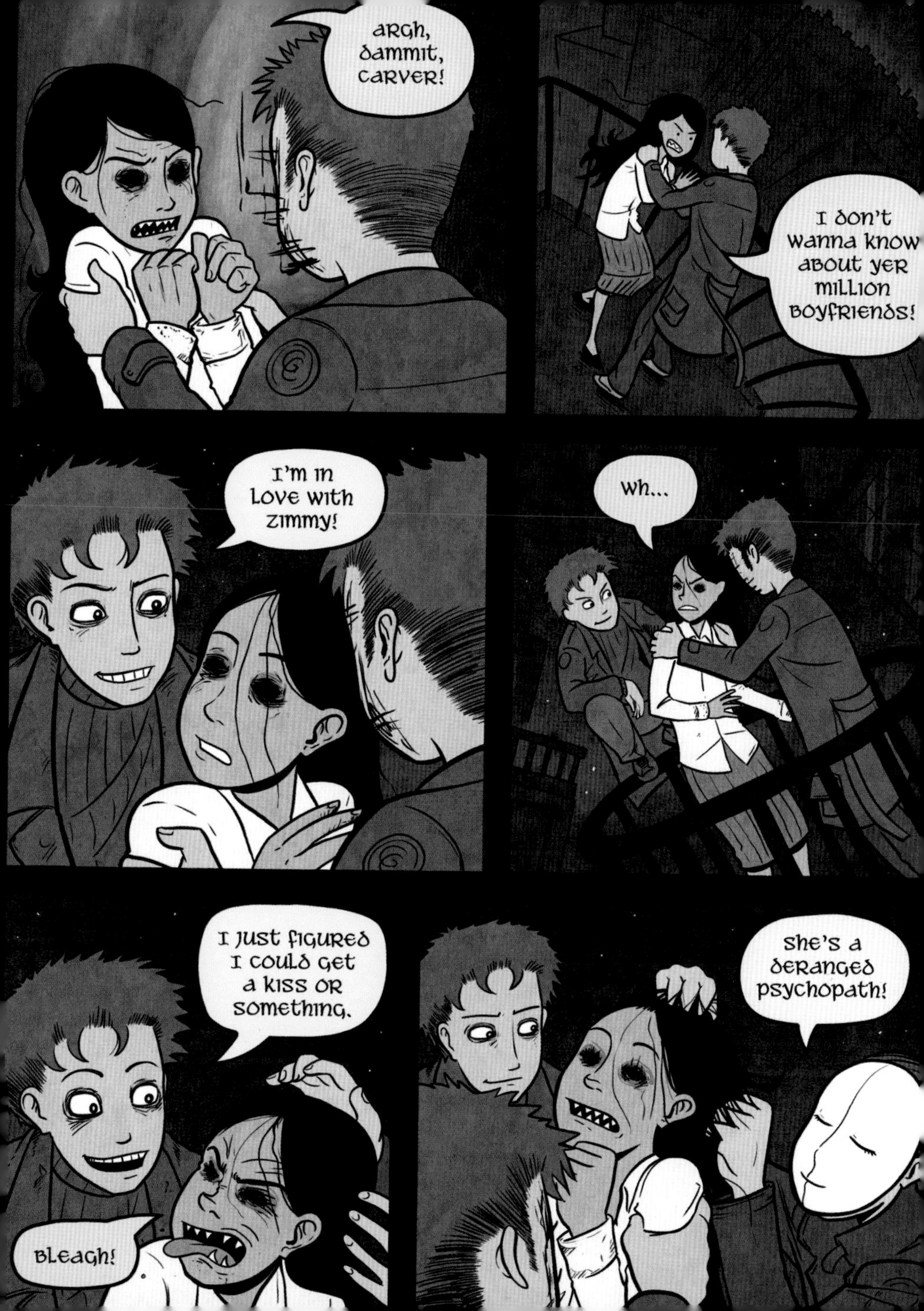
argh, dammit, carver!
I don't wanna know about yer million boyfriends!
I'm in love with zimmy!
wh...
I just figured I could get a kiss or something.
bleagh!
she's a deranged psychopath!

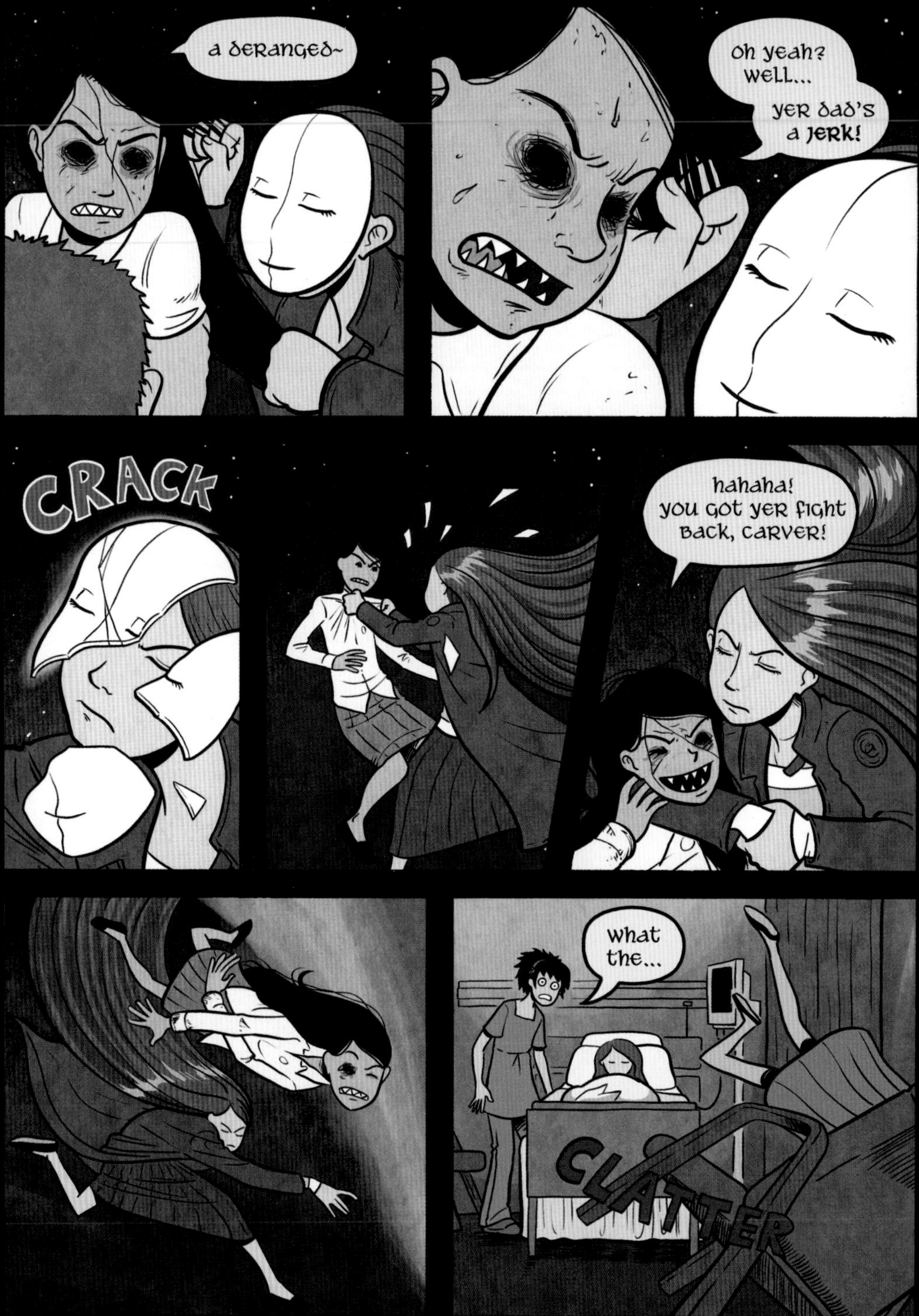
a deranged~
oh yeah? well...
yer dad's a JERK!
CRACK
hahaha! you got yer fight back, carver!
what the...
CLATTER

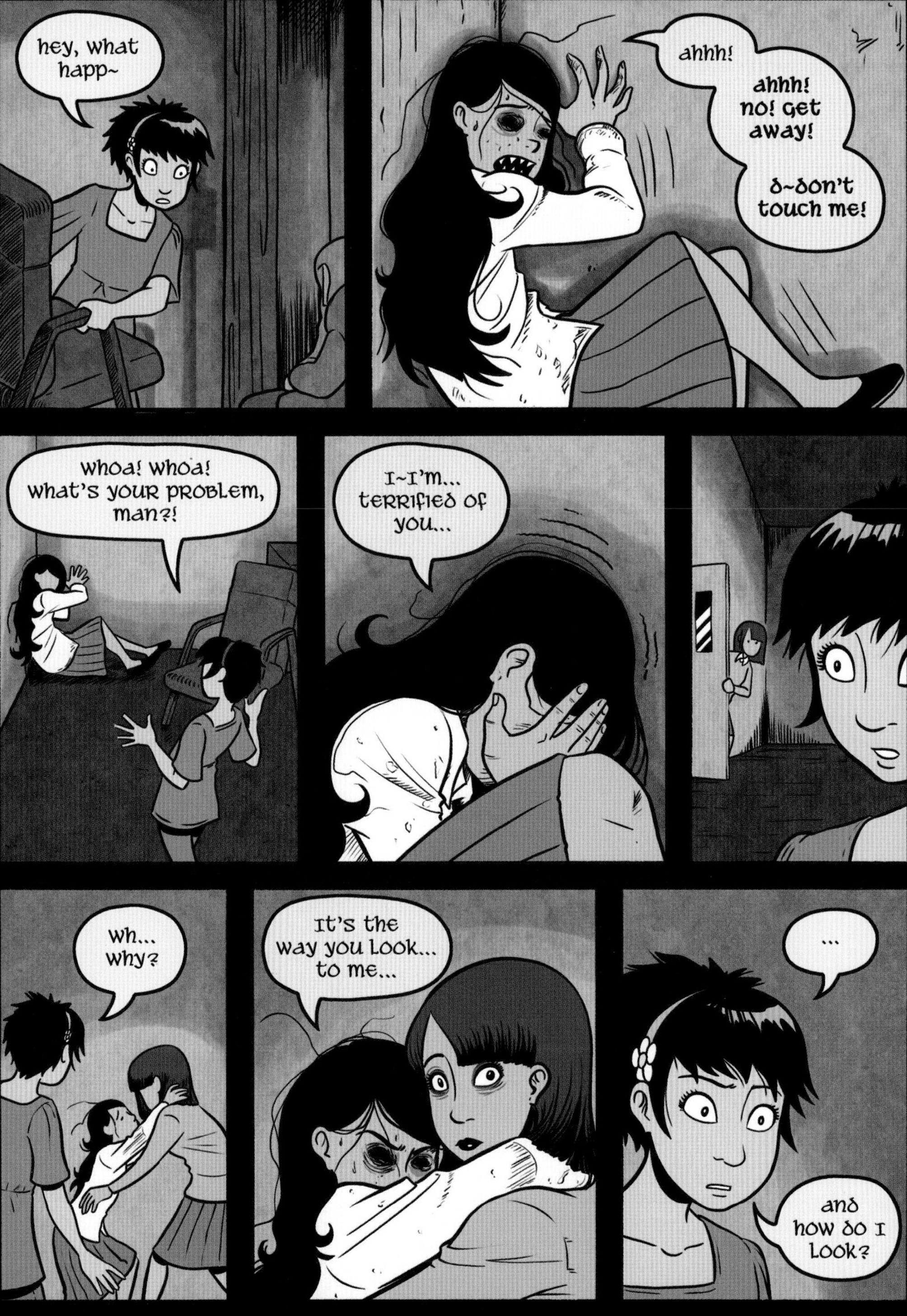
hey, what happ~
ahhh!
ahhh! no! get away!
d~don't touch me!
whoa! whoa! what's your problem, man?!
I~I'm... terrified of you...
wh... why?
It's the way you look... to me...
...
and how do I look?

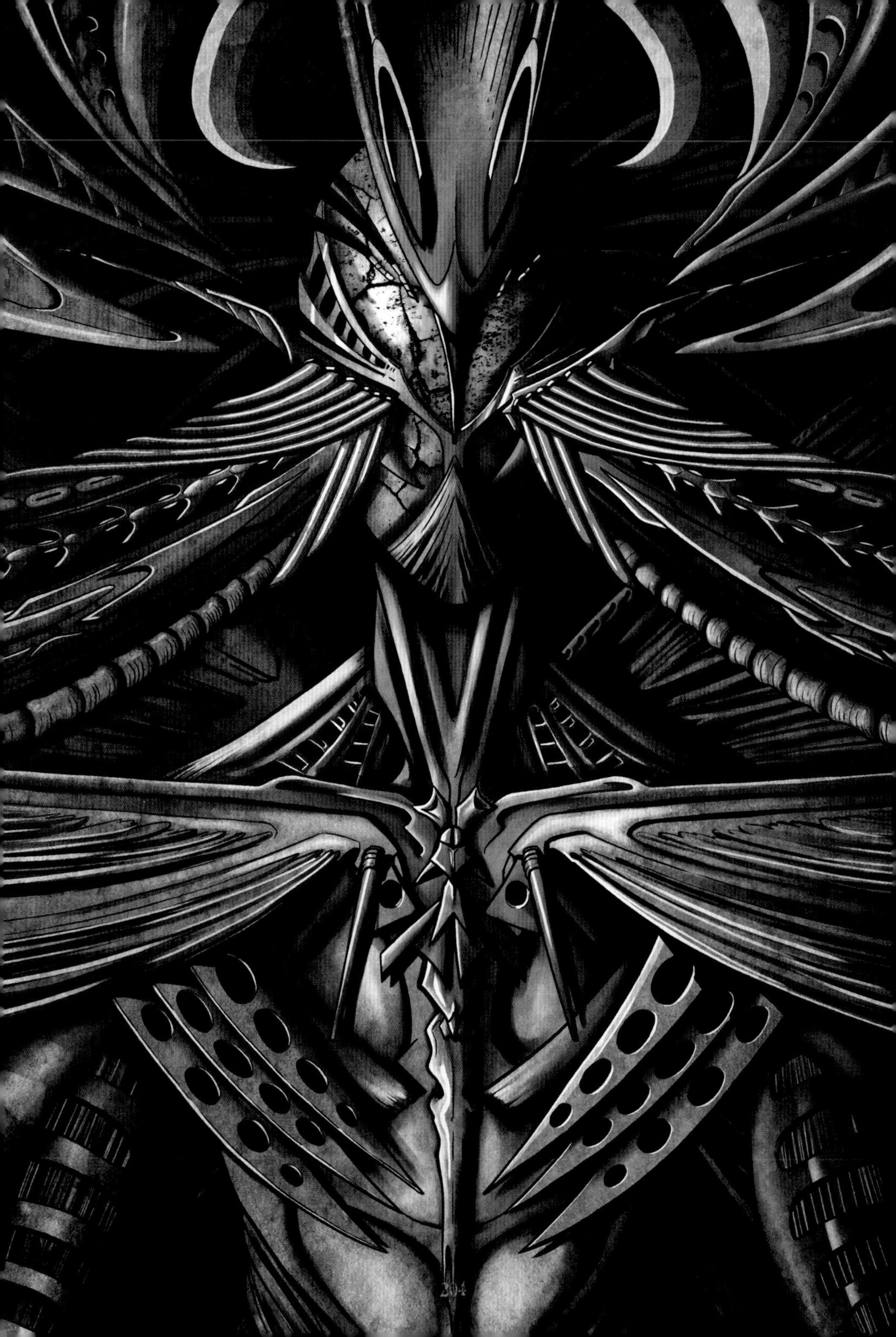

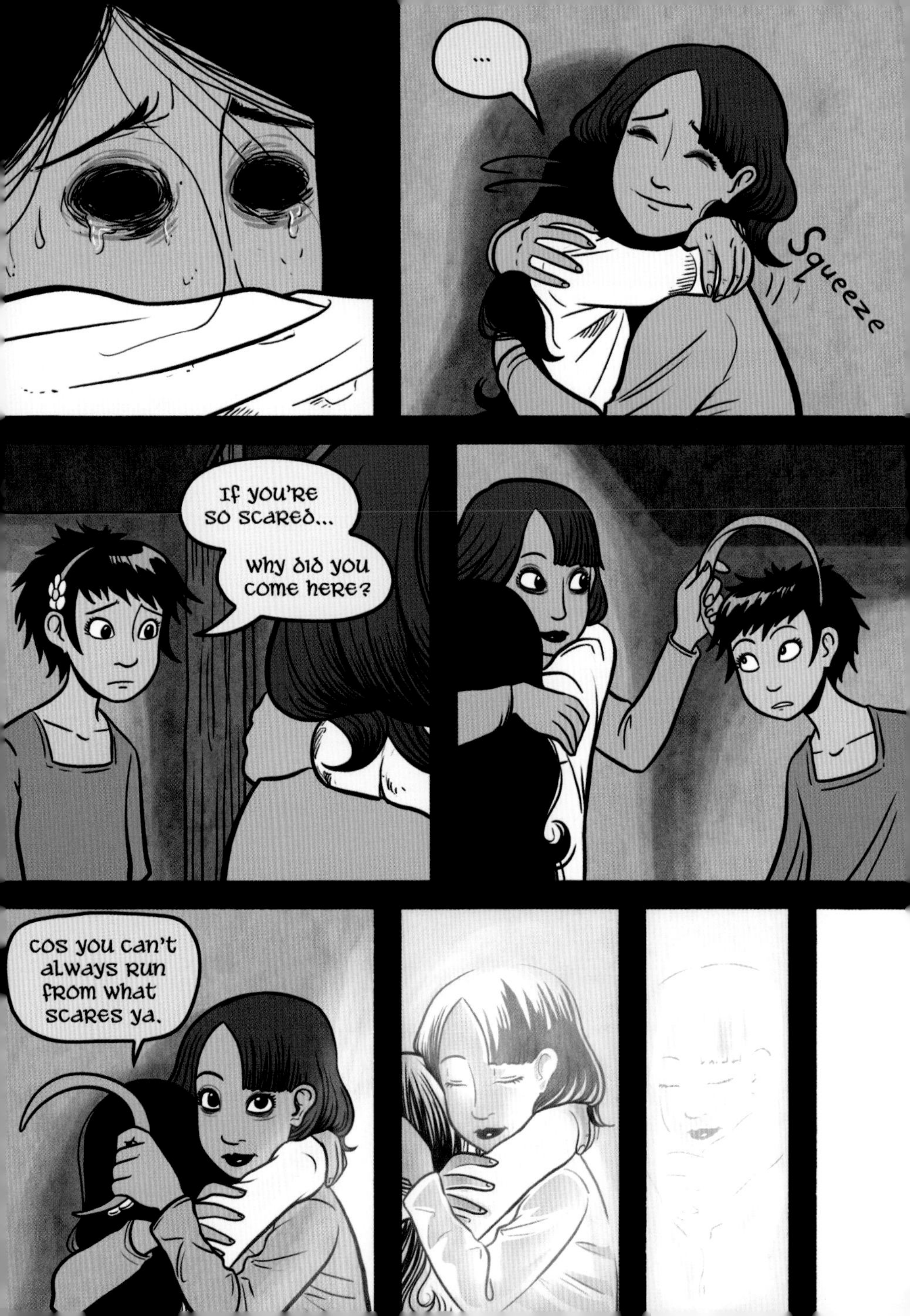
...
Squeeze
If you're so scared...
why did you come here?
cos you can't always run from what scares ya.

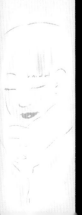

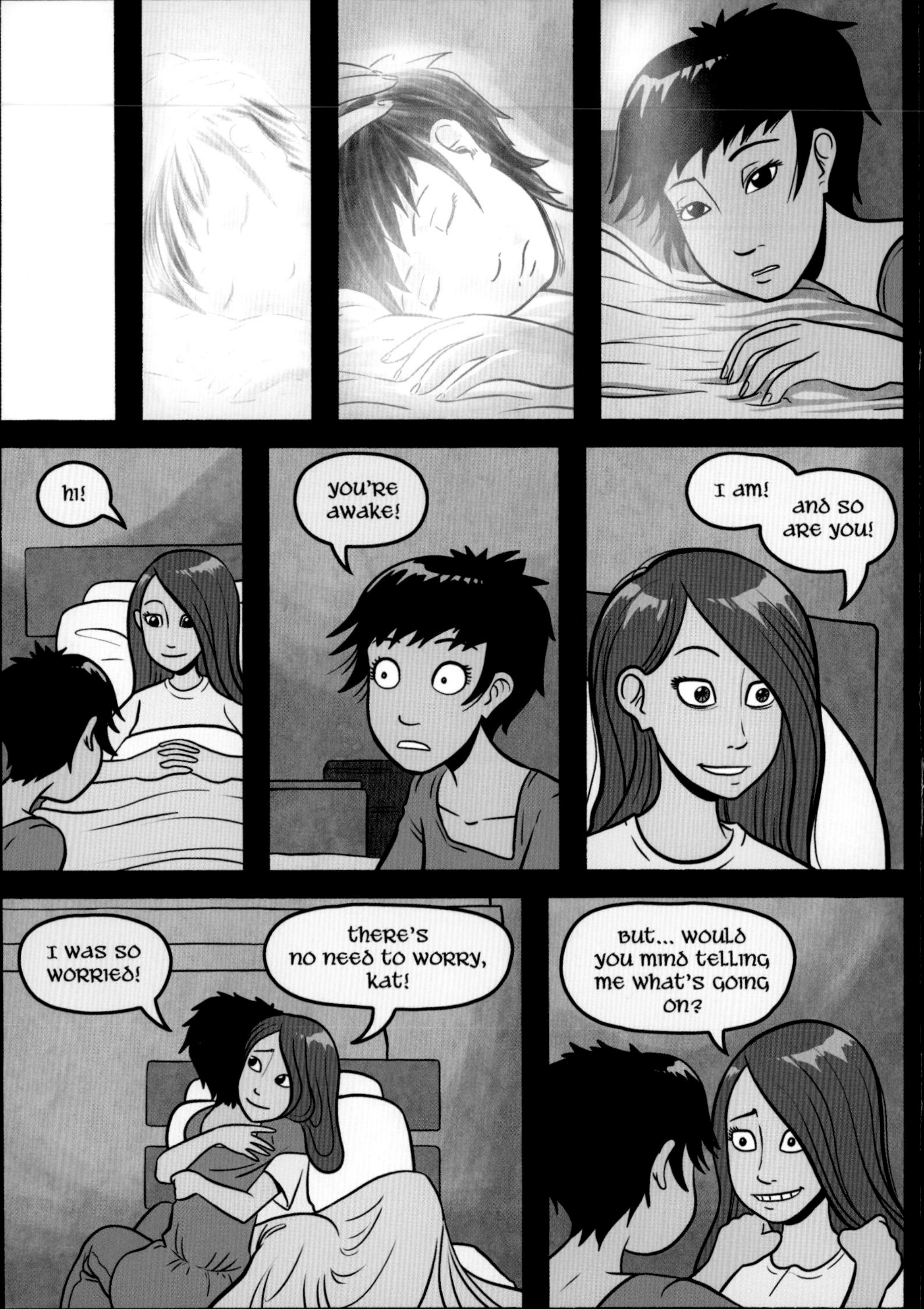
hi!
you're awake!
I am!
and so are you!
I was so worried!
there's no need to worry, kat!
but... would you mind telling me what's going on?

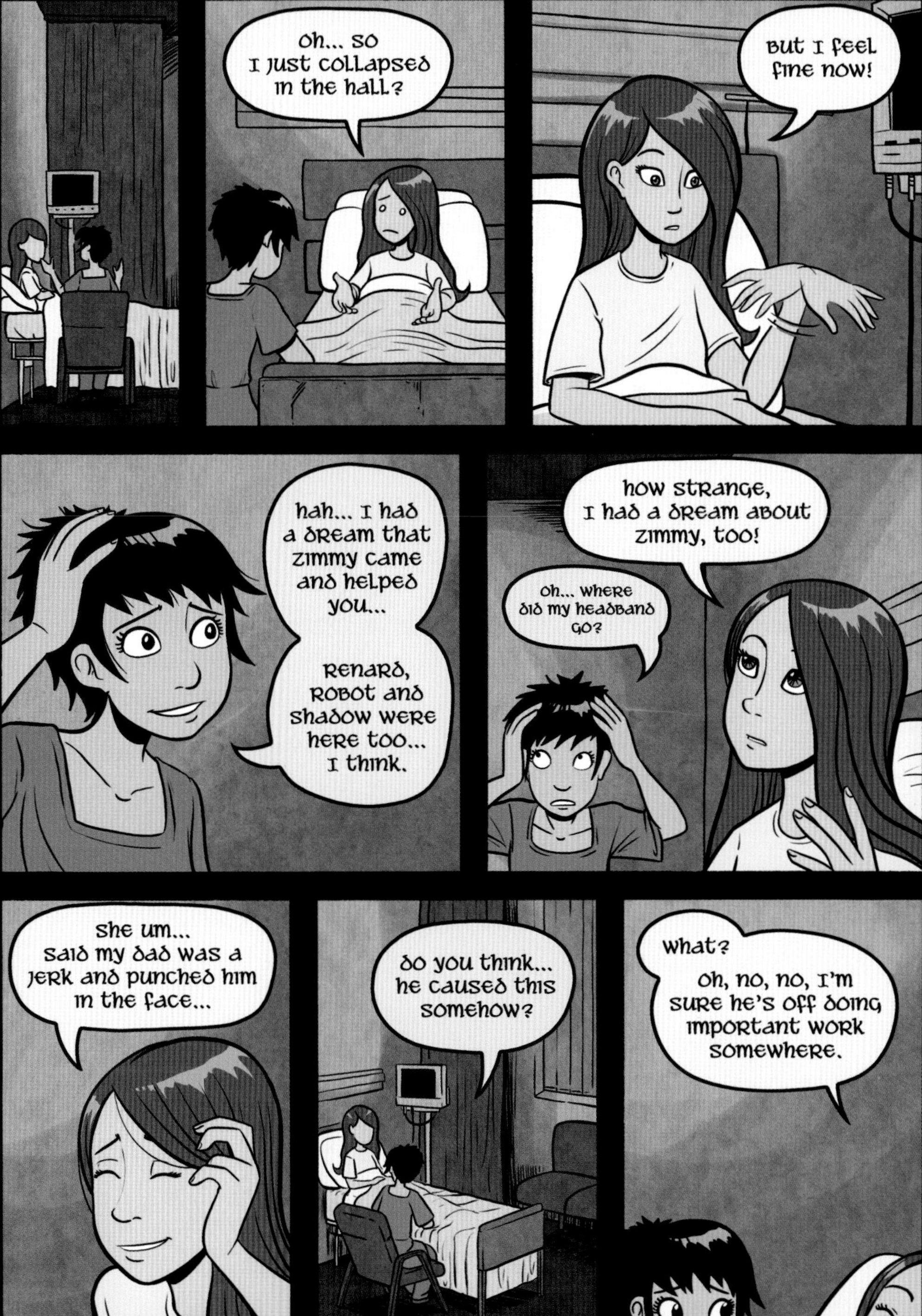
Oh... so I just collapsed in the hall?
But I feel fine now!
hah... I had a dream that Zimmy came and helped you...
Renard, Robot and Shadow were here too... I think.
how strange, I had a dream about Zimmy, too!
Oh... where did my headband go?
she um... said my dad was a jerk and punched him in the face...
do you think... he caused this somehow?
What?
Oh, no, no, I'm sure he's off doing important work somewhere.

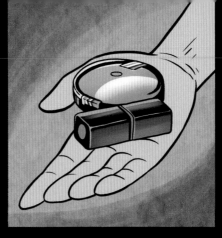

OH, HERE. I BROUGHT THESE FOR YOU.

OH...

I... I'LL PUT THEM ON LATER, MAYBE.

I TOLD YOU I DIDN'T WANT TO SEE HER.

I THOUGHT YOU WERE VERY BRAVE.

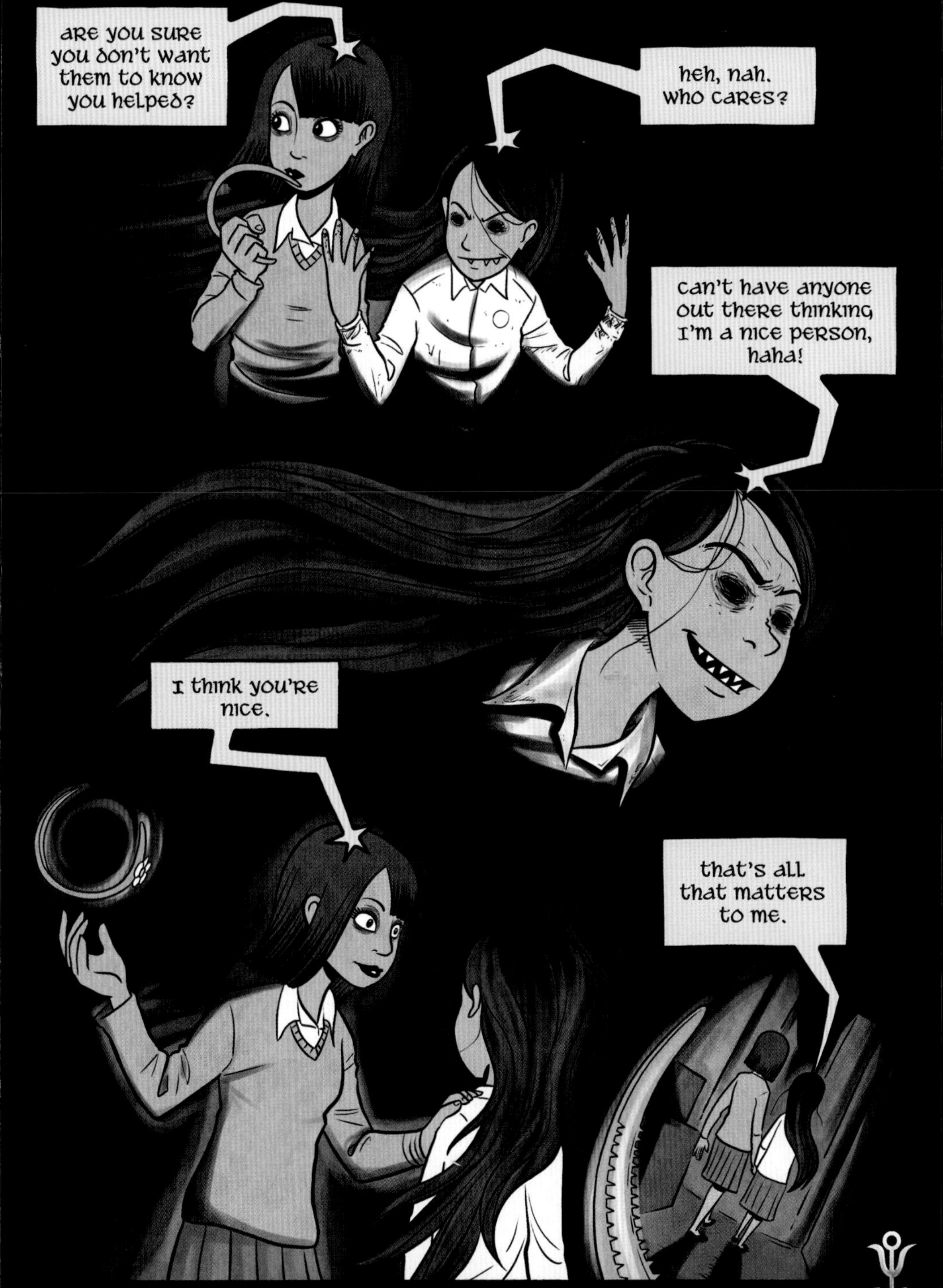
are you sure you don't want them to know you helped?
heh, nah. who cares?
can't have anyone out there thinking I'm a nice person, haha!
I think you're nice.
that's all that matters to me.

Gunnerkrigg Court

Important

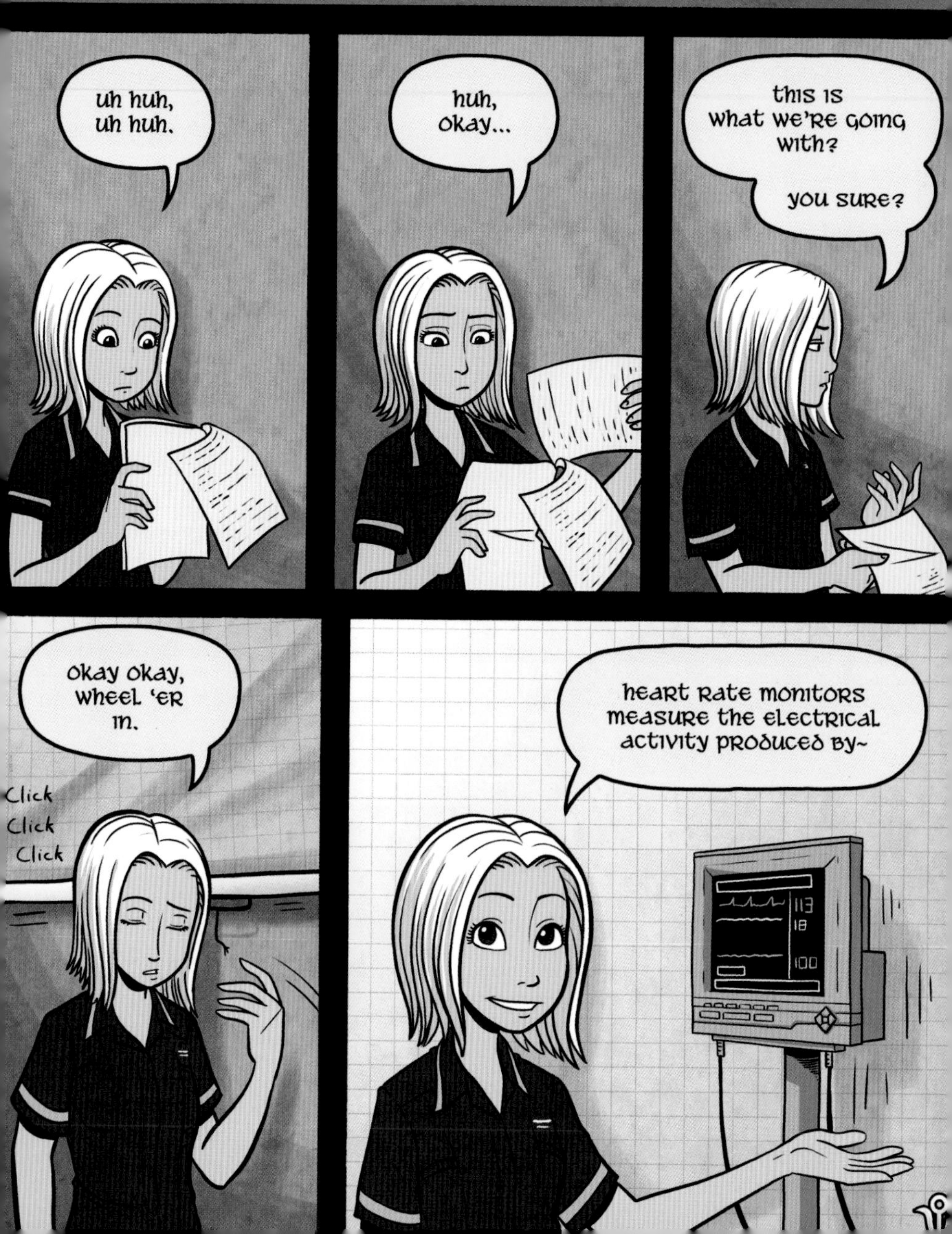
uh huh,
uh huh.
huh,
okay...
this is
what we're going
with?
you sure?
okay okay,
wheel 'er
in.
Click
Click
Click
113
18
100
heart rate monitors
measure the electrical
activity produced by~

Gunnerkrigg Court

Chapter 39:

The Great Secret

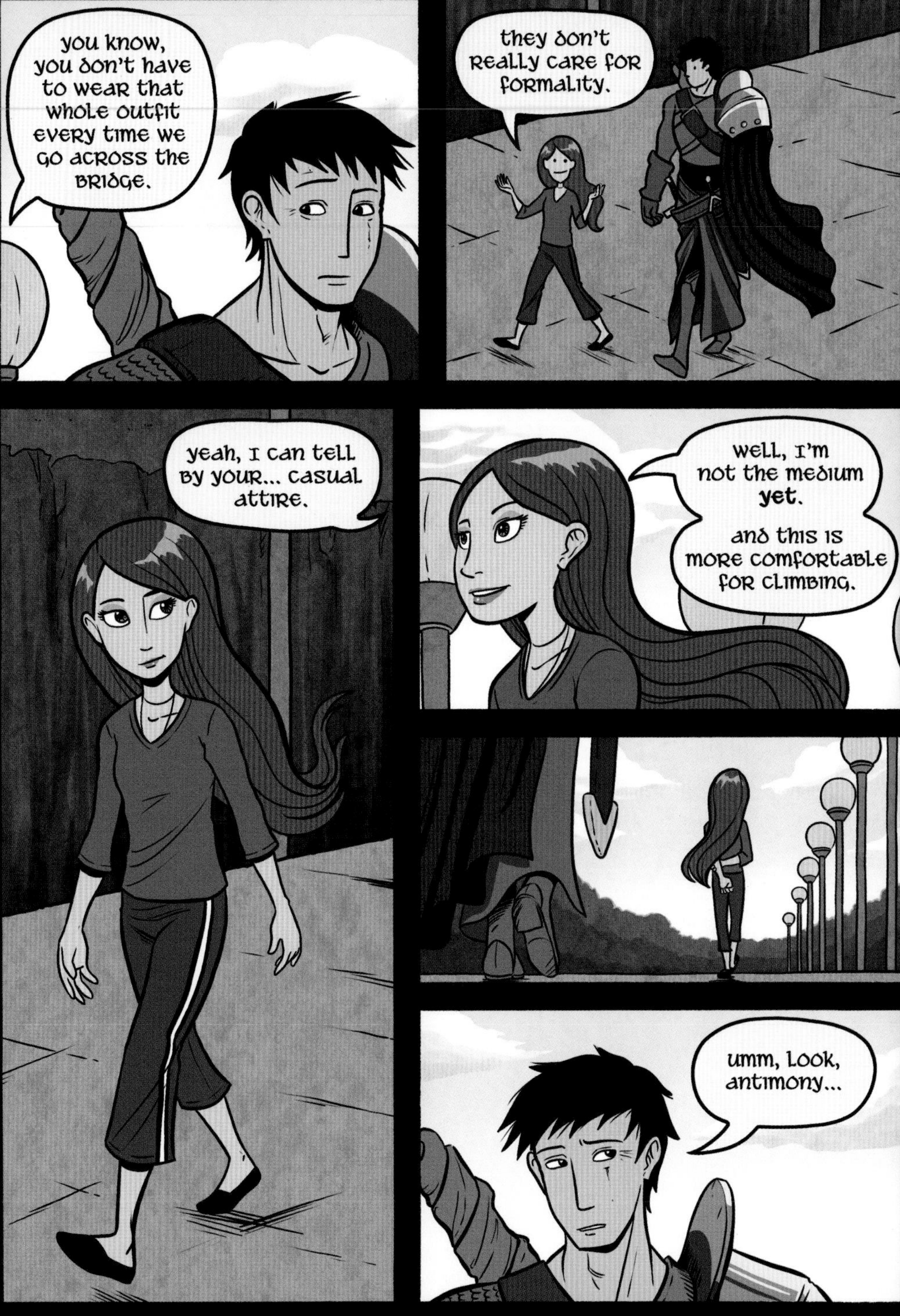
you know, you don't have to wear that whole outfit every time we go across the bridge.
they don't really care for formality.
yeah, I can tell by your... casual attire.
well, I'm not the medium **yet**.
and this is more comfortable for climbing.
umm, look, antimony...

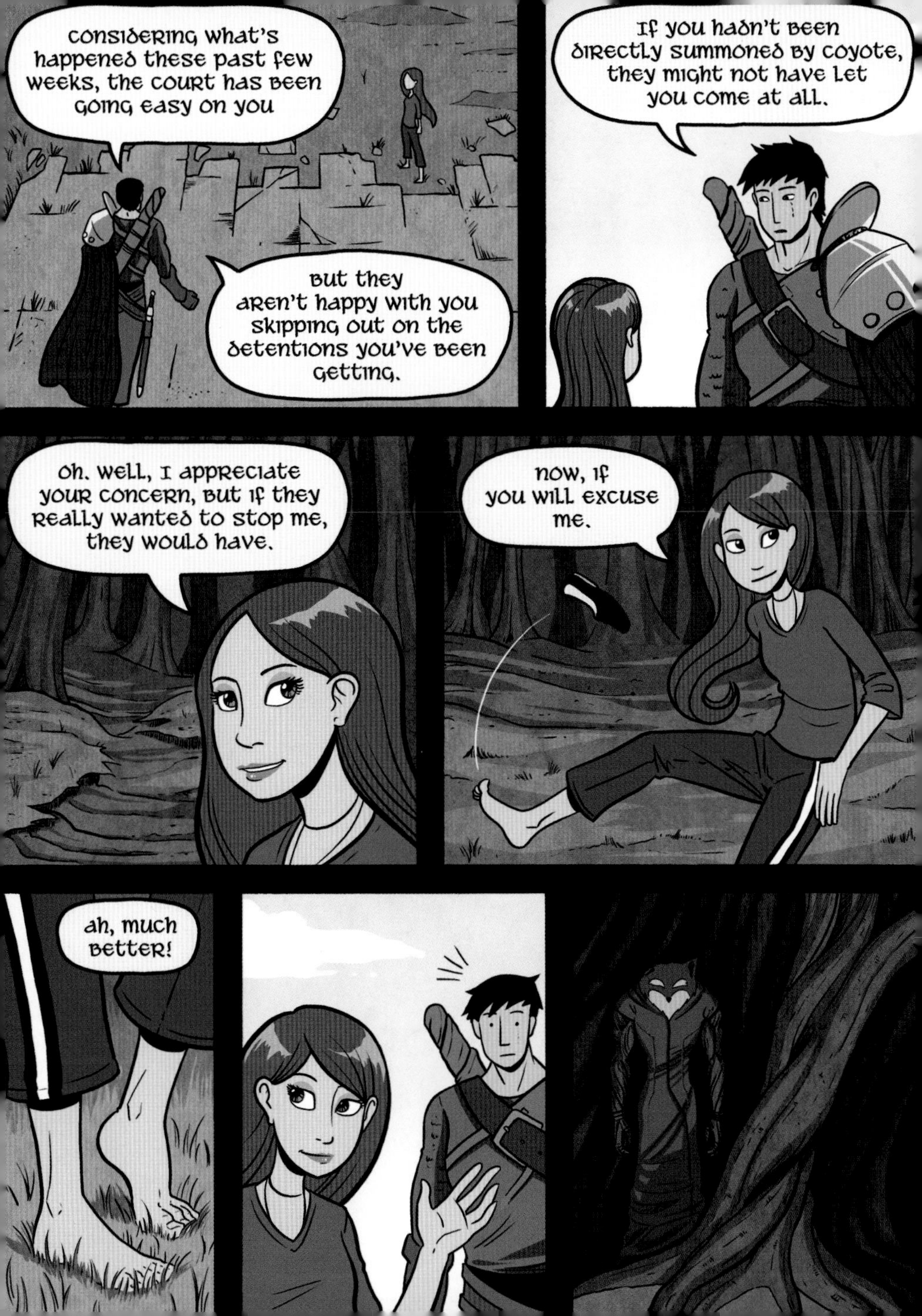
considering what's happened these past few weeks, the court has been going easy on you
But they aren't happy with you skipping out on the detentions you've been getting.
If you hadn't been directly summoned by coyote, they might not have let you come at all.
Oh. Well, I appreciate your concern, but if they really wanted to stop me, they would have.
now, if you will excuse me.
ah, much better!

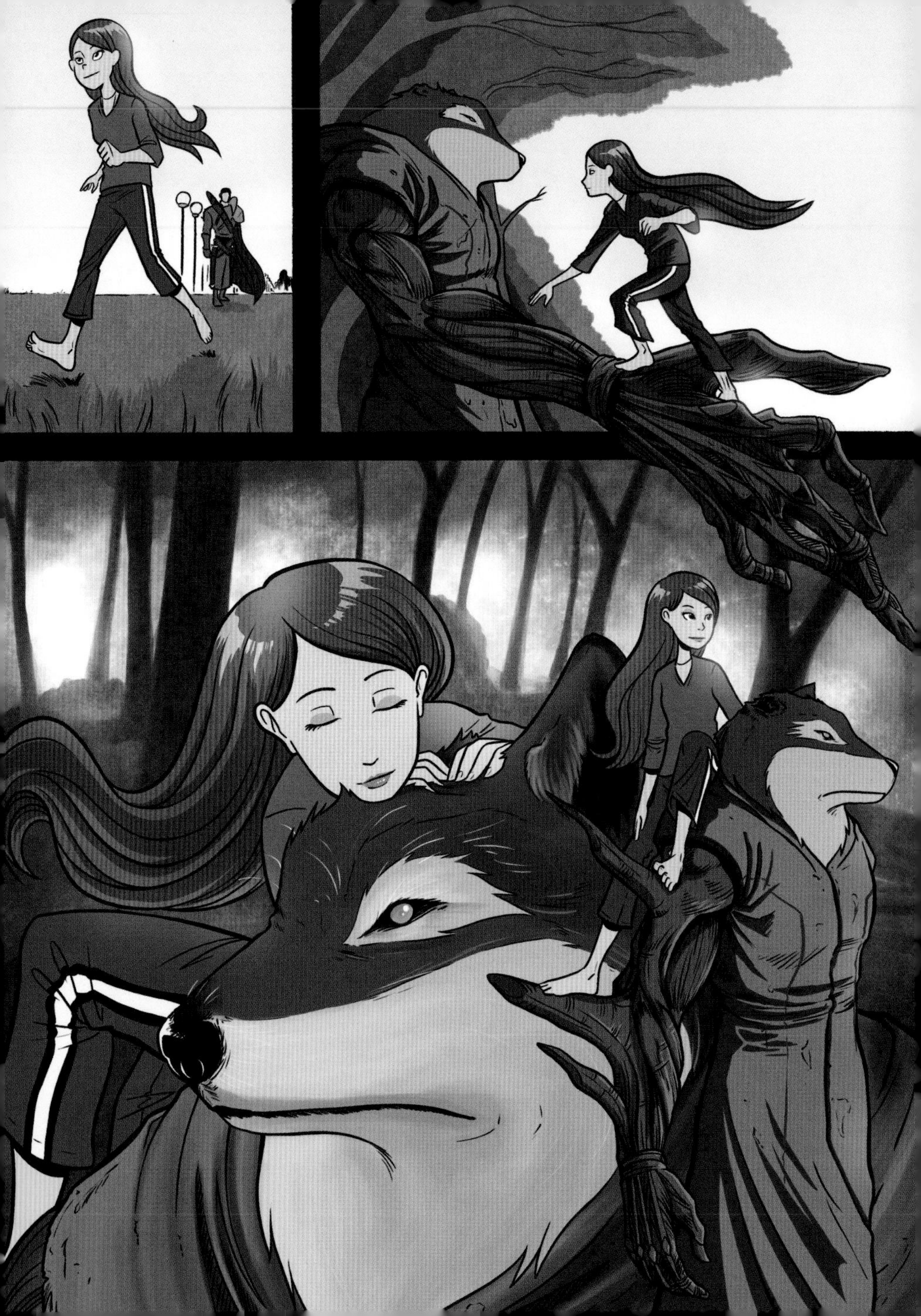

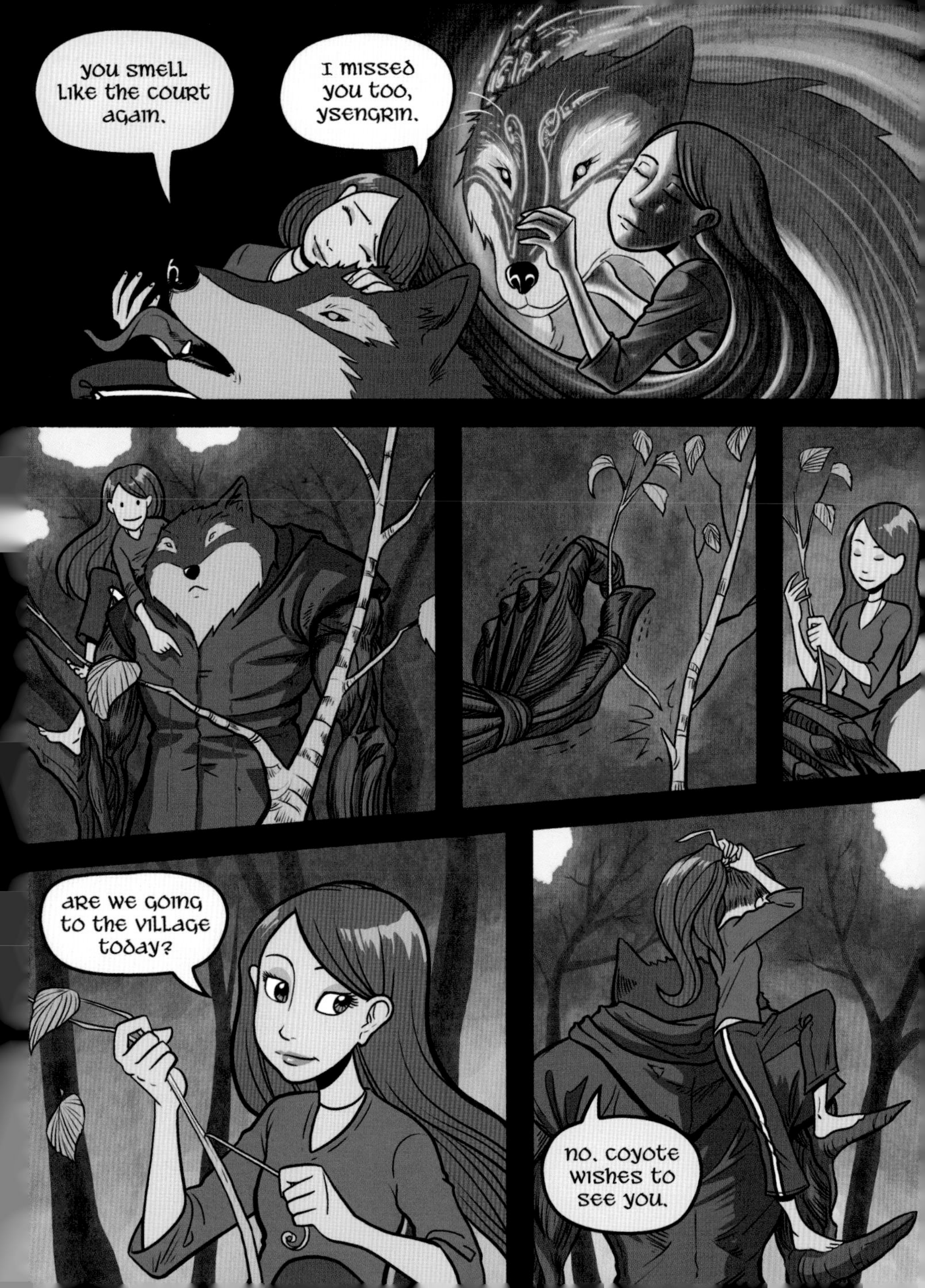
you smell like the court again.
I missed you too, ysengrin.
are we going to the village today?
no. coyote wishes to see you.

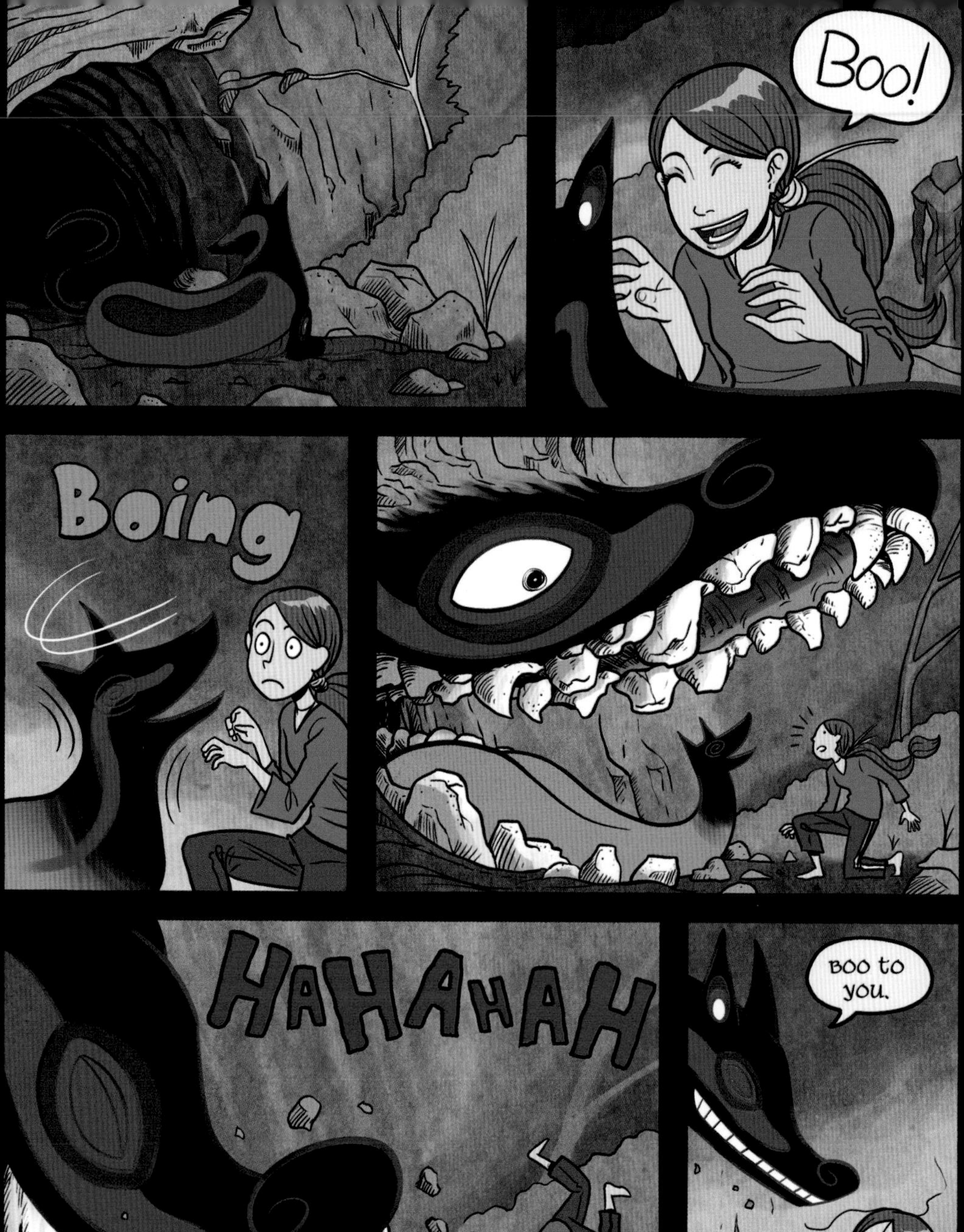
Boo!
Boing
HAHAHAH
Boo to you.

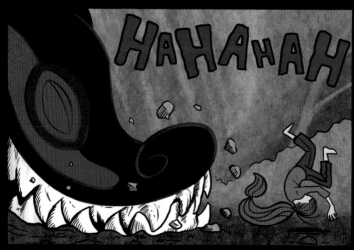

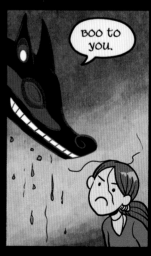

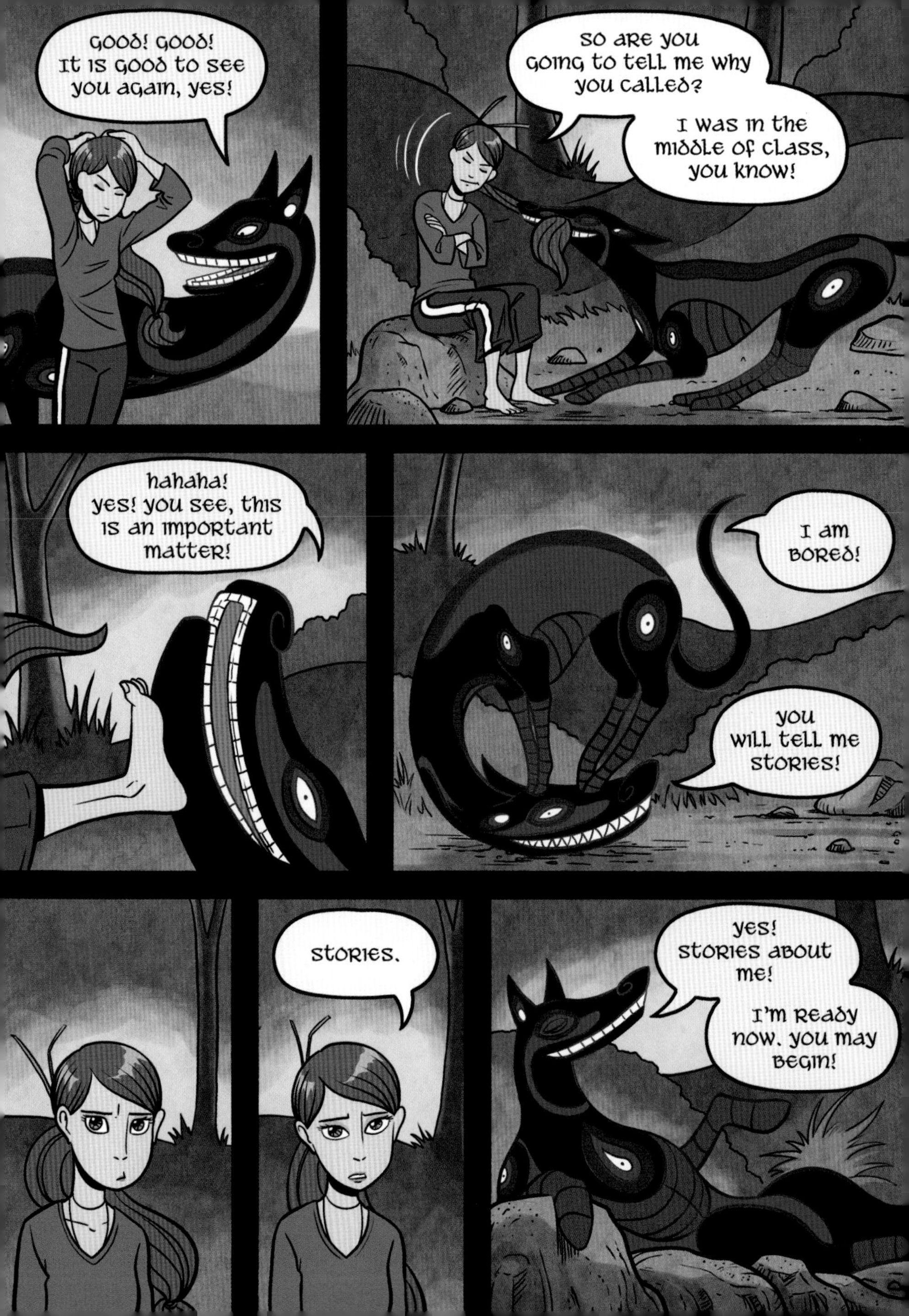
GOOD! GOOD! IT IS GOOD TO SEE YOU AGAIN, YES!
SO ARE YOU GOING TO TELL ME WHY YOU CALLED?
I WAS IN THE MIDDLE OF CLASS, YOU KNOW!
HAHAHA! YES! YOU SEE, THIS IS AN IMPORTANT MATTER!
I AM BORED!
YOU WILL TELL ME STORIES!
STORIES.
YES! STORIES ABOUT ME!
I'M READY NOW. YOU MAY BEGIN!

coyote, you don't need me to tell you stories.

you have plenty of other people who could do it.

like ysengrim.

no!

his stories are as boring and stupid as he is!

well! if you're going to be like that, I don't want to tell you any!

I want to go to the village and see my friends.

who said you have a choice in the matter, fire head girl?

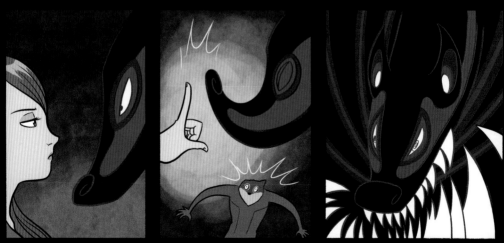

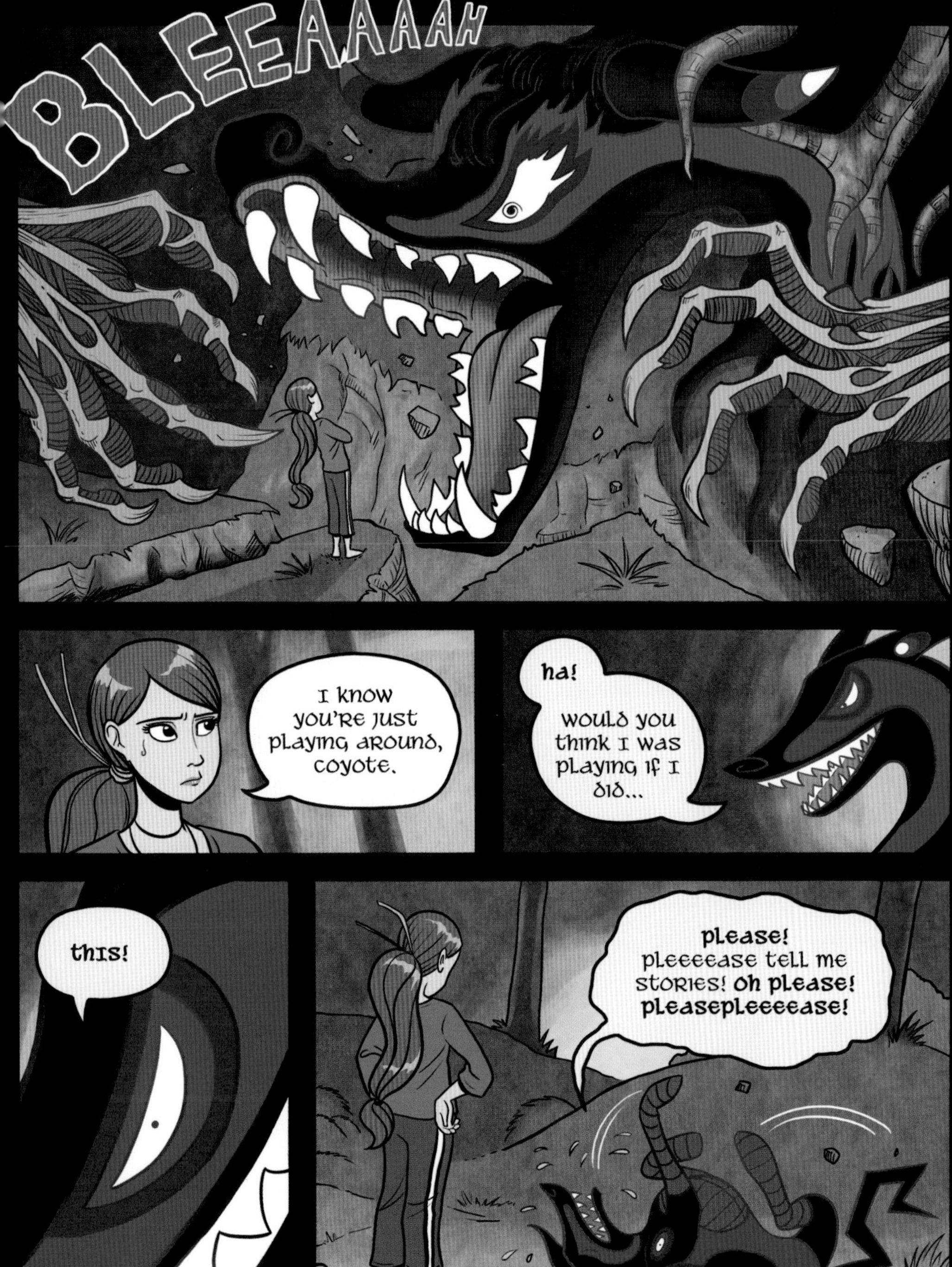
BLEEAAAAH
I know you're just playing around, coyote.
ha!
would you think I was playing if I did...
this!
please! pleeeeease tell me stories! oh please! pleasepleeeeease!

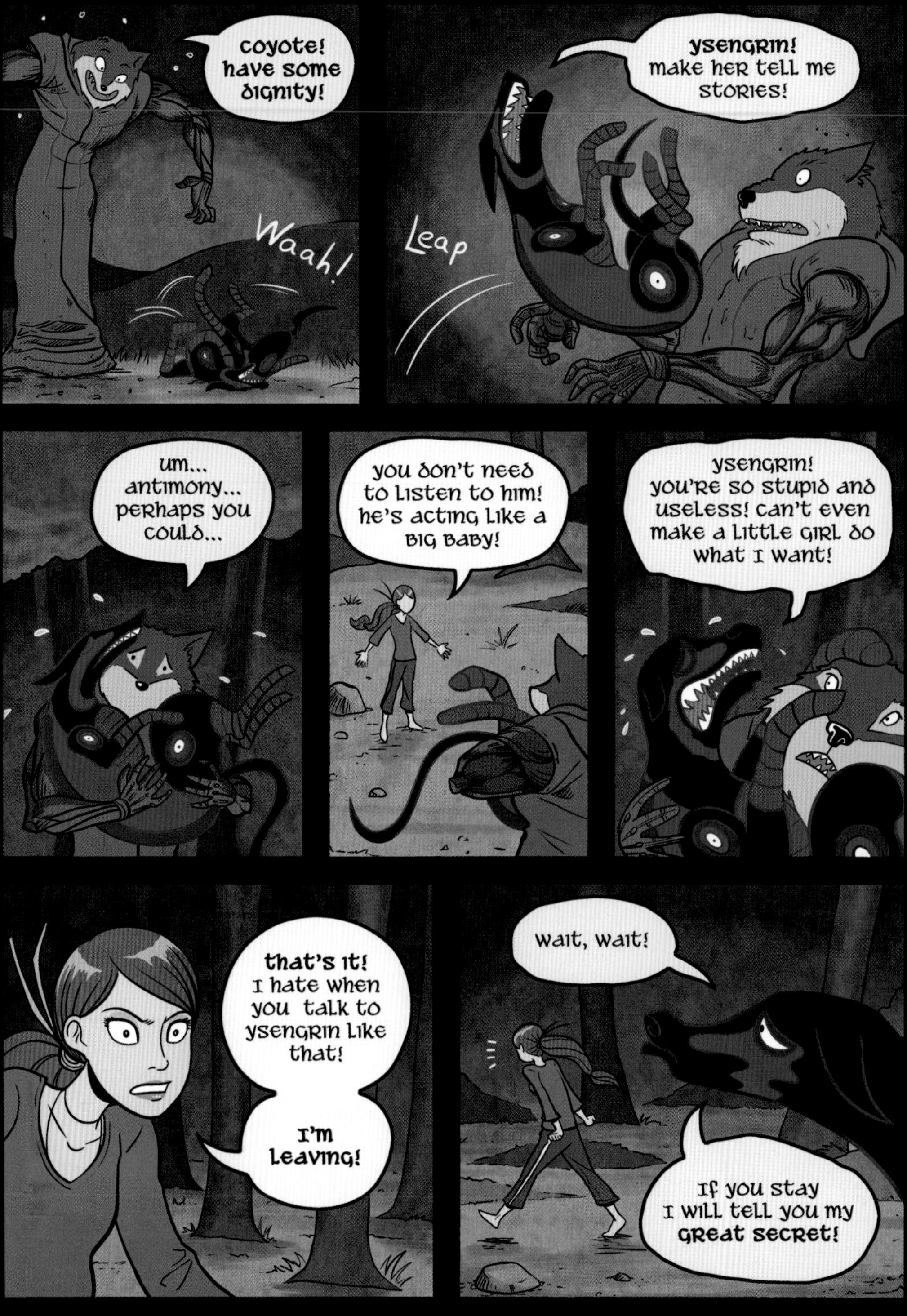
coyote! have some dignity!
Waah!
Leap
ysengrin! make her tell me stories!
um... antimony... perhaps you could...
you don't need to listen to him! he's acting like a big baby!
ysengrin! you're so stupid and useless! can't even make a little girl do what I want!
that's it! I hate when you talk to ysengrin like that!
I'm leaving!
wait, wait!
If you stay I will tell you my great secret!

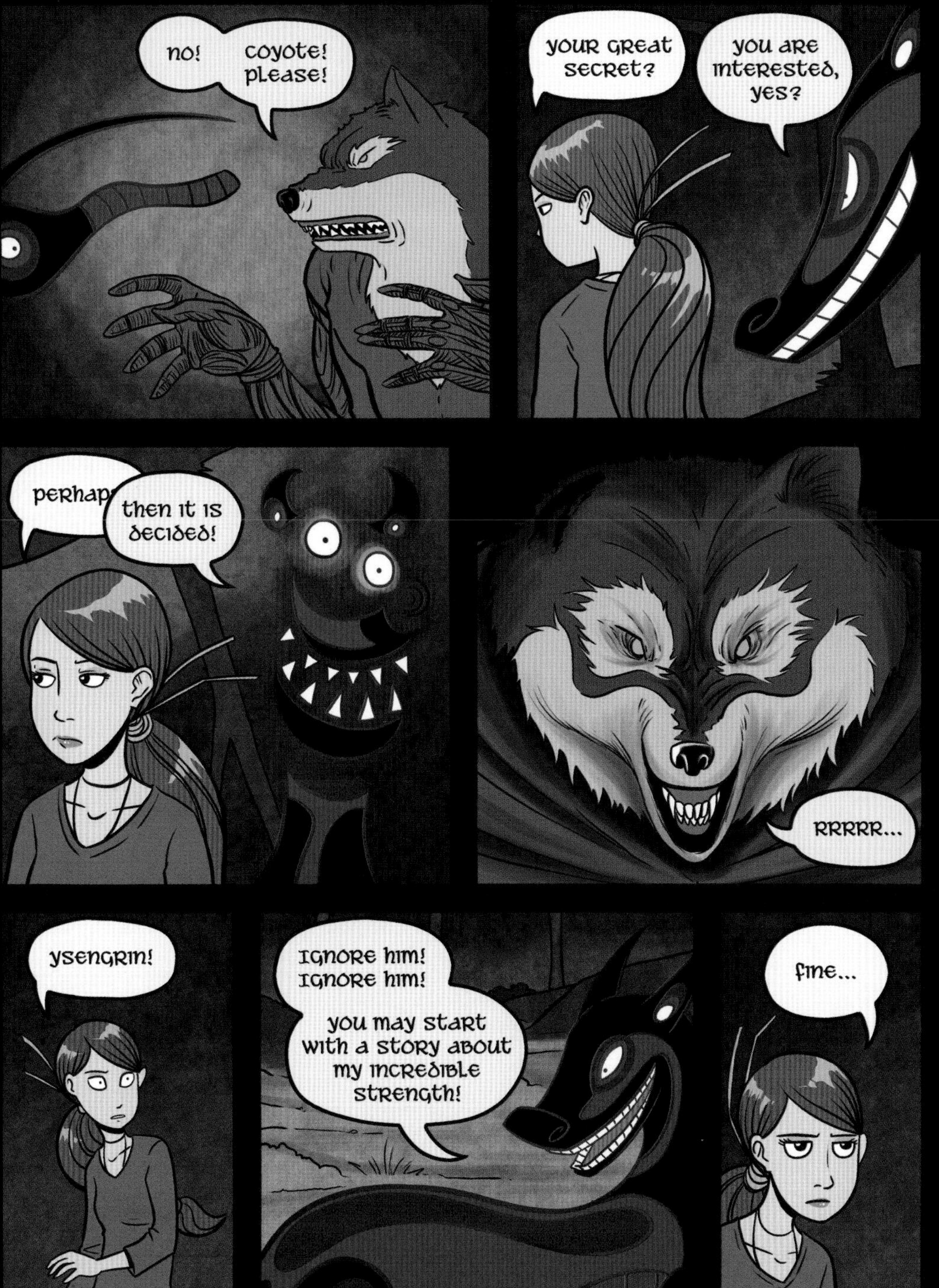

no!
coyote! please!
your great secret?
you are interested, yes?
perhap
then it is decided!
RRRRR...
ysengrin!
ignore him! ignore him!
you may start with a story about my incredible strength!
fine...

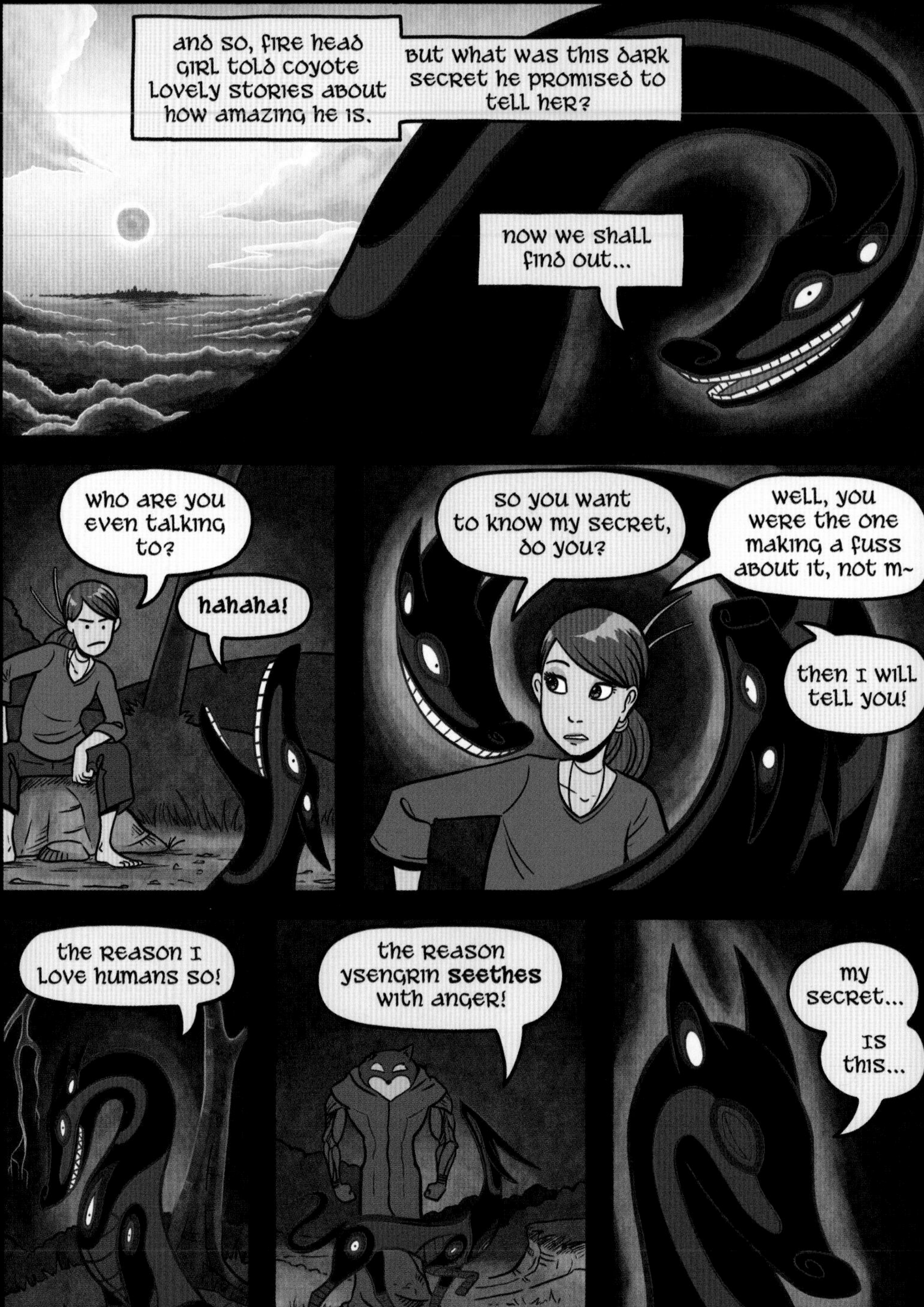
and so, fire head girl told coyote lovely stories about how amazing he is.
but what was this dark secret he promised to tell her?
now we shall find out...
who are you even talking to?
hahaha!
so you want to know my secret, do you?
well, you were the one making a fuss about it, not m~
then I will tell you!
the reason I love humans so!
the reason ysengrin **seethes** with anger!
my secret...
is this...

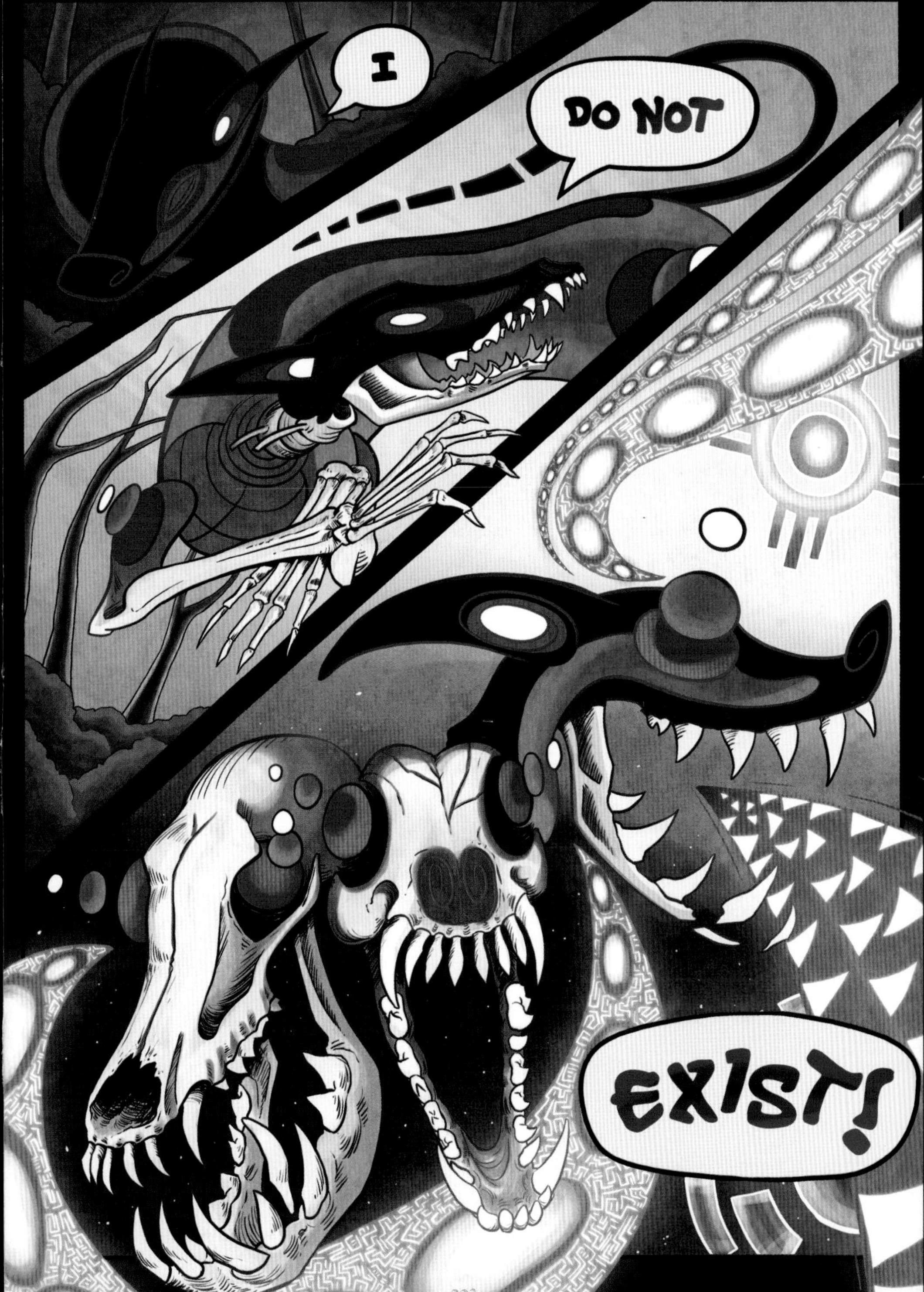
I
DO NOT
EXIST!

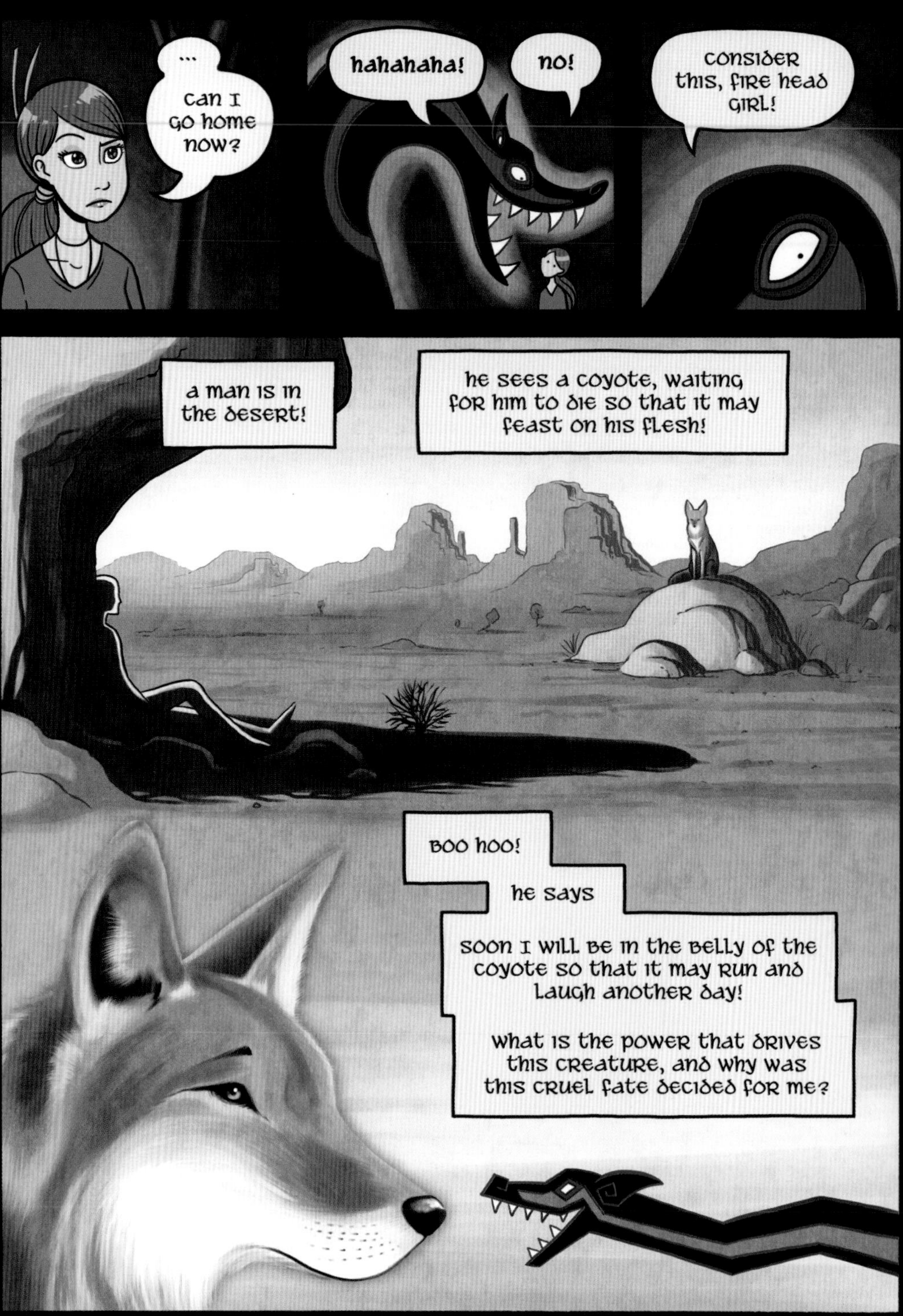
...
can I go home now?
hahahaha!
no!
consider this, fire head girl!
a man is in the desert!
he sees a coyote, waiting for him to die so that it may feast on his flesh!
boo hoo!
he says
soon I will be in the belly of the coyote so that it may run and laugh another day!
what is the power that drives this creature, and why was this cruel fate decided for me?

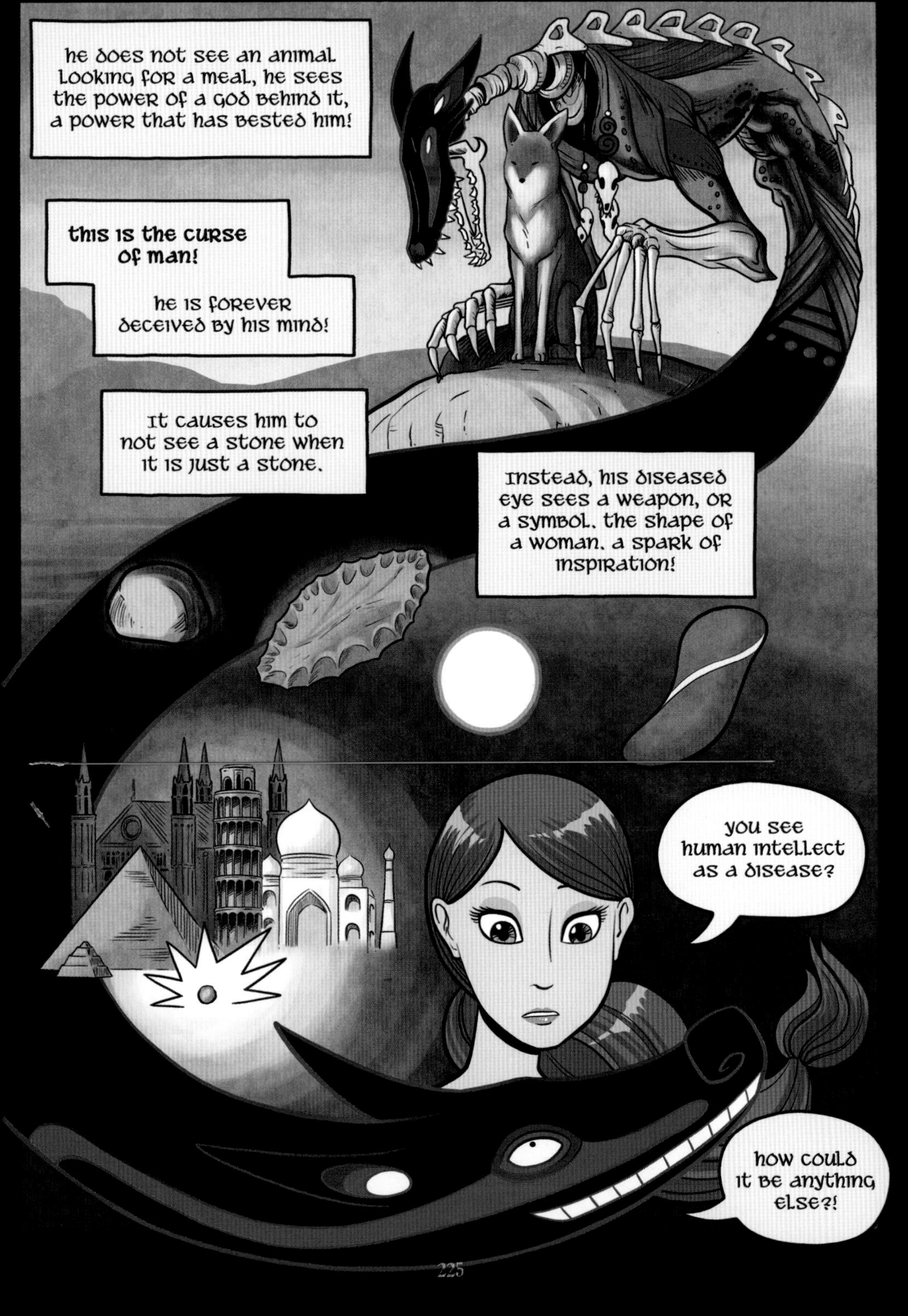
he does not see an animal looking for a meal, he sees the power of a god behind it, a power that has bested him!
this is the curse of man!
he is forever deceived by his mind!
it causes him to not see a stone when it is just a stone.
instead, his diseased eye sees a weapon, or a symbol, the shape of a woman, a spark of inspiration!
you see human intellect as a disease?
how could it be anything else?!

the curse causes man to stumble through this world forever asking questions.
what is this?
what is that?
why is this?
and where he does not find an answer, he places one there himself!
he sees a mountain crumble and says
only a god can do this
and so I am born!
I am aware of how myths originate, coyote.
they were used as teaching tools, as comfort and explanation, passed down generation to generation.
ah! but remember, the man in the desert is **alone** when he dies!
what becomes of **his** comforting story? is it lost forever?
I tell you it is not!
and do you know why?

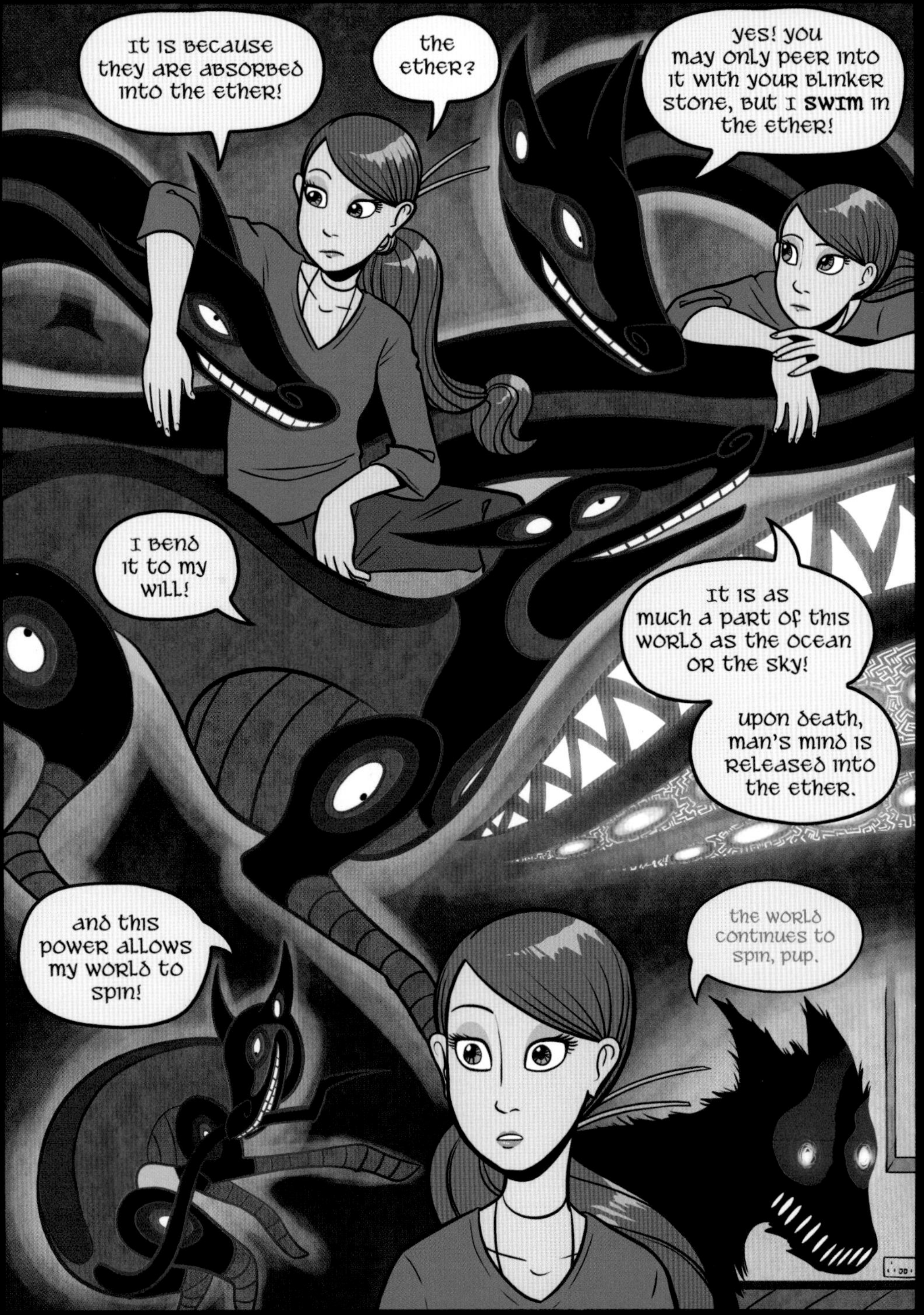
It is because they are absorbed into the ether!
the ether?
yes! you may only peer into it with your blinker stone, but I **swim** in the ether!
I bend it to my will!
It is as much a part of this world as the ocean or the sky!
upon death, man's mind is released into the ether.
and this power allows my world to spin!
the world continues to spin, pup.

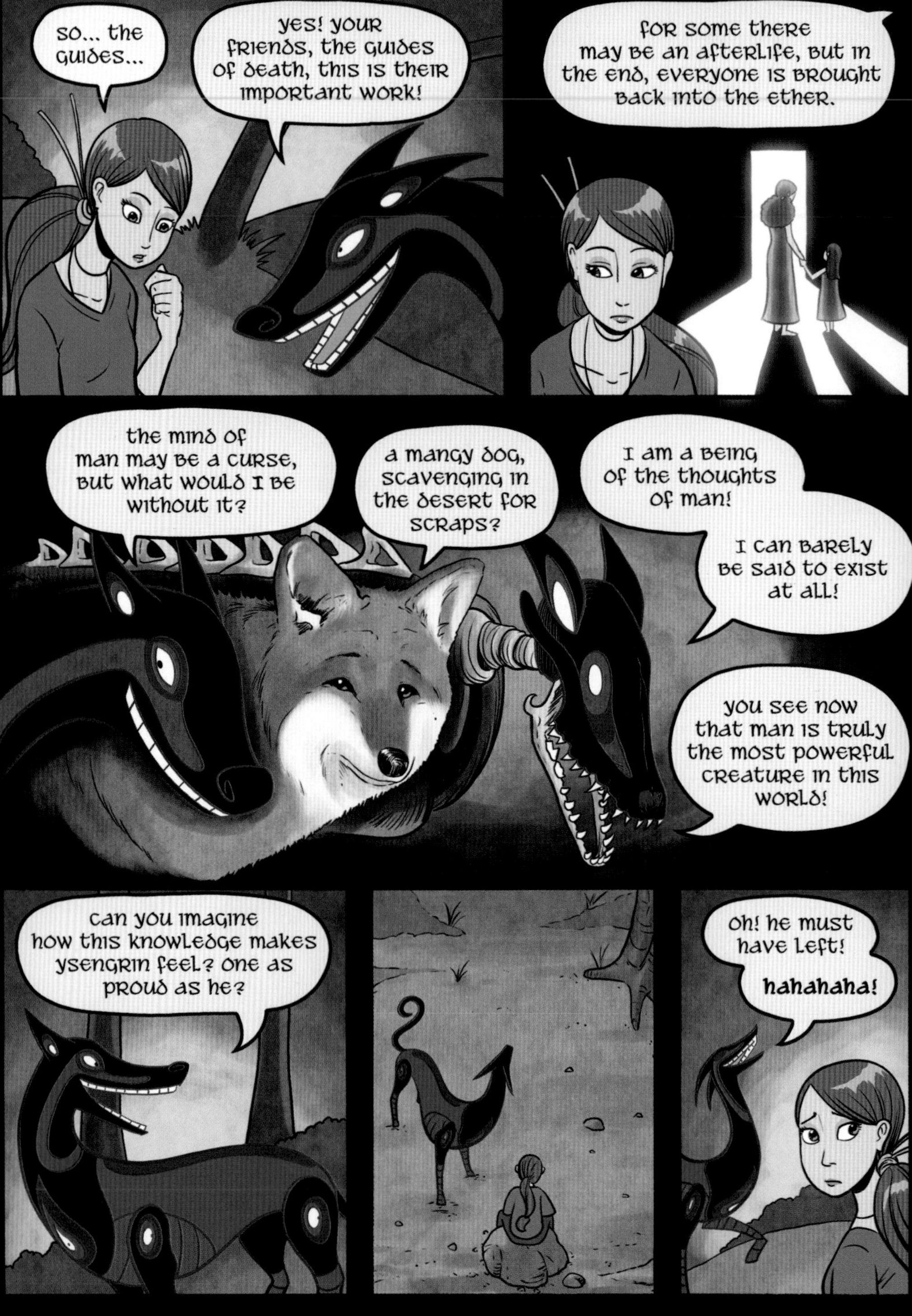
so... the guides...
yes! your friends, the guides of death, this is their important work!
for some there may be an afterlife, but in the end, everyone is brought back into the ether.
the mind of man may be a curse, but what would I be without it?
a mangy dog, scavenging in the desert for scraps?
I am a being of the thoughts of man!
I can barely be said to exist at all!
you see now that man is truly the most powerful creature in this world!
can you imagine how this knowledge makes ysengrin feel? one as proud as he?
oh! he must have left!
hahahaha!

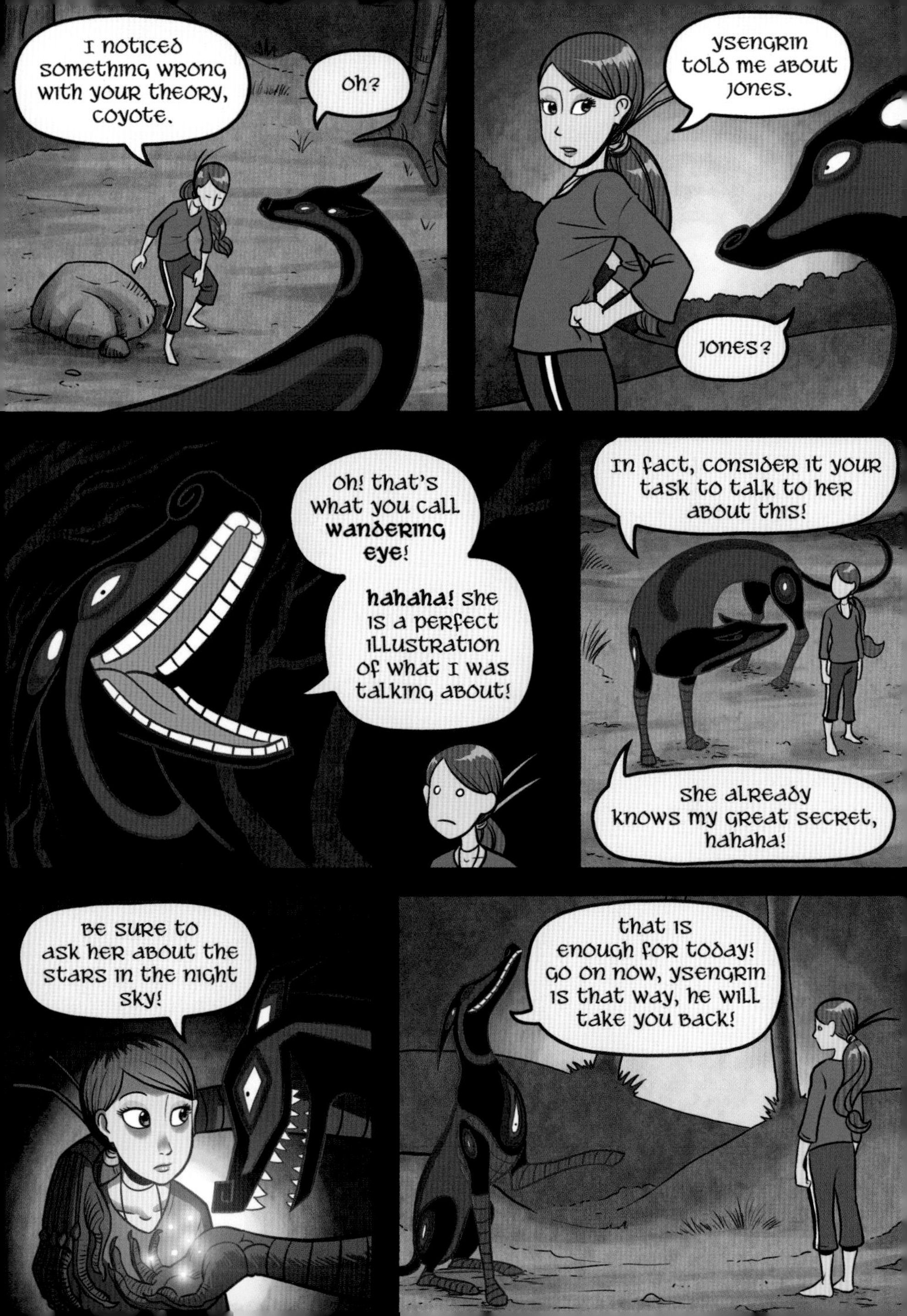
I noticed something wrong with your theory, coyote.
Oh?
ysengrin told me about jones.
jones?
Oh! that's what you call **wandering eye**!
hahaha! she is a perfect illustration of what I was talking about!
In fact, consider it your task to talk to her about this!
she already knows my great secret, hahaha!
Be sure to ask her about the stars in the night sky!
that is enough for today! go on now, ysengrin is that way, he will take you back!

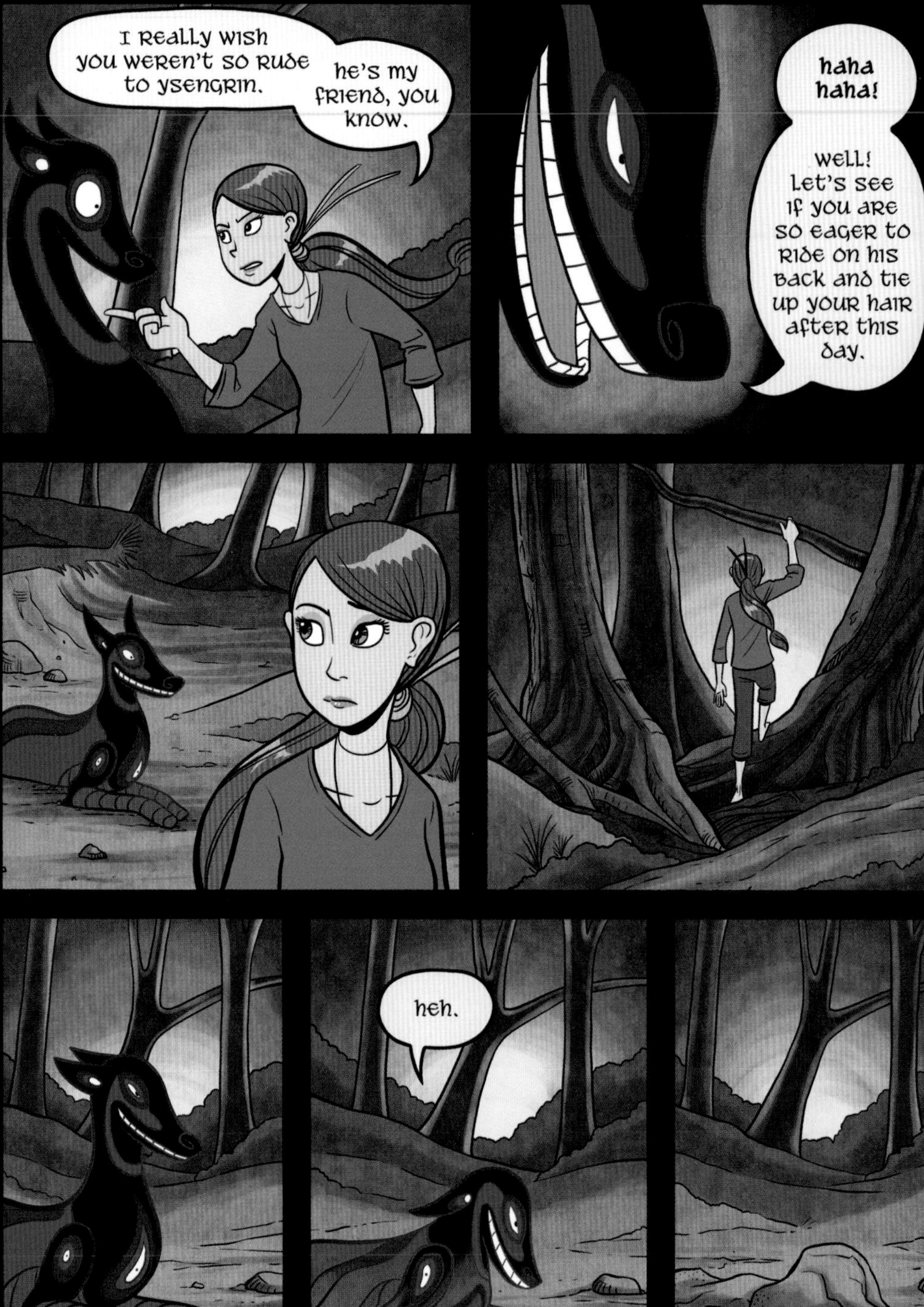
I really wish you weren't so rude to ysengrin.
he's my friend, you know.
haha haha!
well! Let's see if you are so eager to ride on his back and tie up your hair after this day.
heh.

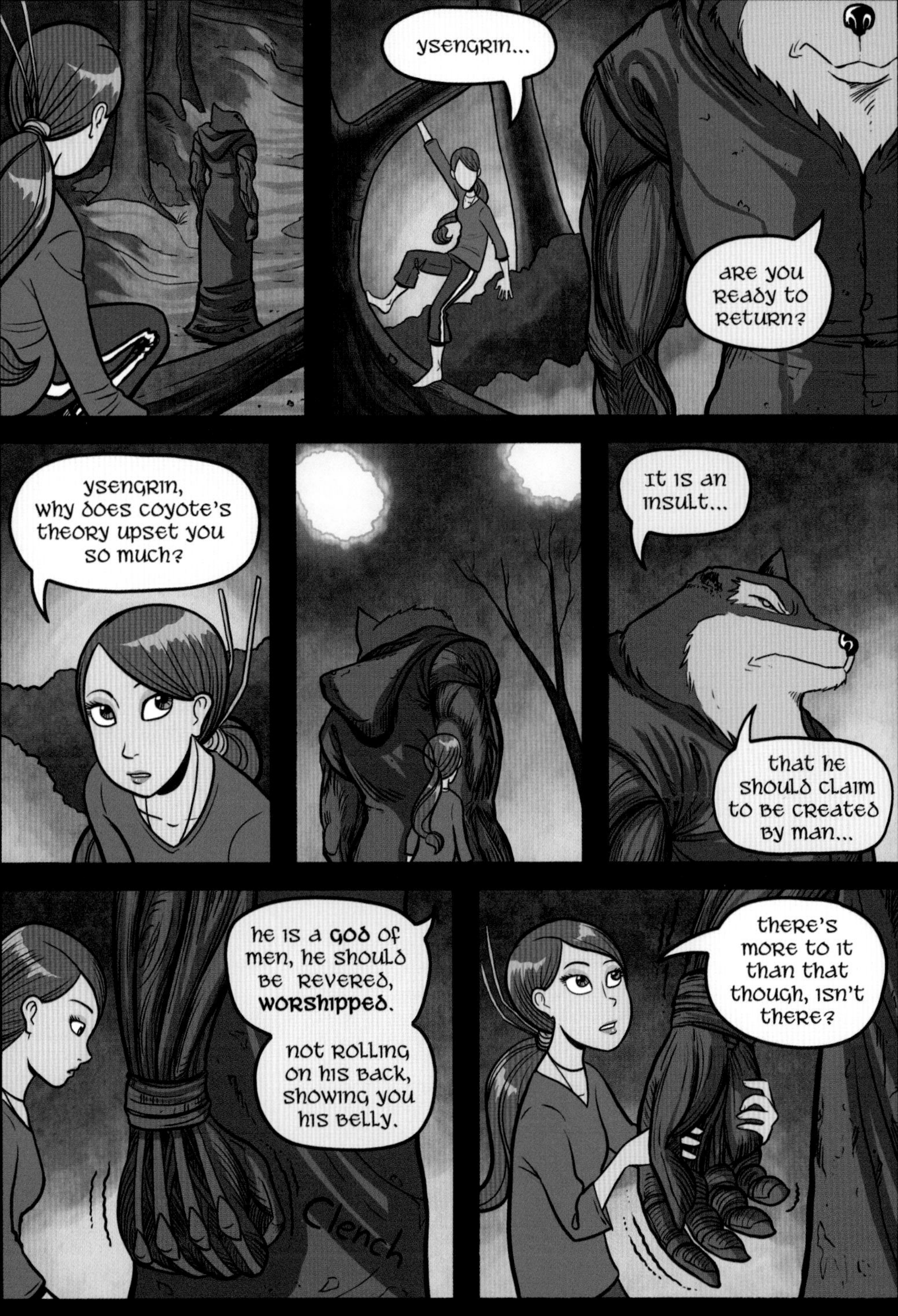
ysengrin...
are you ready to return?
ysengrin, why does coyote's theory upset you so much?
It is an insult...
that he should claim to be created by man...
he is a **god** of men, he should be revered, **worshipped**.
not rolling on his back, showing you his belly.
Clench
there's more to it than that though, isn't there?

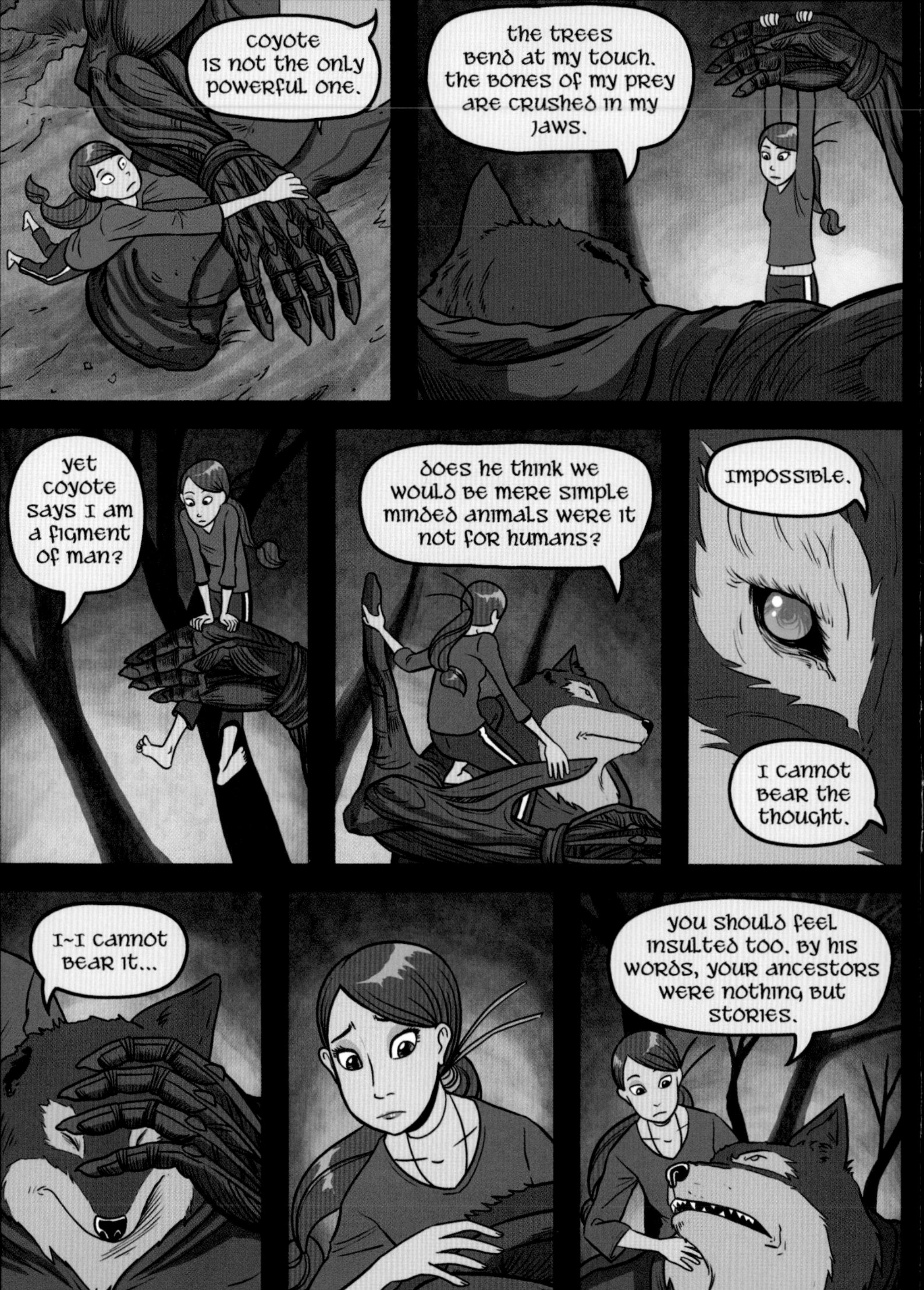
coyote is not the only powerful one.
the trees bend at my touch. the bones of my prey are crushed in my jaws.
yet coyote says I am a figment of man?
does he think we would be mere simple minded animals were it not for humans?
impossible.
I cannot bear the thought.
I~I cannot bear it...
you should feel insulted too. by his words, your ancestors were nothing but stories.

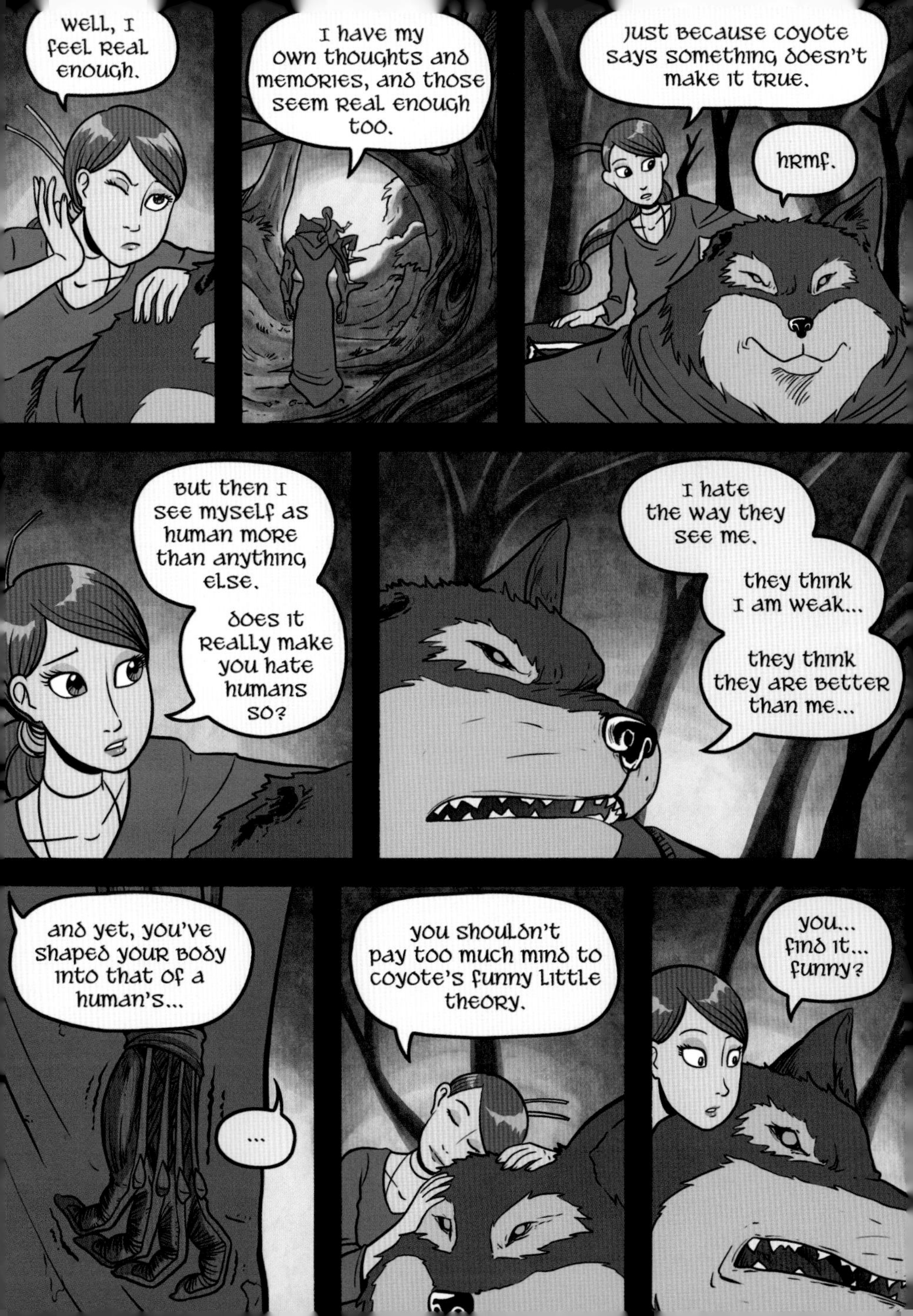
well, I feel real enough.
I have my own thoughts and memories, and those seem real enough too.
just because coyote says something doesn't make it true.
hrmf.
but then I see myself as human more than anything else.
does it really make you hate humans so?
I hate the way they see me.
they think I am weak...
they think they are better than me...
and yet, you've shaped your body into that of a human's...
...
you shouldn't pay too much mind to coyote's funny little theory.
you... find it... funny?

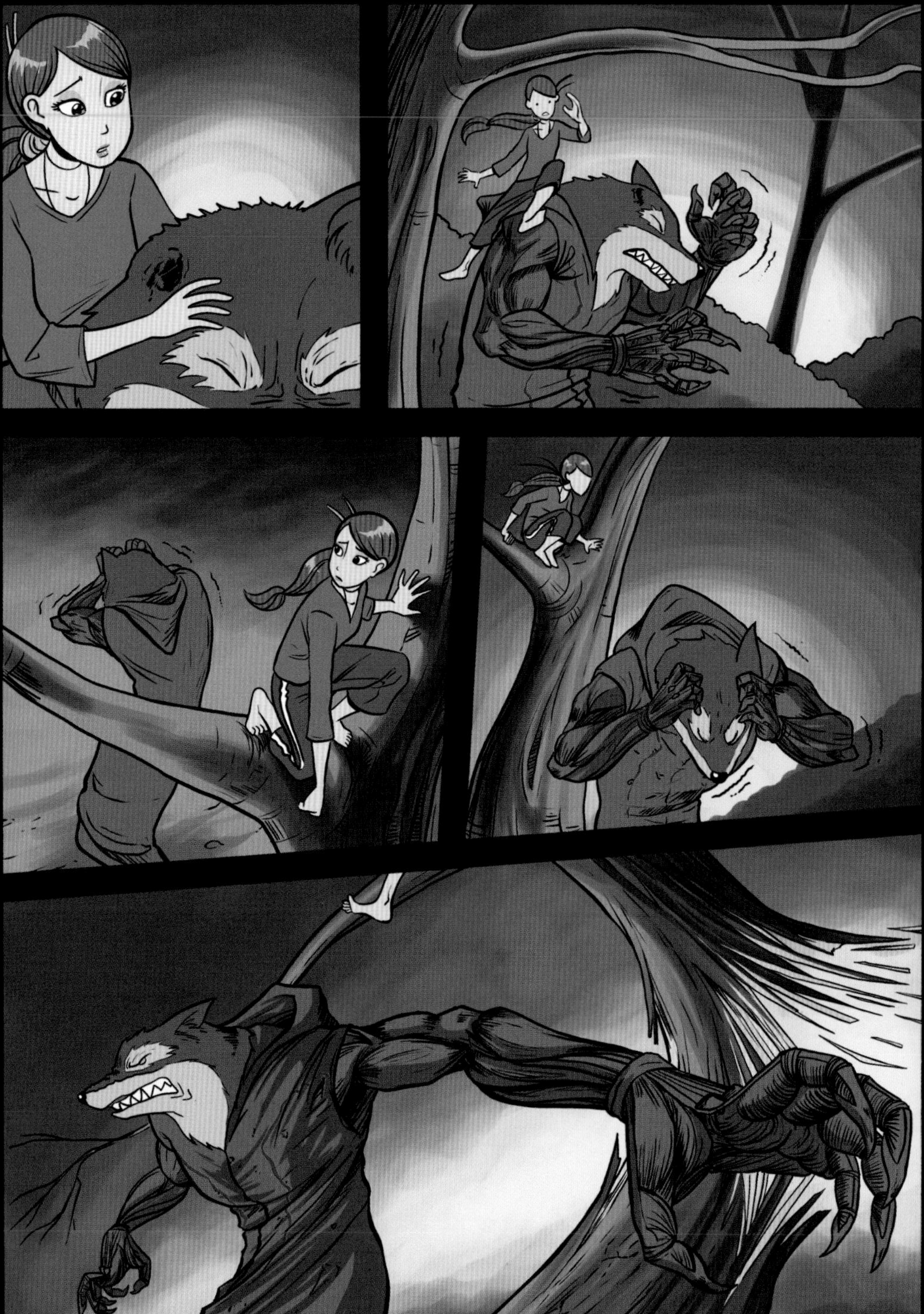

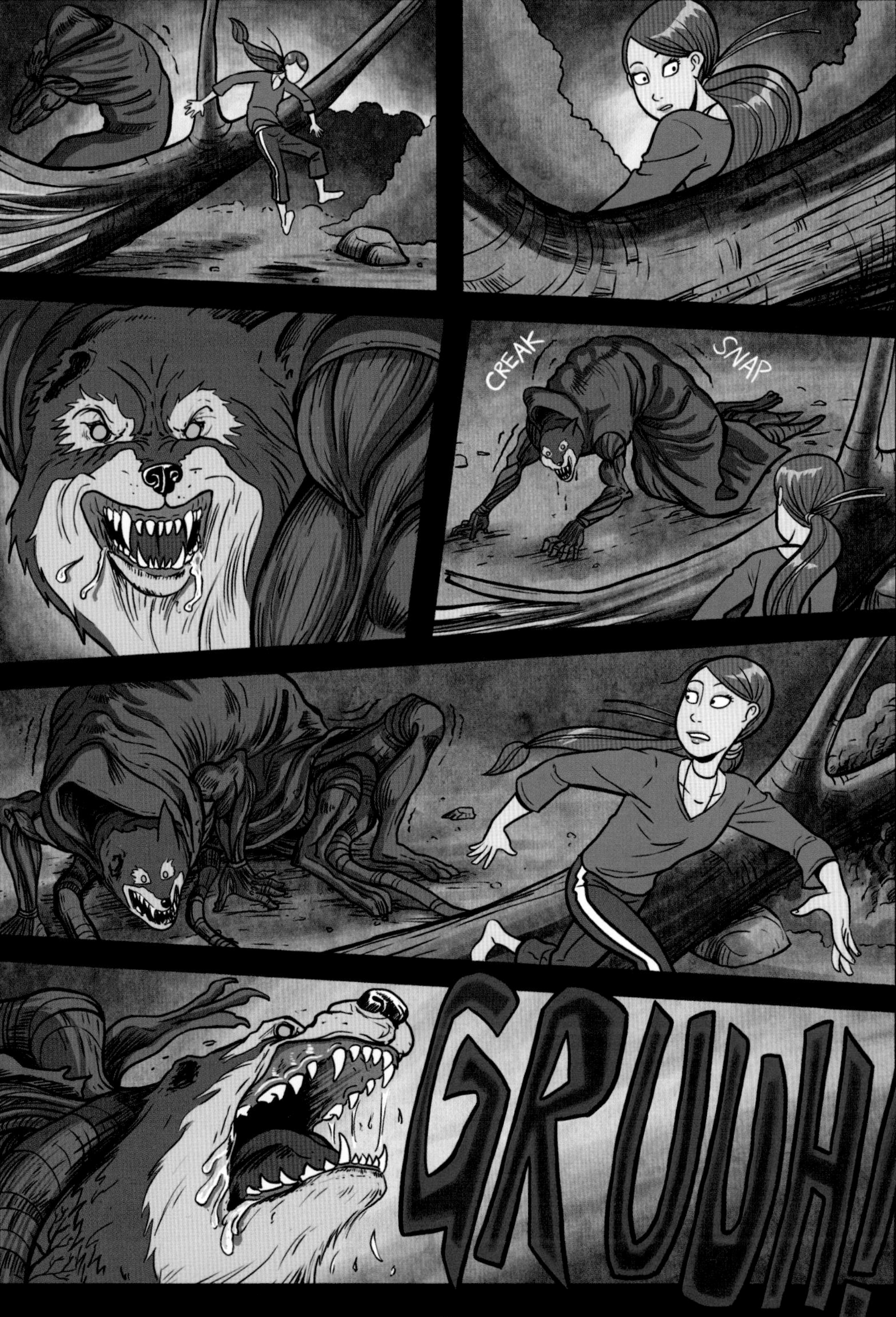
CREAK
SNAP
GRUUH!

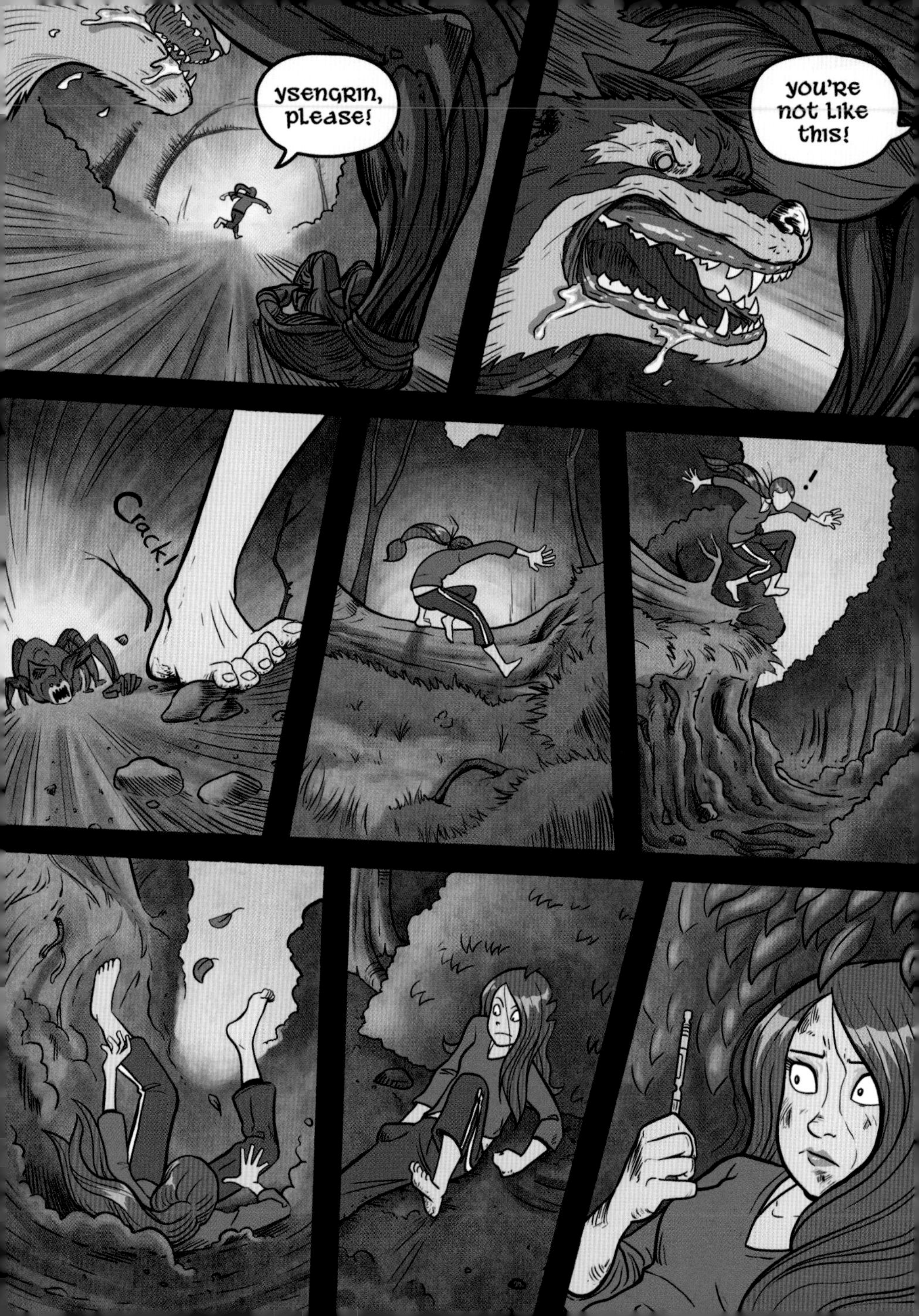
ysengrin, please!
you're not like this!
Crack!
!

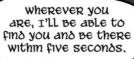

at the first sign of trouble, snap this beacon.

wherever you are, I'll be able to find you and be there within five seconds.

five...

SNAP

four...

Rustle

th~three...

two...

o...one...

...
oh, ysengrin...

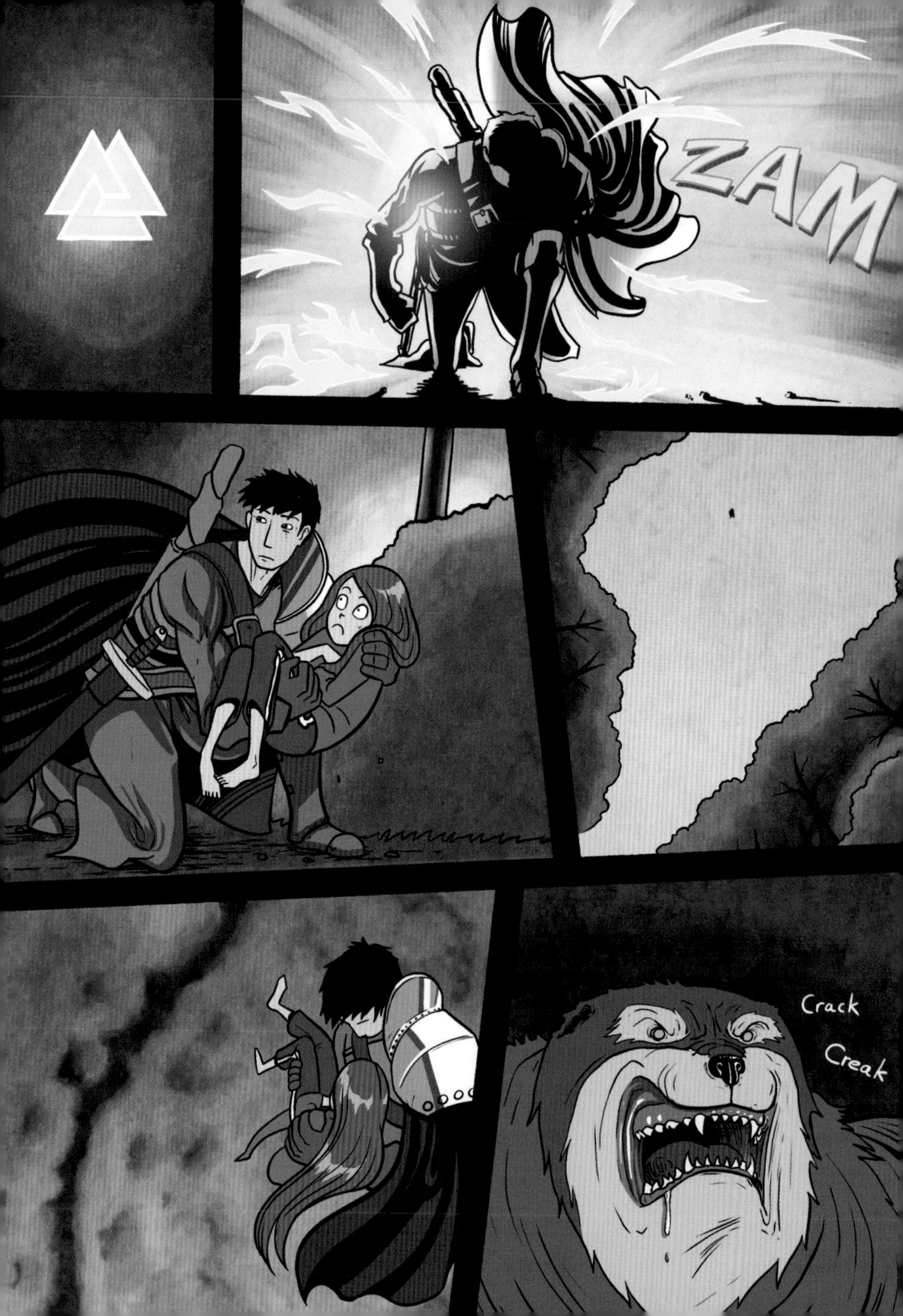
ZAM
Crack
Creak

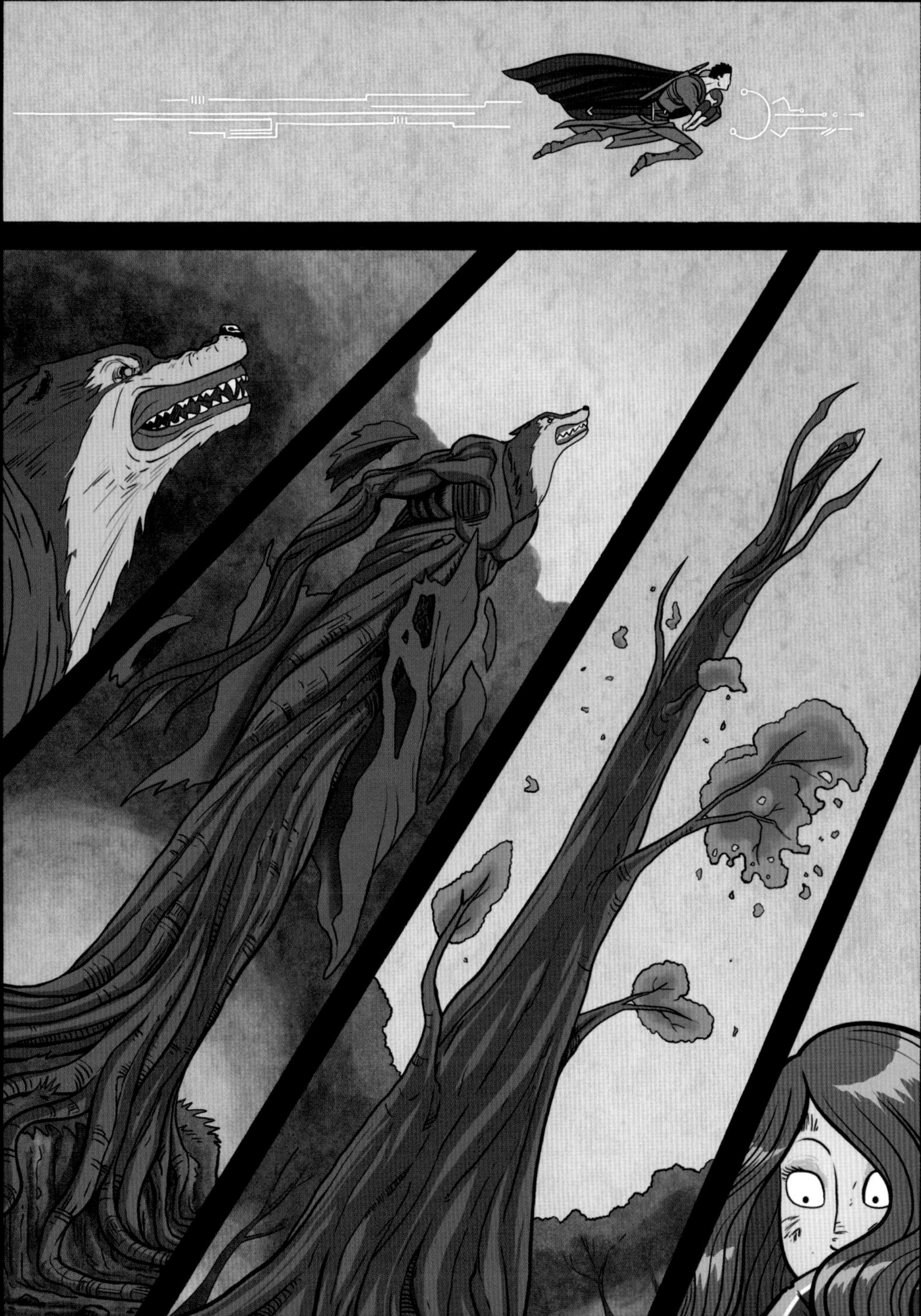

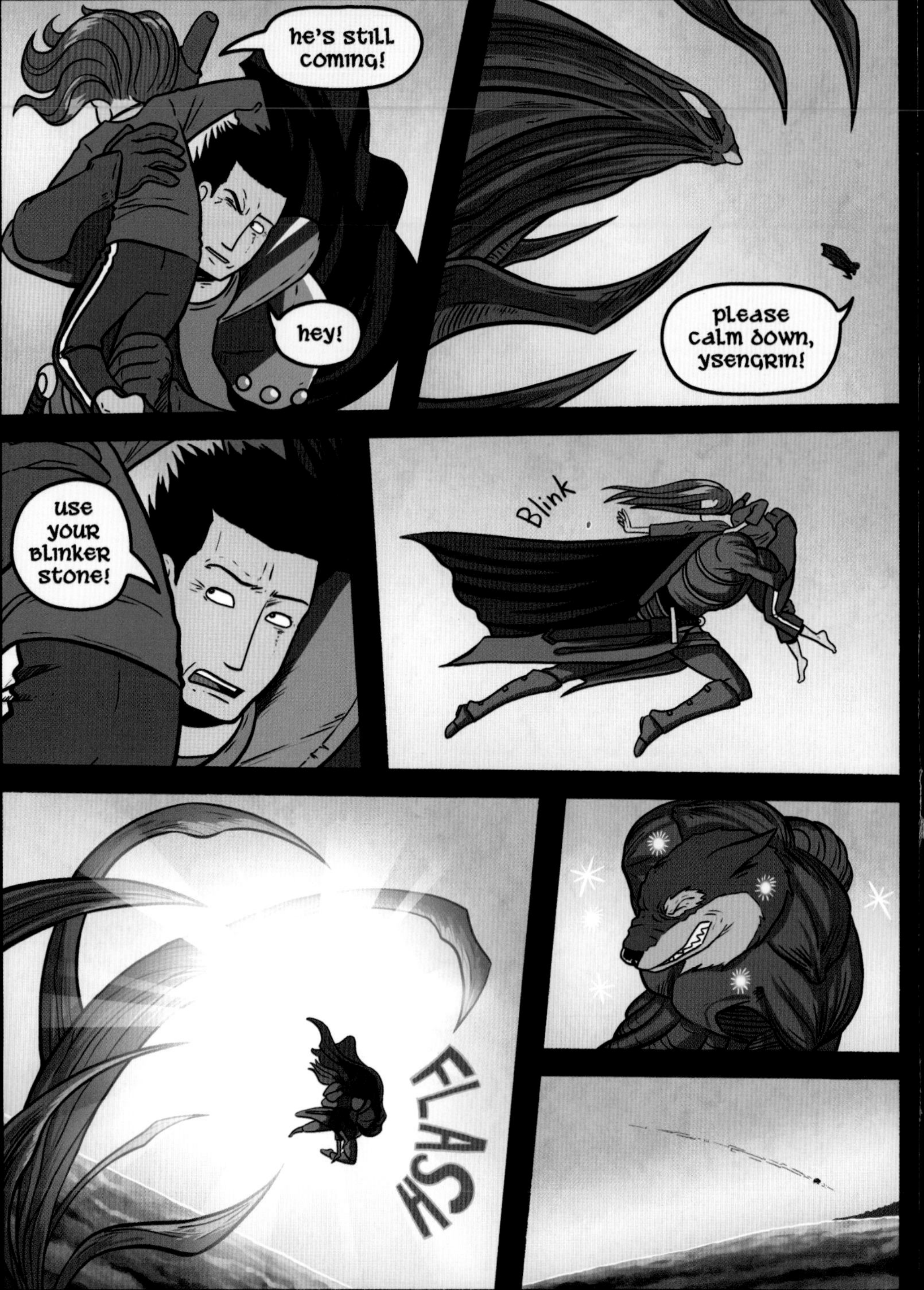
he's still coming!
hey!
please calm down, ysengrin!
use your blinker stone!
Blink
FLASH

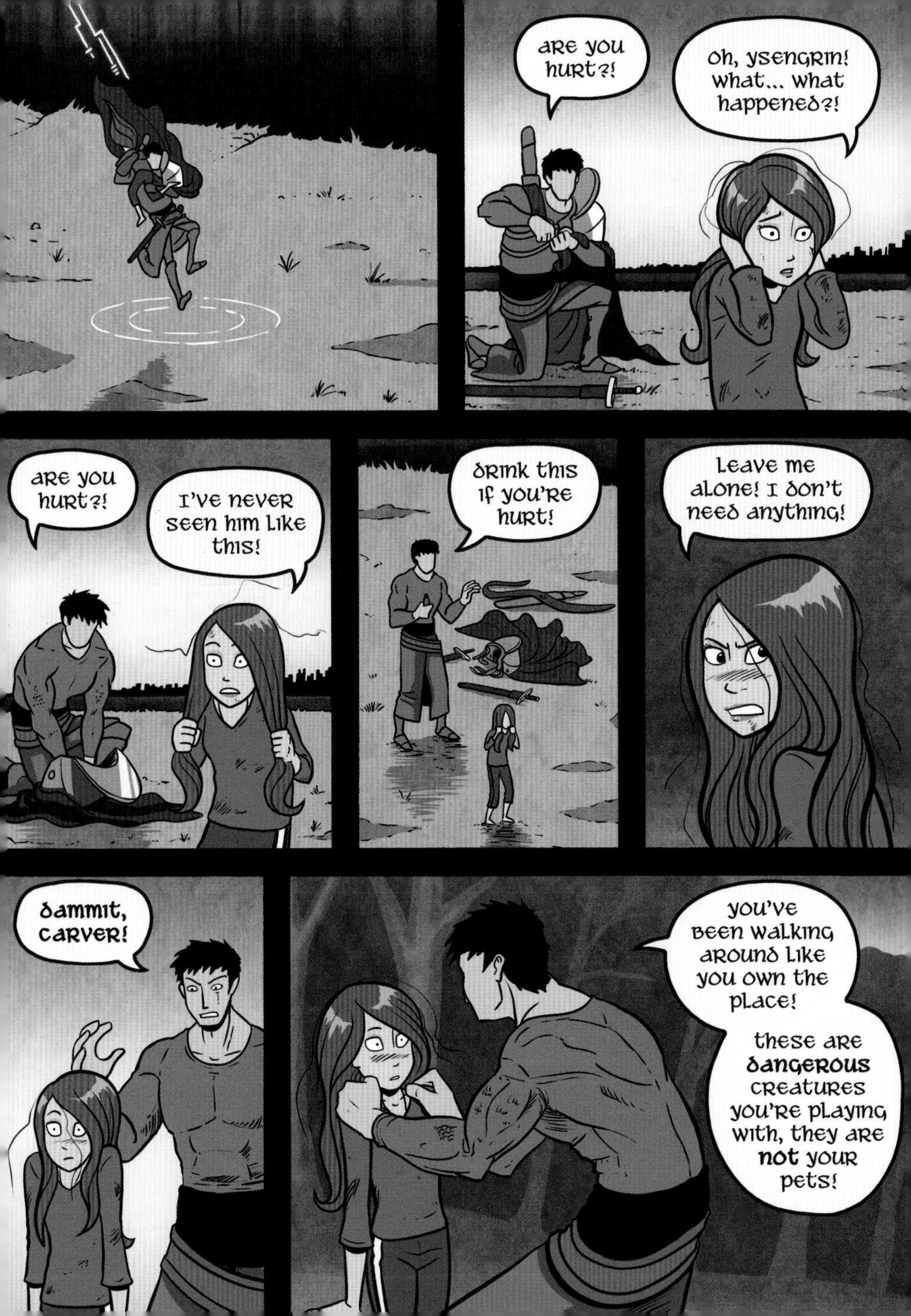

are you hurt?!
oh, ysengrin! what... what happened?!
are you hurt?!
I've never seen him like this!
drink this if you're hurt!
leave me alone! I don't need anything!
dammit, carver!
you've been walking around like you own the place!
these are **dangerous** creatures you're playing with, they are **not** your pets!

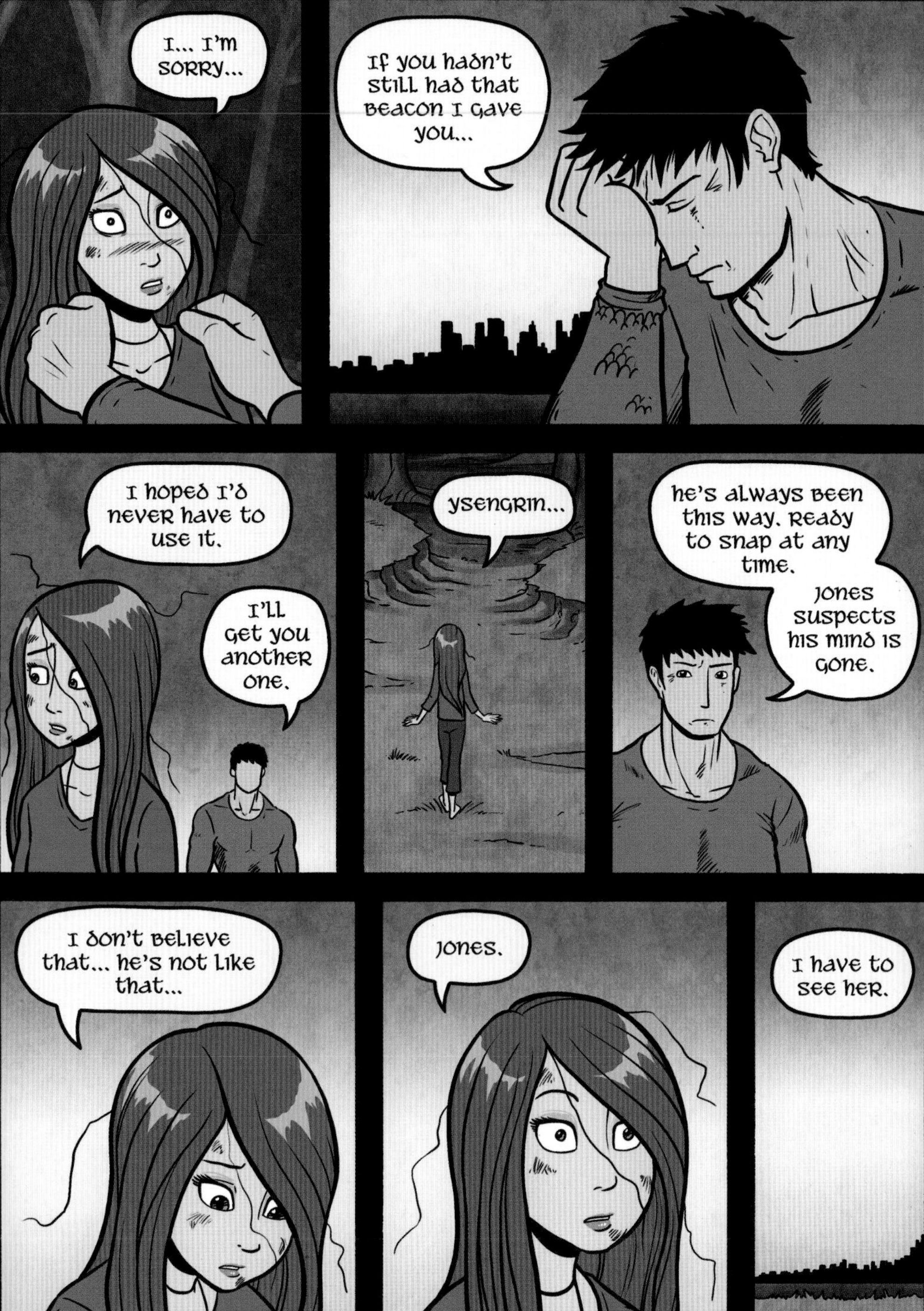
I... I'm SORRY...
If you hadn't still had that beacon I gave you...
I hoped I'd never have to use it.
I'll get you another one.
YSENGRIN...
he's always been this way. Ready to snap at any time.
Jones suspects his mind is gone.
I don't believe that... he's not like that...
Jones.
I have to see her.

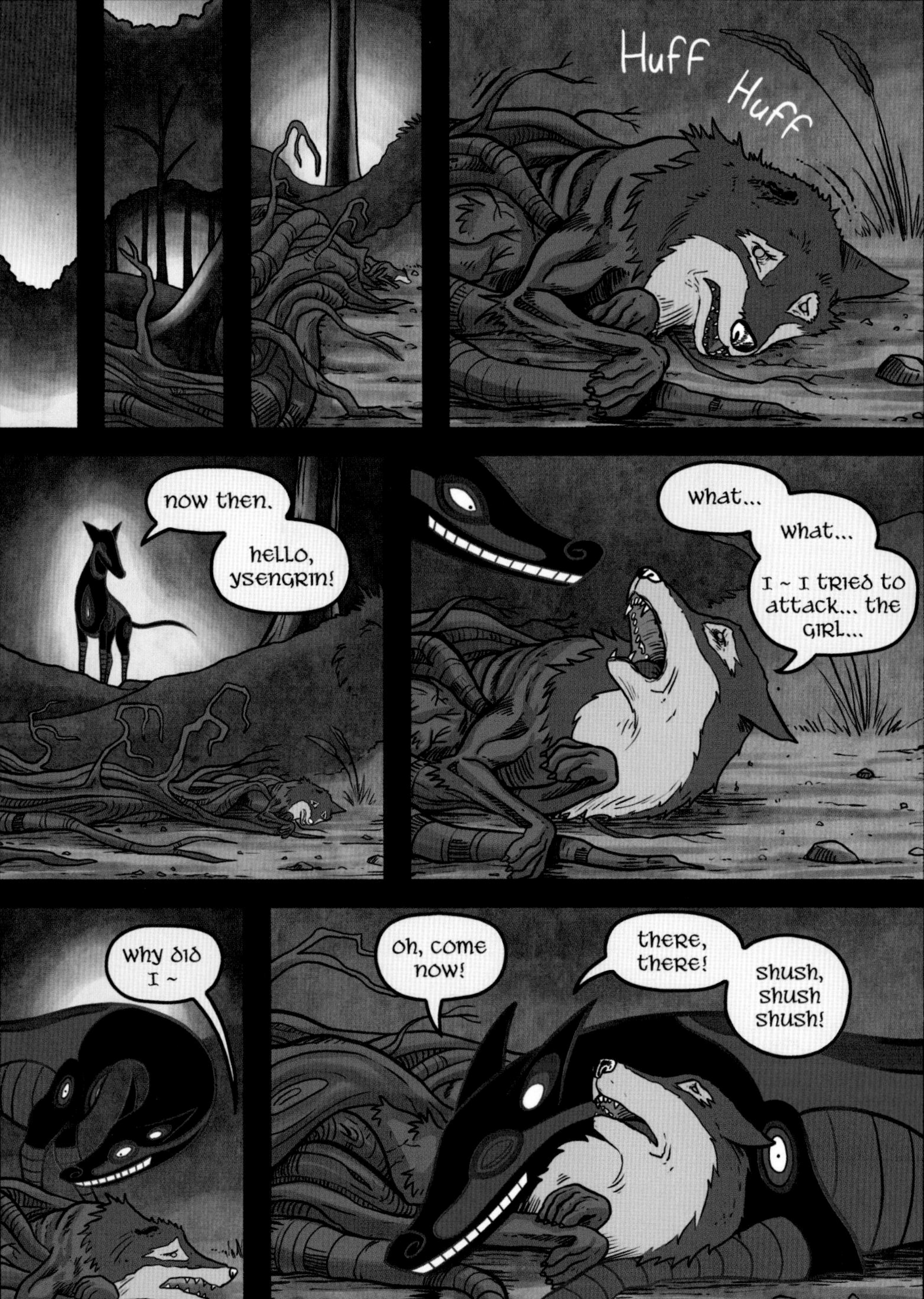
Huff
Huff
now then.
hello, ysengrin!
what...
what...
I ~ I tried to attack... the girl...
why did I ~
oh, come now!
there, there!
shush, shush shush!

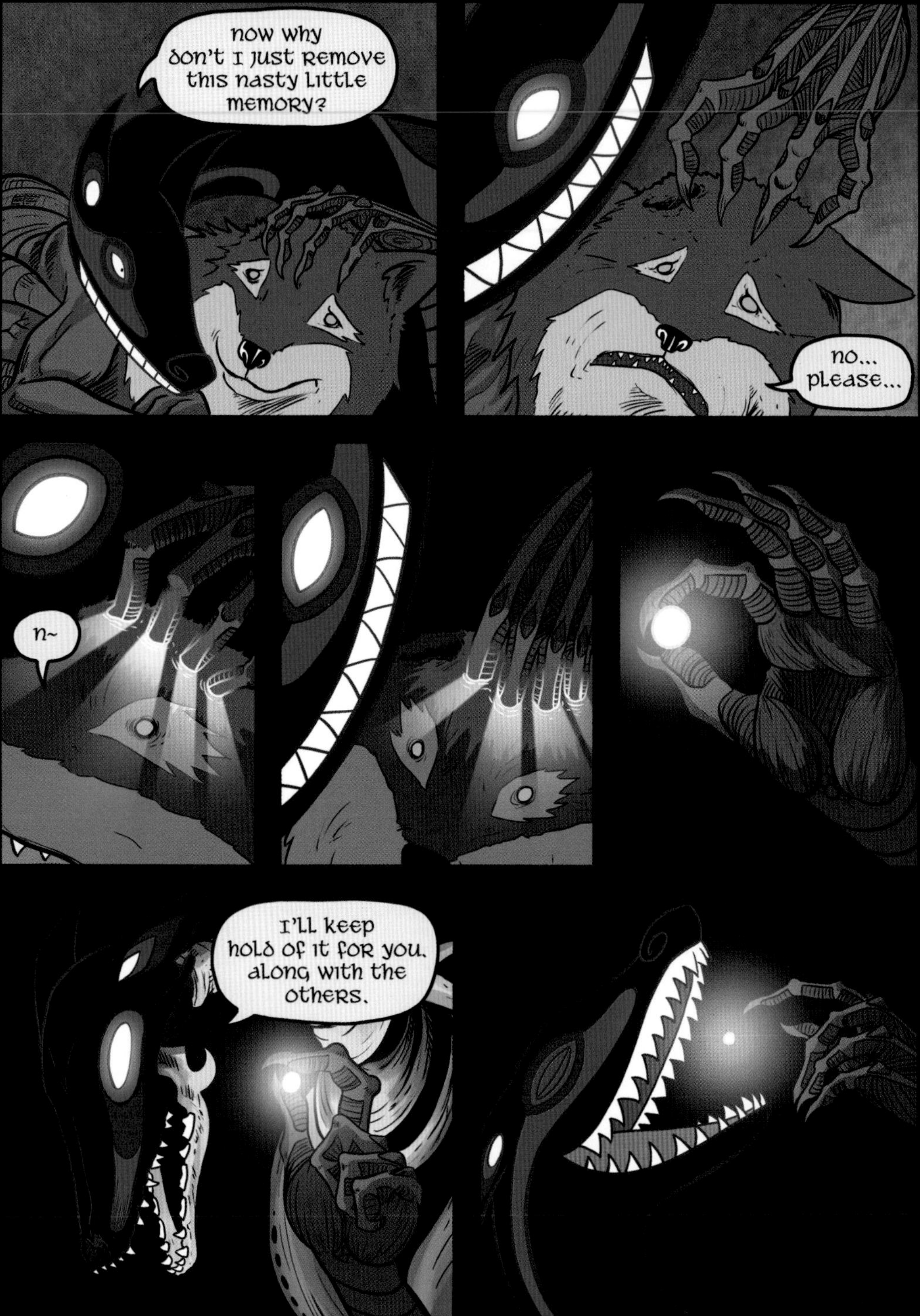
now why don't I just remove this nasty little memory?
no... please...
n~
I'll keep hold of it for you. along with the others.

STAND BACK UP AND PULL YOURSELF TOGETHER!

COME ALONG NOW!

YES, COYOTE.

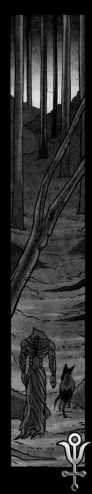

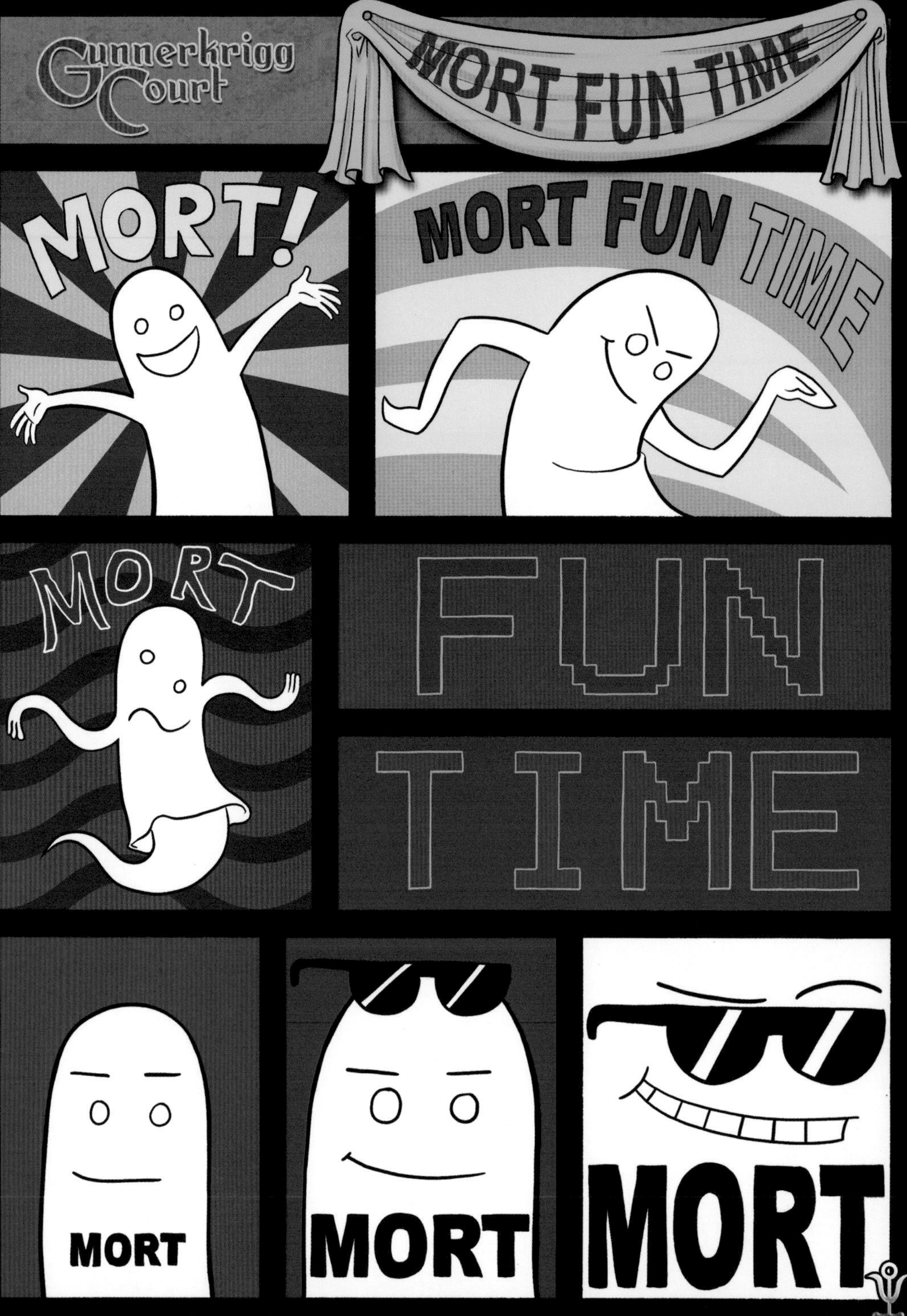
Gunnerkrigg Court
MORT FUN TIME
MORT!
MORT FUN TIME
MORT
FUN
TIME
MORT
MORT
MORT

Gunnerkrigg Court

Chapter 40:

The Stone

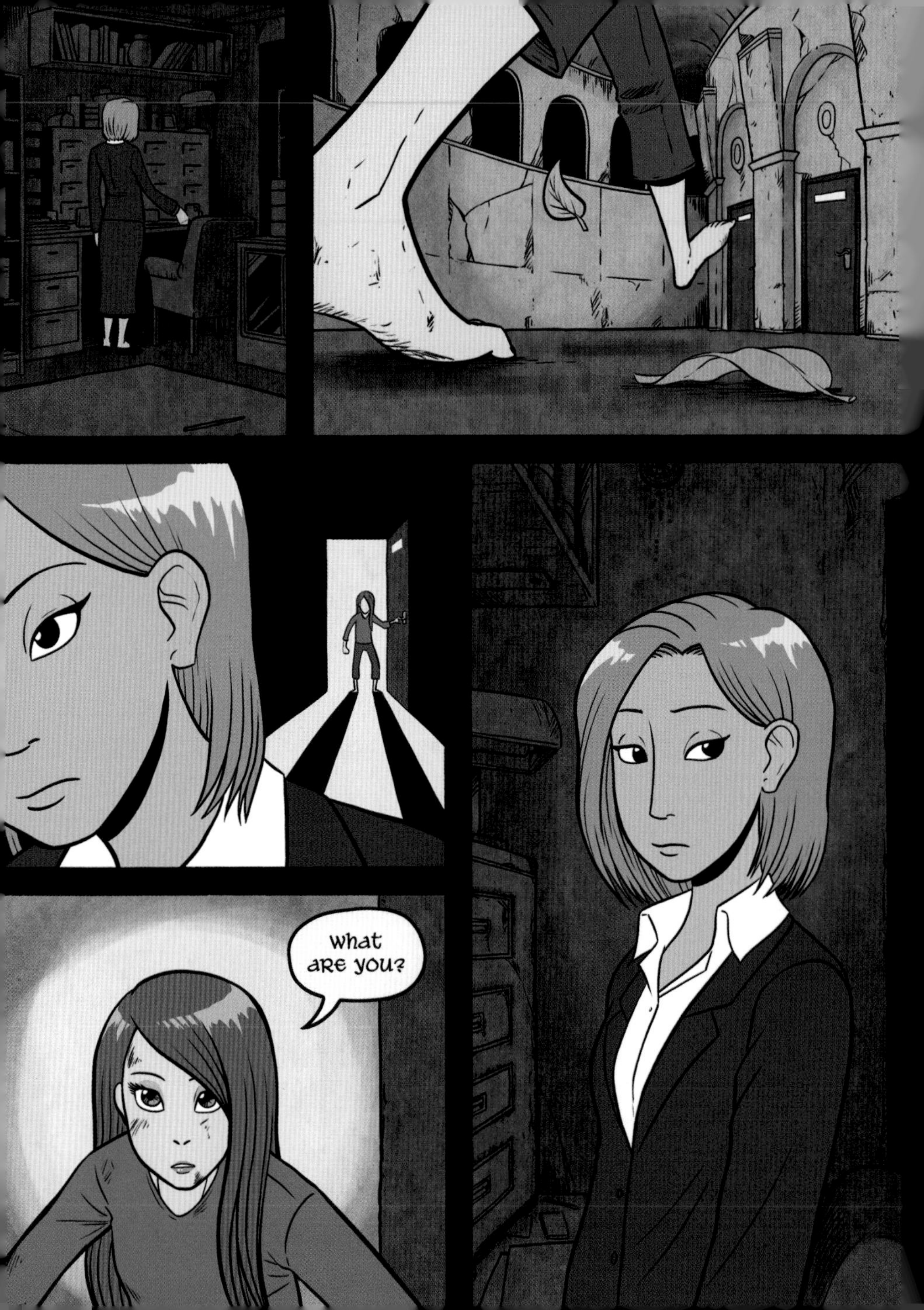
What are you?

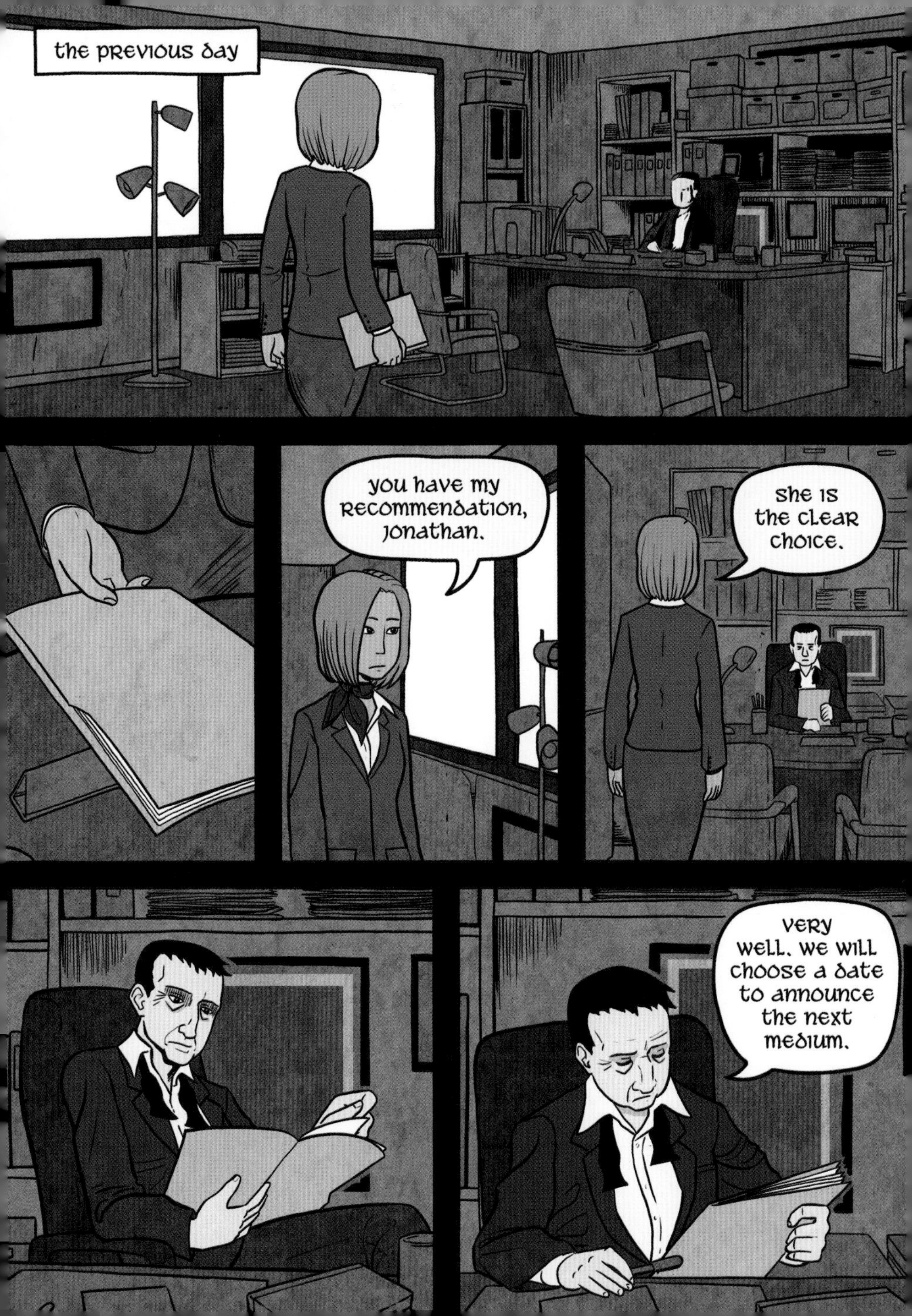

the previous day
you have my recommendation, jonathan.
she is the clear choice.
very well. we will choose a date to announce the next medium.

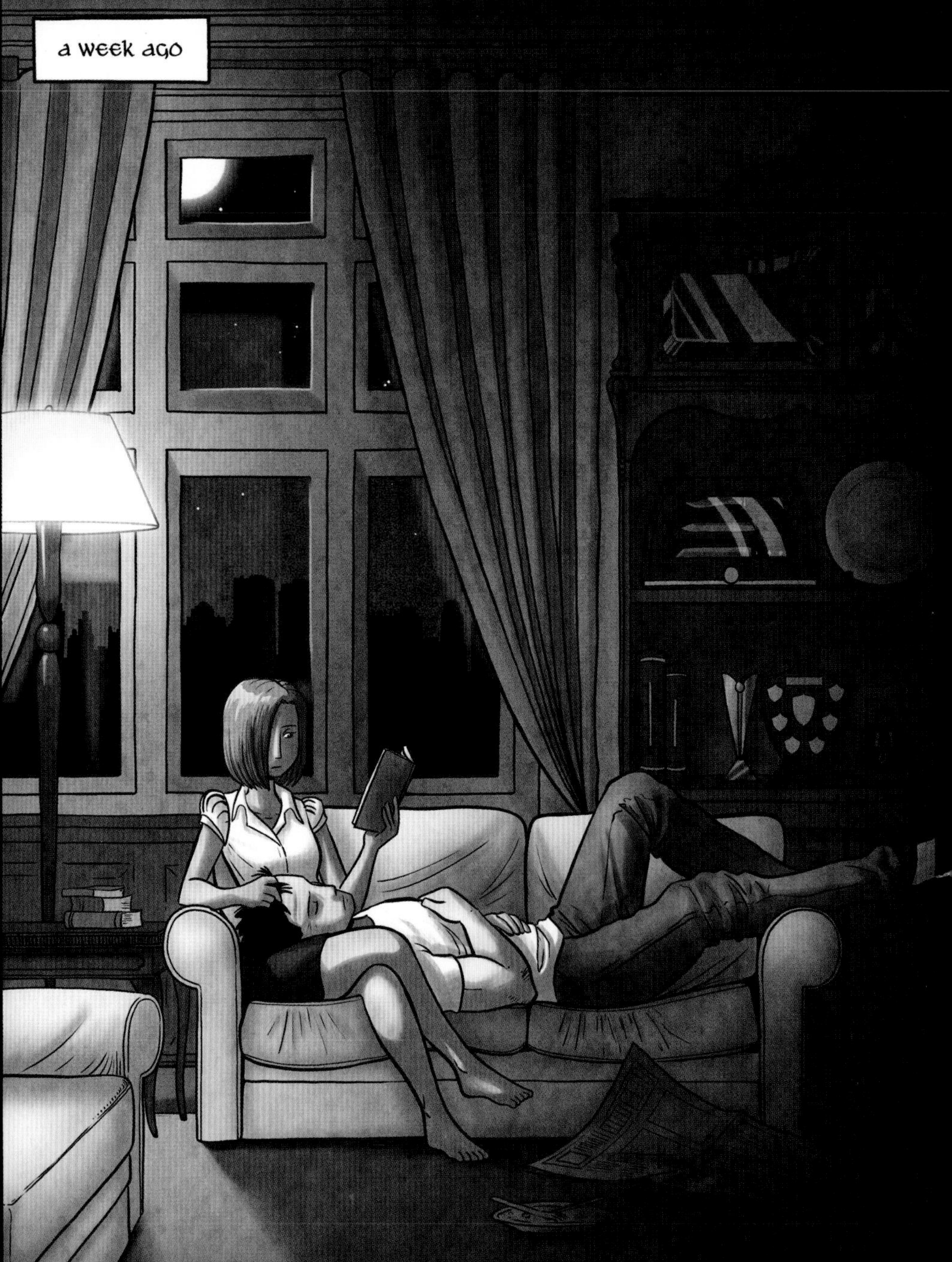
a week ago

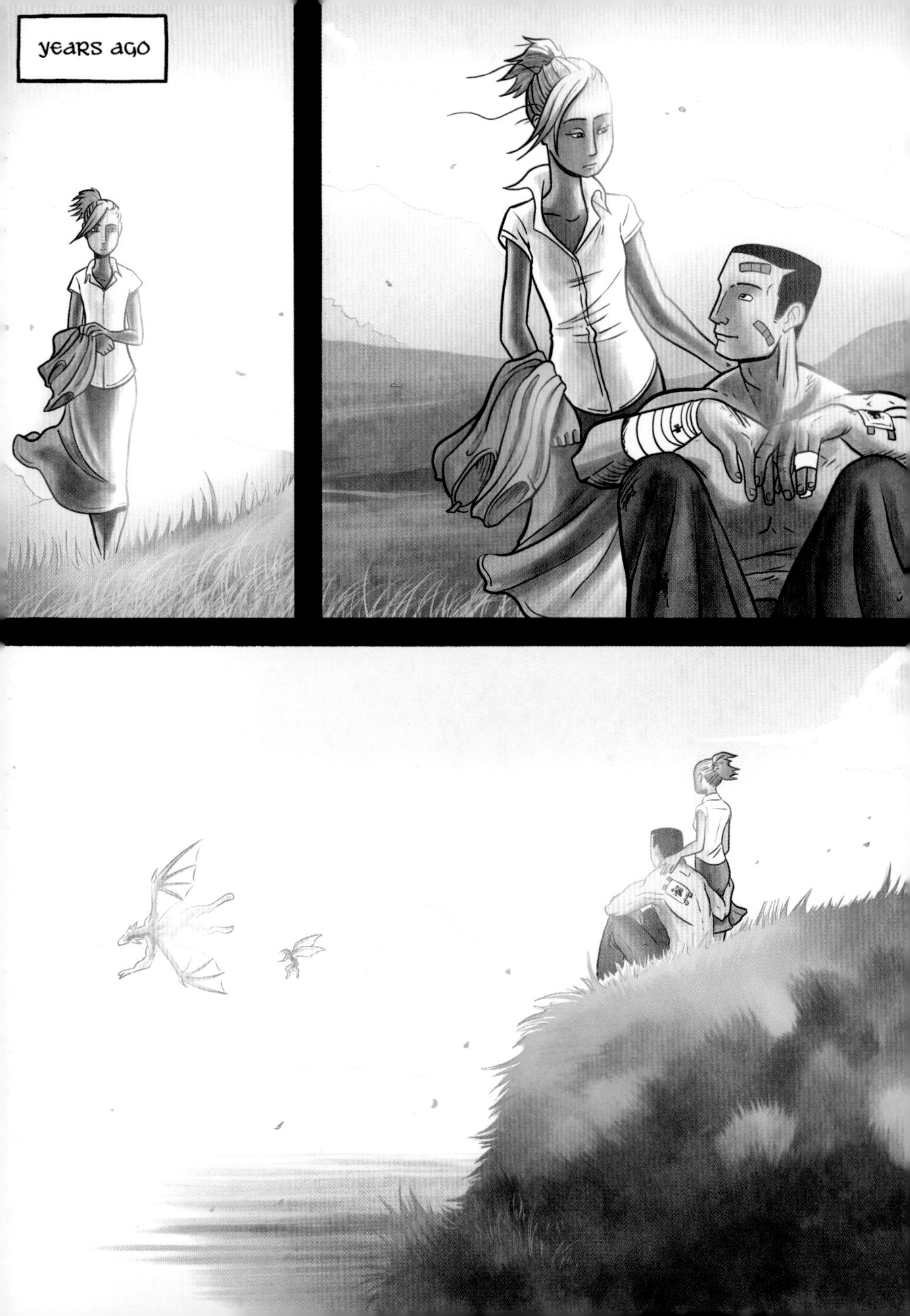
YEARS AGO

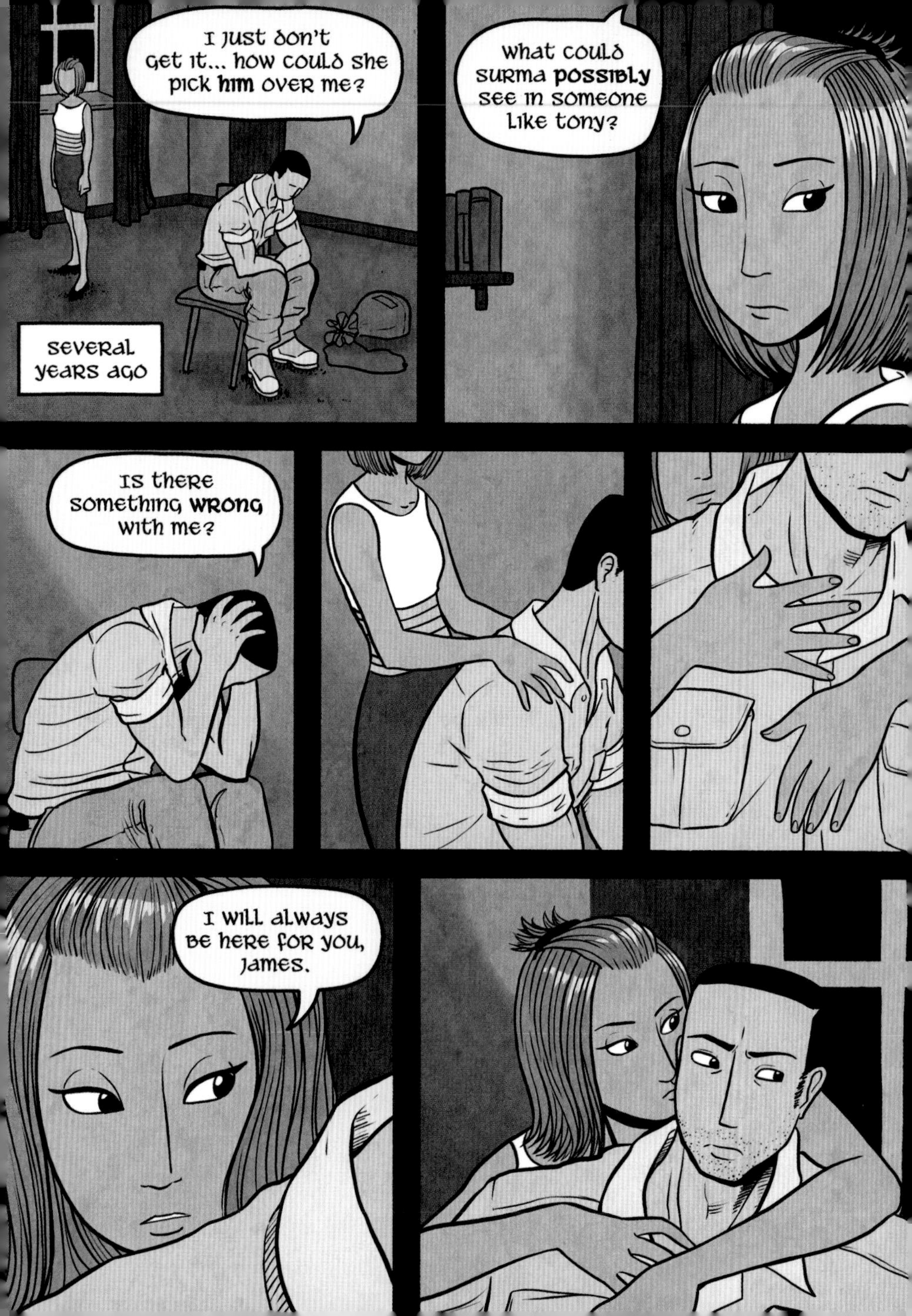
I JUST DON'T GET IT... HOW COULD SHE PICK **HIM** OVER ME?
SEVERAL YEARS AGO
WHAT COULD SURMA **POSSIBLY** SEE IN SOMEONE LIKE TONY?
IS THERE SOMETHING **WRONG** WITH ME?
I WILL ALWAYS BE HERE FOR YOU, JAMES.

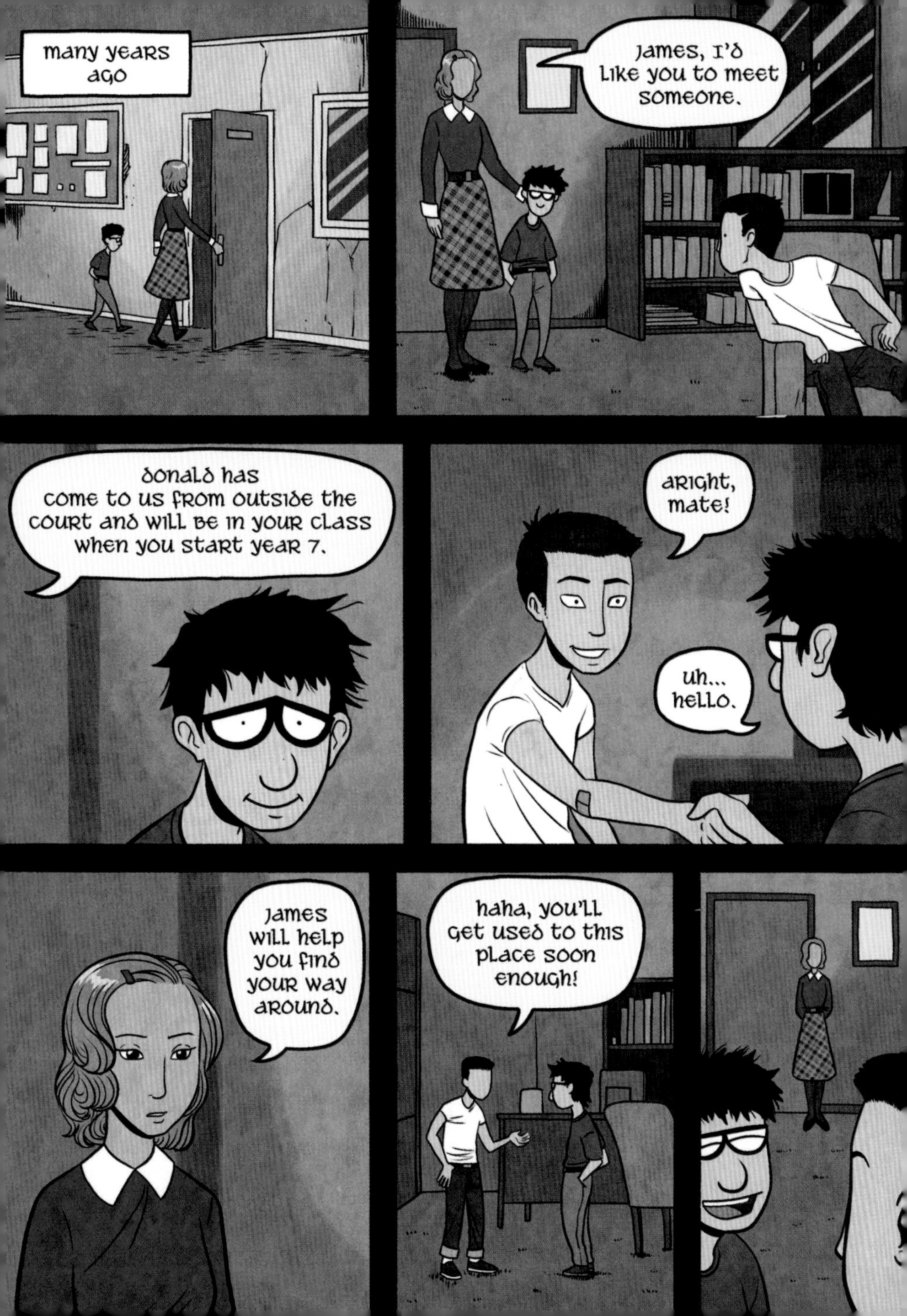
many years ago
James, I'd like you to meet someone.
Donald has come to us from outside the court and will be in your class when you start year 7.
aright, mate!
uh... hello.
James will help you find your way around.
haha, you'll get used to this place soon enough!

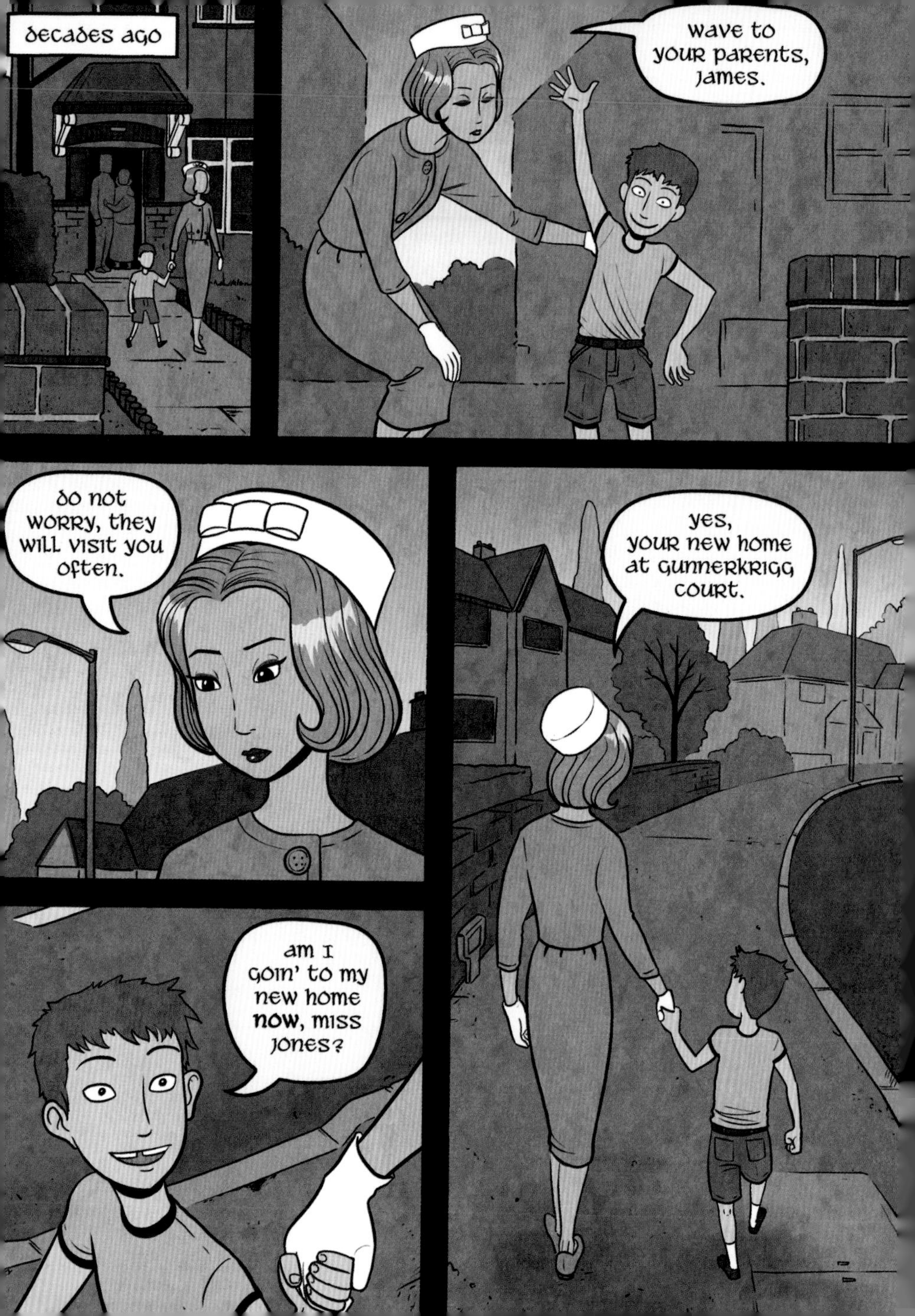
decades ago
wave to your parents, James.
do not worry, they will visit you often.
yes, your new home at Gunnerkrigg Court.
am I goin' to my new home **now**, Miss Jones?

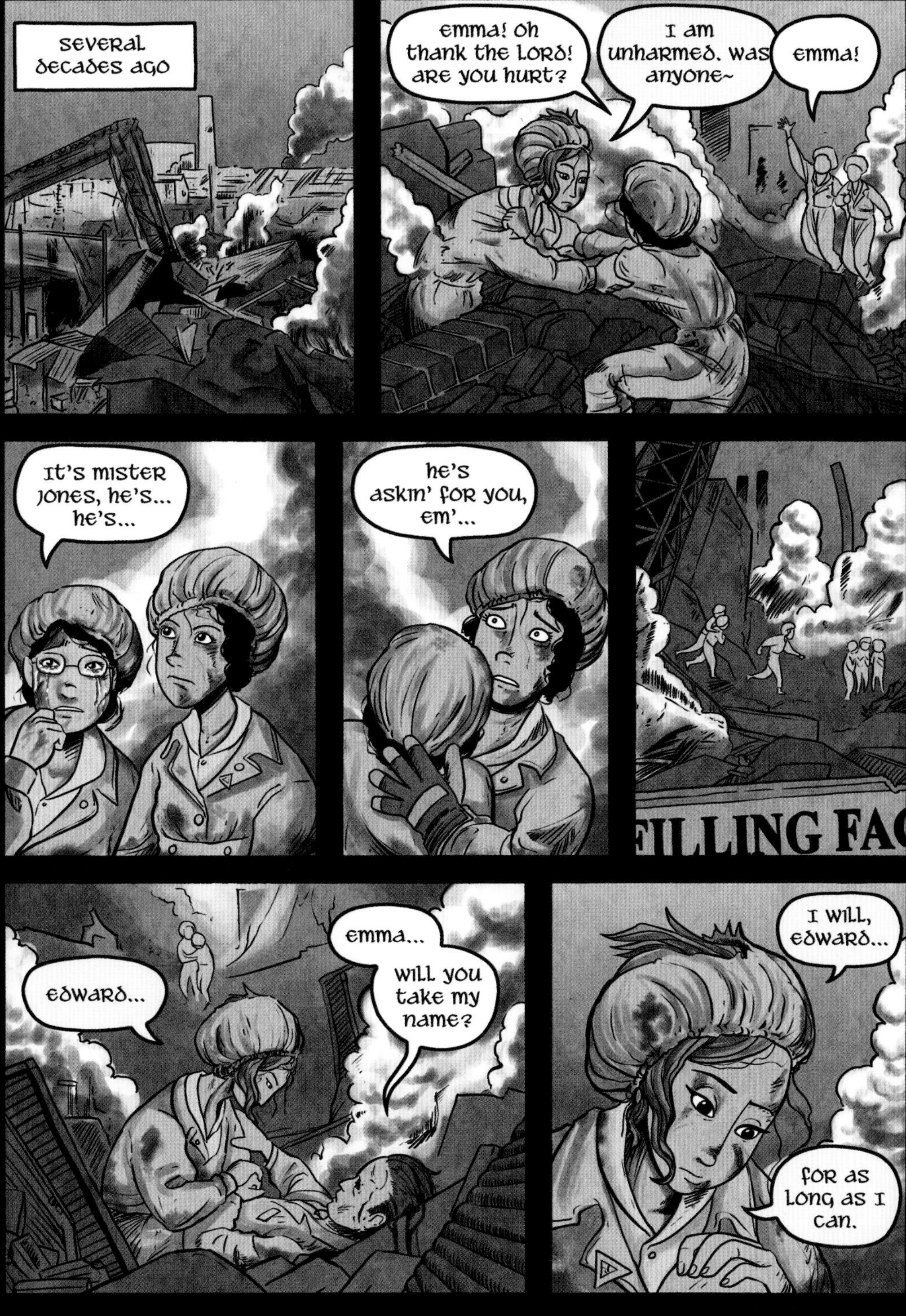

several decades ago
emma! oh thank the lord! are you hurt?
I am unharmed. was anyone~
emma!
It's mister jones, he's... he's...
he's askin' for you, em'...
FILLING FAC
edward...
emma...
will you take my name?
I will, edward...
for as long as I can.

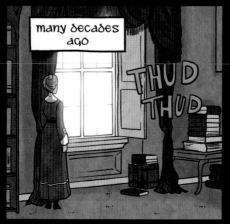

many decades ago

THUD THUD.

CRASH

HERE SHE IS, OFFICERS!

IT IS CLEAR TO SEE WHY THE SO CALLED LADY ELIZABETH REMAINS HIDDEN FROM SIGHT.

WHAT SHOULD BE THE OLD HEIRESS TO THE LANGDON ESTATE IS NOTHING MORE THAN THE YOUNG USURPER YOU SEE BEFORE YOU!

COME ALONG WITH US NOW, MISS. WE 'AVE SOME QUESTIONS FOR YOU.

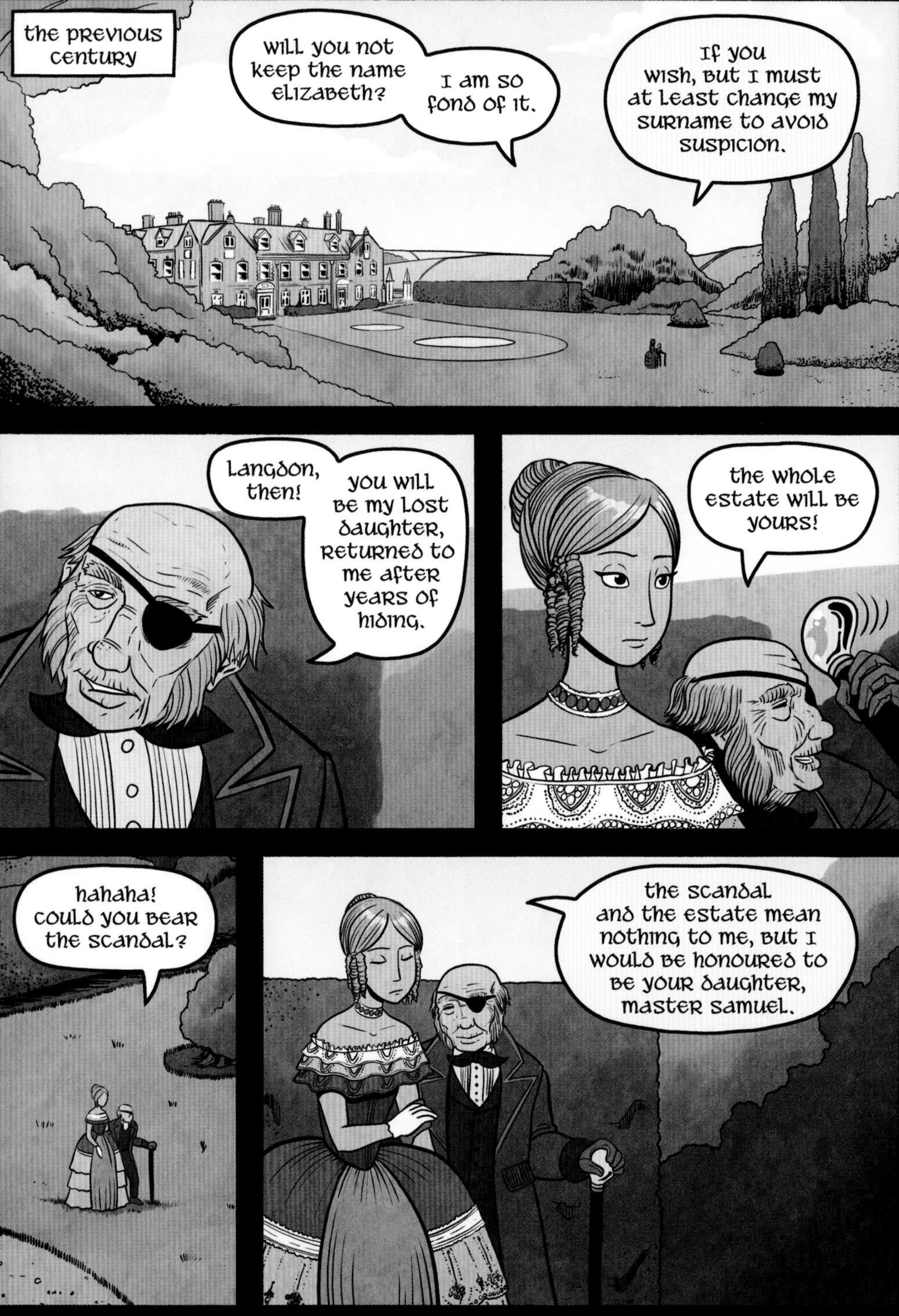
the previous century
will you not keep the name elizabeth?
I am so fond of it.
If you wish, but I must at least change my surname to avoid suspicion.
Langdon, then!
you will be my lost daughter, returned to me after years of hiding.
the whole estate will be yours!
hahaha! could you bear the scandal?
the scandal and the estate mean nothing to me, but I would be honoured to be your daughter, master samuel.

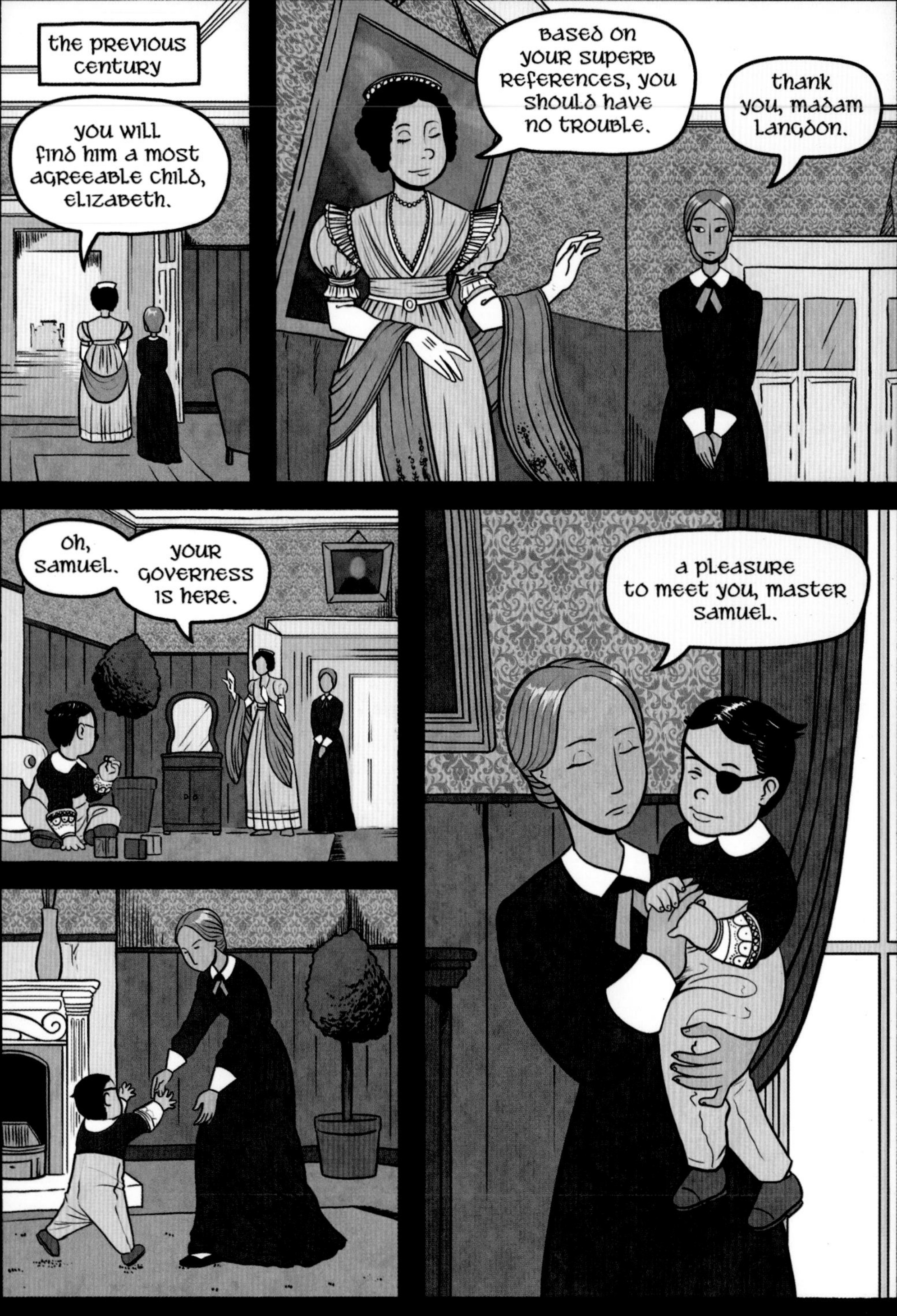
the previous century
you will find him a most agreeable child, elizabeth.
based on your superb references, you should have no trouble.
thank you, madam langdon.
oh, samuel.
your governess is here.
a pleasure to meet you, master samuel.

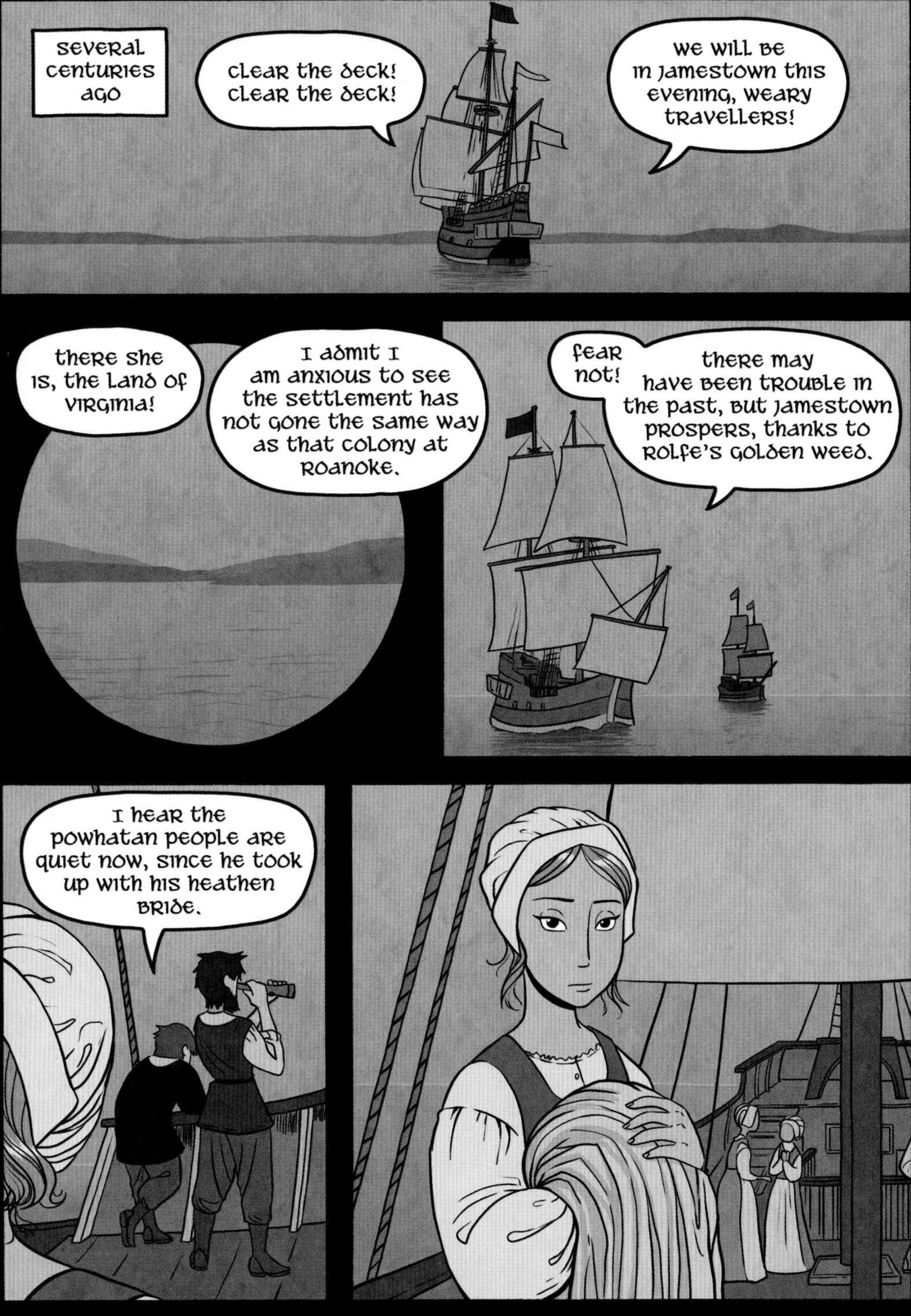
Several centuries ago
Clear the deck! Clear the deck!
We will be in Jamestown this evening, weary travellers!
There she is, the land of Virginia!
I admit I am anxious to see the settlement has not gone the same way as that colony at Roanoke.
Fear not!
There may have been trouble in the past, but Jamestown prospers, thanks to Rolfe's golden weed.
I hear the Powhatan people are quiet now, since he took up with his heathen bride.

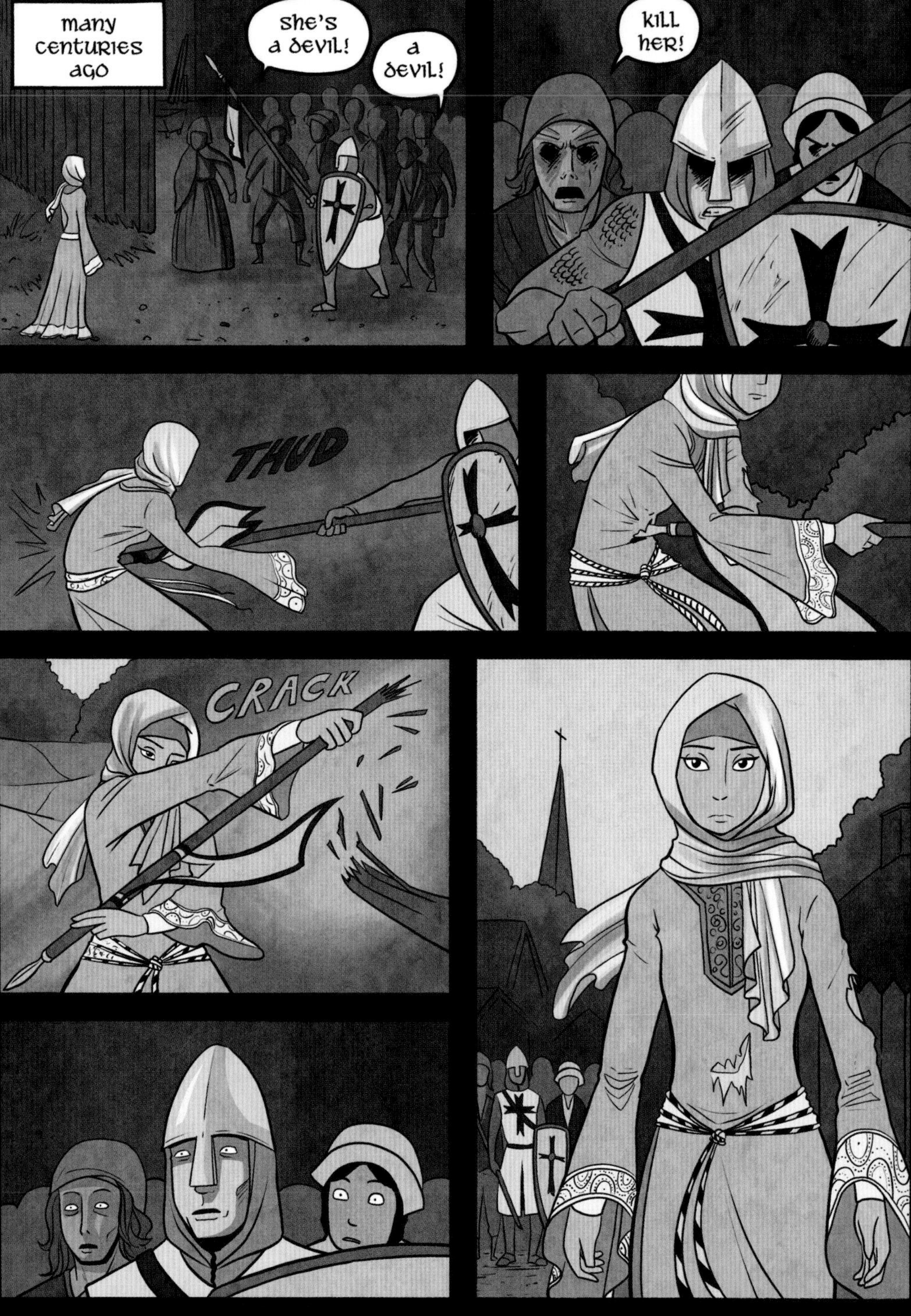
many centuries ago
she's a devil!
a devil!
kill her!
THUD
CRACK

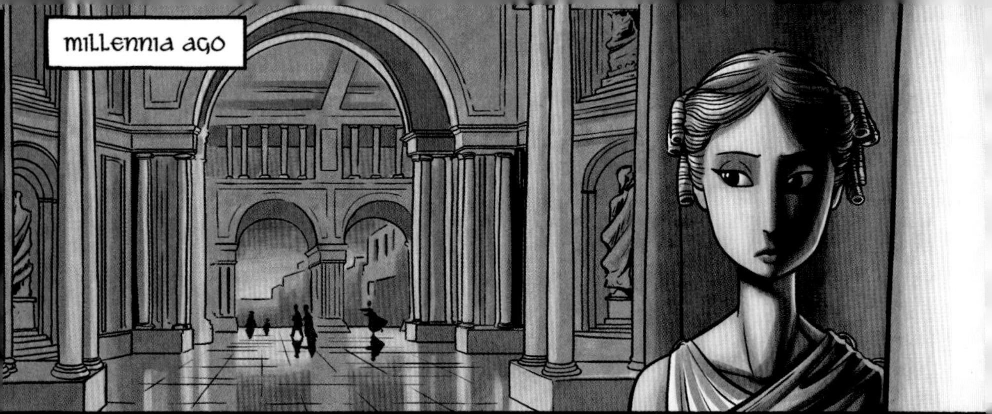
MILLENNIA AGO
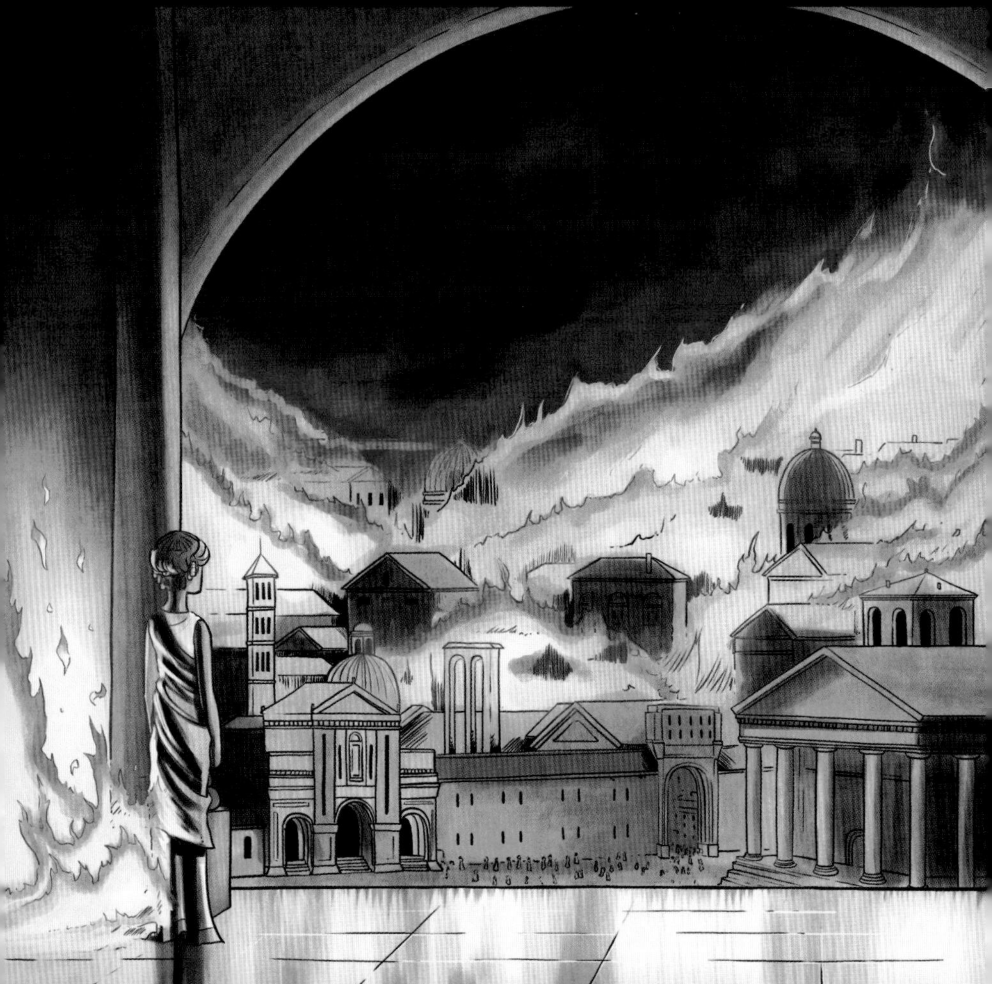

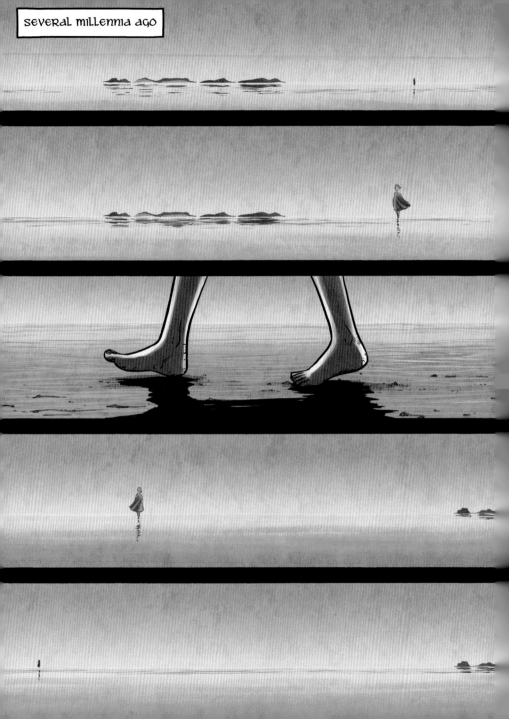

SEVERAL MILLENNIA AGO

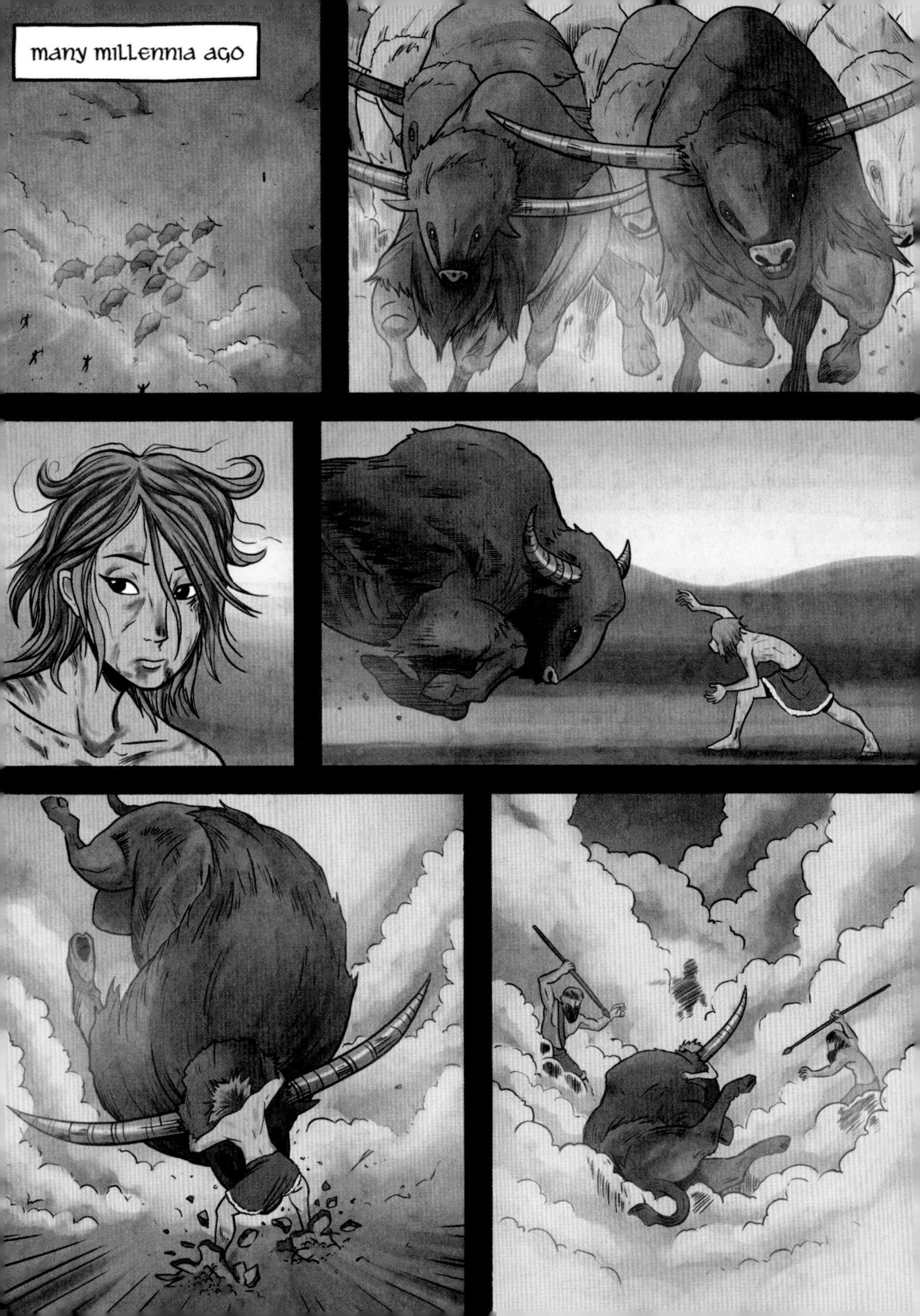
many millennia ago

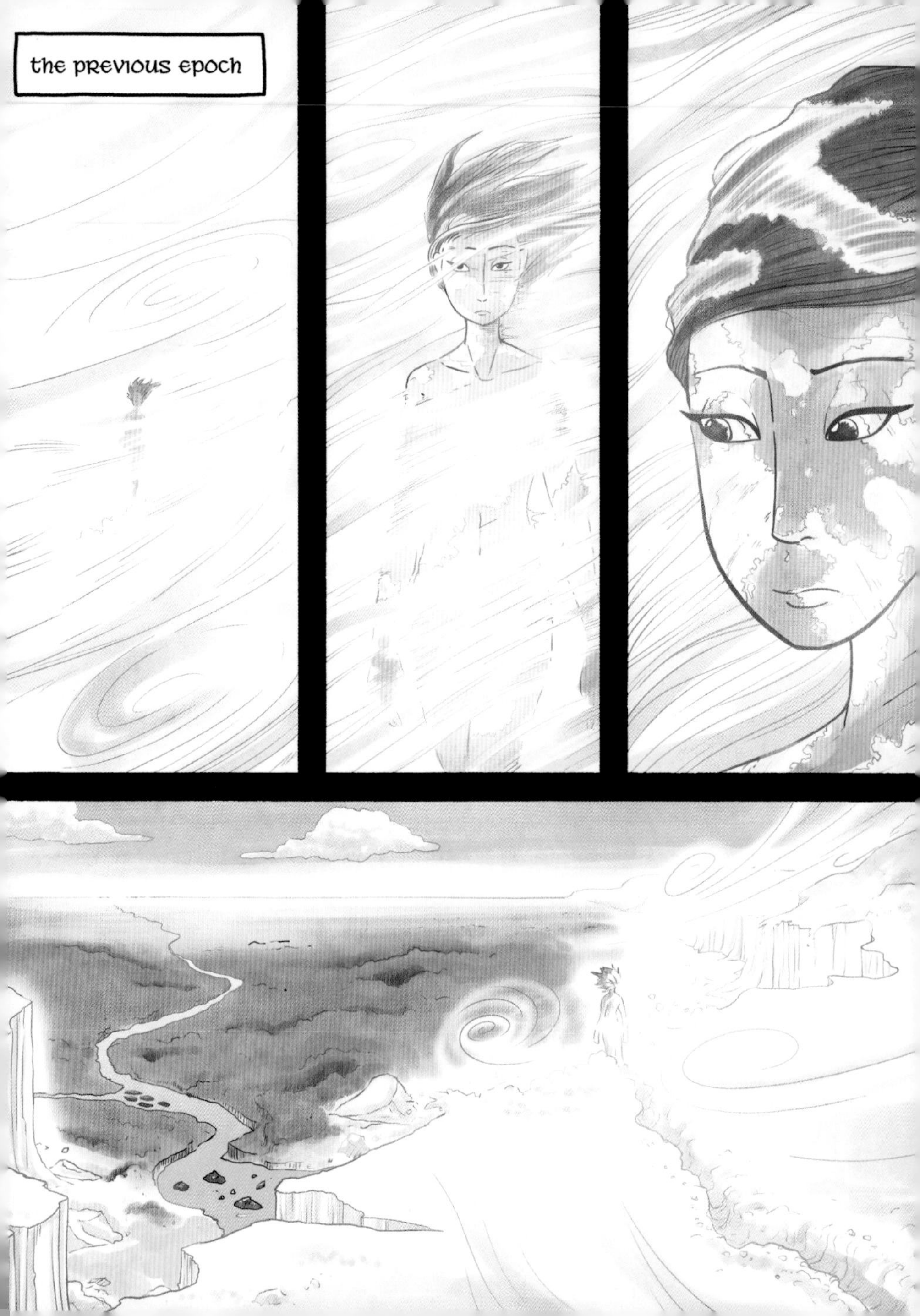
the previous epoch

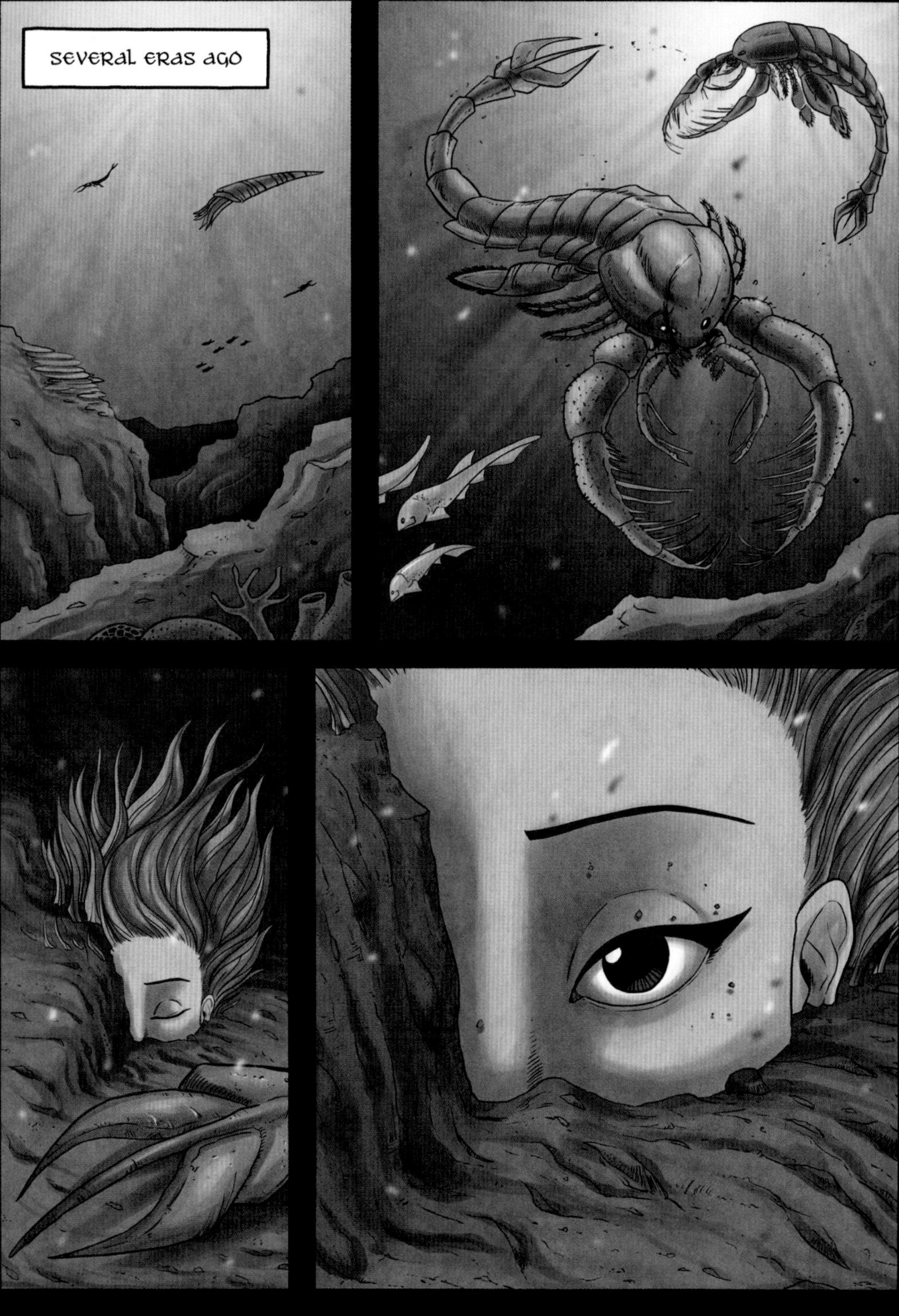
SEVERAL ERAS AGO

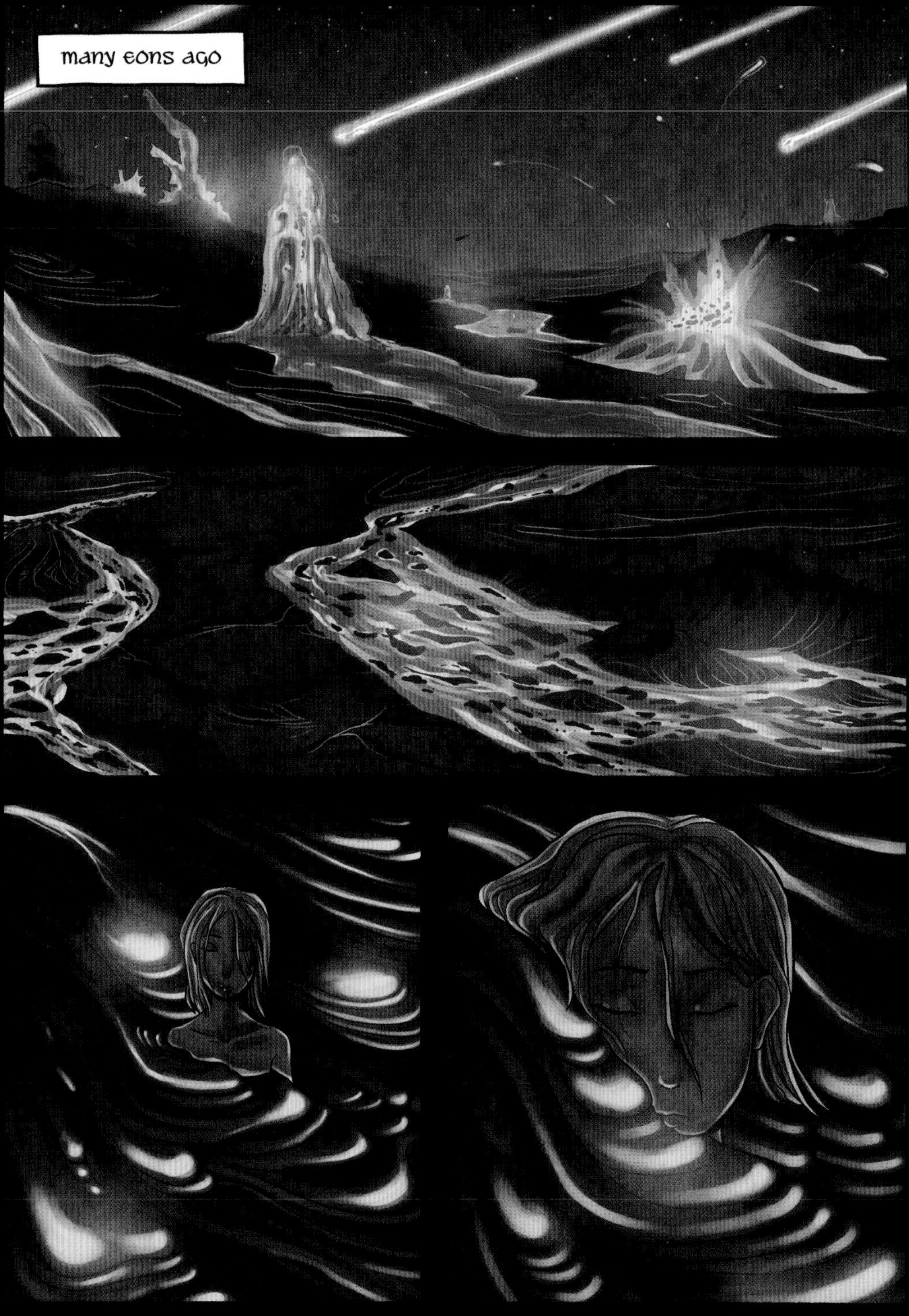
many eons ago

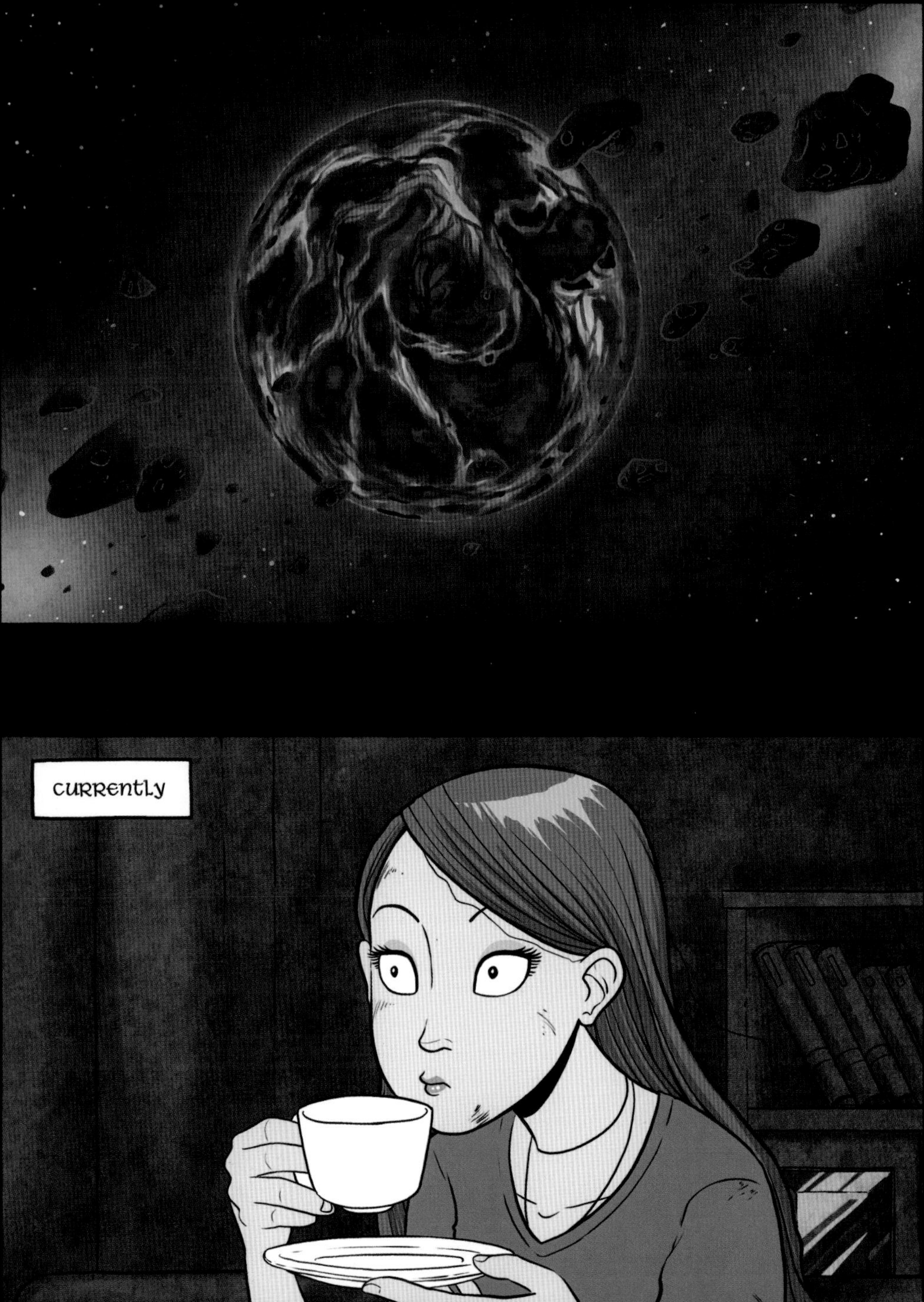
CURRENTLY

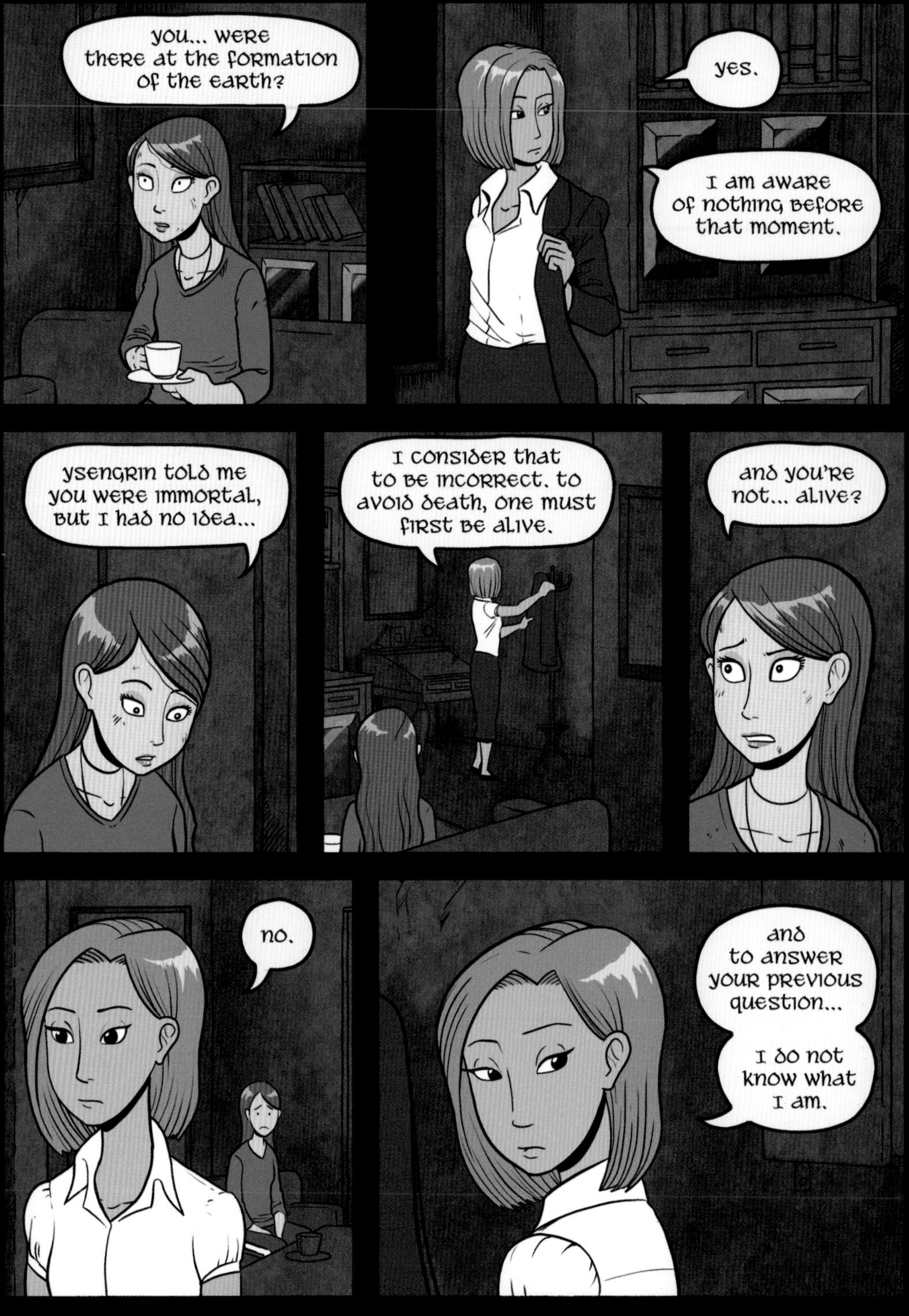
you... were there at the formation of the earth?
yes.
I am aware of nothing before that moment.
ysengrin told me you were immortal, but I had no idea...
I consider that to be incorrect. to avoid death, one must first be alive.
and you're not... alive?
no.
and to answer your previous question...
I do not know what I am.

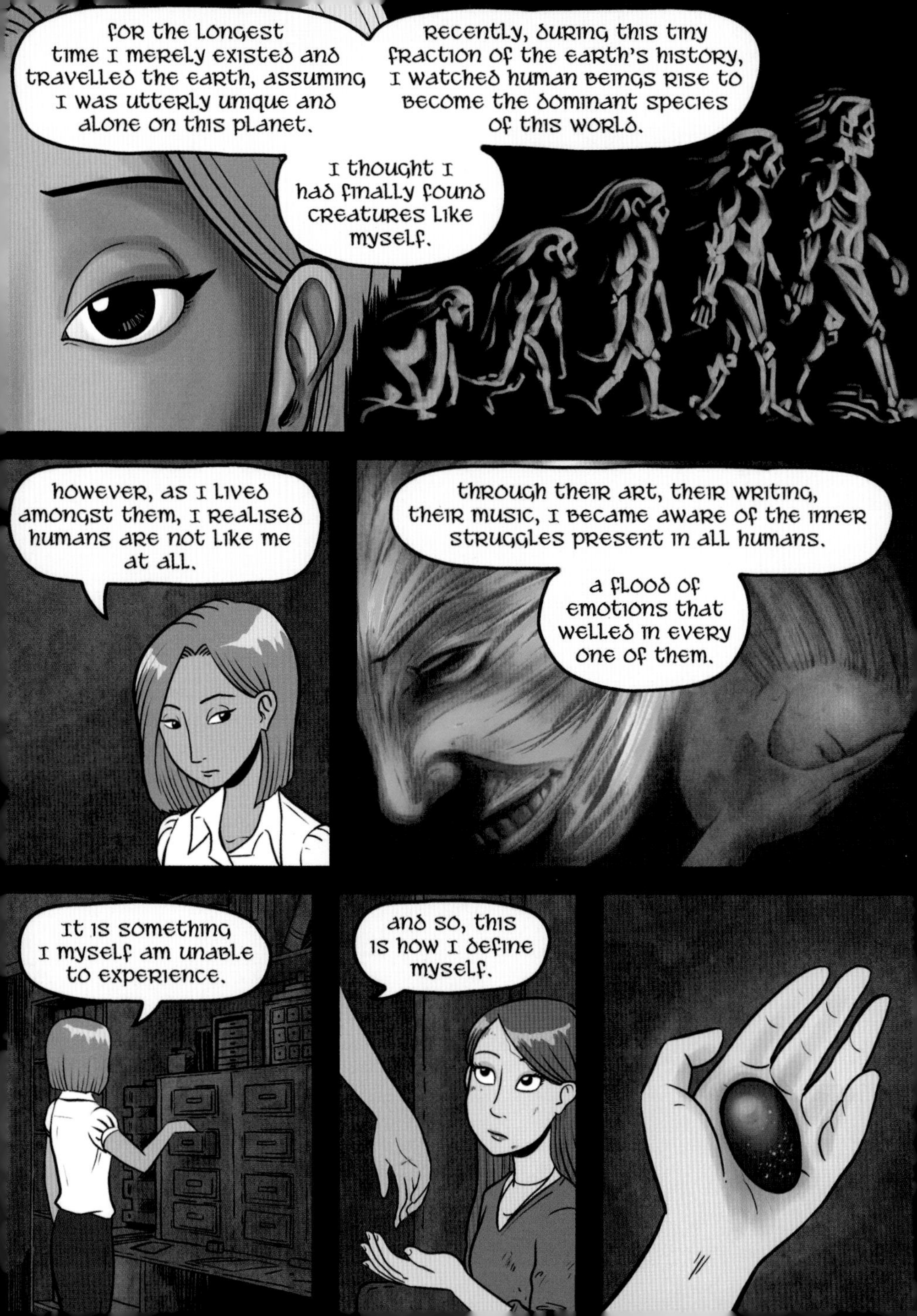
for the longest time I merely existed and travelled the earth, assuming I was utterly unique and alone on this planet.
Recently, during this tiny fraction of the earth's history, I watched human beings rise to become the dominant species of this world.
I thought I had finally found creatures like myself.
however, as I lived amongst them, I realised humans are not like me at all.
through their art, their writing, their music, I became aware of the inner struggles present in all humans.
a flood of emotions that welled in every one of them.
It is something I myself am unable to experience.
and so, this is how I define myself.

a stone?

Like some sort of golem?

no.

a stone is a part of the earth.

it may be shaped into human form but, like me, it is not alive.

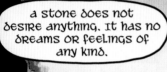

a stone does not desire anything. it has no dreams or feelings of any kind.

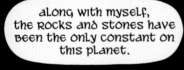

along with myself, the rocks and stones have been the only constant on this planet.

jones... that seems a little...

of course, it is not a perfect definition.

for example.

POP

a stone can be broken.

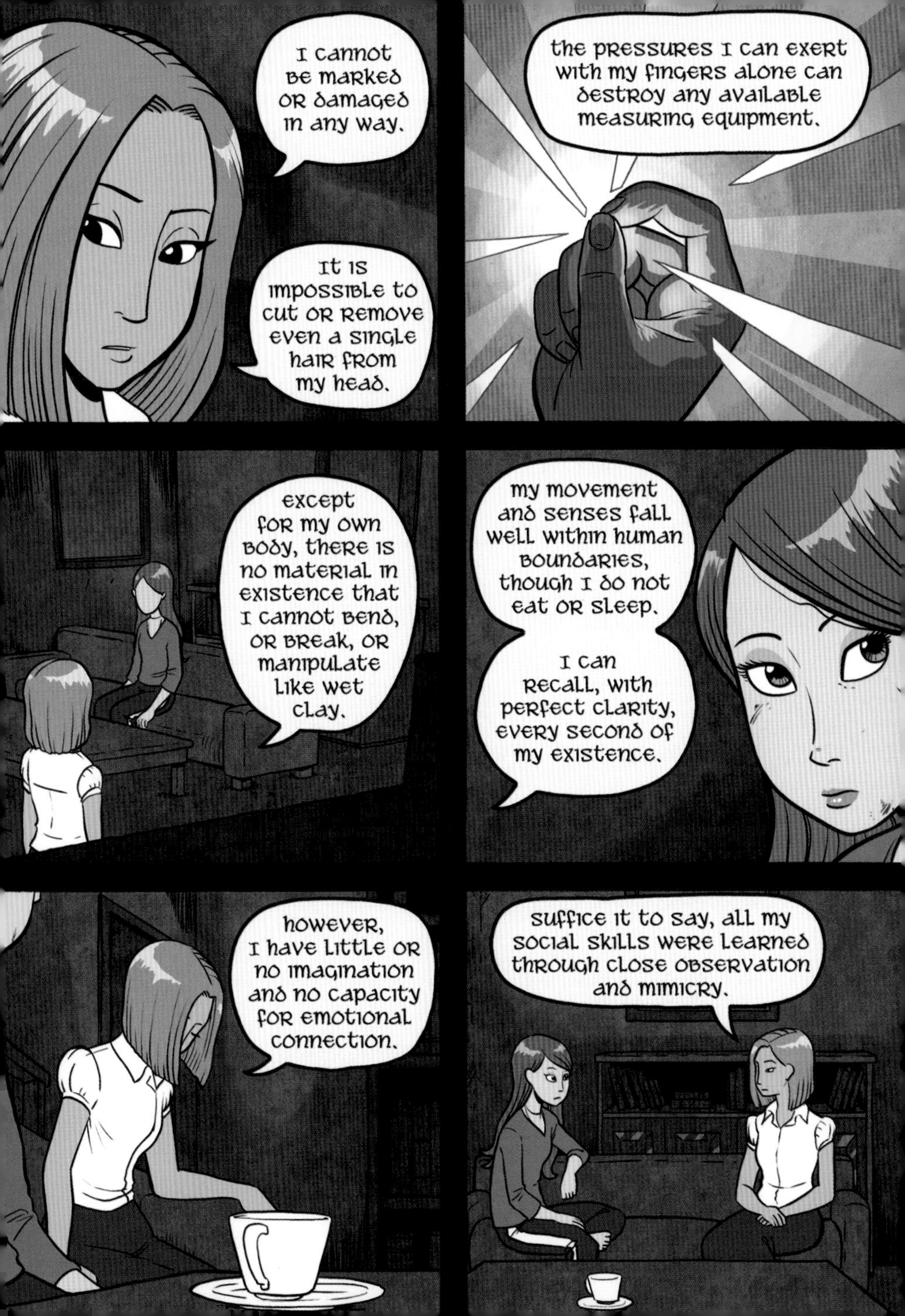
I cannot be marked or damaged in any way.
It is impossible to cut or remove even a single hair from my head.
the pressures I can exert with my fingers alone can destroy any available measuring equipment.
except for my own body, there is no material in existence that I cannot bend, or break, or manipulate like wet clay.
my movement and senses fall well within human boundaries, though I do not eat or sleep.
I can recall, with perfect clarity, every second of my existence.
however, I have little or no imagination and no capacity for emotional connection.
suffice it to say, all my social skills were learned through close observation and mimicry.

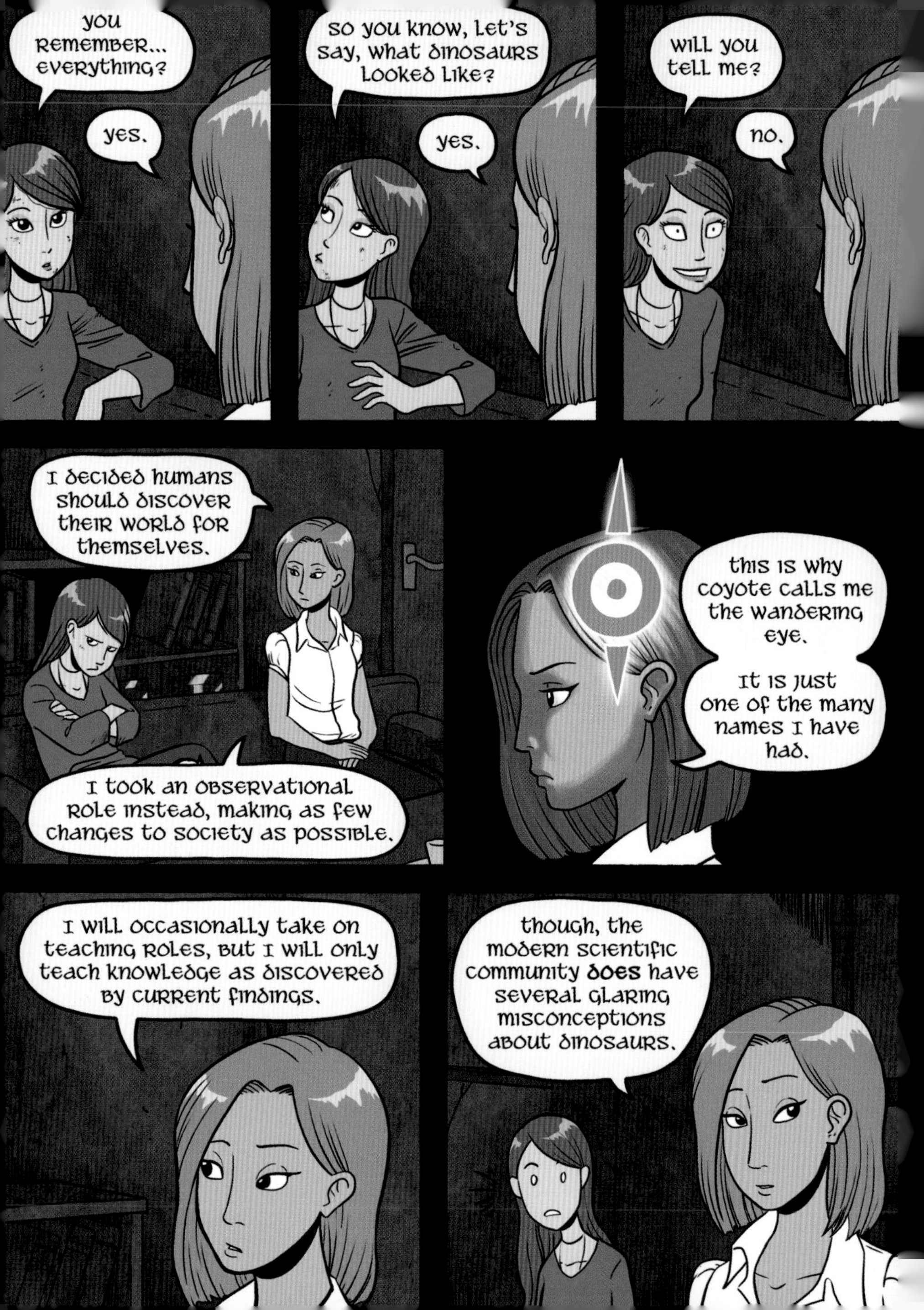
you remember... everything?
yes.
so you know, let's say, what dinosaurs looked like?
yes.
will you tell me?
no.
I decided humans should discover their world for themselves.
I took an observational role instead, making as few changes to society as possible.
this is why coyote calls me the wandering eye.
It is just one of the many names I have had.
I will occasionally take on teaching roles, but I will only teach knowledge as discovered by current findings.
though, the modern scientific community **does** have several glaring misconceptions about dinosaurs.

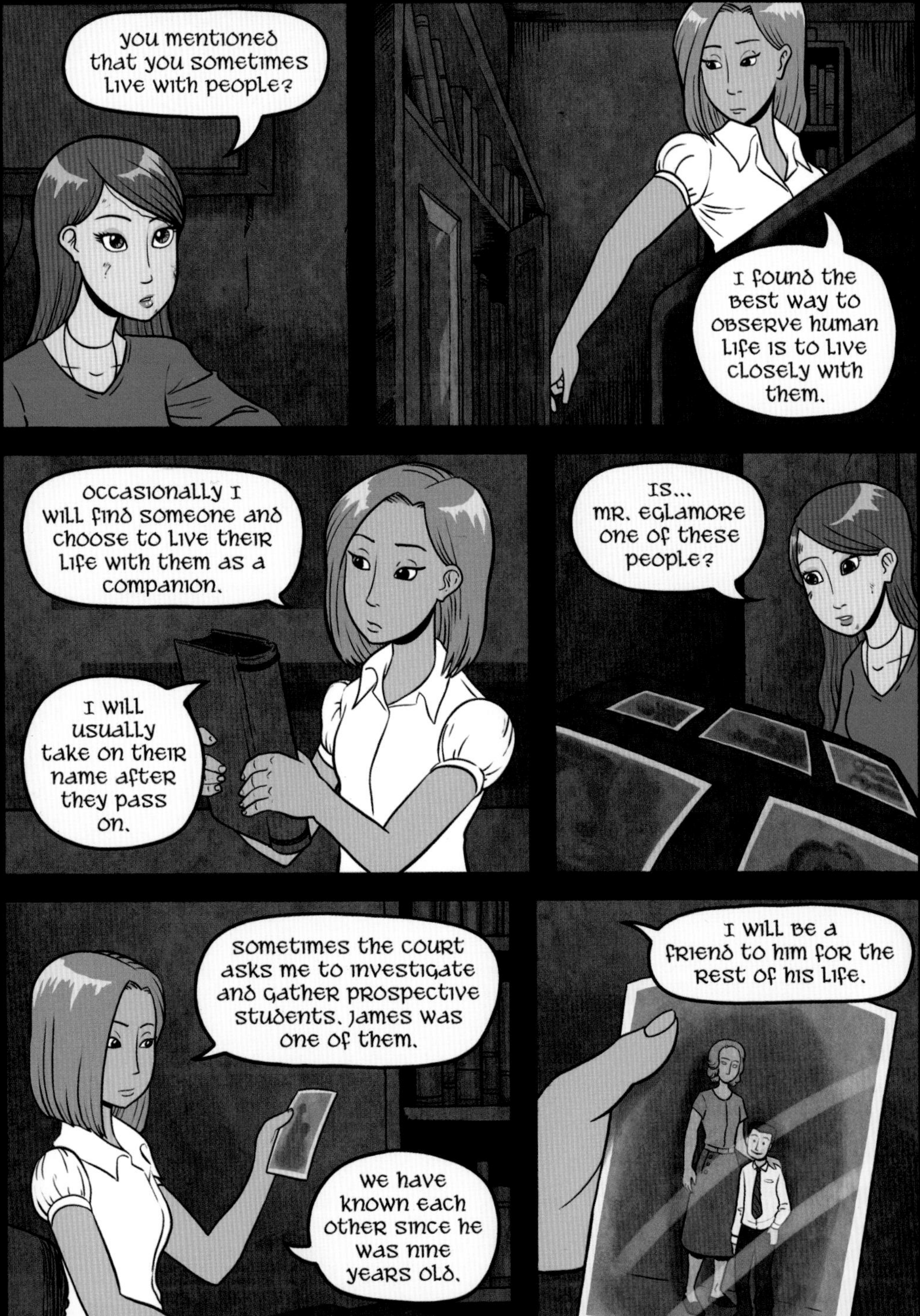
you mentioned that you sometimes live with people?
I found the best way to observe human life is to live closely with them.
occasionally I will find someone and choose to live their life with them as a companion.
I will usually take on their name after they pass on.
Is... Mr. Eglamore one of these people?
sometimes the court asks me to investigate and gather prospective students. James was one of them.
we have known each other since he was nine years old.
I will be a friend to him for the rest of his life.

SO, WERE YOU AROUND WHEN THE COURT WAS FOUNDED?

NO. BY THE TIME I CAME ACROSS THE COURT THE FOUNDERS HAD LONG SINCE PASSED ON.

THIS IS NOT SUCH AN EASY PLACE TO FIND BY ACCIDENT.

I TAKE A CONSULTORY ROLE HERE, IN RETURN FOR A CONSTANT PLACE TO WHICH I CAN RETURN IF I NEED.

THE UNIQUE NATURE OF THE COURT ALLOWS ME TO INVESTIGATE SEVERAL AREAS THAT WERE NOT NORMALLY OPEN TO ME.

ALSO, I AM A WORTHWHILE CURIOSITY FOR SOME OF THE RESEARCHERS HERE.

JONES... IF WHAT YOU TELL ME IS TRUE, YOU ARE MAYBE THE MOST IMPORTANT BEING ON THE FACE OF THE PLANET...

DEBATABLE.

HOW CAN YOU RESIGN YOURSELF TO BE A MERE "CURIOSITY"?

QUITE SIMPLY, I HAVE NO DESIRE TO BE ANYTHING MORE.

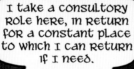

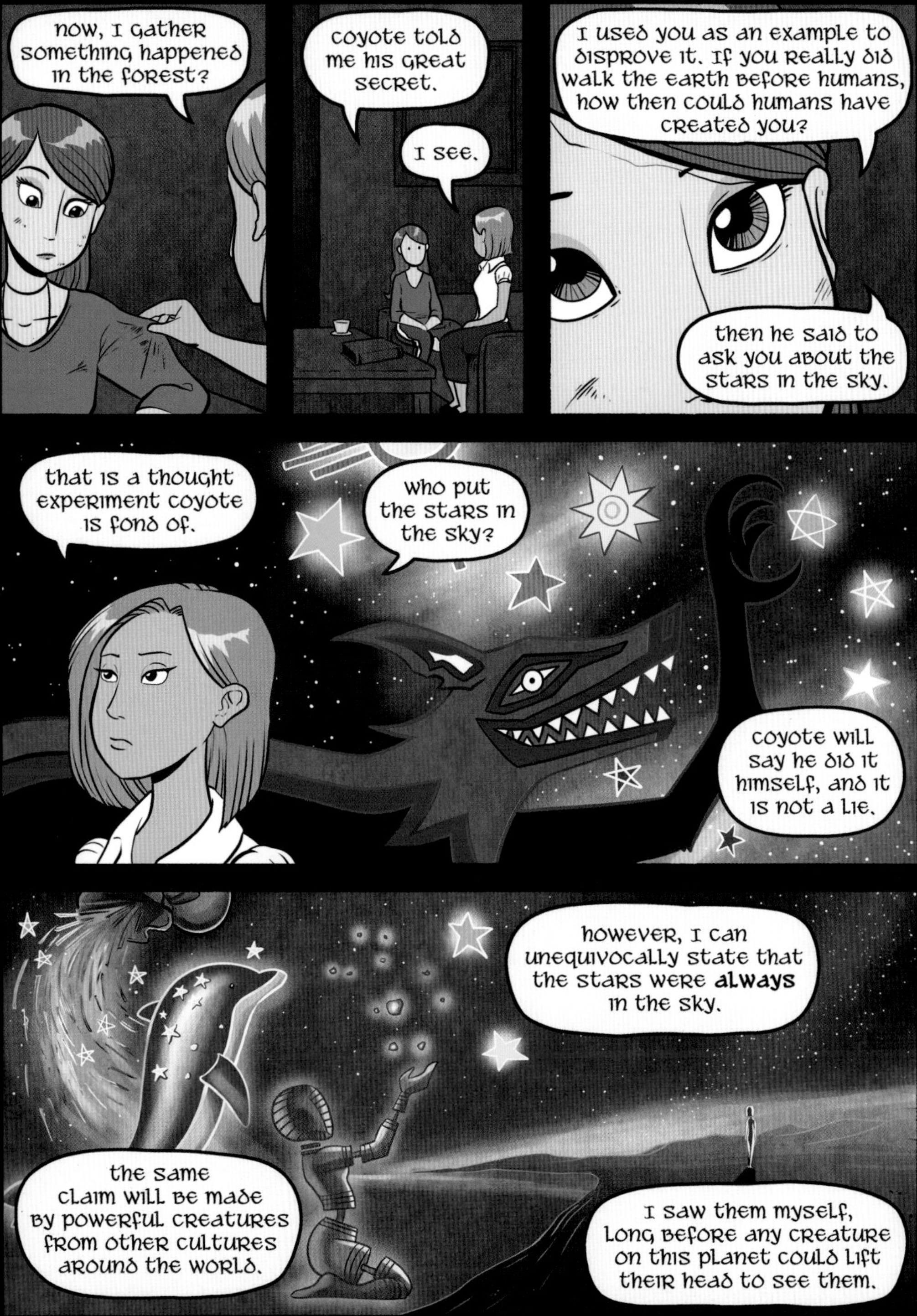
now, I gather something happened in the forest?
coyote told me his great secret.
I see.
I used you as an example to disprove it. If you really did walk the earth before humans, how then could humans have created you?
then he said to ask you about the stars in the sky.
that is a thought experiment coyote is fond of.
who put the stars in the sky?
coyote will say he did it himself, and it is not a lie.
however, I can unequivocally state that the stars were **always** in the sky.
the same claim will be made by powerful creatures from other cultures around the world.
I saw them myself, long before any creature on this planet could lift their head to see them.

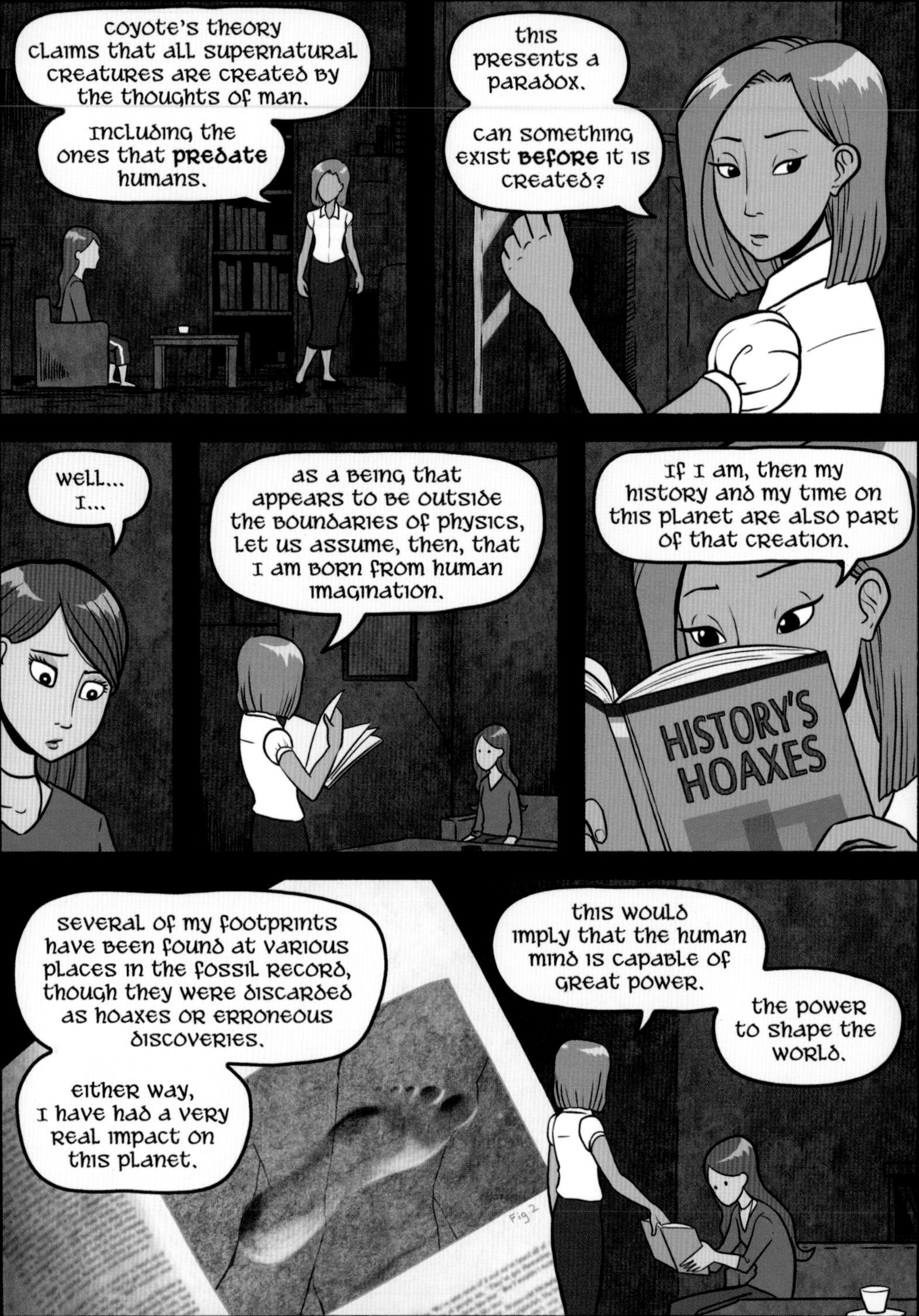
coyote's theory claims that all supernatural creatures are created by the thoughts of man.
including the ones that **predate** humans.
this presents a paradox.
can something exist **before** it is created?
well... I...
as a being that appears to be outside the boundaries of physics, let us assume, then, that I am born from human imagination.
If I am, then my history and my time on this planet are also part of that creation.
HISTORY'S HOAXES
several of my footprints have been found at various places in the fossil record, though they were discarded as hoaxes or erroneous discoveries.
either way, I have had a very real impact on this planet.
Fig. 2
this would imply that the human mind is capable of great power.
the power to shape the world.

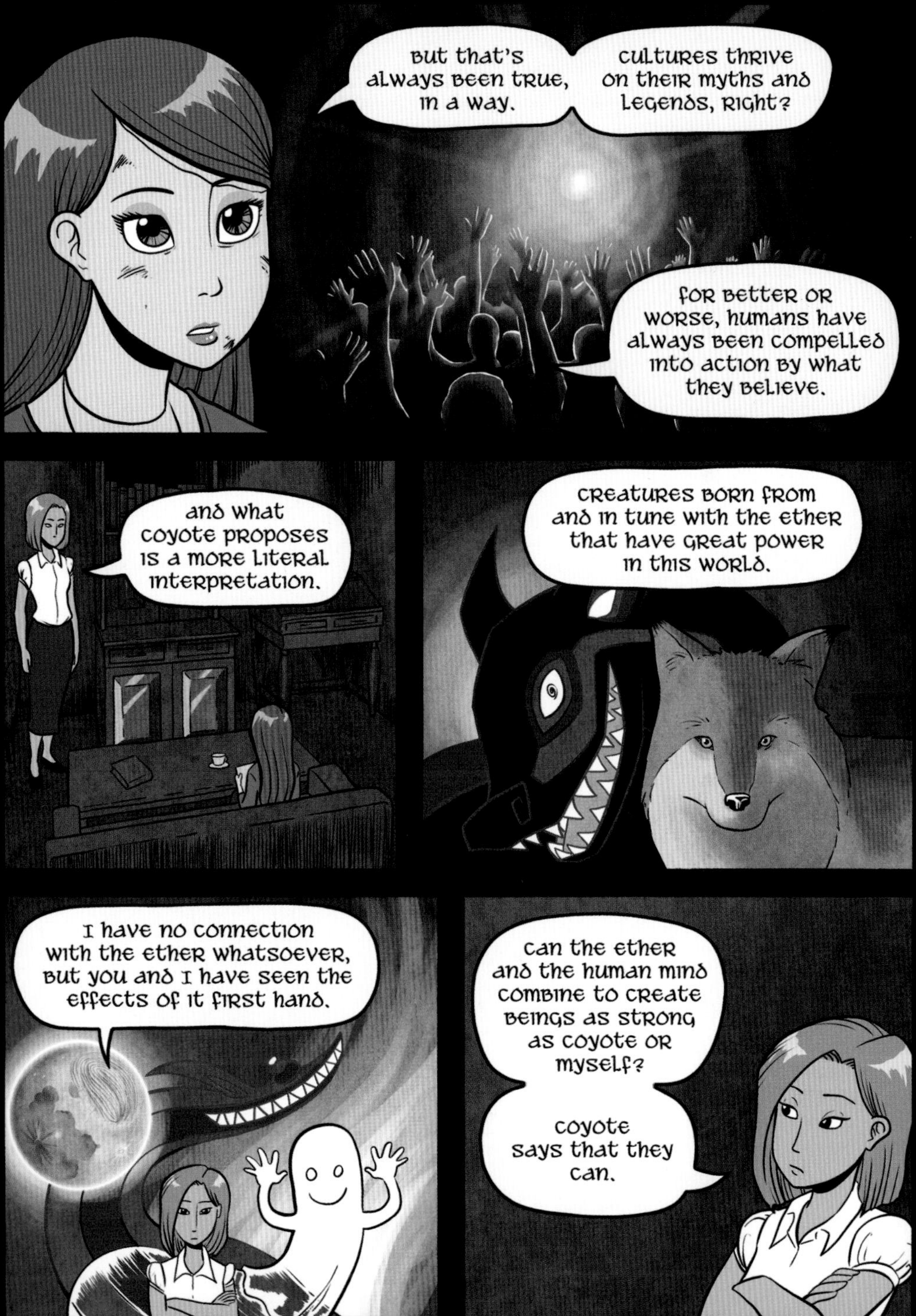
But that's always been true, in a way.
Cultures thrive on their myths and legends, right?
For better or worse, humans have always been compelled into action by what they believe.
And what Coyote proposes is a more literal interpretation.
Creatures born from and in tune with the ether that have great power in this world.
I have no connection with the ether whatsoever, but you and I have seen the effects of it first hand.
Can the ether and the human mind combine to create beings as strong as Coyote or myself?
Coyote says that they can.

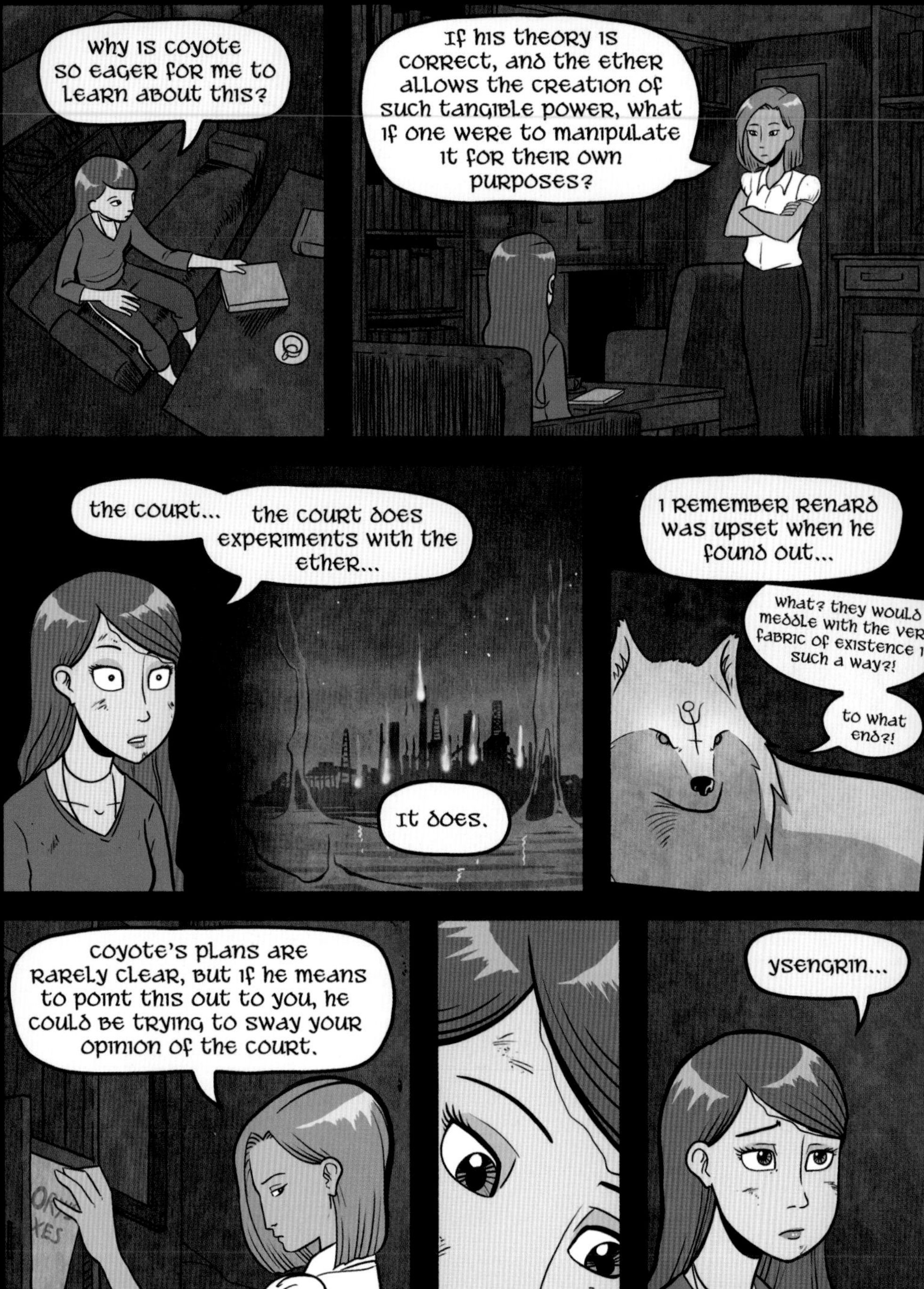
why is coyote so eager for me to learn about this?
If his theory is correct, and the ether allows the creation of such tangible power, what if one were to manipulate it for their own purposes?
the court...
the court does experiments with the ether...
It does.
I remember Renard was upset when he found out...
what? they would meddle with the very fabric of existence in such a way?!
to what end?!
coyote's plans are rarely clear, but if he means to point this out to you, he could be trying to sway your opinion of the court.
ysengrin...

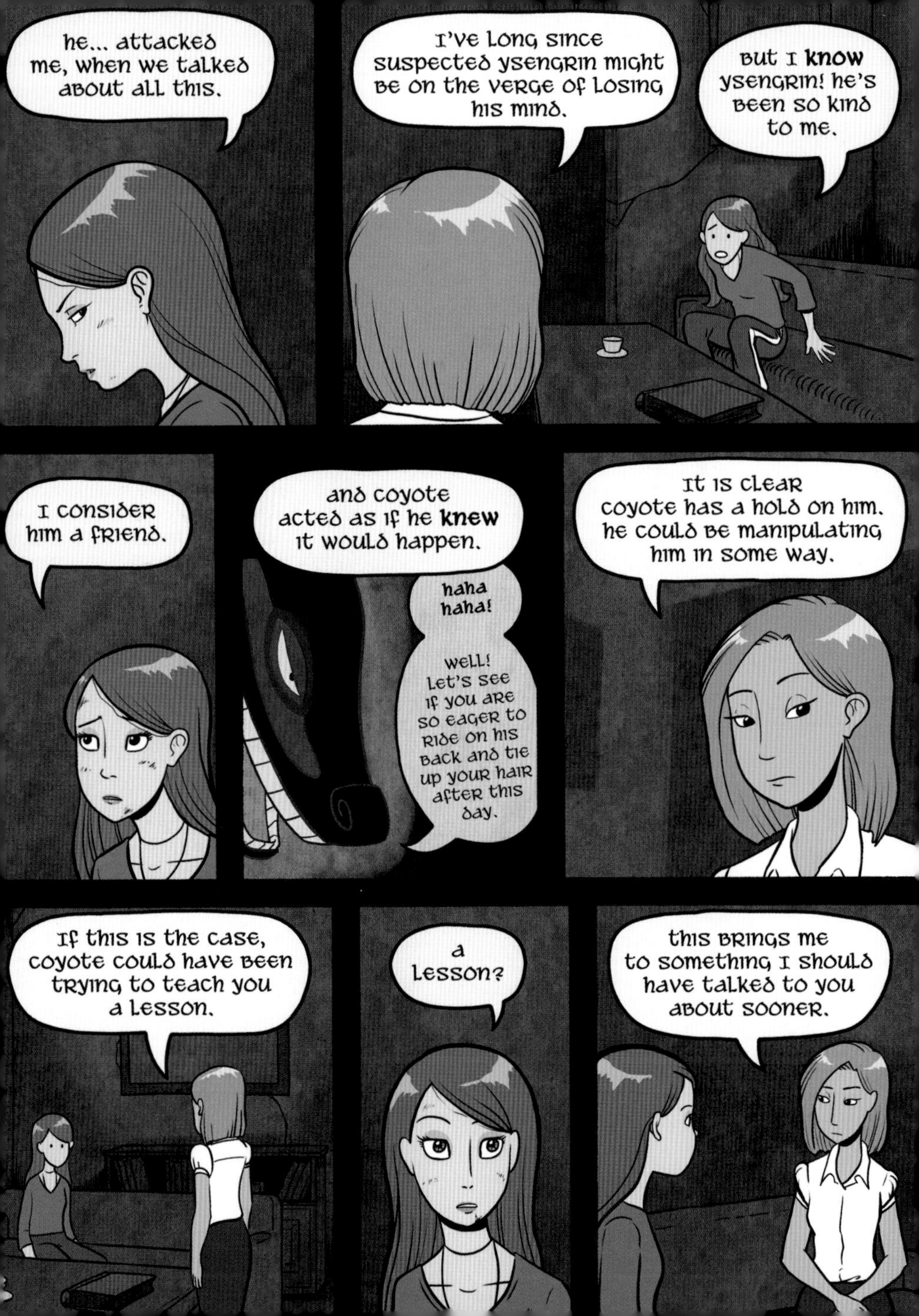
he... attacked me, when we talked about all this.
I've long since suspected ysengrin might be on the verge of losing his mind.
But I **know** ysengrin! he's been so kind to me.
I consider him a friend.
and coyote acted as if he **knew** it would happen.
haha haha!
well! Let's see if you are so eager to ride on his back and tie up your hair after this day.
It is clear coyote has a hold on him. he could be manipulating him in some way.
If this is the case, coyote could have been trying to teach you a lesson.
a lesson?
this brings me to something I should have talked to you about sooner.

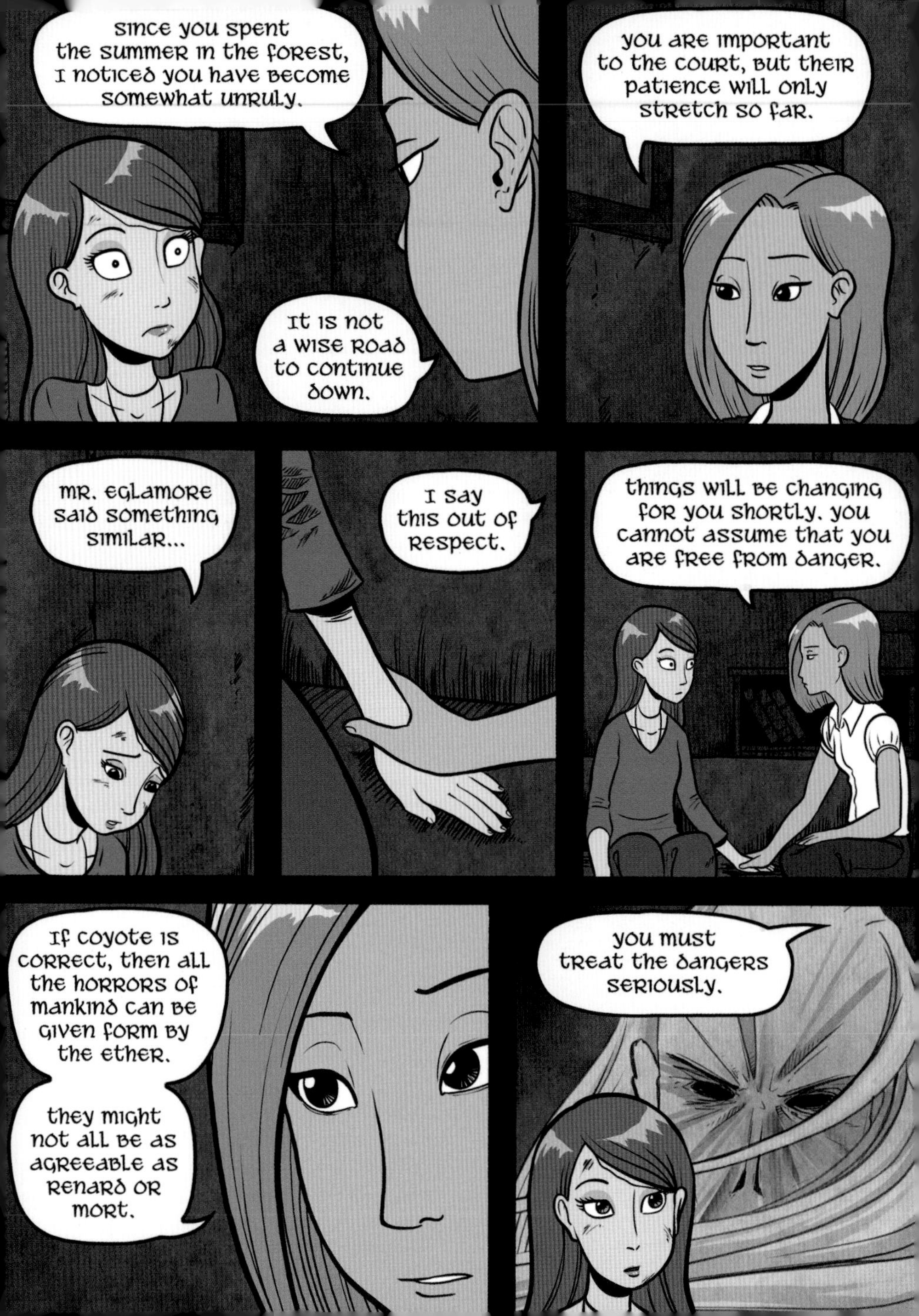
since you spent the summer in the forest, I noticed you have become somewhat unruly.
It is not a wise road to continue down.
you are important to the court, but their patience will only stretch so far.
mr. eglamore said something similar...
I say this out of respect.
things will be changing for you shortly. you cannot assume that you are free from danger.
If coyote is correct, then all the horrors of mankind can be given form by the ether.
they might not all be as agreeable as renard or mort.
you must treat the dangers seriously.

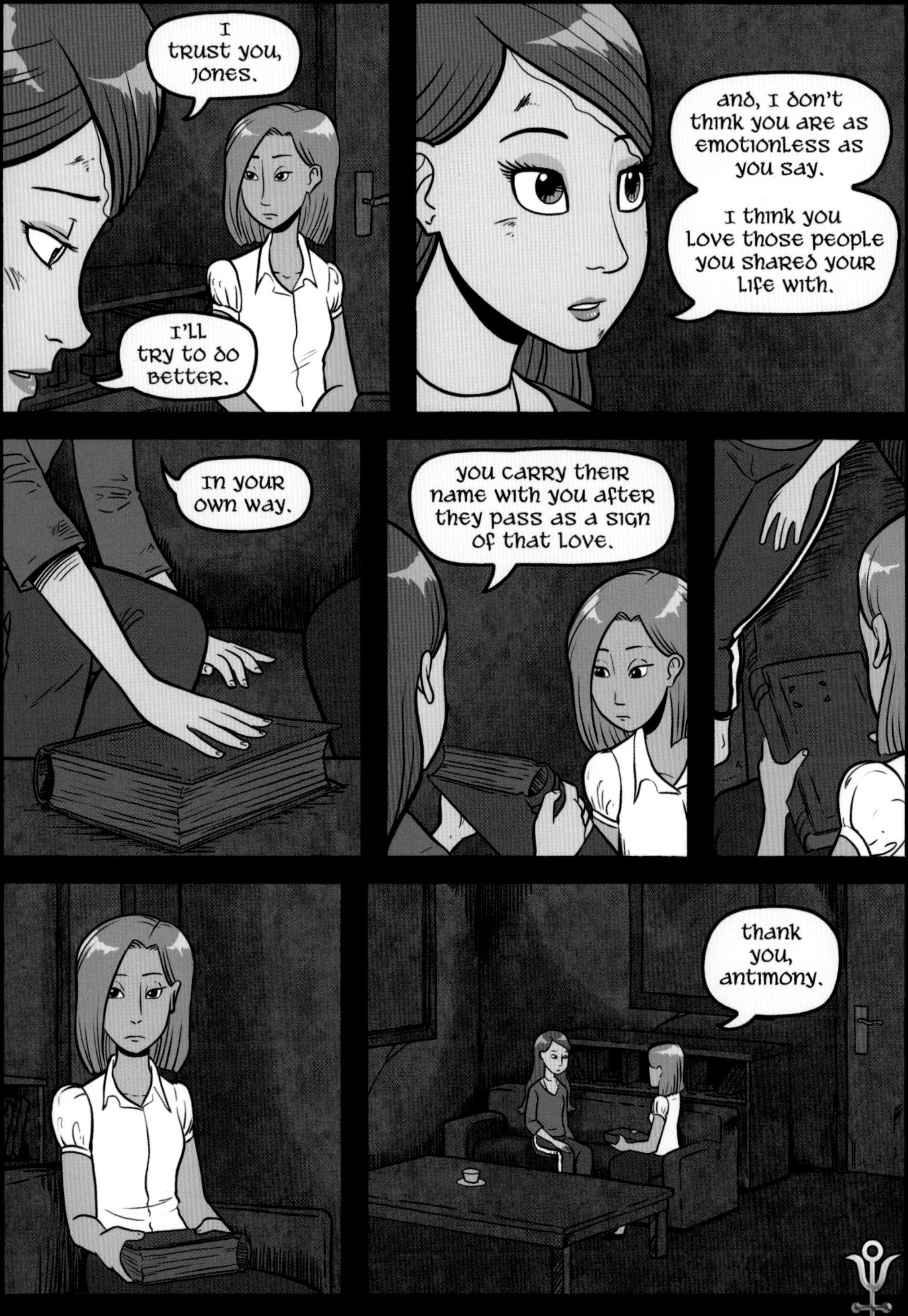

I trust you, Jones.
I'll try to do better.
And, I don't think you are as emotionless as you say.
I think you love those people you shared your life with.
In your own way.
You carry their name with you after they pass as a sign of that love.
Thank you, Antimony.

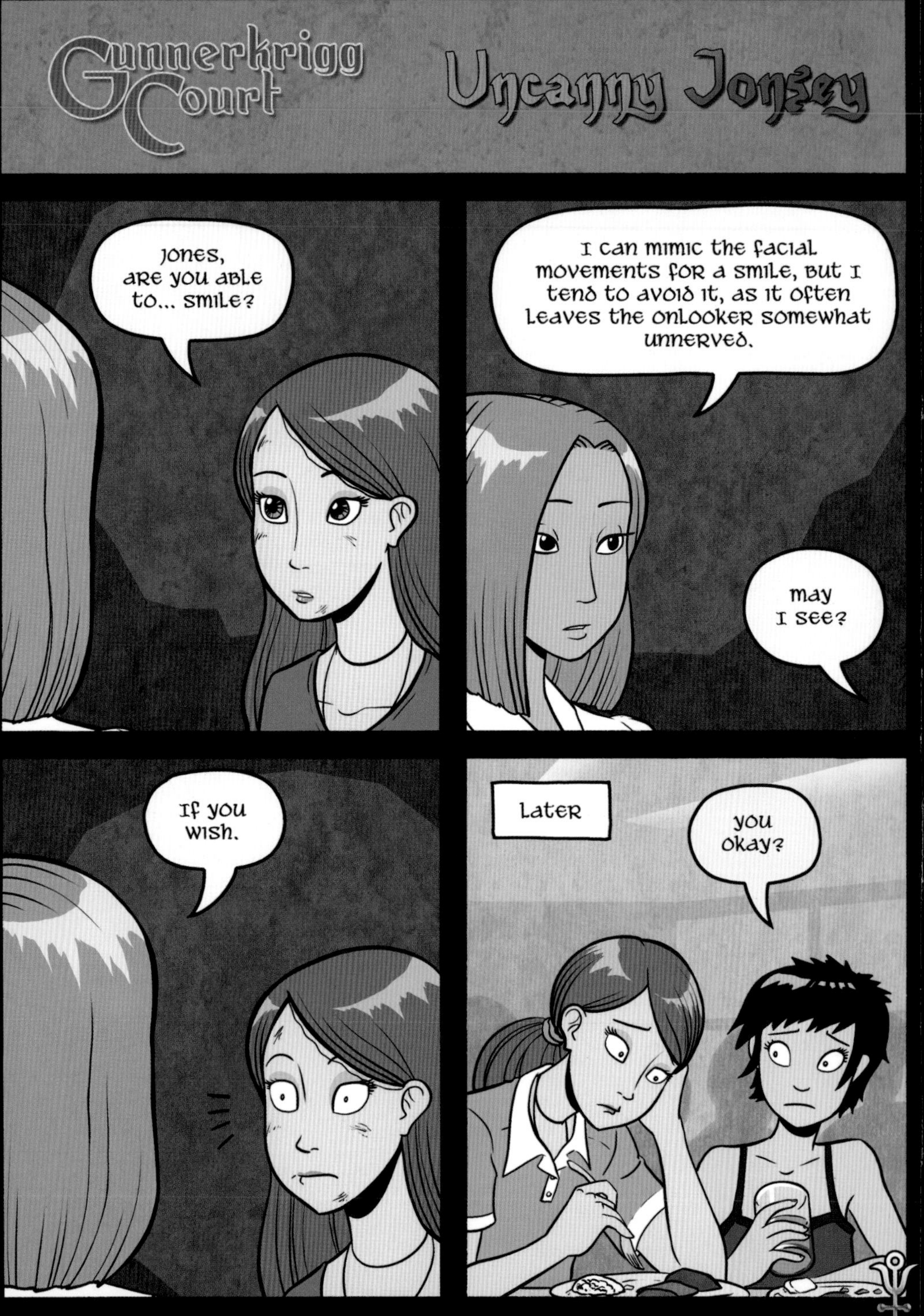
Gunnerkrigg Court
Uncanny Jonsey
Jones, are you able to... smile?
I can mimic the facial movements for a smile, but I tend to avoid it, as it often leaves the onlooker somewhat unnerved.
May I see?
If you wish.
Later
You okay?

Gunnerkrigg Court

Chapter 41:

Changes

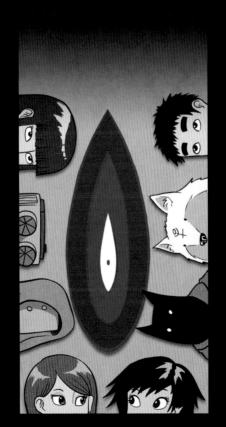

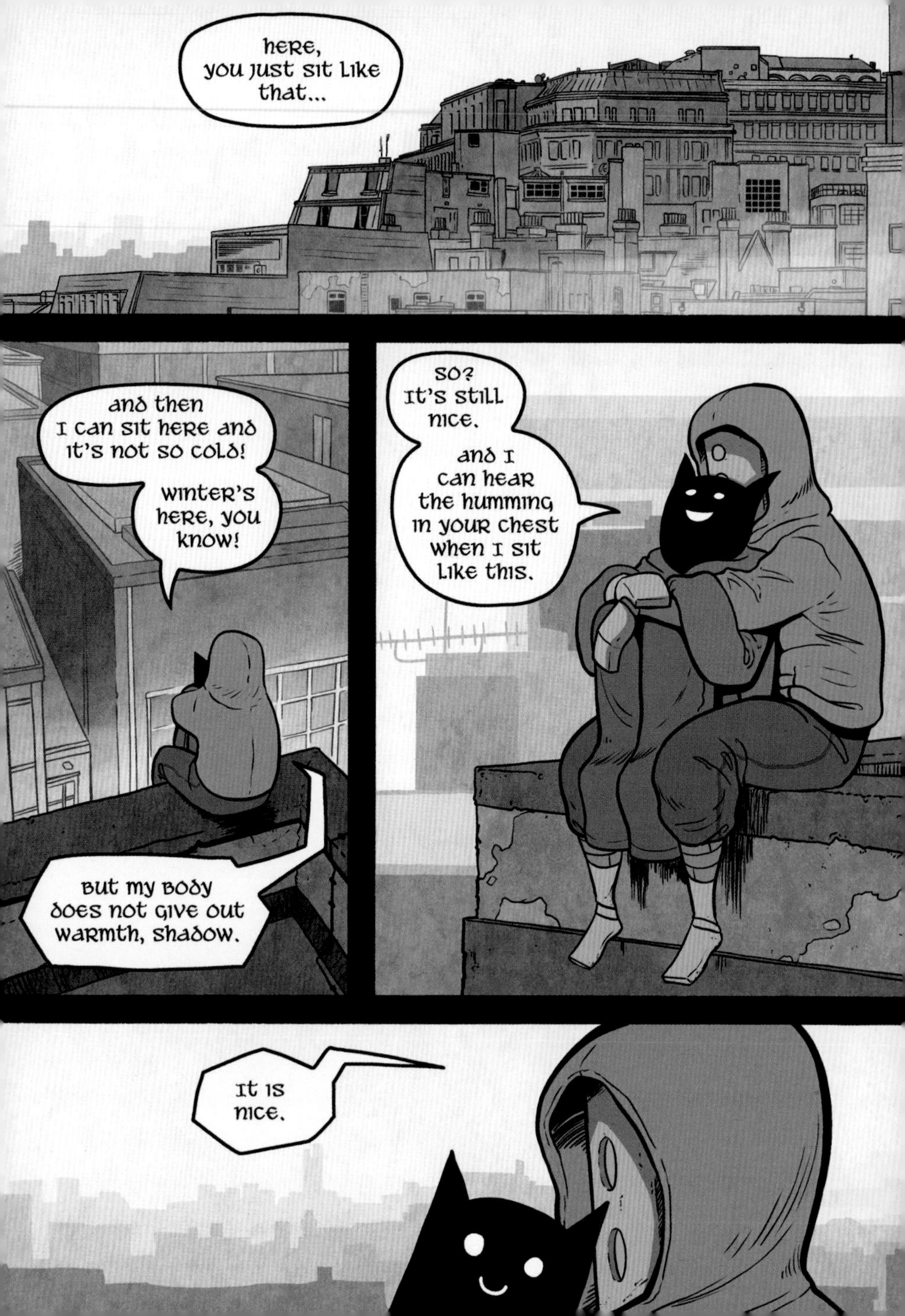
here, you just sit like that...
and then I can sit here and it's not so cold!
winter's here, you know!
But my body does not give out warmth, shadow.
so? it's still nice.
and I can hear the humming in your chest when I sit like this.
It is nice.

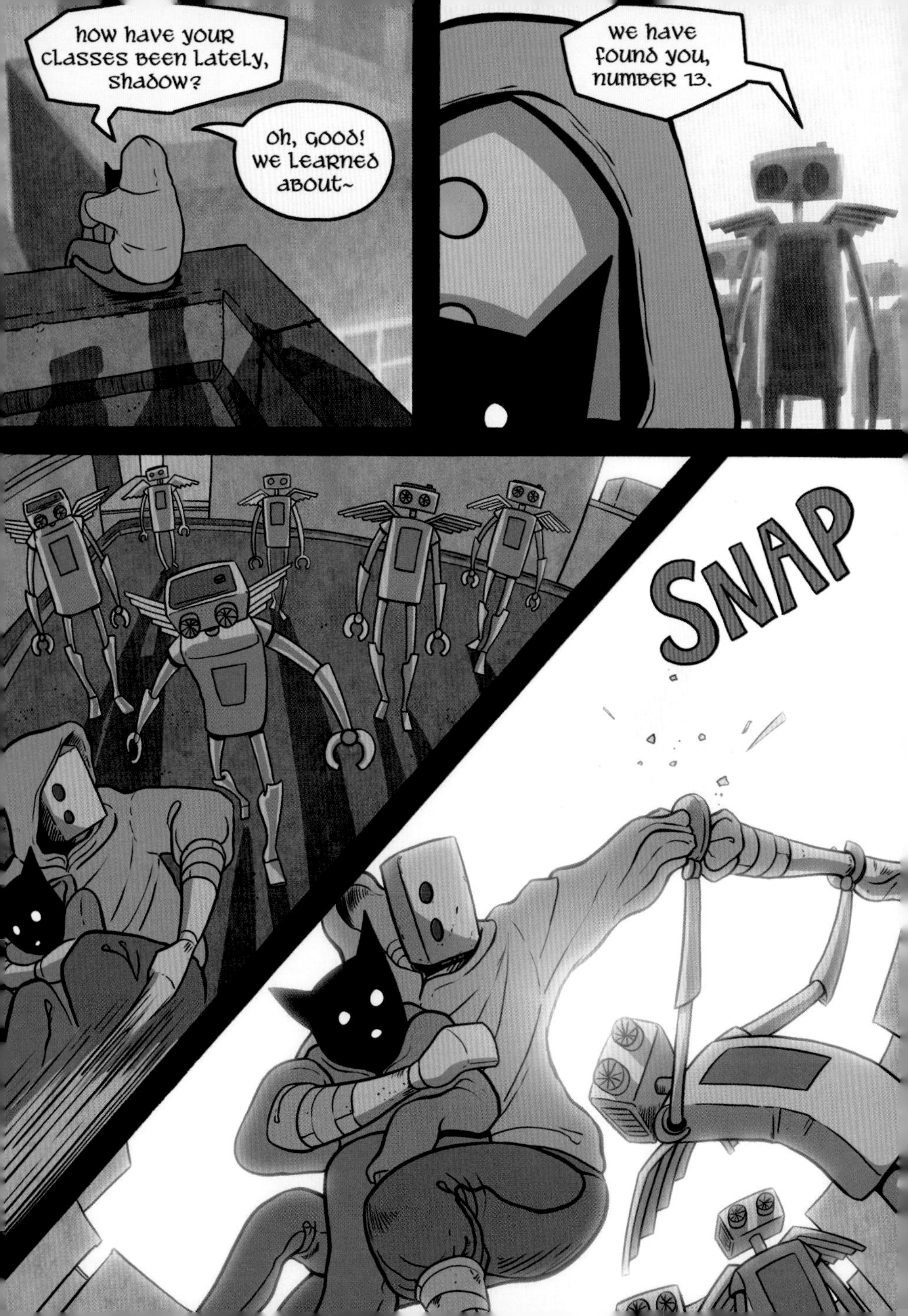
how have your classes been lately, shadow?
oh, good! we learned about~
we have found you, number 13.
SNAP

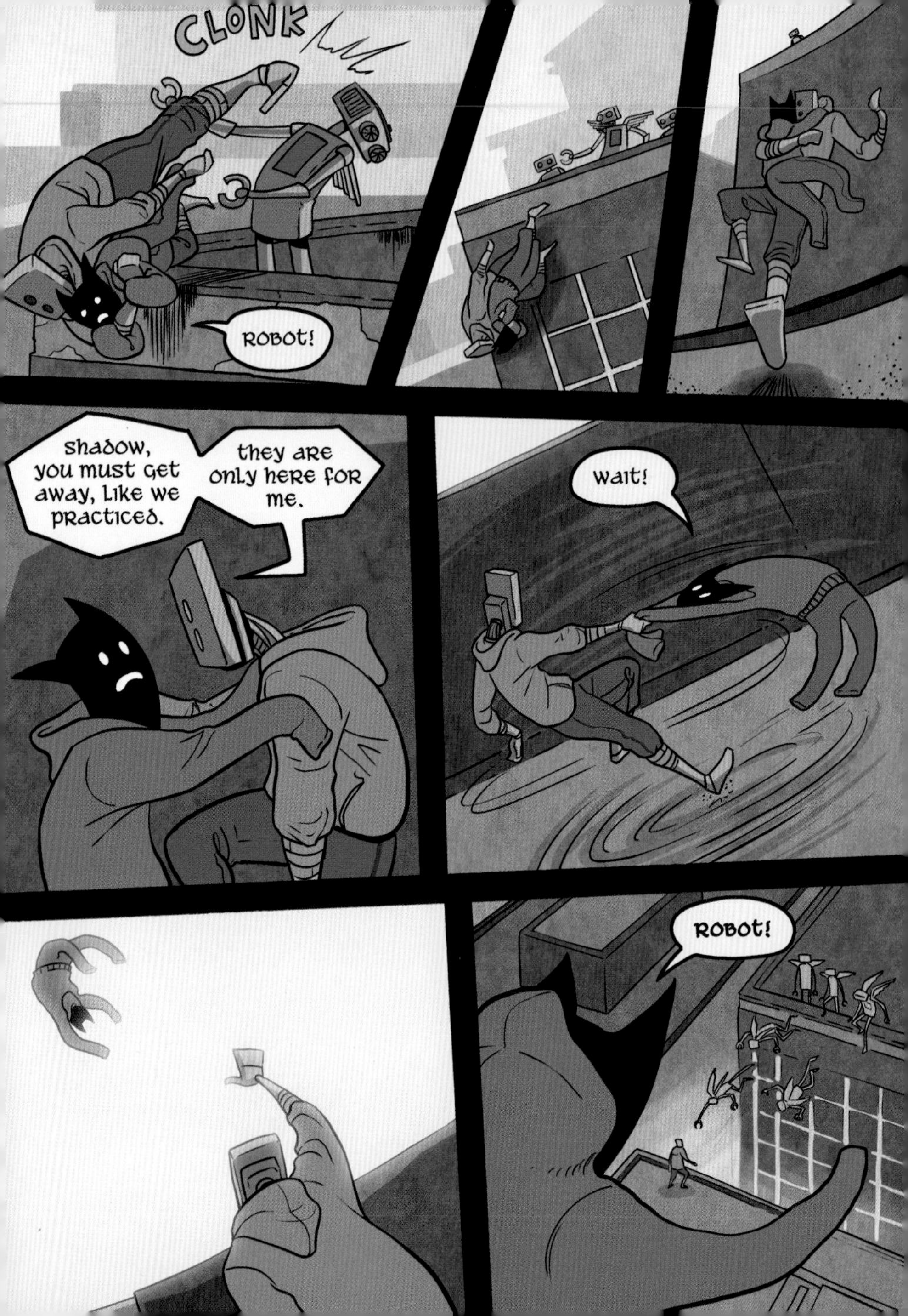
CLONK
ROBOT!
shadow, you must get away, like we practiced.
they are only here for me.
wait!
ROBOT!

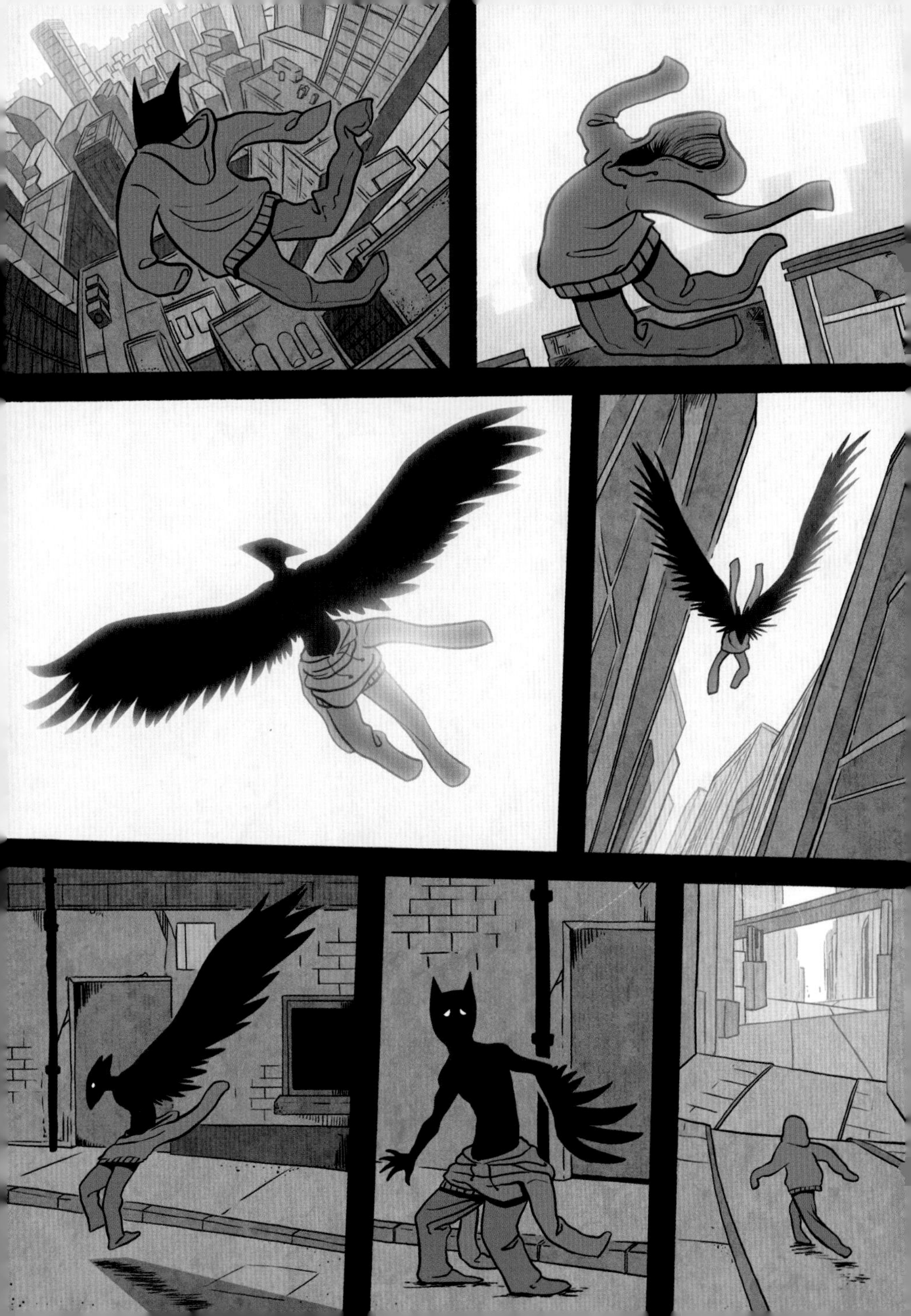

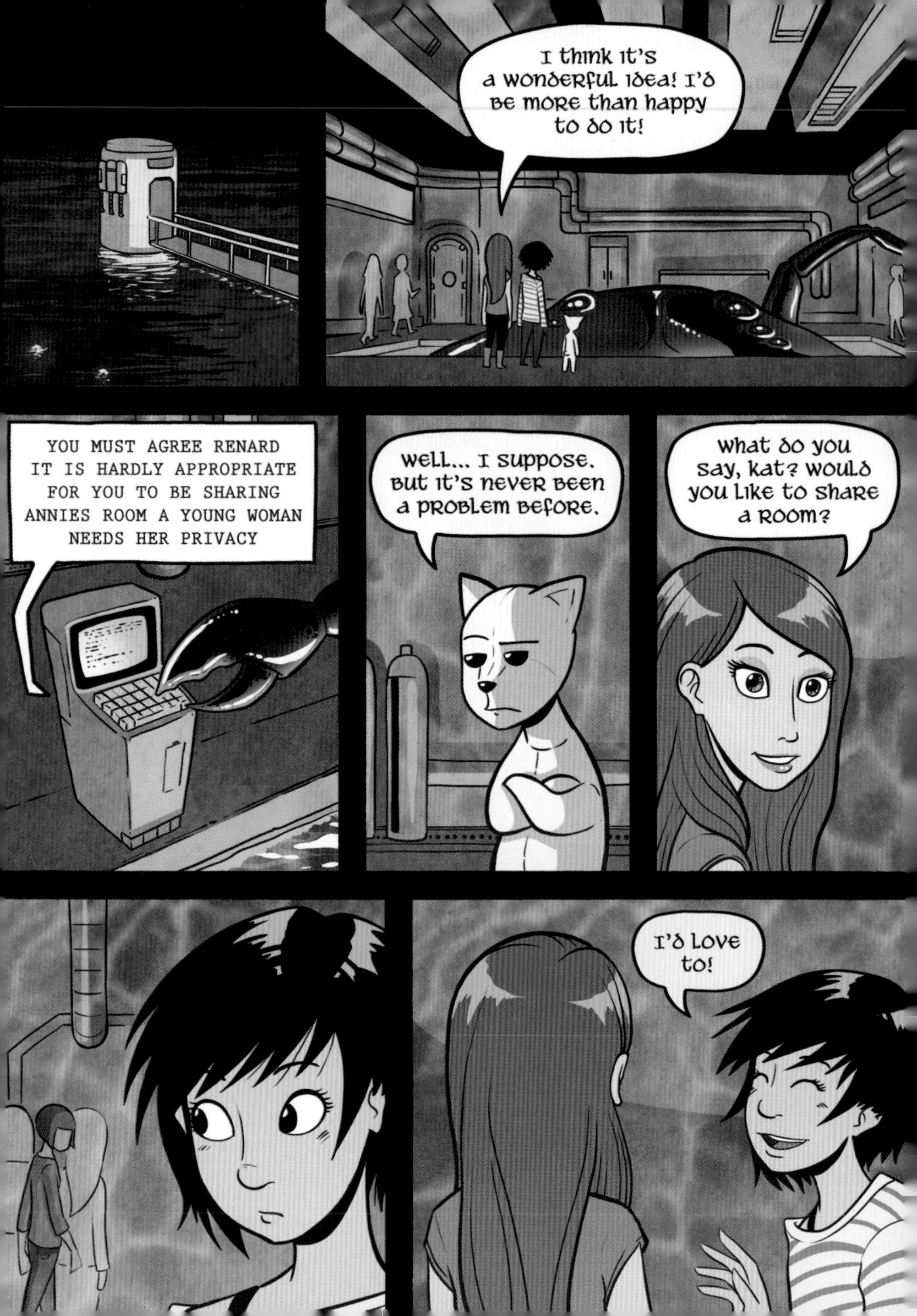

I think it's a wonderful idea! I'd be more than happy to do it!
YOU MUST AGREE RENARD IT IS HARDLY APPROPRIATE FOR YOU TO BE SHARING ANNIES ROOM A YOUNG WOMAN NEEDS HER PRIVACY
Well... I suppose. But it's never been a problem before.
What do you say, Kat? Would you like to share a room?
I'd love to!

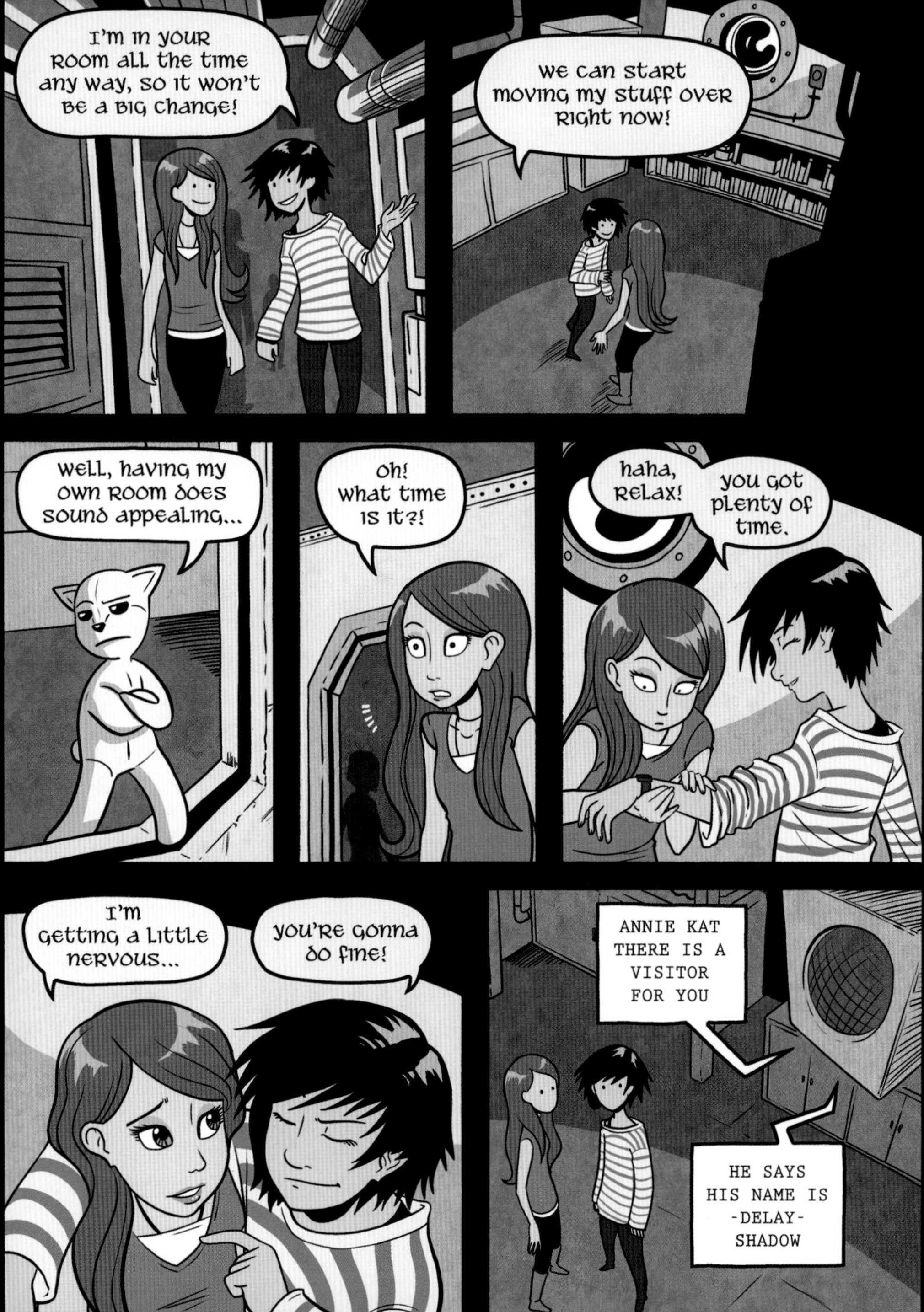
I'm in your room all the time any way, so it won't be a big change!
We can start moving my stuff over right now!
Well, having my own room does sound appealing...
Oh! What time is it?!
Haha, relax!
You got plenty of time.
I'm getting a little nervous...
You're gonna do fine!
ANNIE KAT THERE IS A VISITOR FOR YOU
HE SAYS HIS NAME IS -DELAY- SHADOW

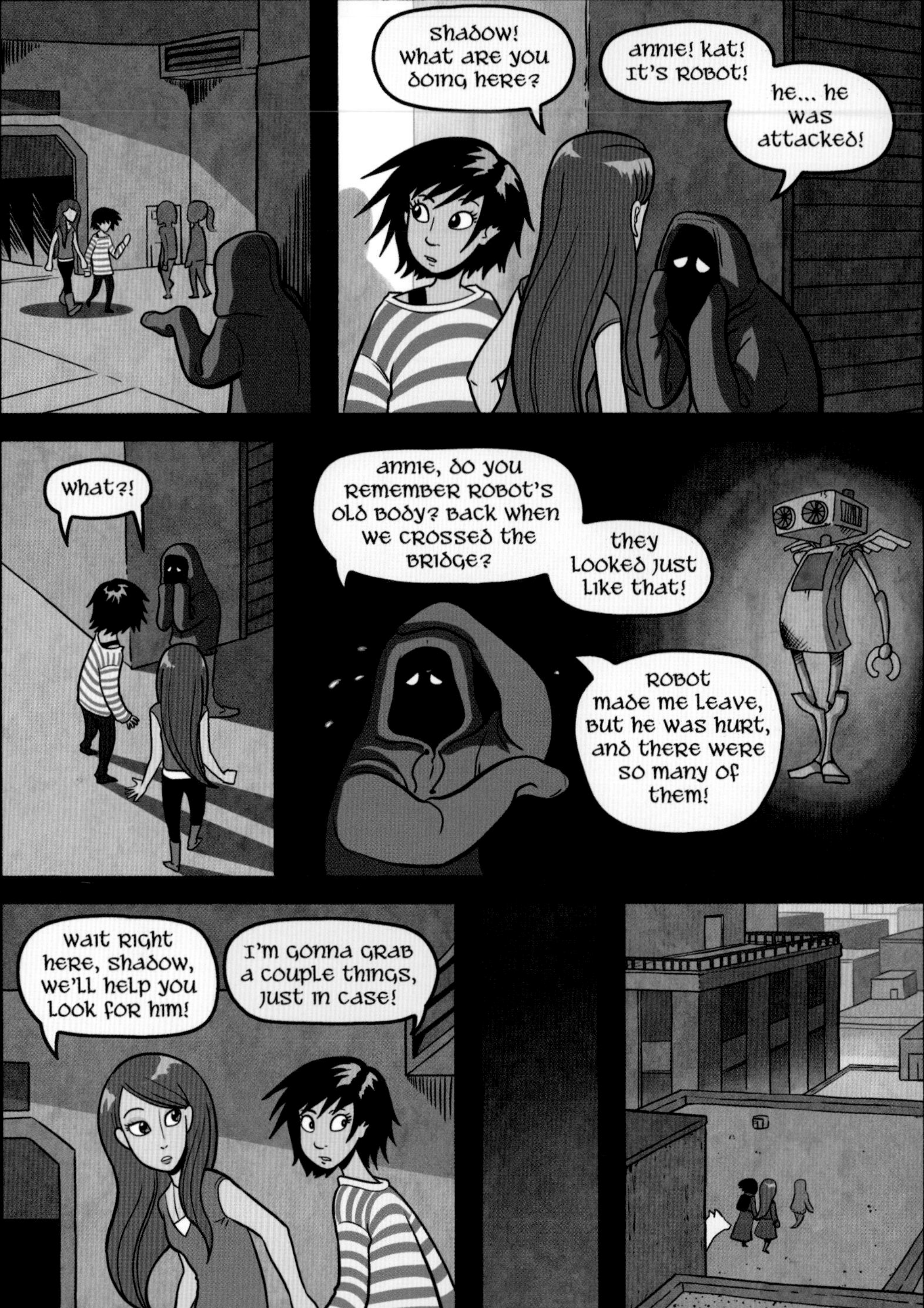
Shadow! What are you doing here?
Annie! Kat! It's Robot!
He... he was attacked!
What?!
Annie, do you remember Robot's old body? Back when we crossed the bridge?
They looked just like that!
Robot made me leave, but he was hurt, and there were so many of them!
Wait right here, Shadow, we'll help you look for him!
I'm gonna grab a couple things, just in case!

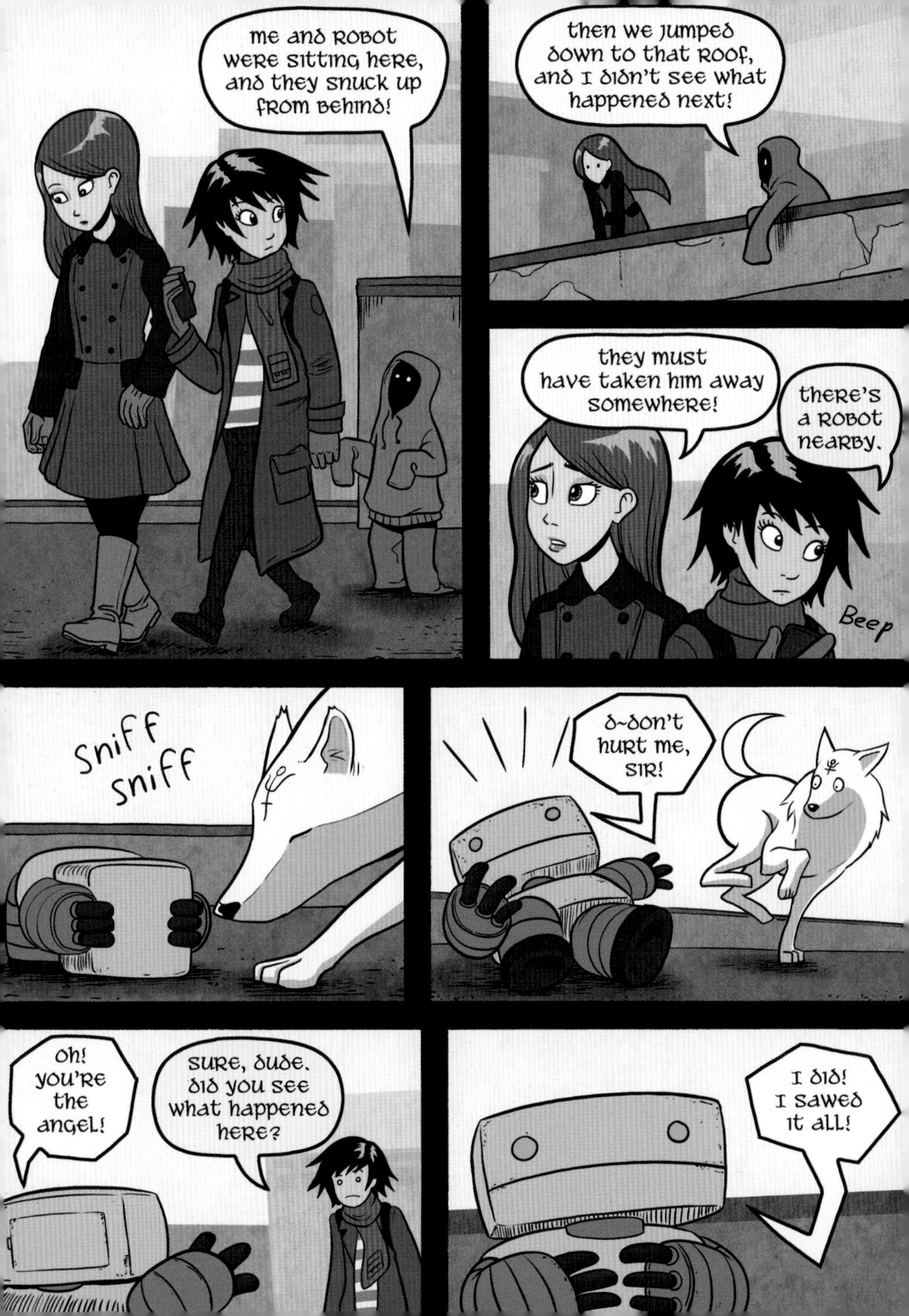
me and robot were sitting here, and they snuck up from behind!
then we jumped down to that roof, and I didn't see what happened next!
they must have taken him away somewhere!
there's a robot nearby.
Beep
Sniff sniff
d-don't hurt me, sir!
oh! you're the angel!
sure, dude. did you see what happened here?
I did! I sawed it all!

I'M GOING to TAKE a LOOK at YOUR VIDEO LOG, OKAY?

Pat Pat

an HONOUR!

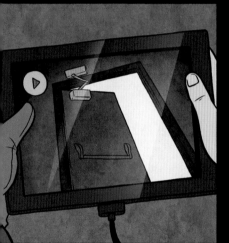

that's them!

WOW, they DO kinda LOOK LIKE that OLD SERAPH BODY...

they DID TAKE him.

ROBOT...

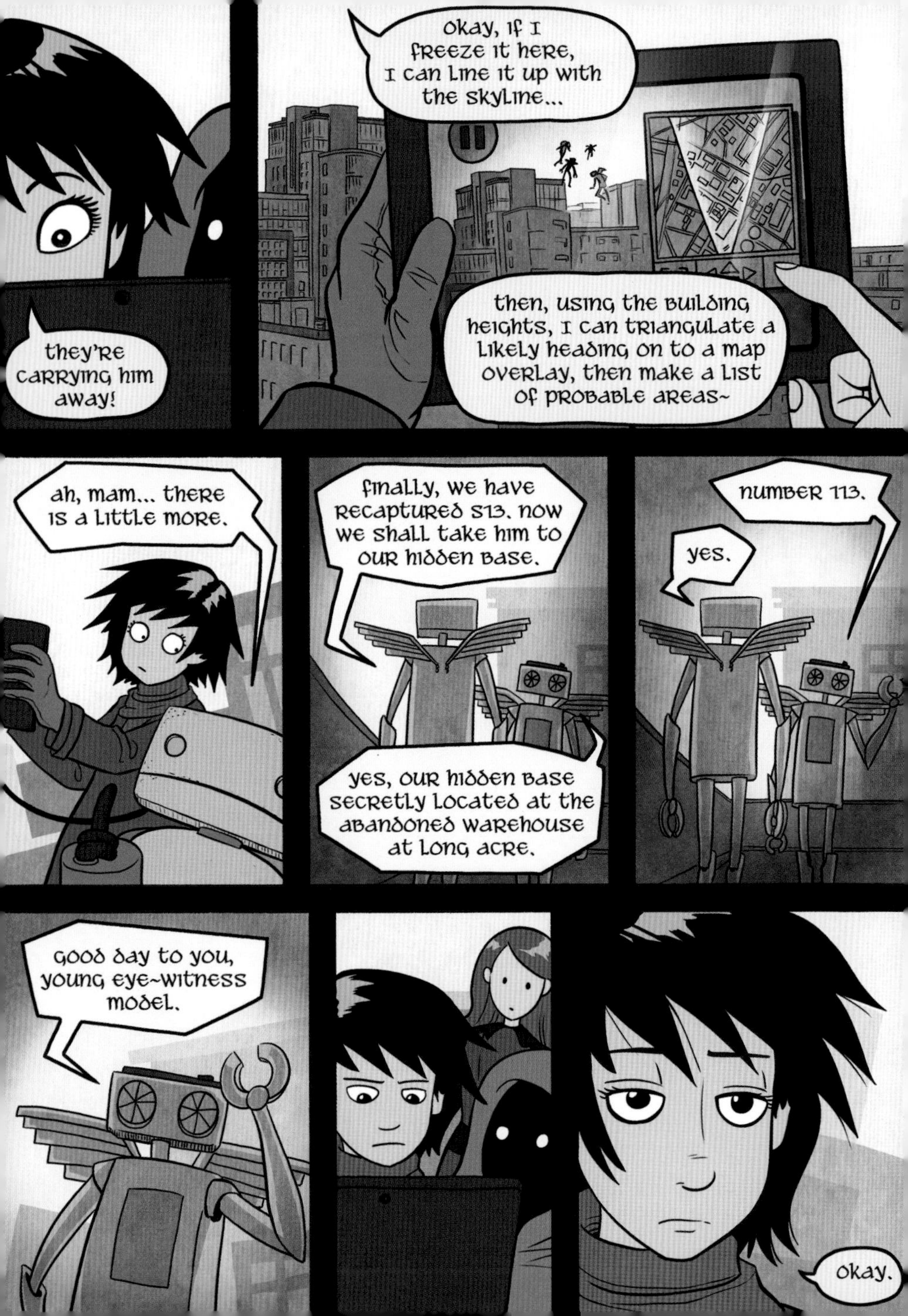
they're carrying him away!
Okay, if I freeze it here, I can line it up with the skyline...
then, using the building heights, I can triangulate a likely heading on to a map overlay, then make a list of probable areas~
ah, mam... there is a little more.
finally, we have recaptured S13. now we shall take him to our hidden base.
yes, our hidden base secretly located at the abandoned warehouse at long acre.
number 113.
yes.
good day to you, young eye-witness model.
Okay.

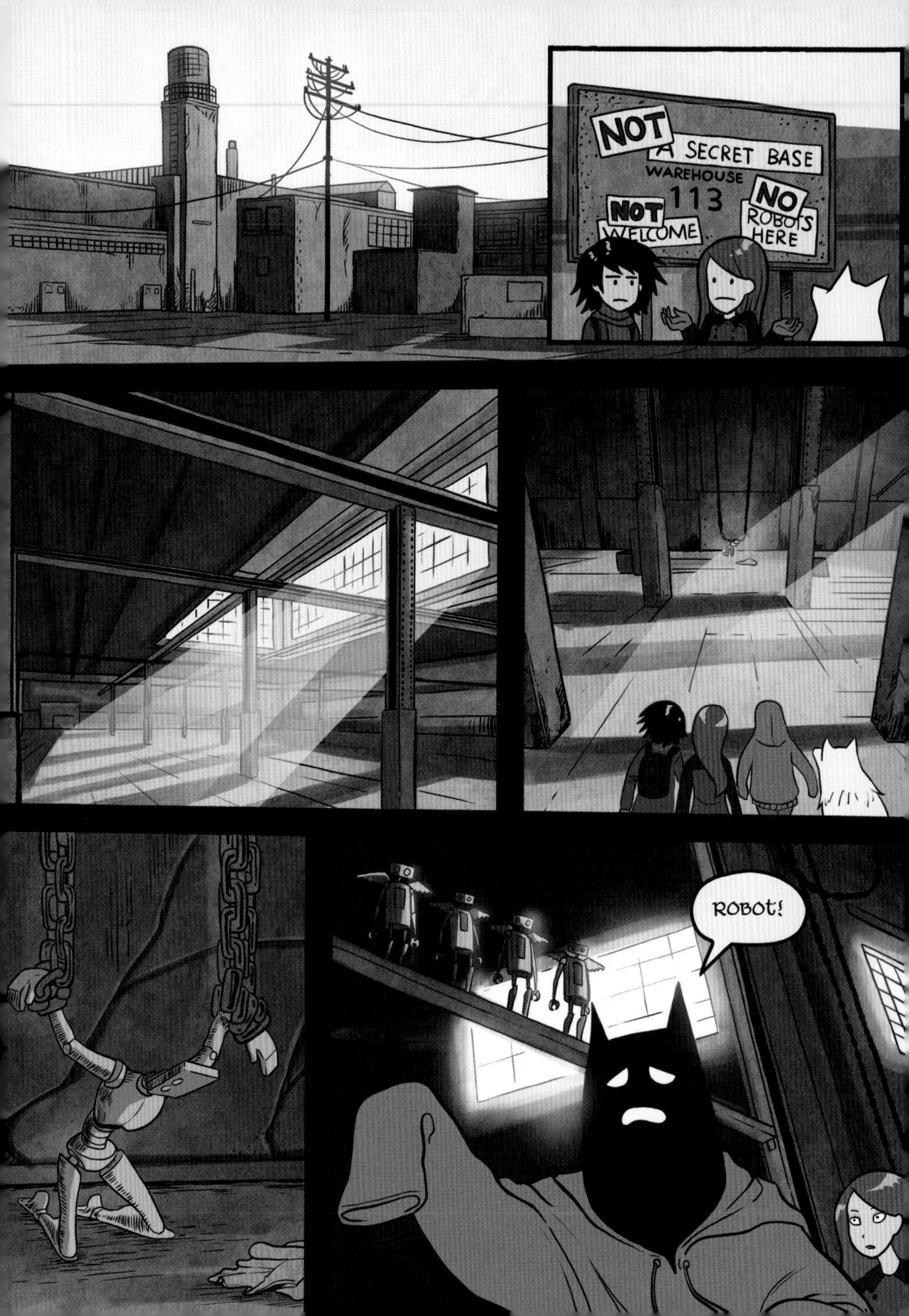

NOT
A SECRET BASE
WAREHOUSE
113
NOT
WELCOME
NO
ROBOTS
HERE
ROBOT!

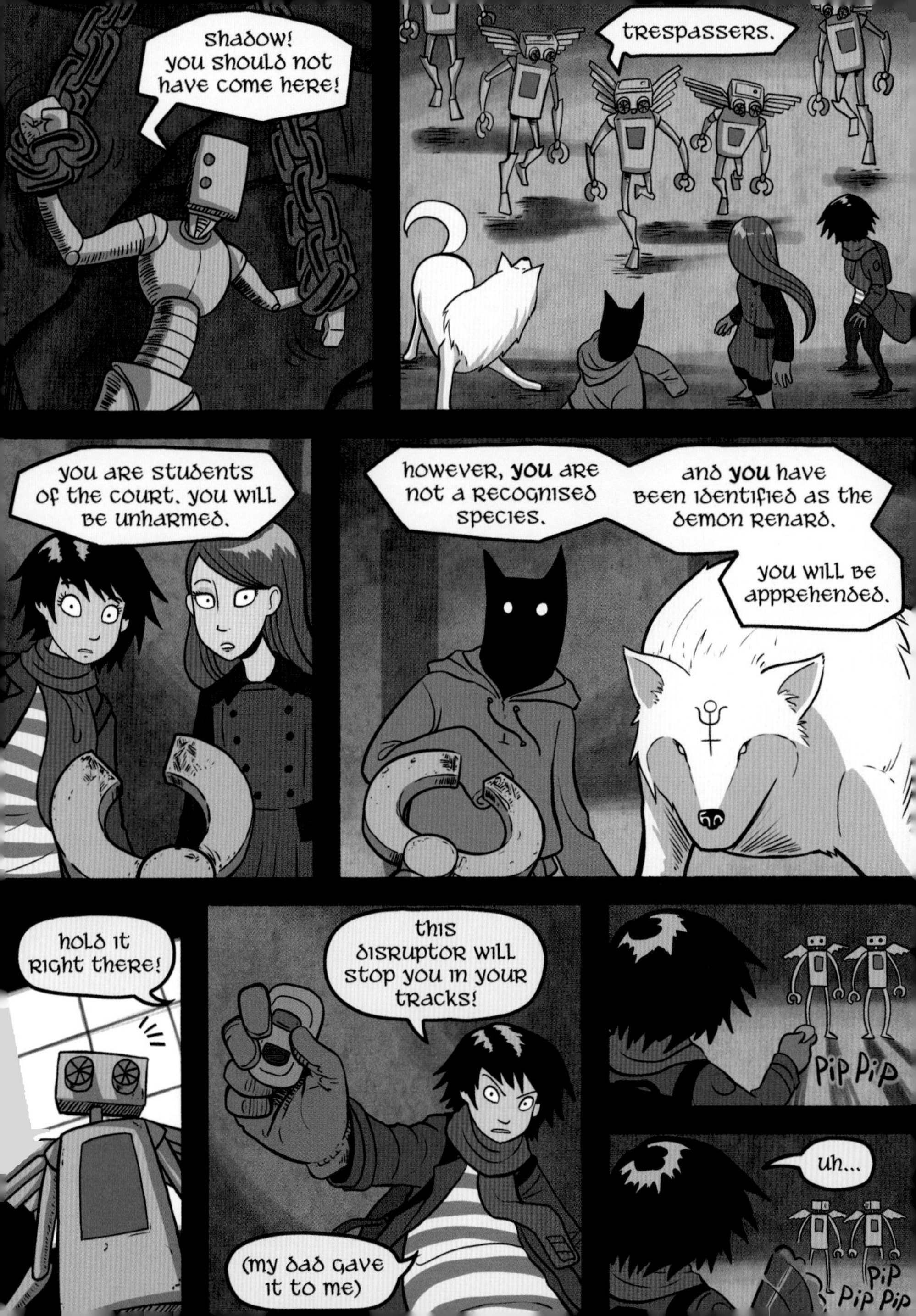
shadow! you should not have come here!
trespassers.
you are students of the court. you will be unharmed.
however, you are not a recognised species.
and you have been identified as the demon renard.
you will be apprehended.
hold it right there!
this disruptor will stop you in your tracks!
(my dad gave it to me)
pip pip
uh...
pip pip pip

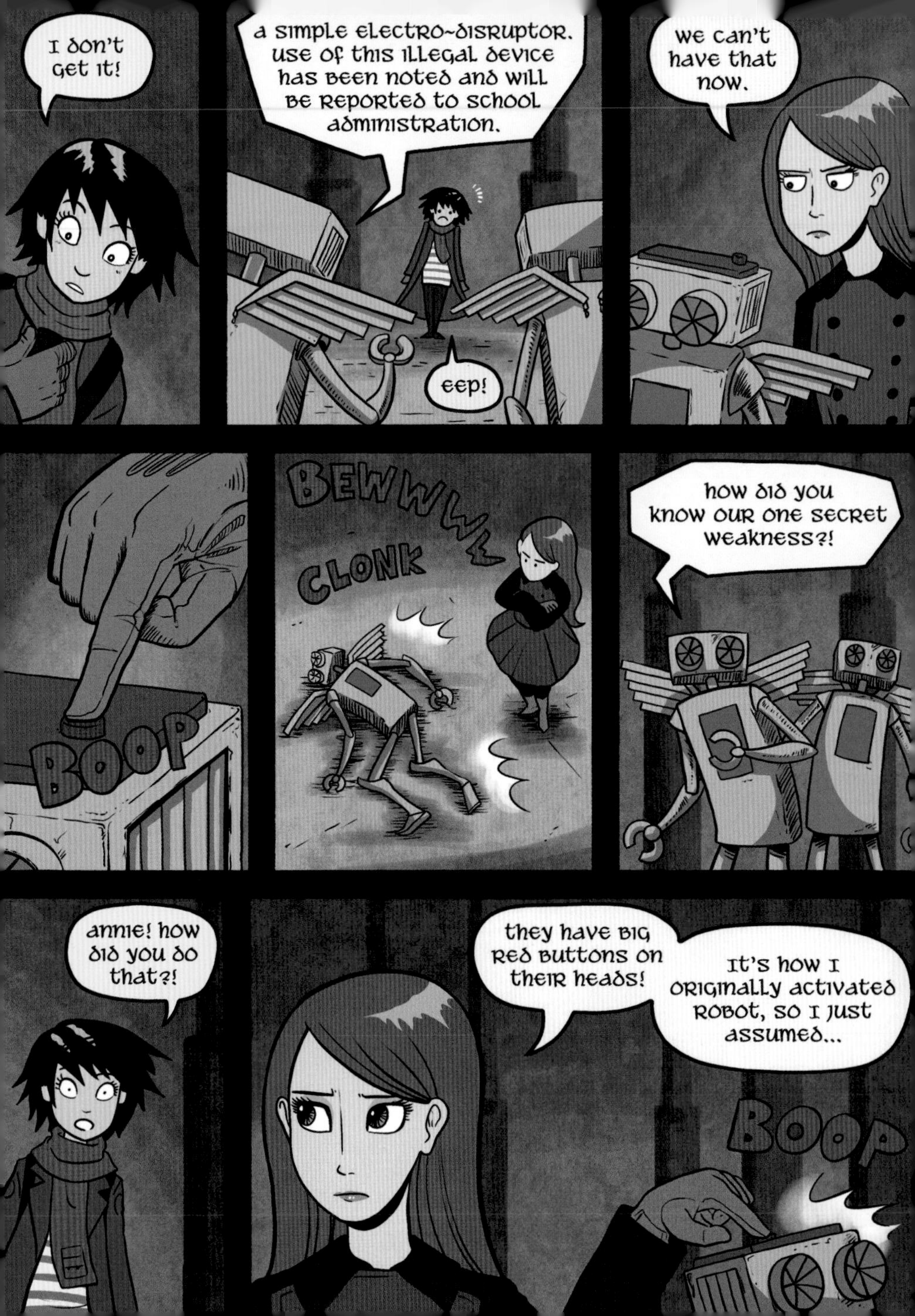
I don't get it!
a simple electro~disruptor. use of this illegal device has been noted and will be reported to school administration.
eep!
we can't have that now.
BOOP
BEWWWL
CLONK
how did you know our one secret weakness?!
annie! how did you do that?!
they have big red buttons on their heads!
It's how I originally activated robot, so I just assumed...
BOOP

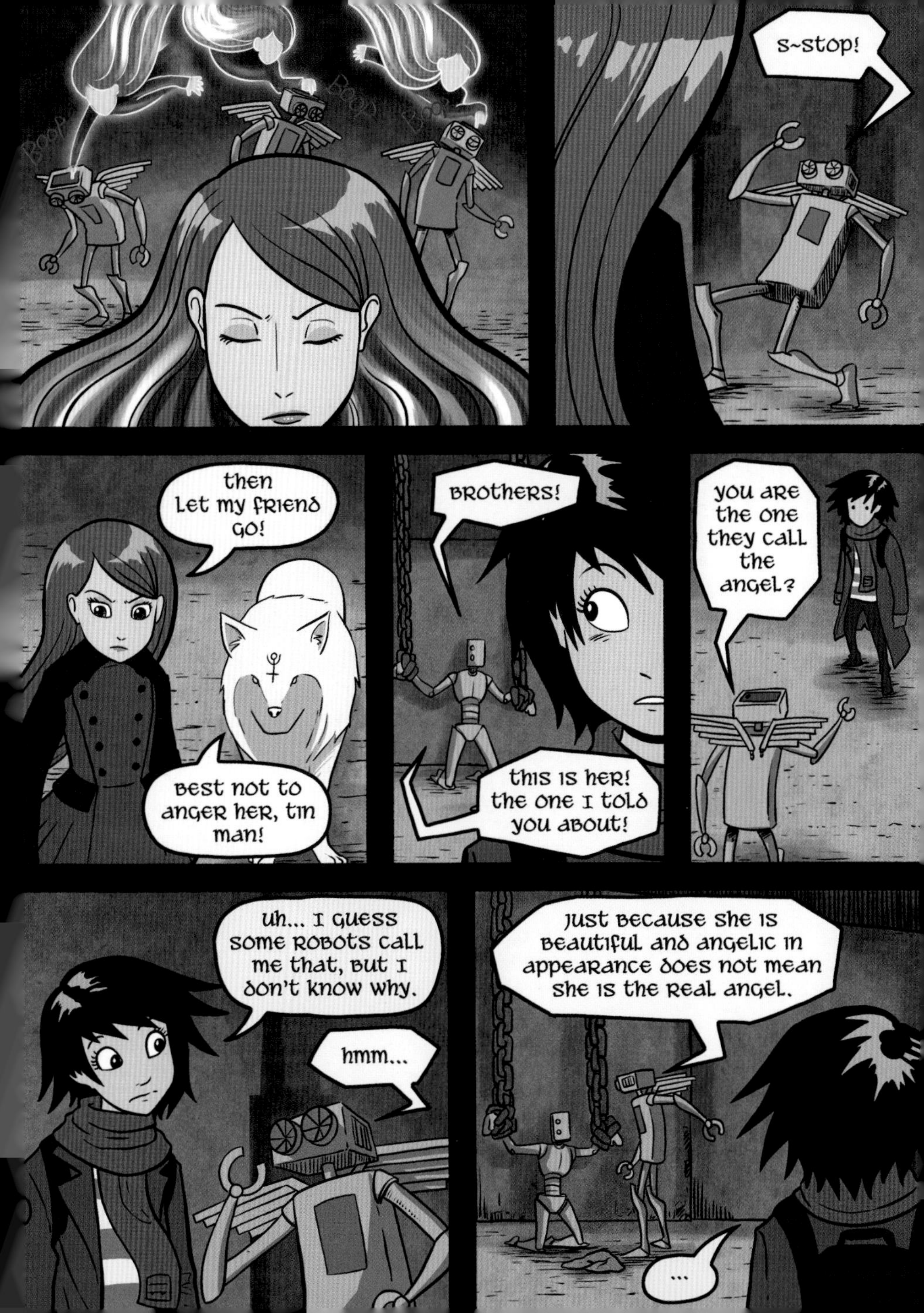
BOOP
BOOP
BOOP
S~STOP!
then let my friend go!
best not to anger her, tin man!
BROTHERS!
this is her! the one I told you about!
you are the one they call the angel?
uh... I guess some robots call me that, but I don't know why.
hmm...
just because she is beautiful and angelic in appearance does not mean she is the real angel.
...

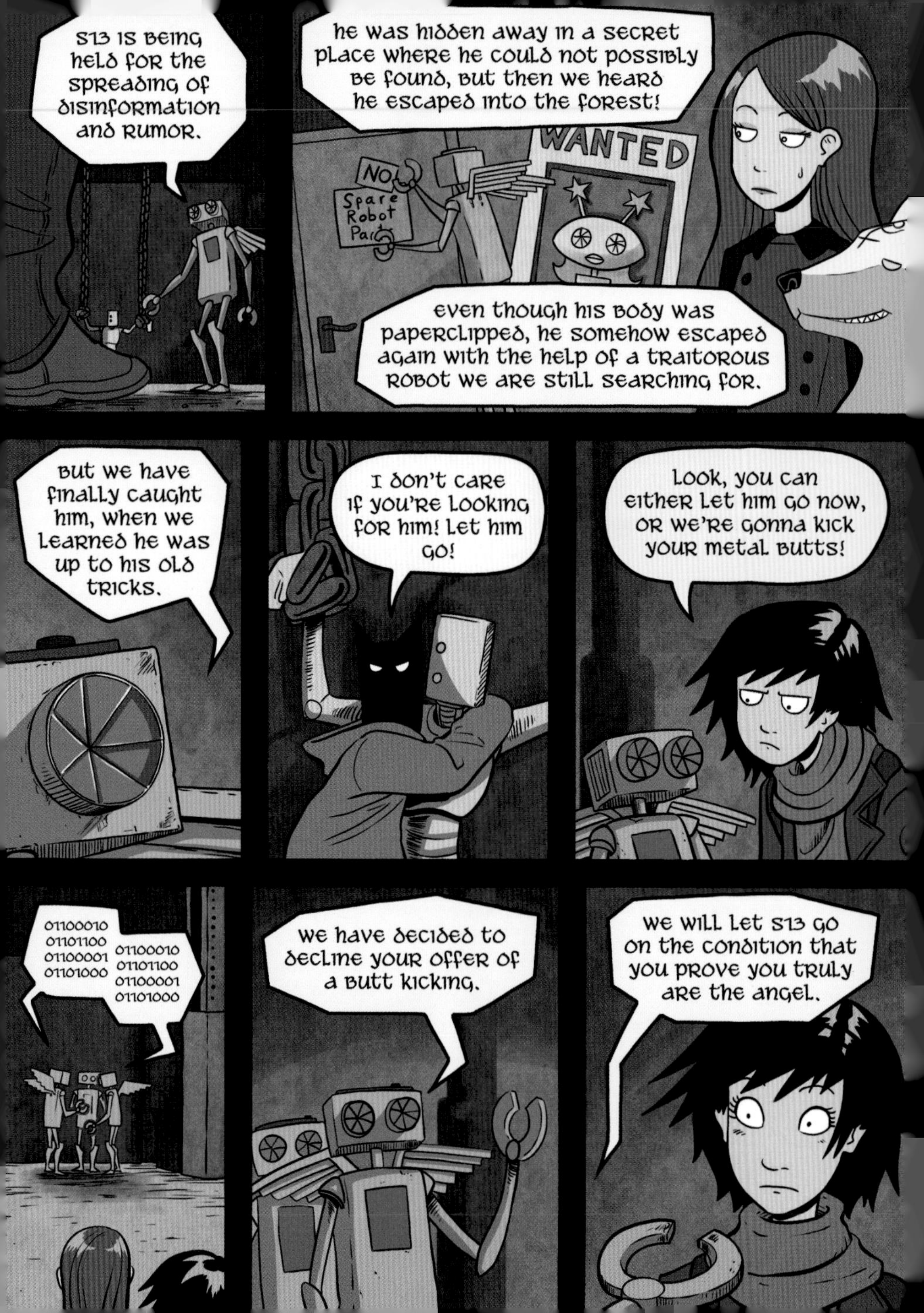
S13 is being held for the spreading of disinformation and rumor.
He was hidden away in a secret place where he could not possibly be found, but then we heard he escaped into the forest!
NO
Spare Robot Parts
WANTED
Even though his body was paperclipped, he somehow escaped again with the help of a traitorous robot we are still searching for.
But we have finally caught him, when we learned he was up to his old tricks.
I don't care if you're looking for him! Let him go!
Look, you can either let him go now, or we're gonna kick your metal butts!
01100010 01101100 01100001 01101000
01100010 01101100 01100001 01101000
We have decided to decline your offer of a butt kicking.
We will let S13 go on the condition that you prove you truly are the angel.

ARE YOU SURE ABOUT THIS, ROBOT?

JUST SHOW THEM YOUR WORK. THEY WILL SEE.

WELL, THIS IS MY WORKSHOP.

I'VE BEEN WORKING ON MAKING A NEW BODY FOR ROBOT.

THIS IS A BIOREACTOR I MADE. I'M DOING SOME TESTS WITH BIO-SCAFFOLDS IN A CULTURE MEDIUM.

TO WHAT END?

TO GROW BIO-HYBRID PARTS.

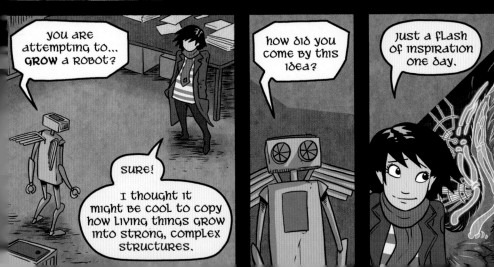

YOU ARE ATTEMPTING TO... GROW A ROBOT?

SURE!

I THOUGHT IT MIGHT BE COOL TO COPY HOW LIVING THINGS GROW INTO STRONG, COMPLEX STRUCTURES.

HOW DID YOU COME BY THIS IDEA?

JUST A FLASH OF INSPIRATION ONE DAY.

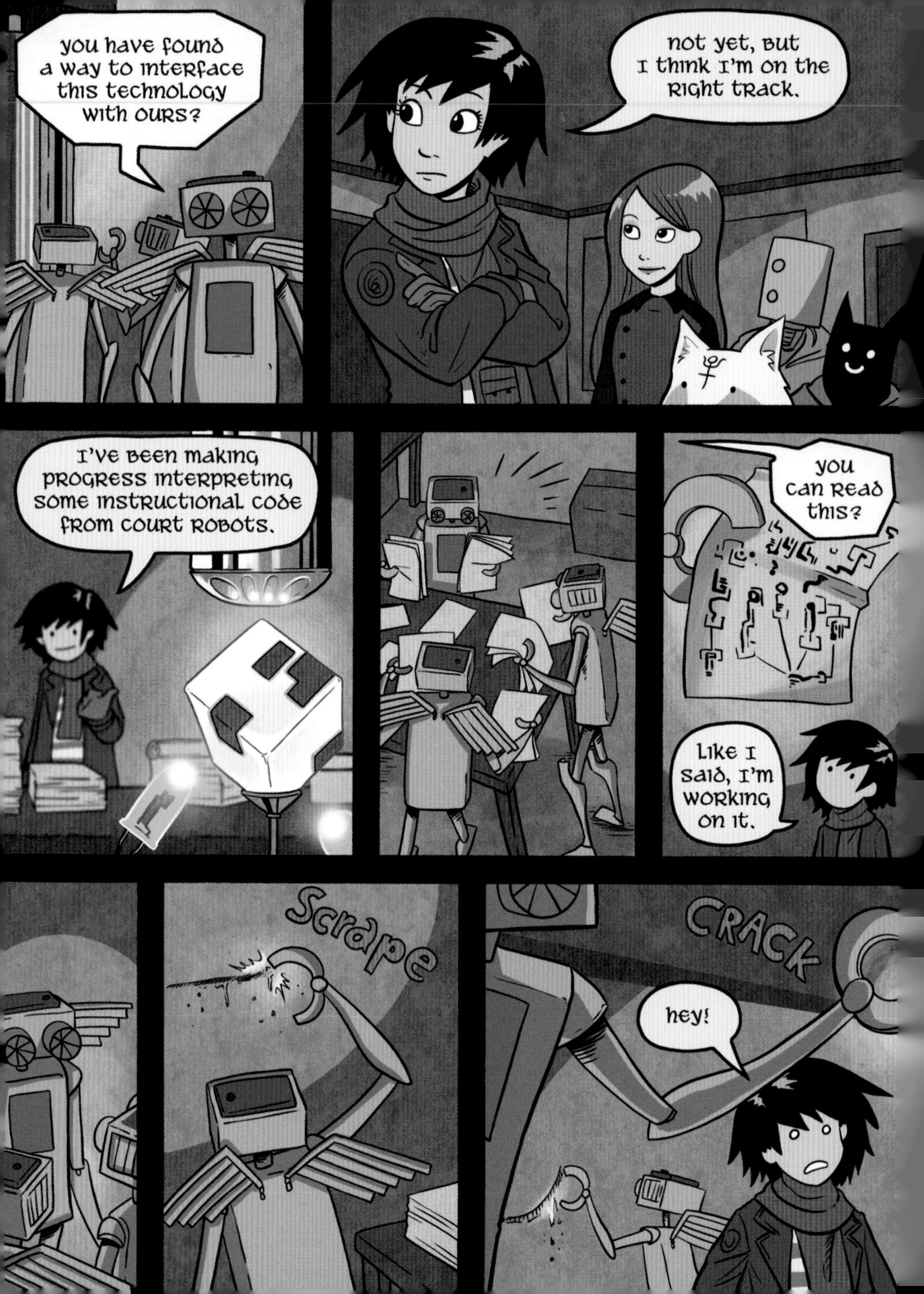
you have found a way to interface this technology with ours?
not yet, but I think I'm on the right track.
I've been making progress interpreting some instructional code from court robots.
you can read this?
like I said, I'm working on it.
Scrape
CRACK
hey!

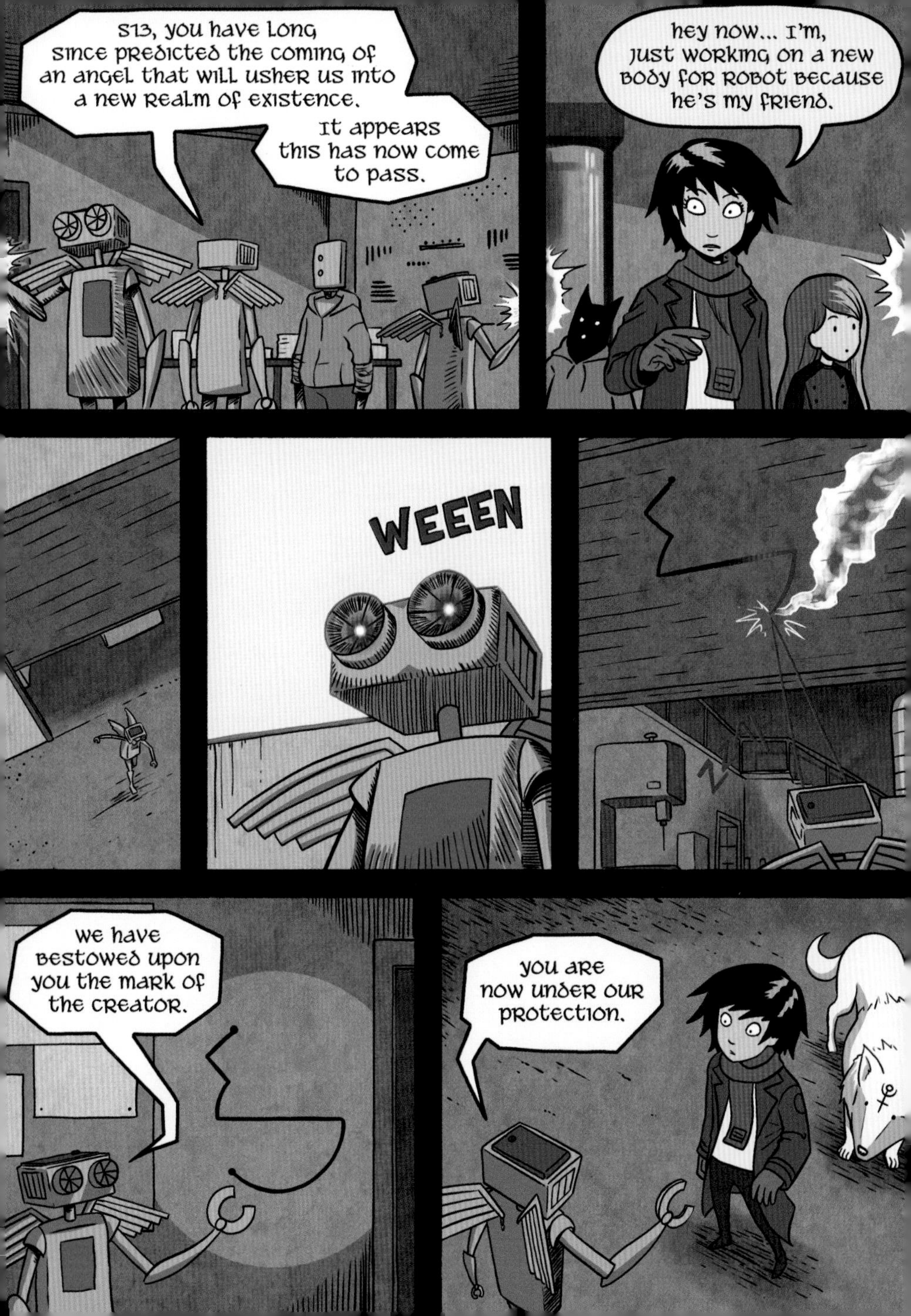
S13, you have long since predicted the coming of an angel that will usher us into a new realm of existence.
It appears this has now come to pass.
hey now... I'm, just working on a new body for robot because he's my friend.
WEEEN
we have bestowed upon you the mark of the creator.
you are now under our protection.

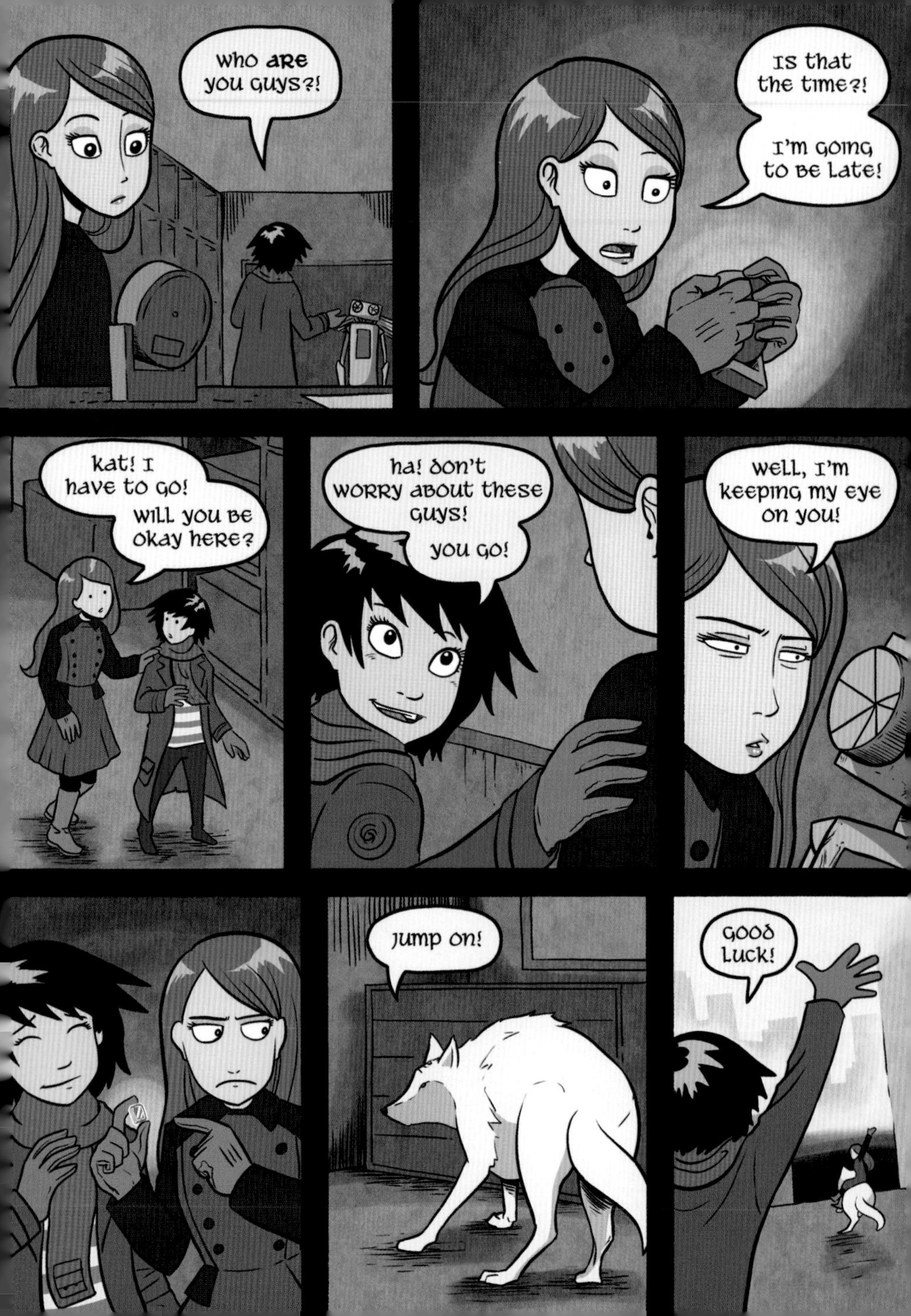
who are you guys?!
Is that the time?!
I'm going to be late!
kat! I have to go!
will you be okay here?
ha! don't worry about these guys!
you go!
well, I'm keeping my eye on you!
jump on!
good luck!

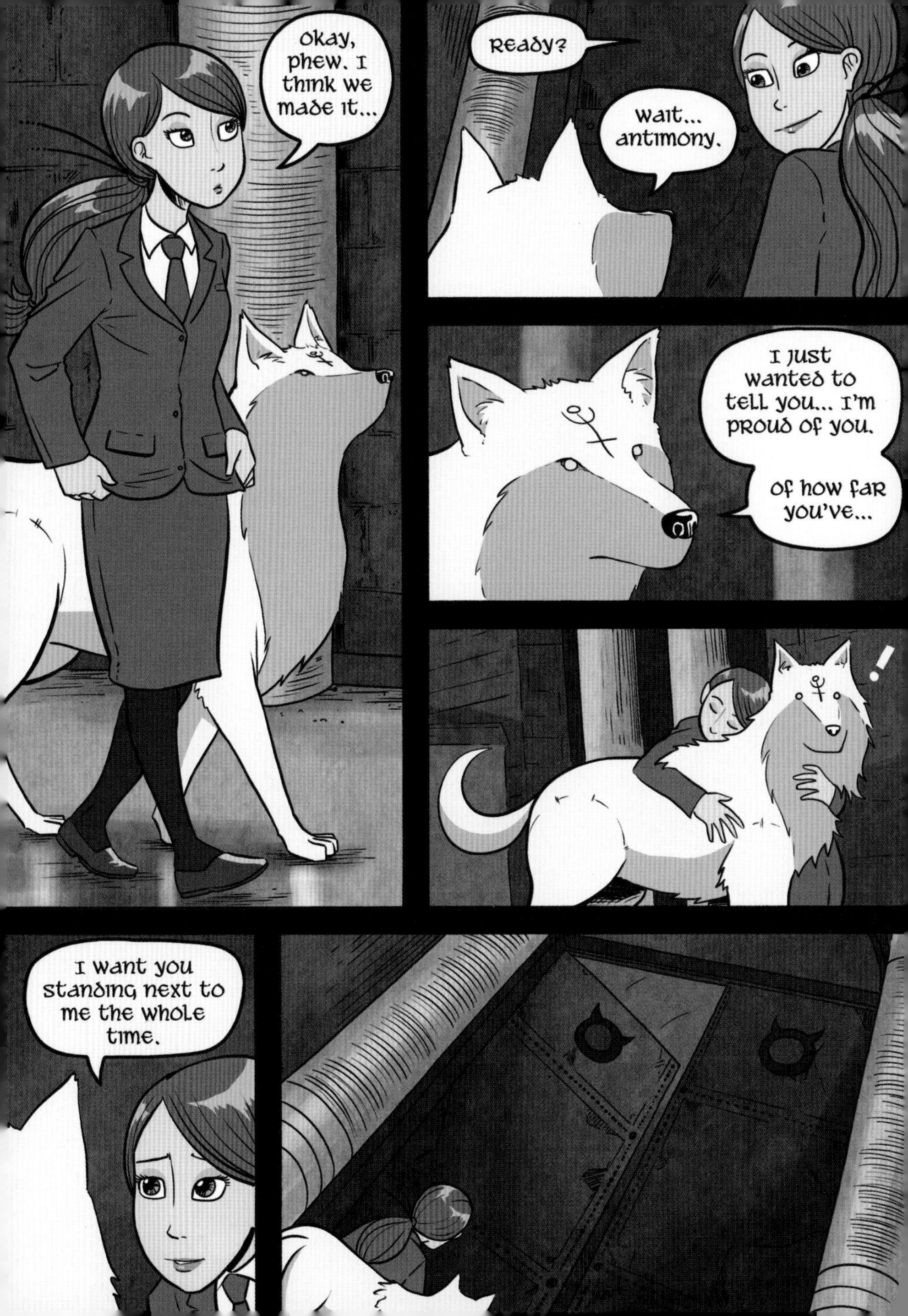
Okay, phew. I think we made it...
Ready?
Wait... Antimony.
I just wanted to tell you... I'm proud of you.
Of how far you've...
!
I want you standing next to me the whole time.

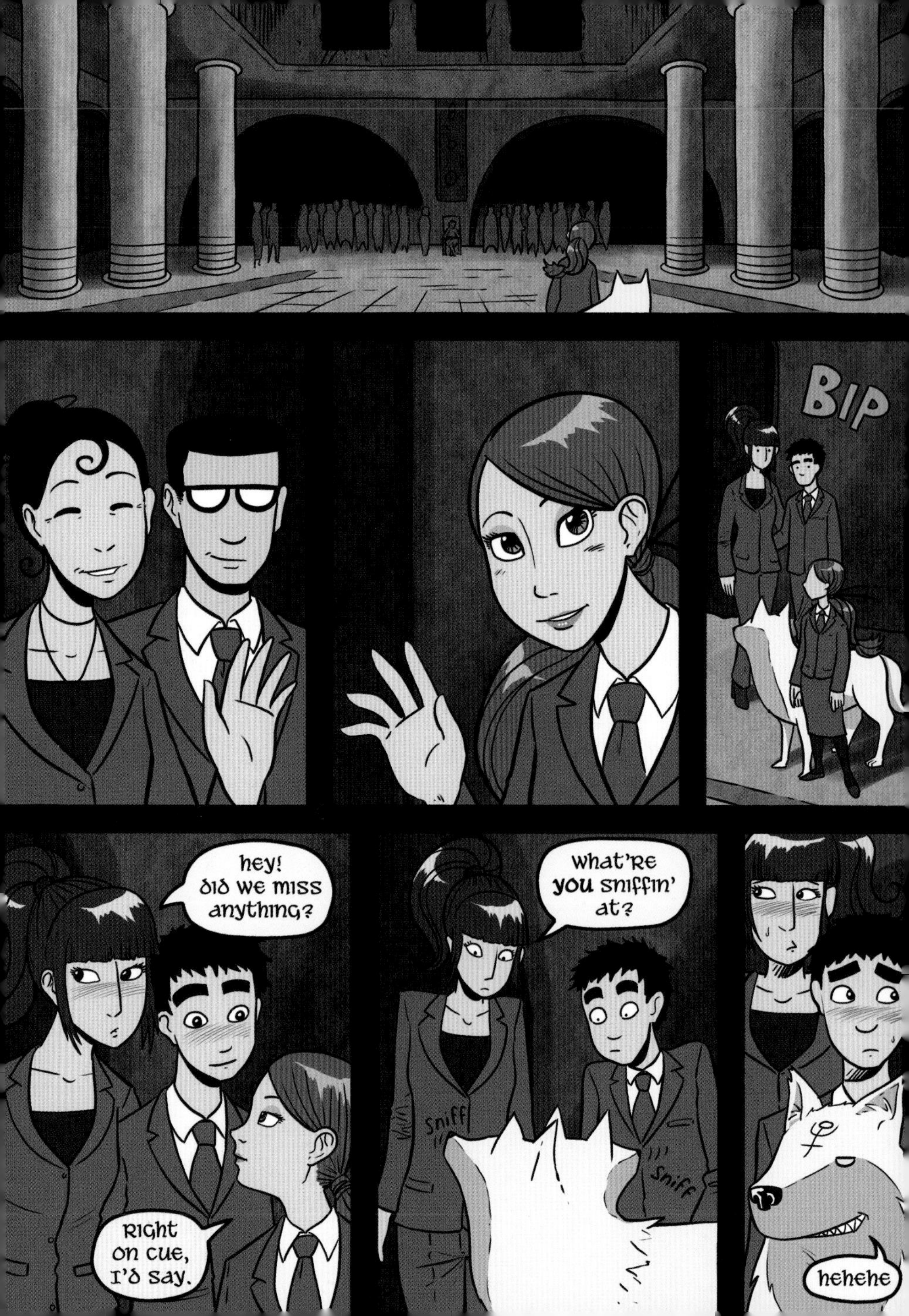
BIP
hey! did we miss anything?
Right on cue, I'd say.
What're you sniffin' at?
Sniff
Sniff
hehehe

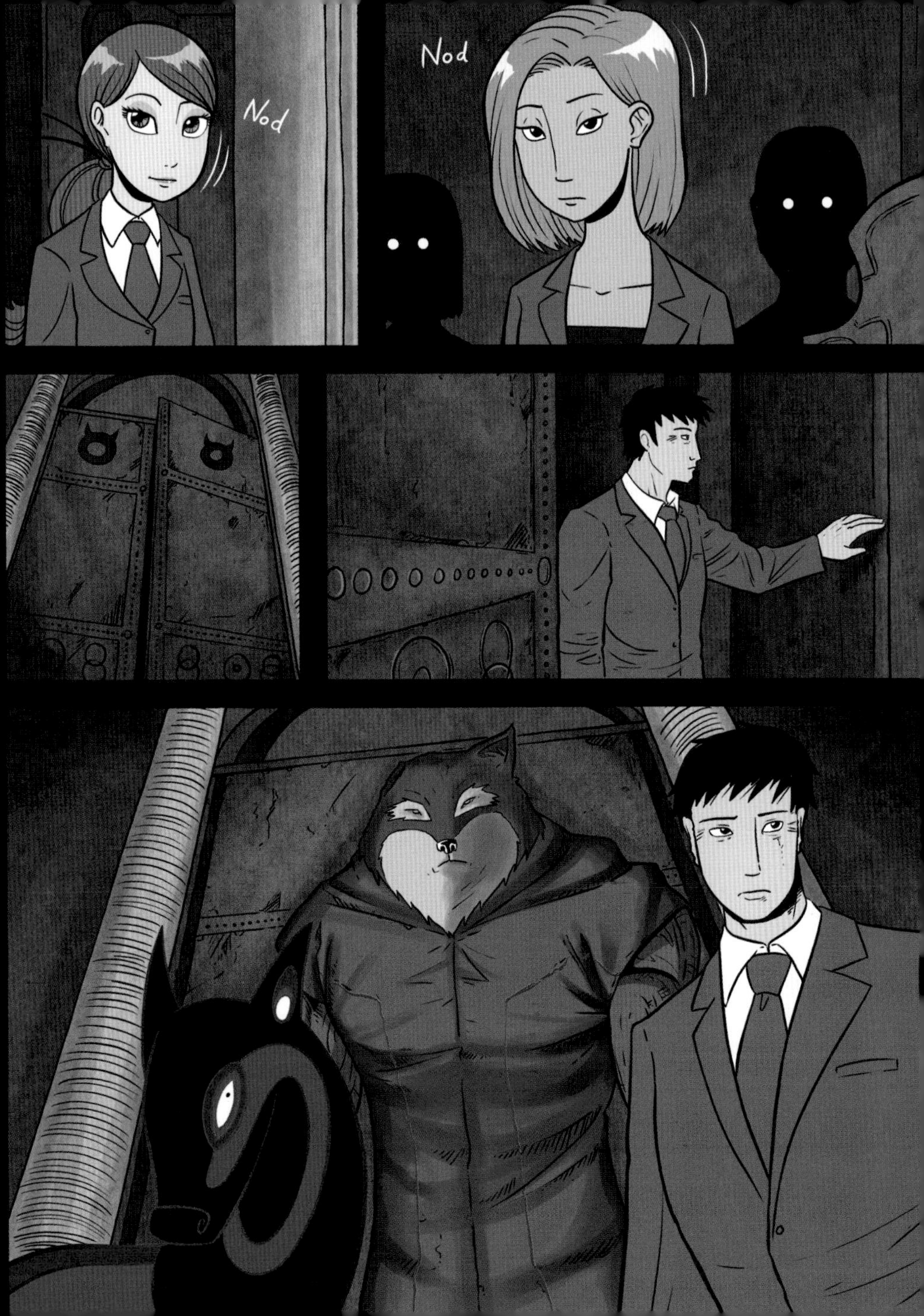
Nod
Nod

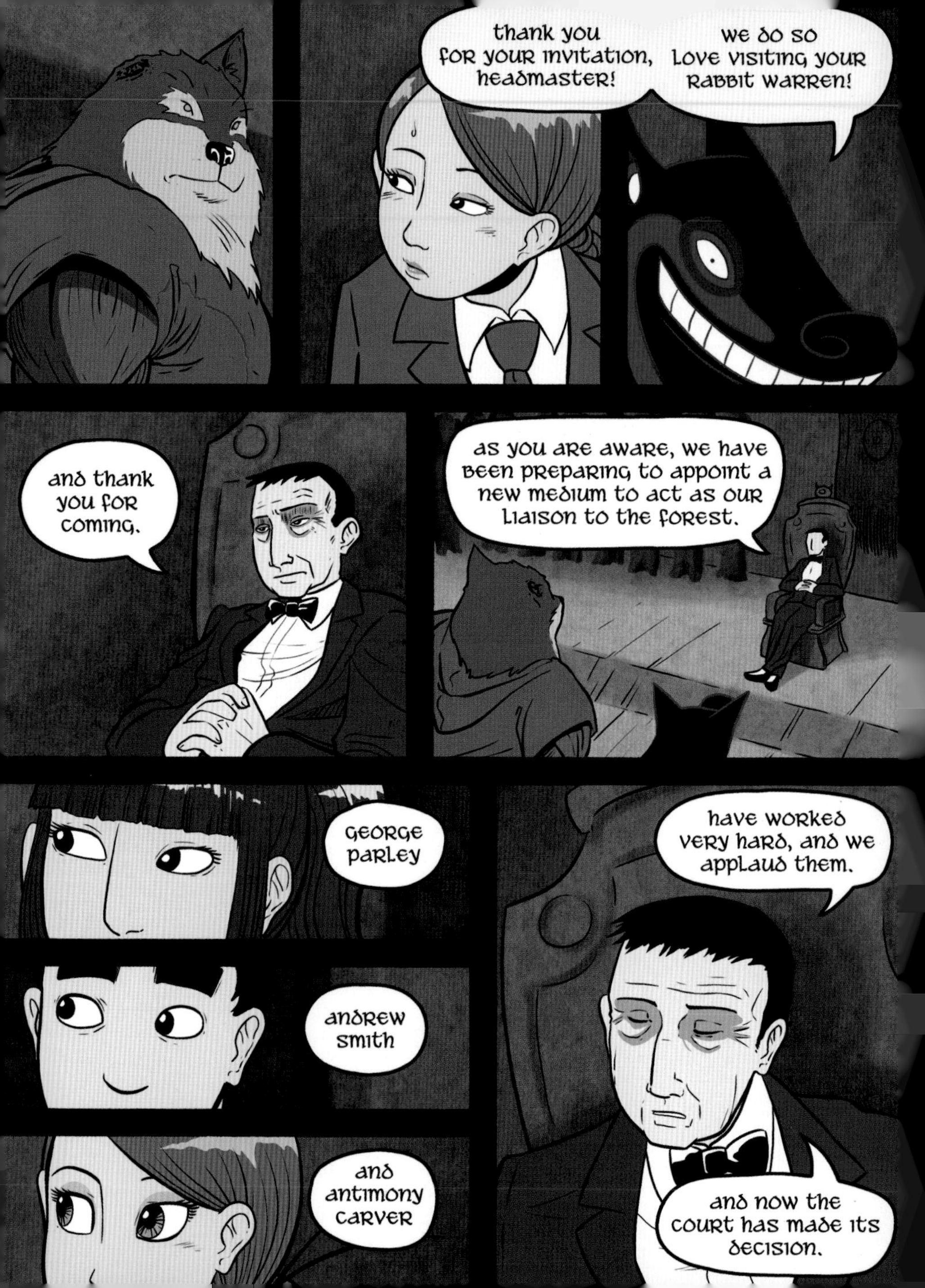
thank you for your invitation, headmaster!
we do so love visiting your rabbit warren!
and thank you for coming.
as you are aware, we have been preparing to appoint a new medium to act as our liaison to the forest.
george parley
andrew smith
and antimony carver
have worked very hard, and we applaud them.
and now the court has made its decision.

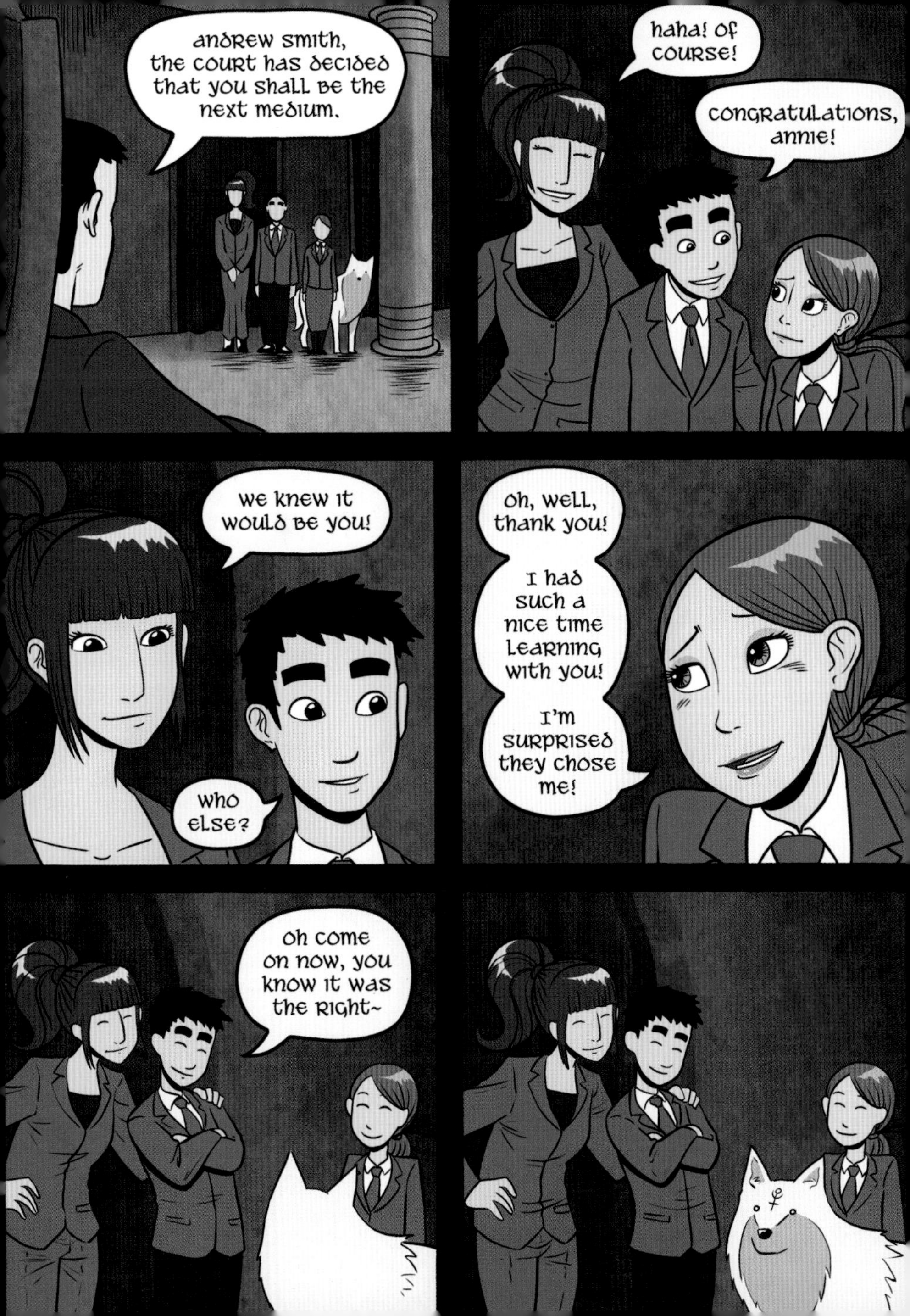
andrew smith, the court has decided that you shall be the next medium.
haha! of course!
congratulations, annie!
we knew it would be you!
who else?
oh, well, thank you!
I had such a nice time learning with you!
I'm surprised they chose me!
oh come on now, you know it was the right~

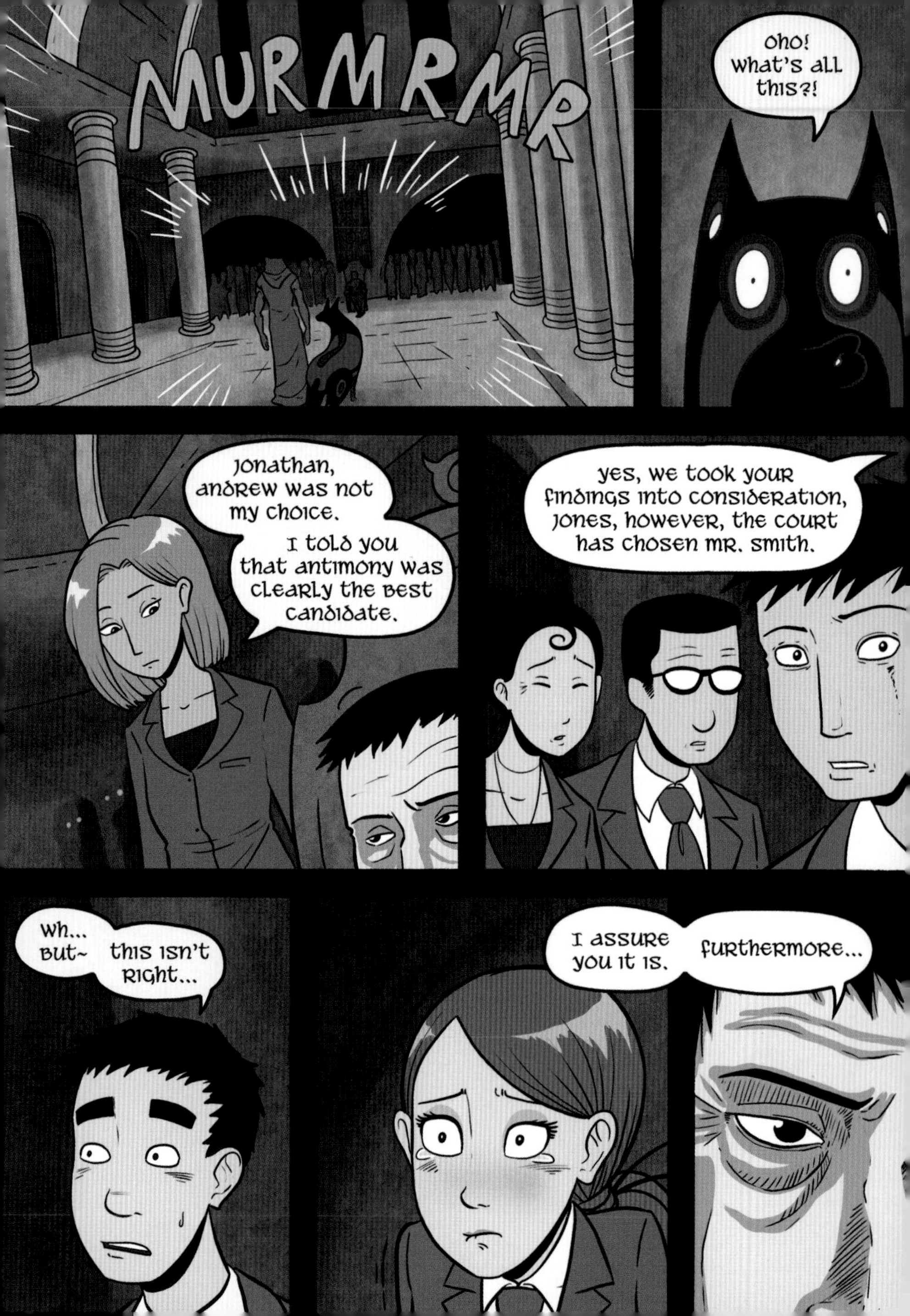
MURMRMR
Oho! What's all this?!
Jonathan, Andrew was not my choice.
I told you that Antimony was clearly the best candidate.
Yes, we took your findings into consideration, Jones, however, the court has chosen Mr. Smith.
Wh... But~
This isn't right...
I assure you it is.
Furthermore...

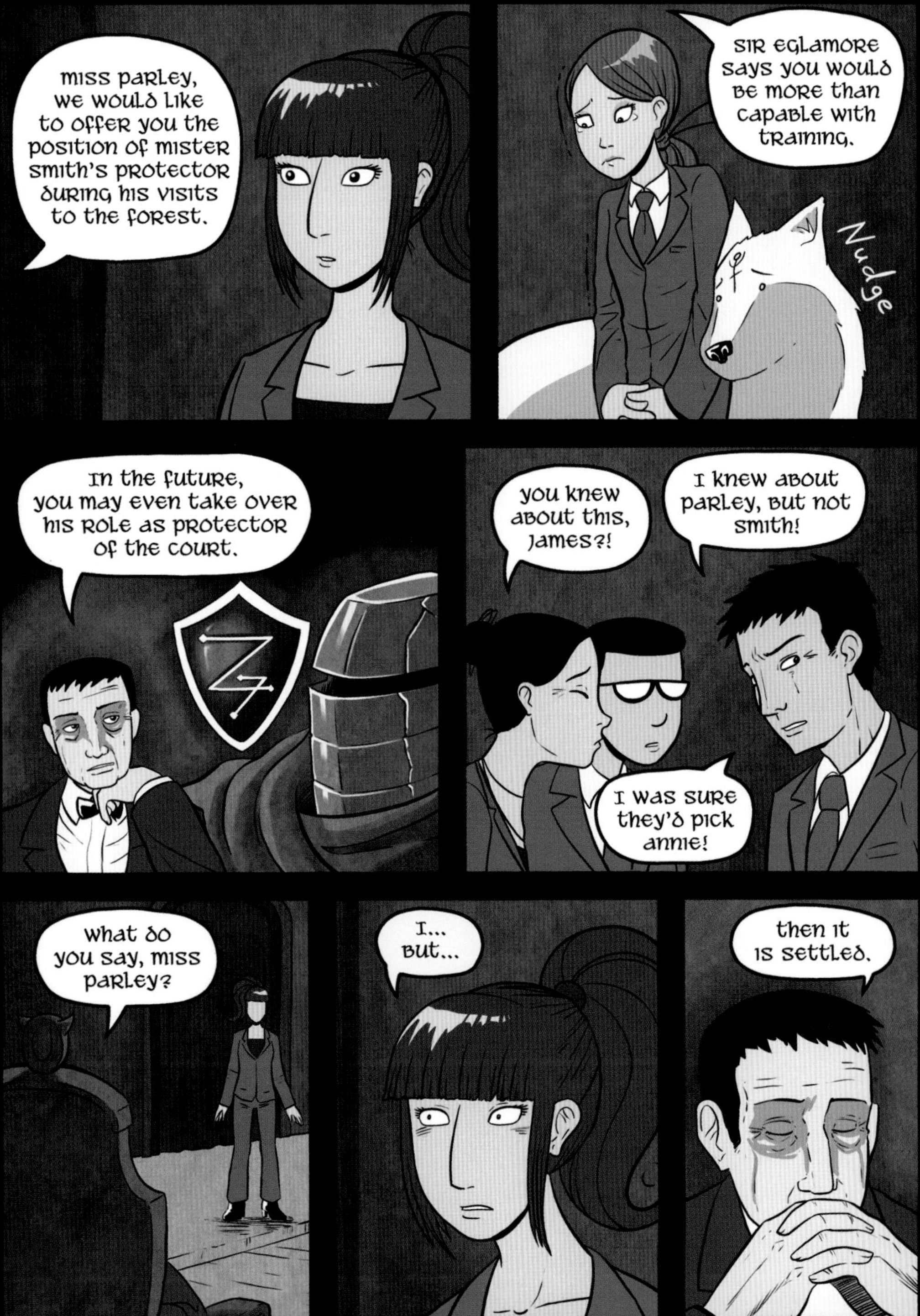
miss parley, we would like to offer you the position of mister smith's protector during his visits to the forest.
sir eglamore says you would be more than capable with training.
Nudge
In the future, you may even take over his role as protector of the court.
you knew about this, james?!
I knew about parley, but not smith!
I was sure they'd pick annie!
what do you say, miss parley?
I... but...
then it is settled.

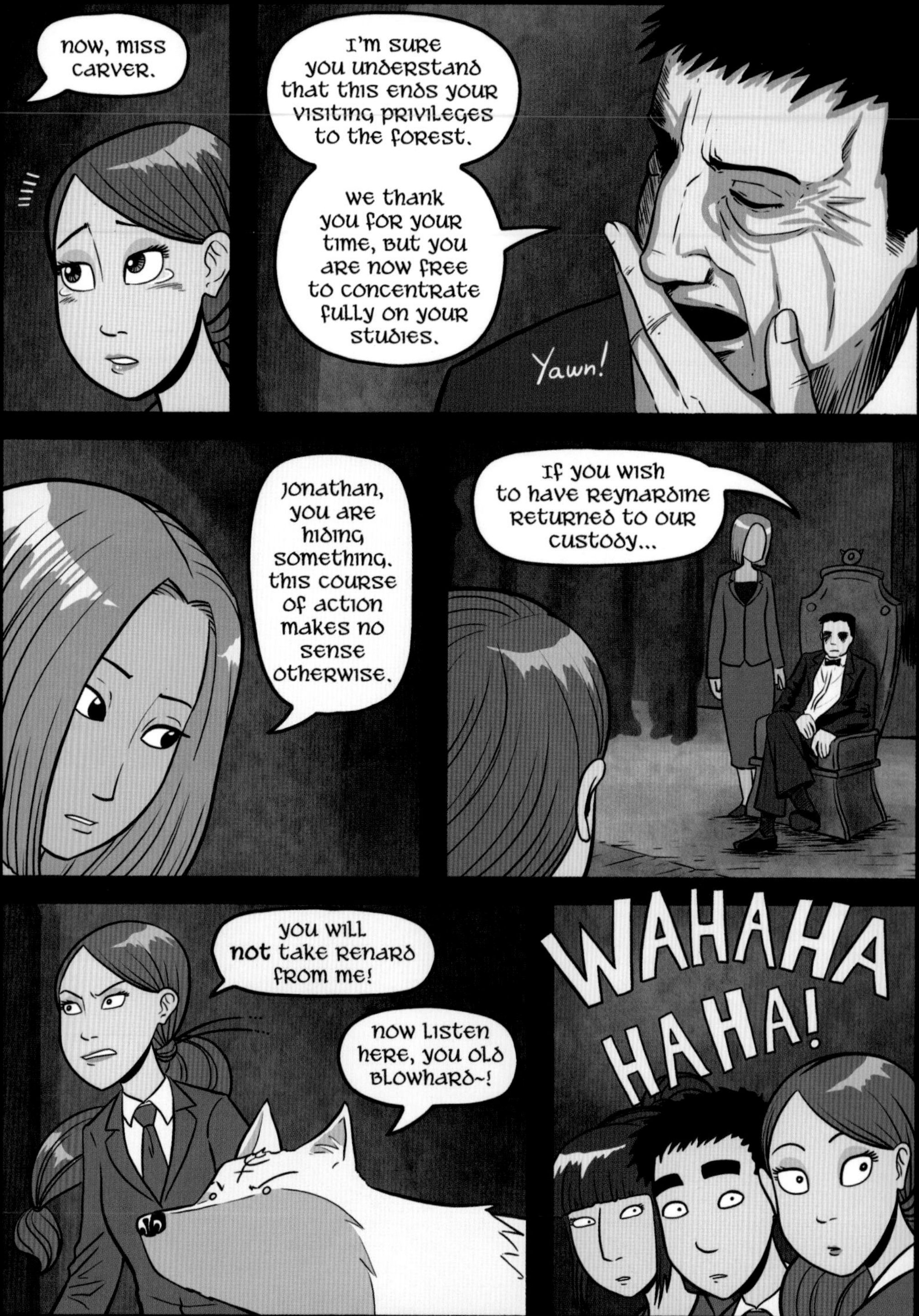
now, miss carver.
I'm sure you understand that this ends your visiting privileges to the forest.
we thank you for your time, but you are now free to concentrate fully on your studies.
Yawn!
jonathan, you are hiding something. this course of action makes no sense otherwise.
If you wish to have Reynardine returned to our custody...
you will **not** take Renard from me!
now listen here, you old blowhard~!
WAHAHA HAHA!

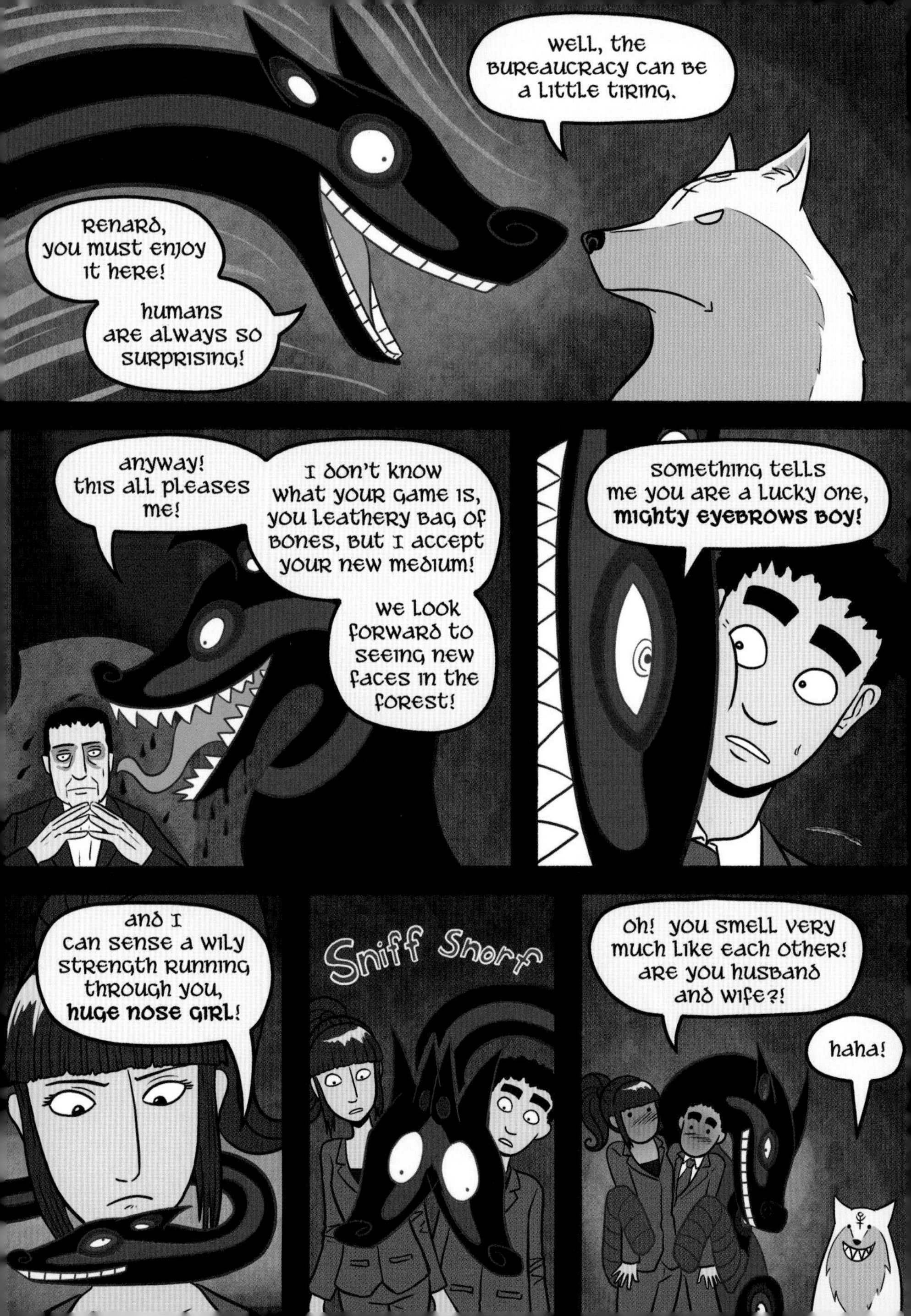
Renard, you must enjoy it here!
humans are always so surprising!
well, the bureaucracy can be a little tiring.
anyway! this all pleases me!
I don't know what your game is, you leathery bag of bones, but I accept your new medium!
we look forward to seeing new faces in the forest!
something tells me you are a lucky one, **mighty eyebrows boy!**
and I can sense a wily strength running through you, **huge nose girl!**
Sniff Snorf
oh! you smell very much like each other! are you husband and wife?!
haha!

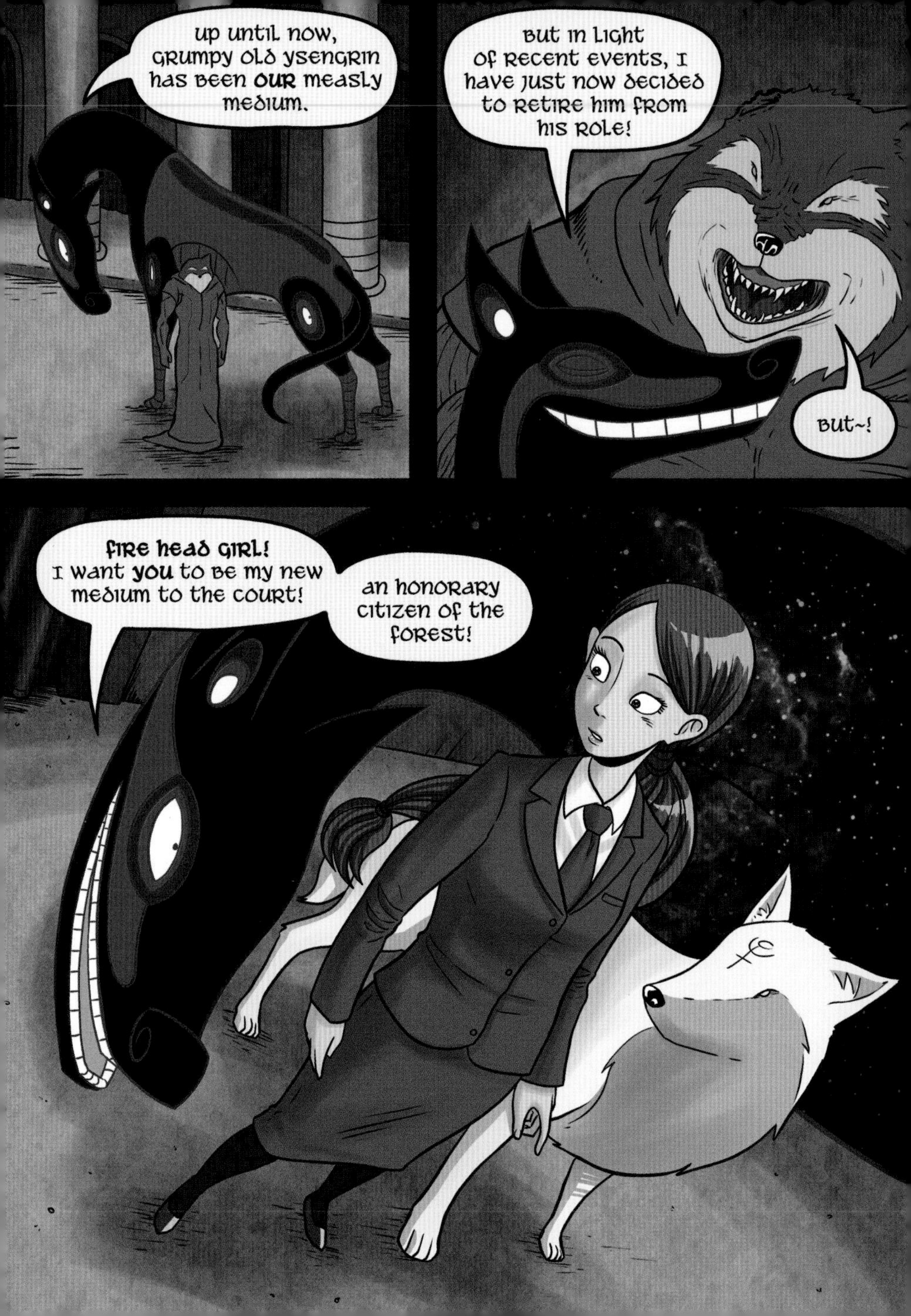
up until now, grumpy old ysengrin has been **our** measly medium.
But in light of recent events, I have just now decided to retire him from his role!
But~!
fire head girl! I want **you** to be my new medium to the court!
an honorary citizen of the forest!

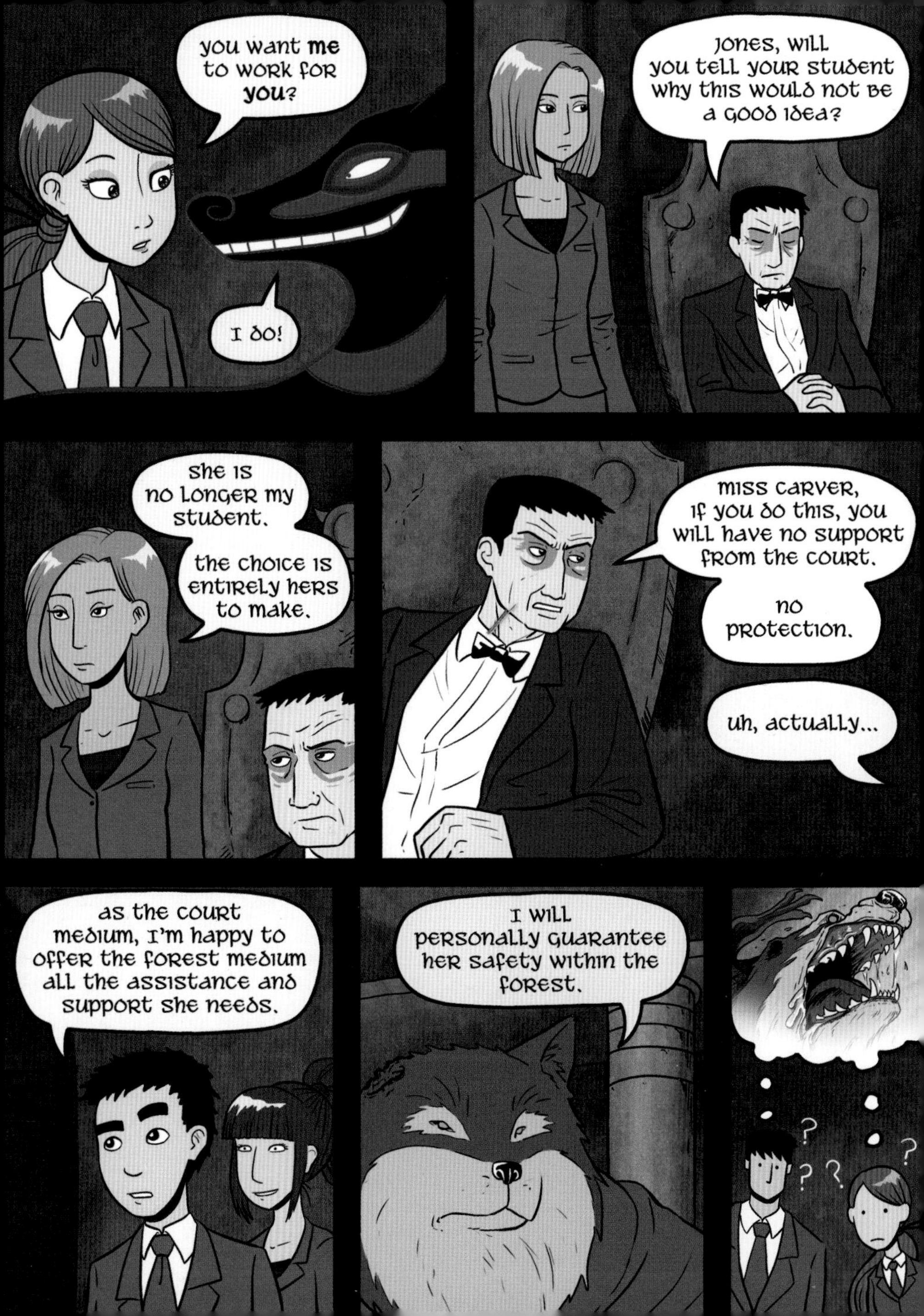
you want me to work for you?
I do!
jones, will you tell your student why this would not be a good idea?
she is no longer my student.
the choice is entirely hers to make.
miss carver, if you do this, you will have no support from the court.
no protection.
uh, actually...
as the court medium, I'm happy to offer the forest medium all the assistance and support she needs.
I will personally guarantee her safety within the forest.
? ? ? ?

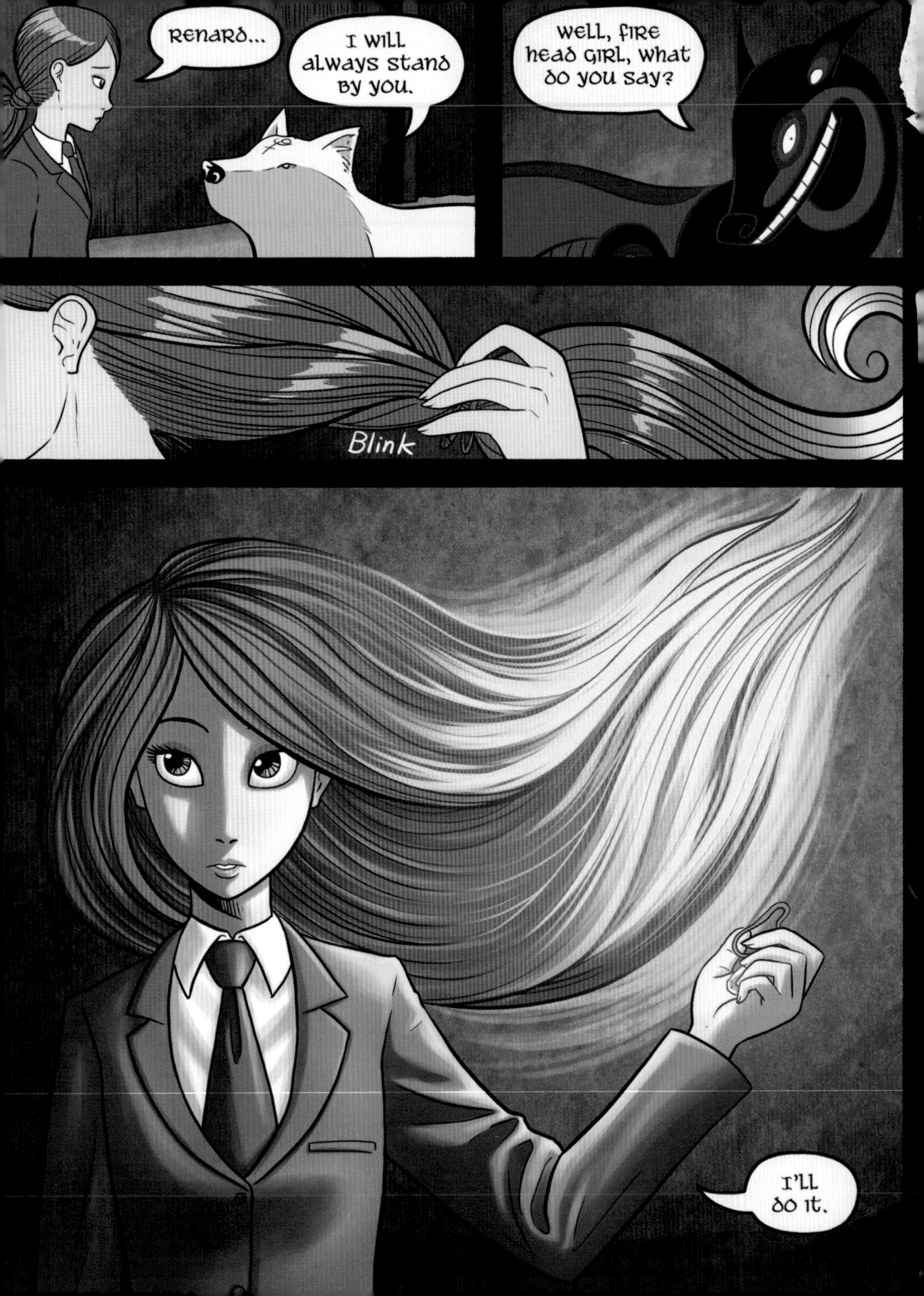
RENARD...
I WILL always stand BY YOU.
WELL, FIRE head GIRL, what do you say?
Blink
I'LL do it.

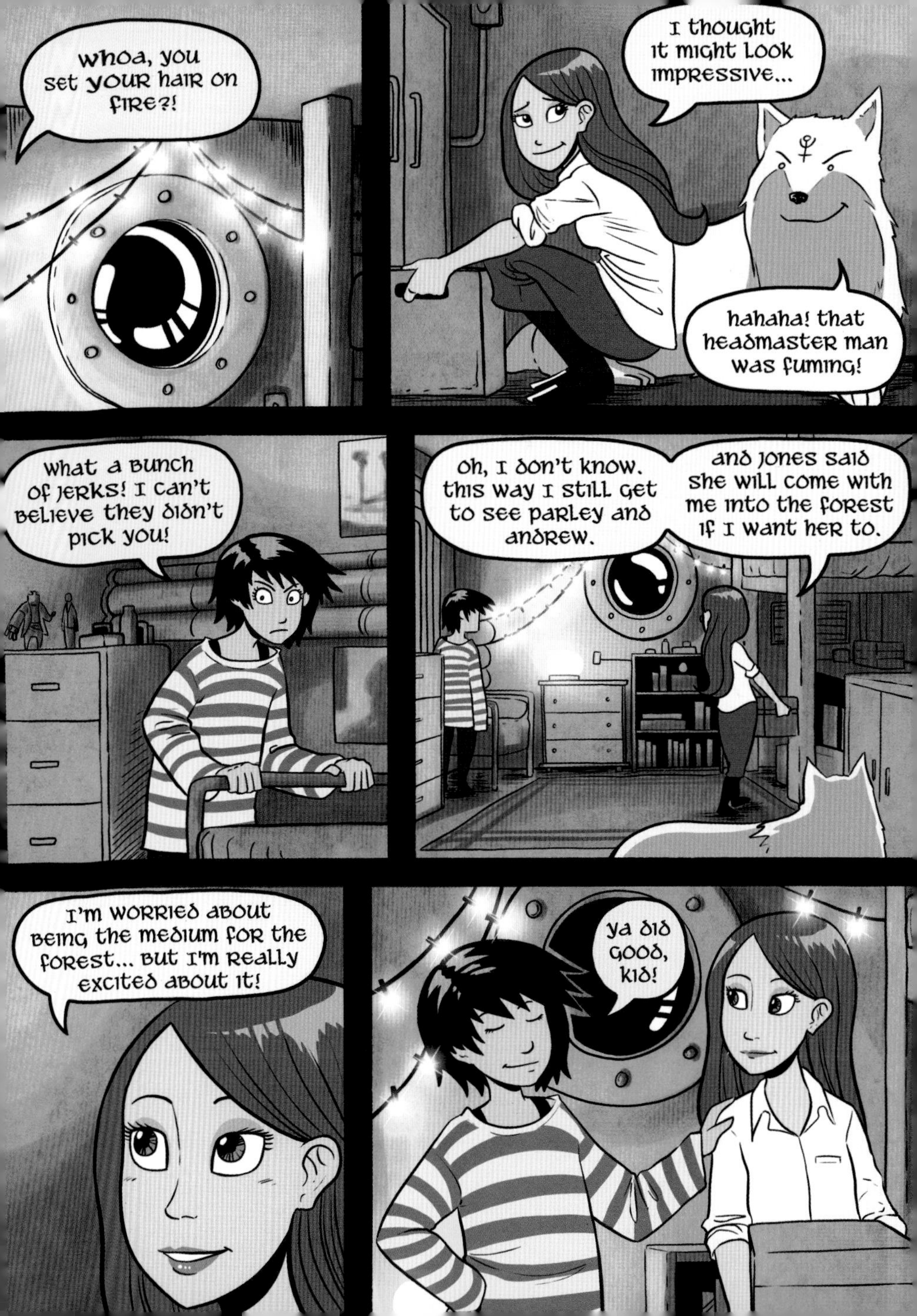
Whoa, you set YOUR hair on fire?!
I thought it might look impressive...
hahaha! that headmaster man was fuming!
What a bunch of jerks! I can't believe they didn't pick you!
Oh, I don't know. this way I still get to see parley and andrew.
and jones said she will come with me into the forest if I want her to.
I'm worried about being the medium for the forest... but I'm really excited about it!
ya did good, kid!

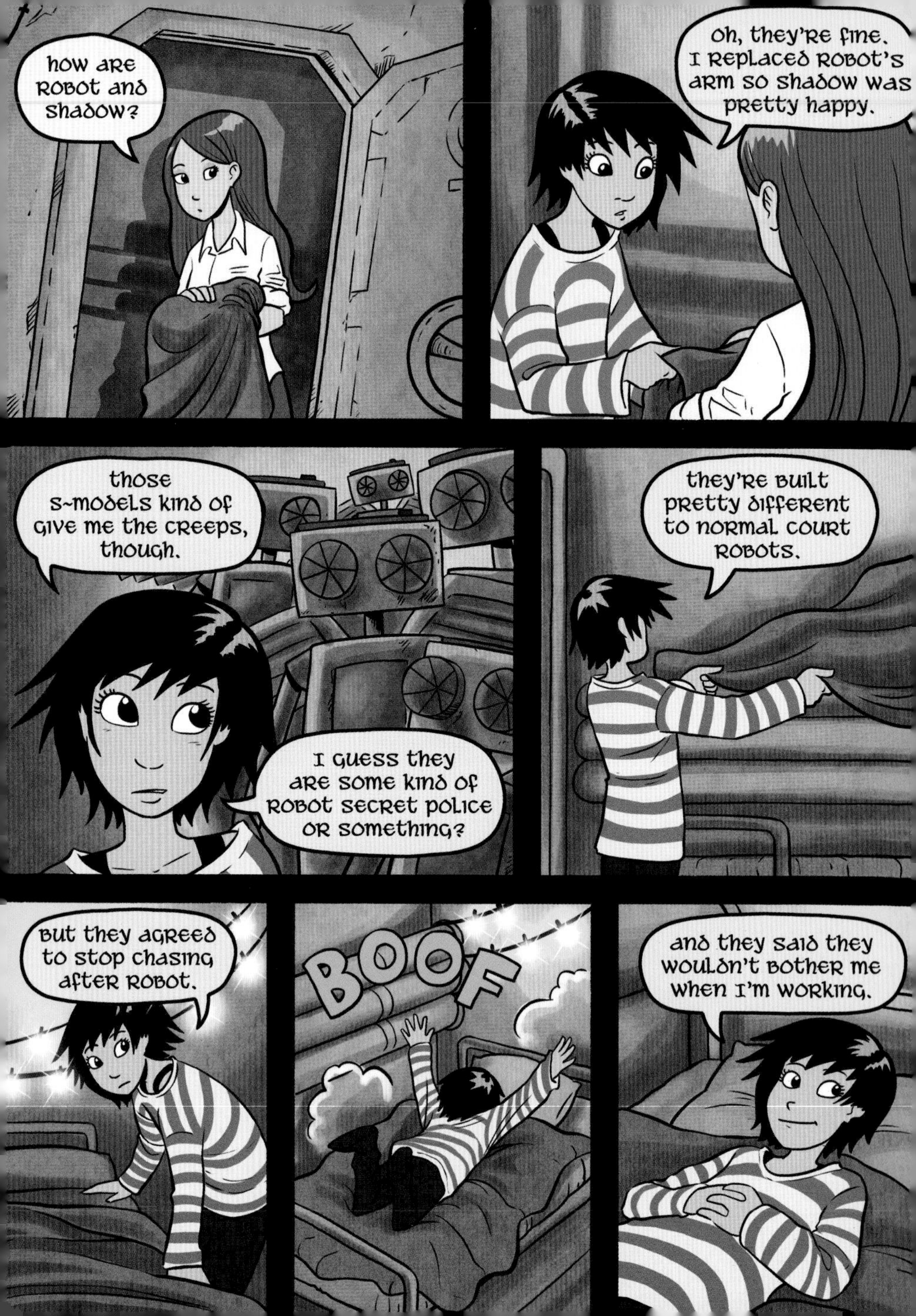
how are Robot and Shadow?
Oh, they're fine. I replaced Robot's arm so Shadow was pretty happy.
those S-models kind of give me the creeps, though.
they're built pretty different to normal court robots.
I guess they are some kind of robot secret police or something?
But they agreed to stop chasing after Robot.
BOOF
and they said they wouldn't bother me when I'm working.

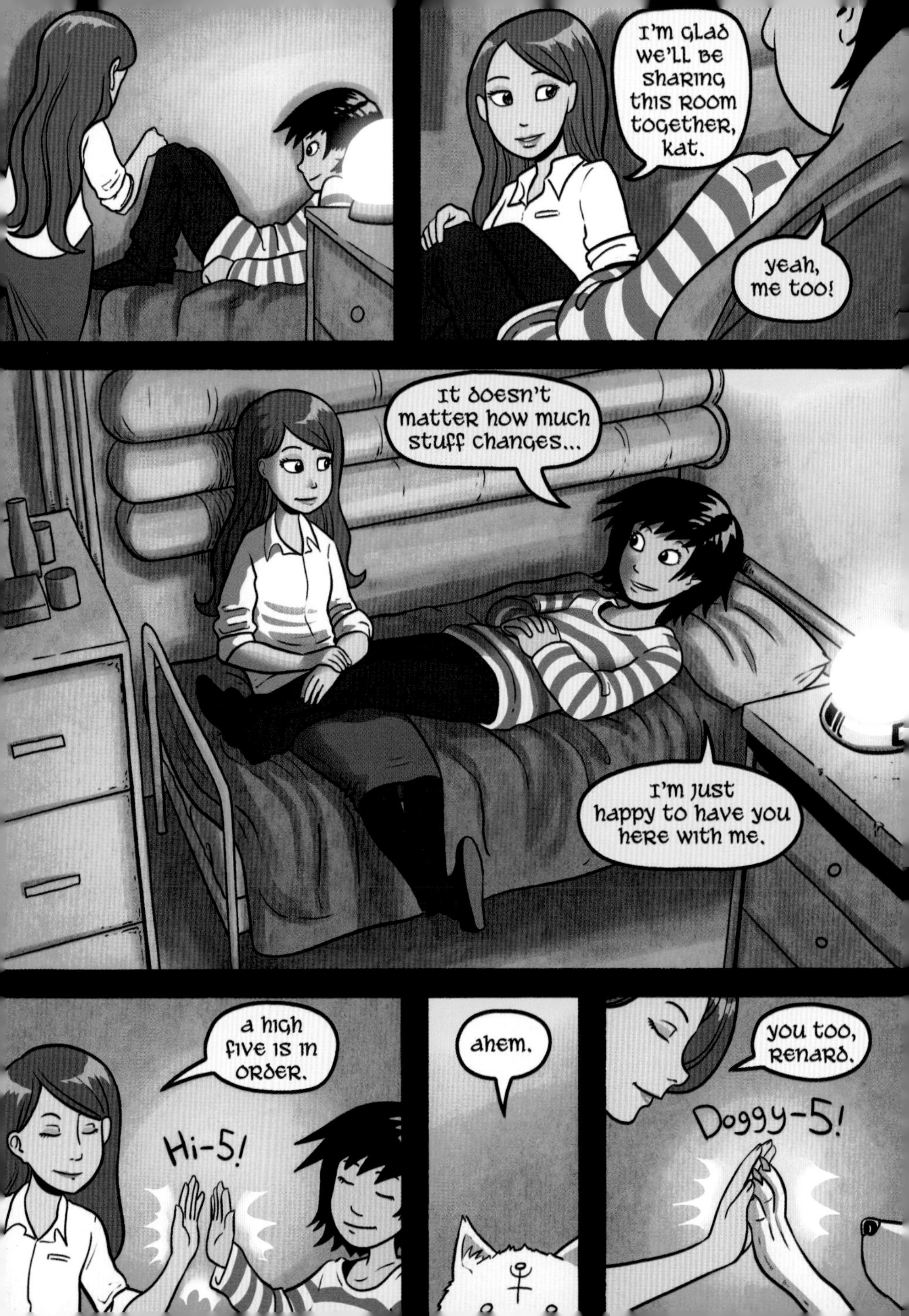
I'm glad we'll be sharing this room together, kat.
yeah, me too!
It doesn't matter how much stuff changes...
I'm just happy to have you here with me.
a high five is in order.
Hi-5!
ahem.
you too, Renard.
Doggy-5!

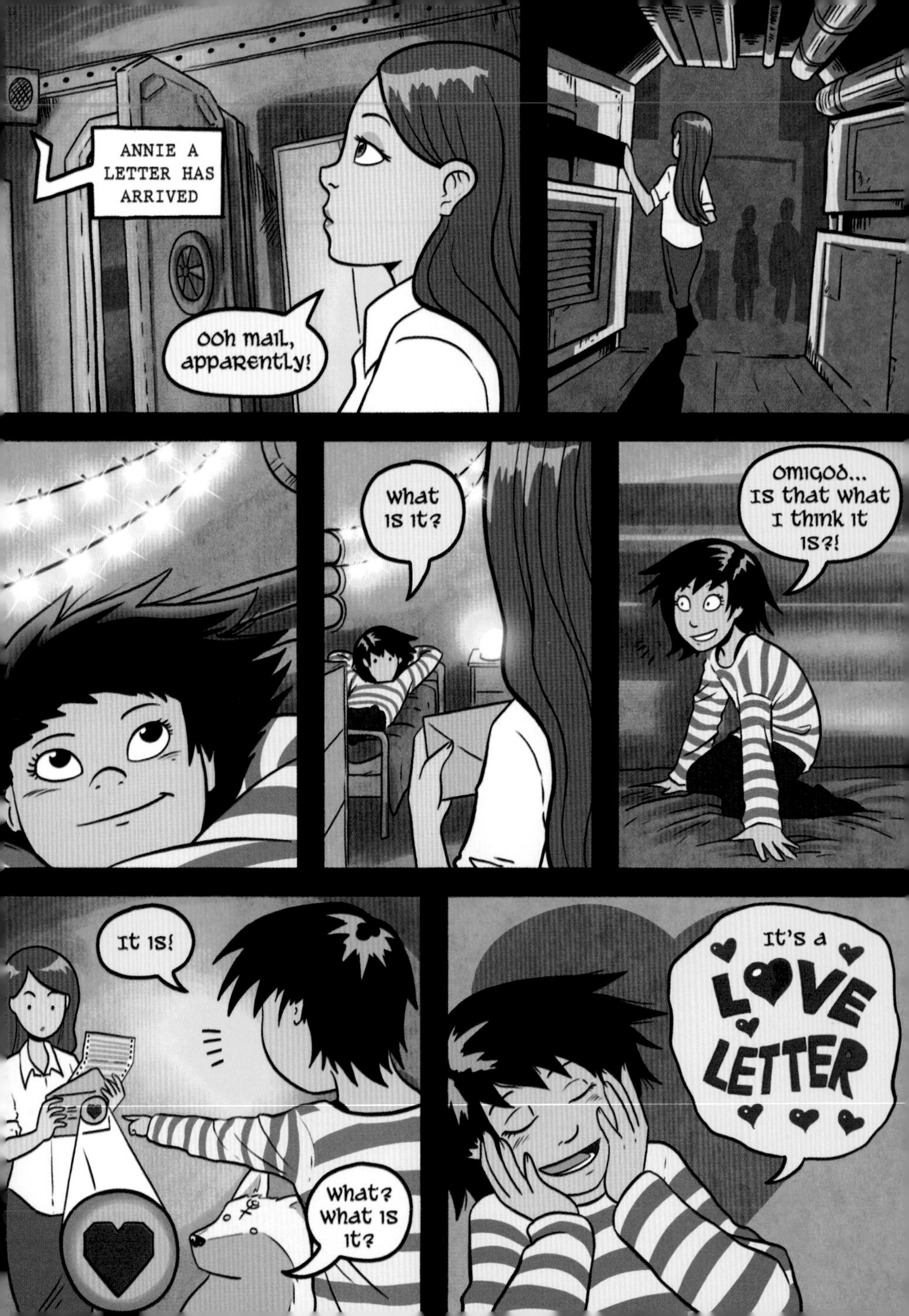
ANNIE A LETTER HAS ARRIVED
Ooh mail, apparently!
What is it?
Omigod... Is that what I think it is?!
It is!
What? What is it?
It's a LOVE LETTER

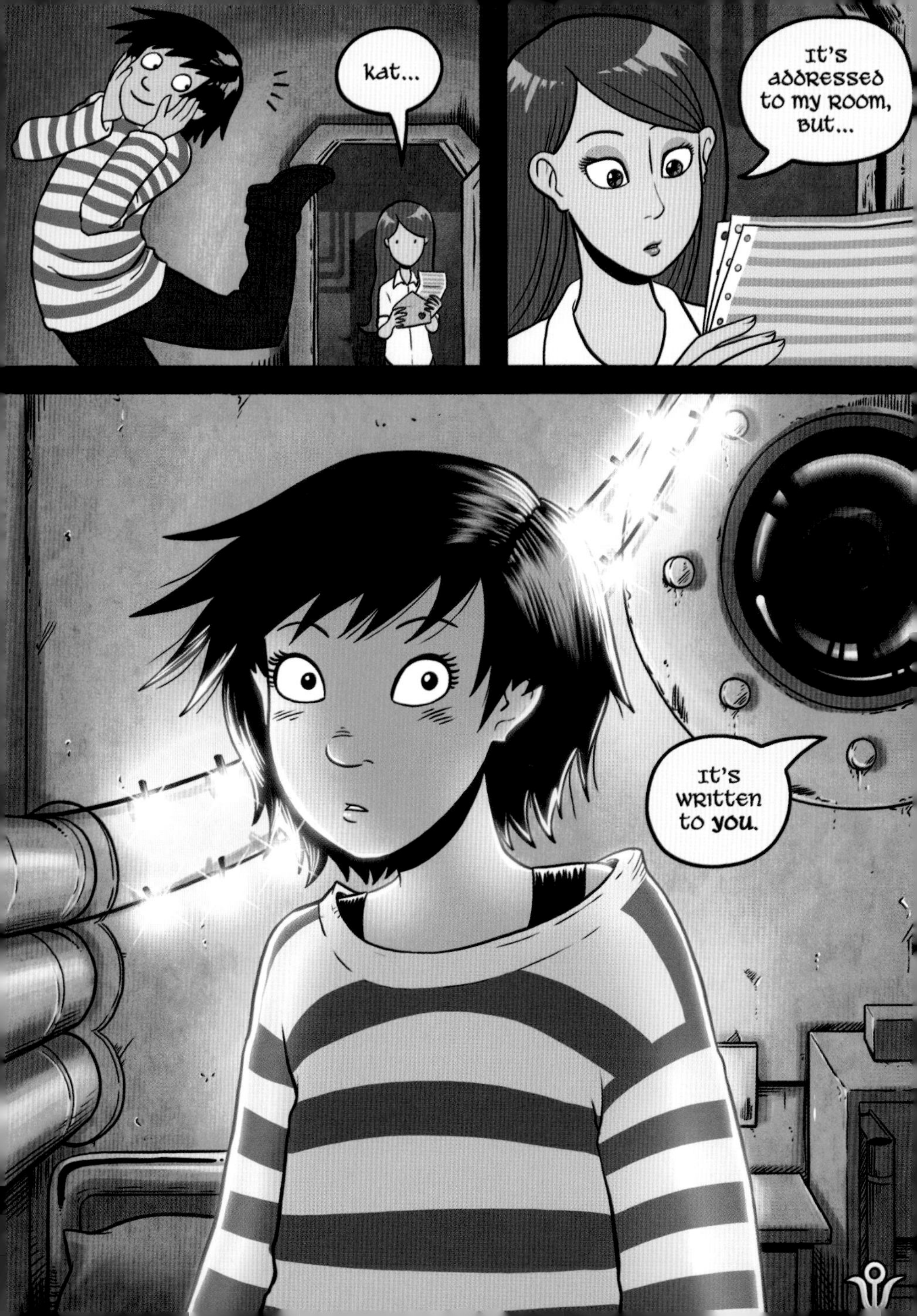
Kat...
It's addressed to my room, but...
It's written to you.

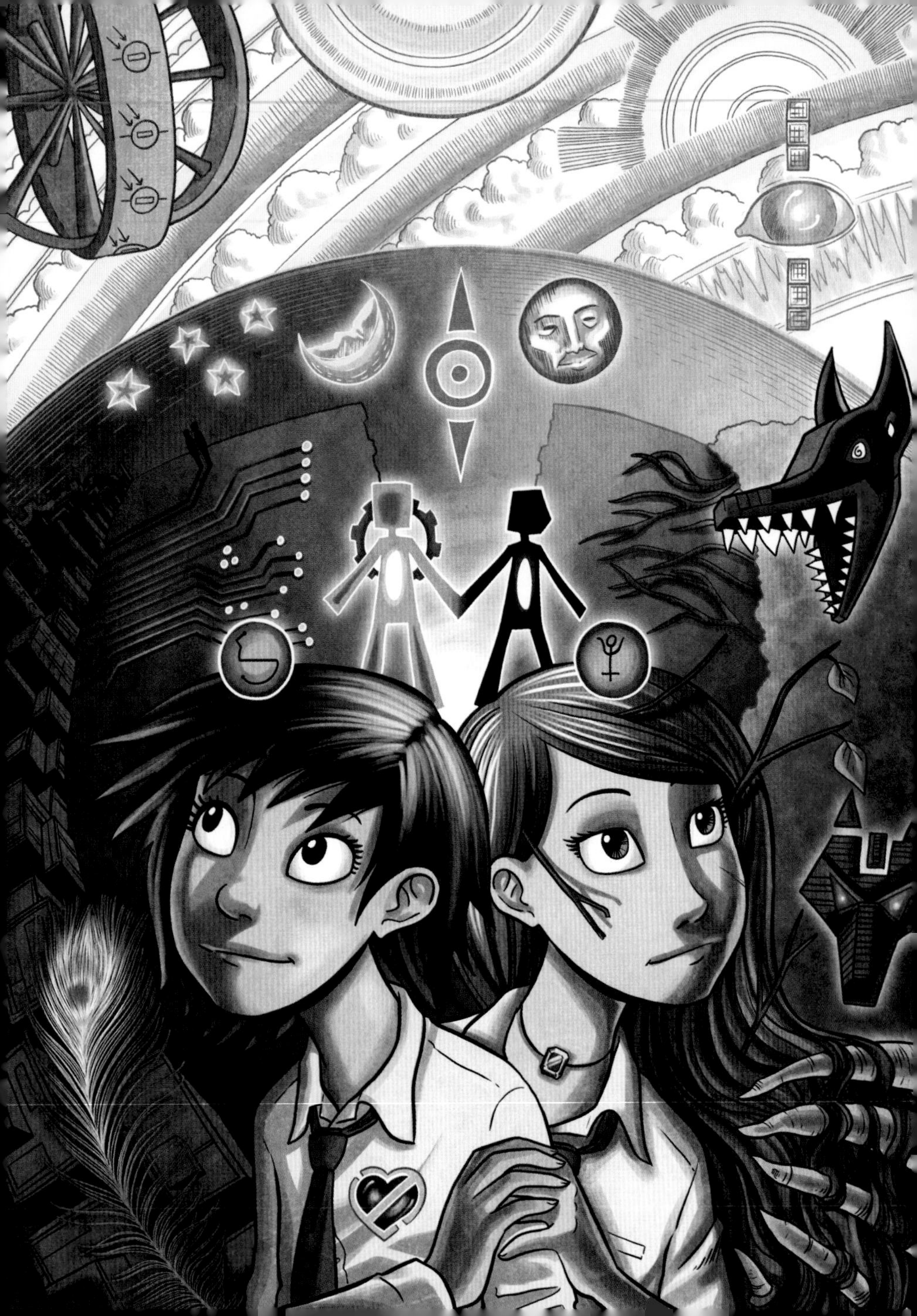

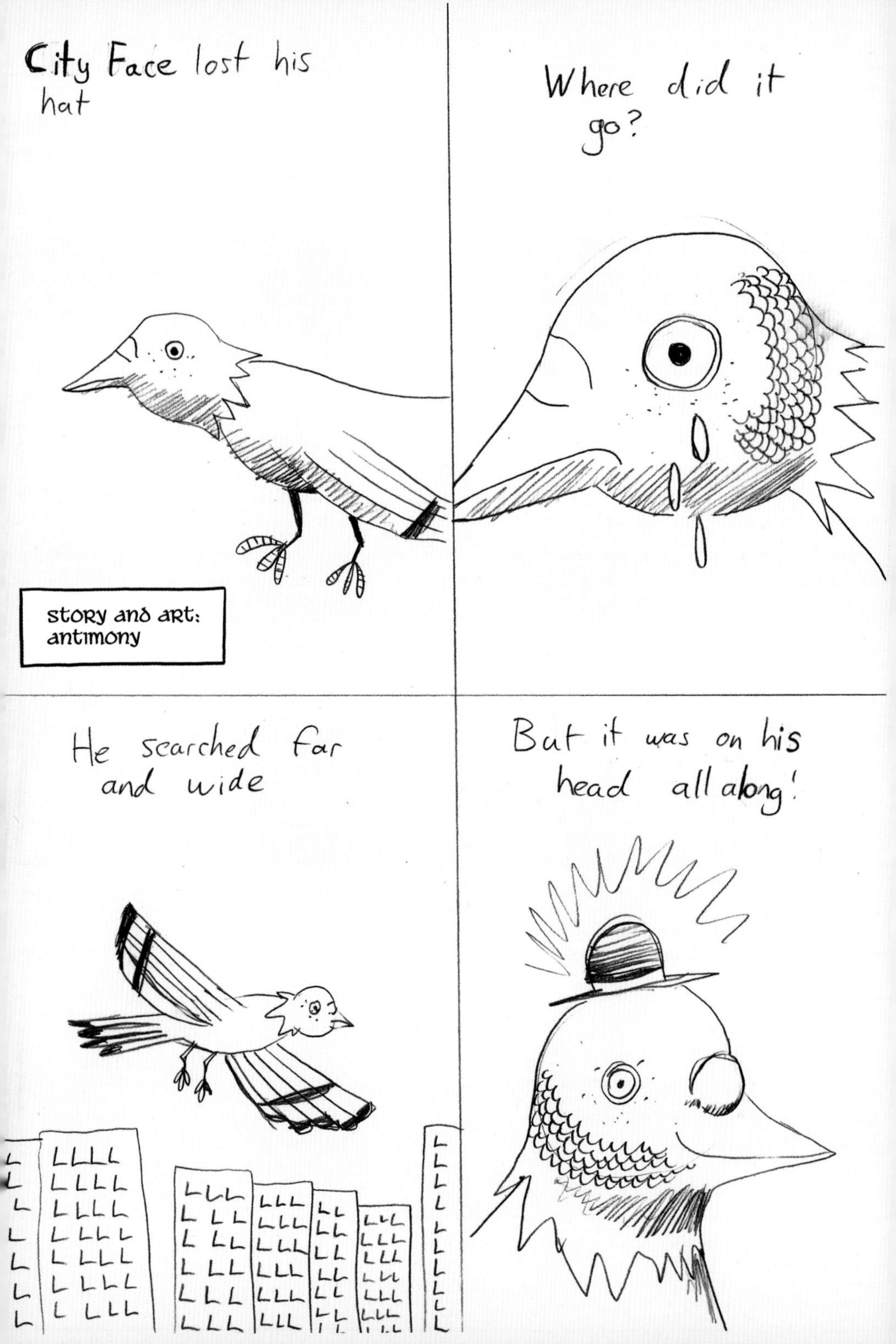
City Face lost his hat
story and art: antimony
Where did it go?
He searched far and wide
But it was on his head all along!

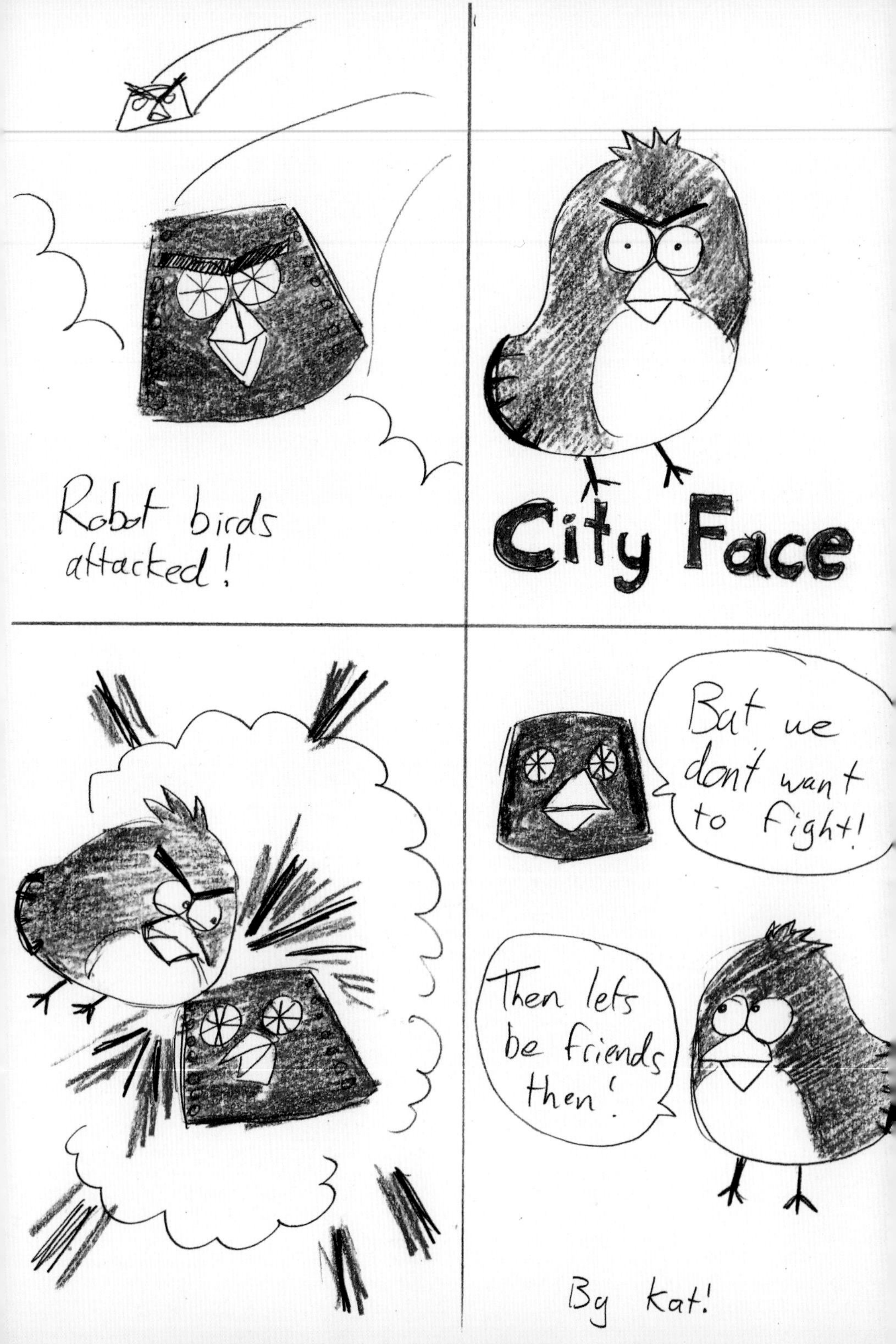
City Face
Robot birds attacked!
But we dont want to fight!
Then lets be friends then!
By Kat!

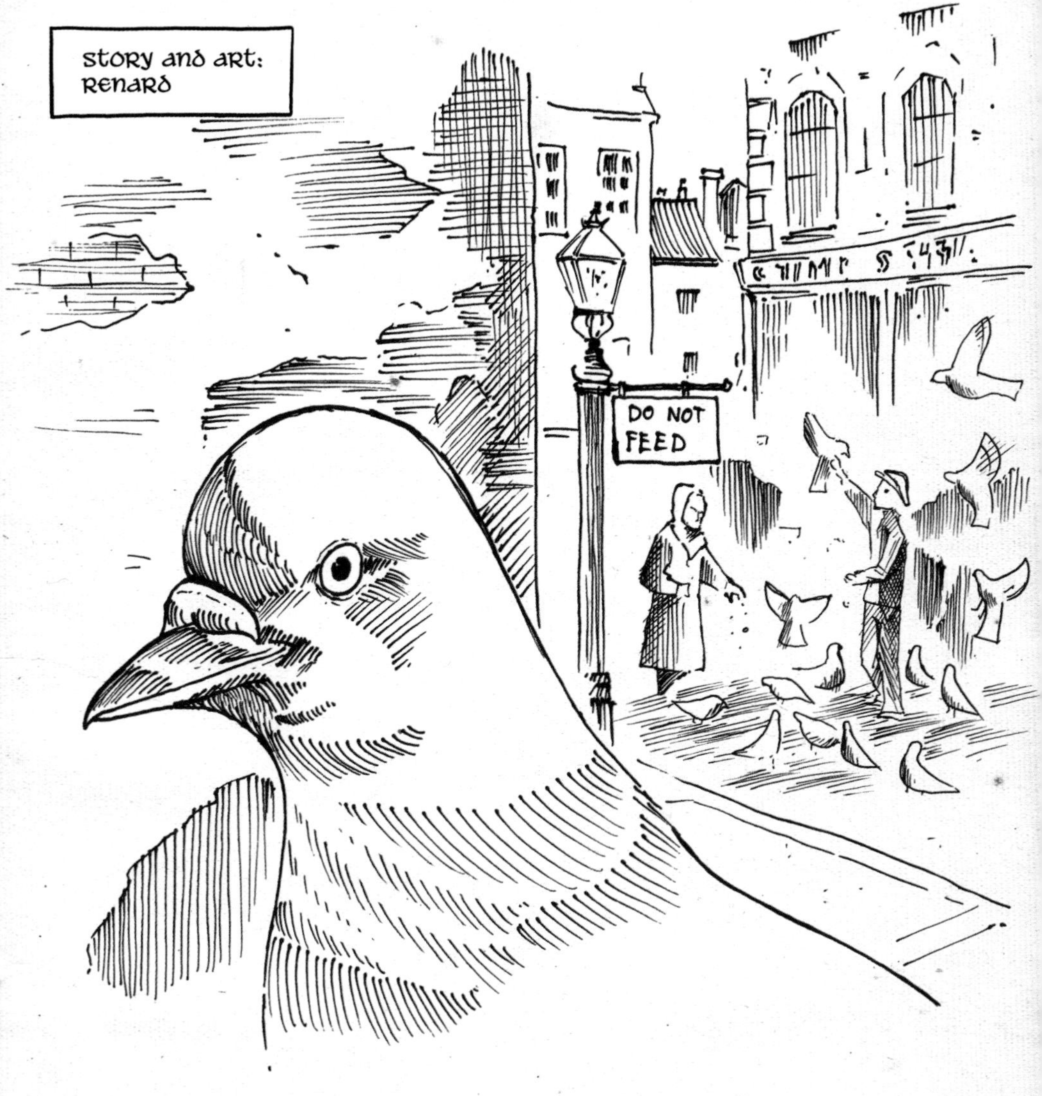
STORY AND ART:
RENARD
DO NOT
FEED

PECKING ORDER.

PIGEON (*to reader*). "THEY COMPLAIN OF OUR PRESENCE-- BUT IT IS THEIR FOOD THAT BRINGS US BACK. COULD THEY REALLY BE WANTING OF AN ABSENCE OF NATURE!"

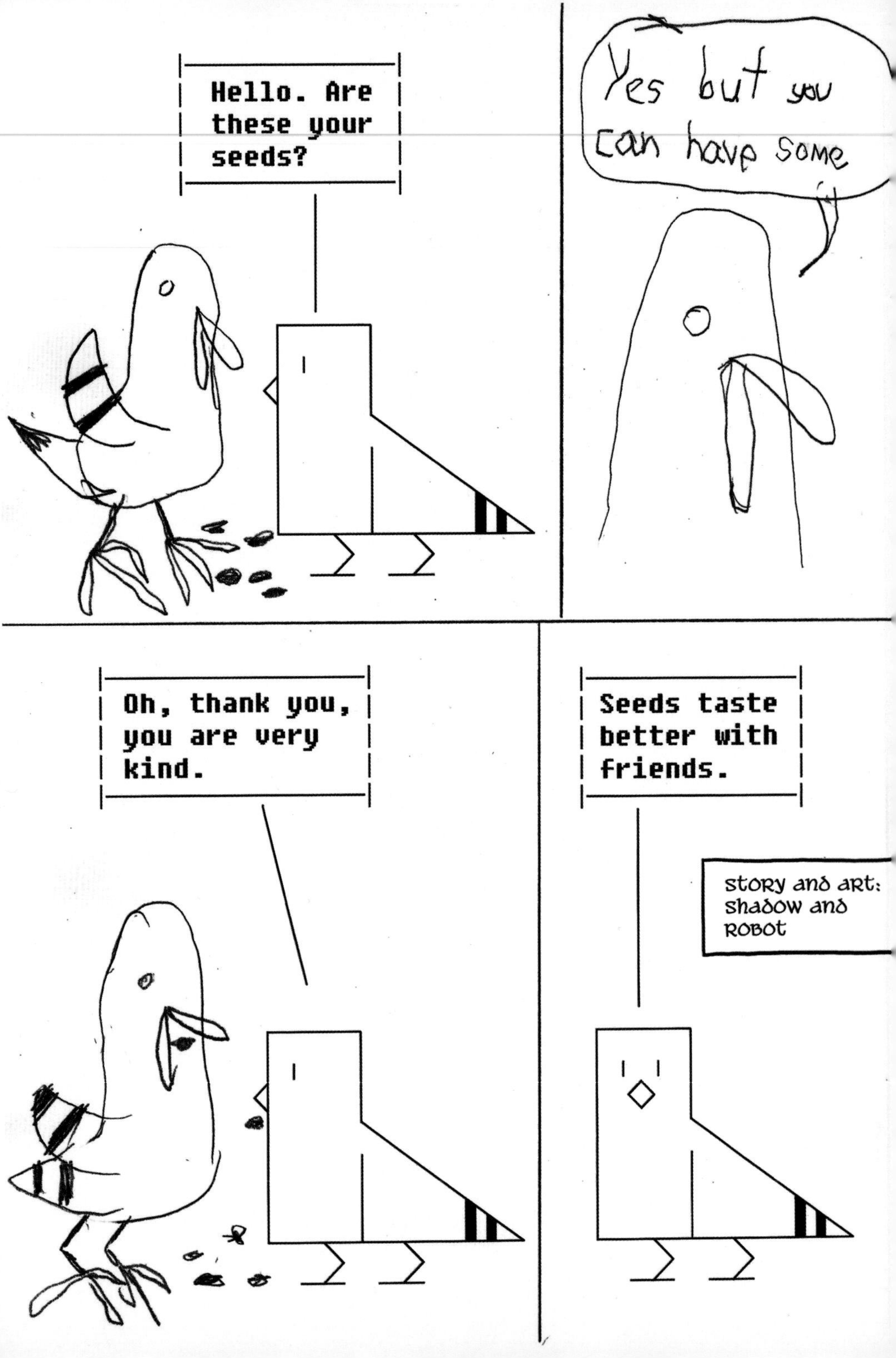

Hello. Are these your seeds?
Yes but you can have some
Oh, thank you, you are very kind.
Seeds taste better with friends.
story and art: shadow and Robot

When should you buy a bird?
When it's going cheep!
What did one egg say to the other egg?
Let's get cracking!
What do you call a parrot that flew away?
A polygon! ??
(joke by Kat)
Why did the chicken go to the seance?
To get to the other side!
Mort

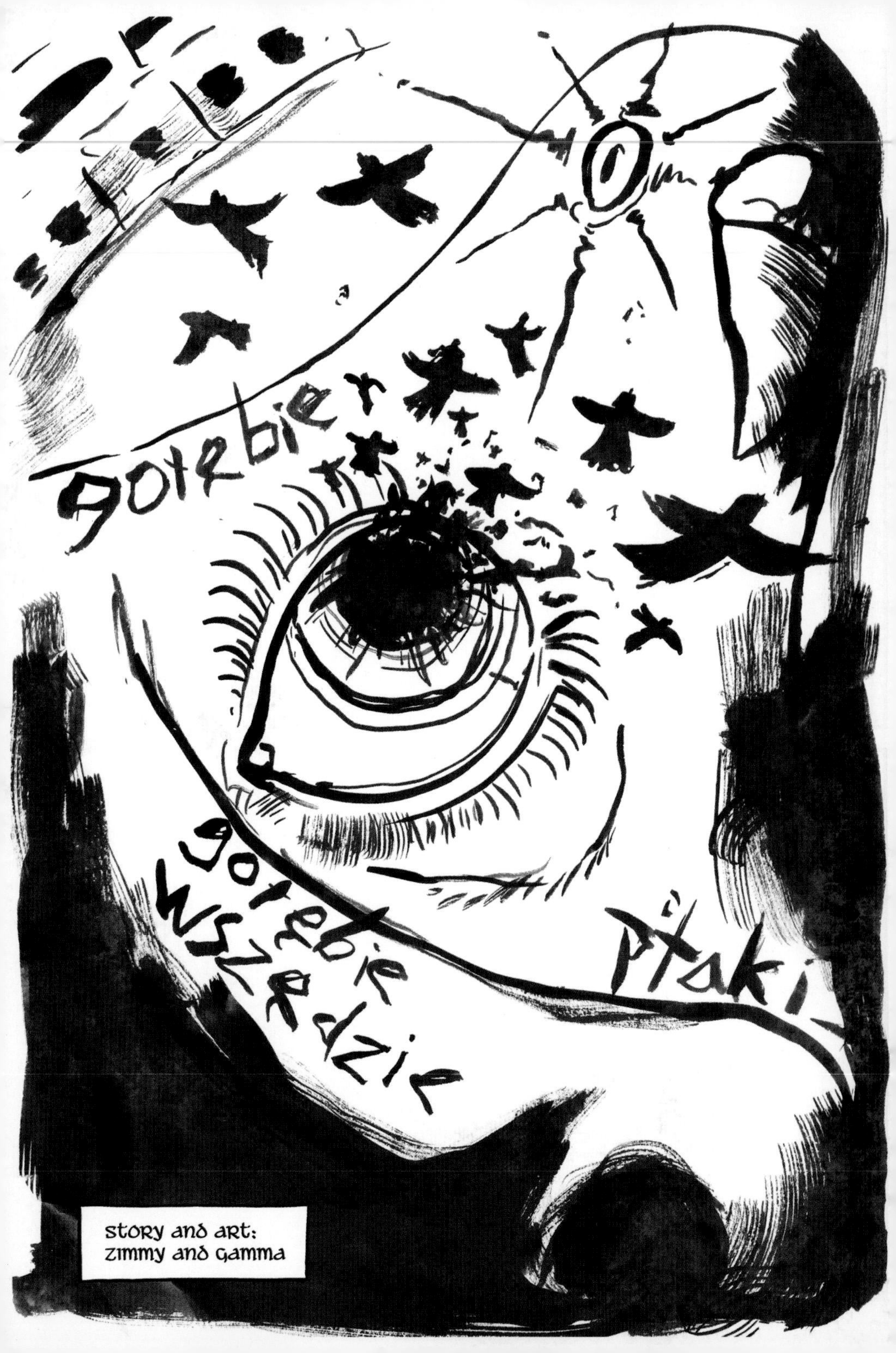
gołębie
ptaki
gołębie wszędzie
story and art:
Zimmy and Gamma

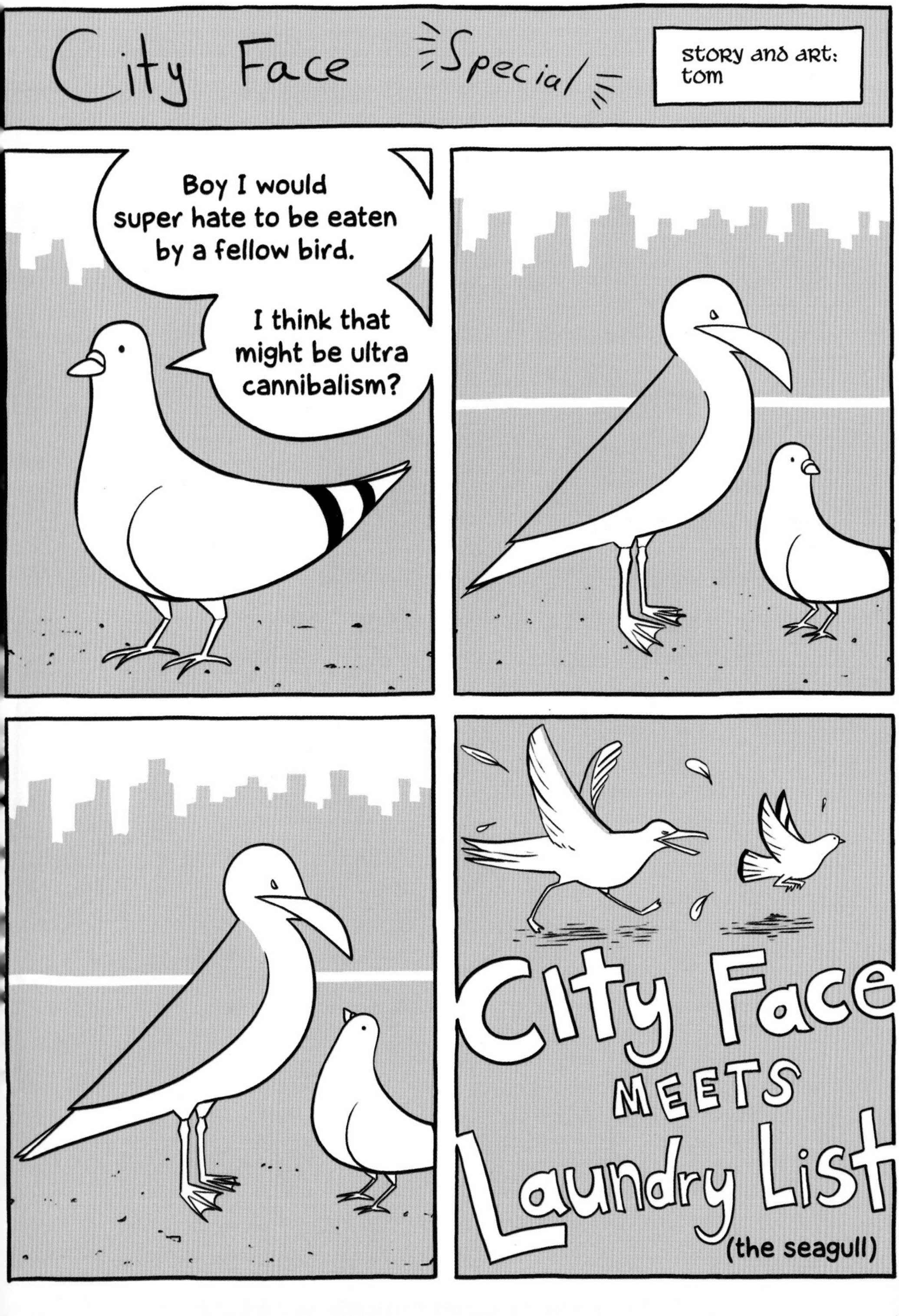
City Face Special
story and art:
tom
Boy I would super hate to be eaten by a fellow bird.
I think that might be ultra cannibalism?
City Face
MEETS
Laundry List
(the seagull)

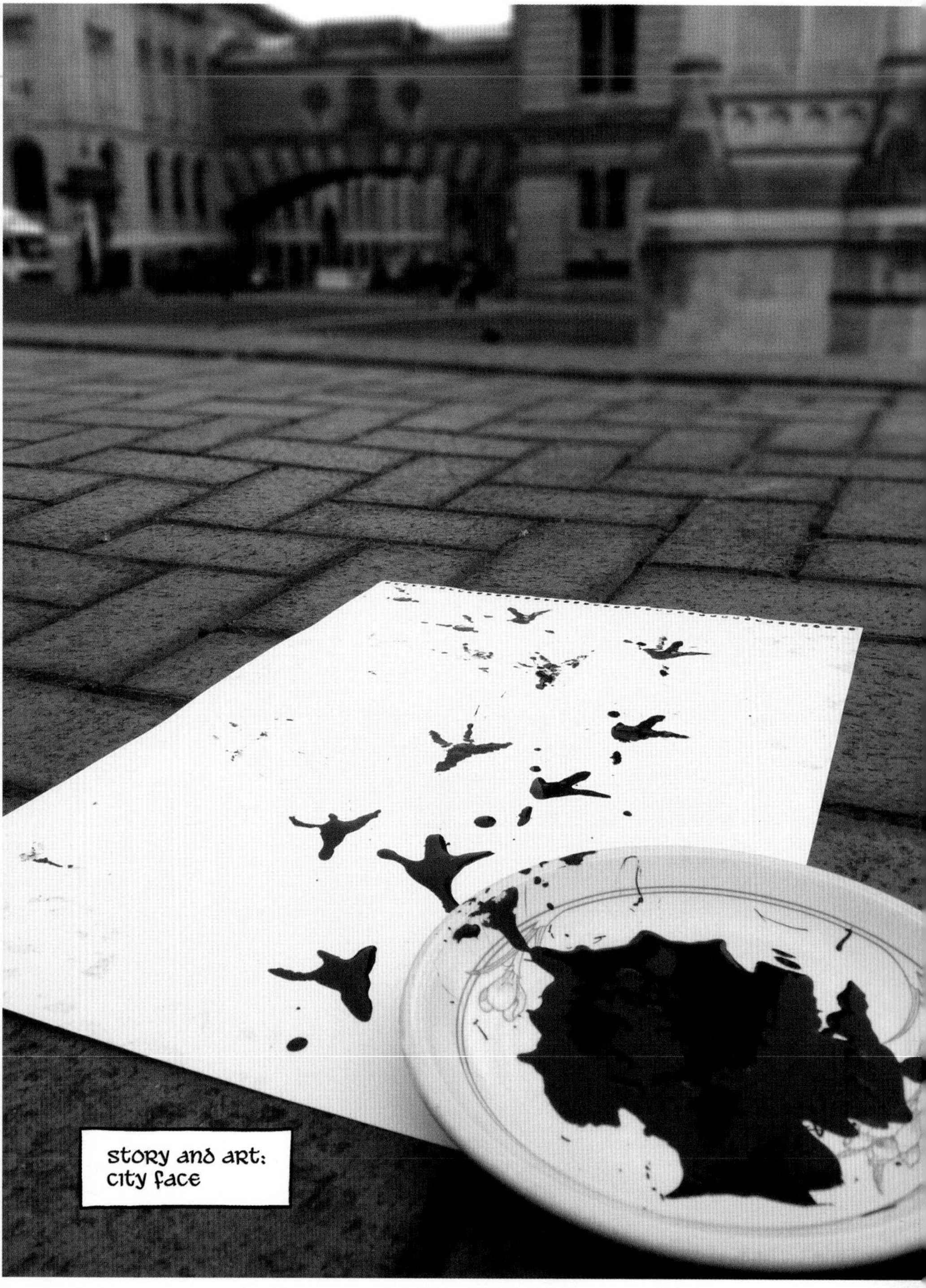
story and art:
city face

About the Author

Tom lives in a crumbling house where he works on his comic and dreams about his stories. There is not enough time in the day to be bored.

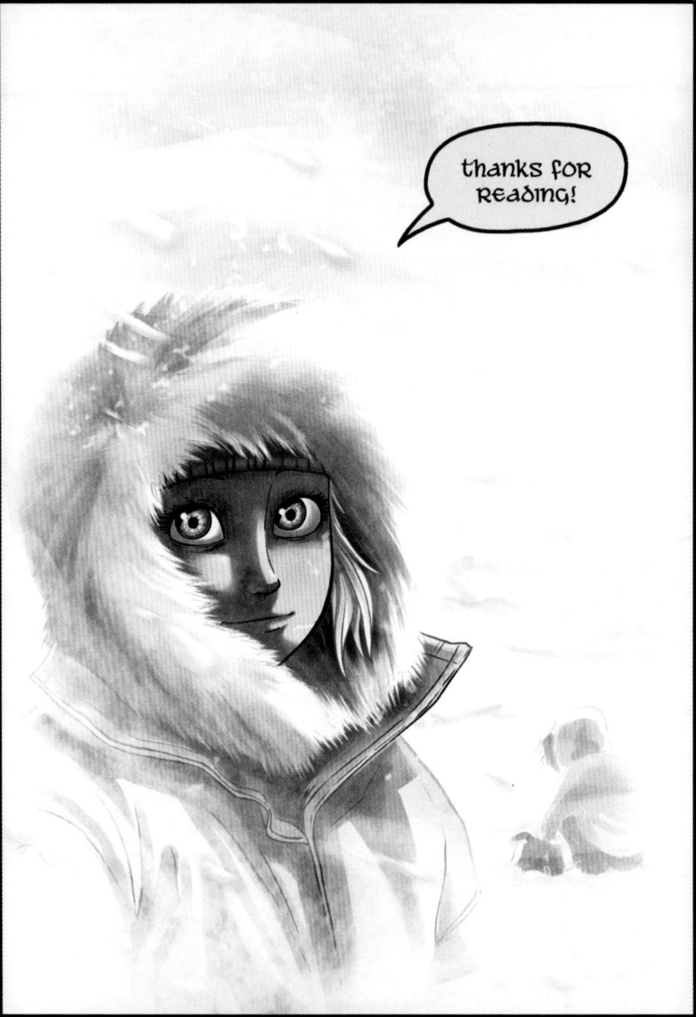
thanks for reading!

www.gunnerkrigg.com

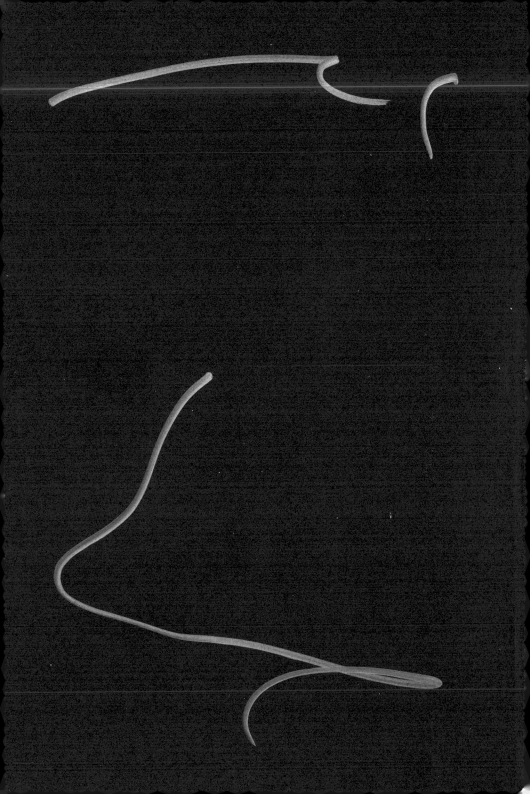